SWORD CATCHER

CASSANDRA CLARE

SWORD CATCHER

TOR

First published 2023 by Del Rey

First published in the UK 2023 by Tor
an imprint of Pan Macmillan
The Smithson, 6 Briset Street, London EC1M 5NR
EU representative: Macmillan Publishers Ireland Ltd, 1st Floor,
The Liffey Trust Centre, 117–126 Sheriff Street Upper,
Dublin 1, D01 YC43
Associated companies throughout the world
www.panmacmillan.com

ISBN 978-1-0350-3751-3

1 3 5 7 9 8 6 4 2

A CIP catalogue record for this book is available from the British Library.

Endpaper map: Sarah J. Coleman/Inkymole

Printed and bound by CPI Group (UK) Ltd, Croydon, CR0 4YY

Visit **www.panmacmillan.com** to read more about all our books
and to buy them. You will also find features, author interviews and
news of any author events, and you can sign up for e-newsletters
so that you're always first to hear about our new releases.

For Josh

Who rules Castellane, rules the whole world.

—Proverb

SWORD CATCHER

PROLOGUE

It began with a crime. The theft of a boy.

It was not presented as a crime. Indeed, the man in charge of the whole enterprise was a soldier, the Captain of the Arrow Squadron, charged with protecting the King of Castellane and seeing to it that the Laws he made were carried out.

He had an exceeding dislike of criminals.

His name was Aristide Jolivet, and as he lifted his hand to rap sharply on the door of the orphanage, the large, square-cut amethyst on his left hand gleamed in the light of the moon. Etched into it was a lion, the symbol of the city. It appeared to be roaring.

Silence. Jolivet frowned. He was not a man who liked to wait, or was often made to do it. He glanced behind him, where the narrow path cut into the cliffside fell away to the sea. He'd always thought this an odd place for an orphanage. The cliffs that rose above Castellane's northern bay were jagged, dotted with scars like the face of a pox survivor, and dusted with a thin layer of loose, gravelly scree. It was easy to lose one's footing up here, and a dozen or so people did every year, tumbling from the cliffs into the green sea below. None made it to shore afterward—for even if they survived the fall, the crocodiles lurking beneath the surface of the water knew the meaning of a scream and a splash.

Yet, somehow, the Home of the Orphans of Aigon managed to prevent most, if not all, of their charges from being devoured. Considering the usual fate of parentless children on the streets of the city, these were good odds. A place at the Orfelinat was a coveted one.

Jolivet frowned and knocked again. The sound echoed, as if the stones themselves were chiming. The granite façade of the Home flowed out from the cliff's face, encircled by a single gray-green wall. The Orfelinat did not sit atop the cliffs but rather was part of them. It had once been a fortress of sorts, back in the time of the old Empire. In fact, the door upon which he was knocking was etched with faded words in the old language of Magna Callatis. They meant nothing to him. He'd never seen the point in knowing a language no one spoke anymore.

The door swung wide. The woman on the other side, wearing the blue and white of a Sister of Aigon, looked at Jolivet with wary recognition. "My apologies for the wait, Legate," she said. "I did not know you'd be returning today."

Jolivet inclined his head politely. "Sister Bonafilia," he said. "May I enter?"

She hesitated, though Jolivet did not know why. The question was merely a formality. If he wanted to enter the Orfelinat, there was nothing she or any of the Sisters could do to prevent him.

"I thought," she said, "that when you came before, and then left, it meant you had not found what you wanted here."

He looked at her more closely. Sister Bonafilia was a neat-looking, small woman, with bony features and rough hands. Her clothes were plain, many times washed and worn again.

"I came before to see what there was to see," he said. "I reported my findings to the Palace. I am back on their orders. On the *King's* orders."

She hesitated a moment more, her hand on the doorpost. The

sun had begun to set already: It was winter, after all, the dry season. The clouds massed on the horizon had begun their transformation into roses and gold. Jolivet frowned again; he had hoped to complete this errand before dark.

Sister Bonafilia inclined her head. "Very well."

She stepped back to let Jolivet over the doorstep. Inside was a hall of hollowed granite, the ceiling decorated with faded tiles in green and gold, the colors of the old Empire, now gone a thousand years. Holy Sisters in their worn linen dresses hovered by the walls, staring. The stone floor was worn past smoothness by the passage of years; it now dipped and swayed like the surface of the ocean. Stone steps led upward, no doubt to the children's dormitories.

Several children—girls, no more than eleven or twelve—descended the stairs. They stopped, wide-eyed, catching sight of Jolivet in his gleaming uniform of red and gold, his ceremonial sword at his side.

The girls scampered back up the stairs, silent as mice under the fixed gaze of a cat. For the first time, Sister Bonafilia's composure began to fray. "Please," she said. "Coming here like this—it will frighten the children."

Jolivet smiled thinly. "I need not stay long at all, if you will cooperate with the King's orders."

"And what are those orders?"

Kel and Cas were playing pirate battles in the dirt. It was a game they had invented, and required few tools save sticks and several prized marbles, which Kel had won from some of the older boys at card games. Kel was cheating, as he usually did, but Cas never seemed to mind. He gave the game his full concentration anyway, locks of his dark-blond hair falling into his freckled face as he scowled and plotted his ship's next move.

Only a few minutes ago, Sister Jenofa had shooed them, along with most of the other boys in their dormitory, out to the garden.

She did not say why, only urged them to amuse themselves. Kel had no questions. Usually at this hour he would be at the washbasin, scrubbing his face and hands with harsh soap in preparation for dinner. "A clean soul in a clean body," Sister Bonafilia liked to say. "Health is wealth, and I wish you all to be rich."

Kel pushed his hair back. It was getting long; soon enough, Sister Bonafilia would notice, seize him, and lop it off with kitchen shears, muttering to herself. Kel didn't mind. He knew she had a special affection for him, as she often went out of her way to sneak him tarts from the kitchen, and only yelled at him a little bit when he was caught climbing the more dangerous rocks, the ones that jutted out over the ocean.

"It's getting dark," Cas said, squinting up at the sky, which was deepening to violet. Kel wished he could see the ocean from here. It was the one thing that never bored him, looking at the sea. He'd tried to explain it to Cas—how it always changed, was a different color every day, the light slightly altered—but Cas only shrugged good-naturedly. He didn't need to understand why Kel did the things he did. Kel was his friend, so it was all right. "What do you think they want us out here for, anyway?"

Before Kel could answer, two figures emerged from beneath the archway that connected the walled garden to the main fortress. (Kel always called it a fortress, not an orphanage. It was much more dashing to live in a fortress than in a place you went because nobody wanted you.)

One of the figures was Sister Bonafilia. The other was familiar to most inhabitants of Castellane. A tall man, wearing a brass-buttoned coat printed over the breast with the sigil of two arrows at odds with each other. His boots and vambraces were studded with nails. He rode at the head of the Arrow Squadron—the King's most highly trained soldiers—as they paraded through the city on feast days or at celebrations. The city folk called him the Eagle of the Fall, and indeed he resembled a sort of raptor. He was tall and wiry, his bony face marked with multiple scars that stood out white against his olive skin.

He was Legate Aristide Jolivet, and this was the second time Kel had seen him at the Orfelinat. Which was strange. To his knowledge, military leaders did not visit orphanages. But less than a month ago, the boys had been playing in the garden, as they were today, when Kel had glanced over toward the fortress and seen a flash of red and gold.

He had always been fascinated by Jolivet, who often figured as a villain in his games with Cas—a pirate and thief hunter who, once he caught hold of an innocent criminal, would lock them up in the Tully prison and torture them for information. Not that Kel or Cas ever broke, of course; a snitch was the worst thing you could be.

Regardless, Kel had recognized Jolivet immediately and scrambled to his feet. By the time he raced to the fortress, Jolivet was gone, and when he asked Sister Bonafilia if the Legate had been there, she'd told him not to be ridiculous and to stop imagining things.

Now a silence fell over the boys in the garden as Jolivet, standing at attention, scanned the scene with his pale eyes, his gaze resting here on that boy (Jacme, engaged in pulling strips from the powderbark tree), there on another (Bertran, the eldest of the group at ten). They passed over Cas and came to rest on Kel.

After a long, unnerving moment, he smiled. "There," he said. "That's the one."

Kel and Cas exchanged a puzzled look. *Which one?* Cas mouthed, but there was no time for discussion. Instead there was a hand on Kel's arm, hauling him to his feet.

"You must come." It was Bonafilia, her grip tight. "Don't make trouble, Kel, please."

Kel was annoyed. He was not a troublemaker. Well, there had been that business with the explosive powder and the north tower, and the time he had made Bertran walk the plank off the garden wall and the idiot had broken a bone in his foot. But it was nothing that couldn't have happened to anyone.

Still, Sister Bonafilia's face was worryingly drawn. With a sigh, Kel handed his marble off to Cas. "Take care of it till I get back."

Cas nodded and made a show of tucking the glass bauble into a vest pocket. Clearly he did not think Kel would be gone more than a few minutes. Kel didn't think so, either—though he was beginning to wonder. The way Sister Bonafilia steered him hastily across the garden didn't sit right. Nor did the way the Legate examined him once he got closer, bending down to peer at Kel as if he were seeking the answer to a mystery. He even tilted Kel's face up by the chin to more closely examine him, from his black, curling hair to his blue eyes to his stubborn chin.

He frowned. "The boy is grubby."

"He's been playing in the dirt," said Sister Bonafilia. Kel wondered why adults seemed to enjoy exchanging observations about things that were obvious. "Which he does often. He likes being muddy."

Kel felt the first stirrings of alarm. He wasn't dirtier than any of the other boys; why was Sister Bonafilia looking and speaking so oddly? He kept his mouth shut, though, as they departed the garden, the Legate marching ahead, Bonafilia piloting Kel through the old fortress at speed. She was muttering under her breath. *Aigon, you who circle the earth with waters, who hold sway over swift-traveling ships, grant unto your daughter the safety of her charge.*

She was praying, Kel realized, and felt that alarm again, sharper this time.

As they reached the front hall, he saw with surprise that the front doors were open. Through them, as if framed in a portrait square, he could see the sun sinking rapidly into the ocean. The sky cast a hot glow over the tin-blue water. At the horizon he could see the towers of drowned Tyndaris, tinted the color of wine.

The scene distracted him, and Kel lost a bit of time, as sometimes happened when he looked at beautiful things. When he was aware again, he found that he was standing among the craggy rocks outside the Orfelinat, flanked by Sister Bonafilia on one side and Jolivet on the other, his red-and-gold uniform glowing like the vanishing sunset.

There was also a horse. Kel stared at it in horror. He had seen horses at a distance before, of course, but never one so close up. It seemed enormous, rising to the sky, its lips curling back over hard white teeth. It was black as night, with rolling black eyes.

"That's right," said the Legate, taking Kel's silence for admiration. "Never ridden a horse before, I'd warrant? You'll like it."

Kel did not think he would like it. He found himself not minding when Sister Bonafilia pulled him close to her side, as if he were a child. (Kel did not think of himself as a child. Children were something else, carefree and silly, not like orphans at all.)

"You must say he will be treated well," burst out Sister Bonafilia in the voice she rarely employed, the one that made orphans burst into tears. "He is so young, to be taken for Palace work—" She straightened her back. "He is a child of Aigon, and under the protection of the God, Legate. Remember it."

Jolivet bared his teeth in a grin. "He will be treated like family, Sister," he said, and reached for Kel.

Kel took a deep breath. He knew how to fight and scratch and kick. He had already drawn back his foot to deliver a vicious kick to the Legate's shin when he caught sight of the look on Sister Bonafilia's face. He could not quite believe the message he read in her eyes, but it was there, as clear as the outline of a tallship on the horizon.

Do not struggle or cry out. Let him take you.

Kel went limp as Jolivet lifted him away. Deadweight. It didn't seem to faze the Legate, though, who swung Kel up onto the monstrous horse's back. Kel's stomach turned over as the world went upside down; when it righted again, he was seated squarely on the beast's saddle, lashed in place by wiry arms. Jolivet had swung himself up behind Kel, his hands gripping the reins. "Hold tight," he said. "We're going to the Palace to see the King."

Possibly he meant to make it sound like a jolly adventure, but Kel didn't know, or care. He'd already leaned over the side of the horse and vomited all over the ground.

x x x

After that, their departure from the Orfelinat was precipitous. Jolivet muttered darkly—some of the sick had gotten on his boots—but Kel felt too miserable and ill to care. There was a great deal of swaying, and of Kel being certain that every time the horse moved its head it was planning to bite him. He remained in this state of high alert as they passed down the cliffs to the Key, the road that ran along the docks, against which lapped the dark waters of the harbor.

Kel was convinced that he would never, at any point, develop an affection for the horse he was sitting on. Still, the view from its back was impressive as they cut through the city. He had spent plenty of time looking *up* at the crowds thronging the city streets, but for the first time now he looked *down* at them. All of them—rich merchants' sons in gaudy fashions, innkeepers and dockworkers trudging home from work, sailors from Hanse and Zipangu, merchants from Marakand and Geumjoseon—made way for Jolivet as he passed.

It really was rather thrilling. Kel began to sit up straighter as they turned up the wide boulevard of the Ruta Magna, which ran from the mouth of the harbor to the Narrow Pass, slicing through the mountains that separated Castellane from its neighbor-kingdom of Sarthe. He had nearly forgotten he had ever felt sick, and his excitement only grew as they neared the Great Hill that loomed over the city.

Cliffs and hills ringed the port city, and Castellane huddled in the bottom of the valley like a hedgehog reluctant to poke its nose out of the safety of its lair. But it was not a city in hiding. It sprawled—and how it sprawled—from the western seas to the Narrow Pass, every bit of it crowded and noisy and dirty and shouting and full of life.

Like most citizens of Castellane, Kel had lived his life in the shadow of the Great Hill but had never expected to set foot upon it, much less make his way to the top, where the Palace of Marivent stood. The Hill—really a range of low limestone peaks covered with a tangle of scrub pine and lavender—was where the nobility lived, their vast estates dotted up and down the slopes. *The rich live high, and the poor live low,* Kel had once heard Sister Bonafilia say. It wasn't a metaphor. The richer you were, the bigger your house and the closer to the Palace, which occupied the highest point in the city.

The nobles liked their pleasures, and sometimes the sounds of their revels drifted down to the city at night. People would wink at one another in the streets and say things like, "It looks as if Lord Montfaucon has started drinking again," or "So Lady Alleyne has rid herself of her third husband, has she?" When you were rich, everyone knew your business and delighted in it, even though they didn't actually know you at all.

They turned off the Ruta Magna and rode through the darkened city streets until they reached the foot of the Hill. Castelguards in red uniforms crowded around the path here; their job was to prevent undesirables from accessing the Hill. Jolivet held Kel firm in the saddle while they rode through the checkpoint, the torches of the guards blazing as they stared curiously at the boy. They must have been wondering if the Arrow Squadron had caught a very small criminal, and, if so, why they were bothering to bring him to Marivent. Most lawbreakers, regardless of age, were destined for a short ride to the gallows of the Tully.

One of the guards dipped a slightly mocking bow. "The King awaits you."

Jolivet just grunted. Kel was getting the impression he didn't talk much.

The path to the Palace wound steeply up the slope through a terrain of lavender, sage, and sweetgrass that turned the mountain deep green in summers. As they reached the top of the mountain, the massive horse puffing, Kel glanced down and saw the city of Castellane spread out before them—the crescent of the port, the lighted ships in the harbor like scattered match tips. The canals of the Temple District. The neat lines of the Silver Streets. The white dome of the Tully, the glow of the clock at the top of the Wind-tower, where it brooded over the city's largest square. The walled area of the Sault, where the Ashkar lived. The Ruta Magna cutting across the city like a dueling scar.

He must have been staring, because Jolivet shook him. They were passing through the North Gate of the Palace, where guests entered. The pennants fastened to the gate-tops indicated which foreign dignitaries were visiting, if any. Right now the blue banner of Sarthe, with its white eagle, fluttered in the salt wind.

Up close, Kel could see that the texture of the white walls was rough, not smooth, and they glittered with bits of crystal. A boy could climb a wall like that, if he was agile and determined. Rough rock meant handholds and footholds. Kel had always been good at scrambling over the rocks in the harbor. He dreamed of joining the Crawlers one day: pickpockets of the Warren who, it was rumored, could clamber up any wall regardless how smooth.

Jolivet shook him again. "Sit up straight, Kellian Saren," he said. "You're about to meet the royal family."

"The *what*?"

Jolivet chuckled. "That's right. The King and Queen of Castel-lane wait on your pleasure."

Kel wasn't sure what reaction Jolivet expected. Excitement, per-haps? Instead Kel immediately curled up like a pillbug. Jolivet yanked him upright as they clattered into a massive square courtyard.

Kel had a blurred impression of arched palisades, with the bulk of the Palace rising behind them. Everywhere were the Castel-guards, charged with protecting the Palace itself, in red-and-gold livery, bearing torches of perfumed wood, which released scented smoke and bright sparks into the sky. Servants, their tunics bearing the lion blazon of the royal family, were rushing to and fro with salvers of wine, fruit, and chocolates; others bore flowers and ar-rangements of peacock feathers bound with golden twine.

Kel could hear laughter and chatter from inside the Palace. Two great bronze doors had been thrown open to the courtyard and the soft evening air. A tall man, not dressed in livery, stood in the arch of the doorway, watching Kel and his captor with narrowed eyes.

Jolivet hauled Kel down from the saddle like a costermonger tossing a sack of onions from a cart. He set Kel on his feet and placed his big hands on the boy's shoulders. There was a touch of puzzlement in his expression as he looked down. "Do you understand what's going on, guttersnipe? You're here to do a service for the King of Castellane."

Kel coughed. His throat still hurt from being sick. "No," he said.

"What do you mean, no?"

The King was a nearly mythic figure in Castellane. Unlike the Queen, he rarely left the Palace, and when he did, it was for ceremonial events: the Marriage to the Sea, the yearly Speech of Independence in Valerian Square. He reminded Kel of the lion on the flag of Castellane: golden and towering. He certainly didn't seem like someone who would talk to orphan brats with no connections to speak of.

"No, thank you," Kel said, mindful of the manners Sister Bonafilia had tried to teach him. "I'd rather not talk to the King. I'd rather go home."

Jolivet raised his eyes to the sky. "Gods above. The boy is simple."

"Aristide?"

A soft voice. Soft voices were like soft hands: They belonged to noble folk, the sort who didn't have to shout to be listened to. Kel looked up and saw the man from the doorway: tall, thin, and bearded, with thick gray hair and aquiline features. Sharply jutting cheekbones shadowed hollow cheeks.

Kel realized suddenly why the man wasn't in livery. He wore a simple gray cloak and tunic, the usual dress of the Ashkar. Around his throat hung a silver medallion on a chain, finely etched with a pattern of numbers and letters.

Kel wasn't entirely sure what being Ashkar meant, but he knew they were not like other people. They were able to do small kinds of magic, even though most magic had disappeared from the world after the Sundering, and they were famous for their physicians' ability to heal.

Because they did not acknowledge Aigon or the other Gods, by Law they must live within the gates of the Sault. They weren't allowed to roam freely in Castellane after sundown—which must mean this man was the only exception to that rule: the King's Counselor. Kel had heard of him only vaguely—a shadowy sort of figure who advised the Court. Counselors were always Ashkar, though Kel did not know why. Sister Jenova had said it was because the Ashkar were cunning by nature. But she had said other, less kind things, as well: that they were dangerous, devious, different. Though when Cas had gotten scalding fever, Sister Jenova had run right to the Sault and roused an Ashkari physician—forgetting, apparently, about all the times she'd said they couldn't be trusted.

The man spoke curtly. "I'll take the boy. Leave us, Aristide."

Jolivet raised an eyebrow. "Good luck to you, Bensimon."

As Jolivet sauntered away, the Ashkar man—Bensimon—crooked a finger in Kel's direction. "Come along."

And he led Kel into the Palace.

Kel's first impression was that everything in Marivent was enormous. The corridors of the Palace were wide as rooms, the staircases grander than tallships. Hallways sprouted in a thousand different directions like branches of coral.

Kel had imagined that everything inside would be white, as it was outside, but the walls were painted in marvelous colors of blue and ochre, sea green and lavender. The furniture was delicate and jewel-like, as if shiny beetles had been scattered about the rooms. Even the shutters, carved and painted with images of flowering gardens, were finely wrought. It had never occurred to Kel that the inside of a building, no matter how grand, could be as beautiful as a sunset. It calmed his racing heart, somehow. Surely terrible things could not happen in a place so lovely.

Unfortunately, he had little opportunity to stare. Bensimon seemed unaware he was escorting a child and did not slow his pace to match Kel's. Instead, Kel had to run to keep up. It seemed ironic, considering he wasn't the one who wanted to be wherever they were going.

Light blazed from torches bolted at intervals along the wall, each at a level higher than Kel could have reached. At length they came to a massive pair of double doors covered in gold-leaf panels, each carved with a scene from Castellane's history: the fleet's defeat of the Empire's ships, the sinking of Tyndaris, the King presenting the first Charters to the Council, the building of the Windtower Clock, the fires of the Scarlet Plague.

Here, Bensimon finally paused. "We are entering the Shining Gallery," he said. "Not quite the throne room, but a ceremonial place. Be respectful."

Kel's first impression on entering the Shining Gallery was of blinding whiteness. He had never seen snow, but he had heard talk of trade caravans trapped in thick drifts of the stuff when they tried to cross the icy peaks north of Hind. White, they had said—everywhere whiteness and a cold that could snap your bones.

In the Gallery, the walls were white, the floor was white, and the ceiling was white. Everything was made of the same white stone as the Palace walls. At the far end of the room, which seemed as vast as a cavern, was a raised dais on which a long table of carved and gilded wood groaned under the weight of crystal glasses, alabaster plates, and delicate porcelain cups.

Kel realized he was hungry. *Blast.*

Bensimon shut the doors behind them and turned to face Kel. "In an hour," he said, "this room will be full of the noble families of Castellane." He paused. "I assume you know of the Council of Twelve? The Charter Houses?"

Kel hesitated, despite his anger at being called ignorant. Maybe it would be better to let Bensimon think he was ignorant. Maybe they would send him back home. But Bensimon would likely guess he was pretending. Everyone in Castellane knew of the nobles on the Hill, and particularly the Charter Families. Their names and their positions were as much common knowledge as the names of the city's streets.

"Cazalet," he said. "Roverge. Alleyne. I can't name them all, but everyone knows about them. They live on the Hill. They have Charters"—he remembered Sister Bonafilia's lessons, screwing up his eyes as he reached for the words—"which are, um, special permissions from the King to control trade on the Gold Roads." (He did not add that Bonafilia had described this as "a rotten plan to make the wealthy more wealthy, of no benefit to the common merchants of Castellane.")

"And over the seas, yes," said Bensimon. "Remember, each House has its own Charter—House Raspail runs the trade in timber, Alleyne in silk. A Charter is itself a valuable thing, granted by the King, or revoked at his pleasure." He sighed, scrubbing his hands through his cropped hair. "We have no time for a lesson, though. I understand that you don't want to be here. That is unfortunate. You are a citizen of Castellane, correct? But you have Marakandi heritage, perhaps, or Hindish?"

Kel shrugged. He'd often wondered the same, given that his light brown skin was a shade darker than the olive tone common in Castellane, but unlike some of the other children in the Orfelinat, who knew their backgrounds, he had no answers. "I was born here. I don't know about my parents. Never met them."

"If you were born here, then you owe the King and the city allegiance," said Bensimon. "You are"—he wrinkled his brow—"ten years old, correct? You must be aware of the existence of the Crown Prince."

From somewhere in the back of his mind, Kel dredged up the name. "Conor," he said.

Bensimon's eyebrows rose into his hairline of thick gray curls. "*Prince* Conor," he corrected. "Tonight, a delegation from Sarthe will be visiting Marivent. As you may or may not know, there has been unrest between our kingdoms for quite some time."

Sarthe and Castellane were neighbors and quarreled often over taxes, goods, and access to the Gold Roads. Most of the sailors at the docks referred to Sarthians as "those bastards on the border."

Kel supposed that was what unrest meant.

"As always, the King—ever with the best interests of the citizens of Castellane at heart—is seeking peace with our neighbors. Among the political, ah, *treasures* of our city is our Crown Prince Conor. It is always possible that, at some point in the future, the King may wish to form an alliance between his son and one of the royal family of Sarthe. For that reason, it is important that, even at his young age, Prince Conor attend tonight's banquet. Unfortunately, he is indisposed." He looked closely at Kel. "Are you following me?"

"The Prince is sick, so he can't go to a party," said Kel. "But what's that got to do with me?"

"The Prince cannot be seen to be absent from tonight's affair. Therefore, you will take his place."

The room seemed to turn upside down. "I'll do *what*?"

"You will take his place. He isn't expected to speak much. You are about his height, his age, his coloring—his mother the Queen is Marakandi, as you no doubt know. We will clean you up, dress you as a prince should be dressed. You will sit quietly through dinner. You will not speak or draw attention to yourself. You may eat as much as you like as long as you do not make yourself sick." Bensimon crossed his arms over his chest. "At the end of the night, if you have performed satisfactorily, you will be given a purse of gold crowns to take back to the Sisters of Aigon. If not, you will earn nothing but a scolding. Do you understand the arrangement?"

Kel understood arrangements. He understood being given a coin or two to run a message for the Sisters, or the prize of an apple or candy for picking up a package from a tallship and delivering it to a merchant's house. But the concept of a gold crown, much less a purse of them, was beyond comprehension.

"People will know what Con—Prince Conor—looks like," said Kel. "They won't be fooled."

Bensimon slipped something out of his pocket. It was a hammered-silver oblong on a chain, not dissimilar to the one the adviser wore around his own neck. Etched into it and picked out by the flame of the firelight was a delicate pattern of numbers and letters. This was Ashkari magic. Only the Ashkar knew how to manipulate and combine letters and numbers in ways that wrung enchantment from their design; only the Ashkar, in fact, could perform any sort of magic at all. It had been that way since the Sundering.

With little ceremony, Bensimon dropped the chain over Kel's head, letting the tablet slip below the collar of his ragged tunic.

"Will this make me look like the Prince?" asked Kel, trying to peer down his own shirt.

"Not quite. What it will do is make those who look at you, and already see a boy who resembles our Crown Prince in complexion and size, more inclined to *regard* you as Prince Conor. To hear his voice when you speak. Your eyes are wrong," he added, half to himself, "but it does not matter; people see what they expect to see, and they will expect to see the Prince. It will not physically change your features, you understand? It will simply change the vision of those who look at you. No one who really knows who you are will be fooled, but all others will."

In a way, Kel did understand. There were tales of the way magic had once been before the Sundering, when a spell could blow a mountain apart or transform a man into a dragon. Magic now—Ashkari magic, talismans and charms and poultices, for sale in Fleshmarket Square—was a shadow of a shadow of what had once been. It could incline and convince and direct, but it could not change the substance of things.

"I would suggest," said Bensimon, "that, at this juncture, you speak."

Kel tugged awkwardly at the chain around his neck. "I don't want to do it," he said. "But I ain't got no choice, have I?"

Bensimon smiled thinly. "You do not. And don't say *ain't*. It makes you sound like a mudrat from the Warren docks."

"I *am* a mudrat from the Warren docks," Kel pointed out.

"Not tonight," said Bensimon.

Kel was brought to the tepidarium: a massive chamber with two stone-bound pools sunk into the middle of a marble floor. A rose window looked out over the nighttime glow of Castellane. Kel tried to keep his eyes on the horizon as he was poked, prodded, and scrubbed with vicious thoroughness. The water ran dark brown into the drain.

Kel thought about whether he trusted this Bensimon and decided he did not. Bensimon said the Prince was sick—indisposed—but Jolivet had come to the Orfelinat a month ago. He couldn't have known then that the Crown Prince would take ill tonight and need a stand-in.

Nor did the idea that he'd be sent home at the end of the night with a bag of gold make much sense. There was a well-known tale in the Maze about the Ragpicker King, the most famous criminal in Castellane. It was said that he'd once invited three rival criminals to his mansion and fed them a splendid dinner, offering them a partnership in his illegal empire. But none of them had been able to agree on anything, and at the end of the night the Ragpicker King had regretfully poisoned his guests, on the grounds that now they knew too much about his business. (He paid for glorious funerals for all three, however.)

Kel could not help but feel that he had already been told a great deal that he ought not to know, and was about to learn more of the same. He tried to think of what he would do were he playing a part in a game with Cas, but could imagine no better strategy than keeping his head down.

After the bath, he was dusted, perfumed, shod, and dressed in a steel-blue satin tailcoat with silver links at the cuffs and collar. He was given velvet trousers as soft as mouse's fur. His hair was trimmed and his eyelashes curled.

When he finally went to look at himself in the mirror that covered the whole west wall, he thought, with a sinking feeling, that if he ever stepped out in the streets of the Maze looking like this, he'd be beaten six ways by the Crawlers and run up the flagpole outside the Tully.

"Cease shuffling your feet," said Bensimon, who had spent the past hour watching the goings-on from a shadowed corner of the room, like a hawk planning its descent onto a family of rabbits. "Come here."

Kel approached the adviser as the rest of the Palace servants melted away like mist. In a moment, he was alone in the room with Bensimon, who grabbed him under the chin, tilted his head up, and surveyed him unceremoniously. "Tell me again what you're doing tonight."

"Being C—Prince Conor. Sitting at the banquet table. Not saying much."

Apparently satisfied, Bensimon let Kel go. "The King and Queen know who you really are, of course; don't worry about them. They are well used to playing parts."

Somehow Kel's imagination hadn't gotten this far. "The King is going to pretend I'm his son?"

Bensimon snorted. "I wouldn't get too excited," he said. "Very little of any of this is about you."

That struck Kel as a relief. If everyone important ignored him, maybe he could make it through the night.

Bensimon led Kel back into the warren of corridors that seemed to make up the interior of the Palace. They took a back set of servants' stairs down to a small but elegant room full of books; there was a tall golden door at the far end of the room, through which Kel could hear music and laughter.

For the first time, Kel's heart jolted with real longing. *Books.* The only reading material he'd ever had were a few shabby novels donated to the Orfelinat by charitable patrons, satisfying tales of pirates and phoenixes, sorcerers and sailors, but of course they didn't *belong* to him. The study books—histories of empires fallen, the building of the Gold Roads—were kept locked up by the Sisters, brought out to be read from during classes. He'd been given an old book of tales by a boatswain once, in return for running a message, but Sister Jenova had confiscated it. According to her, sailors only read two things: murder stories and pornography.

These books were as beautiful as the sun sinking behind Tyndaris. Kel could smell the scent of the leather that bound them, the ink on their pages, the bitterness of the stamping mill where the paper was made.

Bensimon was watching him with narrowed eyes, the way a professional gambler eyed a mark. "You can read, then. And you like it?"

Kel didn't have to reply. Two people had swept into the room, surrounded by Castelguards, and he was stunned into silence.

Kel's first thought was that these people were the most beautiful he had ever seen. Then he wondered if it was just because they were so fastidiously groomed, and their clothes were so lovely. He didn't know the words yet for silk and satin and cloth-of-gold, but he knew when things looked rich and soft, and shimmered in firelight.

The King was familiar: unsurprising, since his face was on every coin in Castellane. On the coins he was in profile, gazing to the right—toward unconquered Sarthe, went the tale. But the coins did not show the breadth of him, his barrel chest or wrestler's arms. He made Kel quail with his sheer size and presence. His eyes were light, high-set, his beard and hair a pale mixture of blond and early silvering.

The Queen had dark, flowing hair like the Fear River at night-fall, and smooth russet-brown skin. She was slim and tall, her hands heavy with rings, each set with a different, glimmering stone. Ropes of gold circled her neck and wrist, and her hair was dressed with pins in the shape of golden lilies. She had been a Marakandi princess, Kel remembered, and gold was a symbol of good luck in that country.

The Queen regarded Kel with the dark eyes that had been the subject of a thousand poems and ballads. The citizens of Castellane were competitive about the beauty of their Queen, and wanted it widely known that she was more beautiful than the Queens of Sarthe or Hind. The Queen of Hanse, Kel had been told, looked like a constipated waterfowl in comparison with Queen Lilibet of Castellane.

"That's the boy?" she asked. Her voice was rich, sweet as sugared rosewater.

"Quite," said Bensimon. He seemed to have a real fondness for the word. "Are you ready, Highnesses?"

The Queen nodded. The King shrugged. And the Castelguards threw open the golden door as the music in the Gallery turned to a processional tune. The King passed slowly through, the Queen following. Neither of them glanced back.

Kel hesitated. He felt his hair ruffle; Bensimon had placed something on his head: a golden circlet. He felt the adviser's hands linger over his head, almost like a blessing.

Bensimon grunted, then gave Kel a shove. "Go *after* them," he ordered, and Kel stumbled through the golden door, into the blinding light.

Kel noticed two things at once. First, Bensimon had been right: The Gallery was now full of nobles. Kel had never seen so many in one place. He was used to a glimpse of a decorated carriage rolling through the cobbled streets, perhaps a gloved hand dangling languorously from an open window. Sometimes a noble in velvets and jewels might be found on a tallship, arguing with the captain about whether or not to sell shares in the ship's next voyage. But that was a rare sighting, like the sighting of a salamander. He had never imagined being surrounded by them—either nobles *or* salamanders.

The second thing was the room itself. He now understood why it had seemed so white. It was clearly kept blank, an untouched canvas waiting for the painter's brush. The walls, which had been bare, were now decorated with jewel-toned frescoes depicting the glories of Castellane. Kel did not know how it was possible. (Later, he would find out they were transparent screens, lowered over the walls, and not paint at all.) *Look*, they said, *how grand a place is our city, and how great.*

The floors had been covered with thick Marakandi rugs, and along the east wall curtains had been drawn away to reveal a pillared arcade. In between the pillars were potted trees painted gold, their leaves gilded and apples and berries of colored glass hanging from their branches. Above the arcade, a gallery of musicians played, all of them in the Palace colors of red and gold. The great hearth was the same, but now a fire blazed in it, large enough to roast a dozen cows.

The inhabitants of the Hill had come to line a sort of shining pathway to the high table, smiling and inclining their heads as the royal family progressed through the room. In the tepidarium, Bensimon had told Kel to keep his head up and glance to neither the right nor the left, but Kel could not stop himself from looking.

The men wore brocade coats and high boots of incised leather; the women were floating clouds of silks and satins, bows and lace, their hair swept up and pinned through with ornaments of all shapes: golden roses, silver lilies, gilt stars, brass swords. Such finery was the stuff of the society drawings one could buy from artists in Fleshmarket Square, where the daughters and sons of merchants went to learn of the scandalous doings of the noble Houses, and imagine marrying into one.

Bensimon had fallen into step beside Kel, the crowd of nobles thinning out as they reached the high table. It looked much as it had before, though yet more decoration had been added. Peacock feathers dipped in gold paint drooped over the sides of gilded epergnes, and a ribbon of lilies laced together with golden chains snaked down the center of the table. Their scent—waxy, too-sweet—filled the room.

In a daze, Kel allowed himself to be guided by Bensimon toward one of the three tall chairs grouped in the middle of the table. The Queen was on Kel's left; on his right, a pretty girl about his own age, wearing pale-yellow silk, her dark-blond hair in tightly curled ringlets.

Kel shot a look at Bensimon, almost of panic: Why had they sat him next to another child? An adult might have ignored him, but the blond girl was already looking at him with a lively curiosity that indicated she knew Prince Conor fairly well.

Bensimon raised an eyebrow and was gone, taking a place just behind the King's chair. The blond girl leaned across her plate to whisper to Kel.

"I heard you were sick," she said. "I didn't expect you'd be here."

It was a lifeline. Kel caught at it. "The King insisted," he said, in a low voice. Hopefully that was how the Prince referred to his father? Kel knew Bensimon had said that the talisman would make him sound like the Prince as well as look like him, but surely it could not change the words he said. He chose them carefully, thinking as he did so of all the times he and Cas had played at being highborn adventurers, how they had modeled their speech on that of the nobles who they'd read of in books. "I was offered no choice."

The blond girl tossed her curls. "You *are* ill," she said. "Usually you would have made a fuss about coming, or be joking about it at least."

Kel put that away in the back of his mind. The Prince was someone who had no trouble kicking up a temper, and liked to make jokes. So they had that in common. It was useful information.

"Antonetta." The woman seated opposite them spoke under her breath, her eyes on the blond girl. "Do sit up straight."

Antonetta. So that was the girl's name, and the woman must be her mother. She was very beautiful, with coils of fair hair and a great deal of pale bosom swelling over the bodice of a raw-silk dress the same color as her daughter's. Her attention rested on Antonetta only for a moment, though, before she was engaged in conversation with a black-bearded man with clever eyebrows.

"Who's that man?" Kel muttered to Antonetta, who was now sitting rigidly upright. "The one flirting with your mother?"

It was a bit of a daring thing to say, but Antonetta grinned—as if she expected this sort of comment from Conor Aurelian. "You don't recognize him?" she said incredulously. She was folding her napkin on her lap; Kel mimicked her movements. "That's Senex Petro d'Ustini, one of the ambassadors from Sarthe. Next to him is Sena Anessa Toderino."

Of course. Kel should have recognized them immediately: a man and a woman, both in Sarthian dark-blue. Senex Petro's sapphire earring glittered against his olive skin, while Sena Anessa had a great deal of hair piled in knots on her head and a long, patrician nose.

Farther down the table sat another boy around Kel's age. He looked Shenzan, with straight black hair and a mischievous face. He winked at Kel, who liked him immediately, though he knew the wink was meant not for him, but for Prince Conor.

"I see Joss is trying to get your attention," said Antonetta, making a face at the boy. It wasn't an unfriendly face, more a teasing one. "He's probably miserable having to sit next to Artal Gremont."

Antonetta must mean the heavyset, thick-necked man on Joss's left. His hair was chopped short, as if he were a soldier, and he wore the armband of a gladiator, which looked a little ridiculous over the damask silk of his tunic. Kel had heard his name before. Though he was a noble, he amused himself battling some of Castellane's most famous fighters in the Arena. Everyone—save Gremont, perhaps, who was in line to inherit the tea and coffee Charter—knew the games were rigged in his favor.

"Lady Alleyne," said Senex d'Ustini to Antonetta's mother. "Your gown is truly magnificent, and is that not Sarthian *sontoso* embroidery upon the cuffs? You are, indeed, a walking endorsement for the glories of the silk trade."

Lady Alleyne? House Alleyne held the silk Charter. Which meant Antonetta, who was currently playing with her fork, stood to inherit the richest of all the Charters. Kel felt a little sick to his stomach.

"Silk has other uses besides fashion," Antonetta interjected. "The Ashkar use it in bandages and thread. One can make sails from it, and in Shenzhou it is used instead of paper to write upon."

Sena Anessa chuckled. "Very clever, Demoselle Antonetta—"

"Too clever," said Artal Gremont. "No one likes a clever girl. Do they, Montfaucon?"

Montfaucon was apparently the man sitting across from him. He was spectacularly dressed in pink velvet and silver braid, his skin a dark, rich brown. "Gremont," he began, sounding irritable, but did not finish his sentence, for the food had arrived.

And what food it was. Not the mush and stews they served in the Orfelinat, but roast capons with white cabbage, ducks stuffed with curried plums, herb and cheese tarts, whole grilled fish dressed with oil and lemon, and Sarthian dishes like pork basted with rose-water on a bed of noodles.

You may eat as much as you like as long as you do not make yourself sick, Bensimon had said.

Kel went to work. He was hungry half the time anyway, and he was starved right now, having emptied his stomach on Jolivet's boots. He tried to copy what the others were doing with his cutlery, but hands were faster than knives and forks. When he sank his fingers into a slice of cheese and sage tart, he saw Bensimon glare at him.

Antonetta, he noted, was not eating, but was looking down at her food with a furious expression. The glamorous Montfaucon winked in her direction. "When beauty and wisdom can be married together, that is the ideal, but in the usual course of events the Gods gift one or the other. I do think our Antonetta might be one of the lucky exceptions."

"One cannot have everything, or the Gods would come to envy mortals," said another man, this one with cold eyes. He had narrow features and light-olive skin, and reminded Kel of illustrations in his schoolbooks of Castellani nobles going back hundreds of years. "Is that not what happened to the Callatians? They built their towers too close to heaven, challenged the Gods with their accomplishments, and for it their Empire was destroyed?"

"A dark view, Roverge," said a kind-looking older man. He was pallid, like someone who spent a lot of time indoors. "Empires tend toward entropy, you know. It is difficult to grasp so much power. Or so I was taught in the schoolroom long ago." He smiled at Kel. "Have you not been taught the same, Prince?"

Everyone turned to look pleasantly at Kel, who nearly gagged on a mouthful of tart. Wildly, he imagined what would happen the moment they realized he wasn't the Crown Prince. He'd be surrounded by the Castelguard. They'd drag him from the Palace and toss him over the walls, where he'd roll down the mountain until he splashed into the ocean and was eaten by a crocodile.

"But Sieur Cazalet," said Antonetta, "are you not the master of all the wealth in Castellane? And is not wealth also power?"

Cazalet. Kel knew the name: The Cazalet Charter was banking, and gold crown coins were sometimes called cazalets on the street.

"See?" said Artal Gremont. "Too clever."

Kel plastered a smile upon his face. He could not make his mouth stretch very far, which was likely fortunate; it gave him the aspect of smiling coolly, rather than enthusiastically. Enthusiasm, as he would later find, was deemed suspicious in a prince. "I am still learning, of course, Sieur Cazalet," he said. "But it is said by the sages that he who desires all, loses all."

Bensimon's mouth quirked, and a look of real surprise went over the Queen's face, quickly hidden. Antonetta smiled, which Kel found pleased him.

The King reacted not at all to this pronouncement by his pretend son, but the russet-haired delegate from Sarthe chuckled. "It's nice to see your son is well read, Markus."

"Thank you, Sena Anessa," said the Queen. The King said nothing. He was regarding Kel shrewdly over the rim of his tall silver cup.

"That was nicely said," Antonetta whispered to Kel. Her eyes shone, making her look twice as pretty. Kel's stomach tightened again, in an unfamiliar and this time not unpleasant way. "Perhaps you are not so ill after all."

"Oh, no," Kel said fervently. "I'm extremely unwell. I might forget anything at any moment."

The adults had gone back to their own conversation. Kel could hardly follow it—too many names he didn't know, both of people and things, like treaties and trade agreements. That was, until Senex Petro turned to the King with a bland smile and said, "Speaking of outrageous demands, Your Highness, is there news of the Ragpicker King?"

Kel's eyes widened. He knew the name of the Ragpicker King; everyone in the city of Castellane did, but he would not have thought the nobles familiar with it. The Ragpicker King belonged to the streets of the city, to the shadows where the Vigilants did not dare to go, to the gambling hells and dosshouses of the Maze.

Once, Kel had asked Sister Bonafilia how old the Ragpicker King was. She had replied that he had always existed, as long as she had been aware to know it, and indeed there was something timeless about the figure he cut in Castellane, striding through the shadows all in black, with an army of pickpockets and cutpurses at his beck and call. He did not fear the Arrow Squadron or the city watch. He feared nothing at all.

"He is a criminal," said the King, his rough voice uninflected. "There will always be criminals."

"But he calls himself a king," said Petro, still with the same easy smile. "Does that not seem a challenge to you?"

Sena Anessa looked anxious. It was almost, Kel thought, like someone in the schoolroom throwing a punch. One waited to see if the punch would be returned or ignored. Friends of the one doing the punching fretted. Going on the attack was always a risk.

But Markus only smiled. "He is no threat to me," he said. "Children play the game of Castles, but it is no challenge to Marivent. Now, shall we discuss the issues I had raised earlier, about the Narrow Pass?"

Sena Anessa looked relieved. "An excellent idea," she said, and voices along the table began to chime in with comments about trade and the Great Southwestern Road that might as well have been spoken in Sarthian for all that Kel understood them.

Antonetta tapped Kel's wrist with the dull edge of her knife. "They're bringing dessert," she said, gesturing for Kel to pick up his cutlery. "You were right. You *are* forgetful."

Kel was mostly full anyway, or so he thought until the sweets appeared. Plums and peaches soaked in rosewater and honey, flower petals crystallized in sugar, glasses of sweet-sour iced sherbet, mugs of sweetened chocolate and cream, custards studded with pomegranate seeds, and plates of marzipan cakes decorated with colorful pastel icing.

The musicians played a soft tune as the last silver platter was brought out, bearing a magnificent cake in the shape of a phoenix, lavishly frosted with gold and bronze, each shimmering wing perfect down to the last feather. As they set the cake upon the table, it burst into flame, to a chorus of admiring noises.

Kel could not see what was admirable about setting a perfectly good cake on fire, but he knew he was supposed to look impressed when a piece of the phoenix dessert was placed in front of him, shimmering on a gold plate. It was sponge cake in hard, shining icing, like the carapace of a beetle.

He almost didn't want to eat it. It had always seemed one of the greatest tragedies of the Sundering to him that not only had the world lost almost all magic, but that creatures like phoenixes and dragons, manticores and basilisks, had vanished overnight.

Still. He picked a piece of icing off the cake in front of him and put it in his mouth. It seemed to explode in flavors stronger than any he had ever experienced, a thousand times the sweetness of apples, mixed with spice and the perfume of flowers. He pressed his tongue against the back of his teeth, half dazed with the savor of it.

He wished he could close his eyes. Everything seemed both as if it were fading and too clear at the same time. He could hear his own heart beating, and beyond that the voices of nobles chattering and laughing, with a sound like knives tearing through silk. He knew that, under the laughter, they were dueling with their words, insulting and challenging and praising one another in a language he knew, but did not understand.

Through the fringed curtain of his lashes, he saw the King looking at the phoenix cake. There was a sort of weary loathing on his face that surprised Kel. Certainly a monarch could not feel so strongly about pastry; the King must be thinking about something else.

Kel slipped further toward sleep as the night went on; apparently there was only so long that being terrified could keep one awake. Eventually he slipped his knife into his lap. Every time he found himself drifting off, he would close his hand around it and the pain would jolt him back awake.

The banquet did not seem to end so much as fade away. First one group left, and then another. Joss Falconet waved to him as he departed alone. Antonetta kissed his cheek, which set his heart tripping faster and made him blush hard enough that he could only hope no one noticed.

The music softened into silence. The peacock feathers, drowned under their weight of gold paint, drooped like the heads of sleepy children. The fire had burned down to cherry embers by the time everyone was gone from the room save the royal family and the King's adviser.

And Kel.

"Well, I thought that all went rather well, darling," the Queen observed. She was still seated at the table, delicately peeling the green skin from a sweet dalandan with her long fingers. "Considering how difficult the Sarthians like to be about every little detail."

The King did not reply. Instead he stood up, looking down at Kel. It was like being regarded by a giant. "The boy is peculiarly literate," he said. His voice was gravelly, deep as a drowned city. "I thought he would have little knowledge save what he had picked up on the streets."

"He is from one of Your Highness's orphanages," said Bensimon. "They have books, teaching. Royal generosity at work."

"He ate like a starveling thing," said the Queen, separating the coral flesh of the dalandan from its white core. Her voice was sandpaper and honey. "It was unseemly."

"He recovered from the mistake," said Bensimon. "That is important. And he did well with Antonetta Alleyne. She is a friend of Conor's. If she did not notice the difference, then who would?"

Kel cleared his throat. It was strange to be talked about as if he were not there. "I'd like to go back now."

The Queen lifted her eyes from her fruit. The King and Bensimon both looked silently at Kel. He tried to imagine rising to his feet, stretching out a hand, and saying, *Thank you, but I am leaving now.* He could bow politely, perhaps. Someday this would be a story he would tell—his one night of seeing what power looked like up close. Of realizing that it had a feeling like velvet against your skin at one moment, and the edge of a blade the next.

But he knew better than that. This was never meant to be a story he could tell.

"Back?" said the Queen. "Back to your filthy orphanage, is that it? Not very grateful." She licked her thumb. "Bensimon. You said he would be grateful."

"He does not yet know the true purpose of his visit," said Bensimon. "If you find him acceptable, I will explain it to him. He will then, I expect, be very grateful indeed."

The Queen frowned. "I don't think—"

"He is acceptable," said the King. "As long as Conor agrees."

He snapped his fingers. "Make your explanations, Mayesh. I will be in the Star Tower. It is a clear night."

With that, he turned on his heel and left. The Queen, a darkly rebellious gleam in her eye, departed flanked by Castelguards, without another look at Kel.

It was as it had been before, no one in the room but Kel and the King's Counselor. Though now, the remains of food were scattered across the table. The musicians had gone, the fire burned down to ash.

Kel curled and uncurled his hand under the table. It was sticky with blood. He looked at Bensimon. "You said . . . I would be going back."

"I did not know if the King would find you acceptable or not," said Bensimon. "It seems he did. Get up. We are not done yet."

Kel hated it when adults said *we* when what they meant was *you*. He frowned as he once again followed Bensimon through the winding corridors of the Palace. Many of the torches had been put out; he could no longer see the contents of the Palace rooms and stumbled as they made their way up a massive stairway, which seemed to curve in on itself like the whorl of a seashell.

Another few turns and Bensimon was leading him down a marble hall and into a grand room. This room, at least, was lit, and decorated in soft hues of fawn and blue. A velvet-draped bed stood in one corner, and next to it, a smaller bed, which puzzled Kel. Was one bed for a parent and the other a child? Yet there were no other signs of children: The furniture was polished mahogany with ivory pieces set in; the paintings on the walls depicted Lotan, the Father of the Gods, with his three sons: Ascalon, Anibal, and Aigon. War, death, and the sea. An iron spiral staircase led up through an opening in the ceiling.

Spread across a nearby table was a clutter of different weapons. Kel knew nothing about weapons and could not have named most of them, though he guessed some to be daggers and others, short-swords. They had delicately incised handles of ivory and jade, studded with gems in different colors.

There was a slight commotion at the door. Kel looked up to a swirl of Castelguards outside, like an incursion of flames. In their midst was a boy, who passed through the door and closed it firmly behind him.

Bensimon straightened up; he did not seem surprised. "Prince Conor."

Kel felt his stomach drop. Here was the boy he'd been impersonating. A boy who had clearly never been sick. He gathered, now, that it had all been a test—and that this was somehow the final part.

The Crown Prince was all in steel blue, just like Kel. He was not wearing a circlet, but Kel would have known him for a prince regardless. He was tall for his age, with his mother's fine features, and there was a sort of leaping flame behind his eyes and laughing expression on his face that made Kel want to smile at him, which was startling enough in itself. He knew the boy ought to be terrifying—he was royalty—and he was, and yet Kel wanted to smile at the Prince all the same.

Though he had no more years than Kel, Conor seemed worlds older as he crossed the room with a light step and said, "How was it, then? Being me?"

An unexpected ache bloomed like a flower behind Kel's rib cage. *I want to be like him,* Kel thought. *I want to walk through the world as if it will reshape itself around my dreams and desires. I want to seem as if I could touch the stars with light fingers and pull them down to be my playthings.*

It was strange to want something you had never known you wanted.

Kel just nodded, as if to say that it was all fine. Conor tilted his head to the side, like a curious robin. He came closer to Kel and, without any self-consciousness, took his hand and turned it over.

Conor made a startled noise. Across Kel's palm were the weals of multiple knife slashes.

"I was trying to keep myself awake," Kel said. He was looking at his hand next to Conor's. His own skin was a shade darker from exposure to the sun, and Conor's palms were smooth and free of scars or blisters.

"Yes, I saw," said Conor. "I was watching, tonight. From behind a screen."

He let go of Kel's hand.

"That is a quite impressive determination, really," said Bensimon. "And a resistance to pain."

Conor's gaze was steady, clear, and gray. *Your eyes are wrong*, Bensimon had said. "Leave us, Mayesh," he said. "I would talk to Kel alone."

Kel rather expected the Counselor to put up a fight. Instead, Mayesh Bensimon seemed to be hiding a smile. "As you wish," he said, and swirled from the room in a cloud of gray cloak.

When he was gone, Kel rather missed him. Bensimon was the person he had known longest in the Palace. Prince Conor, though Kel had spent the night pretending to be him, was a stranger. He watched as Conor went over to the table and picked up one of the daggers and then another. Perhaps this was the end of things, he thought with some dismay. The journey, the peculiar ritual of dinner, and now the Crown Prince would stab him to death.

"Do you like weapons?" Conor said. "I could give you a dagger, if you liked."

Kel felt inordinately pleased to have correctly identified the presence of daggers. Still, this did not seem promising. "To do what with?" he asked, suspiciously.

Conor smiled crookedly. "I don't know what you like, you see," he said. "I'm trying to think how to convince you to stay."

"Stay? Here? In the Palace?"

Conor sat down on the edge of the smaller bed. "My father fostered in the kingdom of Malgasi," he said. "They have a tradition there. When a prince turns ten years old, he is given a sort of—

bodyguard. *Királar,* they call him. Sword Catcher. He is meant to stand in for the prince, to—to protect him from danger. He learns to walk and talk like him, to dress like him. He is made to look like him."

"Made to look like him?" Kel echoed.

"Talismans, charms. Posy-drops to change the color of his eyes." He sighed. "I am not making it sound very pleasant, but I told myself I would be honest with you. There is no point not being. You would find out, eventually."

"You want me," Kel said, slowly, "to be your Sword Catcher?"

Conor nodded. "My father could order you, but I do not want someone reluctant. I want someone who *wants* to do it. And not someone torn from their family, either. That is why—you are from an orphanage?"

Kel nodded. He was too stunned to speak.

Conor relaxed minutely. "That is good. Jolivet did not lie to me, at least." He looked at Kel. "What do you think?"

"I think," Kel said, "that it sounds dangerous, and probably difficult. I think if you are looking for someone who *wants* to do it, that may also be difficult."

Conor exhaled painfully. "As you say."

He looked deflated, which brought home the peculiarity of the situation. Kel had not known what to expect of a meeting with the Crown Prince of Castellane, but he had certainly not expected him to be *depressed.* "Well, you could *try* to convince me," he said. "Tell me, what about it would be good?"

Conor looked up, his eyes brightening. "Really?" He sat up straight. "Well, you would live in the Palace. You would have whatever you wanted, most of the time. Within reason, but any clothes or books or—well, really anything. If you saw it in a shop window, I would get it for you. Unless it was a jade elephant or something else enormous."

"That does seem impractical," Kel said gravely, fighting a grin.

"We would learn together," said Conor. "Jolivet isn't the most agreeable fellow, but he's the best sword-trainer out there. You would become an expert fighter. And my tutors are teaching me everything there is to know; they would teach you, too. You would speak a dozen languages, know the history of all Dannemore, the patterns of the stars, all the Great Equations."

Despite himself, something kindled inside Kel. It was small and bright, a distant signal fire. It startled him. He had not expected to feel truly tempted.

"You would never be hungry," Conor said softly. "And you would never be lonely. You would sleep here, beside me, and we would always be together. And your life would be extraordinary."

Kel leaned back against the table. *Extraordinary*. He knew the word—from lessons, mostly.

Conor leaned forward in excitement. "You would meet royalty from all over, people descended from famous heroes. You would watch the greatest dancers dance, hear the best musicians. You would see things hardly anyone ever sees. You would travel the whole world."

Kel thought of the *White Rock* near the Orfelinat; that had been the ship he sailed with Cas across imaginary oceans. He thought of the marbles they used to weight down their map in the endless game of where-do-you-want-to-go. They had both always known they would never see those distant lands.

"See the world," he said. "With—you?"

Conor nodded eagerly. "Most of the time you won't be pretending to be me. You'll be given another identity. The name of a noble. And when I become King, you stop being the Sword Catcher. After that, you will become like Jolivet, the leader of Castellane's finest soldiers. The Arrow Squadron. And one day, you can retire in honor and wealth."

Honor sounded boring; wealth less so.

"But perhaps you had something else you wished to do? Like becoming a merchant, or a guildmaster?" said Conor, uncertainly. He looked tired. Kel had not thought rich boys ever looked weary like that. "I won't keep you here against your will. I told my father that."

I told my father. That he meant the King was strange enough, but even stranger, Kel saw that Conor's hands, laced together as they were, were shaking. He really did need him, Kel thought in shock. He had never been needed before. Cas was his friend, but Cas didn't *need* him, and neither did Sister Bonafilia or the others. Parents needed their children, but he had never had parents. He had not known what it meant to be needed by someone else: that it made you want to protect them. To his own surprise, he wanted to protect this boy, the Prince of Castellane. Wanted to stand between him and a forest of bristling fléchettes. Wanted to stare down and demolish any enemy that wished Conor Aurelian harm.

It was the first thing he had *wanted* to do since he had come through the Palace gates. Well, besides eat.

Perhaps you had something else you wished to do? Like becoming a merchant, or a guildmaster? When Kel turned sixteen, the Orfelinat would eject him, penniless, into the world. It existed to help children—and only children. Untrained, largely untutored, on the streets of Castellane, there would be nothing for him. Even sailors were trained from a young age. He could scrape by as a lamplighter, or a ship's boy if he was lucky, and would be poor as dirt. Or he could be a criminal—pick pockets or join the Crawlers, the highest he had ever dared to dream—and wind up dangling from the gallows of the Tully.

He took a deep breath. "Extraordinary, you say?"

And Conor began to smile.

CHAPTER ONE

I don't see why I have to get married *now*," complained Conor Darash Aurelian, Crown Prince of Castellane, Duke of Mara-kand (an honorary title he had inherited from his mother), and Potentate of Sarema (a small, deserted island near Taprobana that had been claimed by Castellane some decades ago when a merchant ship planted the lion flag upon its few feet of shoreline; as far as anyone knew, the flag was still there, leaving Castellane's claim to the rocky protuberance uncontested).

Kel just smiled. Conor was looking dramatically aggrieved, which did not actually mean he was feeling dramatically aggrieved. Kel knew Conor's expressions better than he knew his own. Conor might be annoyed about the pressure to get married, or he might be annoyed about the speech the Queen had ordered him to give in Valerian Square today (the reason he and Conor were currently jammed into a carriage with blacked-out windows, boiling hot and squashed between velvet cushions, with Jolivet and Mayesh glaring at them from the opposite seats). Or he might not be annoyed at all, and simply be indulging his flair for the dramatic.

Either way, it wasn't Kel's problem. He wasn't the one trying to talk Conor into a politically advantageous match. In fact, he was against the whole idea. He was quite comfortable with the way things were, and Conor marrying would upset the balance.

"Then don't get married," growled Jolivet. He was dour as ever despite being decked out in full uniform—miles of gold braid, scarlet tunic and trousers, and a helmet so profoundly ceremonial that while he was currently carrying it in his lap, the plumes brushed his chin. Mayesh Bensimon, beside him, looked like a ragged gray crow by comparison: He wore his plain Counselor's robes, his curling white hair spilling over the collar. But then, as an Ashkar, he was only permitted to wear blue or gray in public, which vastly limited any potential sartorial splendor. "That cousin of yours in Detmarch can be King of Castellane, and you can take yourself off to head up the army. Give General Archambault a rest on the border."

Kel held in a laugh. It was true that when a Castellani royal family had more than one heir, the second was usually trained up to become the leader of the army. If Conor had had a sibling, he could have swapped places with them, though Kel could not imagine Conor doing any such thing, even in theory. He hated insects and dirt, and the army, as far as Kel understood, involved a great deal of both. Besides, he was young—only twenty-three—and had years to get married and produce an heir. Mayesh and Jolivet were just being anxious, like clucking old hens.

Conor raised an eyebrow. "Nonsense," he said. "I am far too good looking to risk spoiling my looks in battle."

"Scars can be charming," Kel noted. "Look at Montfaucon. Always surrounded by adoring courtiers."

"If only one could be assured one would go off to fight and return only with a dashing cut on the cheek," said Conor. "The more likely outcome—a pike to the face—is less attractive. Anyway, it's not as if there's a war going on now." Conor always moved his hands expressively when he spoke—a habit Kel had spent years learning and copying. The little bit of light in the carriage glinted off Conor's rings as he gestured. He was richly dressed, as befitted a prince about to address his people. Third-best crown—a gold circlet etched with wings—fine wool trousers, and tooled-leather jerkin, the leather cut out in small diamond shapes to show the silk and metallic thread of the shirt beneath. It was horrendously hot, which Kel knew since he was wearing the same thing.

"There is no war currently," said Mayesh. "And consolidating alliances with other countries via marital connection is one way of making sure it stays that way." He opened the leather notebook on his lap. Inside were dozens of portraits and sketches done on various kinds of paper, all sent from hopeful courts and holdings across Dannemore and beyond. "Princess Aimada d'Eon of Sarthe. Twenty years old, speaks six languages, mother was a famous beauty, docile—"

"Docile means dull," said Conor. He had pulled off one of his rings and was tossing it from hand to hand. It sparked in the dimness of the carriage as it flew, like a colorful firefly. "And what do I care what her mother looks like?"

"Perhaps they are offering two for the price of one," suggested Kel, and saw Conor smile. There were various aspects to the job of being Sword Catcher that went beyond Kel simply putting himself between the Crown Prince and possible harm. Conor was usually surrounded by people telling him what to do in a fearfully serious manner; Kel felt himself tasked with providing some balance.

Mayesh was not amused. "I believe," he said, "the suggestion is that the daughter, like her mother the Queen, will one day also be a great beauty."

"Is she not one now?" Conor took the paper from Mayesh. "Red hair," he said. "I loathe red hair. Besides. Sarthe."

Jolivet snorted. Before Castellane had gained its independence, it had been the port city of Magna Callatis, a vast Empire now split into the three separate kingdoms of Sarthe, Valderan, and Castellane. Valderan had been its verdant south, and even now contained most of the farms from which Castellane sourced its food. Castellane had been its shipyard and harbor. And Sarthe had been its capital, containing the once Imperial city of Aquila. It was common knowledge that Sarthe yearned to build the old Empire up again.

They longed especially for Castellane's harbor, for they were land-locked, forced to pay steep fees to Valderan for access to the coast.

"He has a point," said Jolivet. "Why give Sarthe a foothold here?"

"Why, indeed?" Mayesh drew out another sheet of paper. "Here we have Princess Elsabet Belmany, of Malgasi."

"Malgasi," Jolivet said, thoughtfully. "A useful ally. Especially since your father fostered at their Court."

"They trade richly in spices, fur, and silks, with reserves of arable land that would mean we were no longer dependent on trade with Valderan for crops," Mayesh noted, though there was a curious lack of enthusiasm in his voice.

"Arable land," said Conor. "Never have more romantic words been spoken. So many ballads written about beautiful women with vast tracts of arable land."

"If that's what they're calling it now," said Kel, and Conor grinned before taking the sheet of parchment from Mayesh.

"You needn't talk about land as if it's nothing," grumbled Jolivet. "In trade we are indeed a great power. But in land, we are only a few square miles of city and marsh."

"But what square miles they are," said Kel, peaceably, and Mayesh smiled. Conor held up the piece of parchment he'd snatched to show Kel the portrait of an intense-looking young woman with pale skin and black hair, her forehead bound with a gold circlet surmounted by a ruby phoenix. Elsabet Belmany.

Kel frowned. "I feel as if I've heard her name recently—"

Conor snapped his fingers. "Yes. Some sort of scandal. House Belmany is highly disliked by the folk of Malgasi; it seems an unpleasant situation to involve oneself in."

Jolivet made an exasperated noise. "There are anti-monarchists in Castellane as well, Conor—"

Kel scratched at a bit of the black paint on the carriage window as Conor and Mayesh argued about whether House Aurelian was or was not universally beloved. Through the clear spot of glass, Kel could see that they were on the Ruta Magna. The last section of the Great Southwestern Road that ran from Shenzhou to Castellane, the Ruta Magna cut through the mountains from the Narrow Pass, crossed the city, and ended at the harbor. Kel often wondered what the other end of the Great Road looked like. He knew it dead-ended in Shenzhou's capital, but did it become the main thorough-fare of that city, as it had in Castellane, or did it simply fade into a scatter of streets, like a river bleeding into a floodplain?

Conor always told him he was odd for wondering about such things. But Kel dreamed often of the far-flung corners of the world. From their window in Marivent, he could see the harbor and the great ships returning from Sayan and Taprobana, from Kutani and Nyenschantz. Someday, he told himself. Someday, he would find himself aboard one of those tallships, sailing across the raveled blue silk of the ocean. Hopefully with Conor beside him, though until now Conor's promise that they would one day travel the world had yet to materialize. Not through any fault of Conor's, Kel knew; House Aurelian had kept its Prince unusually close.

"Oh, very well," Mayesh snapped. He showed annoyance rarely; Kel turned with mild surprise to see that the Counselor had taken out a new sheet. "If Malgasi displeases, here we have Prince Floris of Gelstaadt. Young, handsome, will one day control the largest banking empire in the world."

Conor's general preference was for women, but it was by no means a rule. If Conor married another man, a woman of good breeding would be chosen to be the Lady Mother who would bear Conor's child, nurse it, and give it over to the two kings to raise. It had been the situation with Conor's grandparents—a Prince of Cas-tellane and a Lord of Hanse—and was generally not uncommon in Dannemore. Marriages between two queens were rarer but not un-heard of, either.

"Banking empire?" Conor stuck his hand out. "Let me see."

Kel looked over the Prince's shoulder as he perused the sketch. The boy in it, depicted leaning against an alder tree, was good looking, with flax-colored hair and the blue eyes common to Gelstaadt—a tiny country whose liberal banking laws had made it one of the richest in Dannemore.

Conor glanced up. "What do you think, Kel?"

The atmosphere inside the carriage changed subtly. Kel, who had spent the past decade attuning himself to nuances of social interaction, felt it. He was the Sword Catcher, the Prince's servant. It was not his place to give an opinion, at least not in Jolivet and Mayesh's view. (It was, perhaps, one of the few things they agreed on.)

Kel was not sure why he should care. All who worked in the Palace were loyal to the Blood Royal, but he was loyal above all other things to Conor. It was the choice he had made long ago, as a small, grubby boy in borrowed clothes, facing the Prince of Castellane. Who had offered him an extraordinary life, and had given him that and more—an extraordinary friendship to go along with it.

"I think," Kel said, "that either someone has drawn that tree very small, or Floris of Gelstaadt is a giant."

"Good point," said Conor. "I hardly want to marry someone who looms over me. How tall is he, Mayesh?"

Mayesh sighed. "Seven feet."

Conor shuddered. "Mayesh, are you trying to torment me? An unpopular Princess, a giant, and a redhead? Is this your idea of an amusing jest? It is taking years off my life. This may be treason."

Mayesh held up a new sheet of parchment. "Princess Anjelica of Kutani."

Conor sat up, finally interested. Kel couldn't blame him. The painting was of a dark-skinned girl with a cloud of black hair and luminous amber eyes. A cap of golden mesh set with star-shaped diamonds was her crown, and more gold glimmered at her wrists. She was luminously beautiful.

"Kutani?" said Jolivet, sounding dubious. "Would Castellane be able to afford such a dowry as they would certainly demand?"

Kutani was an island kingdom, a center of the spice trade—

cardamom, pepper, saffron, ginger, and cloves: All grew or were traded there, making the kingdom spectacularly rich. According to Joss Falconet, whose House was granted the spice Charter, the island air was scented with cardamom, and the trade winds blew across beaches soft as powder.

"So true," said Mayesh, setting the paper aside. "Probably not."

Conor's eyes flashed. "We are rich enough," he said. "Give me that back."

They had turned off the Ruta Magna onto a narrow lane behind the city's central square, where a plaza was formed by four of the oldest buildings in the city. All were clad in white marble, veined with quartz that glittered in the sun; all boasted broad steps, columns, and arched porticoes in the style of the bygone Callatian Empire.

Valerian Square had once been the Cuadra Magna, the central hub of the Imperial port city. At each cardinal point stood a massive structure dating from the time of the Empire. To the north, the Tully; its steps were guarded by marble lions, their mouths wide open as if to catch criminals in their jaws. To the west was the Convocat; to the south, the Justicia. To the east, the Porta Aurea, the triumphal arch erected by Valerian, the first King of Castellane; citizens fondly called it the Gate to Nowhere.

Castellane had something of a confusing relationship with its past. Today marked the yearly anniversary of Castellane's independence from Magna Callatis. The Castellani had fierce pride in their city-state, feeling it to be the most superior place in Dannemore. Yet they also prided themselves on their descent from Callatians, and on what they had kept from the time of the Empire: everything from the hypocausts that heated the public baths to the courts and the Council of Twelve. Independent but also tied to the glories of a domain long past; sometimes Kel thought he was the only one who observed the contradiction.

Kel and the others drew up behind the Convocat, where a hidden entrance would allow them to pass into the building without being seen. The lane had been closed off to all but royal traffic at both ends. As Kel swung down from the carriage, he saw a group of small children peer out from the shadows, wide-eyed. They were ragged—barefoot and scrubby, freckled by the sun. He thought of two small boys under a powderbark tree, playing at pirate battles, and flipped a copper coin in their direction. "Present my greetings to the Ragpicker King!" he called.

The smallest of the boys gave a frightened gasp. "They say he's here today," he said. "Somewhere in the crowd."

"As if you'd know what he looked like," scoffed a girl in a tattered pinafore. "You ain't never seen him."

The smaller boy puffed up angrily. "I does know," he protested. "He goes round all in black, like Gentleman Death come to take your soul, and his carriage wheels are stained with blood."

Rolling her eyes, the older girl pulled the boy's ear decidedly. The boy yelped, and the children vanished back into the shadows, giggling.

Kel chuckled. As a child, he'd thought of the Ragpicker King as the trickster God of pickpockets. Later, he began to understand that the Ragpicker King was a practical, not a mythological figure, however mysterious. He ran smuggling operations of elegance and size, owned gambling hells deep in the Warren, and had his fingers in trade from the harbor to the Great Road. The Palace could do nothing to rid the city of his presence. He was too powerful, and besides, Mayesh said, it was better not to create a vacuum of power at the top of any organization. Unlawful order was, after all, an improvement on lawful chaos.

Jolivet snapped his fingers. "Come along, Kellian," he said, and the group of four crossed the deserted street and entered the Convocat. It was dark and cool inside, the marble acting to shield the interior from the heat. Kel found himself walking beside Mayesh as Jolivet strode beside Conor, speaking to him intently.

"That was cleverly done, in the carriage," admitted Kel. "Show him three candidates he won't want to marry, then show him one he will and tell him he cannot have her."

"It is both your task and mine," Mayesh said, "to know the Prince better than he knows himself."

"Only you have other tasks, and I have merely the one. You must also know the King and Queen."

Mayesh made a gesture that seemed to indicate agreement without commitment. "I only offer them counsel. So it has always been."

This was manifestly untrue, but Kel didn't feel like arguing. It was better not to delve too deeply into any discussion of the King and Queen, especially when it came to the King. Conor was giving the yearly Speech of Independence today because the Queen would not appear—she loathed public speaking—and the King could not.

Markus Aurelian, the great scholar, the philosopher-king. His wisdom was a point of pride in Castellane. He did not appear often in public, it was said, because he was busy with his learning, his great discoveries in the fields of astronomy and philosophy. Kel knew this was not true, but it was only one among many secrets he kept for House Aurelian.

They had reached the central chamber of the Convocat, where broad marble pillars upheld an arched roof. The mosaic floor, which depicted a map of Dannemore before the breakup of the Empire, had once been colorful. Now it was worn down to a faint shadow by the passage of time and countless feet.

Once, there had been seats here; once, the King had sat in session with the Charter Families, discussing Law and trade and policy. Kel could dimly recall when this had still been the case, before the King had retreated to the North Tower with his telescopes and astrolabes, his maps of stars, his sextants and spheres. Before the King had turned his attention to the skies and forgotten the world below them.

But there was no point thinking about that now. Several of the

Arrow Squadron were approaching. They gleamed in red and gold, like Jolivet, though they sported considerably fewer tassels and less fringe. The leader, a gray-haired man named Benaset, said grimly, "Legate. Sir. There's been an incident."

Benaset explained: A dockworker, found in the crowd with a crossbow strapped to his back. Probably nothing, of course; there was every possibility he was unaware of the Law that forbade going armed to an appearance of one of the Royal Blood. The Tully would uncover the truth, certainly. In the meantime—

"We will need the Sword Catcher," said Benaset. "Is he prepared?"

Kel nodded. Tension had spread through his shoulders, tightening his muscles. Stepping in for Conor was not a rare occurrence. It was always a flip of the coin, as the guards were more than cautious. It was not even the danger he minded, he thought, as he drew his talisman from his pocket and looped it around his neck. (It lay cold against his throat; for reasons he could not guess, the metal never warmed from contact with his skin.) But he had relaxed today. They were nearly at the square; he could hear the crowd. He had let himself assume he would not be needed.

He had been wrong. As quickly as he could, he began to run down the words of the speech in his mind. *I greet you, my people of Castellane, in the name of the Gods. Today—*

Kel frowned. Today something. *Today Castellane was born.* No. That wasn't it.

"I don't think it's necessary," Conor said, interrupting Kel's reverie. "One drunken idiot wandering around with a weapon hardly means an assassination attempt—"

"It is necessary, Monseigneur." Kel knew that flatness in Jolivet's voice, and knew what it meant. The Legate had the power to restrain the Prince physically, vested in him by the King, if such action was required. "This is why you have a Sword Catcher."

Conor threw up his hands in disgust as Kel came over to him. They locked eyes; Kel shrugged minutely, as if to say: *It doesn't mat-*

ter. With a sigh, Conor slipped the crown from his head and held it out to Kel. "Try to look handsome," he advised. "Don't disappoint the people."

"I'll do my best." Kel settled the crown on his head. His rings were paste jewels, but the crown—that was real. That belonged to House Aurelian. It seemed to carry a weight beyond the physical heft of bullion. He looked up, blinking: The Arrow Squadron had thrown the doors open wide, flooding the interior of the Convocat with bright sunlight.

Kel could hear the roar of the crowd, like the rush of the sea.

Conor held out his hand. Kel grasped it, and Conor pulled him close. This part was ritual, muscle memory. Kel had done it countless times, though he still felt a faint shiver up his spine as he looked at Conor. As he felt the weight of the gold circlet on his brow.

"I am the Prince's shield," he said. "I am his unbreakable armor. I bleed that he might not bleed. I suffer that he might never suffer. I die that he might live forever."

"But you will not die," said Conor, releasing his hand. It was what he always said—not part of the ritual, but habit nonetheless.

"Unless Lady Alleyne gets her hands on me," said Kel. Lady Alleyne had a wealth of ambitions, most of them focused on her only daughter. "She's still angling for you to marry Antonetta."

Jolivet scowled. "Enough," he said. "Mayesh, you will remain with the Prince."

It was less an order than a question; Mayesh indicated that he would, and Kel joined Jolivet in the long walk to the doors. The noise of the crowd grew louder and louder still until Kel stepped through the doorway to the covered loggia beyond, all its arches brilliant with white marble. He heard the crowd take an indrawn breath as he moved to stand at the top of the white cascade of steps that led down to the square, as if they all saw him at once, all breathed in at once.

Kel stood at the top of the Grieving Stairs and looked around the square as they chanted Conor's name. The crowd spanned wealth and class and occupation: from dock laborers in rough cambric, their children perched on their shoulders to get a better view, to shopkeepers and publicans. Rich merchants had driven their shining carriages into the square and gathered in groups, dressed in bright colors. On the steps of the High Temple stood the Hierophant, the high priest of Castellane, carrying a staff topped with a milky Sunderglass orb. Kel eyed the old man sideways—it was unusual to see the Hierophant away from the Temple, save for great occasions such as state funerals or the Marriage to the Sea, when the King or Queen of Castellane would board a boat wreathed in flowers and hurl a golden ring into the ocean, to seal the bond between Aigon and the House of Aurelian.

Closest to the steps sat the Charter Families, atop a dais that had been erected before the lions of the Tully, each family beneath a pennant bearing the sigil of their House: a ship for House Roverge, a wreath for Esteve, a silk moth for Alleyne.

Kel swept one last glance over the crowd, catching sight of a shining black carriage with scarlet wheels. Against it leaned a slender, long-legged figure all in black. *He goes round all in black, like Gentleman Death, come to take your soul, and his carriage wheels are stained with blood.* Could it be the Ragpicker King, come to see the Prince speak? Kel supposed he could, if he felt like it. As a child, he'd asked Conor why the Palace didn't simply arrest the Ragpicker King.

"Because," Conor had said, looking thoughtful, "he has too much money."

Enough. Kel knew he was letting his nerves direct his imagination. *Concentrate,* he told himself. *You are the Prince of Castellane.*

He closed his eyes. Against the darkness, he saw blue sea, a ship with white sails. Heard the sound of waves, and the call of gulls. Here, where the western stars drowned with the turning of the world, he was alone in the quiet, with the horizon beckoning. The ship rocked beneath him, the mast at his back. No one knew this place but him. Not even Conor.

His eyes snapped open. He reached out his hands to the crowd, the thick velvet of his sleeves falling back, the rings gleaming on his fingers. The crown was heavy, a bar of iron across his forehead. He said, "I greet you, my people of Castellane, in the name of the Gods," his voice amplified by the talisman at his throat. It echoed through the square.

My people . . . Many in the crowd brandished the red-and-gold flag of Castellane—the ship and the lion. The sea and the Gold Roads. There was a rug worked into the shape of the land of Dannemore in the Palace library. Conor walked upon it sometimes in bare feet: now in Hind, now along the Gold Roads, now returning to Castellane. So the world was to a prince.

"Today," Kel said, and the words rose up in him, unbidden but remembered, "is the day of our freedom, the birth of our city-state. Here, among these streets, did the people of Castellane lay down their lives that they might never again kneel to an Emperor, nor bow down at the feet of a foreign power. Here did we become what we are—a shining beacon to all the world, the greatest city in Dannemore, in all the world—"

The crowd roared. The sound was like thunder, like a storm growing closer and closer until it seemed it would shudder the sky apart. In this moment, it did not matter that Kel was not truly their Prince. The cheering lifted him up as if he walked the sky roads like lightning-struck Elemi.

Their excitement seemed to catch along his bones as if his marrow were filled with black powder. He felt it as a fire rising, becoming a blaze within his blood. It was overwhelming, to be so loved—even if the love was not truly directed at him. Even if it was an illusion.

"Very good," said Conor, when Kel had come back into the Convocat. The crowd, whipped up into a frenzy—in part by the appearance of the Crown Prince, but also, it had to be admitted, by the free alcohol provided by the Palace—was still roaring outside. Tan-

kards were being given out at booths hung with red-and-gold banners as the noble families packed up their belongings and hurried
back to the Hill. Soon enough the patriotic crowd would become a
raucous and celebratory mob. "I liked the part about the heart and
soul of Castellane being . . . what was it? Ah, yes. The citizens. Ex-
temporaneous?"

"I thought we rehearsed it." Kel leaned back against a pillar,
feeling the cool marble against his back, his neck. He was very hot
all over, suddenly, though he had not felt the sun when he'd stood
atop the Grieving Stairs. "People like to be complimented."

"Are you all right?" Conor, who had been sitting with his back
against a pillar, scrambled to his feet. Jolivet and Mayesh were deep
in conversation; the Arrow Squadron paced up and down the room,
silent as guards always were. Conor usually forgot they were there.
"You look . . ."

Kel raised his head. He and Conor were of the same height; Kel
was sure somehow Mayesh had made sure of that, as he had made
sure that Kel's eyes, over the years, had turned the color of tarnished silver. "Yes?"

"Nothing. Sunstruck, perhaps. It will do you good to get into
the dark." Conor put a hand on Kel's shoulder. "Today is a day of
celebration. So let us celebrate. Go and change your clothes in the
carriage, and we will head to the Caravel."

"Right." Kel sighed. As he often did after public appearances as
Conor, he felt an exhaustion deep in his bones, as if he had been
stretched into a peculiar position for hours. He wished for nothing
more than to return to the Palace and collapse into bed. "Joss Falconet's party."

"Why the reluctance?" The corner of Conor's mouth curled up.
"It has been too long since we visited the Temple District."

The Temple District was a neighborhood of pleasure houses; it
had earned its name because most brothels kept a house shrine to
Turan, the God of desire. Kel half wished to ask if they could go
some other evening, but it was clear Conor was looking forward to

the party—and besides, Kel himself had some business in the Caravel quite apart from the usual, and tonight would be as good a time as any to conduct it.

"Nothing," Kel said. "Only Falconet's gatherings can be . . . excessive."

Conor chucked him lightly under the chin. "Excessively enjoyable. I've already asked Benaset to bring the horses around. You can ride Asti."

Beneath the light tone, Conor sounded anxious. He knew Kel didn't want to go; the offer of Kel's favorite horse was a bribe. For a brief moment, Kel wondered what would happen if he refused, said he would return to the Palace with Bensimon and Jolivet. Spent the evening in a dark room with cold blue wine and a map of the western seas.

The answer was: Not much. But Conor would be disappointed, and he would still need someone to accompany him to the Caravel. Conor could not ride out into the world alone, unprotected; he must always be defended. If Kel returned to the Palace, Conor would be assigned a guard from the Arrow Squadron to watch him, and would be accordingly miserable. And if Conor was miserable, Kel would be miserable. Not because Conor would take it out on him; he wouldn't. But the knowledge that he had let Conor down would eat away at him like caustic.

Kel slipped the crown from his head. He held it out to Conor, the gold circlet dangling from his fingers. "Very well," he said, "but do not forget your crown, Monseigneur, lest they treat you disrespectfully at the Caravel. Unless," he added, "being treated disrespectfully is what you're paying for tonight?"

Conor laughed, the anxiety vanishing from his eyes. "Excellent. We will have a memorable evening, I think." He turned to wave his crown breezily at Bensimon and Jolivet, who gazed at the two young men with matched expressions of stony disapproval. "We bid you good afternoon, gentlemen," he said. "Should you wish to find us, we will be in the Temple District, offering the appropriate prayers."

There has always been magic.

It is a force of nature, like fire, water, and air. Mankind was not born knowing how to use magic, just as they were not born knowing how to create fire. It is said the secrets of magic are whispered of in the higher air, where those who have the ability learn the incantations that, in the right hands, become spells.

We do not know who codified the first spells or committed them to writing. Such knowledge has been lost. But we do know that every chant or conjuration has always included the One Word, the ineffable name of Power, without which a spell is only empty speech. Without the Word, there is no magic.

— *Tales of the Sorcerer-Kings*, Laocantus Aurus Iovit III

CHAPTER TWO

I'm sorry." Not looking the least bit sorry, Dom Lafont—a nervous little man with black-rimmed spectacles perched on a warty nose—shook his head. "It isn't possible."

Lin Caster placed her hand flat on the wooden counter that separated them. The Lafont Bookshop in the Scholars' Quarter was a dusty little place, the walls festooned with old prints and sketches of Castellane and famous historical figures of days past. Behind the counter, shelves of books stretched away: some bright and new, in fine colored leather jackets, some plain, bound galleys produced by the Academie to aid students in their coursework.

It was one of those—a treatise on hereditary illnesses by Ibn Sena, a teacher of medicine—that Lin itched to get her hands on. She craned her neck, trying to pick out exactly which of the bound manuscripts on the shelves it was, but the shop was too dimly lit.

"Dom Lafont," Lin said, "I have been a good customer of yours. A *frequent* customer. Is that not the case?" She turned to her friend Mariam Duhary, who was watching the interaction with worried eyes. "Mariam, tell him. There is no good reason that prevents him from selling me a book."

"I am aware of that, Domna Caster," Lafont protested. "But there are *rules*." He wiggled his nose like a rabbit's. "What you are asking for is coursework for the medical students at the Academie. You are not a student at the Academie. If you had a letter from the Justicia, perhaps—"

Lin wanted to slam her hand down on the counter. The man was being ridiculous. The Ashkar, as he knew perfectly well, could not attend the Academie as students, or apply to the Justicia for relief. These were Laws—bad Laws, that made her stomach twist, her blood run sour in her veins. But they had been the way of things since the founding of Castellane. "For students," she said, making an effort to be calm, "these manuscripts are free. I am offering to pay. Name your price, Dom Lafont."

Dom Lafont spread his hands wide. "It is not a matter of money. It is a matter of *rules*."

"Lin is a physician," Mariam said. She was a small girl, birdlike in her delicacy, but her gaze was firm and searching. "As you know. She cured your gout last fall, did she not?"

"It still comes back sometimes," he said sourly. "Every time I eat pheasant."

Which I told you not to do, Lin thought.

"Lin merely seeks to acquire wisdom that will allow her to heal more of the sick, and relieve their suffering," said Mariam. "Surely you cannot object to that."

Lafont grunted. "I know even your own people do not think you should be practicing medicine," he said to Lin. "I know you have no business pawing through knowledge not meant for your sort." He leaned across the counter. "I suggest you stick to what you know—your little amulets and magic trinkets. Don't you have enough *wisdom* already, you Ashkar?"

In that moment, Lin could see herself in the shopkeeper's eyes. Someone powerless, someone clearly different, almost foreign. And yes, she wore, as the laws of Castellane required, the traditional colors of the Ashkar: a gray dress, a blue jacket. And around her throat, the traditional symbol of her people: a hollow golden circle on a chain. Lin's had been her mother's once.

But more than that marked her out. It was in her blood, in the way she walked and talked, in something invisible that she sometimes felt hovered about her like a fine mist. She was knowably, clearly, Ashkar—alien in a way the sailors who thronged the port of Castellane simply weren't. Travelers had a clearly delineated role and place. The Ashkar did not.

Don't you have enough already, you Ashkar? It was what all Castellani felt to some degree. The Sundering had destroyed all magic, erased it from the world. All save the small spells and talismans of *gematry*, the ancestral magic of the Ashkar. Because of that, Lin's people were hated and envied in equal measure. Because of that, special Laws applied to them. Because of that, they were not allowed out of the Sault, the walled community in which they were required to live, once the sun had gone down. As if they could not be trusted in the shadows.

Lafont shook his head, turning away. "There is a reason books like this aren't meant for hands like yours. Come back if you'd like to buy something else. My door will be open."

The world seemed to darken before Lin's eyes. She took a deep breath, her small hands knotting into fists—

A moment later she found herself outside the bookstore, being steered down the street by Mariam. "Mariam, what—?"

"You were going to hit him," Mariam said breathlessly. She had come to a stop between a lodging house for students and a shop selling ink and quills. "And then he would have called the Vigilants, and you'd have been fined, at least. You know they aren't sympathetic to the Ashkar."

Mariam, Lin knew, was right. And yet. "It is *unbelievable*," she fumed. "That inbred bigot! He didn't object to my knowledge when he wanted me to treat him for free, did he? And now it's *Keep your filthy hands off our books*. As if knowledge belonged to any one type of person—"

"Lin!" Mariam interrupted in a whisper. "People are staring."

Lin glanced over. Across the street was a tea shop, already crowded with students enjoying a day free of lectures. A group had gathered around a weathered wooden table outside to drink *karak*—a heavily spiced tea with cream—and play cards; several *were* looking over at her, seemingly amused. A handsome student with a mass of ginger hair, wearing a paper crown, winked in her direction.

What if I asked one of them to buy me the book? Lin thought. But no; it wouldn't work. *Malbushim* tended to be suspicious of the Ash-kar, and even Dom Lafont would see through such a ruse so soon after she'd made her attempt. She returned the young man's wink with a steady glare. He put a hand over his heart as if to indicate she'd wounded him and turned back to his companions.

"We ought to get back home," Mariam said, a little anxiously. "The streets will be a madhouse in an hour or two."

This was true. Today Castellane's independence was celebrated, with speeches, music, and parades stretching on into the night. Visits to temples to give thanks were conducted in the mornings; by the late afternoon, the Palace would have begun distributing free ale to the populace and the celebrations would become considerably rowdier. By Law, all Askhar had to be locked inside the Sault by nightfall; it would not do to be caught out in the jam-packed streets.

"You're right." Lin sighed. "We'd best avoid the Great Road. It'll be packed. If we cut through these back streets, we'll reach Valerian Square."

Mariam smiled. She still had dimples, though she had grown so terribly thin that even her made-over clothes seemed to hang on her. "Lead the way."

Lin took Mariam's hand. It felt like a bundle of twigs in hers. Cursing Lafont silently, she set off, guiding her friend through the steeply tilting, cobblestoned byways of the Student Quarter, the oldest part of the city. Here narrow streets named after Imperial philosophers and scientists wound around the stately dome of the university. Built of ash-colored granite, the pillared dome of the Academie rose like a storm cloud over the steeply gabled rooftops of the shops and lodging houses frequented by students and their tutors.

On an ordinary day, students in their uniforms of rusty black would be dashing by between lectures, with leather satchels of books slung across their backs. There had been a time Lin had wondered what it would be like to study at the Academie, but its doors were closed to the Ashkar, and she'd had abandoned that dream.

Still, the Scholars' Quarter had a hold on her imagination. Colorful shopfronts sold items of interest to students: paper and quills, ink and measuring tools, inexpensive food and wine. The ancient buildings seemed to lean together like tired children, exchanging secrets. In her mind, Lin imagined what it must be like to live in a lodging house, among other students—staying up late to read by the light of a tallow candle, ink-stained desks on wobbly legs, narrow diamond-paned windows with views of Poet's Hill and the Great Library. Hurrying to morning lectures with a lighted lamp in hand, part of a crowd of eager students.

She knew it was unlikely to be so romantic in real life, but nevertheless, she liked to imagine the atmosphere of dusty books and companionate study. She had learned a great deal at the Physicians' House in the Sault, from a series of stern and unsmiling male teachers, but one could not have described it as convivial.

Glancing around now, one could sense the festive atmosphere in the air. Windows had been thrown open, and students clustered on balconies and even rooftops, chatting animatedly over bottles of cheap wine. Lamps of red and gold, the colors of Castellane, had been hung on ribbons threaded from balcony to balcony of the windows overhead. Brightly painted shop signs swung in the breeze; the air here was scented with paper and ink, dust and candle wax.

"You're still angry," Mariam observed as they crossed Historians' Way. She and Lin stepped aside to let a group of clearly inebriated students stagger by. "You're all red. You only turn that color when you're furious." She bumped her shoulder against Lin's. "Was it a particularly important book? I know Lafont said it was coursework, but I can't imagine there's anything the Academie could teach that you don't already know."

Loyal Mariam. Lin wanted to squeeze her hand. Wanted to say: *I need it because of you. Because you have been getting thinner, and paler, all year; because none of my remedies have made you even a little bit better. Because you cannot clamber up a ladder or walk the length of a street without losing your breath. Because none of my books can tell me what is wrong with you, much less how to treat it. Because the knowledge we had before the Sundering is half lost, but I cannot abandon hope without trying everything, Mariam. You taught me that.*

Instead, Lin shook her head. "It was what he said, that even my own people don't want me to be a physician."

Mariam looked sympathetic. She knew better than nearly anyone else how hard Lin had struggled to convince the elders of the Sault that she, a woman, should be allowed to learn medicine. They had finally permitted it, not believing she would pass the physician's exam. It still gave her pleasure to remember that her scores had been higher than those of any of the male students. "It was not the whole Sault, Lin. There were many who wanted you to succeed. And think how much easier it will be for the next girl who wants to be a physician. You forged the way. Do not mind the doubters."

The idea pleased Lin. It would be lovely to have more female physicians in the Sault. People she could trade knowledge with, discuss treatments, patients. The male *asyar* ignored her. She'd hoped they would accept her after she passed her exams, and then again after her first year of practice, but their attitude had not changed. A woman had no business doctoring, whether she was good at it or not. "I'll do my best not to mind them," she said. "I *am* awfully stubborn."

"Oh, indeed. You're as stubborn as your grandfather."

Lin would usually have objected to being compared to Mayesh, but they had just reached the Biblioteca Corviniana, the Great Library, and a chatter of voices had burst out all around them.

The Library had been built two hundred years past by King Estien IV, and thus was a relatively new building in the quarter. Its stone doors were closed today, but a wide marble courtyard opened out in front of it, crowded with people. Estien, a patron of philosophers, had ordered that raised squares of marble be erected outside the Library for the purposes of debate. Any citizen of Castellane was allowed to climb upon one and hold forth on any topic they chose, free from accusations of disturbing the peace—as long as they did not stray from their perch.

There was, of course, no rule that anyone had to *listen*, and thus the various speakers tended to shout their opinions as loudly as possible. A tall young woman wearing the green-lined cloak of a student of science was shouting about the unfairness of the Academie, expecting foreign students to pay for their own lodging when the Castellani were housed at no expense. This drew friendly boos from a group of drunken students who were singing a bawdy version of the anthem of Castellane.

Nearby, a blond young man in a tightly buttoned black tunic was loudly denouncing the monarchy. This drew more interest, as criticizing the royal family was dangerous business. Most of the scholars at the Academie were the children of merchants and guild-masters, shopkeepers and traders. The nobility employed private tutors, rather than sending their children to the free university. Still, loyalty to the crown and the Charter Families ran deep.

"Hey! You, there!" someone shouted, and the blond young man raised an inquiring eyebrow. "Just saw the Vigilants coming around the corner. You'd better hie off if you don't want to wind up in a crocodile's belly."

The young man gave a bow of thanks and leaped down from his marble podium. A moment later he had vanished into the crowd.

Mariam frowned. "I don't think anyone was really coming."

Lin glared around, but there was no way to tell who had shouted at the anti-monarchist. The shadows were lengthening, though, the Great Library casting its pillared reflection across the courtyard. They could not afford to keep dawdling.

They turned onto Vespasian Way, an avenue lined with university lodgings. Through open doors, Lin could see students in their black cloaks running up and down steep sets of stairs, laughing and calling to one another. Someone on a balcony overhead was playing a *vielle;* the melody of their lament drifted through the air, rising and falling like a gull over the harbor water.

> *May she have the courage*
> *to have me come one night there*
> *where she undresses*
> *and make me a necklace of her arms.*
> *Otherwise, I will die.*

"Musicians really do make being in love sound awful," said Lin. "Just endless moping away, all alone because no one can put up with you."

Mariam laughed softly. "How can you be so cynical?"

"Not to mention, apparently love makes you poor, and sickly," Lin went on, ticking off the list on her fingers, "and terribly likely to die young, in a very small room with bad lighting."

"If it was that awful, no one would do it."

"You don't have a choice, I hear," Lin said as they turned onto Yulan Road, where the Student Quarter dead-ended in a wide thoroughfare lined with Shenzan lane houses, terraced and surrounded by low walls with iron gates. Shenzan traders and sailors had settled here in the time of the Empire, their traditions blending over time with those of Castellane. "Love just happens to you, whether you like it or not; otherwise there wouldn't be so many songs. Besides, people do all sorts of things that are bad for them. I ought to know."

The lane houses had given way to shopfronts selling everything from jade sculptures and cheap jewelry to fireworks and paper lan-

terns, painted with symbols for independence, luck, and *Daqin*—
the Shenzan name for Castellane. Delicious steam wafted from the
doors of white-painted noodle shops, where Shenzan sailors and
students enamored of cheap, delicious food rubbed shoulders at
long rosewood tables.

Lin's stomach growled. Time to get home; she was sure there
was a whole honey cake in the pantry. Nearly whole, at any rate.

She ducked down an alley topped with a stone arch, narrow
enough that she and Mariam had to walk single-file. She could see
over some of the low walls into the gardens of the lane houses,
where chrysanthemums and poppies bloomed. Giggling came from
overhead: Families were already sitting on the roofs of their houses,
from which they could command a view of the red-and-gold fireworks that would later explode like falling stars over the harbor.

When they emerged finally from the alley, Lin cursed under her
breath. She must have taken a wrong turn. She had meant to cut
past Valerian Square, behind the Justicia. Instead they had emerged
from the side streets into the middle of a cheering crowd facing the
Convocat.

By the Goddess, she thought, her heart sinking. *No.*

She turned to see Mariam gazing around, wide-eyed. The
square was packed as tightly as a trader's caravan. "But I thought—"

"We were going to avoid the square. I know," Lin said grimly.
Nearby, several carriages had circled together. Their doors were
thrown open, and girls in fashionable clothes—merchants' daughters, their brightly colored boots showing beneath the lace hems of
their frocks—were leaning out, giggling and calling to one another.
Lin caught something about a princess and a kingdom, and two
names she recognized: Conor Aurelian, and Counselor Bensimon.

Outside the Sault, there was no Ashkar with as much power as
her grandfather, Mayesh Bensimon. Within the walls, his power
was matched by that of the Maharam, but here, among the *malbushim*, the only Ashkar whose name they knew was Mayesh's. For
Mayesh stood at the shoulder of the King, at the side of the Prince.

He advised, he counseled, he listened to their fears and desires and dreams. He mapped a path for them to follow. No one stood closer to the throne save perhaps Legate Jolivet, the head of the royal army.

All through the spring there had been rumors that Prince Conor would marry soon. Lin knew her grandfather would be at the heart of deciding what alliance he would make, what advantage it would confer on Castellane. It seemed these girls knew that, too. Everyone did.

Taking hold of Mariam's sleeve, Lin began to push her way through the crowd, past wine-smelling shopkeepers and loudly singing guildmasters. Something struck her lightly on the shoulder; it was a thrown flower. A yellow aster, the symbol of House Aurelian. More crushed flowers were littered in the square, their gold petals ground to a fine dust.

Lin swerved to avoid the massive raised dais on which sat the Charter Families with their banners, and received several filthy looks from those who seemed to believe she was trying to get closer to the Convocat. She could hear Mariam complaining that she wanted to stop, to *look*, but Lin's heart was beating too fast. She couldn't wait to get through the crowd to the other side, before—

A gasp went through the crowd. Mariam stopped dead and tugged on Lin's hand. With a sense of resignation, Lin turned to see that the stairs of the Convocat were no longer empty. Prince Conor Aurelian had appeared atop them and was gazing out at the crowd.

Long ago, Lin's grandfather had brought her to a King's Speech here in the square. He had arranged for her to sit upon the dais, among the Charter Families, as King Markus spoke. Lin had understood nothing of his speech about taxes and trade, but she had loved the spectacle of it: the cheering crowd, the clothes, Queen Lilibet all in green, her throat circled with emeralds as large as the eyes of crocodiles. The young Prince at her side, his thick black curls just like hers, his mouth drawn down in a scowl.

Mayesh had seated Lin next to a fair-haired girl with fat curls and a thin mouth. Antonetta, her name had been. She hadn't said a word to Lin, but Lin hadn't minded. She was enjoying looking at it all too much.

That was, until she had become aware of the eyes that rested on *her*. And not just the nobles—who had been gazing sideways, discreetly—but those in the crowd: the merchants and shopkeepers and ordinary people of Castellane. They had all been staring at the Ashkari girl, up on the dais with the nobles as if she were just like everyone else. As if she were *better*.

It was the first time she recalled such stares—stares that told her she was peculiar, out of place, a curiosity. Not like everyone else. She had been a child, yet they had looked at her with open suspicion. Not because of who she was, but because of *what* she was.

All that flashed through her mind now as Prince Conor, his curling black hair held back by a winged golden circlet, came to the top of the steps to face the crowd. Lin had not seen him since all those years ago, when he had been a child, as she had. He had the same arrogant tilt to his chin even now, the same hard mouth. His frown was narrow as a razor.

Mariam sighed. "He *is* awfully good looking."

Lin knew that, objectively, this was true. Girls sighed over the portraits of the sons of the nobility sold at the weekly market in Windtower Square. And Prince Conor, she knew, was more popular than any other. Sketches of him, with his raven-dark hair and sharp cheekbones, sold for more than similar portraits of graceful Joss Falconet or scowling Charlon Roverge. Although it was more than just looks, Lin thought cynically; Falconet was handsome, but Conor was nearer to the throne, to power.

But she could not force herself to agree with Mariam. There was something about the harshness of the Prince's looks she did not find appealing. He had not spoken yet but was looking over the crowd with a keen consideration. Lin thought she felt his gaze brush over her, though she knew it was only her imagination. She knew there was little point in hating Conor Aurelian. She was like an ant to him. He could step on her and never notice.

But she thought of her grandfather and hated him nonetheless.

"I cannot like him, Mariam," she said. "My—Mayesh chose him, chose all the Aurelians, over his own family. Over Josit and me."

"Oh, I don't think that's true." Mariam looked troubled. And, in the open sunlight, paler than ever. Lin fretted silently to herself. "You know it wasn't so simple."

But it was. Lin still remembered sitting with her brother in their small bedroom, listening to Mayesh arguing with Chana Dorin in the kitchen. *Chana, you must understand. I cannot take them. My duty is to the Palace.*

"And his clothes are ridiculous," Lin said. "The Prince's, I mean." She hoped this would distract Mariam, who loved fashion more than anything. Lin and Mariam had been schooled together as children, but Mariam had been deemed too fragile in constitution to continue her education. Without much reluctance, Mariam had stepped away from intensive studies, turning her considerable skill with needles into her trade.

In a short time, she had learned all there was to know about sewing and fabrics, about the differences between *altabasso* and *soprariccio*, between raw silk and *mockado*. She set up a stall in the market square, and soon enough rich women (and men) all over the city were cooing over her chemises with fine blackwork embroidery at the necklines and cuffs; over bodices of velvet and silk damask, and silk kirtles as fine and sheer as fishing nets. She made visits to the Hill to dress Demoselle Antonetta Alleyne, whose frothy, lace-covered dresses took weeks to complete. Her loom and needle were rarely still, and she often mourned that Lin was usually in her physician's uniform and had little use for fine gowns.

Mariam eyed the Prince thoughtfully. "I wouldn't say *ridiculous*," she said. "They are of a certain style. It is called *sontoso* in Sarthian. It means an intensity of richness."

Richness, indeed. The Prince's fingers gleamed with a dozen jeweled rings, sparking light when he moved. His boots and jerkin were of rich incised leather, his shirt of crimson silk, bright as blood. The royal sword, Firefly, was buckled at his waist with a strap of gold and ivory brocade.

"It means . . ." Mariam took a deep breath and shook her head, as if to clear a fog. "It means that everything must be of the finest work. Look at his jacket. It is pomegranate velvet from Sarthe, woven with real gold thread so thin and fine it makes all the fabric shimmer like metal. The work is so delicate that a Law was passed forbidding the making of it, for it often made the workers mad or blind."

"If it's illegal, how does he have a whole jacket of it?" Lin demanded.

Mariam smiled faintly. "He *is* the Prince," she said, just as Conor Aurelian stretched out his hands to the crowd and began to speak.

"I greet you, my people, in the name of the Gods," he said, and though Lin knew better, though she hated him, it seemed that when he spoke the sun shone out slightly brighter. His voice was rich and deep and soft as the pomegranate velvet he wore.

The crowd began to surge forward, pressing Lin and Mariam tightly toward the steps of the Convocat. Adoration shone on their faces.

That is power, Lin thought. *The love of the people. He holds them in his hands, and they love him for it.* It was almost strange, though she had grown up in the shadow of Marivent and House Aurelian. But there was nothing close to a king or queen in the Sault. Power in the Sault was split between Mayesh himself—who acted as a bridge between the Ashkar and the outside world, protecting those inside the walls from the forces outside them—and Davit Benezar, the Maharam. Half priest, half lawmaker, the Maharam ruled over the community of the Sault, presiding over every birth and death, every wedding, and every punishment.

Neither position was inherited: The Maharam was appointed by the Exilarch, the closest thing the Ashkar had to royalty. The Exilarch, who traveled the Gold Roads from Sault to Sault, traced his lineage in a direct line from Judah Makabi. Makabi had been chosen by the Goddess herself to lead her people: The *Book of Makabi* was one of their holiest texts.

Mayesh's power was far more secular. It was tradition for the Court to have an Ashkari Counselor, who was chosen by the Palace, and had been so since the time of the Empire.

Prince Conor was still speaking, his words rising and falling, strumming the chords of independence, of freedom, of Castellane. The crowd surged like a wave intent on crashing at the Convocat steps; some gazed at the Prince with tears in their eyes. *He could change the Law with a word*, Lin thought. *He has the power to decide what is and is not forbidden. And somewhere, in the shadows of the Convocat, my grandfather is standing. If he were another man, he could take up my cause with the Palace.*

Mariam cried out softly, stumbling as the crowd shoved them. "Lin! There is something wrong—"

Lin swung toward her friend in alarm. Mariam had her hand pressed to her throat, her eyes wide and frightened. Her cheeks were flaming red, and the blood at the corner of her mouth was as red as the Prince's silk.

"*Mariam*," Lin breathed; leaping forward, she was just in time to catch her friend around the waist. "Hold on to me," she said as Mariam slumped against her. "Hold on to me, Mari—"

But Mariam had become deadweight; she bore Lin to the ground with her, and Lin crouched over her, terrified, as the crowd around them murmured and backed away.

Lin tore the scarf from her hair and folded it, sliding it under Mariam's head. Mari was breathing hard, her lips tinged faintly with blue. Lin's chest tightened with panic; she did not have her physician's satchel with her, or any of the tools of her doctor's trade. She was surrounded by *malbushim*—some were staring, but most were ignoring her and Mari. They would believe it was not imperative upon them to help Ashkar. The Ashkar were meant to help themselves, but Lin had no idea how she could get Mari back to the Sault like this—

The crowd parted. Lin heard shouts and the scrape of carriage wheels on stone. She looked up and saw, ringed in a haze of bright sunlight, a carriage the color of flames, red and gold. The blazon of Castellane, the golden lion, snarled from its painted place on the door.

A Palace carriage.

She blinked up at it, dazed. Felt Mari's hand on her wrist, heard her murmur a question, and then the driver clambered down from his seat perched at the front of the carriage. He had gray hair and wore the livery of the Arrow Squadron; he bent down to lift Mari, who cried out weakly.

Lin sprang to her feet. "You're hurting her—"

"Mayesh Bensimon's orders," the man said crisply. "To take you both back to the Sault. Or would you rather I left you to walk?"

Mayesh. Lin knew she ought not be surprised—who else would have sent a Palace carriage for her? She said nothing as the man brought Mari into the carriage, laying her down across a velvet-upholstered seat.

She glanced up toward the top of the Grieving Stairs. She half expected to see Mayesh there, lurking in the shadows behind the Prince, but there was nothing: only Conor Aurelian, his hands out-stretched to the crowd. She thought he glanced at her for a moment as she climbed into the carriage after Mariam, but there was too much of a distance between them. Surely she was imagining things.

The man slammed the door after her as Lin sat down and drew Mari's head into her lap. Mari's eyes were closed, blood crusted at the corners of her mouth. Lin stroked her hair as the carriage began to move, and only then realized she had forgotten something in the square.

Glancing out the window, she saw her bloodstained scarf, flut-tering like a broken bird's wing on the pavement. Something about the sight of it seemed unlucky. She shuddered and looked away.

Many ask now whether there was a time when everyone performed magic, but the answer is that there was no such time. It is true that there was once no body that controlled magic, no great authority that ruled how people could use it. But that does not mean everyone is born with the talent for it.

The great scholar Jibar has said that it is best to think of magic like music. Some have aptitude for it, while some have the ability to learn it note by note. The greatest users of magic, those who rise to become sorcerers, have both.

— *Tales of the Sorcerer-Kings*, Laocantus Aurus Iovit III

CHAPTER THREE

The streets were full of revelers, clogging up the passageways. Usually respectable merchants' daughters danced in the roads, their hair whipping like ribbons; the doors of taverns were propped wide, spilling roisterers onto the cobblestones. Music drifted down from wrought-metal balconies overhead, along with handfuls of stiff colored paper cut into the shapes of phoenixes, swords, ships, and other symbols. A crown cut from yellow paper had tangled itself in Asti's reins; a girl in a white dress threw red hearts from an open window. Conor caught one out of the air and tucked it in a shirt pocket. Conor wore an unremarkable black Valdish cloak, his favorite disguise for wandering the city streets without being recognized; its hood was pulled up, covering his face. Kel wondered what the girl would think if she knew she'd given her paper heart to the Prince himself.

The young men entered the city, unrecognized and without guards. Or so Conor seemed to think; Kel suspected guards in the shadows watched them as they went. Jolivet's Arrow Squadron, ready to intervene in the case of danger. But it was only a suspicion, and Kel did not voice it. It mattered too much to Conor to believe that he was free, if only for a few hours.

It was the sort of night that usually charged Kel with burning energy, left his veins humming with the contemplation of possibility. He wondered if it was the same energy that seized sailors as they approached the horizon and whatever might lie beyond it: uncharted islands, buried gold, ruins from the time before the Sundering.

They passed into the Temple District and turned toward Hourglass Street, where many found their own golden ruin in the night. Here there had once been an alluvial plain, reclaimed before the Empire fell and covered over with a skin of bricks bound together with gypsum and quicklime. The area was crisscrossed with canals; the water in them, fed by underground streams, ran a sluggish dark green beneath arched metal bridges.

Signs hung in front of the gabled "shops" that lined Hourglass Street. Each bore a painting indicating what sort of distraction one might find inside. Most were simply bodies twined together in some form of erotic congress. Others required deciphering: a female figure peering through a door, a man with a rope around his neck, a young woman carrying a flowering vine while another woman knelt at her feet.

Kel could remember the first time he had been here with Conor. Perhaps they had been fifteen. They had both been nervous, with Conor trying hard to hide it. He had said: *Pick which one you like.*

Kel had realized Conor didn't know which place to select, either, or what to ask for. He was leaving it to Kel, because it didn't matter if Kel seemed inexpert or ill at ease. So Kel had picked the Caravel, because he had liked their sign: a tallship with white sails, an open book beneath, its pages forming the waves on which the ship charted its course. He had introduced himself and Conor to the madam, Domna Alys Asper, who had been more than delighted to welcome them. To be able to boast the patronage of the Crown Prince would surely bring other clients to her door. She had given them each a gold hourglass, emblazoned with a ship. These, she had explained, were theirs to keep, and to use each time they visited.

In the Temple District, the cost of pleasure was measured in turns of the hourglass. One could have as many hours as one liked with a courtesan, enjoying their company and skills, as long as one could pay for each hour. Thus Hourglass Street had gained its name, and that night Kel had lost his virtue, over the course of two turns, to a red-haired courtesan named Silla.

Domna Alys had been correct about Conor, too. In the years since, the Caravel had become a favored gathering place for members of the noble families on the Hill. Where Conor went, so went the fashions for everything from clothes to amusements. Never mind that Kel had been the one to choose the Caravel; there was no need for anyone else to know that. Besides, Kel had become quite fond of Domna Alys over the years. Why shouldn't she profit?

She was there tonight, hurrying to greet them as they left Asti and her brother, Matix, in the care of Caravel's discreet footmen. Red and gold lamps dangled from thin metal wires above the front door; brothels, too, could be patriotic. Alys waved them inside the small entryway, smiling. "Monseigneur!" She glowed with pleasure at the sight of Conor. "And my young lord." She bowed to Kel. "What an unexpected delight. Your friends, I think, have already arrived."

Falconet, then, and whoever he'd brought with him. Kel sighed inwardly.

"A welcome visit, Domna," said Conor. "After a wearying day, what better resting place than here?" He produced the red paper heart from the inside of his jacket and offered it to Alys. She smiled and tucked it into her bodice.

Domna Alys was the sort of woman whose beauty gave no clue to her age. Her skin was smooth, her cheeks flushed a pale rose, her eyes wide, blue, and enhanced with the expert application of kohl and shadow. Coils of black hair were dressed high at the back of her neck, and her dress fell in elegant pleats to her ankles, revealing brocaded slippers. She was, Kel thought, just that bit *too* fashionable to be a merchant's wife, and not quite richly dressed enough to be a noble. She knew a great deal about everything that happened in the city, from the Hill to the Maze, and she kept it to herself. A madam who gossiped about her clients would not have a business for long.

She led them into the main salon, where the carcel lamps had all been lit and fresh flowers trembled in long-necked glass vases. The furniture was black lacquer inlaid with greenstone from Shenzhou, and carved screens from Geumjoseon showed images of dragons, manticores, and other extinct creatures. The room smelled heavily of jasmine and incense—a rich scent Kel knew would linger on his clothes for hours.

Joss Falconet, already draped across a green velvet sofa, waved to them in desultory fashion. He was the youngest of the Council members, having gained the spice Charter seat upon the death of his father two years ago. He was handsome, with high cheekbones and the smooth black hair of his Shenzan mother. Two courtesans shared the sofa with him already: a dark young man playing with the lace at the cuffs of Falconet's scarlet velvet coat, and a blond woman leaning against his shoulder. Around his neck gleamed a chain of rough-cut rubies set in silver bezels. When he was pleased by a courtesan, he would pull one free and gift it to them. It made him very popular.

"Excellent," Falconet drawled. "Finally someone to play with."

Kel sank into a carved jade chair. It wasn't the most comfortable item in the room, but he had no intention of relaxing just yet. "You seem to have plenty to amuse yourself with, Joss."

Falconet smiled and indicated the rosewood table before him. On it a game of Castles had already been half set up; there was a pack of cards there, too. Falconet was an inveterate gambler and could usually convince Conor into a game. If there was no game handy, one could find them betting on which noble would fall asleep first at a banquet, or when it would next rain. "I did not mean that kind of amusement, Kel Anjuman. I am looking for a challenge, and courtesans are hardly a challenge—no disrespect meant, my dears—as they are inclined to let me win. Castles, Prince?"

Conor sank into a black armchair. "Of course." His eyelids were half lowered, as if he were tired, or suspicious of something. Behind hung a mural displaying scenes from an orgiastic celebration; the setting seemed to be the marble steps of a temple, on which a crowd of young worshippers were in the act of coupling. A woman with spilling golden hair wrapped her legs around the man arched above her, her face a mask of ecstasy; a man pinned another against a leaning column, one hand between the other's legs; a woman, her hair wound with scarves, knelt to pleasure her female companion.

Alys looked from the painting to Conor, and smiled her cat's smile. "Refreshments, Monseigneur?"

Conor nodded, eyes already on the Castles board. A silver bell was rung, and a few moments later the doors were flung open. The room began to fill with courtesans. Some carried platters of silver and laid them down on the low rosewood tables. Oysters, shining like pearl earrings, shimmered on beds of ice; fat cherries lay beside pomegranates bursting with seeds. Cups of rich drinking-chocolate were dusted with gold and saffron. Kel caught Conor's quick, amused look: All the foods were, of course, aphrodisiacs, intended to stoke sexual hunger.

He could hardly blame Alys; after all, she didn't make her money from card games played in her salon. As she left the room, she laid a hand on Kel's shoulder. He could smell the myrrh in her perfume as she said in a low voice, "That meeting you wished me to arrange— is now a good time for it?"

Kel nodded.

Alys patted his cheek. "On my signal, go to the library," she said, and swept from the room in a swirl of skirts.

Kel turned to see if any in the room had noticed his interaction with Alys, but none seemed to have; they were concentrated on Conor. Courtesans had begun to perch themselves on the Prince's chair like birds in the boughs of a wind-bitten tree. Others circulated within the room, chatting among themselves. The Caravel had become one of the most expensive pleasure houses in the Temple District since House Aurelian had begun patronizing it, and its courtesans reflected the taste of its customers. All were beautiful in one way or another, and all skilled and patient. Both men and women were dressed simply, in white, like Temple sacrifices in the old days. The white clothes against all the black lacquer was a striking sight, duochrome as the face of the Windtower Clock.

A girl with red hair brought Kel a cup of chocolate; he looked at her quickly, but she was not Silla, of whom he was still fond. The last time they had come to the Caravel, Silla had told him she had saved enough money to set up her own house down the street from the Caravel. Perhaps she had already done it?

Conor captured one of Falconet's pieces and chuckled. Kel noted it in the back of his mind, where his awareness of Conor always lived. He wondered if mothers were like this about their children—always knowing where they were, if they were wounded or pleased. He did not know; he had little experience of mothers.

Falconet, unmoved by his loss, stretched back to kiss the blond girl hanging on his left shoulder. She leaned in, her hair falling like a veil across the velvet nap of his jacket. By this time, several other wealthy patrons had arrived. Kel recognized only one of them: Sieur Lupin Montfaucon, who held the Charter for textiles. An aesthete and bon vivant, his voracious appetite for food, wine, sex, and money was known to everyone on the Hill. He was dark-skinned and elegant, with several dueling scars: one on his cheekbone, and another at the base of his throat. When younger, he had set the fashion for every young man at Court, having started crazes for everything from lynx-fur trousers to paper hats. He was now somewhere in his thirties and, Kel suspected, more than a little bitter about ceding his position as tastemaker to Conor.

He bared his teeth at the half-finished Castles board. "What are the stakes? Gold would seem dull for you, Falconet."

"Money is never dull," said Conor, not taking his eyes off the board. "And not all money is gold. Currently we are playing for shares in the latest dye fleet."

"That will annoy Roverge," said Montfaucon, speaking with

some satisfaction of the family who held the dye Charter. Most of the Charter Families, though forced to work together in the Council, disliked the others, like feral cats defending their territory.

"I will play the winner," Montfaucon added, tossing his gold *broccato* jacket across a chair back. "Though I would prefer cards."

"You could play Kellian," said Conor, not looking up.

Montfaucon glanced at Kel. While Joss seemed to like him well enough, it was always clear that Montfaucon did not. Perhaps his jealousy of Conor expressed itself through disliking his constant companion. After all, to *dislike* the Blood Royal was treason. But Kel, even when posing as the Prince's cousin, was not royal. His only claim to lineage was through Marakand, not Castellane.

Kel smiled pleasantly. "I do not think I would present much of a challenge for Sieur Montfaucon."

It had taken Kel years, back in the beginning, to learn all the Court's honorifics: *Monseigneur* for a prince, *Your Highness* for a king or queen, *Sieur* for a nobleman, *Chatelaine* for a married noblewoman, and *Demoselle* for one as yet unmarried. Most of the nobles, having been told he had lately come from Marakand, had been patient with him. Only Montfaucon had once slapped him, for forgetting the *Sieur*; now that Kel was an adult, he continued to use it, deliberately. He knew it was an annoyance Montfaucon could do nothing about.

"Nor, would I imagine, do you own any fleet shares, Amirzah Anjuman," said Montfaucon. He used the Marakandi term for a nobleman to refer to Kel; it was probably intended to annoy, though it did not work. It only amused Kel to wonder what Montfaucon would think should he ever discover he was conferring a nobleman's title on a mudrat from the gutters. One who might not be Marakandi, either. Over the years Kel had grown used to being addressed as if his background were the same as Conor's. Not that it mattered. Being who he was, he had no history to unwrite.

"I do not. It is a shame," Kel said. "But I see others are arriving; perhaps one could be interested in a hand of red-and-black."

Indeed, the room was slowly filling up with young nobles from the Hill, and a few wealthy merchants. Falconet rose to his feet to greet them, ceding his position at the Castles board to Montfaucon. Kel kept a discreet eye on Conor as a group of newcomers surrounded a young, Hindish courtesan, who had before him a stack of telling cards. He was reading fortunes for nobles and courtesans alike.

Once, years ago, a fortune-teller had come to the Palace, brought by Lilibet to enhance some festivity or other. Conor had argued that she should read Kel's fortune, too. She had taken his hands and looked into his eyes: In that moment, he had felt she could see through him, as if he were made of Sunderglass. "You will live a life of brilliant strangeness," she had said, and then tears had come down her cheeks. He had hurried away, but always remembered: the words, her tears.

Brilliant strangeness.

He had always wondered what the fortune-teller had told Conor; Conor had never revealed it.

A movement at the door caught Kel's attention. It was Charlon Roverge—his elegant tunic straining over his broad shoulders—escorting Antonetta Alleyne and two other noble young ladies: Mirela Gasquet and Sancia Vasey, whose family did not have a Charter, but had grown wealthy from landholdings in Valderan.

Startled, Kel looked directly at Antonetta. It was something he did not often do. Fortunately, she did not appear to notice: She was looking around the room, a blush coloring her cheeks. She wore a dress of pink lace with fashionably puffed sleeves, a heart-shaped gold locket at her throat.

It was not unheard of for ladies from the Hill to visit the Temple District. It was a delicate dance in which they stood well back and giggled at the scandalous goings-on while never partaking of the lascivious pleasures on offer. Still, until this night, Antonetta—no doubt due to her protective mother—had never been one of them.

Falconet shot Kel an amused look. "I'd invited Antonetta," he said, in a low voice, "but I didn't think she'd *come*."

"I'd guess Charlon talked her into it," Kel said. "She would always do anything if we dared her to, as I recall."

This was true. As children, they had all been friends—Joss and Charlon, Conor and Kel and Antonetta. They had raided the Palace kitchens and played in the mud together. Antonetta had been fiercely independent then, furious at even the suggestion that she could do less than the boys. She was always longing to prove herself, to climb the highest tree, ride the fastest horse, be the one who snuck into the kitchens to purloin treats, risking the infamous wrath of Dom Valon.

When they were fifteen, she had vanished from their little group. Conor had only said to Kel, "It was time," and Kel had been miserable and Joss indifferent and Charlon angry, until some time later, when Antonetta made her debut at a ball as one of the Hill's marriageable young ladies. Her hair had been curled as it was now, tight corsets constricting her movements, her formerly bare and dirty feet now laced into satin slippers.

Kel remembered that debut now as he watched Antonetta smile up at Charlon. She had hurt Kel quite badly that night. Later, Montfaucon had replaced her in their group and begun to introduce the other three to the pleasures of the city. Games and tree climbing had been left behind, for good.

Whether Antonetta knew she was the subject of discussion now, Kel could not be sure. She'd sat down on a velvet chair, her hand against her chest, her mouth open as she took in the room. A picture of wide-eyed naïveté. Heavy-lidded, Roverge leaned on the back of her chair, watching a group of courtesans dance below the painted mural, their movements slow and sensual. He seemed to be trying to point out their activities to Antonetta, but she was watching Conor.

Conor seemed oblivious; he was deep in conversation with Audeta, a freckled girl from Valderan perched on the arm of his chair. Her eyelids were painted in stripes of gold and scarlet that flashed as she blinked.

"If Lady Alleyne catches wind that Charlon brought her precious daughter to the Temple District, she'll tear out his ribs and make a musical instrument out of them," said Falconet, sounding as if the prospect amused him.

"I'll talk to Charlon," said Kel, and was off across the room before Falconet could stop him. As he got closer to Charlon, he saw that the Roverge heir was playing with a strand of Antonetta's dark-gold hair. Ten years ago, she would have turned around and pinched him savagely; now she sat calmly, ignoring him. Looking at Conor.

"Charlon." Kel clapped his friend on the back. Not that Charlon was a friend he would have selected himself, but Conor had known him since the cradle and he was firmly planted in Kel's life. "Good to see you." He inclined his head in Antonetta's direction. "And Demoselle Alleyne. This is a surprise. I would have thought your delicate nature and spotless reputation would have kept you far from a place like this."

Something flashed across Antonetta's face—a brief flicker of annoyance. Kel savored it. It was like a glimpse behind an actor's mask, truth hidden by artifice. A moment later it was gone, and Antonetta was smiling the smile that made him grit his teeth. "You are *so* lovely to be concerned about me," she said brightly. "But my reputation is safe. Charlon will look after me, won't you, Charlon?"

"Quite," said Charlon, in a tone that made Kel feel as if spiders were marching up his spine. "Her virtue is safe in my keeping."

Antonetta. He almost wanted to say something, to warn her—but she was already rising to her feet, smoothing down her dress. "Oh, a fortune-teller!" she exclaimed, as if she'd just noticed. "I *adore* getting my fortune told."

She hurried over to join the crowd around the young man with the cards.

"You won't get her into bed, Charlon," said Kel. "You know her mother wants her to marry Conor. And she seems amenable enough to it."

"Conor won't have her," Charlon said, with a lopsided grin. He

had light brown hair and a pale complexion, a reminder that his
mother had been from Detmarch. "He needs to make a foreign alliance. When her dreams come crashing down, I'll be there to wipe
away her tears."

Kel glanced over at Conor, who had pulled Audeta into his lap.
They were sharing the fruit of a cherry, passing it from his mouth
to hers. Matters might have escalated from there had Alys not appeared, all apologies, tapping Conor on the shoulder. After a moment of discussion, he rose and followed her from the room, leaving
Audeta to turn her attentions to Falconet.

As she left the room, Alys dropped a nearly invisible nod in
Kel's direction. *Wait for my signal,* she'd said, and he wondered if
she'd distracted Conor for his benefit. Surely not; she would not
manufacture business with the Prince if she did not truly have any.

With a last glance at Antonetta—her head bent over the fortune-
teller's cards as Sancia squealed at her side—Kel rose to his feet and
made his way quietly out of the salon, heading for the back stairs.
On the landing two young men were pressed up against a wall, kissing; neither noticed Kel as he went by. He kept going, ever upward,
until he reached the last landing and a familiar, unremarkable door.

The first time Kel had seen the library at the Caravel, he'd been
surprised. He'd expected whips and blindfolds hanging from the
walls, but had found a wood-paneled room full of books, small tables and chairs, the smell of ink and leather and tallow. Small,
diamond-paned windows were tucked beneath gables; carcel lamps
hung from metal hooks beside them, casting a saffron light. A
wooden archway led into a second room, where the rarest books
were kept.

"We have the largest collection of books dedicated to the arts of
pleasure in all of Dannemore," Alys had said, with some pride. "Our
customers may scan their pages and choose any scenario or act that
delights them. No other house offers such."

Kel wandered to the stacks now, trailing a finger over the leather
bindings. *A Brief History of Pleasure.* (He wondered why that would

be better than a lengthy history of the subject, which surely would
be more suitable.) Many were from other lands, and Kel's gaze
skipped over the spines, translating: *The Mirror of Love, The Perfumed Garden, The Secret Instructions of the Jade Bedchamber.*

"You came," said a voice behind him. "Alys said you would, but
I rather wondered."

Kel rose, turning, and saw a young man about his own age leaning in the archway, his expression open and curious. He was younger
than Kel had expected, and pretty as a girl, with pale-gold hair and
dark-blue eyes. Kel wondered for a moment if he had Northern
blood—which would mean Alys did, too, though it showed less in
her. "You're Merren Asper?" Kel said. "Alys's brother?"

Merren nodded pleasantly. "And you're Kel Anjuman, the
Prince's cousin. Now that we have identified each other by our rel-
atives, come and talk," he said, advancing into the room and pulling
out one of the chairs surrounding a long table. He gestured for Kel
to sit, too.

Kel complied, studying Merren. He wore the unofficial uniform
of a student at the Academie, Castellane's university: faded black
jacket, a loose white cravat at the throat, worn old shoes, and too-
long hair. Up close, he could see the resemblance to Alys in Merren's blue eyes and delicate features. A faint scent rose from his
clothes, not unpleasant: something sharp and green, like the freshly
cut stems of plants.

"Your sister tells me you're the best chemist in all of Castellane," said Kel.

Merren looked pleased. "Does she?" He ducked under the table
and reemerged with a bottle of wine. He peeled away the wax stop-
per from the bottle before discarding it on the table. Imprinted into
the wax was a pattern of grapevines: the symbol of House Uzec. It
was impossible to get away from the Charter Families, Kel thought.
"Would you like a drink?"

"I'm not sure," Kel said. "Your sister also says you're the best
poisoner in all of Castellane."

Merren looked offended. He took a swig from the bottle, coughed, and said, "I am a *student* of poisons. They are all chemical compounds, after all. It doesn't mean I go about madly poisoning people—especially not my sister's clients. She would murder me."

This seemed true. Alys protected her business as a mother might protect a child. Besides, Merren had drunk from the bottle himself. Kel held a hand out. "All right."

The wine was crisp as an apple and spread a pleasant warmth through Kel's chest. *Well chosen, Uzec.* "I didn't realize the Academie offered courses on poison."

"They don't. Technically, I am a student of chemistry and botany. Where it comes to poisons, I am self-taught." Merren smiled as brightly as if he were discussing the study of poetry or dancing. "As a scholar once said, the only difference between a poison and a remedy is the dose. The deadliest poison is not fatal in a single grain, and milk or water can be lethal if you consume too much of it."

Kel smiled a little. "Yet I am sure those who seek you out are not trying to purchase milk or water."

"They want different things. Compounds for dyes, soaps, even shipbuilding. Anything, really." Merren looked thoughtful. "I am a poison-maker because I find the components of poison interesting, not because I find death interesting."

"What is interesting about poison?"

Merren looked down the neck of the wine bottle and said, "Before the Sundering, mages could kill with a touch, a look. Poison is the closest we have now to such power. A real poisoner can create a venom that takes years to work, or place a toxin on the pages of a book so that the reader is envenomed by each page he turns. I can poison a mirror, a pair of gloves, the hilt of a sword. And poison makes us equal. A dockworker, a noble, a king—the same dose kills them all." He cocked his head to the side. "Who do *you* want to poison?"

Under the saffron light, Merren's hair was the color of the brocade on Montfaucon's jacket. In another time, another life, Kel might have been a student alongside someone like Merren. Might have been his friend. But a glass wall existed between Kel and all those outside a small circle who knew who he truly was. He could not breach it. And he was here on Palace business, he reminded himself, whether the Palace knew it or not.

"No one," Kel said. "Chemistry offers more than just poisons, does it not? It offers remedies and cures—and antidotes." He sat back in his chair. "One of the Castelguards, Dom Guion, was poisoned last week. By a lover, they say, a noblewoman of Sarthe. Now, I am not that concerned about the ill-considered affairs of Castelguards, but the emergence of a new poison, one in use by the nobles of Sarthe, a country that does not like our country—a venom that might be used against Princes—*that* concerns me."

"You are worried for your cousin?"

Kel inclined his head. Worrying about Conor was his job. No, keeping Conor *alive* was his job, and that meant more than simply standing in front of crowds pretending to be him while half expecting an arrow to the chest. It meant thinking about who might want to harm Conor, and how.

In this sense, his job overlapped with Jolivet's. But Jolivet's only comment on the death of the Castelguard had been that one should avoid entanglements with Sarthian women. Meanwhile, Kel had prickled with anxiety. The idea that there was some new threat out there bothered him.

"Well," said Merren, "it wasn't a new poison. It was, in fact, quite an old one, often used during the time of the Empire. *Cantarella*, it is called. Many have thought the formula lost, but—" He waved a hand expansively—"not me, of course."

"So you know the poison. Is there an antidote? I'd like to buy it from you, if it exists."

Merren looked as pleased with himself as a mother cat with a litter of kittens. "It does. But I have to ask—you live at the Palace, don't you? I would assume that the chirurgeons there could get anything they wanted. Poisons, antidotes, remedies—"

"There is one doctor, the Royal Surgeon," said Kel. "He is a minor son of the Gasquet Charter Family. He is also an idiot." Kel had never managed to discover where Gasquet had come by what medical knowledge he had. The Palace denizens tended to steer clear of his treatments unless they were unavoidable; Gasquet was a great fan of bleeding, and kept an unfriendly colony of leeches in his private apartments. "Not only a terrible physician, but knows nothing of what you call remedies. Says the best cure for poison is prevention, and Conor should simply avoid eating food unless someone tastes it first."

"And the Prince doesn't want to do that?"

Kel thought of Conor, downstairs, his lips stained with wine and cherries. "It's not a practical solution."

"I suppose not," Merren said. "Besides, many poisons show their effects over time. A taster is only useful if the poison is meant to be instant."

"Perhaps when you leave the Academie, you could replace Gasquet. He certainly needs replacing."

Merren shook his head. "I'm against the monarchy," he said cheerfully. "Though monarchies in general," he added hastily, "not House Aurelian in particular. And it is only a philosophy. The only king I like the sound of is the Ragpicker King."

Kel couldn't help but smile. "You are against kings but for criminals, then?"

"He's a good sort of criminal," said Merren, serious as a child asking whether it was true that the Gods lived in the clouds. "Not like Prosper Beck."

Kel had heard of Prosper Beck. The area just behind the docks was called the Maze: a labyrinth of flophouses, pawnshops, cheap food stalls, and crumbling warehouses that, at night, became venues for illegal boxing tournaments, duels (also illegal), and the buying and selling of various contraband. It was a place the Vigilants themselves refused to go after dark. Kel had always assumed the denizens of the Maze answered to the Ragpicker King, but in the past few months he had heard the name Prosper Beck whispered about; rumor held that someone new was controlling the Maze.

Outside, the Windtower Clock chimed eleven and Merren frowned. When he turned to look out the window, Kel could not help but note the carefully mended tears in his jacket. Montfaucon, it was said, never wore the same article of clothing twice. "It grows late," Merren said. "The *cantarella* antidote—I can have it ready by Seaday. Ten crowns for four doses—two of poison, two of antidote."

He said *ten crowns* as if it were an enormous sum, and Kel reminded himself that, for most people, it was. "That's fair," Kel said. "We should arrange a place to meet. I assume you have lodgings in the Scholars' Quarter? What's the address?"

"Chancellor Street, across from the Lafont Bookshop," said Merren, and closed his mouth sharply, as if he had not meant to let that information out. "But we shouldn't meet there. I know a tea shop—"

There was a knock on the door. Domna Alys's partner, Hadja, peeked her head into the library. A band of colorful silk held back her cloud of curling dark hair.

"Sieur Anjuman," she said, inclining her head in Kel's direction, "the Prince awaits you outside."

Kel scrambled to his feet. This was not at all part of his plan; by his calculations, Conor ought to have been distracted for at least another few hours. "Is something wrong? Why would he be leaving?"

Hadja shook her head, setting her gold earrings to swinging against her russet-brown skin. "I've no idea. I didn't speak with him. One of the Hindish girls passed me a message."

Kel felt in his pocket for his coin purse and tossed five crowns to Merren. "Half now, half when I pick up the doses. I'll see you then."

"Wait—" Merren began, but Kel was already out the door. He loped downstairs, cutting through the main room of the Caravel, where the hanging tapestries had been drawn back to reveal the raised dais of a stage. Props were being brought out; it seemed a performance was soon to take place. Odd that Conor would have chosen to miss it.

Still puzzling, Kel made his way outside, into the fading warmth of the night. He glanced up and down Hourglass Street. Light spilled in dancing squares onto the cobblestones, and laughing groups strolled by the canal water. In the distance, a black carriage rattled toward the Caravel; someone inside was singing a loud and drunken song. A light wind spun discarded paper into miniature funnels.

There was no sign of Conor, or the horses. Kel frowned. Perhaps Conor had grown tired of waiting for him; it would not be entirely out of character. Kel had half turned to go back inside the Caravel when he heard the screech of wheels. He spun around. Whoever had been singing inside the black carriage had stopped. It swung toward him, wheels skipping over the cobblestones.

They were painted blood red.

The body of the carriage skidded sideways, blocking Kel's path. Black curtains shaded the windows; he could not see who was inside. He turned, ready to flip himself over the low stone wall along the canal—he'd take his chances in the water—but wine had made him slow. A hand caught the back of his jacket. He was jerked back, half flung through the open door of the carriage and onto the seat.

Kel scrambled up as the door slammed shut behind him. He was not alone. There was someone else in the carriage—two someones— and a flash of something silver. Eyes still adjusting to the dark, Kel saw metal gleam, and felt the point of a knife rest against the hollow of his throat. He closed his eyes.

For that moment, there was only silence, darkness, his own breathing, and the knife at his throat. Then the driver, overhead, shouted hoarsely; a moment later, the carriage jerked forward, flying over the cobblestones into the night.

x x x

"In times of old, the wrath of the Sorcerer-Kings scorched the earth," Lin read, "for they had taken to themselves power that is not meant for men to have, but only Gods. Their fury boiled the seas and brought down mountains. The land was marked with Sunder-glass where magic had scarred it. Each person on earth ran before them in terror—save Adassa, the Queen of Aram. She alone rose against them. Knowing she could not destroy them, instead she destroyed magic itself, rendering them powerless. All magic was taken from the earth, save that which Adassa had set aside for the use of her people alone: the magic of *gematry*. And Adassa passed into the shadowed realm, where she became a Goddess, the light of the Ash-kari people, who are her Chosen ones."

Lin closed the book. Mariam, a small figure half buried beneath a massive pile of bedcovers, smiled faintly. "I always like the parts where Adassa is a woman best," she said. "Before she becomes the Goddess. She had her moments of weakness and fear, like the rest of us."

Lin put the back of her hand against Mariam's forehead. It was cool now, to her relief. Mari had been crying out, feverish and de-lirious, by the time they had arrived back from Valerian Square that afternoon. There had been some consternation among the guards at the gates of the Sault over the appearance of a Palace carriage, but they had helped Lin carry Mariam inside. She'd brought her friend directly to her own house and settled her into bed in Josit's room; her brother was away on the Gold Roads, after all, and she knew he would not have minded.

It had taken some arguing with Chana Dorin, who thought Mariam would be better treated at the Etse Kebeth, the House of Women. But Lin was used to arguing with Chana. Lin pointed out that she was a physician, that no one knew her skills better than Chana, and that here, in Lin's small whitewashed home, Mariam would have peace and quiet and constant attendance.

It was Mariam who had put an end to the battle; she'd turned over on the bed and, between bouts of coughing, announced: "Honestly, the two of you will still be fighting over me when I am dead and gone. Chana, let me stay here with Lin. It's what I want."

So Chana had succumbed. She'd helped Lin get Mariam into a clean nightgown, and wrapped her hands and forehead in wet cloths to break her fever. Lin had brewed evening primrose into poultices and placed them on Mariam's chest to reduce inflammation; she'd fashioned tisanes of cinnamon and turmeric to make her cough, of ginseng, lemon, salt water, and honey to open her lungs, and spikenard to soothe her. When—despite the cloths—Mariam's fever rose, Chana had gone to the physick garden to fetch willowbark to bring it down.

Mariam's fever had broken after midnight, as fevers often did. The end often came in the late watches of the night, but so did healing: Life and death both struck in the shadowed hours. When Mariam had woken, restless and aching, Lin had decided to read to her from a book of the old tales she'd found on the windowsill. She and Mariam had loved the stories when they were small: tales of Adassa, of her bravery in defeating the Sorcerer-Kings of old, of her cleverness in keeping back a small part of the magic that had been destroyed by the Sundering and holding it for her people. It was because of her that the Ashkar could still work even small magics; without the Goddess, they would be as bereft as others.

"Do you remember when we were children?" Mariam asked. "We both thought we were certain to be the Goddess Returned. We would dress up in blue robes and try to cast spells. I spent several whole afternoons trying to move bits of sticks and paper with my magic."

That was a long time ago, Lin thought. Not quite her earliest memory. Far, far back she could recall her mother and father; both traders on the Gold Roads, they had smelled of cinnamon and lavender and faraway places. She recalled them swinging her between them while she laughed; recalled her mother cooking, her father holding baby Josit up, his chubby hands reaching for the clouds.

She did not recall learning that they were dead. She knew it must have happened, that someone would have told them. She knew she had cried, because she had understood what was happening, and that Josit had cried because he did not. Bandits had overtaken her parents' caravan near Jiqal, the desert that was all that remained of what had once been Aram. Their waggon had been seized, their throats slashed, their bodies thrown into the Road to be picked over by vultures. Though surely no one had told her *that;* still, she had overheard whispers: Such a terrible thing, people said. Such bad luck. And who would take the children?

Children were precious to the Ashkar. They represented the survival of a people who had no homeland, and thus had been in danger of extinction since the Sundering. It was assumed Lin and Josit's one surviving relative, their maternal grandfather, would take them in. Lin had even heard envious muttering. Mayesh Bensimon, the Counselor to the King. Save the Maharam, he was the most influential man in the Sault. He owned a grand house near the Shulamat. A lucky life they would have with him, surely.

Only he had not wanted them.

She recalled sitting in her bedroom with Josit in her lap, listening to Davit Benezar, the Maharam, arguing with Mayesh in the corridor outside. *I cannot do it*, Mayesh had said. Despite the words he was saying, the sound of his voice was, briefly, comforting to Lin. She associated it with her parents, with feast nights when the whole family gathered and Mayesh read aloud, as the candles burned, from the *Book of Makabi*. He would ask Lin questions about Judah Makabi, the wandering of the Ashkar, and the Goddess, and when she got the answers right he would reward her with *loukoum*, a sweet candy of rosewater and almond.

But: "No, no, no," he said to Benezar. "My duties will not allow for raising children. I do not have time, nor attention. I must be at the Palace every day, at any hour they call me."

"Then step down," snapped the Maharam. "Let someone else

counsel the King of Castellane. These children are your blood and flesh."

But Mayesh had been curt. The children would be better served in the community. Lin would go to the Etse Kebeth, and Josit to the Dāsu Kebeth, the House of Men. Mayesh would look in on them from time to time, as their grandfather. That was the end of it.

Lin still recalled the pain of being separated from Josit. They had pulled him wailing from her arms to take him to the Dāsu Kebeth, and though he was only a street away from her, she felt his absence like a wound. Like the Goddess, she thought, she had been wounded thrice, each name a scar of fire beneath her heart: mother, father, brother.

Chana, who headed the House of Women with her wife, Irit, tried to console Lin and make her comfortable, but Lin's rage would not allow it. She was like a wild thing, clambering up into trees from which she could not be fetched down, screaming and smashing plates and glasses, tearing her own skin with her nails.

"Make him come," Lin sobbed, when Chana, at her wit's end, took her only pair of shoes to stop her running away. But the next day, when Mayesh did come to her in the physick garden, bringing an expensive gold necklace from the Palace as a gift, she only flung it at him and ran back inside the Women's House.

That night, as Lin lay shaking on her bed, someone came into her room. A small girl with smooth dark braids wound around her head, pale skin, and short, spiky lashes. Lin knew who she was. Mariam Duhary, an orphan refugee from Favár, the capital of Malgasi. Like Lin and several others, she lived here in the House of Women. Unlike Lin, she didn't seem to mind.

She climbed onto the bed beside Lin and sat quietly while Lin thrashed and hit her pillow and kicked at the walls. Eventually, kicking and thrashing in the face of so much quiet patience became unrewarding. Lin settled into silence, glaring up at Mariam through her tangled hair.

"I know what you're feeling," Mariam said. Lin got ready to snap; *no one* knew what she was feeling, even if they all claimed they did. "My parents are also dead. When Malgasi turned against the Ashkar, they sent the *vamberj*—the wolf-masked soldiers—to hunt us down. They would call out through the streets: *Ettyaszti, mosze-gyellem nas.* Come out, wherever you are. They caught my mother on her way to market. She was hung in the main square of Favár, for the crime of being Ashkar. My father and I fled, or the Malgasi would have killed us, too. We traveled the Gold Roads until he grew too sick. We came here, traveling through the night. My father had said things would be better for us in Castellane. But by the time we arrived in the morning, he was dead in the back of the waggon." Her voice was matter-of-fact as she recounted these horrors, so much so that Lin fell silent. "Everyone wants to tell you that it isn't so bad, but it *is*. You will be so sad that you will feel like you will die. But you won't die. And with every day that passes, you will get back a little piece of yourself."

Lin blinked. No one had spoken to her like this since her parents' death. There was something extraordinary about it.

"Besides," Mariam added, "you're lucky."

Lin sat up, angry, kicking at her covers. "What do you mean, I'm lucky?"

"You've got a brother, don't you?" said Mariam. In the shadows, the gold circle that hung on a chain around her neck gleamed darkly. The words of the Lady's Prayer looked like scratches. "I have no one but me. I am the only Duhary in Castellane. Maybe the only one in the world."

Lin noticed that Mariam did not mention Mayesh. She was glad. She realized in that moment how foolish she had been, demanding that Mayesh visit her. Mayesh waited on the pleasure of the King, not the whim of his grandchildren. He did not belong to Lin. He belonged to the Palace.

Mariam had drawn the shawl from around her thin shoulders and handed it to Lin. It was a pretty thing, of fine cambric and lace.

"Take this," she said. "It makes a very satisfying sound when you rip it. Whenever you feel everything is unfair and awful, tear a piece off."

And she tore the shawl in half. For the first time in weeks, Lin smiled.

After that, the girls were inseparable. Mariam was sister and best friend all in one. They took lessons together, played together, and helped each other with tasks like cleaning the kitchen and planting the physick garden, where all the Sault's herbs and medicinal flowers were grown. Lin thought of Mariam, with some envy, as graceful and delicate in her sensibilities; she never seemed to want to dig in the dirt, wrestle with the other children, or clamber up into the chestnut trees with Lin and Josit. Lin envied her decorum but knew perfectly well she could not change her own nature. She herself was always dirty and knee-skinned from playing; she loved to climb the Sault walls and stand at their very edge as the Shomrim did, her toes jutting over the side, the harbor and the crowded streets of the city swaying below.

When Lin turned thirteen, she realized Mariam was not simply uninterested in roughhousing as Lin previously thought. She began to see, with a more adult eye, that Mariam was not delicate, but rather fragile. Fragile and ill. Her pale skin bruised easily; a short walk would leave her short of breath. She had fevers that came and went, and often she'd be up all night coughing, while Chana Dorin sat with her, giving her ginger tea.

"There's something wrong with her," she'd observed to Chana Dorin one day, when the older woman was plucking leaves from a feverfew plant in the physick garden. "Mariam. She's sick."

"So now you notice," was all Chana said.

"Isn't there something you could give her?" Lin had demanded. "Some kind of medicine?"

Chana had sat back on her heels, her patched skirt spreading around her in the dirt. "Don't you imagine I've tried everything?" she snapped. "If the physicians could help her, Lin, they would."

Something about her tone made Lin realize that Chana was angry because she, too, felt impotent, powerless to help the girl in her care. Whatever had killed Mariam's father, it seemed, was going to kill her, too, unless someone did something about it.

Lin decided that someone would have to be her. She had gone to Chana and told her that she wanted to study healing. The boys her age who planned to be physicians had already begun their training. She would need to catch up if she was to learn everything there was to know about medicine and cure Mariam.

"Please," Mariam said now, snapping her out of her reverie. "You look half dead from tiredness. Go take a nap. I'll be fine, Linnet."

Hardly anyone ever called Lin by her full name. When Mariam did, though, it sounded like family in Lin's ears. A mother's sternness, a sister's exasperation. She touched Mariam's thin cheek. "I'm not tired."

"Well, I am," Mariam said. "But I can't settle. Some hot milk and honey—"

"Of course. I'll get it." Lin set the old book down on the nightstand and headed to the kitchen. She was already thinking about what else she could put in the milk that would be covered by the flavor of honey. Her mind ticked through remedies for inflammation. *Pine bark, frankincense, cat's claw*—

"How is she?" Chana's voice brought Lin out of her reverie. The older woman was seated at Lin's scrubbed pinewood table with a mug of *karak*. Her iron-gray hair hung long and straight about her shoulders; her dark eyes, set in a nest of fine, raying wrinkles, were sharp as needle tips.

Several pots were boiling away on the stove behind her. Like most houses in the Sault, Lin's had a single main room that combined the functions of sitting room, dining room, and kitchen. All houses in the Sault were small—square, whitewashed boxes, a function of the limited space within the walls.

Inside, Lin had done what she could to make the space hers, using items Josit brought back from the Gold Roads on his infrequent visits. A painted mirror from Hanse, wooden toys from Detmarch, a chunk of striped marble from Sarthe, a celadon horse from Geumjoseon. The curtains were Hindish fabric, a fine linen with a multicolored woven border. Lin did not like to think of her brother out on the Roads, but the fever for traveling had been in his blood since he was born. She had learned to accept his absences, his wandering, the way you accepted things you had no choice about.

She turned back now to glance into his room. She was not surprised to see Mariam already asleep, her arm flung across her face. She closed the door quietly and came to sit with Chana at the table.

"She's dying," Lin said. The words tasted as bitter as failure. "Not quickly, but she's dying."

Chana got up from the table and went into the kitchen. Lin stared unseeingly ahead as Chana clanked about with the kettle.

"I've tried everything," Lin said. "Every talisman, every tisane, every remedy in every book I could find. She was better for a while—a long while. But now nothing is working."

Chana returned to the table with a dented mug of steaming tea. She pushed it across the scrubbed wood toward Lin before folding her hands—big, capable hands, strong looking, with knobbed knuckles. But Lin knew those hands were capable of incredibly delicate *gematry* work; Chana Dorin made the best talismans in the Sault.

"Do you remember?" Chana asked, watching as Lin took a sip of the hot liquid. It burned a pathway into her stomach that reminded her how long it had been since she'd eaten. "When I first brought you to the Maharam and told him he must allow you to study medicine?"

Lin nodded. It had been the first time she had been inside the Shulamat. Every Sault had its heart: the Kathot, its main square, and in the Kathot, the Shulamat. A combination of temple, library, and courthouse, the Shulamat was where the Maharam presided over religious ceremonies and heard small cases brought before him: a dispute between two neighbors, perhaps, or an argument among scholars over the interpretation of a passage in the *Book of Makabi.*

She had always thought the Shulamat was the most beautiful building in the Sault by far, with a domed roof covered in shimmering blue *tesserae* and walls of creamy marble. One could see the roof even from outside the gates, like a piece of sky fallen to earth.

Lin could remember how small she had felt climbing the stairs of the Shulamat. How tightly she had held Chana Dorin's hand as they passed through, and how her heart had soared once they stood in the main room, beneath the inverted bowl of the golden dome. Here the mosaic-work stunned with its beauty. The floor was tiled in patterns of green vines and fat red pomegranates; the walls were deep blue, against which patterns of stars were picked out in golden *tesserae*—the constellations as seen from Aram, she would learn years later. A great chest of silver held the hand-copied scrolls of the *Book of Makabi;* a thick cloth of gold draped the Almenor, the great altar. Woven into the cloth were the words of the first Great Question, the same words etched into the charm around Lin's throat:

How shall we sing our Lady's song in a strange land?

On a raised dais beneath the dome sat the Maharam. He had been younger then, though to Lin he had always seemed old. His beard and hair were pure white, his pale hands swollen at the joints. His shoulders were bent beneath his dark-blue *sillon*, the ceremonial robe of the Ashkar. Around his neck gleamed a large circular pendant that bore the Lady's Prayer. The Book of Makabi instructed all Ashkar to bear some version of the Prayer with them wherever they went: Some embroidered it into their clothes, while many others preferred to wear the words as a charm: a bracelet or a pendant. Something that kept it always close to their skin.

The Maharam had greeted Chana Dorin with an expression of sympathy for the recent death of her wife, Irit, which Chana waved away with her usual stubborn refusal to hear anything that smacked to her of pity. It seemed clear the Maharam had known Chana was coming and even what she would ask, though he heard her out patiently enough. Lin's ears burned as Chana told him how clever she was, how quick-minded, and what a ready student of medicine she would make. She had not been so praised in years.

When she was done, the Maharam had sighed. "I do not believe it is a good idea, Chana."

Chana stuck her jaw out. "I don't see why not. The Goddess was a woman, before she ascended. She was also a healer."

"That was in the time before the Sundering," the Maharam had said. "We had magic then, and Aram, and freedom. Now we are without a home, guests in the city of Castellane. And not always welcome guests." His gaze came to rest on Lin. "If you were a physician, my girl, you would have to traverse this city alone, often at night. And men of the *malbushim* are not like men in the Sault. They are not bound to respect you."

"I can protect myself," Lin had said. "All the boys in the Dāsu Kebeth are afraid of me."

Chana had snorted, but the Maharam had not been amused. "I suppose your grandfather put you up to this," he'd said to Lin.

"Davit, no," Chana had protested. "Mayesh is quite against the idea, in fact."

Davit. So the Maharam had a name. He responded to hearing it with a shrug. "I will think on it, Chana."

Lin had been crushed, sure they'd been brushed off. But Chana, brisk as always, had only told her not to mope. The next day a messenger had come from the Shulamat, bearing the news that the Maharam had given his approval. Lin could study to be a physician, as long as she passed every test. No mistakes would be allowed, and no second chances.

Now, remembering the exuberance of that day, the way she and Mariam had danced around the physick garden, Lin managed a smile. "I remember."

"I always counted it as a great victory," Chana said.

"I never understood why the Maharam agreed to it," said Lin. "He must be fonder of you than he lets on."

Chana shook her head, setting the colorful beads of her neck-
laces to swaying. "Not at all. He agreed to annoy your grandfather,
that's all. He and your grandfather cannot stand each other."

"Then I suppose I ought to be glad Mayesh was against my becoming a physician," Lin said. "So typical of him. He was allowed
to choose to be Counselor, but the Goddess forbid I have a hand in
my own destiny."

"Is he so bad?" Chana set her mug aside. "I had hoped, Lin, that
when you grew to adulthood, you could find some peace with your
grandfather. He did send that carriage for you and Mariam today,
did he not?"

Lin shrugged, uncomfortable. "It was not meant as a kindness.
He was simply showing his power." *And that he made the right decision*, she thought, *choosing the Palace and its opportunities over Josit
and me.*

Chana did not respond. She was examining the books flung
across the table—the *Book of Remedies*, the *Seventeen Rules*, the *Sefer
Refuot*, the *Materia Medica*. Well, not quite examining them, Lin
thought. She was staring as if she could bore a hole through the
pages with her eyes. "Linnet," she said, "there is something I ought
to tell you."

Lin leaned forward. "What is it, Chana? You're scaring me."

"Your grandfather was never opposed to you becoming a physician. When I consulted him, he merely said it was your decision,
not one for him to help or hinder. I told the Maharam otherwise
because I knew it was the only way to get him to agree to allow it."

"Mayesh said it was *my* decision?"

"Yes," Chana said. "I should have told you before. I didn't realize you even still remembered what I said that day, much less that
you were still angry with Mayesh for it. There is much he has done
that has earned your anger, Lin, but that was one thing he did not
do."

"Why . . ." Lin began, slowly. "Why does the Maharam hate
him so much?"

Chana took a swig of cold *karak* and made a face. "You know of the Maharam's son?"

"Yes. Asher." Lin thought back. She did not remember the boy, but the stories about him persisted. "He was exiled, wasn't he?"

Exile. The worst punishment the Sault and its council of elders could dole out. To be exiled was to be stripped of your identity. You were no longer Ashkar, forbidden to ever speak to or see your family, your friends, your spouse. Cut off from everything you had ever known, you would be driven from the gates to fend for yourself in the world of the *malbushim*, without family, money, or a place in the world.

"He was," Chana said heavily. "You would have been perhaps five years old when it happened. He delved into what is forbidden." She gazed at the fire, now sunk into saffron embers. "He believed that the magic that existed before the Sundering had not all been lost forever. That he could awaken it, access it, learn to practice it."

Lin's heart gave an odd little thump. "He was exiled just for trying to learn about magic? He was only a boy, wasn't he—fifteen or sixteen? It seems like a mistake, not a crime."

"He did more than just learn about it," said Chana. "He tried to use it. Do you know what bone conjuring is?"

Lin shook her head.

"His mother had died a year or so before," said Chana. "He was trying to bring her back. Even before the Sundering, such things were forbidden." She crossed her arms over her broad chest. "Your grandfather was the only one of the elders to speak up against his exile. He told the Maharam he would regret it forever if he banished his only son, his only remaining family, from the Sault. The Maharam has never forgiven him for it."

"Do you think he does regret it? The Maharam?"

Chana sighed. "I think he had no choice but to do what he did. He adored Asher, but the boy could have done nothing worse in his father's eyes. In all our eyes. The world was nearly destroyed once by such dangerous magic. Mayesh should have known better than to say such things."

Lin was silent. What, she wondered, had Asher Benezar done, precisely? Read books? Attempted spellwork? Like everyone in Dannemore, Lin knew of the Sorcerer-Kings whose battles had scorched the earth, leaving scars of Sunderglass behind—a constant reminder of the dangers and evils of magic. But she did not know how they had done it. How had magic been performed? The knowledge had been lost, she thought, along with the power.

"Lin," said Chana. "What are you thinking?"

Lin stood up, crossing the room to the window. Outside she could see the winding cobblestoned street; over the tops of the nearest houses, the dome of the Shulamat rose, glimmering under the moonlight. And all around, of course, the walls, rising to cut off her view of Castellane. Only the Hill was visible, high and distant, and the white glow of Marivent—the Palace—like a second moon. "I am thinking," Lin said, "that if there was a chance for me to heal Mariam using magic, I would be tempted just as Asher was."

"We—the Ashkar alone—*have* magic. We have *gematry*. We have talismans. They are what we are allowed to use, and they assist us greatly. Lin, you know that."

"I do know that. I also know that in the days before the Sundering, physicians mixed magic and science to wondrous effect. They could knit broken bones instantly, heal a shattered skull, stop the growth of tumors—"

"Enough." Chana cut her off, her tone coldly forbidding. "Keep such thoughts out of your head, Lin. The Maharam was willing to exile his own son for seeking such knowledge. Do not imagine he would be any kinder to you."

But power cannot remain untrammeled forever. As the knowledge of the One Word spread through Dannemore, magic altered from a force anyone with the talent and will could master to a jealously guarded secret gathered in the hands of a few powerful magicians. Those magic-users quickly rose to political prominence. They named themselves kings and queens, and began to lay out the borders of their territories. Tribes became towns, towns became cities, and land became kingdoms. And thus the age of the Sorcerer-Kings began.

—*Tales of the Sorcerer-Kings*, Laocantus Aurus Iovit III

CHAPTER FOUR

Most people, Kel knew, would panic with a blade at their throat. He didn't like it much himself, but he could feel all the years of Jolivet's training paying off: all the times Jolivet had run him through his paces over and over, teaching how he must learn to stand unmoving between Conor and an arrow, Conor and a sword, Conor and a dagger's point. He had learned not to flinch at the touch of sharpened metal, even when it cut his skin.

He did not flinch now, only kept his eyes closed. His talisman was safely put away; surely they could not think he was Conor. Nobles were kidnapped sometimes, when traveling, for money, but that didn't happen within Castellane. Not because the nobility was beloved, but because of the punishment—imprisonment in the Trick, the prison tower where those who had committed treason waited to be executed. Torture that lasted weeks, whatever remained afterward fed to the crocodiles in the harbor—was dreaded, and with good reason.

"I thought he'd twitch a bit more," said an amused, female voice. "He's been well trained."

"Legate Jolivet's hand, I'd wager," said the second voice. This one was male, low and oddly musical. "Tsk, tsk." Something slapped away Kel's hand as he felt for the carriage door. "It's locked, and even if it weren't, I would not recommend hurling yourself out. Such a fall, at this speed, could well be fatal."

Kel sat back. The carriage seats were comfortable, at least. He could feel velvet and leather under his hands. He said, "If you wish to rob me, go ahead. I have not seen your faces. Take what you want and let me go. If you wish to harm me otherwise, be aware I have powerful friends. You will regret it."

The man chuckled, the sound rich and dark as *karak*. "I took you *because* you have powerful friends. Now open your eyes. You are wasting my time, and I will not take kindly to it if you persist."

The point of the knife dug deeper into the hollow of Kel's throat, a painful kiss. He opened his eyes, and saw at first only darkness inside the carriage. Light began to glow, and Kel realized the source was a Sunderglass pendant on a chain, dangling from the carriage roof. Kel stared at it: Such objects were rare, and few could afford their like.

It gave off a soft but potent light, in which Kel finally saw his two companions clearly. The first was a young Chosean woman with long black hair, divided into two braids. She wore a silk tunic and trousers the color of foxgloves and bracelets of milky violet chalcedony on her wrists. In her right hand was a long dagger with a handle of white jade, its point resting against Kel's throat.

Beside her was a very tall, very slender man dressed in black. Not Merren's rusty student black; this man's clothes were rich and expensive looking, from his velvet frock coat to the blackthorn cane upon which he rested his left hand. A gold ring bearing the sigil of a bird—a magpie, Kel thought—gleamed on his finger. His eyes were the only thing about him that was neither black nor white. They were a very dark green, and seemed to hold a strange light inside them. He said, "Do you know who I am?"

He goes round all in black, like Gentleman Death come to take your soul, and his carriage wheels are stained with blood.

"Yes," Kel said. "You're the Ragpicker King." He didn't say, *I thought you'd be older.* He guessed the man in front of him was perhaps thirty.

"And you're wondering what I want with you," said the Ragpicker King. "Sword Catcher."

Adrenaline shot through Kel's body. He forced himself to remain motionless, the point of the knife still leveled against his throat.

The Ragpicker King only smiled. "Let me be more clear, Kellian Saren. You were given to Conor Aurelian of House Aurelian at the tender age of ten, under the Malgasi custom of the *Királar,* the King's Blade. It is your job to protect the Prince with your own life. In dangerous situations you take his place, aided by a talisman that you are"—he narrowed his eyes—"not currently wearing. Though I would not be fooled either way. I know who you really are." He folded his long pale hands over the top of his cane. "Is there anything you'd like to add?"

"No," Kel said. There was a strange feeling in the back of his throat. A sort of pressure. He wanted to swallow hard, as if against a bitter taste, but he suspected his companions would take it as a sign of nervousness. "Nothing."

The girl with the blade looked sideways at the Ragpicker King. "This is dull," she observed. "Perhaps I should—"

"Not yet, Ji-An." The Ragpicker King studied Kel's face. Kel kept his expression neutral. Lights came and went around the edges of the black-curtained windows. Kel guessed they were somewhere in the Silver Streets, the merchant neighborhood that bordered the Temple District. "You are wondering, Sword Catcher, why I have an interest in you. Your business is Palace business, and my business is with the streets of Castellane. Yet sometimes—more often than you might guess—they intersect. There are things I wish to know. *Need* to know. And I could use your help."

"We could all use something," Kel said. "That doesn't mean we'll obtain it."

"You're awfully rude," observed Ji-An, her hand steady on the dagger's handle. "He's offering you a job, you know."

"I have a job. We've just been discussing it."

"And I want you to keep your job," said the Ragpicker King, crossing his impossibly long legs. "So think of what I am offering as a partnership. You help me, and in return, I help you."

"I don't see how you could help me," Kel said, half distracted— the peculiar feeling remained in the back of his throat, halfway between a scrape and a tickle. It wasn't painful, but it was strangely familiar. *When have I felt it before?*

"It is your duty to protect the Prince," said the Ragpicker King, "but not all threats come from foreign powers or power-hungry nobles. Some threats come from the city. Anti-monarchists, criminals— not the gentlemanly sort like myself, of course—or rebellious merchants. The information I possess could be valuable to you."

Kel blinked. None of this was quite what he had expected—not that he had anticipated being kidnapped tonight in the first place. "I will not spy on the royal family for you," he said. "And I do not see why you would be interested in general gossip from the Hill."

The Ragpicker King leaned forward, his hands folded atop his cane. "Do you know the name Prosper Beck?"

Odd that Prosper Beck should come up twice in one night. "Yes. Your rival, I imagine?"

Ji-An snorted, but the Ragpicker King seemed unmoved by the comment. He said, "I wish to know who is funding Prosper Beck. I can tell you it is not just *unusual* for a criminal so wealthy and well connected to simply appear in Castellane, like a sailor stepping off a ship; it is *impossible*. It takes years to build oneself up in a business. Yet Prosper Beck came from nowhere and has already moved to control the Maze."

"Surely you are more influential than Beck. If you want the Maze back, take it."

"It is not so simple. Beck is hard to find. He operates through intermediaries and moves his headquarters from place to place. He bribes the Vigilants with vast sums. Most of my Crawlers have de-camped to work for him." That was interesting, Kel thought. The Crawlers were famous in Castellane: skilled climbers who could shimmy up and down walls with the speed of spiders. They crept in through the upper windows of the rich and robbed them blind. "Someone is backing him, of that I am sure. Someone with a great deal of money. You make your way among the nobility, passing as a noble yourself. You should have little trouble finding out if one of them is financing Beck's enterprises."

"One of the *nobility*? Why would they bother funding a minor criminal?"

The carriage jounced over a patch of rough road, and Kel felt a wave of dizziness. The Ragpicker King was regarding him with a sort of bored curiosity, as if Kel were a bug he had seen many times before that was now exhibiting an unusual behavior.

"Let me ask you something, Kellian," he said. "Do you *like* them? House Aurelian, I mean. The King, the Queen. The Prince and his Counselor. The Legate."

For a long moment there was only silence, save for the sound of the carriage wheels rattling over stones. Then words spilled from Kel's mouth, unplanned, unconsidered. "One does not ask if one *likes* the Blood Royal. They simply are," he said. Like the harbor or the Narrow Pass, like the dark-jade canals of the Temple District, like Marivent itself. "It is like asking if one *likes* the Gods."

The Ragpicker King nodded slowly. "That was an honest an-swer," he said. "I appreciate it."

Was it Kel's imagination, or did the Ragpicker King put a spe-cial emphasis on the word *honest*? That strange pressure was still there—in Kel's chest, his throat, his mouth. He remembered now the last time he had felt it, and he felt anger growing like a vine twining through his veins, his nerves, setting them alight.

"In the spirit of further honesty," said Gentleman Death, "King

Markus. Is it true his absences are not due to his being engaged in study, but rather due to illness? Is the King dying?"

"It is not a question of illness," Kel said, and thought of the Fire on the Sea, the burning boat covered in flowers, and that was the moment he was sure. Without another word, he brought his left hand up, in one smooth, swift motion, and wrapped it around the blade of Ji-An's knife.

She did exactly what he had predicted she would, and jerked the knife back. Pain shot through his hand as the blade opened his skin. He welcomed the pain, clenching his hand to invite it in deeper. He could feel blood wetting his palm as his mind cleared.

"*Ssibal*," Ji-An hissed. Kel knew enough of the language of Geumjoseon to recognize this as profanity. He grinned as his blood welled in fat drops through his fingers and splashed onto the brocade interior of the carriage. Ji-An turned to the Ragpicker King. "This crazy bastard—"

Kel began to whistle. It was a common tune on the streets of Castellane, called "The Troublesome Virgin." The lyrics were bawdy in the extreme.

"He's not crazy," said the Ragpicker King, sounding as if he could not decide whether to be irritated or amused. "Here, Sword Catcher. Take this."

And he held out a handkerchief of fine black silk. Kel took it, wrapping it around his injured hand. The cut wasn't deep, but it was long, an ugly slash across his palm.

"How did you guess?" said the Ragpicker King.

"That you drugged me?" Kel said. "I've been dosed with *scopolia* before. Jolivet called it Devil's Breath. It makes you tell the truth." He finished tying the handkerchief bandage. "Pain counteracts it. And certain thought patterns. Jolivet taught me what to do."

Ji-An looked intrigued. "I want to learn that."

"I suppose it was in the wine Asper gave me," Kel said. "He works for you, then?"

"Don't blame Merren," said the Ragpicker King. "I talked him into it. Bribed him, actually. He'll still provide you that antidote, if you want it. He doesn't like misleading people."

But drugging them is apparently acceptable, Kel thought. Not that there seemed any point in an argument about relative morality with the biggest criminal in Castellane. "Is our business finished, then? I'm not going to tell you what you want to know."

"Oh, I didn't think you were." The Ragpicker King's eyes gleamed. "I admit I was testing you. And you passed. Excellent stuff. I knew a Sword Catcher would be a fine addition to my team. And not only because of your access to the Hill."

"I am not," Kel insisted, "going to be part of your team."

Ji-An pointed the blade at him again. "He won't cooperate," she said to the Ragpicker King. "You might as well let me kill him. He has a killable face."

Kel tried not to look at the carriage door. The Ragpicker King had said it was locked, but he wondered: If he hurled himself against it, would it hold? A fall from a moving carriage could kill him, but so could Ji-An.

"We aren't going to kill him," the Ragpicker King said. "I believe he will come around. I am an optimist." He leveled a green gaze, the color of crocodile scales or canal water, on Kel. "I will say one last thing. As Sword Catcher, you must go where the Prince goes, do as he does. Even if you can snatch an hour or so in a day for yourself, you are not free. Your choices are not your own, or your dreams. Surely that cannot be what you hoped your life would be. Everyone was once a child, and every child has dreams."

"*Dreams*," Kel echoed bitterly. "Dreams are a luxury. When I was a child in the Orfelinat, I dreamed about things like dinner. An extra piece of bread. Warm blankets. I dreamed I would grow up to be a thief, a pickpocket, a Crawler. That perhaps, if I were lucky, I would go to work for someone like you." His tone was mocking. "Branded by seventeen, hanged by twenty. I knew no other choices.

And here you are, offering me a chance to betray those who offered me better dreams. Forgive me if I am not tempted."

"Ah." The Ragpicker King tapped his fingers against the head of his cane. They were very long and white, flecked with small scars like burns. "So you trust them? The Palace, the nobles?"

"I trust Conor." Kel chose his words carefully. "And the Palace is familiar to me. For years I have learned its rules, its ways, its lies and truths. I know the path through its labyrinths. I do not know *you* at all."

The sardonic smile had left the angular face of the Ragpicker King. He drew back the window curtain and tapped lightly at the glass. "You will."

The carriage began to slow, and Kel tensed. The Ragpicker King didn't seem like the sort who took well to being turned down. He imagined being tossed into a ravine, or over a cliff into the sea. But when the door of the carriage swung open, he found himself looking at the front door of the Caravel, the lighted lamps glowing above its entrance. He could hear canal water lapping against stone, smell smoke and brine on the evening air.

Ji-An regarded him down the length of her blade. "I really think we should kill him," she said. "It's not too late."

"Ji-An, dear," said the Ragpicker King. "You are an expert at killing people. It's why I employ you. But I am an expert at knowing people. And this one will come back."

Ji-An lowered her knife. "Then at least swear him to secrecy."

"Kel can feel free to tell Legate Jolivet he listened to my criminal proposals. It will go much worse for him than for me." The Ragpicker King made a small, shooing gesture with his scarred fingers, in Kel's direction. "Go on. Get out. Or I might start to think you enjoy my company."

Kel began to clamber out of the carriage. His legs felt numb, his hand aching. He had not realized until this moment how sure he had been that he would end up fighting for his life tonight.

"One more thing," added the Ragpicker King as Kel leaped down to the pavement. "When you change your mind—and you will—come directly to the Black Mansion. The password *Morettus* will get you through the door. Recall it. And do not share it."

The Ragpicker King reached out to swing the carriage door shut. As he did, Ji-An glanced at Kel and put a finger to her lips, as if to say: *Hush.* Whether she was swearing him to secrecy regarding the password or his meeting with the Ragpicker King, Kel didn't know, nor was he sure it mattered. He had no intention of telling anyone about either.

Kel made his way back into the Caravel to find the main salon only half as crowded as before. Many of the guests must have already selected a partner for the night and gone upstairs. Someone had upended the Castles board, and half-empty glasses were littered on every surface. The tread of boots and slippers had ground chocolate and cherries into the carpet. The fortune-teller had gone, as had Sancia and Mirela, but Antonetta Alleyne remained, perched on a silk divan. She was chatting away to a courtesan with pale-purple curls, who looked enraptured by whatever she was saying. Kel wondered what on earth the two of them could possibly have to say to each other.

Montfaucon and Roverge had remained in the salon, but Falconet was gone, as was Conor. No one noticed Kel's entrance; they were all staring at the far side of the room where the hanging tapestries had been drawn back. They revealed the raised dais of a stage, on which a silent performance was taking place.

Kel leaned against the wall, in the shadows, and tried to gather his thoughts. He was familiar with the stage and the sort of "plays" the Caravel put on. Most depicted a bawdy version of Castellane's history. Those remaining in the salon sprawled in their brocaded chairs, watching as a naked man in a white skull-mask drew a woman—dressed in the stiff, frilled costume of two centuries before—down on a black-draped bed in the stage's center.

Alys, Kel thought. Had Alys known, when she arranged his meeting with her brother, that Merren worked for the Ragpicker King? Had she known he planned to drug Kel to make him more likely to betray his secrets when kidnapped? The thought was unsettling. Kel had trusted Alys for a long time. But it also seemed unlikely. Alys valued Conor as a client, and would be unlikely to do anything that would drive the Crown Prince and his entourage of nobles away from her establishment.

On stage, Death had stripped his partner of her clothes, leaving her in only a filmy petticoat. He began to bind her wrists to the black bed with long ribbons of scarlet silk. Kel was aware of eyes on him. He'd been trained to know when he was being watched, after all. Antonetta Alleyne was looking at him, her expression unreadable, one of her hands playing with the locket at her throat.

"It's meant to be the Scarlet Plague, I think," said a voice at Kel's shoulder. "Death takes a lover while the bodies lie in the streets. The red ribbons are the malady. She will make love to Death and die of it."

Kel turned in surprise to find Silla standing at his shoulder. She was a tall girl, nearly his height, narrow-waisted and slim-shouldered, a laced green velvet bodice making the most of her small breasts. Her skirt was slit, showing her long legs. She had freckles and blue eyes and a generous, wide-mouthed smile that had initially drawn him to her. Someone who smiled like that, he had thought, would be kind, would overlook his inexperience, would laugh with him as he learned what to do and how to do it.

He had been right, too, which was why he was still fond of her. He grinned at her now, shoving his misgivings to the back of his mind. "You get the Scarlet Plague from making love to Death?" he said. "I do not recall this as part of my lessons concerning this particular historical period. The drawbacks of Palace tutelage. They focus entirely too much on the wrong things."

"I should say so." Silla slid an arm around his waist. On stage, the man had divested his partner of her petticoat. She was naked save for the ribbons at her wrists and ankles and the spill of her long dark hair. Death drew off his mask and crawled across black velvet to lower himself upon her, her pale body arching up to his. Someone in the audience cheered, as if they were watching a sporting match in the Great Arena.

"I ought to find Conor," Kel murmured, though it was not what he wanted to do. Silla was soft and warm against his side, and he could not help but think how she could make him forget—forget what the Ragpicker King had said to him, forget his own foolishness in being duped by Merren Asper, forget his suspicions of Alys. Of Hadja, who had brought him the false message that had lured him outside. Had she known it was a trick?

"The Prince went upstairs with Audeta," said Silla. "He is enjoying himself. You need not worry." She laced her fingers through Kel's, her eyes darkening. "Come with me."

Silla knew he would not partake in pleasure in front of the nobles of the Hill, or the Charter Families, for the same reason that he would not drink to excess or indulge in poppy-drops in their company. To lose oneself in pleasure was to lower one's guard. Even alone with Silla or another courtesan, he could not manage it entirely. There was always some part of him holding back.

And yet. He was aware of Antonetta still looking at him, and he could not help himself. He drew Silla toward him, his hand curling under her chin, lifting her face to his. He kissed her red mouth, tasting the salt of her lip paint, savoring the moment she opened her lips to his, inviting him in. As he cradled her face in his hands, he could feel Antonetta's gaze on him, knew she was watching. He had thought it would bother him, but it only sent a greater heat crackling through his veins. *You have come here to be scandalized, Antonetta*, he thought. *So be scandalized.*

It was Silla who finally broke off their kiss. She purred softly, laughing against his mouth, even as he noted distantly that Antonetta was no longer looking at them. She was staring determinedly toward the stage.

"You're eager as a boy tonight," Silla murmured. "Come."

Taking his hand, she led him from the room. As he went, he paused to glance back at the salon as Silla led him through a small archway at the end of the room. He glimpsed Montfaucon, eyes on the stage, hand on the head of the young man who knelt before him, his head moving rhythmically over Montfaucon's lap. *He was the one who had been telling fortunes before*, Kel thought. And Montfaucon was not the only noble being so serviced: The room was full of moving shadows, flashes of skin here and there, the sound of breath, caught. There seemed something hollow and sad about all of it, and he felt a little foolish for having tried to scandalize Antonetta with kissing. Far more scandalous things were going on all around them as Kel followed Silla into the shadows.

Through the archway were a number of curtained alcoves. Silla led him into one of them, its walls plush with rose velvet, before drawing the curtain behind them. Scarlet tapers burned above them in bronze holders. Silla beckoned him close, lifting her face to be kissed.

They had done this often enough that their bodies knew the dance. She arched into Kel as his mouth explored hers, but he wanted more than kissing. He could not have oblivion, but he would take forgetting, even for a short time. He slid his hands up under her bodice, her breasts rounding into his palms. If she felt the bandage on his right hand, she gave no sign. She moaned softly, her fingers trailing down his chest, finding the waistband of his trousers.

"So pretty," she whispered. She rocked her hips against him. He was hard already, and her movements sent small shocks of pleasure through him—each shock like a sip of brandewine, slowing the racing of his mind, erasing the voice of the Ragpicker King. "Some nobles let themselves get soft, like unrisen dough." She slid her hands up under his shirt. "Not you."

Kel supposed he had Jolivet to thank for that. Nobles *could* let themselves get soft; they had no need to fight, to defend themselves or anyone else. *But I am the Prince's shield. And a shield must be iron.*

Silla's fingers were on the fall of his trousers, working at the buttons. Kel let his eyes drift half shut. He knew his body was feeling pleasure. It was as familiar and unmistakable as pain. He tried to focus on it, to bring his mind into the moment. Into Silla, her skin painted pale pink by the rose light of the alcove, her hair soft and thick, scented with lavender. She ran her finger around the inside of his waistband, laughed. "Velvet-lined?"

He licked her lower lip. "They're Conor's."

She tilted her head. "Then I'd better not tear them." She slipped her hand down, stroked him, her palm hot against his skin. "Does he ever let you borrow other things?" she whispered, and he realized she was still talking about Conor. "Like his crown? I think you'd look awfully handsome in a crown."

I wore the Aurelian crown earlier today. But he could never tell her that. It struck him that if the Ragpicker King and Ji-An knew he was the Sword Catcher, did Merren know as well? And what of Alys? And Hadja? Who *else* knew?

Gray hell, stop it, he told himself. *Be here now.* Silla would not mind if he pushed her skirts up, took her against the wall here. Easy enough to hold her up. They'd done it before. He needed to fall into her, into the drowning pleasure of the act. He took hold of her hips just as the velvet curtain tore back, revealing Antonetta Alleyne, framed in the archway.

Antonetta's hand flew to her mouth. "Oh," she said. "Oh *dear.*"

"What the *hell*, Antonetta?" Kel jerked his trousers into place and began to button them hastily. "What's wrong? Do you need someone to take you home?"

Antonetta was still blushing. "I'd no idea—"

"What did you think we were doing in here, darling, reciting poetry to each other?" drawled Silla. Her corset had come unlaced, but she made no move to fix it. "Or were you hoping to join us?" She smiled a little. "Which would be up to Kellian."

"Don't talk to her like that," Kel said; it was a reflex, but Silla's eyes narrowed in surprise. His response made him even angrier at Antonetta. He turned back to her. "If you're desperate to go home, Domna Alys would have arranged a carriage for you—"

"It's not that," Antonetta said. "I was on my way up to the library and I saw Falconet. He was in a panic. He sent me to fetch you." She frowned. "It's Conor. He needs you. Something's wrong."

Kel's blood turned to ice water; he heard Silla take a surprised breath. "What do you mean, something's wrong?" But Silla was already pressing his jacket into his hand; he did not even remember taking it off. He kissed her forehead, shrugged it on; a moment later he was following Antonetta through the main room and up the stairs. "What's happened?" he demanded in a low voice. "Silla said Conor was with Audeta—"

"I don't know," said Antonetta, not looking at him. "Joss didn't tell me. Just to fetch you."

These words spiked Kel's alarm. Falconet being desperate enough to send Antonetta after him portended nothing good.

"I wouldn't have expected you to be the sort to hire courtesans," said Antonetta as they reached the landing. "I don't know why. Silly of me, I suppose."

"It is silly," said Kel, a bite to his tone. "I have no prospects among the sons and daughters of the Hill—your mother has made that clear enough."

He almost thought he saw Antonetta flinch. But he must have imagined it. She was already staring down the corridor. They were on the third floor, where the courtesans' rooms were, and halfway down the hall was an open door—Audeta's room, presumably. Sitting on the floor beside it was Conor. Red spatters stained the floor around him. His head had fallen back against the wall; his left arm looked as if he'd pulled a scarlet glove up to his elbow. Falconet knelt beside him, looking—unusually for Joss—at a loss as to what to do.

"Conor—" Antonetta started forward, but Kel saw Falconet

shake his head. He caught Antonetta by the elbow, drawing her back.

"Better not," he said. "Wait for us downstairs." He hesitated. "And remember, Domna Alys can take care of anything you need." *Or take care of you, if you're uneasy.* But he didn't say that. Antonetta was an adult. She made her own choices, at least as much as her mother allowed. Kel had been her protector once, but she had been very clear on the night of her debut that he was no longer wanted in that capacity.

She bit her lower lip—it was a habit of hers—and looked worriedly down the hall at Conor. "Take care of him," she said to Kel, and vanished down the steps.

Of course I will. It's my duty. But it was more than duty, of course; anxiety raced through Kel's blood like fire as he made his way to Conor and knelt down beside Falconet at his side. Conor was still, improbably, wearing his crown, the gold wings snagged among his black curls. He jumped when Kel put a hand on his shoulder. Slowly, his gray eyes focused. "You," he said, in a slurred voice. He was very drunk—much drunker than Kel would have expected. "Where were you?"

"I was with Silla."

The ghost of a smile flashed across Conor's face. "You like her," he said. His voice held an odd, disconnected quality, and Kel's stomach tightened. What else might Conor say, in this state, regardless of the fact that Falconet was standing well within earshot?

"Yes, well enough." Kel stayed still while Conor's fingers marched up his arm and bunched themselves at the collar of his shirt. "But I've had my fun. You're not well. Let's get you home."

Conor lowered his eyes. His long black lashes brushed his cheeks; Queen Lilibet had always predicted he'd lose those as he grew older, but they remained—a disarming mark of innocence that had not caught up with the rest of an otherwise not-innocent face. "Not to the Palace. No."

"*Conor.*" Kel was very aware of Falconet watching them. He looked up and glared at Joss, who stepped away and stuck his head through the open door of Audeta's room. A moment later Audeta appeared in the doorway, wrapped in a blanket. The scarlet and gold paint on her lids had smeared all around her eyes. She looked tearful, and young.

Conor twisted his fingers in Kel's shirt. Kel could smell the blood on him, like cold copper. Audeta said, in a small voice, "It was the window. He hit the window—" She shivered. "Broke it with his hand."

Kel took Conor's hand. It was mazed all over with small cuts, and a deeper one to the side of his hand that was more concerning. *We both injured our hands tonight*, he thought, and it didn't seem strange, but fitting, somehow.

He untied the black handkerchief from his own hand and began to wrap it around Conor's. The wound on his palm had stopped bleeding anyway. "Joss," he said. "Go downstairs. Take Audeta with you. Play it off as if nothing has happened."

Falconet said something to Audeta in a low voice. She disappeared back into her room. "Are you sure?" Falconet said, looking at Kel with thoughtful eyes.

"Yes," Kel said. "And make sure Antonetta gets home. She oughtn't to be here."

Montfaucon or Roverge would have said, *What do you care about Antonetta?* or *I don't take orders from you.* They would have tried to hover about, hoping to hear something scandalous. *At least it had been Falconet with Conor,* Kel thought. He liked to know things, as everyone on the Hill did, but he did not gossip for the sake of it. And though he recognized Kel had little power, he knew that Conor listened to him, and that was a sort of power in itself.

Falconet indicated with a nod that he would do as Kel asked. Audeta emerged from her room, wearing a yellow silk wrapper, her lids repainted. She headed downstairs with Falconet, looking back anxiously at Conor as she went. Kel hoped Falconet would be able to convince her to keep the incident to herself. If anyone could, it was Falconet.

"All right, Con." Kel gentled his voice. This was the way he had talked to Conor years ago, when Conor woke in the dead hours of darkness with nightmares. "Why would you punch the window? Were you angry at Audeta? Or Falconet?"

"No." Conor was still hanging on to Kel's shirt with his unbandaged hand. "I thought I could forget, with them. But I couldn't."

Forget what? Kel remembered a few minutes ago, with Silla, telling himself to forget, to *be here now.* But Conor . . .

"Is this about you getting married?" Kel guessed. "You know, you don't have to if you don't want to."

The crafty expression of the very drunk passed across Conor's face. "I think I do," he said. "I think I might have to."

Kel was taken aback. "What? They cannot force you, Con."

Conor plucked at Kel's sleeve. "It's not that," he said. "I've made mistakes, Kel. Bad mistakes."

"Then we'll fix them. Anything can be fixed. I'll help you."

Conor shook his head. "I've been trained, you know, to fight a certain kind of war. Tactical strategy and battle maps and all that." He looked earnestly at Kel. "I cannot fight what I cannot find, or see."

"Conor—"

"This is my city," Conor said, almost plaintively. "It is my city, isn't it, Kel? Castellane belongs to me."

Kel wondered if they could get out by the back stairway. Avoid the salon and any potential encounters with other people. Especially with Conor rambling like this.

"Conor," Kel said, gently, "you're drunk, that's all. You're the Prince; Castellane is yours. Her fleets and caravans are yours. And her people love you. You saw that today."

"Not," Conor said, slowly, "not—all of them."

Before Kel could ask what he meant, there were footsteps on the stairs; someone was coming. The footsteps turned out to be Alys. She pursed her lips in concern when she saw Conor but did not seem surprised. Perhaps Falconet had told her. Perhaps he had been like this when she'd pulled him away, earlier. Before tonight, Kel would have asked, but he could not trust Alys now.

Nevertheless, he let her guide them out the back entrance, where their horses had already been brought around by the footmen. She was apologetic—had the Prince not enjoyed himself tonight? Kel found himself reassuring her, even as he thought of Merren and wanted to demand what she'd known.

But Conor was there. He might be drunk, but he wasn't insensible. Kel kept his questions to himself, bidding Alys a stiff goodbye as Conor swung himself onto Matix, his injured hand held close against his chest.

Kel had gotten Conor home drunk many times before, and he had no doubts he'd manage it again tonight. Conor had always been a skilled rider, and Asti and Matix knew their way to the Palace. He and Conor would go home, and they would sleep, and in the morning there would be Dom Valon's hangover cure, followed by training and light disapproval with Jolivet, then visits from the nobles, and all the usual furnishings of an ordinary day.

He wondered if Conor would remember how he had cut his hand, or what he'd said to Kel, a thing he'd never said before: *I've made mistakes, Kel. Bad mistakes.*

Another voice cut past the memory of Conor's words. *Your choices are not your own, or your dreams. Surely that cannot be what you hoped your life would be. Everyone was once a child, and every child has dreams.*

But the Ragpicker King was a liar. A criminal and a liar. It would be a fool's errand to listen to him. And Conor said all sorts of things when he was drunk. There was no point placing too much weight on them.

Up ahead, Conor called for him to go faster; they were nearly to Palace Street, where the land began to slant up toward Marivent. Kel glanced down and saw the paper crown that had been tangled in Asti's reins. It was already coming to pieces; after all, it had never been meant for anything but show.

The time of the Sorcerer-Kings was a time of immense prosperity. Great cities rose up, and clad themselves in marble and gold. The Kings and Queens built for themselves palaces and pavilions and hanging gardens, and there were great public structures: libraries and hospitals and orphanages, and acadamies where magic was taught.

But only those who attended the academies, whose attendance was strictly controlled, were allowed to perform High Magic, which required the use of the One Word. Low magic, which could be done without using the Word, flourished among the peasantry, especially among traders, who traveled between kingdoms. Low magic consisted of combinations of words and numbers etched upon amulets, and was tolerated by the Sorcerer-Kings only because of its limited power.

— *Tales of the Sorcerer-Kings*, Laocantus Aurus Iovit III

CHAPTER FIVE

As Kel had predicted, the day after the visit to the Caravel was uneventful. Conor woke with a vicious hangover. Kel took himself off to the kitchen to retrieve Dom Valon's famous morning-after cure: a vile-looking substance made with eggs, red pepper, hot vinegar, and a secret ingredient the head cook refused to divulge. After downing it, Conor had stopped complaining about his headache and started complaining about the taste of it instead.

"Do you remember anything about last night?" Kel asked as Conor dragged himself out of bed. "Do you remember telling me you'd made a terrible mistake?"

"Was the terrible mistake punching Charlon Roverge?" Conor had peeled the black kerchief from his hand and was making a face. "Because if I did, I think I broke my hand on his face."

Kel shook his head.

"Must have smashed a glass, then," Conor said. "Don't summon Gasquet; he'll just make it worse. I'm going to go boil myself in the tepidarium until the water turns into royal soup."

He stripped off his clothes and made his way, naked, across their rooms to the door that led to the baths. Kel wondered if he should point out to Conor that he still had his crown on, and decided not to. It wasn't as if hot water and steam were going to do it any harm.

When he was younger, Kel had assumed that one day he would be given his own room—near Conor's, certainly, but still separate. That hadn't happened. Jolivet had insisted that Kel continue to sleep where Conor slept, in case something happened in the night. And when Kel had asked Conor about it, saying surely Conor also wanted privacy, Conor had said he wasn't looking to be alone with his thoughts, unless Kel really *wanted* his own room, in which case Conor would make sure he got it. There had been genuine hurt in his voice, though, and Kel had dropped the topic.

Queen Lilibet, after all, shared her apartments with her ladies-in-waiting, keeping a golden bell beside her bed to summon them to her side. Master Fausten had slept on a cot outside King Markus's door in the Star Tower since the Fire on the Sea. And the rooms Kel shared with Conor were vast, encompassing not just the room where they slept, but the library upstairs, the roof of the West Tower, and the tepidarium. Being alone wasn't impossible, so Kel decided he'd been unreasonable to ask in the first place.

Kel, who had already bathed, began to dress, ignoring the stinging in his right hand. There were three wardrobes in the apartments: one, the largest, for Conor's clothes. One for the sets of clothes required for public appearances and other events at which Kel might need to take Conor's place at a moment's notice, containing two of everything, matching: frock coats, trousers, even boots. And the third for clothes that were Kel's own, inflected with the style of Marakand. For after all, wasn't he Amirzah Kel Anjuman, the Queen's cousin? Lilibet had taken some delight in making sure his wardrobe reflected that. Silk tunics in jewel tones with loose sleeves, colorful scarves, and long tapered coats of gold or bronze brocade, their sleeves slashed to show green silk beneath. (Green was the color of the Marakandi flag, and Lilibet wore it almost exclusively.)

Kel dressed in black today, with a green tunic buttoned over: The loose sleeves were useful, as they concealed the daggers secured to his wrists with leather buckles. As far as he knew, Conor had no special plans for today, but it was always good to be prepared.

They ate breakfast in the courtyard of the Castel Mitat. Marivent was not in fact one large castle, but a scatter of different small palaces, or castels, dotted among richly planted gardens. The story was that this had made the Palace easier to defend—even if an army were to get past the walls, they would have to siege multiple fortresses—but Kel did not know if that were true, or if it simply reflected the fact that kings and queens over the centuries had found it easier to add new buildings than to expand the Castel Antin, the oldest of the palaces, which contained the throne room and the Shining Gallery.

The Castel Mitat sat dab in the middle of Marivent; it was a hollow square, surmounted by the sturdy West Tower, which looked out over Castellane and its harbor. Half in sun, half in dappled shade cast by arbors of climbing vines, its courtyard glowed like a jewel box. Orange and red poppies and grandiflora hung from vines like drop earrings of polished coral. In the center of the courtyard was a sundial tiled in scarlet and green, representing the marriage of Lilibet and Markus. The green of Marakand, the red of Castellane.

According to the sundial, it was closer to noon than morning, but as far as Conor was concerned, that still meant breakfast. Bread, honey, figs, and soft white goat's cheese, alongside cold game pie. And wine, of course. Conor poured a glass and held it up to watch the sunlight strike through the liquid, turning it to stained glass.

"Perhaps we should go back to the Caravel," Kel suggested. He was picking at a fig; he found he had not much appetite. "Since you've forgotten yesterday anyway."

"I haven't forgotten *all* of it," said Conor. He had left off his crown, or lost it in the tepidarium. There were shadows smudged beneath his gray eyes. Once they had had eyes of different colors, but that had been changed long ago. "I recall Falconet doing some truly scandalous things to Audeta. She seemed to like them. I ought to ask him how—"

"Well, then, if you enjoyed yourself, all the more reason to return. With Falconet, if you like." *Which will allow me to seek out Merren and demand some answers.*

"I prefer not to wear the same thing twice in a row, or do the same thing two nights running." Conor turned the glass in his hand. "If you're missing Silla, we can always have her brought here."

Where I have no bedroom to myself? No, thank you, Kel thought. But that was not fair. Conor required him close by. It would be that way until Conor himself was married. Which reminded him—

"So were you really thinking of getting married? Malgasi, Kutani, Hanse . . ."

Conor set his glass down with a thump. "Gods, no. What's gotten into you?"

He really doesn't remember, Kel thought. It was both a relief and an annoyance. He would have liked to know what had bothered Conor so much he'd put his hand through a window. Perhaps whatever Falconet had done with Audeta had been very, *very* peculiar.

"I *was* thinking," Conor said, his eyes bright. "Before I get married, I'd like to see more of the world. I'm the Crown Prince of Castellane and I've never been farther away than Valderan. And Valderan is mostly horses."

"Excellent horses," Kel pointed out. Asti and Matix had been gifts from the King of Valderan. "And arable land."

Conor chuckled. So he remembered that, at any rate. "I recall I promised you travel, a long time ago," he said. "An extraordinary life."

You would see things hardly anyone ever sees. You would travel the whole world.

They'd often spoken of the places and things they'd like to see—the floating markets of Shenzhou, the towers of Aquila, the silver bridges that connected the six hills of Favár, the Malgasi capital—but it had always been in a distant, theoretical sense. The little travel he had actually done with Conor had not been much like his dreams of ships and blue water, gulls flying overhead. Traveling with royalty was an organizational nightmare of horses and caravans, trunks and soldiers, cooks and bathtubs, and rarely managing to go more than a few hours a day before having to stop and set up camp.

"My life is already fairly extraordinary," said Kel. "More than most people know."

Conor leaned forward. "I was thinking," he said. "What about Marakand?"

"Marakand? Over the Gold Roads?"

Conor dipped his left shoulder in an elegant shrug. "Why not? Marakand is half my heritage, is it not?"

Kel bit thoughtfully into an apricot. Lilibet had been insistent that her son remain conscious of the roots that bound him to her home country. He—and Kel, of course—had been tutored in the language of Marakand until they were both fluent. They knew the history of the royal family of Marakand and the Twin Thrones, now occupied by Lilibet's brothers. They knew the history of the place, the names of its most significant families. But Conor had never expressed interest in traveling there before. Kel had always suspected that Lilibet's passion for the place had left Conor feeling ambivalent about a country that would, despite his connections there, always regard him as a foreign Prince.

"Darling!" The Queen swept into the courtyard, dressed in rich emerald satin, the waist of her dress lashed tight, long skirts brushing the dusty ground. With her were two of her Court ladies. Their dark hair was tucked up under fern-green caps, their eyes downcast. "How are you? How was yesterday?"

She was speaking to Conor, of course. She preferred to go on as though Kel didn't exist unless it was necessary to acknowledge him. It was much the way she treated her ladies, who stood at a polite distance, pretending to admire the sundial.

"Kel gave a very fine speech," said Conor. "The populace was duly impressed."

"That must have been disappointing for you, darling. Jolivet is so over-cautious." She had come around behind Conor's seat and ruffled her ringed hand through his hair as she spoke, the emeralds on her fingers shining among his black curls. "I am sure no one wishes you harm. No one could."

A muscle in Conor's cheek twitched. Kel knew he was holding himself back; there was no point correcting Lilibet, or telling her that no member of a royal family was likely to be universally beloved. Lilibet preferred her own version of the world, and disagreement only sparked sulking or anger.

"What have you just been speaking of, my dear? You did seem quite animated, just now."

"Marakand," Conor said. "Specifically, my desire to pay the land a visit. It's ridiculous that I've never been there, considering the connection I have to the place. You and Father represent the alliance of Marakand and Castellane, but I am the one who must carry it on. They should know my face."

"The satraps know your face. They visit every year," Lilibet said, a bit absently. The satraps were the Marakandi Ambassadors, and their visits tended to be among the highlights of the Queen's schedule. She would gather with them to hear gossip from the faraway Court in Jahan, and afterward, for weeks, she would talk of little but Marakand: how everything was better there, more cleverly done, more beautiful. Yet in all the years since her marriage, she had never returned. Kel wondered if she knew that her memories were more idealistic fantasy than reality, and did not want them spoiled. "But it's a lovely idea."

"I'm glad you approve," said Conor. "We could leave as early as next week."

Kel choked on his apricot. "*Next week?*" Just readying a royal convoy—with its tents and bedding, horses and pack mules, gifts for the Court at Jahan, and food that would not spoil on the road—would take longer than that.

"Conor, don't be ridiculous. You can't leave next week. We have a reception for the Malgasi Ambassador. And after that, there is the Spring Festival, and the Solstice Ball—"

Conor's expression had shut like a door. "There is always some festivity or another, *Mehrabaan*," he said, deliberately using the formal Marakandi word for "mother." "Surely I must be allowed to miss a few of them in pursuit of such a valuable goal."

But Lilibet's lips had pursed—a sign that she was digging in her low, pointed heels. It was true that there was always a festivity on the horizon; the one thing Lilibet truly seemed to enjoy about being Queen was planning parties. She would obsess for weeks or months over the decorations, the color scheme, dancing and fireworks, food and music. The night Kel had come to Marivent as a child, he had thought he had arrived at a rare magical banquet. Now he knew they happened every month, which took some of the enchantment out of the whole thing.

"Conor," Lilibet said, "it is admirable that you wish to strengthen Castellane's international ties, but your father and I would appreciate it if you saw to your responsibilities at home first."

"Father said that?" Conor's voice was brittle.

Lilibet ignored the question. "In point of fact, I would like to see you oversee the Dial Chamber meeting tomorrow. You've sat in on enough of them; you ought to know how they're handled."

Interesting. The Dial Chamber was the room in which the Charter Families had met for generations to discuss trade, diplomacy, and the current state of affairs in Castellane, with the King or Queen always present to direct the course of the discussion, for the final word on any decision was House Aurelian's. For the past years Lilibet, with Mayesh Bensimon at her side, had represented the King at the meetings—always with a look of dispassionate boredom on her face.

Now she wanted Conor to take her place, and from her expression, it did not look as if arguing the point would do any good.

"If Father could—" Conor began.

Lilibet shook her head, the ornate loops of her glossy, still-black hair trembling. Kel sensed that she was looking at him out of the corner of her eye—for all her pretense that he didn't exist, she was wary of what she said in front of him. "You know that's not possible."

"If I lead the meeting alone, there will be gossip as to why," Conor said.

"Darling," said Lilibet, though there was little warmth in it, "the way to fight gossip among the nobles is to show them you have a firm grasp on power. That is what you must do tomorrow. Seize control; do not let it fly out of your hands. Once you've shown that you can do that, we can discuss a journey to Marakand. Perhaps you could go on your honeymoon."

With that, she swept away, the hem of her green skirt leaving a path in the dust like the dragging tail of a peacock. Her Court ladies hurried after her as Conor sat back in his chair, his expression set.

"The Dial Chamber meeting will be fine," Kel said. "You've been to a hundred of them. It's nothing you can't do."

Conor nodded vaguely. It occurred to Kel that this might mean he'd be left on his own tomorrow afternoon, perhaps into the evening. It depended on how long the meeting went, but all he needed was to get to Merren Asper, threaten the truth out of him, and return. Merren was clearly an academic, not a fighter; it couldn't take that long.

"You'll come with me," Conor said. It wasn't a request, and Kel wondered if Conor truly noticed the difference between asking Kel to do things and telling him. But then, did it matter? It was not as if Kel could say no, in either circumstance. And resentment was pointless. It was more than pointless. Resentment was poison.

"Of course," Kel said, with an inward sigh. He'd just have to try to get away at another time. Perhaps tonight. As far as he knew, Conor had nothing planned.

Conor did not seem to hear him. He was gazing into the distance, unseeing, his palms flat on the table before him. It was only then that Kel realized that though Lilibet must surely have noticed the raw red wounds on Conor's right hand, she had said not one word about them.

"Zofia, darling," Lin said, "do take the pills, won't you? There's a good girl."

The good girl in question—a ninety-one-year-old ball of wild white hair, fragile bones, and mulish temper—glared at Lin out of her one good eye. The other was covered with an eye patch; she had lost it, she claimed, during a sea battle off the coast of Malgasi. The battle had been with the royal fleet. Zofia Kovati had been a pirate, as feared and dreaded in her day as any man. She still possessed an appearance of great fierceness, with her nest of pure white hair sticking out in all directions, a mouthful of false teeth, and a collection of brass-buttoned military coats she wore over full-skirted dresses in the style of decades past.

Lin switched tack. "You know what will happen if you don't take them. I'll have to send a Castellani doctor to look at you, since you don't trust me."

Zofia looked gloomy. "He'll put the pills up my bum."

Lin hid a smile. This was likely; doctors of the *malbushim* were obsessed with suppositories for reasons she could only guess at. Partly, she supposed, because they had not mastered injections into the blood, as the Ashkar had, but she could not explain the rest of it, not when swallowing pills was a perfectly good way of getting medicine into the system.

"Oh, yes," Lin said. "He will."

She grinned as Zofia snatched the pills out of her hand and swallowed them down with only a slight grimace. The foxglove would treat, though not cure, Zofia's failing heart and the swelling in her legs. Lin left her with a bottle of more pills and strict instructions regarding when and how to take them—instructions she had given before, but Zofia seemed to enjoy the ritual, and Lin did not mind. She would have stayed for tea today, as she often did, had she not been late for her next appointment.

The day was warm and bright, perfect for traversing the city.

When she had first started seeing patients in Castellane, Lin had worried about criminals, cutpurses, and Crawlers. The Ashkar regarded the city outside the Sault walls as a dangerous and lawless place. She was sure she would be set upon and robbed, but she had gone mostly unhindered through the streets, rarely troubled by more than curious looks.

Once, in the Warren, after delivering a baby, she had made her way home late at night, under a green-tinted spring moon. A skinny young man, a knife flashing in his hand, had slipped from the shadows between two buildings and demanded her physician's satchel; she had clutched it away from him, instinctively—the items inside were precious and expensive—when a dark shadow had dropped from a balcony above them. A Crawler.

To her great surprise, the Crawler proceeded to disarm the young man and send him on his way with a sharp warning and a sharper kick to the ankle. The would-be thief had scuttled away while Lin blinked in surprise.

The Crawler, whose hooded jacket hid his face, had grinned, and Lin had caught a flash of metal as he turned his head. A mask? "Compliments of the Ragpicker King," he said, offering her a half-mocking bow. "He is an admirer of physicians."

Before Lin could respond, the Crawler had vanished, scrambling up the nearest wall with the quick spidery movements that had earned the Crawlers their name. Lin felt safer after that—quixotic, she knew, to feel safer because of a criminal, but the Ragpicker King was a fixture in Castellane. Even the Ashkar knew he controlled the streets. And much to her own surprise, Lin's rounds of patient appointments had turned out to be her favorite part of being a physician.

After Lin had passed her last medical examination, she had expected to begin seeing patients immediately. But other than Mariam, no one in the Sault seemed interested in availing themselves of her services. They avoided her, seeking out instead the male physicians who had scored lower than she had on the exams.

So Lin had expanded her reach into the city. Chana Dorin sold talismans in the city market every Sunday, and spread the word that there was a young Ashkari physician willing to treat ailments for very little money. Josit, then one of the Shomrim—the guardians of the Sault gates—had told every *malbesh* who came seeking a physician of his sister: her skills, her wisdom, her extremely reasonable rates.

Slowly Lin built a stable of patients outside the Sault, from the rich daughters of merchants seeking someone to remove wens from their noses, to the courtesans of the Temple District whose jobs required them to be regularly examined by physicians. Once she had built her reputation, more began to seek her out: from anxious pregnant mothers to the gnarled old men whose bodies had been broken by years of toiling at shipbuilding in the Arsenale.

Illness was a great leveler, she realized. *Malbushim* were just like the Ashkar when it came down to their health: fretting over their own wellness, vulnerable where it came to sickness in their family, frantic or silent in the face of death. Often, as Lin stood quietly while a family prayed over the body of a lost loved one, she would hear their words—*may he pass through the gray door unhindered, Lords*—and she would add some of her own, silently, not just for the dead, but for those left behind. *Be not alone. Be comforted among the mourners of Aram.*

Why not? she always thought. They did not have to believe in the Goddess for her to touch their hearts in their greatest time of need.

Enough; there was no need to sink into morbid thoughts. Besides, she had reached her destination: an ochre, red-roofed building facing onto a dusty square. Long ago, the Fountain Quarter had been a neighborhood of rich merchants' houses built around courtyards, each one boasting one of the grand fountains that gave the neighborhood its name. Now the houses had been split into inexpensive flats of a few rooms each. Their frescoes had faded to muddy swirls, and the gloriously tiled fountains had cracked and gone dry.

Lin enjoyed the faded grandeur of the place. The old buildings reminded her of Zofia: They had once been great beauties, and their bones still revealed that grace beneath wrinkled, liver-spotted skin.

She hurried across the square, her footsteps sending up puffs of saffron dust, and ducked into the ochre house. The ground floor was stone and tile, curving wooden stairs leading up, each step worn and saddled in the middle. The landlady—a grumpy woman who lived on the top floor—really ought to see to fixing them, Lin thought, as she reached the second landing and found the doors there already open.

"Is it you, *Doktor*?" The door swung wide, revealing the wrinkled, beaming countenance of Anton Petrov, Lin's favorite patient. "Come in, come in. I have tea."

"Of course you do." Lin followed him into the room, setting her satchel down on a low table. "Sometimes I think you survive entirely on jenever and tea, Dom Petrov."

"And what would be wrong with that?" Petrov was already fiddling with a gleaming bronze samovar, the most elegant item in the small apartment, and the only thing he had brought with him from Nyenschantz when he'd left it forty years ago to become a trader on the Gold Roads. He'd always had his samovar with him, he'd told her once, as the thought of being caught in an inhospitable region with no tea was insupportable.

Unlike Josit, Petrov seemed uninterested in displaying much in the way of souvenirs from his years of travel. His flat was plain, almost monastic. The furniture was scrubbed birch, his books neatly arranged in shelves along the walls (though Lin, not being able to read Nyens, could not decipher most of the titles). His cups and plates were plain brass, his fireplace neatly swept, and his kitchen always tidy.

Having poured them both tea, Petrov indicated that Lin should join him at the table near the window. Pots of flowers adorned the sill, and a hummingbird buzzed lazily amid the red valerian blossoms.

As she settled herself across from Petrov, tea mug in hand, Lin's gaze went automatically to the carpet in the middle of the room. It was a beautiful item—rich and plush, woven with a pattern of vines and feathers in deep green and blue. It was not the carpet that interested Lin, though, but rather what it concealed.

"Do you want to see it?" Petrov was looking at her with an impish sort of grin, uncharacteristically boyish. Petrov was in his sixties, but looked older, his skin papery, his hands given to the occasional tremble. His skin was pale, like that of most Northerners, and Lin sometimes thought she could see his veins through it. Though his hair was gray, his mustache and eyebrows were black (Lin suspected he dyed them) and tremendous. "If you'd like . . ."

Lin felt a slight flutter beneath her breastbone. She quickly took a sip of her hot tea; it had a smoky taste, which Petrov claimed came from the campfires along the Gold Roads. It was also too sweet, but she didn't mind. Petrov was lonely, she knew, and the tea was a chance to draw out their appointment, to chat and visit. Loneliness, Lin believed, was deadly; it killed people as surely as too much alcohol or poppy-juice. It was hard to be lonely in the Sault, but much too easy to disappear and be forgotten in the chaos of Castellane.

"I have to examine you first," she said. She'd set her satchel down by her chair; she rummaged in it now, and drew out the auscultor—a long wooden cylinder, hollow and polished—and set one end to Petrov's chest.

The old man sat patiently while she listened to his heart and lungs. Petrov was one of her more mysterious patients. His symptoms did not match anything in Lin's studies or books. She often heard crackling noises when he breathed, which ought to have meant pneumonia, but they came and went without fever, leaving her at a loss. Strange rashes often appeared on his skin—today there were red spots on his forearms and legs, as if the vessels beneath the skin had burst for some reason.

Petrov claimed all of it—his breathing troubles, his fatigue, the rashes—were a disease he had picked up on his travels. He did not know the name of it, or who had given it to him. Lin had tried every treatment she knew: infusions, tinctures, changes in diet, powders mixed into his food. Nothing helped save the amulets and talismans she gave him to ease his pain and symptoms.

"Do be careful," she said, drawing his sleeve down his thin arm. "The best way to avoid these painful red spots is to avoid bumps and bruises. Even as small a thing as moving a chair—"

"*Enough*," he muttered. "What, am I supposed to ask Domna Albertine? She scares me worse than a bruise."

Domna Albertine was his landlady. She had a vast bosom and a vaster temper. Lin had once seen her chase a stray goose across the courtyard with a broom, screaming that she would beat it to death and then track down and kill each of its children.

Lin crossed her arms over her chest. "Are you refusing my advice? Is it that you wish for a different physician?"

She let her voice quaver. She had long ago realized that the best way to get Petrov to cooperate was to make him feel guilty, and she used this knowledge ruthlessly.

"No, no." He shook his head. "If I didn't have you treating me, wouldn't I be dead by now?"

"I am sure there are other physicians who could do what I do," Lin said, rummaging in her satchel. "Even in Nyenschantz."

"In Nyenschantz, the doctors would advise me to go out in the woods and punch a bear," rumbled Petrov. "Either it would make me feel better, or the bear would kill me, in which case I would no longer be sick."

Lin giggled. She took several talismans from her bag and set them on the table. Petrov, who had been grinning, looked at her thoughtfully. "Those papers you wanted," he said. "Did you manage to get them?"

Lin sighed inwardly. She should not have told Petrov about her quest to get the Academie manuscript. It had been a moment of weakness; she had known she could tell no one in the Sault.

"No," she said. "No bookshop will allow me even to look at it—not just because I am not a student, but because I am Ashkar. They hate us too much."

"It is not that they hate you," Petrov said, gently. "It is that they are jealous. Magic vanished from the world with the Sundering, and with it much danger, but also much that was beautiful and wondrous. Only your people still possess a fragment of that wonder. It is perhaps not surprising they seek to guard the bits of history they have. The memory of a time they were equal in power."

"They are more than equal in power," Lin said. "They have all the power, save in this one thing." Lightly, she touched the necklace at her throat, the hollow circle with the old words etched onto it: *How shall we sing our Lady's songs in a strange land?* The cry of a people who did not know how to be who they were without a home or a God. They had learned—over the many years they had learned—yet their belonging was still imperfect. Hollow in parts, like the circle itself.

She looked at Petrov closely. "You are not saying you agree with them, are you?"

"Not at all!" Petrov bellowed. "I have traveled the world, you know—"

"I do know," said Lin, teasingly. "You tell me about it all the time."

He glared. "And I have always said you can judge a country by how they treat their Ashkar. It was one of the reasons I left Nyenschantz. Stupidity, closed-mindedness, cruelty. Malgasi, too, is one of the worst." He broke off, waving his hand as if to ward off the idea of evil. "Now," he said. "Would you like to see the stone? As a reward for healing me, eh?"

I helped, but did not heal. Lin only wished she could do more for Petrov. She watched him worriedly as he rose to his feet and crossed the room to his new carpet. He rolled back a corner of it, revealing a square hole in the floorboards beneath. He reached in with a trembling hand and drew out an oval stone, pale gray as a swan's egg.

He stood a moment, looking down at the stone, his fingertip resting lightly on it. Lin tried to recall the first time she'd seen it; he had brought it out to show to her when she'd told him her brother was traveling the Gold Roads. "He'll see wonderful things, many marvels," Petrov had said, and lifted one of his floorboards to bring out his small stash of treasures: a porcelain teapot, streaked with gold; the belt of a *bandari* dancer, its strands interwoven with dozens of coins; and the stone.

He brought it across to her now, placing it gently in her hand. It was perfectly smooth, lacking even the hint of a facet: It was clearly a highly polished stone, and not a gem. Something seemed to flicker in its depths, a play of light and shadow.

It felt warm in Lin's hand, and inexplicably soothing. As she turned it in her palm, images seemed to arise from the smoky depths, coming tantalizingly to the stone's surface, then vanishing just as she was about to recognize them.

"A lovely thing, isn't it?" Petrov said, looking down at her. He sounded a bit wistful, which struck Lin as peculiar—after all, the stone was his; presumably he could look at it whenever he liked.

"You really won't tell me where you got it?" She smiled up at him. She'd asked before, many times: He would only say that he'd acquired it on the Gold Roads. Once he told her he'd fought a pirate prince for it; another day, the tale had involved a Marakandi queen and a duel gone wrong.

"I ought just to give it to you," he said gruffly. "You are a good girl and would do good with it."

Lin looked at him in surprise. There was a peculiar look in his eyes, something at once both sharp and faraway. And what did he mean, she wondered, *do good with it*? What could anyone do with a bit of stone?

"No," she said, handing the stone back to him. She had to admit she felt a slight twinge of regret as she spoke. It was such a pretty thing. "Keep it, Sieur Petrov—"

But he was frowning. "Listen," he said. Lin did as he asked, and heard a faint step on the stairs outside. Well, there was nothing wrong with Petrov's hearing, at least.

"Are you expecting visitors?" Lin reached for her satchel. "Perhaps I have stayed too long."

As she rose to her feet, she could hear the voice of Petrov's landlady, squawking indignantly downstairs.

Petrov's eyes were narrowed, his back straight. In that moment, Lin could imagine him as a traveler on the Roads, squinting into the distance at an ever-receding horizon. "I'd nearly forgotten," he said. "A few friends; we were meant to play cards." He forced a smile. "I will see you at our next appointment, Domna Caster."

It was a definite dismissal. Puzzled, Lin headed for the door; Petrov hurried to open it, jostling against her in the process. Also odd; usually he did not stand on ceremony.

On the way downstairs, Lin passed two men in disheveled sailors' clothes. She could not have guessed at their nationality, other than that they seemed northern, with pale hair and eyes. One glanced at her and said something clearly discourteous to his companion in a language Lin did not know. They both laughed, and Lin left the building feeling disquieted. Petrov was a gentle old soul: What business did he have with men like that?

But in the end, she supposed, it was not her business. Her job was to care for Petrov's physical health. The choices he made otherwise were not hers to judge.

After sword practice and supper, Kel and Conor returned to the Castel Mitat to find that Roverge, Montfaucon, and Falconet had crowded into the Prince's apartments in their absence. They had already broken out the *nocino*—a strong liquor made from unripe green walnuts—and greeted Conor and Kel's return with cheers.

"And we've a surprise for you," said Charlon. "A visitor, upstairs."

Conor narrowed his eyes with interest, but declared that he and Kel must change out of their sweaty practice whites. He directed his friends to wait for him upstairs, atop the West Tower.

Conor hurried to wash and dress mostly in silence. He seemed almost relieved the others had come by—he had a feverish energy to him, as if he were determined to have a good time the way some men might be determined to win a duel or a race.

What he was racing against, Kel wasn't sure. Having washed and dressed in leather and brocade, Conor disappeared upstairs with wet hair, taking the spiral steps at a run. In contrast, Kel dawdled while getting dressed, gauging his options, before deciding that slipping away without anyone noticing would be impossible. Resigned, he made his way to the tower.

Conor had made many "improvements" to the tower in the past years, showing a flair for decoration he must have inherited from Lilibet. The square tower-top was surrounded by parapets, offering a crenellated view of the city and harbor below. Conor had installed canopied divans, piled with cushions, and marquetry tables where metal bowls of fruit and candy had just been laid out by servants, along with chilled bottles of various liquors and meat pies.

The others had sprawled across the divans with glasses of wine, and it was then that Kel saw the visitor Charlon had mentioned. Antonetta Alleyne, seated primly on a sage-green cushioned chair, her legs crossed neatly at the ankle. Her yellow dress foamed with lace and seed pearls and there were ribbons in her hair, though they looked about to come loose in the strong wind off the sea.

Kel felt a wave of irritation—he'd wanted to ask Charlon what it had meant, him bringing Antonetta to the Caravel. Now he could not. He looked toward Conor, who was leaning against Falconet's shoulder while Roverge, having produced an entire bottle of orris-root jenever from somewhere inside his coat, complained loudly that his father, in a temper, had beaten Charlon's favorite serving maid. The temper seemed to have been caused by some kind of es-

calating feud with a family who was refusing to tithe the legally required portion of their ink sales to the Roverges.

"Charlon, enough," said Montfaucon, taking a small jeweled
snuffbox from his pocket. "This is dull. Let us play a game, perhaps."

"Castles?" Falconet suggested. "I could get the board."

"We did that last night." Montfaucon took a pinch of snuff, his
eyes roaming curiously over Antonetta, who had not spoken since
Kel's arrival. Montfaucon had never been part of their little group
as children: He had never known a different Antonetta from the
one who existed now. "Let us wager on something." He tapped the
snuffbox with a green-painted nail and said, "Would you be interested in a wager, Demoselle Alleyne?"

"I brought no money with me, Sieur Montfaucon," she said.
"Silly of me."

"Clever of you," said Conor. "If you haven't any gold, Montfaucon can't take it off you."

Antonetta looked through her eyelashes at Conor. She was shivering, Kel realized. Her silk-and-chiffon dress would be little protection against the night's chill.

"Nonsense," said Falconet. "Montfaucon accepts promissory
notes, don't you, Lupin?"

Charlon had risen to his feet and was thoughtfully observing
the spread of food. "I've an idea," he said just as Conor leaped up
from the divan. He slid his brocaded jacket off his shoulders and
offered it to Antonetta.

The Antonetta of old would have scorned the idea that she was
bothered by cold, but this Antonetta took the jacket with a brilliant
smile and shrugged it over her shoulders. Conor went to join Charlon at the tower's edge, as did Montfaucon and Falconet. Charlon
was bellowing with laughter over something.

Kel, feeling as uneasy as if an ant had crawled into his collar and
was scrabbling about, decided no one would notice if he did not join
in. He was not known as much for games of chance anyway, while
Conor and the others would bet on anything at all—which bird

would alight first on a tree branch, or whether it would rain tomorrow.

He was in no mood for it. He turned and walked a distance away, until he was standing at the edge of the western parapet. From here, he could see the sunset. It was a glorious one, red and gold like the flag of Castellane unfurling across the sky. Below, lamps were being lit in the city, bringing the pattern of the streets to life with a soft glow. Kel could see the hollow ring of the Sault, the spire of the Windtower in Fleshmarket Square, and the dark dots of moored ships, rising and falling atop the hammered-gold sea.

In the back of his mind, the Ragpicker King's voice whispered, asking him about House Aurelian, about the Charter Families. *Do you like them? Do you trust them?*

"Kel?" It was Antonetta who had come up to him, surprisingly silently. Or perhaps he had simply not been paying attention. Not a good habit for a Sword Catcher.

He turned to look at her. It was odd, Kel thought, the way her mother both desperately wanted Antonetta to marry, yet insisted she dress as if she were still a little girl. Her dress had been designed for someone with a girlish figure, and the fullness of her breasts strained the citrine buttons at her neckline in a way they were not designed to be strained.

"You're not interested in joining the game?" she asked. The light of the sunset glimmered off the metallic threads in Conor's jacket. "Although I cannot blame you. They are betting on who can throw a meat pie farthest off the tower."

"Perhaps you had the notion our amusements had become more sophisticated?" Kel asked. "After all, it has been nearly a decade since you graced us with your presence here at the Mitat."

"Eight years." Antonetta looked down at the city below. The sunset's bloody glow tinted the edges of her pale hair.

"Why now?" Kel said. He wondered if anyone else had asked her. "Did Charlon ask you to come?"

"Well, he thinks it was his idea. That's what matters."

There was a shout. Kel glanced over to see that Charlon was making a triumphant gesture, presumably after hurling a pie. Falconet was drinking from a bottle of scarlet *rabarbaro*, a liquor derived from Shenzan rhubarb. Kel thought it tasted like medicine. Conor stood a little distance away, watching his friends with an unreadable expression.

"I was worried about Conor," said Antonetta. "After last night."

Kel leaned against the stone parapet. "You ought to forget that. He was drunk, that's all."

Now Antonetta glanced up at him. "I heard he might be getting married. Perhaps he's sad at the idea of having to marry one of those foreign Princesses."

So that's what this is about. Kel felt an unreasonable frustration go through him. He told himself it was because she seemed to know Conor so little, despite whatever she felt for him. Conor was angry sometimes—furious, frustrated, jealous, operatically disappointed—but not *sad*. Sad did not seem to describe anything he'd ever felt.

"I don't think so," Kel said. "He does not want to get married, and I doubt House Aurelian can force him."

"Because he's a Prince?" Antonetta said. "You'd be surprised. We can all be made to do things. It simply requires finding the right way to push."

Kel was about to ask her what she meant when Charlon called out to her. She leaped down from the low wall without a second glance, crossing the roof to where Falconet was holding out a pie. She took it, smiling that false smile that made Kel think of the painted masks worn every year on Solstice Day.

He remembered all too clearly when he and Antonetta had still been the sort of friends who climbed trees and chased imaginary dragons together. When he was fifteen, he had given her a ring—not a real ring, but grass he had fashioned into a loop—and asked her to be his bandit queen. He had been surprised how hard she had blushed, and later Conor had teased him. "Charlon will be furious,"

Conor had said. "He's been looking at her differently himself—but you're the one she's always liked."

Kel had stayed awake that night, thinking of Antonetta. If she'd liked the ring. If she looked at him any differently than she did at Conor, at Joss. He determined to study her the next time he saw her. Perhaps he could read her thoughts; she had never taken enormous trouble to hide whatever she was feeling.

It never happened. It was not Antonetta he saw next, but her mother. She had rarely taken much note of Kel before, but after a Court dinner, Lady Alleyne had taken him aside and told him in no uncertain terms to stay away from her daughter. She knew they were young, but this was how trouble started, with boys getting ideas above themselves. He might be a minor noble of Marakand, but he had no land or wealth or significant name, and Antonetta was destined for much greater things.

Kel had never felt so humiliated. He told himself that it was not Kel, himself, who had been humiliated, but Kel Anjuman, the part he played. He told himself Antonetta would be furious at her mother's interference. Instead Antonetta had vanished from their group, disappearing into House Alleyne for months, like a prisoner vanishing into the Trick.

Kel never spoke to Conor of what Lady Alleyne had said to him, and Joss, Charlon, and Conor seemed to feel Antonetta's disappearance was only to be expected. Girls, they seemed to feel, went off and did mysterious things in order to become women, who were fascinating, strange entities.

He heard Antonetta giggle, and then she was gliding back across the tower. The sun had almost entirely set, and the stars were not yet out. She was mostly a shadow as she approached him. He was surprised she had come back, but equally determined not to show it. "I don't have," he said, "anything else to tell you about Conor."

"What about you?" She tilted her head to the side. "Marriage, proposals. That sort of thing. You—"

Marriage is impossible for me. It will always be impossible. He said stiffly, "House Aurelian has given much to me. I wish to repay that debt before I think about marriage."

"Ah." She tucked a curl of hair behind her ear. "You don't want to tell me."

"It would be odd for me to confide in you, Antonetta," Kel said. "We hardly know each other now." She blinked; looked away. He said, "I remember the girl I was friends with when we were children. Who was bold and sharp and clever. I miss that girl. What happened to her?"

"You don't know?" She raised her chin. "That girl had no future on the Hill."

"She could have made a place for herself," said Kel, "if she was brave enough."

Antonetta sucked in a breath. "Perhaps you're right. But how lucky for me that bravery, like cleverness, is not much valued in women. Since I lack both."

"Antonetta—"

Kel thought for a moment he had spoken, said her name. But it was Conor, calling, gesturing for her to come over. Saying that they needed an objective observer to judge the winner of the contest.

For the second time, Antonetta stepped away from Kel and went back to the other side of the tower. Charlon threw an arm around her shoulder as she came close, the sort of gesture that might have been intended as friendly, if it had not been Charlon making it. Antonetta, leaning away from Charlon, had turned her attention to Conor, was smiling as she spoke to him. That brilliant false smile that no one but Kel seemed to notice was false.

He remembered the first time he'd seen it, that smile. At the ball her mother had thrown for her debut into the society of the Hill. He had gone with Conor, as Kel Anjuman, and at first he had looked around for Antonetta eagerly, not seeing her in the room.

It had been Conor who tapped him on the shoulder, directing

his attention to a young woman speaking to Artal Gremont. A young woman in a dress of ornately patterned silk, edged everywhere with lace, whose curled blond hair was tied up in dozens of ribbons. Slim gold chains circled her wrists and ankles, and diamond baubles hung from her ears. She seemed to sparkle like something hard and bright, metal or glass.

"That's her," Conor said. "Antonetta."

Kel had felt his stomach drop.

Somehow he had imagined that once she saw them all—and they were all there: Conor and Kel and Joss—she would come back to them, rejoin their group of friends. Complain about her mother. But though she greeted them all with smiles, with fluttering lashes and breathless giggles, there was nothing there of the old camaraderie that they had shared.

At last he had found a moment to speak to her alone, behind a statue bearing a tray of lemon ices. "Antonetta," he'd said. He felt sick with how pretty she was. It was the first time he had really noticed the fine-grained softness of a girl's skin, the color and shape of someone else's mouth. She had become someone new: someone thrilling, someone horrifying in her distance, her difference. "We've missed you."

She'd smiled at him. That brilliant smile he'd later come to hate. "I'm right here."

"Will you come back?" he'd said. "To the Mitat? Will your mother let you?"

Her smile did not change. "I am a little old for those kinds of games now. We all are." She patted his shoulder. "I know my mother spoke to you. She was right. We are not of the same class. It is one thing to play in the dirt as children, but we are too old to close our eyes to reality. Besides." She tossed her hair. "Different things are important to me now."

Kel could hardly breathe. "What kind of—things?"

"It's no concern of yours," she said breezily. "We must both grow up. You, especially, ought to make something of yourself, Kellian."

And she was gone. He watched her for the rest of the night—giggling, flirting, smiling. Clearly untroubled. Just as she was now, as she laid a hand on Falconet's shoulder, laughing as if he had just made the best joke in the world.

Perhaps it was better that she had changed, Kel thought. The old Antonetta could hurt him. The person she had become all those years ago could not. She could not be a gap in his armor, a place of weakness. That was all to the good. He knew the limits of what was available to him, he thought; he had learned them painfully through the years. How could he blame Antonetta for knowing the same?

In the dream, a man was toiling up a long and winding path cut into the side of the cliffs above Castellane. Dark water crashed in the harbor below, exploding into pale foam whitened by the moonlight.

The man wore long robes, made colorless by the night, and a sharp wind whipped at his face. Lin could taste the salt, sharp as blood in his mouth. Could feel the hatred in his heart—cold and bitter and brutal. A hatred that stole away breath, that felt like a vise gripping the chest, crushing and destructive.

The man reached the high point of the cliff path. He looked down at the steep fall below. At the sea, coalescing into a terrifying whirlpool, spinning and vertiginous. If one fell into such a whirlpool, one would be sucked down into darkness before one was even able to scream.

From a pocket in his robes the man drew a book. Pages fluttered in the wind as he raised it over his head and threw it. It hovered for a moment, white as a gull, before plunging downward. It struck the whirlpool, where the waters spun it like a dancer before drawing it down and down . . .

The man stood watching, shaking with rage. "Be thou forever cursed," he hissed, over the sound of the sea. "Be thou loathed in the eyes of the most holy forevermore."

Lin sat bolt upright, gasping, a firestorm exploding behind her closed lids. Opening her eyes, she saw not a churning black sea, but her own bedroom in her own house, lit dimly by the blue glow of dawn.

She willed herself to slow her breathing. She had not had such a dream—so vivid and unpleasant—for many years. Not since the death of her parents, when she had dreamed each night of their bodies abandoned on the Great Road, picked over by crows until only parchment bone was left.

She slid out from beneath her coverlet, careful not to knock any of her papers to the ground. Her neck ached, and her hair was wet with sweat. Opening a window cooled her skin, but she could still see the ocean behind her eyelids, still smell the cold salt on the air.

Lin's medical satchel hung on a chair by the door. She fetched it, and began to rummage through it for a sleeping draught, something that would calm her. It was odd, she thought: What she had seen in her dream was not objectively horrifying. It was more that it had felt so terribly real. And that she had not been herself, Lin, in the dream. She had been someone else—watching a man consumed by hatred, icy and acidic. An Ashkari man, for he had spoken their language, though he had made the words sound ugly. *What would someone have to do*, she thought, *to earn such loathing?* And what did it have to do with the book—was it the book's owner that the man had hated so much?

Stop trying to make sense of it. It's just a dream, she told herself, and then her fingers closed around something cool and hard. Her heart gave a jolt. She drew her hand out of the satchel and saw, rolling in her palm, a hard gray orb.

She sank down with her back against the wall, staring at it. Petrov's stone. It could be nothing else. The feel of it, the weight in her hand, was familiar; as she gazed at it, she seemed to see smoke swirling in its depths. Now and then it formed itself into shapes that seemed almost recognizable, almost like words . . .

But how had it gotten into her satchel? She recalled Petrov jostling against her as he'd opened the door of his flat. He was clever and careful. He could have dropped it into her bag, but why? Because of the men coming up the steps? Was he hiding it from them?

She sat and wondered, gazing at the stone, until the *aubade*, the morning bell, rang out from the Windtower Clock, signaling the start of the working day and the end of the watches of the night.

The greatest lesson that we, citizens of the Empire, can take from the time of the Sorcerer-Kings is that power should not be limitless. It is for that reason that, when an Emperor is crowned, it is whispered in his ear by a priest of the Gods: *Remember that you are mortal. Remember that you will die.* For when we die, we face Anibal, the Shadow God, who judges our actions in life, and any abuse of mortal power will result in eternity in Hell.

But the Sorcerer-Kings had no Gods. And the One Word bestowed on them a great power. Yet that power was limited by mortal strength. Magic required energy, and too great a spell could exhaust the magician, even unto death.

It was then that the Sorcerer-King Suleman invented the Arkhe—the Source-Stone. It allowed magicians to store energy outside themselves. Such energy came from many sources: from a drop of blood fed to the stone each day to more violent methods; the murder of a magic-user provided great power, which could be stored within the Arkhe.

The world darkened. The Sorcerer-Kings grew in murderous ambition. They began to look past their borders and covet what their neighbors had. *Why should I not be the greatest?* each asked themselves. *Why not the most powerful?*

Thus was the world nearly destroyed.

— *Tales of the Sorcerer-Kings*, Laocantus Aurus Iovit III

CHAPTER SIX

It was almost noon. Kel was looking at Conor. Conor was looking at himself in the mirror.

"I dislike this bandage," Conor said. "It's destructive to the integrity of my ensemble."

Kel, sitting on the arm of the sofa, sighed. It appeared Lilibet had noticed Conor's injuries, after all. The Royal Surgeon, Gasquet, had arrived that morning, woken them both up, and insisted on bandaging Conor's hand before the Dial Chamber meeting.

"I doubt anyone will notice," Kel said now.

Conor made a noncommittal noise. He was looking at himself in the pier glass that hung against the east wall. He generally dressed outrageously for Dial Chamber meetings, as if certain that could liven up the proceedings. Today, however, he had chosen to wear shades of black and silver: black velvet cloak, black silk trousers, tunic of silver brocade. Even his crown was a plain silver circlet. Kel was not entirely certain that Conor intended to take the Dial Chamber meeting seriously, but at least his clothes would.

"You see," said Conor, "my outfit is black. This bandage is white. It destroys the symmetry." He glanced over his shoulder. "I can't believe you didn't chase off Gasquet. Aren't you supposed to protect me?"

"Not against your own doctor," Kel pointed out. "Anyway, you know perfectly well what would have happened. Gasquet would have run to the Queen. The Queen would have raised a fuss. And you hate fuss. I was protecting you against fuss."

Conor, clearly hiding a smile, said, "And I expect you to do the same at the meeting. No one fusses like the Charter Families." He pushed a heavily ringed hand through his hair. "All right. Into the den of overdressed lions we go."

They left the Castel Mitat together, Conor humming a popular song about unrequited love. It was a bright, blustery day, the wind tossing the tops of the cypress and pine trees that dotted the Hill, the sky clear enough to see the mountains of Detmarch ranged in razor-sharp formation to the north. To the west, cliffs fell away toward the ocean, its roar audible even at a distance. And to the east, the Star Tower rose from the ramparts of the walls surrounding Marivent.

As they neared the tower, Kel ran through a quick check: slim blades at his wrists, under the sleeves of his plain gray tunic. A dagger at his hip, hilt tucked through his belt, concealed by the fall of his jacket. He had dressed plainly, in dark gray and green, intending to be ignored.

Kel could hear the sound of voices as they passed through the tower gates—guarded on either side by Castelguards—and into the Dial Chamber, where the sound rose to a din.

The Dial Chamber was a circular marble room whose domed roof rose to a central oculus; meetings were generally held at midday, when the chamber was most directly illuminated by the sun. When it rained, a glass dome was placed over the oculus, though rain in Castellane was rare.

The mosaic floor had been designed—in tesserae of blue, gold, black, and scarlet—to resemble a sundial. A great ironwood chair had been placed at the location of each hour's tiled numeral—Roverge at six, Montfaucon at four, Aurelian at twelve. The chairs themselves belonged to the House they represented, and their backs were carved accordingly: Trees adorned the chair belonging to House Raspail, who held the timber Charter; a bunch of grapes for Uzec; a silk moth for Alleyne; the sun and its rays for Aurelian.

Circling the interior of the dome, words in Callatian, the language of the Empire, had been picked out in gold tiles: ALL THAT IS GOOD COMES FROM THE GODS. ALL THAT IS EVIL COMES FROM MEN.

Kel had always felt that this commentary seemed pointed, considering what tended to go on in the Dial Chamber. He wondered if the Charter Families thought the same, or if they even noticed it. They were not the sort of people who spent much time looking up.

The buzz of voices died down as Conor entered the room, followed by Kel. Faces turned toward him as he stalked to the Sun Chair like the pages of a book turning; Kel tried to read their expressions. Conor had attended numerous Dial Chamber meetings, but had never presided over one. Lady Alleyne, resplendent in pink silk, looked pleased, as did Antonetta, sitting beside her on a low stool; every Charter holder was allowed to bring one companion to meetings of the Twelve. Joss Falconet looked encouraging. Benedict Roverge, who had brought Charlon with him, was glowering. Cazalet, who held the Charter in banking, was smooth-faced and unreadable. And Montfaucon, in raspberry brocade edged by pale-green lace, seemed amused by the whole thing.

As Conor took his place in the Sun Chair, he nodded at Mayesh Bensimon, who was seated on the low stool beside him. This still put their heads on the same level, as Mayesh was ridiculously tall. If Kel had expected him to shrink with age, he had been disappointed. As far as he could tell, Mayesh had not changed since Kel had arrived at the Palace. He had seemed old to Kel then, and was still old, but though his gray hair had gone white, no new wrinkles or ridges had appeared on his face. The state medallion around his neck gleaming like a star, Mayesh sat straight-backed, gazing flatly at the Charter holders from beneath brindled eyebrows.

There was nowhere for Kel to sit, which he had expected. He

took his place beside the Sun Chair as Conor sprawled in it, deliberately loose-limbed, as if to say: *Nothing about this meeting seems terribly urgent.*

"Greetings, Monseigneur," said Lady Alleyne, smiling at Conor. She had been very beautiful when young, and was still handsome, her voluptuous curves poured into her tight gown. The upper circles of her breasts spilled from the square neck of her bodice, only barely restrained by a thin layer of white netting. "Alas, we have already lost one member. Gremont is asleep."

This was true. Mathieu Gremont, holder of the Charter for coffee and tea, was ninety-five, and already snoring quietly in his carved chair. Conor, flashing a smile at Lady Alleyne, said, "Hardly a good advertisement for the strength of his merchandise."

There was a low ripple of laughter. Kel caught the eye of Falconet, who looked tired and a bit rumpled. Well, he *had* been up until nearly dawn, drinking with Montfaucon and Roverge atop the West Tower. He winked at Kel.

Ambrose Uzec, whose Charter was wine, looked at Gremont darkly. "It is time for Gremont to pass the Charter on, surely. He has a son—"

"His son Artal is in Taprobana, meeting with the owners of tea estates," said Lady Alleyne. Her shoes, as well as her dress, matched her daughter's: white heels, sprigged with pink silk rosettes. Kel wondered if it bothered Antonetta that her mother so clearly saw her as a miniature version of herself. He knew Antonetta would never show it, if it did. "Important work, surely."

Kel exchanged a look with Conor. Artal Gremont had been sent away amid a swirl of scandal when they had been fourteen years old. Neither of them had ever managed to find out what it was he'd done to be effectively exiled; even Montfaucon did not seem to know.

"Gremont's business is his own," said Lord Gasquet, looking irritable. He, too, was not a young man, and showed no signs of turning his Charter over to one of his gaggle of sons, daughters, or grandchildren. Charter holders always thought they were immortal, Mayesh had said once, and tended to die without making any provisions as to who might inherit their places on the Council. Infighting would then ensue, usually settled by House Aurelian. Only the King or Queen had the power to grant Charters and strip them away.

"I believe," Montfaucon said, ruffling the lace cuffs that spilled over his wrists like pale-green seafoam, "that we were discussing Roverge's latest troubles, were we not?"

"There is no need to make it sound as if I am beset by troubles, Lupin," growled Roverge. Charlon, beside him, nodded sagely. His eyes were only half open; he was clearly suffering a brutal headache from the jenever he'd drunk the night before. His father turned to Conor. "It is a question of tithes, which I seek to put before you, Monseigneur."

Kel's mind began to drift as Conor considered the matter of whether merchants selling colored paper should tithe a percent of their proceeds to the Roverge House, or to House Raspail. Trade was the blood that ran through the veins of Castellane. Every one of the Charter Families had caravans on the roads and ships on the seas, laden down with precious cargo. Their control of specific goods was the source of their wealth and power. House Raspail, for instance, had the Charter for timber, so no bit of wood or paper, nor the smallest carved flute, changed hands without them getting a share of the profit.

That did not mean, however, that it was objectively interesting to anyone else. Kel could not stop his mind returning to the Ragpicker King. In Kel's memory, the Ragpicker King's voice was soft as the nap on velvet.

Conor had been nodding along as Roverge and Raspail argued, his gray eyes sleepy beneath the tumble of his black hair. Now he said, "The tithe on colored paper will be split between your two

Houses, evenly. Understood? Good. What is the next matter at hand?"

"Bandits," said Alonse Esteve, leaning forward. He was an odd one. The Esteve Charter was horses, and Alonse, though in his fifties, had no wife, nor any heirs to inherit his Charter. He seemed far happier with horses than people and was usually in Valderan, where the best horseflesh was bred. "We must discuss the problem at the Narrow Pass. It affects us all."

It was as if he had tossed a lit match into kindling. A loud squabble blazed up as the nobles fell to arguing. It seemed that several caravans had been attacked by teams of well-coordinated bandits while approaching the Narrow Pass that connected Sarthe to Castellane; it was a concern, as there was no other land route into the city, but no one was agreed on a solution.

"If you ask me," said Polidor Sardou, whose Charter was glass, "the thing to do is march the Arrow Squadron into Sarthe. Put them on the back foot. We need to demonstrate our strength, show them we can't be trifled with."

"That risks war with Sarthe," said Falconet languidly. "The Black Guard would be on us like flies."

"No one wants war," said Lady Alleyne, watching Conor out of the corner of her eye. "A stupid and unprofitable way to settle disputes."

"Liorada, that's simply not true," said Montfaucon. "War can be very profitable indeed."

"Perhaps," said Raspail, "we should consider strengthening our alliance with Sarthe. This state of uneasy détente serves no one, really."

"I had heard tell," Falconet said, "of a possible alliance with Sarthe."

All eyes turned to Conor. He sat motionless in his black velvet, his eyes glittering like the rings on his fingers. The light from the oculus cast his face in shadow. It was Mayesh who spoke.

"The matter of the Prince's marriage," he said, "has not progressed to a place at which you need worry yourself about alliances, Falconet. We can all agree, I think, that it is an area in which our Prince should have time to apply due consideration."

This was not, Kel knew, what Mayesh really thought. He wanted to advise Conor and for Conor to take that advice—and sooner rather than later. But his loyalty was to House Aurelian, not the Charter Families. He would place his words between them and Conor, just as Kel placed his body between Conor and danger.

"I recall," said Roverge, "that when this matter arose for King Markus, he placed it before us to hear our voices. There is no pact more binding than a marriage, and pacts between Castellane and foreign powers are a Council matter."

"Are they?" Conor murmured. "Are you all planning on joining me on my wedding night? We shall have to make a list of names, that I might know how many bottles of wine to provide."

Roverge smiled stiffly. "You are young, dear Prince. It is part of your undeniable charm. But when a royal weds, whole nations are joined in the bedchamber."

"How scandalously put," said Falconet.

Cazalet said, "When Markus came to us then, matters with Marakand were different. We were at odds. Now, of course, there is harmony between us."

"But," said Conor, "not all disputes can be solved with marriage. I can only be married once, for one thing."

Kel wished he could lay a hand on Conor's shoulder. He could see that Conor's fingers were curling in on themselves, a nervous habit. He was letting the Council get under his skin. If he snapped, Lilibet would declare that he had failed to show the Council who was in control.

"Indeed," Kel said, striving for a light tone. "This isn't Nyenschantz."

There was a buzz of laughter; the King of Nyenschantz had been

caught promising his daughter's hand in marriage to several countries at once, and been forced to pay out multiple dowries when the
deception was uncovered.

"I know the Princess of Sarthe, Aimada," Falconet said. "She's
beautiful, clever, accomplished—"

Lady Alleyne sat up straight. "Nonsense," she said. "We cannot
treat our Prince so! Marry him off to some awful woman from
Sarthe? I think not."

"Joss, your sister is married to a Sarthian duke," said Sardou
crossly. "You are not objective in this matter. An alliance with Sarthe
would likely benefit your family."

Joss smiled, innocence personified. "That hadn't crossed my
mind, Polidor. I was thinking of Castellane. Our constant state of
unease with Sarthe drains the city coffers, does it not, Cazalet?"

"What about Valderan?" interrupted Esteve. "An alliance with
Valderan could be valuable indeed."

"Think of the horses," said Falconet, dry as salt. "*So* many
horses."

Esteve glared.

"Falconet may not be objective," said Roverge, "but Sarthe *is*
our closest neighbor, and there is something to be said for solving
the bandit problem. I lost a caravan's worth of indigo powder last
month."

Rolant Cazalet took a gold snuffbox from his pocket. "What
about Malgasi?" he said, pinching up some of the mixture of powdered leaves and herbs he kept inside. One could buy such stuff at
the Ashkari stalls in the city market. It was a bit of small magic—like
posy-drops, which the younger nobles dripped into their eyes to
change the shape of their pupils to stars, hearts, or leaves. "Their
wealth, put at our disposal, could expand our Treasury, and the
footprint of our trade—"

"My sources at the Malgasi Court tell me Queen Iren may be
leaving the throne soon," said Montfaucon.

"Odd," said Mayesh. "She has only in this past decade consolidated her power. One does not usually willingly take leave of a position of power."

"Perhaps she is tired of being queen," said Antonetta. "Perhaps she wishes to take up a hobby."

Lady Alleyne looked pained. "Antonetta, you know nothing of power or politics. Keep your mouth shut and your ears open, my girl."

Kel shot Antonetta a glare; he couldn't help it. Why did she put so much effort into seeming ridiculous in public? She had had better and clearer thoughts about politics and trade at twelve, and he seemed the only one to realize that she could not possibly have lost all her sense in the intervening years.

She simply smiled back at him, as she had the night before: a sweet, charming, slightly befuddled smile. It warmed him—though perhaps that was only the annoyance sweeping through his veins.

"It is not Iren's choice to leave the throne. They say she is dying," said Montfaucon. "Which means Princess Elsabet will soon ascend to the throne. We would not need to wait long to have the gold of Malgasi at our disposal."

"How calculating, Lupin," Lady Alleyne murmured. "And how it would delight Lilibet, having another queen here at Marivent. You *have* thought of everything."

"I hear their Court is chaotic and the Belmany rule not terribly popular," said Raspail. "Mayesh, what do your Ashkari connections tell you? Any news from Favár?"

"There are no Ashkar in Favár," said Mayesh, without inflection. "We are forbidden from Malgasi, save to pass through on the Roads."

Kel frowned. Had he known that? He could tell from the expressions of the other Council members that they had not. Shrugging it off, Raspail said, "What about Kutani? If it is only a matter of gold, none has more than they do. And their Princess—"

"Anjelica," Kel said. He could still see her, or the portrait of her—the pale gold of her eyes, the cloud of her dark hair. "Anjelica Iruvai."

"Anjelica, yes," said Raspail, with a snap of his fingers. "Meant to be beautiful. Biddable, too."

"Are there a lot of trees in Kutani?" Falconet wondered aloud. "Mangroves, I suppose—" He broke off, his eyes widening.

Conor stiffened. The room fell silent. Beside Kel, Mayesh Bensimon was rising slowly to his feet. The nobles followed him. One by one: Esteve, Uzec, Roverge, Montfaucon, Alleyne . . . all but the still-sleeping Gremont. As tradition dictated, they stood and bowed, for King Markus had come into the Dial Chamber, and was regarding them with a curious gaze.

The King. Where Kel often thought Mayesh had not changed in the past twelve years, the King certainly had. He was still a big man, with the arms and chest of a stevedore unloading cargo on the docks, but his face had sagged. Great dark bags hung under his eyes, and his fair hair was streaked with white. His large hands, gloved as always in black, hung empty at his sides.

Beside him stood Master Fausten, his constant companion. He had been the King's tutor in Favár, years ago, when Markus had fostered at the Malgasi Court. When the King had moved himself into the Star Tower, he had summoned Fausten to join him in his studies.

Fausten was a small man, with gnarled limbs like an old tree, the result of a childhood illness. He had the dark hair and pale skin common in Malgasi, though most of his hair was gone now, and his bald pate gleamed with the effort of navigating the uneven terrain of Marivent.

Like the King, he was an astronomer, though Kel had always wondered how one could study the stars when one could barely see the masterful fretwork of the sky itself, glittering in silver and gold. He liked to insist that the sun itself was a star, but Kel put that down to his copious consumption of Malgasi brandewine—an evil-tasting mixture of arrack and whiskey.

"Conor, my dear son," said the King. "And my Council." His gaze trailed over the nobles, slightly unfocused, as if he were not entirely sure he recognized each one of them. "I was at my studies when I thought—what was it I thought, Fausten?"

"You spoke of destiny, my King," said Fausten. He was sweating, clearly uncomfortable in the heavy velvet robes he insisted on wearing. They were midnight blue, and on them the constellations of the sky had been picked out in beads of silver: the Swan, the Crown, and Aigon's Sword among them. "And of fate."

The King nodded. "Such meetings as this are foolishness," he said, indicating the whole of the Dial Chamber with a sweep of one gloved hand. "The stars should be consulted when matters of import lie before us, for that is how the Gods speak to us. Squabbling among ourselves nets us nothing, for we see only a fraction of the path laid out."

"We do not all have your skill, Highness," said Mayesh, "in interpreting the will of the stars."

Conor had gone very still. His face was white, his hands clenched on the arms of his chair. Kel laid a hand on his shoulder; it was rigid as steel under his touch.

"Indeed," said Montfaucon. "I do not find them very talkative, myself."

The King turned his unfocused gaze on Montfaucon. "Then you are lucky," he said. "For when I gaze upon the stars, I see the ruination of Castellane. Marivent, our White Lady, tumbled in the dirt. The Ruta Magna running with blood."

There was a soft murmur of mild shock, as if Lady Alleyne had whipped off her bodice, but no one seemed particularly alarmed.

The King turned to Mayesh. "All must be done to avert this fate. The stars . . ."

Between his teeth, Conor hissed, "*Fausten.*"

The little man turned anxiously to the King. "My liege," he said. "We cannot stay. The lunar eclipse tonight, do you recall? When the moon's light is quenched, much will be revealed. We must prepare the telescopes, that any messages of import are not lost."

The King seemed to hesitate. Fausten dropped his voice, murmuring in Malgasi. After a few moments, the King nodded and strode from the room. Fausten, picking up his heavy robes, scurried after him like a sheepdog after a wayward member of his flock.

"There you have it," Conor said, into the ensuing silence. "I will be consulting the stars as regards my future marriage, so there is no further need for discussion on the subject."

"My lord," said Kel. He rarely addressed Conor in this way, but the moment called for it. He had withdrawn his hand from Conor's shoulder, knowing it was a familiarity the Council would look askance at, even from the Prince's cousin. "King Markus was clearly joking. A bit of humor to lighten the mood. Would you not all agree?"

The assembled nobles murmured in assent, recognizing the escape Kel was providing, and relieved enough not to mind, for the moment, the source of it.

"Of course," Conor said. "A joke. My father was being purposefully absurd."

"Have a care," Mayesh said in a low voice, but Conor was spinning the tea glass rapidly in his hand, staring at it as if it held the answers his father sought in the stars.

"There are no other matters to discuss, then?" Conor asked, not looking up. The nobles exchanged glances, but not a one spoke. "Before this meeting is adjourned?"

"Well," said Lady Alleyne. "There is the matter of the Solstice Ball—"

Conor rose abruptly to his feet, green glass sparking in his hand. Kel knew what he was going to do, but had no way to stop it; he flinched as Conor threw the glass as hard as he could. It sailed past Gremont, striking the wall behind him and smashing there, spraying crystalline fragments.

Antonetta gave a little scream before covering her mouth. Gremont sat up, blinking. "What? Is the meeting over?"

Without another word, Conor stalked out of the room. Frowning, Lady Alleyne said, "That child must learn to curb his temper."

"That child," said Kel, "is your Prince, and will one day be your King."

Lady Alleyne rolled her eyes. Coldly, Roverge said, "The dog barks on behalf of its master. Bark somewhere else, little dog."

Kel did not answer. The Charter Families were already rising, ready for departure. And it was hardly his place to argue with Roverge, or any of them. He had said too much already; he could see that in Mayesh's eyes.

He followed Conor out of the room, pausing only to bare his teeth at Roverge as he went. Antonetta watched him anxiously as he went; worried, no doubt, about Conor. Kel could not help but recall what she had said the night before: *We can all be made to do things. It simply requires finding the right way to push.*

Lin was in the physick garden, kneeling in the dirt beside a foxglove plant. She loved it here—the air was fresh and green with the scent of growing, and the sun illuminated the winding paths through the beds of herbs and flowers. Though maintained by the Women's House, the contents of the garden were shared with all the Sault. Here grew the medicinal herbs that had been used by Ashkari physicians for generations. Larkspur, asphodel, and foxglove rubbed shoulders with monkshood and laburnum. Jars in the Physicians' House held that which could not be grown in the Sault: birch and willowbark, ginseng and lotus root.

"I thought I'd find you here." Lin looked up, shielding her eyes with one hand, to see Chana Dorin looming over her. She wore her usual frayed gray dress, a colorful apron tied around her waist. "I suppose you need to use the kitchen?"

Lin tucked her handful of foxglove leaves into her satchel and rose to her feet. Most physicians in the Sault simply placed orders with the Physicians' House for the compounds they needed. Lin had discovered early that her requests were often seen to last, or ignored entirely, leaving her short of medicine. Chana had offered to let her use the kitchen in the Etse Kebeth, the largest in the Sault, to compound her own medicines.

Though she had been angry at first—most physicians did not have to also be their own apothecaries—Lin had discovered an advantage to her situation. It allowed her to experiment, to mix various ingredients together as she tried to create new medicines to treat Mariam. She often thought longingly of what it would be like to have her own laboratory, as the students at the Academie did— but that was impossible. The kitchen would need to do for now.

"I do," Lin said. "I found a reference to an old Hindish compound for treating lung inflammation—"

Chana held up a hand. "No need to explain yourself." She squinted against the sun. "The Goddess Festival is a month away."

Lin raised her eyebrows. It was not like Chana to make idle observations. "Yes?"

"I hoped you would help me make the sachets for the girls." The sachets were small bags of herbs, worn around the neck of those women young enough to be considered as potential vessels for the Goddess. The herbs were for love and luck. Silliness, in Lin's opinion.

"Chana, I'm *so* busy already—"

Chana held up a hand. "Lin, you know perfectly well everyone in the Sault is meant to assist in preparing for the Tevath."

"Not the physicians," Lin said, though she knew many of them did, regardless. The Festival of the Goddess, called the Tevath, was the most important holiday of the year in the Sault. The Ashkar gathered in the Kathot, where the Maharam would recite the story of the Goddess, and of lost Aram. How Queen Adassa snatched life for her people from the jaws of defeat. How she saved for them the magic of *gematry*, so they could make their amulets and talismans. How she had promised she would one day return in the form of an Ashkari girl.

When she was younger, Lin had loved the Festival, as had Mariam. It was a chance to dress up, to be seen as special for a day—as any girl, and *only* a girl, might be the Goddess Returned. It was an opportunity to dance—the graceful dance taught to every Ashkari girl, performed only at the Festival. The Kathot would be alight with lanterns, magical as a forest from a Story-Spinner tale, and there would be laughter and wine, music and *loukoum*, honey cake and flirting.

Now, though, it was a reminder that the majority of the Sault looked at her as if she were peculiar. "But *why* would you want to be a physician?" was the question she heard most often from dancing partners. And the question under the question: Was she still planning on having a family? How could she be a physician and also raise children? Of course she was odd, they would murmur when they thought she couldn't hear them. Terrible what had happened to her parents, but there must have been some reason Mayesh Bensimon hadn't wanted to take the children in. Something wrong with them, perhaps; the girl at least had turned out awfully peculiar.

Lin sighed. "Chana, I wasn't planning on going."

"I *knew* it." Chana pounced on this information like a pigeon on a breadcrumb. "Lin, that just won't do. It's the most important Festival of the year, and the last time you and Mariam will be eligible. The Sault is your home. You cannot withdraw from your people."

They are the ones who have withdrawn from me. It was more than that, though. When Lin was young, she had always tensed during the part of the Festival when the Maharam spoke the words in the Old Language, words meant to call forth the Goddess. *If you are among us, Adassa, show yourself.*

She could not recall the moment when she realized that no one truly expected the Goddess to return. That the hush of expectation was only in her own heart. The Festival was in truth a marriage market, parading girls in their finest clothes past unmarried young men in the hope matches would be made.

"Besides," Chana added, "Mariam has already started working on your dress."

Lin felt a pang of guilt. She had forgotten to tell Mariam she wasn't going—well, to be truthful, she'd been avoiding the issue. "I'm trying to get Mariam well," she said, "which is more important."

"I am not sure Mariam would agree with you," Chana said. "She assumes you're going. She's even asked me if I think Josit might be back with the caravans by then."

Josit. Mariam had come to see him off, months ago, when he'd departed with the Rhadanites for Hind. Lin recalled him leaning down from the waggon, tucking a curl of hair behind Mariam's ear. Mariam smiling up at him. Telling him to bring her back fine cotton in every shade of blue. The way the smile had slipped from her face as the caravan disappeared through the gates. Lin had known what Mariam was thinking: Was this the last time she would ever see Josit?

"Don't try to make me feel guilty about Mariam, Chana," Lin said, wretched. "I'm working night and day trying to find a cure for her. That's more important than a dress."

Chana put her fists on her hips. "That's the trouble with you, Lin. You've stopped seeing Mariam as your friend, your sister. You see her only as a patient. If there was one thing I learned from losing Irit, it is that our loved ones need more from us than doctoring. There are other physicians. Mariam needs her friend."

The words cut, not least because Chana spoke of Irit so rarely. Lin had often wondered if Chana would seek love again, but she did not seem inclined to it. "Has she said that to you?"

"I know the Festival is important to her. I know she has been tirelessly working on dresses for a dozen girls, and a special one for you. All her energy and thought are going toward it. I know she worries this might be the last Festival she ever sees."

"But don't you see?" Lin cried. "Doesn't that mean I should work even harder on a cure, a treatment?"

"I'm not saying you should stop trying to heal her." Chana's voice gentled. "But the mind and the spirit need care, as well as the body. It is good for Mariam to have something she is looking forward to. But if you do not go—" Chana shook her head. "Be her friend, not her healer, for a night. She will be so much happier if you are there."

And with that, Chana turned on her heel and strode from the garden, her bearing as regal as any noble's. Lin sat, feeling miserable, in the shadow of the dwarf mulberry tree. She knew what she ought to do: She ought to *ask* Mariam what she wanted.

Only she was frightened of the answer. What if Mariam wanted Lin to stop searching for a cure? What if she wanted to be left to die in her own time? Lin didn't think she could bear that. Lin's hand tightened at her side; she winced, and realized she was holding Petrov's stone. She did not remember having taken it from her pocket, but there it was, cradled in her palm, the shape and feel of it peculiarly calming.

She turned it over. She could not help but be fascinated by it, by the swirl of darkness within it, like smoke rising from a single point and spreading outward to cover the sky. Each time she looked at it, the shapes inside seemed different, seemed to beckon her understanding.

Stop. She slid it back into her pocket with a hard flip of her wrist. That was enough, she told herself. The stone was still Petrov's; she needed to bring it back to him as soon as she could. Before she got into the habit of using it to comfort herself. Before she no longer could bring herself to return it at all.

Kel found Conor some distance from the tower, in the Queen's Garden. It had been a gift from Markus to Lilibet upon her arrival at Marivent, a quarter century ago. A long white path of crushed seashells led to a walled green space where the Queen had resettled plants and flowers from Marakand, combining them freely with the local flora: lavender flowers and aster mixed with hyacinth and bird-of-paradise; roses climbed the courtyard walls while tulips the color of pale gold glimmered in the sun.

In the center of the garden was a reflecting pool, tiled with emerald tesserae, like a green eye regarding the sky. Conor stood beside it, staring bleakly at the water. As Kel approached he said, without looking up, "I should not have done that."

"Done what? Thrown the glass?" Kel asked, coming to stand by Conor's side. He could see them both reflected in the waters of the pool. Faint ripples caused by the wind made them indistinct, two slim, dark-haired figures, essentially identical. "You woke up Gremont, which is no bad thing."

"I fear," Conor said, "it will not be interpreted as my retaining control over the Council, will it?"

"I cannot predict what the Queen will think. I daresay no one can."

"Perhaps the stars can," Conor said darkly. "As, apparently, they know everything, and care about nothing."

A pause, then, "He is mad," Conor said, without looking away from the pool. "My father is mad, and if what the surgeons say about madness is true, I will be mad one day myself."

Kel did not move. He had heard Conor say this before; the first time had been after the Fire on the Sea. What was meant to be a celebration—the King setting out in the boat covered in flowers to enact the ceremonial marriage between Castellane and the ocean that sustained it—had ended in fire: the boat in flames, the charcoal-black smoke thickening, hiding the figure of the King.

Only those standing on the Royal Docks had been close enough to see that the King had made no move to save himself. Jolivet and the Arrow Squadron, diving into the water, had pulled their sovereign from the flaming wreckage. It had been played off as an accident—some in Castellane believed it to be an assassination attempt—but Kel had heard the King shouting at his guards. *You should have let me burn*, he'd cried out, kneeling on the Royal Docks as water poured from his thick velvet robes. As Gasquet raced forward to wrap his charred hands, though, the King did not seem to feel the pain. *You should have let the fire take me.*

Conor, his wrists and brow wreathed in flowers, had watched, ashen-faced and silent. Since that day, he had said almost nothing of the incident, save in the dead of night, only when he woke screaming from dreams he would not describe. *I have lost him, he has gone mad, and one day I will go mad, too, and also be lost.*

He was not alone: No one on the Hill spoke of it, though the torches in the Star Tower had been replaced with chemical lamps, and the King had worn black gloves ever since, to conceal the burns on his hands.

"The surgeons are often wrong," Kel said. "I would not put too much stock in what they believe."

Conor was silent. He did not need to say: *It is not just what they say, but what everyone believes. Madness is inherited through tainted blood. The child of mad parents will also be mad, and pass that poison down through the generations. If it becomes well known that my father is mad, not simply distracted and dreamy, House Aurelian could be in peril.*

"Besides," Kel added. "I would prefer you not go mad, because then I would also have to learn to imitate all the mad things you'd do."

At that, Conor laughed—a real laugh, not the false one he employed with Montfaucon and the others. His wary stance had relaxed a little—and just in time, Kel thought, for Mayesh had appeared at the garden gate like a watchful gray crow. Of course, after every Dial Chamber meeting, Lilibet would meet with Jolivet and Bensimon in the Shining Gallery to discuss the proceedings.

Conor rolled his eyes. "I expect he will scold me on the way to the gallery," he said. "There's no need for you to come—it will be murderously boring. I believe there's a gathering at Falconet's tonight," he added, turning to follow Mayesh. "Go get drunk. One of us might as well enjoy their evening."

Once the Sorcerer-Kings had harnessed the power of the Arkhe stones, their abilities grew ever greater. With their new strength, they were able to tame the great creatures of magic, born of the Word: the manticores, the dragons, the phoenixes, were forced to do their bidding. While the people cowered, the Kings and Queens battled, and rivers turned to fire as mountains were hurled across the earth. Still their ambitions grew, and the Sorcerer-Kings stole the magic of their own magicians—along with their very lives—to absorb their power into the hungry stones. The suffering of the people was enormous, save in one kingdom: the kingdom of Aram.

—*Tales of the Sorcerer-Kings,* Laocantus Aurus Iovit III

CHAPTER SEVEN

L in made her way through the dusty streets of the Fountain Quarter, her hood pulled up to shield her face from the late-afternoon sunlight. It was one of those days when the hot winds had come boiling over the Arradin mountains to the south, pressing the city beneath it like a butterfly under glass. Pedestrians moved sluggishly, their heads down; women clustered together under broad parasols. Even the ships in the harbor seemed to bob up and down more slowly, as if mired in boiled honey.

Reaching Petrov's house, she ducked into the welcome cool of the stairwell, and took the steps two at a time to the second floor. She knocked loudly and waited; they did not have a scheduled appointment. She had merely hoped to catch him at home, since he rarely went out. "Dom Petrov?"

No response.

She crouched, trying to peer through the keyhole, but could see nothing but darkness. "Dom Petrov—it's Lin. Lin Caster. I need to see you."

She had been leaning against the door. It shifted now, under her weight, swinging open a crack. Lin rose to her feet in surprise. It was certainly not at all like Petrov to leave his door unlocked.

She bit her thumbnail worriedly. What if he was ill? What if he had collapsed, weak from his blood disorder, and could not rise to come to the door? The image decided her. She pushed down on the latch and the door swung open.

She caught her breath as she stepped inside. The small flat was utterly empty, every bit of furniture vanished. Lin turned in a slow circle. Gone were the books, the bronze samovar, even the plants on the windowsill. And on the floor—the plush rug was gone. In its place, a spatter of dark-brown stains.

Dried blood.

Horror made Lin's blood fizz like wine. She was suddenly terribly aware of the stone in her pocket, weighing it down. The floorboard that had concealed Petrov's treasures had been wrenched up, showing an empty black space beneath.

"What are you doing here?"

Lin bolted to her feet. Domna Albertine, Petrov's landlady, loomed in the open door. She was glowering, her dark-gray curls escaping from beneath an incongruously frilly pink velvet cap. Her dress was stained, the material worn and yellowed beneath her arms.

"Well?" she demanded, brandishing her trusty broom, the terror of geese everywhere. She squinted. "Wait, you're that physician, that Ashkari girl."

Lin stood her ground. "Where is he? Where's Petrov?"

"Does it matter? Some friends of his came looking for him the other day. At least they *said* they were his friends." Domna Albertine spat sideways. "I heard some noise, but I like to leave my tenants to their business."

Lin, who knew this was not true, glared.

"I came the next day to collect the rent—Petrov's gone. Blood all over the floor. I mopped it up, but as you see, it stains." She shook her head. "I had to sell his furniture to pay off the cleaning. And his back rent. *Filh de puta.*"

Ignoring the obscenity, Lin said, "I see you pried up the floorboards."

Albertine narrowed her eyes. "They were like that when I got here." She smiled, but it was an unpleasant smile, full of cold contempt. "I know why you're here, *feojh*," she said. It was a nasty epithet for Ashkar, and it made Lin's blood freeze in her body. "You want his books—nasty little magic books, full of illegal spells. I could have reported him to the Vigilants, at any time, but he was an old man and I felt sorry for him. But *you*, prancing all around the city with your dirty little talismans." Her mouth worked, and whitish spittle gathered at the corners. "They ought to get rid of all of you. Burn out the Sault, like they did in Malgasi. *Cleanse* it."

Lin clenched her hands at her sides. "We do no harm," she said, her voice shaking. "You know nothing—"

"I know enough." The landlady's tone was venomous. "Magic is a curse. Your people carry it, like a sickness. Like a plague."

Lin swallowed bile. "I could make a talisman that would make every bone in your body ache," she said, in a low voice. "You would never sleep a peaceful night again."

Albertine recoiled. "You wouldn't *dare*."

"Just tell me what you did with Petrov's books," said Lin, "and I'll leave."

Domna Albertine's hand tightened on her broom handle. But there was fear in her eyes, a sickly sort of fear that was worse than anger. "I sold them to a dealer in the Maze. One of those that buys old junk. Now get out."

Lin caught up her satchel and ran. She could hear Domna Albertine shouting obscenities after her as she sprinted down the stairs and out into the Fountain Quarter.

She was some distance away when she slowed to a walk, her mind whirling. What had happened to Petrov? Who were those men who'd claimed to be his friends, and what had they done to him? She felt hot and sick all over, thinking of the blood on the floor, the amount of it. One could not survive losing that quantity of blood.

Petrov had known those men were coming. He might well have known they planned to kill him. And yet his first thought had not been to run. His first thought had been to preserve the stone.

She began to make her way toward the Sault, a bitter rage still pulsing inside her heart. She wished she could have flown at Domna Albertine, smacked her across the face. But the woman would only have called for the Vigilants, and they would have sided with the Castellani woman, not the Ashkari girl.

Lin slipped her hand into her pocket, touching the stone's cool surface. Calm flowed into her from the point of contact. She wished she could take it out and look at it, but she dared not do so on the public street. It was hers now, and she felt a responsibility to protect it—for Petrov's sake indeed, but also, puzzlingly, for the sake of the stone itself.

Castellane at sunset. Kel walked through the streets; he had borrowed Conor's black cloak, the one that allowed him to enter the city incognito. Its hood was pulled up, his talisman safely stowed in his pocket. It was good to be no one: nameless, faceless, a figure in the crowd.

And it *was* a crowd. He had come down the Hill through the East Gate, down the path that led into a tangled maze of outer streets, and finally to the Ruta Magna, the city's main thoroughfare.

During the day, the Ruta Magna was an elegant shopping street, where the wealthy purchased their goods: fine furniture, bolts of silks, embroidered gloves from Hanse, rugs from Hind and Marakand. At night, the shops bolted their doors, hiding their glass windows behind painted wooden screens, and the Broken Market appeared.

The Broken Market wove its way down the Ruta Magna, eventually disappearing into the shadows of the Maze. While the weekly market in Fleshmarket Square was heavily regulated by the Council, the Broken Market was a lawless event. It had been born as a place to off-load broken or imperfect pieces of merchandise. Chipped cups of Shenzan porcelain, edged in gold; chunks of shattered glass with the edges sanded down, transformed into bracelets and dangling pendants; clock parts and unrepaired doorknobs; ripped lace gloves and torn curtains whose fabric could still be repurposed into dresses and coats.

A place for unwanted things to find new homes, Kel thought, ducking under the sagging awning of a stall selling three-legged chairs and tipsy tables. And, if one grew bored with shopping, there were performers—jugglers and musicians, and the itinerant Story-Spinners who could always be found on a different street corner, recounting the most recent installment of their tales. The most popular tellers gathered large and adoring crowds, desperate for the newest update of stories that sometimes carried on for years.

Having bought a bag of sweet *calison*, a sugary-almond paste beloved by Castellani sailors, Kel made his way northeast, toward the Scholars' Quarter. He passed the gray walls of the Sault as he went; atop their ramparts, he could see the lines of silent Ashkari watchmen, the Shomrim, standing guard. They were motionless as statues, gazing down on the crowds below. Two more Shomrim guarded the metal gates set into the walls through which the Ashkar could pass between the hours of sunrise and sundown.

Kel had known those gates all his life. Into them were etched words in the language of the Ashkar—a language he could not read. As far as he knew, it was not spoken by any outside the Ashkari community. Around the words were carved leaves, fruits, flowers, and small animals. The gates were things of beauty, though they existed to keep the world out—and the Ashkar inside.

As the market receded, Poet's Hill rose above Kel, with the Academie and the Student Quarter clustered around its base. The night was cloudless, the moon bright as a beacon. Hadn't Fausten said something about an eclipse? Or perhaps it had been a politic lie; perhaps he had been equally frantic to get the King out of the Dial Chamber.

I do not find them very talkative, myself.

Kel had seen Conor's flinch, almost imperceptible, and wanted to kick Montfaucon. The King's withdrawal from Palace life had happened so gradually, and so long ago, but that did not mean it had been forgotten. Kel and Conor had still been boys when Markus had begun to spend more and more time in the Star Tower, with Fausten. More time talking about the stars and the secrets they held, about the meaning of destiny and fate and whether the Gods spoke to men through what was written in the heavens.

At first, no one thought this was odd. A man must work his mind like his sword arm, Jolivet often said, and to have a philosopher-king could be a point of honor for Castellane. Had not King Maël designed the Tully gallows, a far more humane method of executing prisoners than the previous practice of tossing them to the crocodiles? And had not King Theodor's knowledge of science helped end the Scarlet Plague?

The Gods smiled down upon kings and made them wise, Jolivet had said, as Conor, with Kel beside him, had stood watching as the instruments of Markus's study were carried into the Star Tower: the gold orrery, the massive brass sextant, the telescope from Hanse and its boxes of accompanying lenses.

What was odd was that the King had followed his things into the tower, and emerged afterward but rarely. The strong, commanding man who had taught Conor to ride a horse and Kel to speak Sarthian had vanished, and this distant, dreamy-eyed ghost, with Fausten always at his side, had taken his place.

The winding streets of the Scholars' Quarter swallowed Kel; the stars above gleamed faintly, washed with moonlight. *The same stars the King studies from his tower,* Kel thought, turning onto Jibarian Way, though he himself had never managed to see any real shape in them. They always seemed to him a scatter of gleaming sand, cast across the sky by a careless hand. No meaning, no design, any more than there was meaning or design in the cracked cobblestones underfoot.

The street slanted up, toward the Academie. Taking advantage of the bright moonlight, students sat out on their balconies, some reading, some drinking in groups, some playing cards or smoking *patoun*, a mix of dried herbs and leaves, which filled the air with a sweet incense. Tea shops and pubs were open and doing a roaring business.

He had reached Chancellor Street. It curved upward, curling around the base of Poet's Hill. The sign for the Lafont Bookshop, gilt painted on wood, swung overhead. Across the street was a tall, narrow building, paint peeling off the sides. Balconies of wrought iron held a medley of weather-worn tables and chairs, while potted plants balanced on sills trailed green fringe down the building's façade. A sign in an upper window depicted a stylized quill pen, the symbol of the Academie. Definitely a student lodging house, then.

Kel dashed across the street and tried the front door. It swung open with a light touch, giving onto a tiny entryway and a perilously steep staircase, very nearly a ladder. The place smelled of stew and of something Kel recognized—a sharp, green scent, like the one that had hovered on Merren's clothes at the Caravel.

Kel took the stairs two at a time, past several small landings, before arriving at a lopsided door. Here, the scent of freshly cut plants was stronger than ever.

Kel elbowed the door open. The lock was weak and broke immediately, nearly spilling him into the flat beyond. It was a small space: a single main room divided up into various areas by their use—a corner with a washbasin and curved, claw-foot bathtub; another with a small brick-and-tile oven and a collection of cooking pots hanging on the wall. Flowers and leaves were scattered across a table whose paint had largely peeled off; beside them sat a large glass phial, carefully stoppered, full of pale-blue liquid.

Wooden shutters gave onto a wrought-iron balcony, where an impressive collection of various plants grew in clay pots balanced precariously on the metal railing. A mattress on the floor was the only bed, its colorful velvet blanket the sole concession to luxury or comfort.

At first glance, Merren Asper seemed nowhere to be found. But the room was warm, almost hot—Kel glanced at the oven, in which a fire burned merrily. A copper pot balanced on top of the stove held a dreadful-looking soup of cut greens and water, which gave off the aromatic steam that scented the place.

Aha. Kel kicked the front door shut behind him. "Merren Asper!" he called. "I know you're here. Show yourself, or I'll start throwing your furniture out the window."

A blond head peeked around a bookcase. Merren Asper opened his blue eyes wide and said, "Er. Hello?"

Kel began to advance on him menacingly. And he had been taught menace by Jolivet, who was a master of the form.

Merren backed away, and Kel followed him. It was not much of a distance. Merren's back hit the far wall, and he glanced around as if seeking a means of escape. There wasn't one, so he tried for insouciance. "Well, anyway," Merren said, waving a hand airily, "how did you, ah, find me? Not that I *mind* . . ."

Insouciance did not impress Kel. It was Conor's go-to when Jolivet or Mayesh was angry with him, and generally meant he knew he was in the wrong.

Kel glared. "You told me where you lived, idiot," he said. "I thought of going to the Caravel to ask your sister how I could find you, then I remembered that I asked you your address and you'd given it, and it was unlikely you'd lied since we'd both drunk the same truth serum. Probably something you should have thought about, no?"

"Probably," Merren said glumly. His eyes darted past Kel, toward the phial of blue liquid on the peeling table. He glanced away quickly, but Kel had already noted the gesture. "I thought you wouldn't trust the wine if I didn't drink it too, but I suppose I didn't consider the consequences. I'm not very good at that sort of thing." He waved a hand again, his fingers marked with old chemical burns. "You know: lying. Deceit." He looked at Kel earnestly. "It wasn't at all personal. Andreyen—that's the Ragpicker King—said you wouldn't come to any harm. That he just wanted to offer you a job. And I thought you'd like working with him."

Andreyen. It had never occurred to Kel that the Ragpicker King had a name. "So you were doing me a favor?"

"Yes!" Merren looked relieved. "I'm glad you understand."

"I've been told I'm very understanding." Kel picked up the glass vessel from the table. He held it up, examining the sky-blue liquid inside. "Not by anyone who knows me well, however."

Merren darted forward to reach for the vessel. "Don't drop that. It's very important—"

"Oh, I plan to drop it," Kel said, "unless you tell me what I want to know. And I don't advise lying. As we've covered, I know where you live."

Merren looked indignant. "I don't see how threats are ethically better than drugging someone with truth serum."

"Perhaps not," Kel said. "But I really don't care that much about retaining the moral high ground."

He strode over to the balcony, holding the vessel in his right hand. Merren yelped like an injured puppy as Kel held it out over the drop to the street below.

"You *can't*," Merren said breathlessly. He had rushed toward the balcony, then stopped, as if uncertain whether approaching Kel would make him more likely to drop the phial or not. "It's for a client. He already paid for the ingredients. My reputation—"

"A poisoner's reputation," Kel said mockingly. "A great concern to me, to be sure." He wiggled the phial, and Merren groaned. "Just tell me—did Alys know when she arranged the meeting between us that it was a sham? That you were planning to sell me out to the Ragpicker King?"

"No! Of course not. She would never have agreed to anything

like that. She'd be so upset with me if she did know—" Merren bit his lip. He was an odd combination, Kel thought. Wise about his chosen field of study, and desperately naïve about everything else. "It was just an interview. There was no plan to harm you, I swear it. I'm a kind person. I don't even eat meat."

Kel glared. "And what about Hadja? She said one of the courtesans had passed her a message, but that wasn't true, was it?"

"She *thought* it was true," Merren said. "Ji-An passed her a false message. Hadja would never keep anything secret from Alys, and Alys would never lie to you." He looked miserable. A small pulse beat at the base of his throat, where the loose collar of his shirt revealed the notch of his collarbone. "Please don't tell your friends to stop going to the Caravel. My sister depends on their business. It would break her heart."

It would empty her coffers, you mean, Kel thought, but he didn't say it. There was something about Merren that made it difficult to be cross with him. There was no malice behind those dark-blue eyes. They were the color of Antonetta's eyes, and in his own way, Merren seemed just as innocent. More innocent, even. Antonetta had grown up on the Hill; she had learned to recognize machinations and backstabbing, even if she did not partake in them herself. Merren seemed as if he would not recognize venality or selfishness if they appeared before him and performed a puppet show.

Kel sighed. "I won't tell them anything. Just—give me the rest of the *cantarella* antidote. And some of the poison, too," he added. "I assume you have it."

Merren nodded.

Kel lowered the vessel to his side. He watched as Merren went over to the bookcase and knelt, pushing some of the tattered volumes aside. When he returned to Kel, he was carrying four phials: two containing a gray powder, and two containing white.

"The gray is the poison, the white the antidote," said Merren. "Both are tasteless. Give a full phial of antidote to anyone who's ingested *cantarella*; it doesn't matter how much." He handed over the phials, which Kel tucked into his jacket, and proceeded to remain where he was, his hand outstretched. It took a moment for Kel to realize what he wanted. Kel handed over the vessel of blue liquid with a mild pang; he would always, he suspected, wonder what it had been.

He'd half expected Merren to seize the vessel and bolt, but he didn't. He took it gingerly and went to set it on a nearby shelf, between a distressingly human-looking skull and a bottle that looked as if it had washed up in the harbor, its label faded and torn. Meanwhile, Kel set a five-crown coin down on the table between them. He saw Merren glance at it when he turned back around, but he didn't reach for the money, only left it lying there.

"Is the Ragpicker King going to continue to bother me," Kel said, "now that I've turned him down? I didn't think one became a well-known crime lord by taking no for an answer."

"He won't bother you again," Merren said. "He needs someone to report on the Aurelians and doings on the Hill, but if it's not you, he'll find someone else. Though no one else has your access."

Kel raised his eyebrows. "Because?"

"Because you're the Sword Catcher," Merren said plainly, and Kel felt his stomach lurch. *Of course he knows*, he thought savagely. Merren was clearly in the Ragpicker King's confidence. But Kel had lived more than half his life jealously guarding the secret of who he really was. He could not help the feeling that things were spinning out of control, the world tilting sickeningly on its axis.

"How many people know?" he snapped. "How many of those who work for the Ragpicker King? Does your sister know that there is no Kel Anjuman?"

Merren shook his head, his eyes worried. "No. Only myself, Andreyen, and Ji-An. And it will stay that way. It does Andreyen no good for you to be exposed."

"Because he still hopes I'll spy for him."

"You should," Merren said, with an unexpected intensity. "He'll treat you fairly."

"The Aurelians treat me fairly."

"I don't know you that well. At all, really. But I can tell that you deserve better than them," Merren said. "No matter how safe you may feel now, the nobles and the royal family will turn on you in the end."

"That the nobles of the Hill are untrustworthy is hardly news to me."

"But you trust the Prince—"

"Of course I trust him." Kel could hear the dangerous note in his own voice, but Merren seemed unaware of it. He plunged on.

"My father was a guildmaster. He was always loyal to the crown. To the Charter Families. But when he needed the Aurelians, they abandoned him."

"Your father?" Kel felt dazed; the conversation had taken a turn he did not expect. "Who was your father?"

"It doesn't matter," Merren said stiffly. "He's dead now."

He walked away from Kel, toward the table, and leaned on it with both hands. Kel half wondered if he should simply leave; their business was concluded, after all. He had the answers he wanted, and the antidote he'd aimed to get.

Yet he couldn't bring himself to do it. Something kept him where he was—not reaching out to Merren, but not leaving, either. He glanced around the flat again. It was true that the space was small and cluttered, but it was also rather cozy. Soft night air spilled through the balcony shutters. Kel could imagine curling up on the mattress under the eaves and reading a book. When it rained, the sound would be close, as if one slept among the storm clouds.

I have never had my own room, Kel thought in that moment. At the Orfelinat, he had slept in a dormitory. At the Palace, his rooms were Conor's. In that moment, Merren's tiny flat seemed like something from a dream.

It still felt like a dream when he crossed the creaking floorboards and put a hand on Merren's shoulder. Merren twisted around to look up at him, clearly surprised. Whatever he had expected from Kel, it was clearly not kindness.

"I won't say the Ragpicker King doesn't lie," Merren said, in a low voice. "But if he says he'll do something, he'll do it. That's a sort of honor that those on the Hill don't have."

I do, Kel wanted to say, but was it true? He kept his promises to Conor, but he would break a promise to anyone else for Conor's sake, in a heartbeat.

Merren was still looking up at him. The firelight burnished his hair to gold, outlined the curves of his mouth, his collarbone. In that moment, Kel knew he could kiss Merren, and Merren would let him. He'd kissed both boys and girls before, though never anyone whose time he hadn't paid for. He could still find oblivion in it, he guessed, and perhaps even a new sort of oblivion: For the first time in his life, he would be kissing someone without Conor's knowledge, in a place Conor did not know he had gone.

And yet.

"I should leave," Kel said abruptly, and half flung himself away from Merren and toward the door. He heard Merren call after him, but he was already out of the flat, racing down the stairs into the darkness of the unlit street. He glanced back as he turned the corner, but could see nothing, only a square of light where Merren's balcony was.

What the hell was I thinking? Kel wondered. His encounter with Merren had not gone at all as he had planned it. He had meant to blast him with righteous indignation, but instead he had felt a painful longing—for Merren's flat, his life, his surprising lack of guile.

Perhaps it was because he had spent the afternoon in the Dial Chamber with a group of people who delighted in tricking each other and the world, who traded vast sums of money they could never spend back and forth to burnish their own self-importance, who discussed Conor's future as if the only thing about it that could possibly matter was its impact on them.

Not a one of them, save perhaps Falconet, had ever treated Kel as if he were a person in his own right. Not a one of them had ever given him as much thought as Merren Asper had when he had told Kel he deserved better.

Kel soon found he had wandered down near the harbor, where the air carried the heavy scent of smoke, brine, and damp wood. He stood on the Key, looking out at the deep roll of the sea, blue-black and shimmering: the same view that had been his in the first years of his life, gazing out from the Orfelinat. The rough hush of the waters was his cradle song, instinctively comforting, like a voice calling his name. Whose voice, he did not know. It had been so long.

The tide was low, revealing the island of Tyndaris, partway between the harbor and the mouth of the sea. Once it had been a spit of land at the mouth of the harbor. A city had grown up there: Tyndaris, small sister of Castellane. Then came the Sundering War, scorching earth and sky with searing bolts of magic. One plunged into the Castellane Sea, which roared like a lion and gathered itself into a massive wave. The people who could fled to the hills, but Tyndaris had no hills, no mountains. It floated at the level of the sea and so the sea reclaimed it. Shattered by the tremor, drowned by the ocean, Castellane's sister sank beneath the waves. Now only its highest points were revealed at low tide: the jagged tops of the tallest towers and the hill on which rested a temple of Aigon, now called the Church of a Thousand Doors.

The temple remained a pilgrimage site, and boats set out from the harbor daily, ferrying the devout. At night, when the crocodiles hunted beneath the black gloss of the waves, deserted Tyndaris seemed to glow upon the ocean's surface, its Sunderglass towers reflecting the light of the moon.

A ghost city, Kel thought. For cities could die. Even Castellane herself would not last forever.

Enough morbid thoughts, Kel told himself. He was done with all this. He would return to Marivent and the life he was used to. He would forget about the Ragpicker King and everything that came with him.

He started back along the Key, where open tavern doors cast patches of light on the cobblestones. Groups of drunken sailors walked arm in arm, singing. As he passed a closed warehouse, its ground-floor windows painted black to block the view of the goods stored inside, Kel felt a stir of unease.

He glanced around. This part of the Key was less crowded; he was surrounded by warehouses and customs offices. Down a narrow alley between a sailcloth-makers and a rope factory, he saw a flicker of movement. He backpedaled immediately, but it was already too late. He was seized, a hand clamping itself over his mouth as he was dragged into the alley.

Jolivet's training kicked in. Kel bent double, twisted, and kicked out. He heard a gasp and a curse. The grip on him loosened. He yanked himself free and darted toward the mouth of the alley, but a figure dropped from above, blocking his way—and then another, and another, like spiders shaken free from a web.

Kel looked up. At least half a dozen more dark figures—all in black, save for strange white gloves—clung to the brick wall of the warehouse. *Crawlers.*

"That's right." Someone grabbed him by the front of his jacket, spun him, and slammed him up against the wall. Kel stared at the figure in front of him: medium height, dressed in a rusty black military jacket. It had to be a century since Castellani soldiers had worn black. This jacket had brass buttons down the front and a hood, pulled up to hide the face beneath. The voice coming from under the hood was a man's, gravelly with the accent of the Maze. "No point running."

Kel took quick stock of the situation. More of the Crawlers surrounded him on either side; there must have been a dozen of them. Their clothes were dark and ragged. Their hands were powdered with a chalky substance, no doubt to make climbing easier. They had rubbed black greasepaint along the tops of their cheekbones, along their noses and chins. The intent was to make them less visible in the moonlight. It also made their faces look like a child's drawing of a skull.

"What do you want?" Kel demanded.

"Oh, come now." The Crawler who had slammed Kel against the wall shook his head. Silver flashed in the shadows; the left upper quarter of his face was covered by a metal mask. His skin was pale, his brown hair cut short. "Did you think we wouldn't recognize you, Monseigneur? You wear this cloak every time you come into the city, thinking it disguises you. A foolish consistency." He flicked the edge of Conor's cloak with his finger. "We know exactly who you are."

Monseigneur.

They thought he was Conor.

"Just because I am alone," Kel said, in his haughtiest tone, "does not mean you can freely lay hands upon me. Not unless you want to die in the Trick."

There was a quick, uneasy murmur, swiftly covered by a bark of laughter from the silver-masked Crawler. "Prosper Beck sent us, Monseigneur. And I'd guess you know why."

Prosper Beck? Kel held himself still, hiding any reaction, but his mind was racing. What business did a minor criminal like Beck have with the Crown Prince of Castellane?

"Beck owns you now, Aurelian," the Crawler continued. "He sent you a message at the Caravel, gave you a chance to pay your debt back last night. But you hid up in that Palace on the Hill, like nothing down here matters at all—"

Last night. Kel couldn't help but think of Conor, smashing his hand through the window, the blood. But it was not enough to fill in the puzzle; only enough for him to know that a puzzle was beginning to emerge.

"I don't know what you're talking about," he said tightly. It was true enough.

"He's disrespecting us, Jerrod," said one of the other Crawlers—a girl with fair hair and a black cloth mask. "He's pretending like he don't know."

It was impossible to see Jerrod's expression. The alley was too dark, and the metal mask too disconcerting. But his voice held a gloating tone. "He knows, Lola."

A big man with a pockmarked face barked a laugh. "No one's likely to forget they owe Prosper Beck ten thousand crowns."

"*Ten thousand crowns?*" The words were startled out of Kel. It was a massive sum. One might buy a fleet with such money.

There was ugly laughter among the crowd, but Jerrod didn't laugh. The mask made it difficult to read his expression, but he seemed to be looking hard at Kel, a realization dawning in his eyes. He caught hold of Kel's chin, forcing him to look up. "You're not him," he exhaled. "You're not the Prince."

"What?" Something silver flashed in Lola's hand; she sprang forward, the moonlight glancing off a long, ragged-edged knife. "Then who in gray hell is he?"

"Let me go." Kel tried to yank himself free of Jerrod's grip, but the other man was stronger than he looked. He could sweep Jerrod's feet, he thought, topple him and kick in his ribs, but that would only bring the rest of his crew down on Kel like a wave. "I'm not who you thought I was, so let me go."

"Can't do that," said the man with the pockmarked face. He had drawn a long razor from his pocket. All through the group weapons began to flash, like stars coming out. It was an oddly beautiful effect for something so dangerous.

"Kaspar's right," said Lola. "We can't let him go. Even if he's just an anonymous mouse, a mouse can still squeak."

She started toward Kel, Kaspar and the others following. Kel flexed his hands at his sides, preparing to fight. Jerrod, to his surprise, hadn't moved. He was still holding on to the front of Kel's jacket.

"Back off, Lola," he said. "And the rest of you. Listen to me—"

Kel heard the sound of a high whine, like an insect buzzing past his ear.

Lola screamed.

Jerrod's head whipped to the side, though he was still holding Kel against the wall. Lola, the blond Crawler, was sprawled in the alley, an arrow protruding from her chest. Blood was already pooling under her, running among the dirty cobblestones.

Kel stared, utterly stunned. Where had that come from? Jerrod pushed Kel back harder against the wall, his eyes narrowed behind his mask. "What the fuck?" he snapped. "There was no one following you—we would have seen—"

"*Jerrod!*" Another Crawler, a young man with gold earrings, reeled back, an arrow through his throat. He clutched at it, sinking to his knees, a red foam on his lips.

Jerrod's mouth worked silently; no words came out. This time Kel took advantage. He lunged, slamming his head into Jerrod's. The edge of the metal mask cut his forehead, but the pain was blunted by adrenaline. Jerrod staggered and Kel twisted away, breaking his hold.

Kel ran for the mouth of the alley. Only a fool picked a fight while outnumbered, and besides, he had no reason to believe the anonymous archer was on his side.

Kaspar, snarling, blocked his way. Without slowing down, Kel hit him, a clean uppercut that sent him spinning back into a stack of wooden boxes. An arrow flew past and struck one of the boxes, sending the stack tumbling.

The Crawlers had begun to panic, swarming up the walls like fleeing ants. Kaspar shoved past Kel, striking him two hard blows to the torso. Kel reeled back, the breath knocked out of him, as Kaspar flung himself at the wall and started to scramble up. Jerrod was kneeling over Lola's body, his shoulders hunched.

Kel began to back toward the mouth of the alley, but something was wrong. His legs weren't obeying him properly. There was a hot, needling pain in his chest. He put his hand to it. It came away red.

Kaspar hadn't just struck him as he'd gone by, at least not with an empty hand. He'd stabbed him. Kel pressed his hand against the wound, trying to keep the blood in. If he could just make it to the Key, he thought, but the alley seemed to be elongating, stretching out before him to the horizon. He could never walk such a distance, and soon enough it did not matter. His legs had given out under him.

He sank to the ground. It was filthy and hard, and stank of fish and garbage. He would have liked very much not to be lying where he was, but his body was not cooperating.

He pressed his hand against his chest. His shirt was as wet as if he'd spilled water on it. The pain was a screw, turning and tightening, pinning him to the earth. He could hear his own breath, rough and hoarse. Brick walls rose above him, between them a thin strip of stars.

And then, blotting out the stars for a moment, the shimmer of a metal mask. Jerrod was crouched over him.

"You might not be the Prince," Jerrod said, his voice strained. "But you're wearing his cloak. I wasn't wrong about that. *Who are you?*"

Kel shook his head, or tried to. *I can't tell you*, he thought, *but it is my job to die for Conor, and now I suppose it is happening. I just didn't think it would be in quite such a stupid way.*

"My apologies," Jerrod said. And he sounded as if he meant it. "It wasn't supposed to happen like this."

Kel almost laughed. It was too ridiculous. But it would have hurt too much to laugh, and his vision was starting to blur. The shadows bled together, and Jerrod was gone. The stars were all Kel could see. He imagined himself on his boat again, far out past the harbor, where the sea and sky were the same color. He could smell salt and hear the lash of the waves. If this was death, perhaps it would not be so bad.

He thought of Jolivet then, shaking his head. He thought of Antonetta, pale with grief—surely she would grieve if he died?—comforting Conor perhaps, her hand on his. And lastly, he thought of Conor, wearing his crown of wings, of what he would say when he found out Kel was dead. Something clever and cutting, no doubt. He thought of Mayesh, saying, *We will do our best to keep you alive*, and he saw a blur of violet, the color of foxgloves. Something flashed, bright, at the corner of his vision. Then he seemed to sink below the surface of the air as if it were water, until darkness was all he could see.

Aram was a kingdom ruled by a young Sorcerer-Queen, Adassa. Her father, King Avihal, had been a clever diplomat, negotiating peace with the other sorcerous Kings and Queens that his land might be spared the ravages of battle. When King Avihal died, he gave his daughter the Source-Stone that had been his, but she was a gentle soul and not a seeker of power. Even her own people feared she might not have the strength for queenship. Her one great ally was the captain of her guard, the loyal Judah Makabi. He stood by her side, advising and counseling, as she struggled to learn the ways of the throne. She will be a great Queen, Makabi assured the people. Only wait. She will bring us to greatness.

There was one other who saw the ascension of the young Queen as an opportunity—the Sorcerer-King Suleman.

— *Tales of the Sorcerer-Kings*, Laocantus Aurus Iovit III

CHAPTER EIGHT

Sitting at her kitchen table, Lin turned Petrov's stone over in her hands. Books and papers were scattered all about, as always—from heavy bound tomes to thin sheets of vellum covered in delicate illustrations of anatomy from the *Book of Remedies*. When Josit was here, he made her put them away as he said they gave him nightmares, full of peeled-back skin and lidless eyes. (Lin knew this was partially her fault. As a child, she had enjoyed terrifying him with tales of skinless *shedim* who carried off troublesome little boys.)

With the shutters closed against the dark night, and the fire lit, the house became a cozy little cave. It was Lin's favorite time for studying, but tonight she could not keep her mind on her books. She could not forget what Chana had said to her in the garden, that she was treating Mariam as a patient, not a friend. That Mariam needed something to look forward to other than a life of dutifully swallowing the tisanes and powders Lin mixed up for her.

The words had made Lin cold inside. She had treated enough dying people to know they often held on to life through sheer force of will, just long enough to see one last beloved face, or realize one last wish. It *was* good for Mariam to have something to look forward to, but what if, once the Festival was over, she let go? Stopped holding on? Would she hold on for Lin, or was that unfair to ask? Would she wait for Josit, to see him again? But who knew *when* Josit would return? All sorts of things could delay a caravan: bad weather, shortages of goods, or problems at the caravansary, the way stations along the Roads.

Ugh. Lin rolled Petrov's stone into her palm. The firelight caught it at strange angles, picking out shapes in the depth of the rock, like shadowy figures concealed by a screen.

Of course she had buckled to Chana's pressure, agreed to attend the Festival and help with the preparations. So much for her stubbornness. Chana knew how to bend her will like a broken branch.

Something seemed to rise to the surface of the stone as she turned it and Lin stared. It almost looked like a letter, or a number, some kind of legible shape—

A loud pounding on her front door sent her scrambling to her feet. It was late; she'd heard the Windtower Clock chime midnight some time ago. Only if a patient was in desperate need would someone trouble her at this hour.

Mariam? Heart pounding, she threw her front door open to find her neighbor Oren Kandel standing on her doorstep. "You're needed at the gate," he said. "There's a carriage waiting."

Lin bit back a sharp comment. Oren had never forgiven her for the fact that he'd offered to marry her, and she'd said no. He was one of the Shomrim now, a gate guard. She saw him often when she came in and out of the Sault, and always greeted him politely. He always glared back with a look that said he wished he could take her medical satchel and toss it over the wall.

He had asked her to dance once, at the Goddess Festival two years past. She'd said no, claiming she was tired. The truth was that there was something about Oren that frightened her. A pinpoint spark of hatred always burning in the depth of his dark-brown eyes. It had only flamed brighter since she'd turned him down that night.

"A carriage?" she echoed. "Is it one of my patients from the city?"

His thin fingers played with the thick metal chain around his neck; it bore the Lady's Prayer on it in fancifully engraved words. "I can't say. I was just told to escort you. And that you should bring your satchel."

"It would help if I knew what the problem was—"

He regarded her sourly. "Don't know."

He was enjoying not telling her what she wanted to know, that much was clear. "Wait here," Lin said, and closed the door in his face. She hurried into her room, where she unfolded her physician's clothes and dressed carefully in the blue linen tunic and trousers, tucking Petrov's stone into her pocket. She bound her hair into a single braid, and fastened the chain of her mother's necklace around her neck. The familiar gold circle felt comforting as it settled into the hollow of her throat. Lastly, she dragged her satchel—always packed and at the ready—out from under her bed.

The moon was high in the sky when she joined Oren outside. He spit a thin stream of brown *patoun* at the ground when he saw her, before setting off without another glance. His pace was long and quick, making no allowance for her shorter stride; Lin was tempted to tell him she didn't need an escort and could make her way to the gates on her own. But he would protest, which would only cost her time getting to her patient.

Whoever they might be. Lin pondered the possibilities—Zofia? Larissa, the retired courtesan whose hypochondria meant she thought every slight sneeze heralded a case of plague?—as she traversed the Sault some yards behind Oren, following the curve of the eastern wall.

Night in the Sault was divided into four Watches. The first one began at sunset, the last ending at dawn, when the *aubade*, the morning bell, rang out from the Windtower Clock, signaling the beginning of the workday. The Ashkar were forbidden to leave the Sault itself during the night hours, save for those physicians whose skills were urgently needed to save a life. Even then, they were required to wear their Ashkari blue or gray, and were often stopped by Vigilants, demanding to know what they were doing outside their walls. *Saving the lives of people like you,* Lin always wanted to snap, but so far she'd managed to hold her tongue.

Then there was Mayesh. An exception to all rules, as usual, he was allowed to come and go freely in the night hours; the Palace needed him, and that superseded all other Laws. But when royal business was done, no matter the lateness of the hour, Mayesh could not remain at Marivent, nor make use of its lavish guest rooms. He was still Ashkar. He would be returned to the Sault like an unwanted package, to seek the solitude of his small house on the Kathot. It would make even a good man angry, and Lin did not think her grandfather was a good man.

She and Oren had reached the city gates, which had been propped open. Mez Gorin, the second gate guard, waited there, his polished wooden staff in his hands. (Staffs had been chosen as the weapons of the Shomrim long ago, since they looked harmless to the *malbushim*, but were deadly in well-trained hands.) Mez, always kind, had a tangle of brown hair and caterpillar-thick eyebrows. He smiled when he saw Lin, and gestured that she should pass through the gates.

She approached, leaving Oren behind to sulk. Lin could glimpse the bustle of the Ruta Magna through the stone arch, which was etched with a line of a prayer in Ashkar: DALI KOL TASI-QEOT OSLOH DAYN LESEX TSIA. *Grant us pardon in this hour, as Thy gates are closed this night.* The lines referred to the gates of Haran, the great city of Aram, but gates, Lin supposed, were gates, all the world round. Through these particular gates, Lin could see a scarlet carriage waiting in the road, its doors blazoned with golden lions.

A Palace carriage. Just like the one that had fetched her and Mariam from the square a few days past, but why on earth was it here now? She stared at Mez, puzzled and incredulous, but he only shrugged and nodded, making a shooing gesture, as if to say: *Go on, then, get in.*

At night, when the city was dark, Marivent glowed upon the Hill like a second moon. In its light, Lin made her way to the carriage—she could see a driver in red livery, perched high on the seat in front—and opened the door, clambering a little awkwardly inside. She was glad for her comfortable tunic and trousers. How noble ladies in all their layers of skirts and petticoats managed these things, she had no idea.

The inside of the carriage was red and gold velvet. Candles in bronze holders were bolted to the inside walls, but only one was lit. And sitting across from Lin, beetle-browed and scowling, was her grandfather Mayesh.

"*Zai?*" Lin cursed inwardly; she had not meant to use the old nickname. "What on earth—?"

The carriage lurched forward, swerving into the traffic on the Ruta Magna. The Broken Market was in full swing, the glare of naphtha torches turning the stalls to indistinct shadows.

"There is a patient who needs your help," Mayesh said mildly. "At the Palace."

"So that's why all . . . this was necessary?" Lin waved her hand as if to encompass the whole of the last fifteen minutes. "Why you had to send Oren, instead of coming to my door yourself? You knew I wouldn't want to treat anyone at Marivent?"

"No," he said. "I assume your Oath of Asaph means something to you. *For a Physician should mind not rank, wealth, or age; neither should he question whether a patient is enemy or friend, a native or a foreigner, or what Gods he worships. To heal is as the Goddess commands.*"

His tone made her bristle. "I know the words," she said. "Had you bothered to attend my Oath-Taking ceremony—"

She broke off at the scratch of a lucifer. It flared up with a small flame, which Mayesh used to light another of the tapers inside the carriage. The new light illuminated Mayesh, and the dark red-brown stains smeared across the chest and sleeves of his usually immaculate robes.

He said, "I sent Oren because the blood would have excited comment. I did not want that."

Lin had gone tense. It was a great deal of blood—a dangerous amount. "Whose blood is it?"

Mayesh sighed. Lin could see two instincts fighting inside him: the first, to tell her nothing at all, as he always had. The second, that he could not hold back if he expected her to treat this mysterious patient. Lin sat without moving, enjoying his conflict. "Sieur Kel Anjuman," he said, at last. "He is a cousin to the Prince."

Surprise stiffened her spine. "The Prince's *cousin*?" she echoed. "Is there not a Palace chirurgeon to treat him? Some Academie graduate with a bowl full of leeches and a leather strap for patients to bite on?"

Mayesh smiled without humor. "You paint an unpleasant portrait, but I assure you the reality is worse. If Gasquet treats him, he will die. Therefore . . ."

"Therefore, me," Lin said.

"Yes. Therefore, you. The Prince will welcome your presence," he added. "He is fond of his cousin."

The Prince is a corrupt idiot, she thought, *and his cousin is probably much like him.*

"And what if I can't heal him?" Lin said. They had left the Broken Market behind and were passing through the streets near Valerian Square. Here the stucco walls were painted with advertisements for public events, from Academie lectures to fights at the Arena. The bright colors swirled together as they passed, a mix of gold and emerald, saffron and scarlet. "What if he dies?"

"Lin—"

"What of Asaph?" she interrupted.

All Ashkar knew the tale of Asaph the physician, after whom the Oath was named. He had been famous, a healer respected inside and outside the Sault for his wisdom and skill. None of that had helped him when he delivered twins for the wife of King Rolant, in the time of the Red Plague. It had been a difficult birth—breech, and the Queen had labored for hours. Thanks to Asaph's skill, one twin had been born alive. The second had been dead—dead in the womb for days, long before Asaph had been summoned. Not that it mattered. He was put to a traitor's death: flung from the Hill into the sea, where he was torn to pieces by crocodiles.

It was not a story that would have endeared the Palace to anyone—especially someone already disposed to dislike the residents of Marivent.

"I am not powerless in the Palace, Lin," Mayesh said. "I will not let anything happen to you."

The words left her mouth before she could stop them. "I am your flesh and blood," she said. She recalled the words of the Maharam, so long ago, the way her grandfather had turned away from them. *They are flesh of your flesh, those children, blood of your blood.* "Yet how long has it been since we have spoken, Mayesh? Months? A year? You have always put House Aurelian and its needs and desires before me, before Josit. Forgive me, then, if I have no reason to believe you will change that now."

Mayesh raised his gray eyebrows. His eyes, despite his age, were clear, their gaze piercing. "I did not realize you thought me such a villain."

"I did not realize you thought of me at all." The carriage had begun to make its way up the steep rise of the Hill, Castellane falling away below. "I suppose you came to me because you think I can be trusted to keep my mouth shut."

"I came to you," Mayesh said, "because you are the best physician in the Sault."

You did not even want me to become a physician, Lin thought. *I never had your support.* And yet—Chana's words, spoke so recently, rang in her mind. *Your grandfather was never opposed to you becoming a physician. There is much he has done that has earned your anger, Lin. But that was one thing he did not do.*

Maybe he meant it, she thought. *Maybe.*

She interlaced her hands in her lap. "Very well," she said. "Tell me of his injuries, this Kel Anjuman."

The story came out as the carriage wound its slow way up the steep rise to the Palace gates. There had been a meeting that day, of the Charter Families. Afterward this cousin of the Prince's had left Marivent for the city. No one knew where he had gone, specifically. (*The Temple District*, Lin thought. Drinking, whoring, like his cousin. What else did nobles do?) Mayesh had been working late into the night, some issue with the Treasury, when he had seen a commotion at the front gate. Arriving there, he had found that Anjuman's unconscious, bleeding body had been dumped at the threshold of the Palace. The guards had not seen who had left him: He had appeared between one moment and the next, they swore, as if carried there by a ghost. Mayesh had been forced to half carry, half drag the young man's limp body to the Prince's apartments, where the extent of his wounds became clear. Soon after, Mayesh had left for the Sault.

Probably stabbed by someone he cheated at gambling, Lin thought. Or a courtesan he'd wronged. But she quickly told herself not to judge this Kel Anjuman. He was her patient, and besides, he was not responsible for Mayesh's injustices toward her. He was not an Aurelian.

By this time they had reached the North Gate of Marivent—the threshold Mayesh had spoken of, where Anjuman had been dumped. It certainly did not look as if acts of high criminality and drama often played themselves out here: It was a quite ordinary stone arch, with lion flags flying from the vaulted top. Torches burned along the ramparts of the white walls surrounding the Palace. They illuminated the night, blotting out the stars.

Lin watched silently as Mayesh leaned from the carriage window, exchanging words with the Castelguards who stood ranged at their posts like stiff wooden statues painted in red and gold. Lin tried and failed to imagine her grandfather kneeling here at the gate, amid the green grass, cradling the body of the Prince's cousin. Getting bloodstains all over his Counselor's robes. It did not seem possible, unless Mayesh was leaving out some part of the story.

And no doubt he was, she thought. If he did not need her help, he would have told her nothing; as it was, he was surely only telling her what he felt he must.

The carriage rattled through the archway. The gate was behind them; they were in the Palace proper. Much as Lin did not want to be excited about it, she felt her pulse jump: She was here. Here, inside Marivent, the beating heart of Castellane.

Long ago, Lin and Mariam had followed the tale of a particular Story-Spinner on the Ruta Magna, an unfolding fable titled *The Taming of the Tyrant*. Lin still remembered the moment the story's heroine had entered the Palace for the first time. How a gasp had run through the listening crowd. Most people lived all their lives in Castellane, with Marivent shimmering above them like a star, knowing they would never enter its gates. Knowing that beyond those gates lay a sort of a magic, of a type that had not been lost in the Sundering. The magic of power, of glamour and riches, luxury and influence. The destinies of nations turned on House Aurelian's whim. That was itself a kind of sorcery.

Various of the smaller palaces rose around them, white in the moon. Lin knew a few of their names, from stories: the Star Tower; the Sun Palace, shaped like a rayed orb; the Castel Antin, where the throne room resided. To the southwest, at the edge of the sea cliffs, rose the black needle of the Trick. Many a Story-Spinner's tale involved a daring escape from the Trick, but in reality no one had ever managed the feat.

They rolled through a second archway, this one a vine-wrapped trellis, and into a courtyard surrounded on three sides by stone walls. Mayesh murmured that this was Castel Mitat, where the Prince lived. The carriage drew to a stop near a tiled fountain and they disembarked quickly.

The moment they were out of the carriage it sped away. Lin only had time to note that the walls of the Castel were set with great, arched windows and embellished with long balconies, before Mayesh hurried them through a double door set below a wall-mounted sundial.

Inside was a steep staircase of old marble, the center of the steps worn to deep indents by the passage of feet through the years. Few lamps were lit. They raced upstairs through the shadows, their footsteps echoing. Nearly empty at this hour, the place felt oddly abandoned, the air catching chill from so much marble cladding.

They reached the final landing and turned onto a hallway of more white stone. Rugs from Marakand unrolled in deep jewel tones all down the passage. Arched windows cast back Lin's own reflection as they approached a pair of double doors made of wood and hammered metal. An intricate pattern of crowns and flames had been etched into their design.

Mayesh put his hand to the door, paused, and looked at Lin. "These are the Crown Prince's apartments," he said. "He shares them with his cousin. They have lived in the same rooms, like brothers, since they were children."

Lin said nothing. It struck her as odd that Conor Aurelian was willing to share his rooms—or share anything, for that matter—but she supposed he liked his cousin's company, and the apartments were surely vast. The Prince likely only noticed his cousin's presence when he felt like it.

Mayesh rapped hard on the door before swinging it open and ushering Lin inside. Tense as a bow strung tight, she stepped into the Crown Prince's apartments.

It was a large space, though not as enormous as she'd imagined. The floor was made of alternating squares of marble as if it were the board of a Castles game: black and white, with an occasional splash of red quartz. There was a raised dais in one corner of the room, on which rested a vast bed with black and white velvet hangings. Another bed, smaller, had been set near the steps of the dais, and all around the room were ranged massive divans piled with cushions gloved in raw Shenzan silk. Marakandi lamps of hammered silver and stained glass shed a warm light over the room, and as Lin's eyes adjusted to it, she saw a tangle of bloody sheets on the smaller bed, where the figure of a young man lay motionless. Beside the bed, another young man, this one wearing black and silver, paced back and forth almost frenetically, muttering what sounded like curses under his breath.

"Conor," Mayesh said sharply, and Lin felt a faint surprise that her grandfather would call the Prince by his given name. She was heartened to hear no sound of fear in his voice. She had always wondered if he was different in the Palace; if the proximity of royal blood and power cowed him. It seemed not. "Where is everyone?"

Prince Conor's head snapped up. He looked nothing like he had in Valerian Square. There was an ashy tint to his light-brown skin, and his features seemed drawn too tight. "I sent them away," he said. "They weren't helping, they—" He narrowed his eyes at Lin. "Is this the physician?"

"Yes," Lin said. She did not offer her name; let him ask for it. As he looked at her, she was aware of a dark thrill through her nerves. The Prince of Castellane was studying her. This was someone who held power in his hand as if it were a child's toy. There was a tangibility to such power; she felt it like the leading edge of a storm.

"She looks very young, Mayesh," he said, his tone dismissive. "Are you sure . . . ?"

He didn't need to say the rest of it. *Are you sure she's the best in the Sault? She's just a girl. Surely there's a wise, bearded old man you could lay hands on who would do a better job.* Lin wondered what the punishment was for kicking a Prince in the ankle. The Trick, no doubt.

She itched to get to the young man lying on the bed. She did not like how still he was. At least the Prince had sent the chirurgeon away; a bad doctor was worse than no doctor.

"Lin is twenty-three," said Mayesh. His voice was even. "And she *is* the best in the Sault."

The Prince rubbed at his eyes. There was black kohl smeared around them. It was a style Lin had seen on nobles before: Both the men and women darkened their eyes, and wore paint on their nails and jewels on their fingers. The Prince's hands glittered with rings: emeralds and sapphires, bands of white and rosy gold. "Well, then," he said impatiently. "Come and look at him."

Lin hurried across the tiled floor to the low bed, setting her satchel down on a wooden table nearby. Someone had placed a silver bowl of clean water there, and a cake of soap. Mayesh must have asked for it. Castellani doctors did not clean their hands before they worked, but the Ashkar did.

She cleaned and dried her hands, then turned to look at her patient. The bed was a mess of bloody, tangled sheets; the young man her grandfather had called Kel lay unconscious among them, though his hands moved occasionally at his sides in the rough, spasmodic twitches that were indicative of being dosed with morphea for pain. Gasquet must have done so before Conor had sent him away.

Anjuman had also been stripped down to his trousers and a cambric shirt, soaked through with blood. Most of it seemed to be on the right side of his abdomen, but there were dark patches over his sternum, too.

She could see the family resemblance between her patient and Prince Conor. They had the same light-brown skin and fine features, the same curling dark hair, though Anjuman's was sweat-darkened and sticking to his neck and temples. Anjuman was breathing hard, his lips purplish blue, and when she briskly lifted his hand, she saw that the beds of his nails were the same color. Though he was gasping for air, his chest rising and falling, he was suffocating.

Everything went very still around her. She knew these symptoms: He was dying. There was little time. "Move out of the way," she said, and thought the Prince's eyebrows rose, but she did not stay to see his reaction. Her brain was ticking ahead like a clock, sorting her next steps, deciding what her patient needed. She took up her satchel, upending its contents onto the bed; she caught up a thin-bladed, sharp knife, and bent over Kel Anjuman.

"What are you doing?" The Prince's tone was sharp. Lin looked up and saw him staring at her, his arms crossed. His smoke-black hair was in tangled disorder, she noted, as if he'd run his fingers through it too many times to count.

"Cutting away his shirt. I need to see the wound," Lin said.

"It's an expensive shirt."

Which is already ruined with blood. Lin paused, the tip of the blade against the cambric. "Between this shirt and your cousin, which one would you say you like better?"

His mouth thinned, but he gestured for her to go on. She sliced away Anjuman's shirt, revealing a long gash along his side. It had bled freely, though it was no longer: His chest and belly were half covered in patches of drying blood. Lin could tell at a glance the gash was shallow enough. It was the puncture wound just to the left of his sternum, surrounded by violet-black bruising, that was cause for concern.

"Hold him down," she said to the Prince, as she gathered what she needed. Her movements were automatic, swift but unhurried. There was a strange calm that came upon a physician in these moments, when quick action was needed to save a life.

"*What?*" The Prince looked stunned, then furious as she slid a bellied scalpel from its leather holder and laid the sharp end between two of Anjuman's ribs. "At least give him some morphea if you're going to cut him—"

"He's had morphea already. And more will stop his breathing," she said. "Blood is pressing on his heart, crushing his lungs. I have to drain it."

"Gasquet was going to put leeches on him—"

"And he would have died." Lin kept her hand steady; still, she was reluctant to cut with no one stabilizing the patient. He was likely too drugged to feel the pain, but if he did, and jerked with movement, the blade would skid, perhaps even nicking an artery. "Are you going to help me or not?"

When the Prince did not move, she glanced toward her grandfather, who stood a few feet from the end of the bed, his face mostly cast in shadow. His arms were crossed; he looked grim, inexorable.

"I could get Jolivet," he said, in response to a swift look from Prince Conor, but apparently that was not a pleasing suggestion. The Prince swore, clambered onto the bed, and put his hands on his cousin's shoulders, holding him firmly against the cushions.

"If you kill him—" he began, but Lin was not listening. Anjuman's lips were cyanotic blue. She began to cut—a short, precise incision—working the tip of the scalpel between his ribs with a practiced accuracy. Blood welled, spilling quickly down his side; his body jerked reflexively, but Prince Conor's arms flexed, keeping him still.

The Prince was stronger than Lin would have guessed.

Among her tools was a bag of treated reeds, hollow and flexible. Lin transferred her scalpel to her left hand and picked one up. The Prince was looking over his shoulder at her, his gray eyes narrow. The lace cuffs of his shirt were smeared with blood.

Lin began to insert the reed, feeding it carefully through the incision. She felt it hit the rib and angled it upward, away from bone, toward the cavity of the chest. She could sense the Prince's gaze on her like the pressure of a knife's tip, sharp and searching. The back of her neck prickled as the reed slid in farther—

There was a rush of air from the wound. A moment later, blood poured through the reed. Lin snatched up a bowl from her satchel, but it was already too late for her clothes: Blood drenched her tunic, wetting her sleeves. She maneuvered the bowl to catch the liquid, vaguely aware of the Prince shouting something at her about how if she was going to bleed Kel, they might as well simply have kept Gasquet.

She ignored him. With the scalpel, she cut the reed so only a millimeter or so protruded from Anjuman's skin. "You can stop holding him down now," she said quietly, and the Prince shot her a blazing look, his hands still on his cousin's shoulders.

"Have you ever done this before?" he asked, in a tone that indicated he felt this was very unlikely. "This ridiculous procedure—"

"I have," Lin said, and did not add that one of the aspects of it that she found most satisfying was how quickly it worked. Kel Anjuman sucked in a breath, and the Prince sat up, looking down as his cousin's eyelids fluttered. Anjuman's face was speckled with blood, but he had stopped gasping. His breaths were deep and regular, his lips no longer blue.

His eyes opened—slowly, as if the lids were weighted. "Conor," he said, tiredly, like a child asking for its mother. "Are you—" He blinked. "Is that you?"

The Prince shot Lin a quick, worried look. "He's still in shock," she said, "but the blood is no longer crushing his heart and lungs. He will live."

She heard Mayesh make a restless movement; she knew he disapproved. It was never a good idea in medicine to promise life. Anything could happen.

"Did you hear that?" the Prince said, catching at his cousin's hand. Their hands were very similar in shape, though the Prince's glittered with rings, and Anjuman's were bare. "You idiot. You'll live."

Anjuman whispered something in response, but Lin was not listening; blood had stopped draining into the bowl. She set it aside, knowing her work was far from done. Anjuman was no longer in danger of suffocating, and that was a relief, but his wounds still required treatment. Puncture wounds especially held a terrible risk of infection, which could take hold deep within muscle tissue. Wounds could swell from within, bursting their stitches, the skin turning black and putrid. Death came soon after.

Now that there was time, she began to organize her spilled

tools, setting out what she would need on the table beside the bed: glass jars of tinctures, ampoules of medication, bandages of soft cotton spun from reeds.

After washing her hands again—turning the water in the bowl to a deep pink—she returned to her patient. She gently probed around his wounds, checking for broken bones, contusions, while the Prince held his cousin's hand in a death grip. "Kellian. Where were you?" he demanded roughly. "Who did this to you? Were you wearing the—your necklace?"

Necklace? Lin wondered. Aloud she said, "Do not interrogate him."

The Prince shot her an incredulous look. "I need to know who did this to him—"

"Not this very moment, you don't." She seized up a towel and began to mop away the dried blood on Anjuman's chest and stomach. As she did, she inhaled and was relieved to find no telltale stench emanating from his wounds; it seemed the viscera had not been punctured. Things were not as bad as she had feared. Still, there was much to be done.

"You said he would be fine—"

"Not if you exhaust him," Lin said sharply. As she cleaned the last of the blood from Anjuman's chest, she saw something gleam at the hollow of his throat. The necklace the Prince had asked about?

"He's strong," the Prince said, not looking at her. "He can endure it. Kel, tell me. What happened? Who would have dared to touch royalty like that?"

"Crawlers," rasped Anjuman. "It was Crawlers. Jumped down on me from a warehouse roof. No chance—" He winced, his gaze flicking to Lin. His pupils were blown wide with pain.

The Prince flushed scarlet along his high cheekbones. "I'll have Jolivet go down into the city. Burn the Crawlers out of the Maze—"

"No," Anjuman said sharply. "They had no idea who I was. Leave it, Conor."

His right hand scrabbled among the bedclothes, fretfully, as if he were searching for something. When he lifted it, she saw that a talisman on a chain hung, jangling, from his fingers. An Ashkar talisman. Mayesh must have given it to him, for healing.

She moved to gently take the amulet from her patient. As her fingers brushed the silver, she felt a sharp pain at her side, like a bee's sting. She jerked her hand away, and the talisman fell back among the bedclothes. Drat. Probably the sting had just been a muscle cramp, but Lin had no attention to give it right now. She could feel the rage emanating from Prince Conor, like heat from a fire. And she could tell it was bothering her patient. Anjuman might be in pain, but the tenseness around his eyes and mouth had nothing to do with physical discomfort.

"Monseigneur. I am going to have to ask you to leave," she said, half to her own surprise.

The Prince's jaw tightened. "*What?*"

Lin stared down at her patient. Now, with the blood cleaned away, she could see the expanse of his chest. He seemed healthy, with good color, his skin drawn taut over hard muscles beneath. But the slashes at his side and chest were not his only wounds. White lines crisscrossed light-brown skin, some thin as pale string, some thick and corrugated. She had seen scarring like this before, but usually only in those who had once earned their living fighting in the Arena.

"This is delicate and careful work," she said, fixing the Prince with a level gaze. "I need to concentrate, and Sieur Anjuman needs to rest."

"It's all right," Anjuman protested, but his free hand was clenched in the bedclothes.

"Hush," Lin said to him. "You must keep calm. And Monseigneur, you will have to ask him questions later. For now, you must leave me alone with my patient."

The Prince seemed torn between shock and anger. His mouth had flattened into a hard line. Lin was aware of Mayesh, watching them with an irritating calm. She was even more aware of the time, minutes ticking by—minutes during which infection could be spreading in her patient's blood.

The stiff brocade of the Prince's shirt rustled as he crossed his arms. "If I am to leave, you will need to promise me you will save his life. He will not die. Not now, and not a few days hence."

It felt like swallowing a cold penny. Lin said, "I cannot promise that. I will do everything I can to prevent infection—"

The Prince shook his head, dark curls falling into his eyes. "I require you to promise."

"It is not me you are making demands of, though you might think so," Lin said. "You are trying to give orders to Life and Death, and they listen to no one, not even an Aurelian."

As the Crown Prince looked at Lin, without speaking, she could see in his face the hardness of a nature unused to refusal. How did her grandfather manage it, she thought, each day spent with people who never heard the word *no*—or if they did, were not required to heed it?

"Conor," Mayesh said. It was gently spoken, not a reprimand. "Let her work. It will be best for Kel."

Prince Conor tore his eyes away from Lin and gazed almost blindly down at his cousin. "If he dies . . ."

He didn't finish, only spun on his heel and stalked out of the room. Mayesh nodded once at Lin and followed him. The door clanged shut behind them, plunging the room into a terrible silence.

Lin could feel her heart pounding somewhere in the region of her throat. What had she just done? *She had just insulted the Crown Prince. She had ordered him out of his own room.* She felt a sickly horror: What had she been thinking? But she could not fall to pieces over it now. Her concentration must be on her patient, who was moving restlessly on the bed.

"Hold still, Sieur Anjuman," she said, bending over him. Like Prince Conor's, his eyes were gray, fringed with velvet-black lashes.

"It's Kel. Not Sieur anything. Kel. And if you come at me with leeches, I'll bite," he said, with an energy that surprised her.

"No leeches." She shook the ampoule and tipped up Kel's head with a finger under his chin. His skin was faintly rough with the beginnings of stubble. "Open your mouth and hold these under your tongue."

He did as she asked, swallowing as the grains of morphea dissolved. Almost instantly, she saw the tight cast of his face ease, the taut line of his mouth relaxing as he exhaled.

Morphea could suppress breath, but he was breathing easier now. And shock could also kill. Pain loosened a patient's hold on life; some raced toward death just to escape agony.

"That," he said, "was surprising."

"The morphea?" she asked, discarding the empty ampoule.

"Not the morphea. You made Conor leave," he said. And, despite everything, he grinned. In that moment, he looked like a mischievous boy, like Josit after he had successfully poached apples from the Maharam's garden. "Not many people can do *that*."

"It was awful." Lin had moved to the table. "I am sure he hates me."

"He only hates being told what to do," said Kel, watching her as she returned with a small metal clamp, an ampoule of lunar caustic, a demiard of water infused with *levona* and *mor*, and a steel needle and silk thread. "Alas," he said, glumly. "Needles."

"If it hurts, tell me. I can give you more morphea."

"No." He shook his head. "No more. I don't mind pain, as long as it's within manageable bounds."

Manageable bounds. That was interesting—a dissonance, like his scars. What did young nobles know of pain, and what amount of it they could or could not manage?

"You said you were bleeding out on the Key." She spoke evenly, calmly, more to distract him than anything else. Having removed the bit of reed still in his side with the clamp, she moved to disinfecting his other wounds with herb-water. She knew it would hurt, despite the morphea. "But you were found at the Palace gates. You had been dumped there—"

He winced, his back arching, and muttered something that sounded like *the arrows*, and then a name, *Jeanne*. So had he been visiting a girl in the city? And been robbed, perhaps, on the way back?

"Yes," he said. "I know who left me outside Marivent. It wasn't the person who stabbed me."

She laid the washcloth aside and reached for the lunar caustic. It would stop any further bleeding. It would also hurt. Kel was looking at her quietly. A surprising level of acceptance, she thought. The richer the patient, the more difficult they generally were, complaining about every discomfort. He really was not what she had expected, this cousin of the Prince.

"Right. That was Crawlers," she said, smoothing the caustic over the wounds. "I was surprised you'd heard of them." They didn't seem the sort of city dwellers of whom nobles would be aware.

He smiled wryly. "We all live in the same city, don't we?"

The bleeding had stopped; the wounds glittered with caustic, a peculiarly beautiful effect. "Do we?" Lin said. "I have lived here all my life; this is the first time I have been on the Hill. Most people will never come here. The nobles and the ordinary people of Castellane—they may all live in the same *place*, but it is not the same city."

He was silent. Sweat had broken out across his skin, pasting his hair to his forehead. The caustic would feel like fire on his skin, Lin knew; she had to do more to ease the pain.

Use me.

Lin started. For a moment she thought Kel had spoken aloud, but it was only a whisper in the back of her head. That second voice that all physicians seemed to have, that advised them in times of urgency.

She quickly reached for a salve made from feverfew, whitewillow, capsicum, and a dozen other ingredients sourced from the corners of Dannemore. It was difficult stuff to make, especially when she had only the kitchen at the Women's House to work in, but it would numb his skin for the stitches.

She began to smooth it gently over his cuts. She heard him sigh; he was looking down at her through half-closed eyes. She capped the salve and reached for her needle and silk. Kel watched her warily—then relaxed as the needle pierced the skin and she began to sew.

"I cannot feel it," he said, wonderingly. "Truly, that is magic."

"It is medicine." She tucked a stray lock of hair behind her ear. *Once, they were the same. No longer.*

"The ordinary folk of Castellane may not come up on the Hill," said Kel, "but the nobles here would be lost without the city. Not only does it provide them their fortunes, it is their playground. They would die of boredom if confined to the Hill."

"You speak as if you were not one of them," Lin said. Taking some herbs from the bag, she sprinkled them on the puncture wound before making another stitch.

"Perhaps I would rather I weren't." Kel glanced down and took on a slightly greenish tinge. "I see you are seasoning me like a chicken."

"The herbs will keep infection away. And don't look."

He yawned. Morphea and blood loss were making him tired, she thought. She concentrated on what she was doing. After a few moments, he spoke again. "When I was younger, I thought the Ashkar must be very dangerous, to be kept within walls."

"When I was young," Lin said, reaching for bandages, "I thought the *malbushim* must be very dangerous, for us to have to keep them out with walls."

"Ah," he said, and yawned again. "Perspective is everything, isn't it?"

Having put away her things, Lin took several hammered-silver talismans from her satchel and slid them between the layers of his bandages. "These will help you heal, and sleep," she said. "What you need is rest, to let your body knit itself together. I will be back in three days to see how you are getting on."

"Wait," he said, as she turned to go. His voice slurred with weariness. "Your name, physician?"

"Lin," she said, as his eyes fluttered shut. "Lin Caster."

He did not respond; he was breathing deep and steady. As she was about to leave, she saw something glitter among the tangle of his sheets. The talisman he had held so briefly earlier. She plucked it free and was just setting it on the nightstand when something unusual about it caught her eye.

She stood for what felt like a long time, looking at it, before placing it carefully in Kel's palm. *Mayesh*, she thought. *Mayesh, what have you done?*

Lin had expected to find her grandfather waiting for her outside the door. He was not there, and neither, to her surprise, were the Castelguards. The corridor was empty save for Prince Conor, sitting in the embrasure of an arched window, gazing stonily out at the city of Castellane. It was little more at this hour than a collection of flickering lights in the distance.

Damn Mayesh for having wandered off. There was nothing Lin wanted less than to be alone with the Prince. But there was no help for it. She approached him, painfully aware of the blood on her tunic, and said, "It is done, Monseigneur."

The Prince looked at her in a sort of daze, as if she were someone long forgotten who had turned up unexpectedly in a dream. Tiredness had scrubbed away the harsh lines of his face; he looked gentle, which Lin knew he was not. "What?"

"I said," Lin repeated, "that it is done—"

He sprang down from the window, swift and graceful; Lin took an involuntary step back. "What does that mean? *Is he alive?*"

"Of course he's alive," she snapped. "Do you think, if he had died, this is how I would choose to relay that information? Kel needs to rest, and eventually to have his bandages changed. But rest first, and dry bedding and clothes. He will get no good sleep lying in his own blood."

He looked at her, his black hair ruffled like the fur of an angry cat.

Name of the Goddess, Lin thought. She had snapped at the Crown Prince. *Again.*

Then he smiled. It was not a cold smile, or a superior one, though it was touched with self-mockery. The relief in his eyes was real. It made him seem human. In the small hours of the night, between the watches of sickness, between fever and recovery, perhaps everyone was a little bit the same. "Such an intemperate doctor," he said, with a touch of amusement. "Am I to understand you are giving me orders again?"

"Well," she said, "I did not think you would change the bedding *yourself.* I just thought that . . . you would want to know what needed to be done."

He only grinned. "Indeed. It seems your grandfather was right. You *are* the best in the Sault—perhaps the best in Castellane."

The grin was disarming. It flashed white teeth and lit his gray eyes to silver. For the first time tonight, Lin could see the Prince of Hearts in him, the one the city sighed over. Something about it irked her, like being stuck with a pin. Perhaps it was that to be the King's son was one kind of power, to be beautiful was another, and to be both was entirely too much power for any one person.

Besides, Conor Aurelian held himself as someone who knew he was beautiful. Even his disarray did not mar his looks. His rich clothes might be crumpled, his sleeves of ivory silk spotted with blood, but his beauty was not the sort that required orderliness. In fact, it benefited from some dishevelment, being the kind that came from strong contrast: black and silver, fine features and untidy dark hair.

"Where is my grandfather?" she inquired, suddenly wanting very much to be away. "I ought to go; he might be waiting for me."

Prince Conor said, "Before you do. Bensimon said you wouldn't require payment, but I'd like you to have this." He slid a ring from his right hand and held it out to her, with the gesture of one bestowing an expensive toy upon a child.

The ring was a plain gold band, set with a flat sapphire. Incised into the sapphire was the rayed sun of House Aurelian. A signet ring.

For a moment, Lin was ten years old again, flinging the gold necklace Mayesh had brought her, with its Aurelian stamp, at his feet. She heard Josit, protesting—*just take it*—and saw the stony look on her grandfather's face as she turned away.

She did not reach out for the ring. "No, thank you. I don't want it."

He looked taken aback. "You don't *want* it?"

The quick flash of memory was gone, but the anger remained. Anger at Mayesh, she knew, but here, made flesh, was the very reason Mayesh had abandoned her, arrogantly offering her what would be a year's salary for herself, but was plainly nothing to him. "What am I meant to do with it?" she asked, her voice brittle as glass. "Sell it at a pawnshop on Yulan Road? I'd be arrested. Wear it? I'd be robbed by Crawlers, like your cousin. It has no value to me."

"It is a beautiful thing," he said. "That has its own worth."

"For those wealthy enough to sit about contemplating an item they can neither eat nor sell," Lin said acidly. "Or do you think I wish to keep it in a box and pine over the time I met the Prince of Castellane and he deigned to tell me I was a halfway-decent physician?"

The moment the words were out of her mouth, she regretted them. His face had gone taut. She was aware suddenly of how much bigger he was than she—not just taller, but broader in the shoulders and larger overall.

He moved toward her. She could feel the force that radiated off him, even as disheveled as he was. A disheveled prince was still a prince, she supposed, with all the careless power that blood and privilege had conferred on him. It was a quality all the stronger for the fact that he had never had to consider that he possessed it, never wonder if there might be some reason for him to hold back.

He could pick her up with one hand, she thought, and toss her against the wall. Break her neck, if he liked. And his power came not from the fact that he had the physical strength to do it, but from the fact that there would be no repercussions for him for the act. No questions asked.

He would not even need to question himself.

He was looking down at her from an uncomfortable height, his gray eyes unwavering. They were like and yet unlike Kel's. But of course they would be. "How—" he began.

A sharp voice cut him off. "Lin!"

She whirled. She had never been so glad to hear her grandfather approaching. He was at the far end of the corridor; Lin hurried toward him, aware of the Prince behind her, his gaze burning a hole between her shoulder blades. She could *feel* him watching her, even as she quickly explained Kel's condition to Mayesh.

Her grandfather nodded, clearly relieved. "Well done," he said. "Now wait for me in the carriage downstairs. I must have a word with the Prince."

Lin did not stay to hear what the word was. She inclined her head in Prince Conor's direction and murmured, "Monseigneur," before making her escape.

The Prince said nothing in response, and offered no farewell, though she noted that he was still holding the signet ring in his hand. He had not put it back on.

Outside, the sky was lightening in the east, over the Narrow Pass. Just before dawn was the coldest time of the day in Castellane. Dew sparkled on the grass, wetting her feet as she approached the waiting carriage. (The driver, a dour-faced Castelguard, gave her a single dark look as she clambered in; perhaps he did not relish being awake so early.)

She was grateful to find that someone had placed a box of heated bricks, wrapped in soft linen, on the bench seat. She retrieved one, rolling it between her palms, letting her skin soak up the warmth. She wondered if Mayesh had requested they be put there.

She thought again of the talisman in Kel's hand. *Mayesh, what have you done?*

There was a rap on the door and Mayesh appeared, folding himself inside the carriage. With his height and long limbs, he made her think of an elongated bird—a heron, perhaps, picking about in the shallows when the tide was exceptionally low.

He glowered at her as the carriage began to move. As they rolled beneath the trellised arch, he said, "Would you prefer to hear the good news first, or the bad?"

She sighed, folding her hands tighter around the hot stone. "Both at the same time."

"Hmph," he said. "You do seem to have worked wonders with Kel. I looked in on him briefly. That ought to dispose the Prince well toward you. *But*," he added, and she assumed this was the bad news, "it seems not. He has forbidden you to return to the Palace grounds."

She jolted upright. "But I *need* to—I must examine Kel again, in no more than three days—"

"Perhaps you should have thought of that." The North Gate passed by above them. They were leaving Marivent. "I cannot help but ask: What did you do to offend Conor so badly? He said, if I recall correctly, that you were a rude and peculiar girl, one he did not wish to see again."

"I did nothing." When her grandfather only raised his eyebrows in response, Lin said, "I refused his offer of payment. I want nothing from House Aurelian."

She turned to stare out the window. As quickly as she had come to the Palace, she had left it. And would, it seemed, not be returning. The heroine of *The Taming of the Tyrant* would be very disappointed in her, but then she had not had Conor Aurelian to deal with.

"Everyone in Castellane accepts something from House Aurelian, every day," said Mayesh. "Who do you think pays the Vigilants? The Fire-Watch? Even in the Sault, it is Treasury money that provides the salary of the Shomrim—"

"To protect us, or to protect them against us?" she said, recalling Kel's words: *When I was younger, I thought the Ashkar must be very dangerous, to be kept within walls.* "Anyway, it does not matter. I may have offended the Prince by refusing his signet ring, but I could have done worse." Her brick had gone cold. She set it down beside her and said, "I could have said I knew perfectly well that Kel Anjuman is not the Prince's cousin."

Mayesh's eyes narrowed. "What," he said, "makes you say that?"

Lin could no longer see their reflections in the window. It had grown too light outside. The sky over the city was turning from black to a pale blue, streaked with feathery gray clouds. There would be movement down at the harbor, and shipbuilders beginning the trek over the rocks to the Arsenale. Seabirds would have begun to circle, filling the air with reedlike calls.

Lin said, "He is covered with scars. Not the kind of scars a noble might get from the occasional duel, or even piffling about drunkenly on horseback. I have seen nothing like these, save on the bodies of those who used to be fighters in the Arena. And don't try telling me he was an Arena fighter when he was twelve." (It had been a decade since King Markus had outlawed gladiatorial combat, calling it inhumane.)

"Oh," said Mayesh, "believe me, I wasn't going to. But I see you haven't finished?" His tone was one of polite inquiry. *Do go on.*

Lin went on. "He had a talisman in his hand. An *anokham* talisman. I know enough of *gematry* to know what it does."

"It is rare magic. Powerful," said Mayesh. "That talisman dates from before the Sundering."

"It is illusion magic," said Lin. "It ties Kel Anjuman—or whatever his name is—to Conor Aurelian. It makes him *look* like Conor Aurelian when he wears it."

"Your study of *gematry* has been more comprehensive than I realized," Mayesh said. He did not sound displeased. Only thoughtful, and a little curious. "Has this been part of your quest to cure Mariam Duhary?"

How do you know about that? Lin thought, but she did not ask. She had only this one chance to question Mayesh about what she had witnessed; she would not squander it. "It has been part of my general studies," she said. "Mayesh." (He looked at her sharply from beneath his heavy brows, but said nothing.) "I didn't take the ring because I didn't want payment from House Aurelian. I do want payment from you, however. I want you to tell me who my patient is."

"Was," said Mayesh.

They had reached the Ruta Magna. The Broken Market had been cleared away as if it had never existed, and the shops were beginning to open. They passed a group of merchants from Sarthe and a Chosean girl with foxgloves pinned in her glossy black hair; all paused to look curiously at the carriage with the royal seal upon the side.

"He isn't *dead*—"

"No, but it does not seem you'll be treating him again. Lin, I am sworn to keep the secrets of the Palace. You know that."

"I could make a great deal of trouble with what I already know," Lin said, almost in a whisper. "Is he a sort of whipping boy? Is he punished in Conor's stead? Or is he a bodyguard? I *will* find out, you know."

"I do know. I'd hoped you would accept the story that Kel is Conor's cousin, for all our peace of mind. But I *suspected* you would not." Mayesh templed his fingers under his chin. "If I tell you this, you must swear a binding oath, that it will go no further than between you and me."

"*Imrāde*," Lin said. "I swear."

"At the Malgasi Court, for many years, there was a tradition," said Mayesh. "When the King had only one son as heir, a boy would be chosen from the city. A neglected child, with no parents, no family that might miss him or complain. They called the boy the *Kirá-lar*, the King's Blade. Here," he said, "we call him the Sword Catcher. Kel was brought to the Palace to serve the Prince when he was ten. And I will tell you what he does."

Dawn had passed by the time Lin had returned, alone, to her little house. Sunlight streamed through the curtains. Everything was where she had left it the night before: papers, books, stone-cold mug of tea.

Utterly exhausted, she drew the curtains and began to undress for sleep. At least she did not have patients to see today; that was a small mercy. The watches of night had ended; the Shomrim would be returning home to sleep their odd daylight sleep. Strange dreams came to Lin when she had been up all night, dreams in which she wandered a world where it was always night, the darkness spangled with gleaming light that was not stars. She wondered if it was the same for the watchmen. Or for Mayesh, who also had not slept.

"Don't you ever wonder?" she had asked her grandfather, after he had explained to her what a Sword Catcher was—and who Kel Saren was, truly. Not the Prince's cousin at all, but his bodyguard, his double, his shield. Even the nobles did not know, he had said. Only House Aurelian. And now, her. "Who his parents are? Who gave birth to him, before he ended up at the Orfelinat?"

Mayesh had barked a laugh. "There is no need to make a mystery of it. There are hundreds of abandoned children in Castellane. One imagines he was unwanted for any of the ordinary reasons."

Unwanted. She, too, had been unwanted, Lin thought, untying the cord at the waist of her trousers. But she had had the Sault, where children were treasure, even those who had no family. Every Ashkari life was valuable. Every Ashkar born repaired the breaking of the world and brought the Goddess closer to returning.

In Castellane, it was different. Unwanted children were vulnerable refuse, prey for the unscrupulous, invisible to the respectable. She thought of Kel Saren, the way his smile had reminded her of Josit. She wondered whether he minded being Sword Catcher, or perhaps, as soldiers did, he accepted the danger of his life with equanimity.

She would find out, she thought. He was her patient. Conor Aurelian could not keep her from discharging her duty to her patient, no matter what he said.

She kicked her trousers off and winced. That pain in her side she'd felt at the Palace—what *was* it? She pulled her tunic up and saw, there on her hip, a red mark like a burn. But what could have burned her? Had a wasp been caught in her tunic? She drew it off and shook it. No insect fell out. Instead, she heard a soft *thunk*.

Of course. Petrov's stone. She reached into the tunic's pocket to pull it out and realized three things immediately: One, there was a hole in the pocket where there had not been before. Two, that the hole was surrounded by scorched fabric, as if the hole were the result of a flame. And three, that the pocket, with the stone in it, had rested just over her left hip when she wore the tunic.

She gazed at the stone. It was unchanged: smooth, round, milky pale. Cool to the touch. Yet somehow, and for some reason, it had burned through the pocket of her tunic and scorched her skin, at the very moment that she was treating Kel Anjuman.

She heard again the whisper in the back of her mind, clearer now. *Use me.* She had thought she was simply remembering to use the salve, but now that she held the stone in her hand, the voice was louder, the memory sharper. And there was that burn, on her skin . . .

She felt as she had before she had ever read a single medical book, when she had desperately wanted to heal but lacked the tools or language. She brushed the stone with her fingertips, knowing she was groping in the dark. Answers existed, but where? Petrov might have had them, but he was gone. His books and belongings had disappeared into the Maze, a place no lone Ashkari woman would dare to go.

When she finally slept, she did not dream of darkness. Instead, she knew she was in a high place, and around her were flames, growing ever closer. The wind howled past her, but did nothing to quench the fire. When she woke in the evening, her muscles ached, as if she had been running through the night.

Suleman set out to charm the Queen. It was not hard for him to do. His hair was black as raven's wings, his body hard as if it had been carved from stone. No other Sorcerer-King was as admired. He arrived in Aram on the back of a dragon and found Adassa to be beautiful as well as young and impressionable. He set about trying to convince her to ally with his own country. He spoke of the power of the Source-Stones and their ability to make land fertile and heal mortal wounds. Adassa fell in love with Suleman, and for some time they were lovers. He showed her how to bring prosperity into Aram using her Source-Stone. But despite all this, she refused to marry him, not wanting to give up the independence of her throne. Eventually he prevailed upon her to visit him in his own kingdom, so that she could see all that might be hers if she agreed to marry him.

— *Tales of the Sorcerer-Kings*, Laocantus Aurus Iovit III

CHAPTER NINE

Drowned deep in morphea, Kel dreamed.

He dreamed he lay in his bed in Conor's room, and Mayesh came, and the King and Queen, and chirurgeons and scholars from all over Dannemore. Fausten was there: He brought out ink and quills, and marked Kel's face, his neck, his bare arms and legs, while Kel tried to speak, to move, and discovered he could not.

The experts examined the marks and spoke in whispered, half-regretful voices about what must be cut away to leave a perfect canvas upon which they could do their work. "All that is here is flawed," said Fausten, his rheumy eyes fixed on a distant point. "Flesh and blood must be sacrificed. Here—" and he placed his hand upon Kel's chest—"is the diamond."

King Markus stepped forward. In his hand was the ceremonial blade Firefly. Gold and silver enamel adorned its hilt; rubies studded the crosspiece like drops of blood. "My son," he said. "This is your task."

And he gave the blade to Conor. Kel tried to whisper Conor's name, to call out to him for mercy, but the universe was tilting away from him. He could not grasp its substance, not even to beg for his life. As Conor raised the blade above his heart, Kel heard the screaming of a phoenix and felt the turning of the world.

"So you went to the Palace," Mariam said, bumping her shoulder against Lin's as they made their way through the market. "And you met the Prince. And his cousin. You saw their *rooms*."

"Mariam, I've told you this story *five times*," Lin groaned. It was true; she had told the story multiple times over the past three days, though she'd kept her word to Mayesh. No mention of Sword Catchers or *anokham* talismans had escaped her lips, nor a word of Crawlers, for that matter.

Mariam had paused at a stall that sold silks and brocades. She had come to the market in search of material with which she planned to make dresses for, it seemed, half the girls in the Sault. The Goddess Festival was a little less than a month away, and Mariam had been flooded with orders. Though the Ashkar must dress plainly outside the Sault, within its walls they could wear whatever they chose, and the Festival was a chance to parade one's finery before the whole community.

She smiled at Lin around a bolt of green cloth the color of a lily pad. "And yet I wish to hear it again. Is that wrong?"

"I'm curious myself," added the stallkeeper, a bored-looking woman with white hair and black eyebrows shaped like inverted V's. "Did you say you'd been to the *Palace*?"

Lin took hold of Mariam's sleeve and dragged her several feet away, into a spot between a jeweler's stall and a watchmaker's. She put her hands on her hips and looked severely at Mariam—though she wasn't actually angry, and she suspected Mariam could tell. How to be angry when Mariam seemed, well, *better*? Whether it was the tisanes Lin had been forcing into her every day, her excitement over the upcoming Festival, or her delight over Lin's trip to Marivent, it was difficult to say. What mattered was that she had a spring in her step and color in her cheeks for the first time in some while.

"What was the Prince wearing?" Mariam said, unrepentant. "Tell me all about his clothes."

Lin made a face at her. It was a bright, breezy day, the kind where the sky looked like the high ceiling of a temple, painted in shades of lapis and white. The soft air lifted the sleeves and hem of Lin's dress playfully, like a kitten seeking attention. "I didn't notice his clothes," she lied. "Perhaps you want to hear more about how I treated my patient's wound? Or would you like me to discuss my concerns about infection? Oh, and pus?"

Mariam stuck her fingers in her ears.

"*Mariam.*"

"I'll take them out when you promise to tell me how handsome the Prince is up close. Did you challenge him with blazing eyes? Did he tell you that he ought to put you in the Trick, but he could never imprison someone so beautiful?"

"No," Lin said, patiently, "because that, Mariam, is the plot of *Taming the Tyrant.*"

"You are absolutely no fun," Mariam declared. "I want more, Lin. I wish to hear about the furnishings in the Palace, and what the Prince was wearing, and the size of his—"

"*Mariam.*"

"—crown," Mariam finished, with a grin that lit up her thin face. "Honestly, Lin. Surely the cut of the Prince's coat can't be a state secret." She pushed a lock of breeze-blown hair behind her ear. "Anyway, you'll see them again when you go back to check on your patient, won't you?"

Lin sighed. She couldn't lie to Mariam, who knew she always, always returned to see how her patients had responded to her care. "I won't be going back," she said. "Mayesh brought me there because they were desperate. But Prince Conor has been clear that I cannot return."

"Because you're Ashkar?" Mariam looked as if she'd been slapped. Lin hurried to reassure her, hating that she could not be more honest. But to tell Mariam that the Prince had forbidden Lin from entering Marivent because he *disliked* her would puncture the fantasy that her friend was enjoying so much.

"No, nothing like that, Mari. Because they have their own chirurgeon, and they do not wish to cause him offense."

"I heard one of my ladies on the Hill talking about him," said Mariam crossly. "She said he was dreadful—" She broke off as the city clock, which adorned the top of the Windtower, loudly chimed the hour of noon. "Oh, dear. We've been here an hour and I haven't bought anything."

"Because you keep bothering *me*," Lin pointed out. "Didn't you say you needed rose silk?"

"Yes, for Galena Soussan. It won't suit her at all, but she's determined. She's got her eye on impressing someone at the Festival, but I don't know who . . ."

Lin tugged on Mariam's left braid. "Darling. We can gossip all we want when we get back home. Go get what you need."

They agreed to meet in an hour's time at the foot of the Windtower, the great spire that cast its long shadow over Fleshmarket Square. (It was one of the few bits of Castellani architecture, along with Marivent and the roof of the Tully, that Lin could see from her house, rising above the Sault walls. Its shape had always reminded Lin of the silver spice boxes that adorned most Ashkari tables.)

As soon as Mariam had hurried off, Lin reached into the pocket of her blue dress and drew out Petrov's stone. Approaching the jeweler's stall, she asked the spectacled man working there whether it would be possible to have it set inexpensively, perhaps into a ring or bracelet?

He took the stone from her, a flicker of what looked like surprise passing over his face. But, "A fine specimen," was all he said, first raising the stone to the light to peer at it, then measuring it with a pair of engraved calipers. He pronounced it to be a sort of quartz, flawed with what he called "inclusions," which Lin took to mean the odd shapes inside the stone. It wasn't worth a great deal, he said, but it was pretty, and he could set it in plain silver for a crown. A brooch, he suggested, would be most practical, and he could do the work now if she was willing to return to the stall in half an hour to retrieve the finished product. Lin agreed, and sallied forth to wander the square while the jewel was set.

Lin loved the weekly market. The great tower with its beautiful clock rose above Fleshmarket Square, and in its shadow stalls and tents sprouted each Sunday morning like colorful mushrooms. One could find just about anything here: ivory fans and cotton tunics from Hind; black pepper and brilliant feathers from Sayan; dried medicinal herbs and rosewood carvings from Shenzhou; pickled cabbage and rice wine from Geumjoseon; fruit paste, *calison*, and toys from Sarthe.

The thought of marzipan made Lin's stomach rumble—a problem very easily addressed in the market. The smells of food filled the air with rich and clashing scents, like a dozen heavily perfumed aristocrats rubbing elbows in a small room: sizzling butter, noodles frying in oil, the spice of chili and the bitter tang of chocolate. The greatest difficulty was in choosing *what* to eat—pork dumplings and candied ginger from Shangan, or rice-cake soup from Geumjoseon? Coconut pancakes from Taprobana or smoked fish from Nyenschantz?

In the end, she decided on a paper cup of honey-sesame sweets, studded with dried raisins. She nibbled on them as she wandered into the part of the market devoted to small animals meant as pets. Silver cages stacked outside a blue tent held sleepy-eyed cats, their engraved metal collars proclaiming names like RATSLAYER and MOUSEBANE. White-faced monkeys on embroidered leashes darted in and out of the crowd, sometimes tugging on the clothes of passersby and begging with wide eyes. (Lin passed one of them a sesame sweet while the monkey-seller was looking the other way.) Peacocks waddled in enclosures, spreading their fans. Lin paused to visit the abode of a white rat she'd always been fond of. He had pink eyes and a whippet tail, and when let out of his cage, he would crawl up her arm and nuzzle her hair.

"If you want him so bad, you ought to just get him," grumbled Do-Chi, the grizzled old man who owned the stall. His family had come from Geumjoseon a generation back and, according to him, had always been trainers of small animals, having once owned a hedgehog circus. "Three talents."

"No chance. My brother would murder me when he gets back. He can't stand rats." Lin stroked the rodent's head through the cage bars with a regretful finger before she bid Do-Chi farewell and moved on to her favorite part of the market—the bookstalls.

Here was all the knowledge in the world—maps of the Gold Roads, *Magna Callatis: The Book of Lost Empire, The Book of Roads and Kingdoms, A Gift to Those Who Contemplate the Wonders of Cities and the Marvels of Traveling, A Journey Beyond the Three Seas, The Mirror of Countries, An Account of Travel to the Five Hindish Kingdoms,* and *The Record of a Pilgrimage to Shenzhou in Search of the Law.*

There were also the sort of travelogues written by nobles when they returned from time abroad filled with a desire to show off to the populace. Lin stopped to look with some amusement through the pages of *The Admirable Adventures and Strange Fortunes of Signeur Antoine Knivet, Who Went with Dom August Renaudin on His Second Voyage to the Lakshad Sea.* It promised to be "A Tale of Sea-Faeries and Seafaring" but Lin knew she had neither time nor attention to devote to it now. She checked, as she always did, for any new medical texts that might have turned up since she'd last come, but found only the anatomies and remedy books she was already familiar with.

On her way back to the jeweler's stand, Lin looped around the far side of the market to avoid the area where red-and-white-striped flags (red for blood, white for bone) advertised Castellani chirurgeons plying their trade. Armed with knives and pliers they would yank out abscessed teeth and sever gangrenous fingers while blood sprayed and onlookers applauded. Lin hated it; medicine wasn't theater.

Her detour took her past the Story-Spinners, each with a crowd around them. A man with a grizzled beard held a group captive with tales of piracy on the high seas, while a green-haired woman in shocking-pink skirts kept an even larger group spellbound with the tale of a girl who fell in love with a dashing soldier only to discover he was the prince of a rival country. *It's always princes*, Lin thought, drifting closer. *No one ever seems to fall into passionate, forbidden love with a lamp-maker.*

"He laid her milk-white body down upon the sands," declaimed the woman in pink, "whereupon he did make love to her, *all night long.*"

The audience broke into applause and demands for more and filthier details. With a giggle, Lin disposed of her now-empty paper cup, and hurried to the jeweler's stand. He presented her with the stone, set in plain silver with a pin in the back. She professed herself delighted, paid, and set off for the Windtower to meet Mariam.

She examined her new brooch as she went. She was not entirely sure what had compelled her to have the stone set. She could still see shapes in it, despite its new setting: It seemed almost as if smoke were coiled within it, waiting to rise.

As she neared the tower, she saw Mariam, waiting beside a hired waggon that she had piled with bolts of shimmering cloth in every color from bronze to duck's-egg blue. Lin fastened her new brooch to the shoulder of her dress and started toward the waggon when a woman stepped in front of her, blocking her way.

She felt a sharp flash of fear—irrational, but instinctive. Most Castellani were indifferent to the Ashkar, but some went out of their way to bother them: to make jokes at their expense, to trip them or knock into them in the street. *At least it never rises beyond the level of bother*, Chana Dorin had said to Lin once. *It's not like that everywhere.*

But the woman in front of Lin was looking at her without hostility, and what seemed to be a mild curiosity. She was young, perhaps a few years older than Lin, with jet-black hair and equally dark eyes. Her padded brocade jacket was the unusual color of violets. Her hair was pinned up neatly at the back of her head with combs carved of semiprecious stone: red jasper, milky pink quartz, black chalcedony.

"You are Lin Caster," she said. "The physician." Her voice rose slightly, giving the statement the air of a question.

"Yes," Lin said, "but I am not working now." She glanced reflexively toward the red-and-white flags in the marketplace, wondering if she should warn the stranger off, but the girl only made a face.

"Ugh," she said. "Barbarians. They would be laughed out of Geumseong, or beheaded for defiling the art of medicine."

Geumseong was the capital of Geumjoseon. Indeed, Lin could imagine that the blood-splattered carnival of surgery practiced in the market would horrify someone used to Geumjoseon medicine, where care and cleanliness were prized.

"I am sorry," Lin said. "If it's an emergency—"

"Not an emergency, quite," said the girl. A gold pendant winked at her throat as she turned to glance at Mariam, who was waving at Lin. "But something of interest to you. It concerns a mutual friend, Kel Saren."

Lin tried to hide her surprise. Mayesh had told her Kel's real name when he had told her of his true occupation. Still, she had the impression that very few people knew it, even those who worked at the Palace.

"He was attacked the other night, by Crawlers," continued the girl. "The way you healed him was impressive. The king wishes to speak to you of it."

Lin was stunned. "The *king*?"

"Yes," the girl said, pleasantly. "The king."

"I don't mean to cause offense, but you don't look as if you work for the Palace."

The girl only smiled. "Not everyone who serves the king wears his livery. Some prefer a more subtle approach." She gestured toward a black carriage some distance away. A driver was perched on the upper seat, dressed in red and looking bored. "Come, now. The king is waiting."

"But," said Lin, "the Prince forbade me from returning to Marivent."

The girl's smile widened. "The wishes of the king supersede those of Prince Conor."

Lin hesitated only a moment longer. The idea that the rarely seen King Markus wished to see her made her more nervous than excited. She could not imagine what he wanted. But beneath that nervousness was the sure knowledge that her return would irritate the Prince, and there would be *absolutely nothing he could do about it.*

She thought of the arrogant way he had waved his signet ring at her, as if he had expected her to kiss the stone in gratitude. "All right," she said. "Just let me bid my friend goodbye."

The girl's eyes narrowed. "You cannot tell her where you are going. This summons is to be kept secret."

Lin nodded her agreement before darting off to tell Mariam of her change in plans. A sick patient, she explained, in the Lark Street district. Mariam was understanding, as she always was; as the black carriage drew away from the square with Lin and her companion inside, Lin glimpsed Mariam chatting away merrily to her waggon driver.

The carriage cut its way through the crowded square, a shark gliding through a crowded shoal of fish. Lin's companion had fallen silent. She was gazing out the window, her face blank of expression.

By the time they turned onto the Ruta Magna, Lin could stand the silence no longer. "Will you tell me your name?" she said. "You know mine. I feel at a disadvantage."

"Ji-An," said the girl. Though Lin waited, she added no family name.

"Are you in the Arrow Squadron?" Lin asked.

"I am not a soldier. I serve the king directly." Ji-An touched a hand to the pendant at her throat. It was shaped like a gold key. "Years ago, the king saved my life. My loyalty to him is absolute."

Years ago? Lin's companion could not be that old—perhaps

twenty-five? And King Markus had been in seclusion for ten years at least. Had he saved her life before she was twelve?

"King Markus saved your life?"

"I didn't say that," said Ji-An calmly.

Lin's heart began to beat faster. The carriage had jounced off the Great Road and onto a smaller street. They were heading into the Warren, the largest neighborhood in Castellane, where trades-people, merchants, and guildmasters mixed with barbers, clerks, and publicans. It was an old quarter; every once in a while a grand white building would rise from among its wood-and-brick neigh-bors, a memento of the days of the Empire. An elegantly tiled cali-darium sat between a noodle shop and a knife sharpener's, while a porticoed temple to Turan, God of love, cozied up to a squat inn called The Queen's Bed.

"This is not the way to the Palace," noted Lin.

"Oh," Ji-An said, her tone pleasant, "did you think I meant the King on the Hill? He is not the king I serve. I meant the King in the City. The Ragpicker King."

The Ragpicker King? Lin's mouth fell open. "You lied to me." She put a hand to the door of the carriage. "Let me out."

"I will," Ji-An said, "if you want me to. But what I told you was true. The Ragpicker King *does* wish to speak to you of Kel Saren. He heard that you healed him and was astonished to learn of your skill."

"Perhaps it wasn't that bad an injury."

"It was," said Ji-An. "I saw his wounds myself. I did not think he would survive them."

"You saw his wounds?"

"Yes. I am the one who brought him to the Palace gates. I knew someone who was injured like that, once. She—the person suffered for many days before they died. But Kel Saren will live."

Lin was still, her hand on the carriage door. She recalled Kel saying, *I know who left me outside Marivent. It wasn't the person who stabbed me.*

She drew her hand back from the door. "But why?" she said. *Why would a Sword Catcher to the Prince know a common criminal, someone who works for the Ragpicker King?* "Why did you save him?"

"Oh, *look*," announced Ji-An. "We've arrived."

And so they had. They had reached Scarlet Square, the center of the Warren, and the Black Mansion was before them, its dark dome, all strange unreflective marble, rising like a shadow above the rooflines of the city.

How strange to dream about a phoenix screaming, when no phoenix still existed in Dannemore. Kel knew they had lived once, and been the companions of Sorcerer-Kings, as had dragons and basilisks, mermaids and manticores. They had been creatures of real magic, created from the now-vanished Word, and had vanished when the Sundering stripped magic from the world.

Still, in his dreams, they cried out, and their cries sounded like children screaming.

Later, in the dream, he was playing a game of Castles with Anjelica Iruvai, Princess of Kutani. She was dressed as she had been in the portrait Kel had seen, which was perhaps not surprising. The coils of her dark hair were caught in a net of silver, spangled with crystal stars. Her lips were red, her eyes soft, the color of honey wine. She said, "It is not unusual to dream of fire when you yourself have a fever."

He saw Merren in his dreams, surrounded by his poisoner's alembics, cross-legged in a circle of hemlock and deadly nightshade. With his threadbare jacket and unkempt blond curls, he looked like a forest spirit, something not quite tamed. He said, "Everyone has secrets, no matter how innocent they may seem."

Kel saw the Ragpicker King, all in black like Gentleman Death, and he said, *"Your choices are not your own, or your dreams, either."*

Lastly, Kel saw the steps of the Convocat, and he stepped out onto them, clothed in Conor's raiment, wearing the crown of Castellane with its sharp wings on either side. He looked across the cheering crowd that filled the square and saw the arrow flying toward him, too quickly for him to move away; it pierced Kel's heart and he fell. As his blood spilled red down the white steps, Conor nodded to him from the shadows, as if to say that he approved.

Kel bolted up in bed, his heart racing, his hand pressed to his chest. He had felt the pain in his sleep, and felt it still—a deep sharp ache to the left of his sternum. He knew it had been a dream, the arrows a mist of morphea and half sleep, but the pain was real and present.

He remembered, in a confusion of images, lying here among wet and bloody sheets. Drifting in and out of waking and sleeping; seeing Conor there, but being unable to speak to him. The look on Conor's face. *I ought to have died in the alley,* Kel had thought, *not here, where he can see me.*

He slid a hand into the collar of his nightshirt, discovering the texture of bandages—wrapping his chest, and bound over his right shoulder, like a sling. There was a thicker patch of them just under his heart. He prodded at the spot and jumped as a stab of pain shot through him.

With the pain came a memory. A narrow black alley, Crawlers on the walls above him. The flash of a silver mask. A hot needle in his side. A glimpse of violet . . .

"Sieur Kel! Stop that!" Kel glanced over to see Domna Delfina, shaking her head until her gray curls flew, rising from her seat near his bed. The senior housemaid was holding a pair of knitting needles, the half-finished project she'd been at work on abandoned in her haste. "You mustn't touch the bandages. Sieur Gasquet says—"

Kel, peevish with fading morphea, poked himself hard in the lumpiest part of the bandage with a forefinger. It hurt. *Genius,* he thought. *Of course it hurts.*

"Gasquet didn't do this. He's terrible at bandaging." Kel's voice scraped out of his throat, dry from disuse. How long had he been asleep?

Delfina rolled her eyes. "If you won't behave, I'll get him myself."

Kel had no desire to see Gasquet quite yet. "Delfina—"

But she had already gathered up her knitting. She was making something very long and narrow, with a great deal of green and purple. A scarf for a giant? Formal attire for an enormous snake? She muttered something dismissive in Valdish and left, leaving Kel to rub his eyes and search his brain for bits of memory.

He knew he must have been in bed for several days. His muscles felt limp, debilitated; he imagined if he stood up, his legs would shake. His memory was beginning to come back, though. He remembered the arrow, the fleeing Crawlers, Jerrod. He thought he could recall a red haze of pain, though pain was difficult to remember in its entirety. One knew one had felt pain, but the experience could not be truly re-created in memory. Probably all to the best.

Then, somehow, he had gotten from the Key to the Palace. He had a strong suspicion regarding the method of his return, but he planned to keep it to himself for now. After that . . . He thought he recalled Mayesh, speaking in Ashkar. And later, a girl with auburn hair and a serious face. Her hands had been gentle, fading pain into memory. *Truly, that is magic.*

It is medicine, Lin had said. Lin Caster—that had been her name. Mayesh's granddaughter. She had healed him. After that, his memory was only flashes of light between dreams. A hand holding his head up, someone spooning salty broth between his teeth. Morphea grains being shaken from an ampoule, placed on his tongue to dissolve like sugar.

There was a bustle in the corridor—Kel heard Delfina's voice, and then the door was thrown open and Conor came into the room. He had clearly come from the stables: He wore his riding jacket and was crownless, his hair a windblown tumble. His face was bright with color. He looked the picture of health, which only made Kel feel more like a chicken that had been recently deboned.

He grinned when he saw Kel sitting up, that slow grin that meant he was genuinely pleased. "Good," he said. "You're alive."

"I don't feel it." Kel rubbed at his face. Even the texture of his own skin seemed strange—he hadn't shaved for days, and the stubble of his beard was rough against his palm. He couldn't recall the last time that had happened. Conor kept himself clean-shaven, so Kel did, too.

"Delfina seemed concerned that you were tearing at your bandages like a madman," said Conor, flopping into the chair beside Kel's bed.

"They itched," Kel said. He felt slightly awkward, which he did not like. He was not used to feeling awkward around Conor. But his memories of the alley behind the Key were coming back, more and more clearly. He could hear Jerrod's voice in the back of his mind. *Beck owns you now, Aurelian.*

He winced. Conor immediately leaned forward, putting his hand under Kel's chin, lifting his face to be studied. "How do you feel? Should I get Gasquet?"

"No need," Kel said. "I need a bath and some food, not necessarily in that order. And then Gasquet can prod at me." He frowned. "The physician who healed me—she was Mayesh's granddaughter?"

"She still is, as far as I know." Apparently satisfied that Kel was in no imminent danger, Conor sat back. His tone was light, but Kel sensed something—a layer of feeling or doubt, just below the surface Conor chose to show the world. Few saw beneath that invisible armor; even Kel could only guess. "An Ashkari physician. Mayesh has been keeping that quiet."

"He never speaks much of the Sault." The memory of Lin grew clearer, firming up around the edges. She had been small, with quick hands and hair the color of fire. A stern voice, like Mayesh's. *I need to concentrate. You are interrupting me. Please leave me alone with my patient.*

No one talked to Conor like that. Interesting. Kel filed the memory away.

"Kellian—what happened to you?" Conor demanded. It was clear he'd been waiting days to ask. "I told you to go get drunk with Roverge, and the next thing I know you get yourself dumped off at the Palace gates like a wounded sack of potatoes. Who left you there?"

"I've no idea." Kel looked down at his hands to hide the lie in his eyes. Several of his fingernails were broken. He remembered scrabbling at the stones in the alley, wet black mold under his fingers. The smell of it, like a dead mouse in a wall. The memory made his stomach clench. "I was in an alley," he said, slowly. "I thought I'd die there. The next thing I remember is waking up in this room."

"What were you doing down in the city?" Conor demanded. Kel supposed it wasn't *demanding*, exactly; Conor simply expected to know where Kel had been because he could not imagine a situation in which Kel had secrets he did not know. It was why Kel had been so angry at the Ragpicker King—and perhaps why he had felt so very odd in Merren's flat. *Now I have secrets that must be kept.*

Conor cocked his head to the side. He had latched on to Kel's hesitation like a hunting dog latching on to the scent of blood. He said, "Now, what would you feel you had to sneak off to do? A duel, perhaps? Over a girl? Or a boy? Did you get some guildmaster's daughter pregnant?"

Kel held his hand up to forestall the flood of half-serious questions. He couldn't imagine trying to explain to Conor about the Ragpicker King. Besides, he had tied up the loose end with Merren; there was no point talking about it now. But he could not lie about what had happened in the alley. "No romance," he said. "No duel. I went to the Caravel to see Silla."

Conor leaned back against a bedpost. "This happened at the Caravel?"

"I never made it there. I was jumped by Crawlers." *Well, at least that's the truth.* He took a deep breath, sending a stab of pain deeper into his chest, like an arrow tunneling home. "Crawlers who thought I was you."

Conor went still. "*What?*"

"They must have followed me, waited until I was alone. I was wearing your cloak—"

"Yes," Conor said. He twisted at a ring on his left hand—a blue signet ring that winked like an eye. "I remember; we had to throw it away. It was ruined. But that isn't enough to assume they thought you were me. Unless—your talisman?"

"I wasn't wearing it. But they called me Monseigneur, and it was very clear who they thought I was."

"That's not possible." Conor spoke evenly. Only his hands betrayed real tension: His fingers had curled up against his palms. "Crawlers don't seek out princes to rob and kill. They're lowlifes. Pickpockets. Not assassins."

"They didn't want you dead," Kel said. He wondered if he should mention the arrows, but decided not to. It would only complicate things. "They only tried to hurt me when they realized I *wasn't* you. What they wanted was money."

"Money?"

"They work for Prosper Beck," Kel said, and saw Conor blanch. "How long have you known you owe him ten thousand crowns?"

Conor jerked upright—a curiously ungraceful movement, a puppet being yanked by its strings. His leather riding jacket spun with him as he crossed the room to the rosewood cupboard he had personally ordered from Sayan. The doors were painted with images of colorful birds and unknown Gods, their eyes circled in gold.

Inside were decanters and bottles of every liquor under the sun. *Nocino*, made from bitter Sarthan walnuts, and bloodroot liquor from Hanse, dark and thick as if it were drawn from human veins. Juniper-scented jenever from Nyenschantz. Sticky white rice-and-honey wine from Shenzhou, and apricot-kernel *vaklav* from the high mountains of Malgasi. The servants had been instructed to keep the cupboard stocked with everything Conor liked, and when it came to alcohol, his taste was various. The cabinet even had a false bottom, where poppy-drops and the odd powders Charlon liked were kept out of sight.

His back to Kel, Conor selected a bottle of *pastisson*, the cheap green anise stuff drunk by every student in the city. A gold label on the bottle bore the image of a viridescent butterfly. He walked back to the bed, seated himself again in the chair, and twisted the cork out of the bottle.

The scent of licorice rose, roiling Kel's stomach. He already felt slightly sick. He could not help but feel that this was far from what a Sword Catcher was designed to do; he did not want to tell Conor unpleasant things that must be reckoned with. That was Mayesh's job, or Lilibet's. Even Jolivet's. Not his.

"I am not telling you this to hold you to account," Kel said, as Conor took a drink from the bottle. "I am telling you because if I do not, next time it *will* be you they follow and threaten, not me."

"I know." Conor looked at Kel with unblinking gray eyes. "I should have told you."

"Does anyone else know? Mayesh, even?"

Conor shook his head. The alcohol was bringing a little of the color back to his face. "I ought to have told *you*," he said, "but I only just found out myself. Do you recall that night at the Caravel? When Alys wanted to speak to me alone?" Conor licked a drop of wine from his thumb. "It seems that bastard, Beck, has been going around Castellane buying up all my debts. Debts to boot-makers, clothiers, wine merchants, even the debt for that falcon I borrowed and misplaced."

"You misplaced it in the *sky*," Kel pointed out. "It flew off."

Conor shrugged. "The Hill runs on credit," he said. "We all run up bills, all over town. We pay them eventually. That's how the system works. When Beck approached Alys, he tried to buy my debt to the Caravel. She refused to sell it. She has a loyal heart."

And a clever brain, Kel thought. By being the first to alert Conor to the situation, Alys Asper had won Conor's loyalty. She had bet on House Aurelian against Prosper Beck, which made sense to Kel. What did not make sense was how many merchants, it seemed, had bet the other way.

For Conor was correct: The lifeblood of Castellane was credit. Trade ran on it. The nobles ran up bills when their fleets were out at sea, their caravans on the Gold Roads, and paid them off when the goods came in. To bet against Conor was to bet against a system that had been in place for hundreds of years.

"Alys," Conor said, "is one of the few who refused. Totaled together, it seems, the rest of my debts equal ten thousand crowns." Kel supposed it made sense; merchants were unlikely to pointedly remind the Crown Prince what he owed. The ten thousand crowns could represent years of spending. "And Beck wants it all. Now. In gold."

"Is that even possible?"

"Not really. I have an *allowance*, you know that." It was true: Conor was paid monthly from the Treasury, by Cazalet, who kept a close eye on Palace expenditures.

"This might be a matter for Jolivet," Kel said. "Have him send the Arrow Squadron into the Maze. Find out where Beck is hiding. Bring him to the Trick."

Conor's smile was bitter. "What Beck is doing is legal," he said. "It's legal to buy up debt, from anyone at all. It's legal to enforce payment by nearly any means. All Laws the noble Houses passed— including House Aurelian." He ran a finger around the neck of the *pastisson* bottle. "Do you know what Beck threatened me with, if I didn't pay him the full amount immediately? Not with violence. He threatened to haul me in front of the Justicia, to force repayment through the Treasury. And he could. You can imagine the scandal then."

Kel could. He thought of what the Ragpicker King had said, that Prosper Beck was likely being funded by someone on the Hill.

Had one of the noble Houses engineered all this, just to humiliate Conor? Or was this just the overreach of a greedy criminal new to Castellane, who did not yet understand how the city worked?

"The Treasury would have to pay off my debt," Conor said slowly, "and you know the Treasury money belongs to the city. The Dial Chamber would be furious. My fitness to be King would be questioned. It would never end."

Kel felt slightly breathless, and the pain was intensifying. It had likely been hours since he'd last had morphea. "Have you tried to negotiate with Beck? Has he asked anything else of you?"

Conor set the bottle of *pastisson* down with a thwack. "It doesn't matter," he said. His face changed then; it was as if a hand had been passed over sand, smoothing it out, erasing any marks that had been visible before. He smiled: that too-quick smile that did not reach his eyes. Now Conor was hiding something from him. "I ought to have paid Beck already. I was being stubborn. I didn't want him to think he could threaten the money out of me. Perhaps at another time, but—" He shook his head. "I don't like it, but there it is. I'll get him paid, and we can forget about this."

"Pay him how, Con?" Kel asked, quietly. "You just said you didn't have the gold."

"I said I couldn't lay my hands on it easily, not that I couldn't get it at all." Conor waved an airy hand; the light from the window caught the sapphire in his signet ring and sparked. "Now stop worrying about it. It will make you heal more slowly, and I can't have that. I need my Sword Catcher back. For the past three days, you've been very boring indeed."

"I'm sure I haven't," said Kel. His mind was whirling. He felt as if he had started out on a long journey only to be told it was over before he had reached the Narrow Pass. He knew he had not imagined the look on Conor's face, the bitterness in his voice. But the pain was radiating through his body, and it was difficult to think.

"Kellian, I have it on good authority that for the past seventy-two hours you've been doing an excellent imitation of a landed trout. I was so bored I had to invent a new game with Falconet. I call it 'indoor archery.' You'd like it."

"It really doesn't sound like I would. I like the indoors, and archery, but I don't feel combining the two would be wise."

"You know what is no fun at all? Wisdom," Conor observed. "How often have you been invited out for a boisterous night of wisdom? Speaking of boisterous fun—a drink before I call the good doctor in to look at you?" Conor asked, lifting the bottle of *pastisson.* "Though I should warn you, Gasquet advises against mixing morphea and alcohol."

"Then I shall certainly do so," Kel said, and watched, half lost in thought, as Conor poured him a glass of cloudy green liquor with a hand that shook so imperceptibly he did not think anyone else would have noticed it at all.

Aram was different from any other land. In other lands, to use magic was to be preyed upon by the Sorcerer-Kings, seeking ever more power to feed their Source-Stones. But in Aram the people were free to use *gematry* to improve their lot. The Queen had no desire to appropriate that magic, and used her own power only to enrich the land. Every market day, the people of Aram could present themselves before the palace, and the Queen would come out and with spells and *gematry* would heal many of the sick. It was not long before the folk of Aram came to love their Queen as a kind and just ruler.

— *Tales of the Sorcerer-Kings,* Laocantus Aurus Iovit III

CHAPTER TEN

Five hundred years past, there had been an outbreak of the Scarlet Plague in Castellane; nearly a third of the population had died. As a physician, Lin had been required to learn about it. The bodies had been burned, as had been the custom, and the choking smoke that resulted had sickened more, until citizens were dropping in the streets.

The King at the time, Valis Aurelian, had ordered the end of corpse burning. Instead, plague pits were dug, and the bodies buried in them and covered with quicklime. Not long after, the plague had ended—though Lin wondered if it hadn't simply worn itself out as epidemics were wont to do. Regardless, Valis got the credit—and his face permanently on the ten-crown coin—and the city got a number of spaces on which it was forbidden to build, as the Law prohibited construction on grave sites. Earth covered the bodies, flowers and trees were planted there, and the houses that faced these green spaces became desirable residences.

And then there was the Black Mansion.

It had been there as long as anyone could remember, rising at the north end of Scarlet Square (which, despite its name, was not scarlet at all, but thick with greenery)—a great house built of smooth black stone with a domed roof, two great terraces on either side, and narrow vertical windows. It seemed to absorb light rather than reflect it. Everyone in Castellane was familiar with the mansion, with its red door like a drop of blood, and they knew who lived there—who had always, it seemed, lived there.

The Ragpicker King.

Lin's pulse sped up as she and Ji-An dismounted the carriage and approached the dark stone house. She had given up any thought of running away or even protesting. She did not like being misled, but she was terribly curious. Everyone in Castellane, she suspected, was curious about what lay behind the walls of the Black Mansion, just as they were curious about the interior of Marivent. How strange, to see inside both structures within the span of three days. She lightly touched the brooch at her shoulder. How strange life had been recently, in every way.

Two guards, dressed in black, stood on either side of the mansion's great front door. They nodded to Ji-An as she ascended, with Lin beside her. A bronze knocker in the shape of a magpie graced the door, but Ji-An did not use it. Lifting her necklace over her head, she used her pendant as a key and ushered them both inside.

Inside, the mansion was less dark than Lin would have expected. The interior walls were polished wood, lit by hanging carcel lamps. A long corridor stretched ahead of them, like a tunnel leading into the heart of a mountain. It was carpeted with thick rugs in deep jewel colors, muffling the sounds of their feet as they walked.

"What do you know of the Ragpicker King?" asked Ji-An as they followed the winding corridor. Doors led off it on either side, all of them closed. Lin could not help but wonder what was behind them.

"What everyone knows, I imagine. That he is a criminal mastermind, of sorts."

Ji-An frowned. "He doesn't like that word, so I wouldn't use it around him."

"What, *criminal*?" Lin wondered how else he might describe himself. A guildmaster of felons? A tycoon of the illicit?

"Oh, no, he doesn't mind *that* at all. But he does object to being called a mastermind. He feels it has the air of pretense."

They had reached a massive room, with glass skylights built into the sloped ceiling. The floor was black marble, and a wide channel, running with water, had been cut through the center. There was no way past save a wooden bridge that arched above the man-made river. Ji-An led the way over, flicking the hem of her robe away from the edges. "If you can avoid it," she said, "do not look down."

Lin couldn't help herself. As she crossed the bridge, she heard a noise—a dank, sucking noise, as of something sliding beneath the water—and looked down.

The surrounding black marble lent the indoor river an opaque quality, but as Lin watched, she saw that the water was not still. It moved, without the eddies or currents of a tide. Shadows darker than its darkness slid noiselessly beneath the surface. One glided close to the bridge, and Lin jumped as a bumpy crest, dotted with a single yellow eye, broke the surface.

Crocodile.

She shuddered, and hoped Ji-An hadn't noticed. She was glad to reach the other side of the bridge and hop down onto the marble bank. Glancing back as they moved away, she saw only flat black water, stirred here and there by peculiar currents.

Distracted, Lin barely noticed as they crossed into a solarium: a glassed-in tangle of hothouse flowers. They had these at the Palace, too; Mayesh had told her of them. In such a place, one could make the delicate plants that did not grow in Castellane's salty earth flourish. Long ago, the Empire had discovered that one could not graze animals on the alluvial plain surrounding their precious harbor; crops like wheat and oats did not grow within the circle of the mountains. So Castellane became a garden of trade. If they could not grow crops, they would grow the money to buy them. They traded roads for wheat, tallships for barley and millet; their apples were banks, their peaches casques of gold.

Yet here, the Ragpicker King had re-created a more temperate climate, redolent of white flowers. Paths of crushed stone wound through the garden, with its roof of glass; benches were set at intervals. Lin tried to imagine the lanky, black-clad form of the Ragpicker King, relaxed on a bench, enjoying his carefully tended hothouse.

She failed.

"Wait here," said Ji-An. "I have an errand to run; I will return to escort you when Andr—when *he* is ready to see you."

"I don't—" Lin began, but Ji-An was already gone, slipping noiselessly through the greenery.

Well, really, Lin thought. It was one thing to be snatched from the market under false pretenses and another to be made to wait around afterward. The Ragpicker King could at least behave as if kidnapping her was a *priority*.

Annoyed, she wandered among the flowers for a time, naming off the ones she knew from botanist's guides. Camellias from Zipangu grew beside the paths, white heads nodding like a group of old men in harmonious agreement. There were blue passionflowers from Marakand, and nodding Hindish poppies, the sap of which could be extracted to create morphea.

After what seemed like an hour, she lost patience. She could not remain here forever. She had patients to see in the afternoon, and Mariam would worry if she did not return for hours.

She slipped out the door of the solarium. She did her best to point herself back in the direction she'd come, but soon found herself in an unfamiliar room. It was large, with a massive fireplace and a great deal of shabby but comfortable-looking furniture—deep sofas and wing chairs whose brocade was fraying along the arms, not at all the sort of thing she'd have expected to find in the home of the Ragpicker King. The ceiling above disappeared into shadow—the famous dome of the Black Mansion? A pendant lamp hung from it on a long metal chain, swaying slightly above her head.

Shelves along the walls held oddments and antiquities: a brass and turquoise honey pot, probably Marakandi in origin. A map written in Malgasi. A jade statue of Lavara, Goddess of thieves, gamblers, and the underworld. And—she saw with some surprise—a silver incantation bowl of Ashkari workmanship. She picked it up, curious: Indeed, engraved around the rim were words in Ashkar. ZOWASAT MUGHA TSEAT IN-BENJUDAHU PAWWU HI'WATI. *Designated is this bowl for the sealing of the house of Benjudah.*

In the Sault, engraved bowls and tablets were often buried at the threshold of a home, to protect the family within from bad luck and evil spirits. Seeing such a bowl here, a holy item scattered among a collection of trinkets, made the hair rise on Lin's arms. And it wasn't as if Benjudah was an ordinary Ashkari name. Only one family bore it—the family of the Exilarch, the Prince of the Ashkar.

"Two long tons of black powder." A man's voice, gruff and irritable and very nearby, broke into her thoughts. "You're sure you can manage it?"

"Calm yourself, Ciprian." The second voice was smooth, low, peculiarly devoid of any identifiable accent. "Of course I can manage it. Though I am tempted to ask why you need quite such a large amount of explosives."

Lin set the bowl down hastily, her hands shaking slightly. She was sure this was a conversation she was not meant to overhear. Two long tons of black powder could blow a city block into the sky. She had only heard of black powder being used to blast holes through rock or to destroy ships. During sea battles, flaming bags of it would be catapulted onto enemy decks, shattering the hulls when they exploded. She had treated sailors who had old burns from the stuff. Was a naval army being supplied? Or, more likely, a band of pirates?

"Because I need to blow something sky-high. Why else?"

"As long as it isn't a someone."

"Not at all. A fleet of ships—actually, how many ships are in a fleet? Let's call it *several* ships," came the reply, just as two men walked into the room where Lin was standing.

She recognized the Ragpicker King immediately. Tall and thin, with legs like the long black spokes of carriage wheels. He wore his customary black, his clothes plain but elegantly cut in a way that would be sure to intrigue Mariam.

With him was a young man with dark-red hair. (Lin was always glad to see another redhead, though the young man's skin was the olive tone of most Castellani, not pale like her own.) His clothes were plain broadcloth, his eyes narrow and black. He was still speaking, a dark intensity underlying his words. "I've told you no one will be harmed," he said. "I've planned it quite carefully—"

Lin had not moved. She stood still, hands clasped, near the shelves of curiosities. Perhaps she ought to have ducked behind a sofa, but it was certainly too late for that now. The Ragpicker King had seen her. His black eyebrows lifted, as did the corners of his mouth.

"Ciprian," he interrupted, "we have company."

The red-haired man paused mid-gesture. For a moment, both men stared at Lin.

Lin cleared her throat. "Ji-An brought me," she said. This was mostly true. Ji-An had brought her to the Black Mansion, if not to this particular room. "But she had an errand to do."

"Probably had to kill someone," said Ciprian, and shrugged when the Ragpicker King gave him a dark look. "What? She's very good at it."

Lin thought of Ji-An's cool eyes and graceful movements and supposed she was not surprised. Someone like Ji-An would clearly do more than simply fetch wayward physicians for the Ragpicker King.

"So you're the physician," the Ragpicker King said.

"Not feeling well, Andreyen?" Ciprian inquired.

"A touch of gout," said his companion, looking not at Ciprian but at Lin, the same amusement playing around his mouth. So it seemed clear he had a name—Andreyen—but Lin could not imagine thinking of him that way. Even up close, he seemed more like a child's tale than a living man. A figure one might follow down a dark road, only to discover he had vanished where the street turned. A golem made of clay and shadows, with bright-burning eyes.

"Ciprian, I'll notify you when your shipment arrives. And by the way, I can guess who those several ships belong to."

Ciprian grinned ferociously. "I'm sure you can." As he left the room, he passed Lin, his shoulder nearly bumping hers. He paused for a moment. He had the sort of gaze that seemed to weigh heavily, Lin thought, like a too-familiar hand on the shoulder. "You're awfully pretty to be a doctor," he said. "Or to be Ashkar, for that matter. Quite a waste, all those girls locked up in the Sault—"

"*Ciprian.*" There was a sharp warning in the Ragpicker King's voice, and the amusement had left his face. "Go."

"Only a jest." Ciprian shrugged, dismissing Lin as easily as he'd noticed her. She waited until his footsteps had faded from earshot before turning to the Ragpicker King.

"Do you really have gout?"

"No." He threw himself into a worn armchair. She wondered how old he was. Thirty, she'd guess, though he had the sort of face that seemed ageless. "And I didn't call you here because I need a physician, Lin Caster, though I am glad to see you've come. I wasn't sure Ji-An could convince you."

"Because you're a criminal?" Lin said. Ji-An had said he didn't mind the word, so why not be honest?

"No, because I've been told she has an off-putting manner— though I've not noticed it myself."

"She told me you saved her life," Lin said. "Perhaps she's nicer to you."

"She isn't, and I wouldn't like it if she was," he said. "So you're the physician who healed Kel Saren?"

"How did you know that?"

He spread his hands wide. They were very long and pale, like the legs of a white spider. "Knowing things that happen in Castellane is a significant part of my occupation. Ji-An had told me she did not think Kel would live, that his injuries were too great for him to survive. What I want to know is—did you use *that* to heal him?"

"Use what?" Lin said, though a part of her guessed what he would say.

"That brooch." He pointed with a languid hand at her shoulder. "Or, to be more specific, the stone inside it."

Her hand flew to her shoulder. "It's only a bit of quartz."

"No." He pushed his chair back until the front two legs came off the ground. "That is what the jeweler in the market told you. But it is not the case."

"How do you know—"

"He works for me," said Andreyen. "He identified the stone as soon as you brought it to him, and sent a messenger to the Black Mansion. Ji-An went to fetch you."

Lin could feel her cheeks begin to heat. There was nothing she hated more than the feeling she had been manipulated.

"I have eyes in the Palace," he went on. "I knew you had healed Kel; that you *also* had a Source-Stone, I did not know. I assumed you knew what it was. That you used it in your medicine. Though—" He let the chair fall back down with a thump. "You are also Ashkar. This sort of magic is forbidden to you. It is not *gematry*; it is the very opposite of that. Source-Stones were invented by King Suleman, the enemy of the Goddess."

"You know a great deal about our beliefs," said Lin tightly.

"I find them interesting," he said. "It is because of your Goddess, the lady Adassa, that there is no more magic in the world— save the low magic your people practice. I have always felt that if we were to find our way back to High Magic, it would be through *gematry*. There is some key there that will unlock the door. But what you have there—the Arkhe, the stone—that is a remnant of High

Magic. It holds a piece of the world before the Sundering." He narrowed his jade-green eyes. "So how did an Ashkari girl get hold of such an object, as priceless as it is forbidden?"

Lin folded her arms across her chest. She was beginning to feel the same way she did when the Maharam questioned her—a certain rebellious instinct to snap, to push back rather than answer. But this was the Ragpicker King, she reminded herself. As casual as his current demeanor was, that did not mean he was not dangerous.

She had seen a crocodile attack a seal in the harbor once; the water had been still and smooth as glass until the moment it broke suddenly into a boiling froth of thrashing and blood. She did not think it would be wise to lie to the Ragpicker King. One did not become the Ragpicker King without an excellent instinct for when others were prevaricating.

"Anton Petrov," she said, and told the story quickly: that he had been her patient, that he had slipped the stone inside her bag, that she feared he was dead. That she had suspected he had known he was going to die.

"Anton Petrov," he said, with some amusement. "I would almost think you were mocking me with a tale, but I can tell a liar." He seemed to note her puzzled look, and smiled. "*Petrov*," he said, "in the language of Nyenschantz, means 'stone.'"

"I think," Lin said slowly, "that he believed himself to be its guardian, in some way." She shook her head. "I do not know why you have told me all this," she said. "You want the stone. I would have given it to you the moment you asked. I will give it to you now."

"You would do that?" The Ragpicker King's eyes were pins of green ice, holding her in place. "So easily?"

"I am not a fool," Lin said.

Something changed then in his face; he was up on his feet before she could say another word. "Keep the brooch. And come with me," he said, and stalked out of the room.

Lin had to hurry to keep up with his long stride. They made

their way through another series of corridors, these tiled in blue, black, and silver, reminiscent of a night sky. She was relieved that they did not again pass through to the grand chamber with its dark interior river.

They reached a half-open door through which a pale smoke drifted. There was an acrid tang to it, like the scent of burning leaves. The Ragpicker King stiff-armed the door open and gestured for Lin to enter the room ahead of him.

Inside, to Lin's surprise, was a laboratory. It was not large, but it was cluttered. A large polished wood worktable was covered with the instruments of science: phials of multicolored liquids, bronze alembics (Lin had seen such things before in the market, where perfumers showed off the distillation of rose petals into attar), tangles of copper and glass tubing, and a mortar and pestle, still filled with half-pulverized dried leaves. An athanor smoldered away in the corner, releasing a pleasant heat.

A number of tall wooden stools surrounded the central table. Seated upon one of them, long legs dangling, was a young man with curling blond hair, in dark clothes like a student's. He was scribbling away with great haste in a notebook propped on his lap.

Lin felt a stab of longing. In contrast, her workshop in the kitchen of the Women's House seemed makeshift and ineffectual. What she could do with the equipment here, the compounds and cataplasms that would be at her fingertips—

Without looking up, the young man pointed at a retort distilling a pale-green liquid into a large glass vessel. "I've managed to dilute the *Atropa belladonna*," he said, "but the concern remains that, for the solution to work, the key ingredient must be present in an amount that would surely prove fatal."

"Belladonna," said Lin. "Isn't that deadly nightshade?"

The young man looked up. He was irrationally pretty, with delicate features and dark-blue eyes. He blinked for a moment at Lin before smiling pleasantly, as if she were someone whose visit he had been anticipating.

"It is, yes," he said. "I suppose I'm used to using the more scientific name. The Academie insists on it." He set his notebook down on the table. "I'm Merren," he added. "Merren Asper."

Asper, Lin wondered. Like Alys Asper, who owned the Caravel? She had provided physical examinations to a number of the courtesans there; Alys made sure they stayed healthy.

"This is Lin Caster, an Askar physician," said the Ragpicker King. He had moved behind Merren, all long dark limbs in motion, like a shadow cast at noon. He had opened a drawer and was rummaging around in it.

Merren brightened. "The Ashkar are master herbalists," he said. "You must have a laboratory like this in the Sault—" he gestured around the room—"or more than one, I suppose."

"There is one," Lin said. "Though I am not allowed to use it."

"Why not?"

"Because I'm a woman," said Lin, and noticed the Ragpicker King glance over at her, briefly.

"Are you a good physician?" Merren asked, looking at her earnestly.

You are *the best in the Sault.* She pushed the intrusive thought of the Prince away and said, "Yes."

"Then that's stupid." Merren picked up his notebook. He did not seem curious, Lin noted, as to why Andreyen had brought her into what was clearly his workshop; nor did he seem to wonder why the Ragpicker King was muttering to himself as he went through a drawer of crumpled papers. Seeming to locate the one he wanted at last, Andreyen gestured for Lin to join him as he spread the paper out, smoothing it across an uncluttered section of the worktable.

"Look at this," he said as Lin joined him. "Do you recognize anything familiar about these drawings?"

Lin leaned in closer, though not to the Ragpicker King. He still frightened her, even in this incongruous setting. On the paper were a series of diagrams, the words written in Callatian, the language of the Empire. Her knowledge of it was limited to medical terms, but it did not matter: The drawings were what leaped out at her. They were sketches of a stone nearly identical to the one Petrov had given her—down to the swirl of smoke within it forming suggestions of *gematry* words and numbers.

She touched the paper lightly. "Is this from before the Sundering?"

"It is a copy of a few pages from a very old book. The works of the scholar Qasmuna."

Lin shook her head; she didn't recognize the name.

"She wrote them just after the great wars," said the Ragpicker King. "She had seen magic leave the world and sought a way to bring it back. She believed that if these vessels of power could be reawakened, magic could be done again."

"And that would be a good thing? For magic to be done again?" Lin said in a low voice.

"You need not fear a return of the Sorcerer-Kings," said Andreyen. "It is only one Source-Stone. The Word is still gone from the world—the unknowable name of Power. Without it, magic will remain limited."

"Limited to you?"

He only smiled.

"There's more of this?" Lin indicated the pages.

"In theory. Most copies of the book were destroyed in the purge after the Sundering. Qasmuna herself was put to death. I've been looking for an edition for years." His keen gaze swept over her. "Just as I've been looking for a Source-Stone."

"Then why don't you want mine?"

"Because I do not want to learn magic myself," said the Ragpicker King. "I have no aptitude. You clearly have aptitude. I believe the stone helped you heal Kel Saren."

Lin saw Merren glance at her, a flicker of curious blue.

"I told you," Lin said. "I did not use it."

"I believe that is what you think," said Andreyen. "But a Source-Stone seeks a hand that will wield it."

Lin thought of the stab of pain she'd felt while healing Kel. The burn on her skin—still there, even now—when she'd returned home. She'd had no conscious sense of using the stone, no sense of a strange power granted. And yet . . .

"And I," said the Ragpicker King, "seek a hand that will wield such a stone."

"A hand that will wield it," Lin said slowly. "Are you saying— You want me to learn magic, and perhaps perform it, in your service?"

The Ragpicker King flexed his long, white hands. "Yes."

"Oh." Lin had been half braced for this moment—the one where he finally told her what he wanted from her—but now that it had come, she found herself stammering. "I don't—I would prefer not to be in your employment. It's nothing personal," she added. "But—you are who you are."

Merren looked up from his notebook. "That was quite diplomatic," he said. "We are all who we are, after all. Ji-An is an assassin, I am a poisoner, and Andreyen dabbles in a bit of everything, as long as it's illegal."

"You are more than a poisoner, Merren, you are a scientist," said the Ragpicker King. "As for you, Lin Caster, I am not asking you to do me a favor with no recompense. I can offer you the use of the laboratory here, since you cannot use the equipment in the Sault—"

"And what about me?" Merren inquired, looking alarmed. "I thought this was my laboratory."

"You would have to share, Merren. It will be good for your character."

"No—Sieur Asper, that's all right." Regret lay like a stone in Lin's chest, but she knew even entertaining the offer was foolish. This was not her world, not her people. She did not belong in the Black Mansion, but within the walls of the Sault or at the bedsides of her patients. "I'm afraid I shouldn't."

"*Shouldn't*," said the Ragpicker King, as if it were a word he found distasteful. "It is your choice, of course. I feel you could do good work here. Qasmuna was not just a scholar, you know. She was a physician. She wished to return magic to the world that it might be used for healing the sick."

Oh. Lin said nothing aloud, but she was sure the Ragpicker King could see the change in her expression. A sort of hunger flared in her, for more than just the laboratory now. For the chance, however small—

"I am not saying it will be easy," said the Ragpicker King. "It took me years even to find these copied pages of Qasmuna's work. But there is one place I've never had access to in my search—the library of the Shulamat. In your Sault." He spread his hands wide. "You might take a look there."

Take a look? Lin almost told him: *That will be impossible, books on magic are restricted, forbidden, unless they are lessons in* gematry. *And even those can only be studied in the Shulamat itself, not taken from the building, or outside the walls of the Sault.*

Instead, she said, "I suppose I could try."

The Ragpicker King clapped his hands together. "Excellent," he said, and in that moment Lin knew: He had never had any doubt that she would agree.

In the end, the Ragpicker King summoned Ji-An to escort Lin from the Black Mansion, assuring her that she would soon enough learn the layout of the place. The labyrinth of corridors were meant to confound any intruder who might find their way inside.

Ji-An gave Lin a sour look before walking her briskly to the front door. "I told you to stay put in the solarium," she said crossly, as the door swung open. "I hope you are not going to be troublesome."

"I don't plan to be." Lin was already out the door. Outside, the afternoon light was dark gold; birds sang in the boughs of the trees that lined Scarlet Square. She felt as if she had passed into the underworld and returned to a city unchanged.

Halfway down the steps, she turned, looking up at Ji-An, who was standing in the doorway of the mansion, framed by scarlet. "Is he a good man?" Lin asked. "Or a bad one?"

Ji-An frowned. "Who? Andreyen? He does what he says he will do. If he says he will kill you, he will kill you. If he says he will protect you, he will protect you." She shrugged. "To me that is a good man. Perhaps others might feel differently."

In Aram, Suleman was profuse with his compliments, telling Adassa he had never seen such a rich land, or such a wise healer and Queen as she was. Even as he spoke his honeyed words, he prevailed upon Adassa to visit him in his own kingdom of Darat, so that she could see all that also might be hers if she agreed to marry him.

She was at first reluctant to go. Her people were anxious at the thought of her leaving, for though Aram was at peace it was surrounded by lands deep in strife. It was Judah Makabi who convinced Adassa, saying, "Be not ignorant of the designs of others, lest you be defeated."

At his insistence, she wore around her neck a talisman of *gematry*, meant to protect her against ill intent.

While in Darat, Adassa was shown many wonders that had been accomplished through the use of magic. Great marble castles higher than the tower of Balal, which was the pride of Aram. There were dazzling rivers of fire that burned night and day, illuminating the sky. Phoenixes wandered the grounds of the palace, shedding sparks like fireflies.

Yet often Adassa was aware of the hard gaze of Suleman upon her. Though he told her he watched her with the eyes of love, she was suspicious. At night when she retired to her chambers, she found that a carafe of water had been placed for her beside her bed; when she gave some of the water to one of the palace cats, the creature was rendered instantly unconscious. Realizing that Suleman meant to drug her, Adassa made her excuses the next day and returned to her kingdom. With a heavy heart, she went to Makabi and asked of him that he journey unto Darat and spy on Suleman to determine his plans, and she laid upon him the guise of a raven that he might travel unseen.

—*Tales of the Sorcerer-Kings*, Laocantus Aurus Iovit III

CHAPTER ELEVEN

Kel had been injured before, of course. In his line of work, it would have been strange if he hadn't. But he had not come so near death before, nor spent so much time abed, drugged with morphea and the peculiar dreams it gave him. The first time he felt strong enough to rise from his bed and traverse the room, he was horrified. His legs felt limp as wet paper. He fell immediately, cracking his knees on the stone floor.

Conor had come quickly to help him up while Delfina, who had arrived to change the bed linens, shrieked and fled the room. She returned—to Kel's annoyance—with Legate Jolivet and a stone-faced Queen Lilibet. The Queen was infuriated that Kel had been attacked at all: Didn't the criminals of Castellane know better than to ambush nobility from the Hill? What were things coming to, and to that end, how long would the Sword Catcher be useless to them? Should Conor cancel the next fortnight's public appearances? When would the Sword Catcher be well again, if ever?

Thanks to the Gods, Jolivet was there. He explained that the Sword Catcher was in excellent physical shape (good news to Kel, who did not feel it) and that there was no reason to imagine he would not make a swift and full recovery. Kel should avoid lying in bed any longer, but take moderate exercise, increasing his effort each day until he felt strong enough for his training to resume as usual. He should also eat a healthful diet of meat and bread, not too many greens, and no alcohol.

Kel, who was on his feet by this point and able to limp to the tepidarium and back, expected Conor to fight this decree— especially the ban on drinking. But Conor only nodded thoughtfully and said he was sure Jolivet knew best: something Kel was fairly sure Conor had never said before in his life. Even Jolivet seemed startled.

But perhaps he should not be too astonished, Kel thought later, as he dressed slowly, hands shaking while he attempted to do up his buttons. Conor had been distracted since Kel had told him of Prosper Beck's demands. Busy wheedling the Treasury for the money? Borrowing it from Falconet? Or more likely, borrowing a little here and a little there to avoid facing down Cazalet? Whatever his plan, he was absent from the Castel Mitat for long stretches during the days, and Kel—for the first time in years—was thrown upon his own company.

Strengthen yourself, Jolivet had said, so Kel began by walking. He was half ashamed at how slowly he paced the mosaic-tiled paths of the Palace gardens, past flowering vines of honeysuckle, under trees heavy with lemons and figs. His chest ached—a deep hurt that made itself known when he breathed or moved too quickly.

He stopped taking the morphea. His body missed it most the first night without it, when he turned restlessly upon his bed, unable to get to sleep. But each day the craving faded, and each day he could walk farther, faster.

He limped through the Night Garden, amid the tightly curled green buds of plants that bloomed only after sunset. He circled the Carcel—the windowless, fortified stone sanctuary where the royal family was hidden in the event of an attack on the Palace. It had not to Kel's knowledge been used in at least a century, and ivy grew thick over the barred iron door.

As there were no prisoners in the Trick, the Castelguards let him climb the winding spiral staircase until he reached the top, where a narrow aisle bisected two rows of empty cells, their Sunderglass doors standing open. He pushed past the pain of it, climbing the stairs once, twice, five times, until he could taste blood in his mouth.

He wandered the cliff paths, where the Hill itself fell away to the ocean, the sea below gray and heaving as a whale's back. The cliff paths were studded with follies—fanciful structures of white plaster made to resemble miniature versions of temples and towers, farmhouses and castles. They contained cushioned benches and were meant to provide rest and shelter for those delicate souls who found the cliff path a wearying trek.

Sometimes on his travels Kel would catch wisps of gossip as servants or guardsmen went by, paying him no attention. Most of it centered on romantic entanglements among those who served the great Houses on the Hill; some had to do with the Palace, or even with Conor. There was no gossip about debts, Crawlers, or cousins of the Prince who might have been recently injured, however. If anyone wondered about Kel's peripatetic ways, he heard nothing about it.

He never saw the King, though smoke spilled sometimes from the high windows of the Star Tower. On occasion, he saw the Queen, usually directing the staff or the gardeners. Once, on his way down the stairs of the Star Tower, he overheard her speaking with Bensimon and Jolivet.

"Old Gremont won't last much longer," Lilibet was saying, "and his wife is not interested in administering a Charter. That son of his must be fetched back from Taprobana lest the family's chair become the object of an internecine struggle."

"Artal Gremont is a monster," Bensimon growled, and then Jolivet cut in, and the argument turned in another direction. Kel went on his way down the stairs, filing away the information to relay to Conor later as a piece of mildly interesting gossip. Whatever Artal

Gremont had done, it was bad enough that Bensimon disliked the idea of him returning, even a decade later.

The next afternoon, on a whim, Kel cut through the Queen's Garden on his way to the stables, meaning to visit Asti. He was passing the reflecting pool when he heard voices, muffled by the high hedges that surrounded the garden. One voice was a woman's; the other was Conor's. He was speaking Sarthian. "*Sti acordi dovarìan 'ndar ben*," Kel heard him say. *Those arrangements should be suitable.*

A moment later, his voice faded. Kel wondered what arrangements Conor was describing, but then, it was Conor's business, and Kel had been walking for hours now. Life in the Palace was a sort of wheel, Kel thought, as he turned his steps toward the Castel Mitat; it went on and on in the same rotations, cutting the same paths of habit and memory into the earth. The fact that he had nearly died was not even a stone in the road. It mattered only to him; it had changed no one but him. In that, he was alone.

Lin was dreaming.

In the dream she knew she was asleep, and that what she saw was not real. She stood upon a high stone tower, whose top was a bare expanse of stone. Mountains rose as black shadows in the distance; the sky was the color of charcoal and blood, the wounded eye of destruction.

In minutes, the world would cease to be.

A man appeared at the edge of the tower's roof. She knew he had not climbed its sheer sides to reach her. Magic had carried him aloft: For he was the Sorcerer-King Suleman, and until today, there had been no greater power than his in all the world.

As he walked toward her, his steps light as a cat's, flames sparked among the folds of his cloak. The wind that blew from the burning mountains lifted his black hair. Lin knew of course of Suleman. The lover of Adassa. Her betrayer. She had never understood why the Goddess had loved him; he had always sounded to her fearful in his power, terrible in his rage. And yet he was beautiful—beautiful as fire and destructive things were beautiful. It was a cruel sort of beauty, but it stirred a fierce longing in her. She rose and turned toward him; she was holding out her hands—

Lin sat bolt upright, her heart hammering, her skin slicked with sweat. She folded her hands over her chest, half incredulous. Had she woken herself out of the dream? Perhaps she had, for she knew how the story ended. She had been dreaming of the last moments before the Sundering. The last moments before Adassa's death.

In minutes, the world would cease to be.

Lin pushed her damp hair back, rising from her bed to pad into the main room of the house, where she had thrown her cloak over the back of a chair. She felt through its folds until she found the hard shape of the brooch. She unpinned it, running her fingers over the stone. In the dim moonlight, it was the color of milk. Its smooth, cool surface calmed the beating of her heart.

You give me strange dreams, she thought, gazing at the stone. *Dreams of the past. Her past.*

Adassa had been a Queen among Sorcerer-Kings. She, too, would have possessed a Source-Stone.

What if—?

A low rap on the front door snapped Lin out of her reverie. Two raps, followed by a pause, then a third rap.

Mariam.

Lin hurried to the door. It was late for Mariam to be awake—she usually tired before First Watch. What if she had been taken ill in the night? But then, surely, it would be Chana at the door, demanding Lin's presence at the House of Women. But when Lin swung the door open, it was only Mariam on her front steps,

In the moonlight, Mariam's face was stark pallor and shadow, the hollows under her cheekbones like bruises. But she was grinning, her eyes bright. "Oh, dear, I woke you up," she said, sounding unrepentant. "I meant to come earlier, but I had to wait for Chana to fall asleep, otherwise she would have given me endless trouble for going out at night. '*You need your rest, Mariam,*'" she said, in a passable imitation of Chana's commanding tones.

"Well, you *do*," Lin said, but she couldn't help smiling. "All right—what is it? Gossip? Galena's run off with one of the *malbushim*?"

"*Much* more important than that," said Mariam, with an air of injured dignity. "You still want to see your patient, the Prince's cousin, again, don't you?"

Lin tightened her hand around the brooch she was holding. "Yes, of course, but—"

"What if I told you I had a solution to your problem?" said Mariam. "Someone willing to help you get into the Palace? Someone who knows when the Prince will be busy?"

"Mariam, how could you possibly—"

"Walk with me to the gates tomorrow morning," Mariam said. "There will be a carriage waiting. You'll see then." As she pulled her shawl around her shoulders, she was beaming. "You trust me, don't you?"

Looking out over the ocean, Kel could see the heat shimmer atop the water like a transparent veil. It would be boiling hot down in the city. Here on the Hill it was cooler, though the flowers hung limply on their vines and the peacocks lay panting in the grass.

It was the second week of his recovery, and Kel had spent the morning exploring the gardens, climbing up and down various sets of steps. He was reminded of his boyhood, when every nook and cranny of Marivent had seemed a place to have a potential adventure with Conor. They had been bandits in the courtyards, and Sorcerer-Kings in the towers; they had dueled at the top of the Star Tower, from which one could see the sun rise over the Narrow Pass.

He was leaving the Star Tower, his tunic wet with sweat, his chest aching, when he found Queen Lilibet waiting for him in the Queen's Garden. Today she wore a pale celadon green—a color that made Kel think of a single drop of green poison dissolving in milk. Bracelets of green sapphire circled her wrists, and a silver band around her forehead held a single emerald between her eyes.

"Sword Catcher," she said, as he crossed the grass. So she was not going to pretend she had not been awaiting his departure from the tower. She must know, as he did, that Conor was attending a meeting at the Alleyne estate, and thought it was an excellent time to corner Kel alone. "A word with you."

As if he had a choice. Kel came closer to the Queen, inclining his head.

"Mayesh has told me," she said, without preamble, "that you were attacked in an unsavory part of the city, after visiting a courtesan."

"Yes," Kel said, keeping his tone courteous. "That is true."

"I am not a fool," said the Queen. "I am under no illusion as to the sort of amusements my son prefers. But you are meant to accompany him when he pursues those amusements. Not to pursue them yourself."

"The Prince had sent me away that evening—"

"It does not matter what he says," Lilibet said sharply. "You cannot be careless with yourself, Kel Saren. You are Palace property. It is not your purpose to die when you are not defending my son." She turned her head to look toward the Castel Mitat. Her hair was matte black, darker than Conor's, the result of a skillful application of dye. "He cannot survive without you."

Kel felt a jolt of surprise. "But he will have to," he said, "if I die for him."

"Then at least he will know your last thought was of him."

Kel did not see how that mattered much. "When he becomes King—"

"Then he will take the Lion Ring and throw it into the sea," said Lilibet. "After that, Aigon will protect him. When a God takes over for you, Kel Saren, then you can lay down your duty. Do you understand?"

Kel was not sure he did. "I will be more careful," he said. "My first thought is always of Conor. Your Highness."

The Queen gave him a hard look before she walked away—one that, Kel sensed, indicated that she suspected there was something he was not telling her. Which was true enough.

It had been an odd conversation. Kel felt uneasy as he walked slowly back toward the Castel Mitat. What had Lilibet meant, that Conor could not survive without him? She did not know the danger Conor was in from Prosper Beck. Was there some *other* danger she dreaded, something of which Kel was unaware?

His musings were cut short by Delfina, hurrying toward him across the Palace lawns. She was bright red under her mobcap, having apparently searched for him all over the grounds. Jolivet was waiting in the Prince's rooms, she said; he wanted to see Kel immediately. Also, she added in an accusatory fashion, the heat had aggravated her skin condition, and she was going to see Gasquet.

"He'll put leeches on you," Kel warned as she hurried off, but she ignored him. He struck out for the Castel Mitat on his own, passing two of the King's old hunting hounds, asleep and snoring in the grass. "You've the right idea," he told them. "Continue as you are."

He couldn't help but wonder what it was Jolivet wanted to talk to him about. Usually if Jolivet sought him out it was about sword practice, but Kel was hardly in shape for that. Perhaps Jolivet or his squadron had learned something about the attack in the alley, in which case Kel could only hope the Legate had not discovered too much.

When he reached the rooms he shared with Conor, he braced himself to find Jolivet waiting for him, his long face glowering beneath his Arrow Squadron helmet. But there was no Jolivet there when he opened the door.

Instead, sitting on a plum-colored silk divan, was Antonetta Alleyne.

Beside her was a slim girl in a loose yellow gown, over which she wore a short capelet of saffron velvet. The hood of the capelet was drawn up, hiding her face. One of Antonetta's maids, Kel assumed.

Antonetta herself wore a robin's-egg-blue gown with puffed sleeves, the puffs secured with white ribbons. Blue powder had been combed through her curls, turning her hair a color darker than her eyes. When she saw him come in, she looked up and for a moment a look of unguarded relief crossed her face.

It was gone a moment later, leaving Kel to wonder if he'd really seen it at all.

"Oh, good," she said, clapping her hands together as if she were at the theater. "You're here. Do come in, and close the door behind you."

"How did you persuade Delfina to tell me Jolivet was here?" Kel said, closing the door but not locking it. "Perhaps she is more trusting than I thought."

"No. Just susceptible to bribery. Most people are."

Antonetta smiled, and Kel could not help but think about what had passed before his eyes as he lay dying in that alley off the Key. His vision of Antonetta, in tears. But here she was, smiling that artificial smile that drove him out of his mind. He said tightly, "But why bother bribing Delfina? I assume you're here to see Conor. He's out—"

"I'm not looking for him," Antonetta said. "In fact, he's meeting with my mother, so I knew he *wouldn't* be here." She winked at Kel. "I brought someone to see *you*." She shook her companion, who had been utterly silent since Kel had arrived, by the shoulder. "Go on, now!"

Kel thought he heard a weary sigh. The young woman beside Antonetta raised her hands and pushed back her yellow hood. Familiar dark-red hair spilled down her back as she looked wryly at Kel.

Lin Caster.

She looked younger than he recalled. He remembered careful

hands, a stern, sweet voice, strangely calming in its evenness. For the first time he noted Lin had a curious face, inquisitive green eyes and decided eyebrows. He supposed she'd always looked this way, and his fever had made him think of her as older, more authoritative. Well, the fever and the fact that she'd thrown Conor out of the room.

"Antonetta," Kel said. "What is this?"

Lin looked up. "I apologize for surprising you," she said, in that rich voice that seemed at odds with her delicate stature. "But you were my patient and I wished to see if you'd healed. Demoselle Alleyne kindly brought me into the Palace—"

"*Smuggled* you into the Palace," said Antonetta, sounding pleased with herself. "The moment I heard that you'd been hurt, and that your physician wasn't returning because she was afraid of Conor, I knew I had to do *something*—"

Lin rose to her feet. It was odd to see her dressed in yellow velvet. Kel knew she was Ashkar—she was Mayesh's granddaughter, she wore the traditional hollow circle on a chain around her throat—and yet, out of the traditional gray clothes, she looked like any Castellani maid or merchant's daughter. No wonder the dress was too big on her, he thought. It wasn't hers.

"I am not *afraid* of the Prince," said Lin. "He asked me not to return." She sounded calm, as if she were oblivious to the danger of ignoring a royal request.

Antonetta giggled at Kel's expression. "It's *such* a wonderful trick we've played on Conor," she said. "Lin did tell me he'd asked her not to come back to Marivent, but I told her not to fret about the Prince's tempers. He loves to be dramatic."

Kel rubbed his temples with his fingers. He was beginning to get a headache. "But—the two of you—how did you meet?"

"Through my dressmaker," said Antonetta.

"Your *dressmaker*?" Kel said. "How in gray hell—"

"You shouldn't swear," Antonetta said reprovingly. "My dressmaker Mariam—"

"Is a friend of mine. She is Ashkar," said Lin. "I told her I had healed the Prince's cousin, Kel Anjuman, after he'd had a bad fall from a horse. I hope that was acceptable."

Her gaze was steady. So she hadn't said anything to her friend about Crawlers; that was a relief.

Antonetta rose to her feet and came over to Kel, her satin slippers making a whispering sound against the marble floor. "Where were you injured?"

Kel made a vague gesture at his torso. "Here. Landed on a fence-post."

To Kel's surprise, Antonetta reached out to brush the front of his shirt with her fingertips. For all her artifice, the warmth of her touch, even through his shirt, was almost too real.

She looked up into his face. Her blue eyes were wide, her cheeks pink, her lips parted. She was achingly pretty. But it was all artifice, Kel thought. *She's practicing a look of fond concern, for whenever it might be useful. For Conor.* It annoyed him, and he did not want to be annoyed at Antonetta. Still, he felt it like a hot irritability under his skin.

"Demoselle Alleyne," said Lin. She had picked up her satchel, which had been concealed behind Antonetta's spreading skirts. "I must ask you to leave, that I may examine my patient."

"Oh, I don't mind staying," said Antonetta cheerfully.

"I'm going to have to ask him to strip down, you see," said Lin.

"I *have* been practicing my life drawing," said Antonetta, "and a knowledge of anatomy is useful to anyone—" She broke off as Kel shot her a dark look. "Oh, all *right*. But it will be very boring in the hallway."

Kel relented a bit. "Perhaps you can act as lookout. Let us know if anyone's coming."

Kel's eyes met Antonetta's, and for that brief moment he knew she was recalling, just as he was, the many times she had been lookout in their long-ago games. He could not have said why he was sure he knew her thoughts, only that he was, and then she was out into the hall, the door closing behind her.

Once she was gone, Lin indicated that Kel should sit down on his bed and remove his jacket and shirt. So she hadn't just been trying to get rid of Antonetta, he thought with wry amusement, doing as he was told.

He shrugged away his coat and unbuttoned the silk tunic underneath. As he slipped it off, Lin looked at him with something close to surprise.

"Sieur Anjuman," she said. "You really do look much better than you did the last time I saw you."

"I should hope so," Kel said. "I believe I was drooling blood at the time, and no doubt groaning incoherently."

"It was not as bad as all that," she said. "Would you have any objection to my examining the wounds to make sure they're healing properly?"

"None, I suppose."

She came close to him and carefully peeled away the light bandages still remaining. Kel felt oddly exposed for a moment, but it was clear Lin was utterly unaffected by the sight of a bare male chest. In fact, she regarded him with a cool impassivity that made him think of Lilibet inspecting a new set of drapes.

"You've healed well," she said, running her fingers over the scar on his side before touching the puckered wound just below his heart. "Very well. Most people would still be in bed. Have you had much pain?"

He told her that it had only been recently that he had stopped the morphea. She was horrified to hear Gasquet had kept him on the dose for so long—"I never allow my patients to take it for more than three days!"—and she unscrewed a jar of salve she had taken from her bag. The room filled with a faint, peppery scent like vetiver.

She bit her lip as she began to smear the salve liberally over not just his new wounds, but the older ones as well. "So many injuries," she said, half to herself.

"I'm very clumsy," said Kel. The salve tingled, flooding his skin with goosebumps.

"No," she said. "You're a Sword Catcher."

His hand shot out; he caught at her wrist. She looked at him in surprise, still holding the jar of salve, but arrested mid-motion.

"*What did you say?*" he hissed.

She drew in a sharp breath. "I'm sorry. I thought Mayesh might have told you that I knew."

He exhaled slowly. "No."

"I recognized your *anokham* talisman." She seemed remarkably calm, considering. "It's very old Ashkari work, not the kind of thing that is made anymore. I won't tell anyone," she added. "Consider me bound to secrecy, as my grandfather is. If I were to tell anyone, it would endanger him."

Kel released her wrist. He ought to be furious, he thought, or panicked. And yet. Perhaps it was the knowledge that the Ragpicker King was aware of his true identity, as were Merren and Ji-An. In truth, Lin's awareness of who he was did not place him on a sharper knife's edge than he already walked. Perhaps it was that some part of him trusted her. She had saved his life; it was instinctual, a sort of recognition.

"Tell me one thing," Lin said, screwing the cap back on the jar of salve. "Do you even remember how you got all those scars?"

Kel, who had been about to reach for his shirt, paused. He touched a scar on his left shoulder, a triangular welt like a dent in his skin. "This came from an assassin at the Court of Valderan, armed with a bow and arrow. And this one, here"—he indicated a spot below his rib cage—"a mercenary with a whip; he'd broken into Antonetta's eighteenth birthday party, looking for Conor. Here"—he stretched to reach his back—"an anti-monarchist with an axe who managed to infiltrate the annual inspection of the cavalry."

"And this?" She touched a patch of raised skin just over his right hip. She smelled faintly of lemons.

"Hot soup," Kel said, gravely. "Not every story is a heroic one."

"You never know," Lin replied, with equal seriousness. She finished rebandaging his injury and patted him lightly on the shoulder. "The soup could have been poisoned."

"I hadn't thought of that," said Kel, and retrieved his tunic with a laugh; it was the first time he had laughed in several days, and it felt like a weight lifted off him.

"Now," she said, looking up at him as he rebuttoned his tunic, and he expected her to give him a piece of medical advice, instruct him to use the salve each day perhaps. "I did not only come here to see if you were healing." She tucked a braid behind her ear. "The other night, when you were hurt, you said something about arrows, and then a name. *Jeanne*."

He looked at her silently.

"But you were not saying *Jeanne*, were you? It was *Ji-An*. She's the one who saved your life that night. She carried you up here—"

"She shot arrows at the Crawlers," he said, shrugging on his jacket. "Killed several. I imagine they're none too pleased about it. Lin, *how do you know all this?*"

"We both know him," she said, quietly. "The Ragpicker King. We both know him, and we both shouldn't. So I thought we could keep each other's secret." She held out a folded square of paper. "I didn't come here because he asked me to," she said, firmly. "I don't even know how he found out I was planning to come to the Palace. But when I was leaving the Sault, a little boy ran up and shoved this into my hands. '*Compliments of the Ragpicker King.*'"

Kel took the paper gingerly, as if it were coated with black powder. "What does it say?"

"I don't know," she said. "It's addressed to you—"

A babble of voices exploded in the hallway. Kel could hear Antonetta's voice, high and distressed, "Oh, *don't* go in there, Conor, please don't—"

And Conor's voice. Familiar, and annoyed. "It's *my room*, Ana," and then Lin was on her feet, and the door was open, spilling Conor and Antonetta into the room.

Conor had clearly ridden Asti from the Alleyne estate; he had on his riding clothes, including a tooled-leather coat in hunter green. The placket and cuffs gleamed with brass studs. He wore no crown, and the wind had whipped his hair into a smoky tangle.

Quickly, Kel palmed the paper, tucking it into the sleeve of his jacket. It was not particularly skillfully done, but then, Conor was not looking at him. He was looking at Lin, and for a moment there was an expression on his face—an unaffected surprise and anger—that startled Kel. Conor rarely showed the truth of what he felt, unless that feeling was amusement.

The look was gone as soon as it had appeared. Calmly, Conor drew off one of his riding gloves and said, "I thought I had made it clear what my wishes were the last time you were here, Domna Caster."

Antonetta stamped a slippered foot. "Conor, don't be angry. *I'm* the one who brought her. I thought it was important for Kel—"

"I'll be the judge of what's important." Conor tossed his riding glove onto the bed next to Kel, who raised an eyebrow at him. Conor ignored this. He also ignored Lin, who was standing with her back straight, her hands folded in front of her. Her cheeks were flaming bright red—anger or embarrassment, Kel did not know—but otherwise she had not reacted to Conor at all.

"Conor." Antonetta tugged at the sleeve of the Prince's jacket. "I heard you'd told her not to come back, but I thought you were joking. You're always so funny." She pouted up at him. "It's not as if you'd be bothered by some little Ashkari girl. Not *really.*"

Conor drew off his second glove even more slowly than the first, seeming utterly absorbed in the task. And Kel realized, with a flicker of surprise, what Antonetta's calculated show of naïveté was capable of. She had deftly disarmed Conor in a way that arguing with him could never have done. Even if he guessed her behavior to be part pretense, there was little he could do now to show his anger without looking a fool, or seeming as if he were truly concerned over the matter of Lin's presence.

Conor tossed the second glove into the corner of the room. "How true, Antonetta," he said, without a flicker of emotion. "You have such a generous heart. Such tolerance for others, regardless of their behavior." He turned to Lin. "Have you finished examining Kel? And determined that competent care has been taken of him? Or is he dying as a result of the Palace's negligence?"

Lin had picked up her satchel. "He's healing very well," she said. "But you knew that."

"Yes," said Conor, smiling coldly. "I did."

Never had Kel felt more like a piece of flotsam, pulled between shifting tides. Conor would not blame him for any of this, he was aware—he had not known Lin was banned from Marivent—yet he could think of nothing he could say to ameliorate the situation. A strange energy seemed to pass between Lin and Conor, like the charge given off by amber when it was polished with cloth. Was it just that Lin seemed not to understand the way she was meant to speak to Conor? That one showed deference to a prince? Or had something happened the night Lin had healed him, something more than her request for Conor to leave the room?

Conor turned to Antonetta, who was regarding Lin and Conor with a look of consideration on her face. Kel, not for the first or last time, wondered what she was really thinking. "I am sure you have more fashionable and interesting things to be doing, Ana," Conor said. "Go home."

Antonetta wavered but stood her ground. "I'm meant to bring Lin back to the city—"

"I'll make sure Domna Caster gets home safely," said Conor. Most would have turned smartly on their heel at his tone; Antonetta looked at Lin, who nodded, as if to say, *It's all right, go ahead.*

At the door, Antonetta paused. She looked back over her shoulder—not at Conor, Kel thought with surprise, but at him.

There was something in her eyes, a sort of guarded playfulness, that said, *I pulled this off, and we both know it.*

But there was nothing he could say aloud. She left, the door drifting closed behind her, and something in Kel wondered: Was this how it was to be now? Antonetta Alleyne, popping in and out of his life with no warning? He did not like the thought. He preferred to be able to prepare himself to see her. Jolivet had taught him for years the dangers of being caught off guard.

"So," said Kel, turning to Conor, "I take it your meeting with Lady Alleyne was cut short?"

But Conor didn't answer. He was studying Lin, who had slung her satchel over her shoulder. "I must go," she said. "I have other patients to see this afternoon." She nodded awkwardly at Conor and said, "You need not worry I will return. Kel requires nothing more from me."

"*Kel?*" Conor echoed. "What a familiar way for a citizen to address a noble."

Lin's eyes flashed. "It must be my terrible ignorance speaking. All the more reason I should leave you to your afternoon."

Conor pushed a hand through his sweat-dampened hair. "I will escort you to the North Gate, then."

"That is not necessary—"

"It is," Conor drawled. "You are Ashkar, but wearing the clothes of a Castellani. I believe those colors, those fabrics, are forbidden to you. It is unlikely anyone would notice or guess, but still a danger."

"*Conor*—" Kel began.

"I may not agree with those Laws," said Conor, "but they are the Laws." His gaze flicked over her. "You have certainly taken a great risk for our friend Kel here. A dedicated physician indeed."

Lin's face was composed, but her eyes burned with anger. "I have my own clothes in my satchel. If I could use your tepidarium, I can change—"

"Then you will be wandering about the grounds as an Ashkar, which will invite yet more questions. I suggest you change in the carriage. Before you reach the city, of course, or you'll be giving passersby an unexpected thrill."

Lin opened her mouth—then closed it again, seeming to realize there was no point in objecting. She followed Conor out into the corridor, pausing only to cast an apologetic look at Kel over her shoulder. He wondered what she was sorry for. Conspiring with Antonetta? Dropping a message from the Ragpicker King into his lap and leaving without an explanation? Still, anyone willing to stand up to Conor had nerve, and he admired that. Shaking his head with a half smile, he took out the note she had given him and scanned the few lines scribbled on the paper in a surprisingly inelegant hand.

I know about the debt and the Crawlers. Come and see me if you wish to protect your Prince.

The Prince was silent as Lin kept pace with him: down the long marble corridor, the curving stairs, out into the bright sunlight. The first night she had come to Marivent it had been dark, nearly moonless, washing the courtyard garden of the Castel Mitat clean of color. Now she saw that it was beautiful: Roses tumbled down trellises that clung to the stone walls like a lover's hand, golden poppies spilled from the necks of stone pots, spiked purple salvia bordered the curving paths that snaked through the grass. A small fountain plashed beneath a tiled sundial; etched on the dial's face was a line from an old Castellani love song: AI, LAS TAN CUIDAVA SABER D'AMOR, E TAN PETIT EN SAI. *Alas, how much I thought I knew of love, and yet how little I know.*

"Now is when you tell me," said the Prince, "that Bensimon failed to tell you I forbade you from returning to the Palace."

Lin had been aware of him, of course, even as she had been looking at the garden. He was leaning now against one wall of the Castel, a booted foot up behind him. His hair was a tangle of black curls, his eyes silver in the sunlight. The color of needles and blades.

She said, "He told me."

The corner of the Prince's mouth twitched—in anger or amusement, Lin could not tell. "I offer you a way out," he said, "and you do not take it. Leaving me to wonder: What is wrong with you, precisely?"

"Only that I am a physician," said Lin. "And as such, I wanted—"

"It does not signify, what you wanted," he said. "When I command you to do something, it is not an idle request. I would have thought your grandfather would have made you aware of that much, at least."

"He has. But Kel is my patient. I needed to see if he was healing properly."

"We are not completely incompetent here at Marivent," the Prince said. "Somehow we have managed all these years without you, and are not all dead as a result." He plucked the bloom of a passionflower from a cascading vine and spun it between his fingers. Smiled at her, but not with his eyes. "When I say, *do not return to the Palace*, that does not mean, *unless you feel like it*. People have been thrown in the Trick for less."

Lin could see the Trick from where she stood: a long, narrow spike of black, piercing the sky. A wave of anger rolled through her. There were no trials for those sent to *La Trecherie*, no Justicia. Only the snap of royal fingers, the whim of a king or queen. *Here is a man*, she thought, *who has never worked for the power he holds. He believes he can demand anything, order anything, for he has never been refused. He is rich and lucky and beautiful, and he thinks the world and everything in it belongs to him.*

"Go ahead, then," she said.

"What?"

"Throw me in the Trick. Call the Castelguards. Put me in a cell." She held her hands out, wrists crossed, as if ready for the shackles. "Bind me. If that is what you want."

His glance trailed from her wrists to her face, lingering on her mouth for a moment before he flicked his eyes away. He was flushed, which surprised her. She would not have thought it possible to shock him.

"Stop that," he said, still not looking at her.

She dropped her hands. "I knew you wouldn't really do it."

There were rings in his left ear, she noticed, small gold hoops that glowed darkly against his light-brown skin. "You are mad to stupidly court such danger," he said. "I wonder that Mayesh chose a mad physician to look after my cousin, granddaughter or no."

Lin could not stop herself. "He is not your cousin."

Now he did look at her, his eyes hard. "What did Mayesh tell you?"

"Nothing. I saw his talisman. It might mean nothing to most Castellani, but I am Ashkar. I can read *gematry*. Kel is the *Királar*. Your Sword Catcher."

The Prince did not move. He was very still, but it was a stillness that contained a dangerous energy. It reminded Lin of serpents she had seen caged in the market square, motionless in the moment before striking. "I see," he said. "You believe you know something that can hurt me. Hurt the Palace. You think that gives you power." He stood up straight. "What is it you want, then? Money?"

"*Money?*" Lin could feel herself shaking with rage. "I would not take your ring when you offered it freely. Why would you think I want money now?"

"Mayesh is aware that you know," he said, half to himself. "He must think the secret safe, with you, then."

"It is. I have no intention of telling anyone. For Kel's sake, and for my grandfather's. Not for yours. The Palace means nothing to me."

She started for the archway, the one that led out of the court-yard. She heard quick footsteps behind her; a moment later the Prince moved to block her way. She could have gone around him, she thought, but it seemed foolish, as if she thought they were play-ing a child's game of catch-the-mouse.

"You hate me," he said. He sounded almost puzzled. "You do not know me at all, and yet you hate me. Why?"

She looked up. He was tall, so much that she had to crane her head back to look at him. She did not think she had been this close to him before. She could see the individual threads of his dark lashes, smell the leather and sunlight scent of him. "Kel is covered in scars," she said. "And while his current injuries may not have the Aurelian name upon them, his old ones do. He was given to you as if he were a *thing*, like an engraved box or a decorative hat—"

"Do you imagine I wear a great number of decorative hats?" inquired the Prince.

"He was only *ten*," she said.

"Mayesh seems to have told you a great deal."

"All of it," she said. "Kel was just a child—"

His face changed, as if a screen had been drawn back, and now she could see what lay behind it. A real anger—cut away from pretense, from disguise. It was a clean anger, burning white-hot. "As was I," he hissed. "I was a child, too. What do you imagine I could have done about it?"

"You could release him. Let him live his own life."

"He does not serve me. He serves House Aurelian, as do I. I could no more free Kel than I can free myself."

"You are playing games with words," said Lin. "You have the power—"

"Let me tell you something about power," said the Prince of Castellane. "There is always someone who has more of it than you. I have power; the King has more. House Aurelian has more. The Council of Twelve has more." He raked a hand through his hair. He was not wearing a crown; it changed him, subtly. Made him look younger, different. More like Kel. "Have you even," he said, "*asked* Kel? Whether he wishes to be other than he is? Wishes Jolivet had never found him?"

"No," Lin admitted. "But surely, given the choice—"

He barked a disbelieving laugh. "Enough, then," he said. He

looked away; when he looked again at her, the screen was back in place. His anger was gone, replaced by only a faint incredulity, as if he could not believe he was here, having this conversation, with Lin of all people. She felt his scorn, as tangible as the touch of a hand. "Enough of this profitless conversation. I do not answer to *you*. Leave, and know that when I say leave, it means *leave and stay away*, not *leave and return when you feel so inclined*. Do you understand me?"

Lin gave the smallest of nods. Barely a movement at all, but it seemed to satisfy him. He spun on his heel and stalked back into the Castel Mitat, his green coat whipping around him like the flag of Marakand.

She was halfway to the North Gate, still fuming, when a carriage drew up alongside her. Lacquered red, with a gold lion blazoned on the door, it was clearly a royal carriage; a Castelguard with a scarred face held the reins of a matched pair of bay horses. "Lin Caster?" he said, looking down at her from his perch on the driver's seat. "Prince Conor sent me. I am meant to take you into the city, wherever it is you wish to go."

Somehow, Lin was sure, this was a pointed gesture. She set her jaw. "That's not necessary."

"It is, actually," said the guard. "The Prince says I must make absolutely sure you leave the grounds of Marivent." He sounded apologetic. "Please, Domna. If you refuse, I could lose my post."

Name of the Goddess, Lin thought. What an absolute brat the Prince was; clearly he hadn't changed at all since his childhood.

"Very well," she said. "But do be sure to tell him that I wasn't the least bit grateful."

The guard nodded as Lin clambered angrily into the velvet-lined carriage. He looked more than a little alarmed but said nothing. Clearly he had decided that, whatever was going on, he wanted no part of it.

In the guise of a raven, Judah Makabi flew through the nights and days to the land of Darat, where he hid himself in Suleman's garden. He saw how, in the palace, all was peace and beauty, while outside its walls the flames of war scored the ground with Sunderglass.

Exhausted, his wings heavy with dust, Makabi the raven listened as the Sorcerer-Kings and Sorcerer-Queens of Dannemore gathered beneath the branches of a sycamore tree and spoke together of their avarice and greed for power. They told one another that they would band together to attack Aram, for its Queen was young and untutored, and could not stand against their combined forces.

"I thought you had intended to seduce her to bring her under your sway," said one of the Sorcerer-Queens to Suleman.

"I find I grow tired of waiting," Suleman replied, and the Source-Stone at his belt flashed like an eye. "Perhaps, if she learns obedience, she will be Queen of Darat one day. But it seems unlikely."

Makabi flew back to Aram with a heavy heart.

— *Tales of the Sorcerer-Kings*, Laocantus Aurus Iovit III

CHAPTER TWELVE

The day after Lin's visit to Marivent, Kel duly presented himself at the Black Mansion, note in hand. Unusually, Conor had asked where he was taking himself off to and, scrambling, Kel had invented a new fighting style that was being taught at the Arena. "Something a Sword Catcher should know about," he'd said, and Conor had agreed. Kel was left to hope that Conor would not demand a demonstration of the technique later.

Kel had often looked down on the Black Mansion from the West Tower; it stood out among the other buildings of the Warren like a dollop of jet-black paint splashed onto an ochre canvas. No one knew who had built the place; it had existed as long as there had been a Ragpicker King to occupy it, which was longer than anyone alive could recall.

He mounted the black stairs to find the famous scarlet door guarded by a mustachioed man so heavily muscled he seemed top-heavy, like an inverted pyramid. He wore an elaborate uniform of red and black, with braiding on the shoulders as if he were a member of the Arrow Squadron.

"Morettus," Kel said, feeling a bit silly, as if he were in a Story-Spinner tale involving spies and passwords.

"Fine," said the guard. He didn't move.

". . . Now?" said Kel, after a long pause.

"Fine." The guard nodded.

"Right," Kel said. "I'm going to open the door now. And go in."

"Fine," the guard said.

Kel gave up. He had his hand on the door latch when it swung open from inside. Ji-An stood on the threshold, a slight smirk on her face. She wore her foxglove-purple coat, her hair pinned up with jade clips. "That was agonizing to watch," she said, gesturing for him to enter the mansion. "You're going to need to learn to be more assertive."

"Does he say anything but *fine*?" Kel asked as soon as the door had shut behind them.

"Not really." They were walking down a wood-paneled corridor that seemed to snake through the interior of the Black Mansion like a vein of gold in a mine. Paintings of scenes from around Castellane hung on the walls between closed doors. "But he once dispatched an assassin with a spool of thread and a butter knife, so Andreyen keeps him around. One never knows."

"What about you?" Kel said.

Ji-An looked straight ahead. "What about me?"

"You saved my life," Kel said. "Why? I didn't get the impression you were fond of me."

"Please don't fuss about it. I was nearby because Andreyen asked me to follow you and report back."

"Did he," Kel muttered under his breath.

"Don't bother being offended. It was very dull, following you. You barely leave Marivent. Then when you finally did, you went to Merren's, of all places. At which point I realized that I wasn't the only one following you."

"The Crawlers," Kel said, and Ji-An nodded. "You could have let me bleed out on the street, though."

"Andreyen wouldn't have liked that," Ji-An said as the corridor opened out into a sort of great room, the kind nobles tended to maintain in their country retreats. Half a dozen armchairs and low sofas were scattered in a haphazard circle beneath a ceiling like an inverted bowl. The furniture was mismatched—a black lacquer cabinet here, a tiled Valdish table there. Merren was sprawled in one of the chairs, reading. Despite the heat of the day outside, a fire burned in the enormous grate that dominated one wall. "Is there some specific reason you've come to talk to Andreyen? I might as well know before I go fetch him, in case it's something he couldn't possibly find interesting."

So the Ragpicker King hadn't told his loyal assassin about the message he'd sent to Kel. Interesting. Perhaps he'd wanted it to be a secret, though why, Kel couldn't imagine.

He thought back over the last few days, the bits of gossip he'd caught wind of as he wandered around Marivent. "Tell him I have a question about Artal Gremont."

The book fell out of Merren's hand and hit the floor with a thump. An incredulous expression passed over Ji-An's face. Kel looked from one of them to the other, wondering what on earth he'd said.

"I'll—go fetch Andreyen," said Ji-An, clearly caught entirely off guard. She glanced back one more time at Kel as she departed the room, eyes wide, rather as if he were a hedgehog who had started spouting off poetry in Sarthian.

The moment she left, Merren rose to his feet, scooping up his fallen book. He looked just as he had the last time Kel had seen him—somehow nervous and graceful at the same time, his fair hair a halo of ringlets, his black clothes shiny with age and patched at the elbows. "Why would you mention Gremont?" he demanded.

Kel threw up his hands. "Just chance," he said. "He's a figure of curiosity on the Hill. He was sent off into what amounted to exile nearly fifteen years ago—"

"It wasn't *exile*," Merren snarled. "He *escaped*. He ought to have hung from the gallows in Valerian Square."

Kel narrowed his eyes. "This has something to do with your father?"

"My father. My sister. My family." Merren's hands were shaking. "You really—no one on the Hill knows what Gremont did?"

"What do you mean, what he did?" Kel began, but Ji-An and the Ragpicker King had come into the room, putting an end to the conversation. Merren sat back down quickly, opening up his book again, while Andreyen settled onto a dark-blue sofa. He was, as always, impeccably dressed in black, his long white hands folded atop his blackthorn cane. His eyes were bright in his narrow face.

He said, "Kellian. I was told you'd recovered well, but I'm pleased to see it. Have you come because I requested you to, or do you really have a question about that toad, Artal Gremont?"

"The former. I came because of the message you sent to me at Marivent," Kel said. "Does Lin Caster work for you, too? Does everyone in Castellane work for you secretly?"

"No," said Andreyen. "Some of them work for Prosper Beck."

Kel couldn't decide whether this was a joke or not. What he did know was that he was the only one in the room standing up—Ji-An had perched herself on a side table—and he was beginning to feel foolish. He sat down in a wing chair opposite Andreyen, who looked pleased.

"The truth is," said the Ragpicker King, "I find very few people qualified to work for me. Ji-An and Merren, of course, have special skills. Lin and I merely have similar interests. You, on the other hand"—he fixed Kel with a steady jade-green gaze—"I still want you to work for me."

"Nothing about that has changed," Kel said quietly. "If this conversation is conditional on my agreeing to work for you . . ."

"It isn't. But much *has* changed. You've been stabbed nearly to death by Beck's Crawlers. If Ji-An hadn't been there, you'd likely be dead."

Kel crossed one leg over the other. It was uncomfortably hot in the room and he longed to shrug off his jacket. "The Crawlers ambushed me because they thought I was Conor," he said. "Beck must be out of his mind if he's sending Crawlers to threaten the royal family." He frowned. "The leader was named Jerrod, Jerrod something—"

"Jerrod Belmerci," said Ji-An. "He's Beck's right-hand man. He protects Beck completely. People often think they can get to Beck through him—and believe me, they've tried—but he's a stone wall."

"Sounds like you might have had some personal experience there," Merren said, grinning at Ji-An. His fury over Gremont seemed to have gone, a shadow banished by sunlight.

Ji-An threw a pillow at Merren. Kel, meanwhile, was lost in thought—thinking of Jerrod, of his silver mask and what it might conceal.

"Not that Beck isn't out of his mind," added Ji-An, "It *is* a peculiar move, and dangerous, positioning oneself to extort royalty."

"Most people wouldn't try to wring money out of House Aurelian," said Merren. "They could just send the Arrow Squadron to burn down the Maze. It almost seems like . . ."

He trailed off. The Ragpicker King looked at him, his gaze inquiring but patient. There was almost a *fondness* to that look, Kel thought in surprise. As if Andreyen simply liked Merren, outside of needing a poisoner on his staff.

"Well," Merren said, "almost as if it's personal."

"I suppose it could be, if Beck's being funded by someone on the Hill," said Ji-An, eyeing Kel.

Kel shook his head. "I've thought about that. It could be any of the Houses, really. They're all ruthless, and they're all rich. And none are likely to confide such business to me. They know I'm close to the Prince, so I'm the last person they'd tell."

"You could search all their homes," said Ji-An, looking delighted at the prospect. "We could break in—"

"Before we go quite that far," said Andreyen, "Kel, can I speak to you in private?"

Kel, surprised, could not help but glance at Merren and Ji-An, who it seemed had been abruptly dismissed. Merren simply shrugged and closed his book before heading out of the room; Ji-An, though, could not conceal a look of hurt. Kel felt a little guilty as she departed with her hands shoved into the pockets of her foxglove jacket.

Once they were gone, Andreyen rose to his feet. Kel wondered if the Ragpicker King planned to lead him somewhere, but no; it seemed Andreyen was only pacing.

"Why *Morettus*?" said Kel. "As a password. They do make us study dead languages up at the Palace, you know. I'm aware it means 'no name' in Callatian."

"Because all Ragpicker Kings have the same last name: no name at all. I am Andreyen Morettus because I have given up the name I had before. It is a reminder that there will always be a Ragpicker King; it is an office, not a specific person." He eyed Kel, picking up a silver bowl that had been sitting on a shelf. Idly, he passed it from hand to hand. "Now. I am going to tell you something that very few people know. How few? A month ago, three people in all of Castellane knew it. Now only two people know, because one of us is dead."

"Died of old age?" Kel said hopefully.

"No, murdered. Poisoned in fact. Not," Andreyen added, with the ghost of a smile, "by Merren." He ran a finger around the rim of the silver bowl. "But before I tell you anything else, know that if you repeat any of this information to anyone—for instance, your friend the Prince—I will have you hunted down and killed."

His raised his eyes to Kel's, and in that moment, Kel saw behind the calm, even kindly veneer of the Ragpicker King—the one who looked fondly at Merren, and responded to threats with amusement—to the cold and ruthless criminal beneath.

Blood on his carriage wheels, Kel thought. Aloud, he said, "You are not making learning this secret very appealing."

Andreyen set the bowl down. "If you do not wish to know it, I won't tell you. But it may be the only thing that will help the Crown Prince."

Kel leaned back in his chair. "I wondered," he said. "Why me?

Why offer me the task of spying for you? You seem to have plenty of informants on the Hill. You knew Lin Caster treated me, you know I've been wandering the Palace grounds; you surely know more than I do about the various political machinations of the Charter Families. What have I got to offer that a dozen others might not?"

Andreyen looked at him silently.

"Is it because putting myself in danger for Conor is my vocation? Because if you suggest that his life is threatened, I must say yes to whatever you ask?"

"Loyalty," said the Ragpicker King.

"Not to you."

"It does not need to be loyalty to me." Andreyen reached inside his black coat and drew out an envelope. "There has been a Ragpicker King in Castellane for as long as there has been a King on the Hill," he said. "I inherited the title from another, just as your Prince will inherit his title from Markus." Kel squinted, but could not see what was written on the envelope; only a blank square faced him. "A wise king knows that there will always be crime," said Andreyen. "As long as there are Laws, people will break them. But criminals are not anti-monarchist by nature. Many of them are quite patriotic."

Kel snorted, and Andreyen gave him a cool look before resuming.

"Most criminals wish only for their businesses to prosper, like any guildmaster or merchant might. A wise king knows that he must encourage the right kind of crime, and thwart the wrong kind."

"So you are a sort of Charter member," said Kel. "But your Charter is crime."

Andreyen looked amused. "You could think of it that way. My Charter is crime. The wrong kind of criminals don't fear the Vigilants or the Arrow Squadron, but they fear me."

"What does this have to do with the King on the Hill—King Markus?" Kel asked. He sensed they were coming closer to the secret Andreyen wished to tell him, though they were still circling it like ravens circling the Star Tower.

"When King Markus inherited his throne, he inherited an ancient contract—between the King on the Hill and the Ragpicker King. The agreement assures that my larger operations will not be touched. I will never be hauled before the Justicia; I will never be dragged to the Tully. In turn, I make sure that the kind of crime that does not threaten the King or the city is allowed to flourish—in a controlled sort of way—and that the kind of crime that is unwanted in Castellane does not. It is an arrangement that has withstood the test of time. It has always remained secret, as it must. But now . . ."

Andreyen turned the envelope over in his hands, and with a jolt, Kel recognized the royal seal: the wax dyed with the royal scarlet, the lion rampant. He strode across the room to Kel, offering him the letter.

This is it, Kel thought. *The secret that could cost me my life.*

But it was a cool, detached thought. He had no choice. Not if, somehow, all this could help Conor.

When he took the letter, he found the paper heavy and stiff—*paper, the Raspail Charter*—and the moment he unfolded it, he recognized the handwriting immediately as the King's.

The message was short, and addressed to the Ragpicker King.

There are few who hold Castellane as precious as you and I do. The city is in danger, I am in danger, and my son is in danger. You and I must meet.

Kel read the few lines several times, as if they might give up more of their import in the repetition. At last, he looked up at Andreyen. "What does this mean?"

"I never found out. I sent back a message with a suggested time for meeting, but it is my belief that the King never received it. The messenger was a Castelguard. That night, he was found dead in his room—"

"Dom Guion," Kel said, remembering. The reason he had gone to Merren in the first place. A Castelguard he could not recall ever having spoken to, and yet because of his death—all this. "It was put about that he was murdered by a jealous lover, a woman from Sarthe—"

"Guion was not interested in women," said the Ragpicker King, "though I doubt many knew that. He was an intensely private person. He had to be. He was one of three people in the city who knew of my contract with Markus. It was something I learned when I first came to the Black Mansion. There is always a messenger." He threw himself back into his chair. "But not now. No messenger has come in Guion's stead; there has been no word for me from the Palace. I believe Markus thinks I never replied to him."

Kel narrowed his eyes. "Are you asking me to be your new messenger? Why not one of your spies who is already on the Hill or in the Palace? Why me?"

"As I told you before," said the Ragpicker King, "loyalty. Not to me, but to House Aurelian. When I first made my offer to you in the carriage, I wanted to see if you would accept it, or remain loyal to the Prince. You passed that test. I believe you will keep this secret, for his sake. And . . . ?"

"And?" Kel said, through his teeth.

"And then there is the Prince's loyalty to you. Guion was murdered. His death was easy to sweep away, to dismiss. Should I choose another of my spies to try to contact the King, who can say if they, too, will not be killed before the objective is reached? Whoever did this is clever—clever enough to know how important you are to the Prince. It is one thing to murder a guard, and another to slay the Prince's cousin, who has hardly left his side for over a decade. They must know that if they harmed you, the Prince would hound them to the ends of the earth. He would never stop seeking revenge."

And Kel knew that was true. Slowly, he turned the letter over in his hands. "King Markus says here that Conor is in danger," he said. "And you believe Prosper Beck is that danger?"

"Prosper Beck was already growing in power when Markus sent me this message. Making sure that I cannot reach the King, nor he me, is in Beck's interest. He is exactly the sort of criminal—chaotic, oblivious to the normal rules of engagement—that the King on the Hill would work together with me to eliminate. The King says his son is in danger, and now Beck is willing to threaten the Prince. No criminal who answers to me would touch a member of the royal family."

Kel said, "If Prosper Beck arranged for your messenger to die, then he must know about this contract. So there were not three people who knew of your arrangement, it seems. There were four."

Andreyen inclined his head as if to say: *very true.* Kel wondered where his preternatural calm came from. Mayesh always said graciousness paired with viciousness was the domain of the nobility, but Andreyen was certainly not that. Then again, it was impossible to determine his class. He stood apart from such things.

"That is what I need you to find out for me," said Andreyen. "Normally, with the assistance of the Aurelian King, it would not be so difficult to discover who Beck is, and how he knows what he knows. But without it . . . I need to understand what the King wished to tell me at that meeting. If there is a thread that can unravel Beck's growing empire, I need to know how to find it and draw on it." He fixed Kel with an unnerving stare. "So. You'll do it?"

There is a great deal about this I don't like, Kel thought. But Andreyen had a point. If Kel didn't talk to the King, there was no way to find out if there was a greater danger Conor was in. If Beck wanted more than just money. Getting rid of Beck was as much in Conor's interest, and thus Kel's, as it was the Ragpicker King's.

"All right," said Kel. "I will speak with the King. But if I get murdered because of it, I swear to Aigon I will come back and haunt you from hell."

"Excellent," said the Ragpicker King. "I look forward to it."

Once a week, the Maharam held receiving hours in the Shulamat. He sat in state, wearing his *sillon*, ceremonial robes thickly fringed at the cuffs and hem with dark-blue thread. Across his lap lay his almond-wood staff—a replica of the one Judah the Lion had carried with him into the desert after the destruction of Aram.

During these hours, the Maharam would answer questions regarding matters of Law, offer blessings on engagements or new babies, and moderate minor disputes that had sprung up in the Sault. Any accusation of a crime, or issue that involved the whole community, would be saved for the annual visit of the Sanhedrin. It was during one of these hours that Chana Dorin had brought Lin to the Maharam to demand that she be allowed to study medicine.

Lin had not come before him again since—until today. And she had not wanted to come before him today, either. But she had been desperate. The previous night she had gone to the House of Women to see Mariam, bringing with her not her physician's satchel but the brooch she'd had made with Petrov's stone in it.

She had tried everything she could think of to awaken the stone in Mariam's presence. All she wanted was for it to flare up as it had at the Palace, but it lay cold and dead in her palm like a toad's eye waiting to be dissected. Thinking words at it did nothing, concentrating did nothing, and praying, alas, did nothing. Eventually Mariam, sensing her distress, had begged her to go to sleep and worry about making the stone work as a healing object later. "After all," Mariam had said, "you still know so little about it."

Which, Lin had to admit, was true, and here was her chance to change all that. So she had waited this afternoon, very deliberately, loitering in the square outside the Shulamat, until everyone else who had come to see the Maharam was finished.

The diamond-paned windows of the Shulamat let in a pale gold light, in which dust motes hovered like wingless moths. The silence was eerie as Lin proceeded up the aisle, between the rows of benches, toward the Almenor, the raised central platform where the Maharam sat.

She approached and made the customary gesture of respect,

folding her two hands over her heart. His silver hair and beard shone like pewter as he inclined his head, acknowledging her.

Lin heard a faint sound. It was Oren Kandel, she realized, sweeping a broom along the rows of empty pews. A sense of irritation prickled along her spine; she wished Oren was not there, and not so clearly eavesdropping.

Still. There was nothing to be done about it.

"I have come," Lin said, "to petition for access to the Shulamat library."

The Maharam frowned. "That is impossible. Access to the library is only for students of the holy texts."

"As a physician," Lin said carefully, "I am asking that an exception be made. A life is in danger—Mariam Duhary's life. And is not the saving of a life a purpose holier than any other, even obedience to the Law?"

The Maharam templed his fingers beneath his chin. "You bring up an interesting question of Law," he said. "I will deliberate upon it."

"I . . ." Lin turned to glare at Oren, who was inching closer with his broom. "I hope that you will not need to deliberate long. Mariam needs my help—*our* help—soon."

"You are passionate about your profession," said the Maharam. "That is admirable. I will do my best to help you." His teeth were yellow when he smiled. "Perhaps you could help me, in return. Your grandfather brought you to the Palace the other night, I understand?"

Lin had not been prepared for this. But of course the Maharam would know; Oren had been at the gate that night, and would have told him. "I had a patient there," she said.

"There are many other fine physicians in the Sault," said the Maharam. "Why bring you? It is not as if you and your grandfather are close. A shame, I have always thought. Did he perhaps wish to discuss with you the matter of who will succeed him as Counselor?

Who he plans to recommend to the Palace? He is not a young man, after all, and must be tiring of his arduous duties."

Oren had given up all pretense of sweeping and was staring openly.

"My grandfather does not confide in me, Maharam," said Lin. "As you observed, we are not close."

Disappointment flashed across the Maharam's face, deepening the net of wrinkles around his eyes. "I see," he said. "Well, it is a complicated matter you have brought before me. It may require the wisdom of the Sanhedrin."

Lin caught her breath. "But—it could be months before they come to Castellane again," she said, forgetting to be politic. "Mariam could die by then."

The Maharam's usually benevolent gaze hardened. "Mariam Duhary is dying of the same disease that killed her father—a disease the best physicians of the Sault could not cure. Yet you think you can do better? Why?"

"I think," said Lin, trying to control her temper, "that for a religion that purports to worship a Goddess, who was once a powerful Queen, there are a great many men making decisions about what I, a woman, can read and do."

His eyes darkened. "I advise you to tread carefully, Lin. You are a physician, not a scholar. Yes, we worship her, but it is from Makabi that we have our Laws, from which none of us are exempt."

"Makabi was not a God," said Lin. "He was a man. I do not believe it is the will of the Goddess that Mariam die so young. I do not believe the Goddess is so unkind."

"It is not a matter of kindness. It is a matter of fate and purpose." The Maharam sat back, as if weary. "You are young. You will understand in time."

He closed his eyes as if in sleep. Lin understood this as a dismissal. She left, pausing only to kick the pile of dust Oren had swept carefully into a corner. She heard him yell as she hurried down the steps, and grinned. Let that be a lesson to him not to eavesdrop.

When Kel returned to the Palace, he found Conor lying on his bed, reading a book. This was not unusual: Conor tended to treat Kel's bed as an extension of his own, and would often drape himself across it when feeling dramatic.

He sat up when Kel came in, and said, "Do you think you'll be ready for practice again soon? Or do you intend to continue this business of wandering about the Palace like a lost soul?"

Kel shrugged off his jacket and went to join Conor on the bed. It had not occurred to him before, but his new habit of rambling about the grounds of Marivent provided a useful excuse for any absences. "I thought we could start up again tomorrow—"

"There's a diplomatic dinner two nights hence," Conor said. "I've been trapped with Mayesh all afternoon, practicing my Malgasi. You ought to come. Sena Anessa will be there, too, and she likes you. I believe she feels she's watched you grow up."

"Dinner with Malgasi *and* Sarthe," said Kel. "Two countries that loathe each other. How could I resist?"

"You'll be fine," Conor said, and Kel knew that, of course, there was no question of resisting. If Conor wanted him to go, he would go; it was his purpose, his duty. He thought briefly of the Ragpicker King and their discussions of loyalty. To the Ragpicker King, Kel's loyalty was a quality that simply made him useful. Andreyen saw that loyalty, but he did not understand it. He did not live in a world of loyalty and vows. He lived in a world of trickery and extortion, a world where power balanced on a knife's edge, ready to tip this way or that. Of course, one could say the same of the Hill, or international diplomacy for that matter. But that, too, was part of Kel's purpose: to be a shield for Conor against invisible arrows as well as visible ones.

Conor had not seemed to notice Kel's silence; he was grinning. "Look what Falconet gave me," he said, and handed Kel the book he'd been reading. It was a slim tome, bound in embossed leather.

Conor watched with a look of amusement as Kel flipped it open and perused the contents.

For a moment, he thought it was simply the same collection of loose portraits Mayesh had shown them the previous day, bound into book form. Then his eyes adjusted. Here indeed were Floris of Gelstaadt, Aimada d'Eon of Sarthe, Elsabet of Malgasi, and many more, but instead of being painted in their finery, they had been depicted stark naked. Princess Elsabet had been drawn draped over a brocade sofa, eating a persimmon, her long black hair brushing the ground.

"Where did Falconet *get* this?" Kel said, staring.

"He had it commissioned, to amuse me," said Conor. "Leave it to Falconet to know exactly the list of royals Mayesh considers eligible. The images are reliant, of course, on the artist's imagination, but they do say there are spies in every Court."

Kel looked at him. "*Every* Court?"

Conor looked thoughtful. "Are you suggesting there are spies here at Marivent drawing naked pictures of me?"

"I *have* seen some of the servants lurking in the shrubberies. Planning to peek through the windows, perhaps?"

"Well, let them bask in my nude glory, then. I've nothing to be ashamed of." Conor flipped a page, revealing an illustration of Princess Aimada of Sarthe, wearing only a few strategically placed peacock feathers. "Not bad."

"She has lovely eyes," Kel said, diplomatically.

"Only you would be looking at her eyes." Conor turned the next page, and there was Princess Anjelica of Kutani. The artist had drawn her with one hand feathered across her bare breasts, half covering them. Her eyes were the same as they had been in Mayesh's portrait: amber-gold, unfathomable. Kel turned the page quickly.

"Give me that back." Conor flipped the book out of his hand and grinned. "Gray hell, look at Florin of Gelstaadt. That tree cannot compete with his absolutely enormous—"

"Bank account," Kel said gravely.

"Surely those proportions *can't* be accurate," Conor said. He stared once more, then tossed the book onto the nightstand. "Falconet may be a bit mad."

"All the best people are," said Kel. "He knows your sense of humor, Con."

But Conor wasn't smiling now. He was looking at Kel through his eyelashes; it was something he did when he wanted to hide the evidence of his thoughts. He said, "What would you say if I told you that I no longer needed a Sword Catcher? That you were free to go where you wanted to go, and do what you liked?"

Something deep in Kel's belly tightened. He was not sure if it was anxiety or relief, lightness or heaviness. He was not sure of anything anymore. He had not been since that first meeting with the Ragpicker King. Slowly, he said, "What makes you ask?"

"Something Mayesh's granddaughter said." Conor flopped back down on the bed and regarded Kel through the tangle of his dark hair. "When I was escorting her out of the Palace."

"You didn't need to ban Lin Caster from the Palace, Con," Kel said. "She wasn't plotting some sort of coup. She's a physician. She feels a sense of duty toward her patients."

"She's maddening," Conor said, moving restlessly on the bed. "I've met sharp-tongued women before, but most know to temper their blades. She speaks as if—"

"As if you weren't her Prince?" said Kel. "The Ashkar have their own banished ruler, you know. The Exilarch."

"I don't think I recalled that," Conor murmured. "Either way—"

"She is Mayesh's granddaughter," said Kel, not sure why he was pushing against this so hard. He often felt it was his purpose not only to protect Conor physically, but to recognize the ways in which he had been given principles to follow only irregularly—a word from Jolivet here, a bit of advice from Mayesh there—and left in neglect to attend them as best he could in an atmosphere that rewarded neither virtue nor empathy nor restraint. Perhaps it was merely that he felt there was no one else to define goodness for Conor, though he was no expert himself. "Do you want her to be afraid of you?"

Conor pushed the hair out of his eyes and fixed Kel with a sharp look. "Afraid of me? She is the furthest thing from afraid of me, Kellian."

"And it bothers you?"

"When I see her, I feel as if I have stood too close to a fire, and hot cinders have flecked my skin with little burns." Conor scowled. "I tried to pay her, the night she healed you. She refused to take the reward I offered—" He held up his hand, showing Kel the blue signet on his right ring finger—"and I cannot help but feel that if she had, my irritation would cease. I dislike owing her."

"Think of it as owing Mayesh," Kel suggested. "We are all used to that."

Conor only scowled more, and Kel decided it was past time to change the subject.

"So," he asked, "what would *you* say, if I told you I no longer wished to be *Királar*? That I wanted to leave Marivent?"

"I would let you go," said Conor. "You are not a prisoner."

"Then there is your answer," Kel said. "If I wanted to leave, I would leave. If you no longer want a Sword Catcher, that is your decision, but not one you ought to make for my benefit." Conor was silent. "I have trained for this, nearly all my life," Kel added. "I am proud of what I do, Conor."

"Even though hardly anyone knows about it?" Conor said, with a crooked smile. "Even though you must be heroic in secret?"

I wouldn't say hardly anyone, Kel thought darkly. Too many people knew his secret for his liking, but that was not something he could share with Conor. "It isn't *that* much heroism," he said. "Mostly it's listening to you complain. *And* snore."

"That is a treasonous statement. I do not snore," Conor said, with great dignity.

"People who snore never think they snore," said Kel.

"Treason," Conor repeated. "Sedition." He stood up and stretched, yawning. "As it turns out, I barely remember a word of Malgasi. Fortunately, I've a new cloak of black swan feathers that ought to distract the ambassadress."

"That sounds expensive," said Kel, and immediately regretted having said it. Conor stopped his stretching and looked at Kel, hard. After a moment, he said, "If you are still worried about the Prosper Beck business, don't be. I'll take care of it."

"I wasn't worried at all," Kel said, but it was not the truth, and he suspected Conor knew it.

This time, when a knock came on the door late in the evening, Lin knew immediately that it was not Mariam. She would have used her code: two quick raps, a pause, then a third. This was the thud of a fist against her door, and she bolted to her feet, suddenly panicked.

She had spent much of the evening, after her rounds in the city, studying the few pages she had of Qasmuna's book and cursing herself for never having studied Callatian. She had a translator's dictionary from her time as a student and had been doing her best with it, skipping from the dictionary to the original. The pages were also not in order, having been torn from their bindings, making it difficult to construct a narrative or even a series of instructions from the pages.

So far Lin had learned only a few rather disappointing things. The Source-Stones had indeed existed, and been invented by Suleman the Great, lord of what was now Marakand. There seemed three ways to fill them with power: One could drain off one's own magical energy into them, like filling a flask with water. One could take power from a magical creature—a dragon or phoenix or hippogryph, something formed from the power of the Word itself. Or one could kill another magic-user and take their energy in the form of blood.

Magical creatures, alas, no longer existed. Lin did not know how one could manage the method of saving one's own magical potential, and her physician's Oath forbade her from killing anyone else, had she even known a magic-user in the first place.

Frustrated, she took out her own stone—she was beginning to think of it as hers, and not Petrov's—and looked into it. *How can I use you?* she thought. *How can you help me heal Mariam?*

For a moment, she thought she saw the odd shapes in the stone rearrange themselves, flowing like the letters and numbers of *gematry*. She thought she could read the old Ashkar word for "heal," buried down deep, a cinder glowing through smoke—

And then the knock came on the door. She scrambled up, sliding the pages of Qasmuna's book—and her notes—carefully under the pillows on the window seat. Then she went to the door.

To her surprise, standing on her stoop and looking diffident, was Mayesh. He seemed to have just come from the Palace, for he wore his Counselor's robes, and around his throat the silver medallion of his status gleamed.

"*Barazpe kebu-qekha?*" he said. May I enter your home? It was a formal request, not the sort usually made by family.

Wordlessly, Lin stood back and let him into the main room of her house. He took a seat at the kitchen table, careful not to disarrange her remaining books and papers.

Lin locked the door and came to sit across from him at the table. She knew she ought to offer him tea at least, but he seemed distracted. She could sense him studying the room, from the various items Josit had brought back from his travels to the cushions her mother had carefully sewed. She did not think he had been in this house since her parents had died, and she could not help but wonder if it made him think painfully of Sorah. Surely there was pain when he thought of his lost daughter? It had always felt an extra injury to her, that in taking himself out of her life, Mayesh had taken from her the last person in the Sault, besides herself and Josit, who truly remembered and loved her mother.

"I heard you managed to get yourself into the Palace," Mayesh said, his words snapping her out of her reverie. "Despite Conor's request to the contrary."

Lin shrugged.

"You are lucky it was only a request," said Mayesh, "and not a royal order."

"What is the difference?"

Mayesh's eyes were red-rimmed. He seemed tired, but then he always seemed tired. Lin could not remember a time she had seen him look as if he did not have the weight of the world on his shoulders. "A royal order is a formal demand made by the Blood Royal. The punishment for disobeying it is death."

Lin kept her expression calm, though her heart skipped a beat. "No one," she said, "should have that kind of power over another human being."

Mayesh studied her. "Power is an illusion," he said. This surprised Lin; she had always assumed him obsessed with power, its dilemmas and possibilities. "Power exists because we believe it does. Kings and queens—and yes, princes—have power because we grant it to them."

"But we *do* grant it to them. And death is no illusion."

"Do you know why the King always has an Ashkari Counselor?" Mayesh said abruptly. "In the time of Emperor Macrinus, the Empire was on the brink of war. It was the good advice of the Emperor's Counselor, a man named Lucius, that brought it back. When Lucius lay dying, the Emperor was distraught: How would he ever find another to advise him so well? It was then that Lucius said to him: All the good advice I have ever given you was first told to me by my friend, a man of the Ashkari people, named Samuel Naghid. Against the advice of his Court, the Emperor brought Naghid into his confidence, and named him his next Counselor. And for thirty years, Naghid guided the Empire, serving first Macrinus and then his son, and the Empire retained its territories and peace. After that, it was considered both wise and lucky to have an Ashkari Counselor to the throne, and the Kings of Castellane keep that tradition."

"I see," said Lin. "What meaning do you take from that? Because to me it sounds as if the wisdom of an Ashkar was trusted only when people believed it came from a *malbesh*."

"That is not the lesson I take from it. The *malbesh* opened the door, but Naghid proved himself, and because he proved himself, the belief continues that an Ashkari Counselor is indispensable—both wise and impartial, for they stand apart from the squabbles of the people. They have the power of the outsider."

"A power that is used to serve the throne?" Lin said, quietly. She half expected Mayesh to fly into a fury. Instead, he said:

"Because there is always an Ashkar close to the throne, the King is forced to look upon us and remember we are human beings. The task I perform protects us all. Not only do I speak for our people, but I am a mirror. I reflect the humanity of all our people to the highest seat in Castellane."

Lin raised her chin. "And you are telling me this because you want me to understand why you chose the Palace over me and Josit?"

Mayesh flinched almost imperceptibly. "I did not choose the Palace. I chose everyone in the Sault."

A knot of pain, presaging a headache, had begun to form between Lin's eyes. She rubbed at it and said, "Why are you telling me this?"

"I was impressed with the way you got yourself into the Palace," he said. "It indicated to me an understanding of the uses of power. You could not get in yourself, so you found someone who could, and you worked your will through them."

It was Mariam's idea, Lin wanted to say. But that would be of no help to Mariam, and might in fact cause trouble.

"But the Prince was furious," she said, instead.

"He was also impressed," said Mayesh. "I know him well. He complained that you were too clever by half. That's a compliment, from Conor. He was furious—"

"Furious is bad."

"Believe me," said Mayesh. "It's good for him." He rose to his feet. "I was also impressed that you did not come to me," he added. "Conor indicated that you seemed concerned with protecting my position. When you said you would tell no one else that you know Kel is the Sword Catcher, he seemed to believe you."

Lin exhaled. She had wondered if Mayesh was aware she had revealed her knowledge. It seemed he was, but if he were troubled by it, he was carefully giving no indication.

"I am your granddaughter," said Lin. "Should I not be assumed trustworthy by association?"

Mayesh only shrugged. "We will see," he said, and went out the door.

After he had gone, Lin went to retrieve the pages she had hidden beneath the window cushions. How strange, she thought, to have had her grandfather in her house—she had imagined the moment so many times. Imagined herself reproaching him, his head hanging with shame. It had, of course, been nothing at all like that. But she found she did not regret the difference.

As she drew out the papers, the pain in her head made her flinch. The papers fell from her hands. She knelt to gather them, half-absentmindedly, her attention on the turmeric tea she'd need to make to prevent her headache from worsening.

She paused. The pages had fallen in such a way that she was able to see something she had not seen before. Two of the torn-out pages were clearly meant to be looked at side by side. What had seemed separate incomplete designs was in fact one design—the same design, like a ten-rayed sun, that she recalled from the covers of more than one book in Petrov's flat.

Frozen, she stared at the pages. Petrov had been obsessed with the stone in his possession. What if he'd also had Qasmuna's book, or one like it?

You want his books—nasty little magic books, full of illegal spells, his landlady had said. *I sold them to a dealer in the Maze.*

The Maze. Just on the other side of the Sault walls, but nowhere an unaccompanied Ashkari woman could go safely. Neither the Vigilants nor the Ragpicker King could protect her there.

It was Mayesh's voice she heard then, in her head. *You could not get in yourself, so you found someone who could, and you worked your will through them.*

Still kneeling on the floor, and despite the pain in her head, Lin began to smile.

Long ago, Kel had trained himself to wake up at dawn for training sessions with Conor and Jolivet. Now that Conor was old enough to refuse to rise at daybreak to practice swordplay, that skill had fallen out of use, but Kel was pleased to discover his internal clock still functioned. He woke as the sun rose over the Narrow Pass, his eyes snapping open.

Pale-gray light streamed through a gap in the curtains. Conor was asleep in his bed nearby. The light that filtered through the draperies around his bed laid a pattern of uneven lines across his bare back.

Kel dressed silently: soft boots, gray clothes that would blend with the dawn. Conor did not stir as he left the room.

Few were afoot in Marivent at this hour. The grass of the Great Lawn was starred with dew, and in the distance, the ships in the harbor bobbed on water that resembled hammered tin.

Servants hurried back and forth like flitting shadows, preparing the Palace for the day. When they saw Kel, they ignored him. It was fortunate, Kel thought, as he approached the Star Tower, that he had been marching himself around the Palace grounds for the past days. No one would question his presence anywhere; they were used to his wanderings.

Still, when he entered the tower, he felt a tightening of his nerves. He had not been inside the tower in years, and the air of it felt peculiar—cool and dry, which was not surprising, but also dusty, as if it had been closed up for a long time. Like the air of a tomb—

though that was foolishness; Fausten came in and out here every day, as did Jolivet and a few of the older servants.

As with most of the other towers, the upper, inhabited part of the Star Tower was reached by a set of narrow spiral stairs. Kel's soft boots allowed him to move soundlessly up them. He tried to look intent upon the simple activity of walking.

The staircase ended at a landing that featured two doors: one of plain wood, the other metal, hammered with a pattern of stars and constellations. Light spilled from around the metal door's edges, providing the strange illusion that it was floating in space.

Years ago, Kel recalled, he and Conor had been playing up and down the steps, and the King had emerged from behind the metal door, benevolent but stern. He was studying the stars, he had told them; they needed to leave him in peace and quiet.

Kel put his hand to the metal door now. It was possible, he thought, that this was merely the King's study and that he slept in the room across the landing. But barely had he touched the door than it swung open, and he found himself in a chamber lit brightly by two orbs of Sunderglass, within which a blue light shone. The room was circular, the roof high above a clear glass turned to silver by the dawn's light. The walls were paneled wood, gleaming a warm brown; the furniture was plain but solid, carved from Valdish chestnut.

A gold-and-silver orrery, displaying the elliptical position of the planets, rested on a desk; the walls were lined with books regarding astronomy, the positions and histories of the stars. A cabinet held a sextant, and telescopes of varying sizes, some made of ivory or studded with gems. Finely drawn wheel charts and maps, showing the position of the stars and the paths of the planets, hung upon the walls. Everywhere were papers, covered in notes made in a close, dark, scribbled hand.

As Kel's eyes adjusted to the light, he started, realizing that what he had taken for an empty chair by the window was, in fact, occupied. It was only that the man sitting in it was as motionless as furniture. He did not seem to be moving at all, not a twitch of muscle, or a breath. Despite the harsh light in the room, he was in shadow.

"Your Highness," Kel said. King Markus did not look at him. He was gazing out the window at nothing, his eyes red-rimmed. He wore his astronomer's robes, though Kel could see they were frayed at the cuffs.

Kel cautiously approached the chair—it was difficult not to think of it as a throne. The back was plain but high, the arms carved with worn scrollwork. As he drew close, he went instinctively to his knees. "Your Highness," he said, again. "The King in the City sent me."

Now the King did look down at him. His gray eyes, so like Conor's, were hazed with confusion. "You are not Guion," he said.

Kel reached into his jacket. Before he had left the Black Mansion, Andreyen had pressed into Kel's hand a small pewter bird. The King would recognize it, he'd said, though Kel was puzzled. It seemed a cheap trinket to him, though the little magpie did seem to be the Ragpicker King's unofficial symbol. The thieving bird.

"The Ragpicker King said you would know me by this," Kel said. "That I have come from him."

The King's eyes were glued to the bird. "Yet—you are the Sword Catcher."

"Yes," said Kel. "But I am also a messenger. The King in the City is concerned he has not had word from you."

"It is I who have not had word from him. I sent a message requesting a meeting." The King tore his eyes from the magpie trinket and stared again out the window. "I should not have done it. The stars prophesied we would not meet. The stars do not lie."

"Perhaps," said Kel. Sweat prickled along his spine—the sky outside was brightening. He could not stay here long. And his knees hurt from contact with the stone floor. "Perhaps what the stars intended was that you tell me what danger faces House Aurelian, and I will bring that message to the Ragpicker King."

The King moved fretfully in his chair. "Fausten tells me this is the destiny written in the stars. But I know it is my sin, my evil, that has brought us to this place."

"What place?"

"This place of debt," said the King, and Kel felt as if a hot poker had jabbed him between his shoulder blades. Could the King know of the money Conor owed Prosper Beck? Surely that could not have been the danger he spoke of. Should the King wish to pay that money back, it would be simple for him. The Treasury was his.

"It is not your fault," said Kel, choosing each word with care. "Your Highness. This is Prosper Beck's fault."

The King looked at him blankly.

"Who is Beck?" Kel whispered. "What does he want? Surely the debt can be paid, ten thousand crowns—"

Hoarsely, the King snapped: "This is no debt to be paid in gold, boy. This is a debt of blood and flesh. It entraps me like the bars of a cage, yet I cannot escape it."

Kel sat back on his heels. "I don't—"

The metal door slammed open. A squat figure barreled into Kel. He found himself hauled to his feet by none other than Fausten. The little man was pale, the bald pate of his head shiny with sweat. He stank of sour sweat and old liquor.

"Your Highness," Fausten gasped. "My apologies. You should not have been troubled by this—this interloper."

The King looked at Kel—no, not at Kel. At what he held in his hand. But Kel had already closed his hand around the magpie trinket. He wrenched away from Fausten, but there was nothing to say. He could not appeal to Markus, who was watching them with haunted eyes. Fausten did not know about the contract between the two Kings in Castellane, and keeping that secret was far more important than Kel's protesting that he had a right to be where he was.

He let Fausten herd him out onto the landing. It galled him not to push back, but he knew it would have accomplished nothing, and Fausten could certainly stir up trouble for Kel if he liked.

Fausten was breathing hard through his nose. "How dare you—"

"I heard a noise while walking the grounds," Kel said smoothly. "I came to assure myself His Highness was well. It was a mistake to assume—"

"It was indeed a mistake," Fausten snapped. When he was angry, his Malgasi accent thickened. "His Highness's welfare is not your concern, *Királar*. The Princeling is your responsibility. Not his father."

"The safety of all House Aurelian concerns me," said Kel, tightening his hand around the tin magpie. Its sharp little wings cut into his palm.

Fausten shook his head slowly. Kel had never noticed how small his eyes were before, how glittering and black. "His Highness," he hissed, "does as I advise. I interpret for him the will of the stars, which he believes in utterly. If the stars told him to imprison you in the Trick, he would do it. You would hardly be the first *Királar* locked away for treachery."

"I have done nothing to warrant that."

"See that you continue to do nothing." Fausten gave Kel a small shove; he was not strong, but Kel, stunned by what he'd just heard, took a step back. "*He szekuti!*"

Get out of here. Do not return.

With that, Fausten spun on his heel and hurried back into the King's study. Kel could hear him muttering in his high, worried voice, assuring the King all was well. "Your Highness, you are agitated. Have a bit of your medicine."

Bile rose in Kel's throat. He flung himself down the steps, puzzled and furious, and out the door of the tower, into the clear air of morning. The sky above was blue and clear, the air free of dust.

His hand ached. He opened it, looked down. He had gripped the Ragpicker King's magpie trinket so tightly in his hand that he had crushed it out of all recognition.

When Judah Makabi returned to Aram, Queen Adassa gave him back his human form, and bade him speak of what he had seen. "Dark news, my Queen," he told her. "You have been betrayed. King Suleman has raised a great army against you, and they will attack Aram in three days' time."

Adassa did not speak, but shut herself up in the great tower of Balal. When she did, unrest stirred in Aram, for the people feared their Queen had forsaken them. But Makabi came out to the front of the palace and said to them: "Do not fear, for our Queen will save us. Have faith. She is ours."

On the morning of the second day Adassa emerged from her tower much changed. She had been a beautiful and gentle girl, but all that seemed burned away, and it was a woman bright and sharp as a blade who went out from her palace and looked upon her people, who had gathered together to hear her speak.

"My people of Aram," she said. "I need your help."

— *Tales of the Sorcerer-Kings*, Laocantus Aurus Iovit III

CHAPTER THIRTEEN

Kel made his way up Yulan Road, his head bent under the bright sun of Castellane. It was nearly noon, and he was beginning to overheat in his green velvet jacket, but such were the sacrifices one made to please the Queen of House Aurelian.

Merren Asper walked by his side, a slim figure in rusty black, seeming lost in thought. *Here I am*, Kel thought, *side by side with a poisoner, off to meet the only man in Castellane who can, in theory, get me close to Prosper Beck. How again did I get here?*

Not that it was a difficult question to answer. The Ragpicker King. Kel had made his usual excuses about training at the Arena, and headed directly for the Black Mansion. He'd found Andreyen in the solarium, admiring the plants. "You talked to Markus," Andreyen had said, the moment he caught sight of Kel's expression. "And I see it did not go well."

Halfway through the story, Merren and Ji-An had joined them, plainly curious. Andreyen had shot Kel a warning look, but he'd already moved past the part of the story where Markus had acknowledged a connection to the Ragpicker King. He repeated the other things Markus had said: that it was his sin and evil that had brought them to this place. That Conor's debt could only be paid in blood. And what he had not said: anything about Prosper Beck.

He told them, too, about Fausten—his defensiveness and his threats. "Maybe *he's* Prosper Beck," Merren had suggested. "Or funding him."

The Ragpicker King had been quick to dismiss this notion. "Fausten has no money to speak of," he'd said. "The influence he wields over the King is his only power. Prosper Beck is a destabiliz-ing force. Fausten likes things as they are." He'd shrugged. "You'll have to try to talk to the King when Fausten is not there."

But Kel had dug his heels in. Perhaps Fausten had been bluffing when he'd threatened the Trick, but Kel doubted it. There had been none of the usual fluttering of diffidence about him. He'd seemed sure, and the horror of what the Trick represented was stronger than he guessed Andreyen would understand.

"The King understands there is danger, of some kind," said Kel, "but I do not believe he has a clear picture of it. His faith in the stars and what they portend is almost religious. He believes in prophecy, not actuality." He hesitated. "I must speak with Prosper Beck in-stead. He knows his own plans; no one else seems to." He'd reached out to brush the yellow petal of a sunflower. "I'll need to find Jerrod Belmerci."

There had been an explosion of argument. Jerrod could not be gotten through; he would never let Kel near Prosper Beck; it would only alert Beck that Kel was looking for him. But Kel had been adamant, and at last Ji-An had reluctantly proffered the information that Jerrod could be found between the hours of noon and sunset at a noodle shop on Yulan Road, where he conducted business on be-half of Beck.

"If you're determined to go," Andreyen had said darkly, "take Merren with you."

"Merren?" Kel had echoed. "Not Ji-An?"

The Ragpicker King's lip curled in amusement. "Don't be rude to Merren."

"I don't think it's rude," Merren had said. "I think it's a good question."

Kel had half expected Ji-An to be offended, but instead she had merely exchanged a quick look with the Ragpicker King. One that told Kel that she understood Andreyen's reasoning. "Poor Merren," she said. "He hates conflict."

"That's true," Merren said, looking glum but resigned. "I do hate conflict."

But here they both were, marching up Yulan Road as the Windtower Clock began to chime noon, the sound of its bells carrying on the breeze from the harbor. Yulan Road was lively now with students in search of a cheap midday meal at one of its many dumpling pushcarts. Gold and white banners hung above carved wooden doors, bearing the names of shops in Castellani and Shenzan: a jeweler's store, a tea shop. Scarlet lanterns of paper and wire, painted with characters for prosperity and luck, dangled from hooks in plaster walls. Similar neighborhoods bearing the cultural imprint of those who had settled in Castellane from Geumjoseon, Marakand, and Kutani dotted the city, though the area around Yulan Road was likely the oldest. Trade in silk had been the first Charter, after all.

Kel had started his trip to the Black Mansion with a plan, one he had not entirely shared with Andreyen. The closer he got to Jerrod and the enactment of the plan, the more he felt tension rise like a bitter taste in the back of his throat.

He pushed the thoughts away. "You're awfully loyal to the Ragpicker King," he remarked as Merren paused to examine the wares of a cart selling medicinal herbs.

"You're awfully loyal to the Prince," said Merren mildly.

"I didn't realize you'd sworn an oath to protect Andreyen," said Kel. "Or that keeping him safe was your duty and vocation."

Merren looked up, squinting against the sun. His hair was bright as new-minted gold. "I owe him."

Despite his jangling nerves, Kel's curiosity was piqued. "For what? Is this something to do with Gremont?"

"Artal Gremont is the reason I became a poisoner," said Merren matter-of-factly. "So I could kill him. Andreyen offered me a place to work. To hide from the Vigilants, if necessary. One day, Artal Gremont will set foot in Castellane again, and I will be ready. And Andreyen will have helped me."

"Gray hell," said Kel. "What did Artal Gremont do to your family?"

Merren's gaze darted away. Abandoning the cart and its wares, he started back up the road, his hands shoved into his pockets. Kel went after him.

"It's all right," Kel said. "You don't have to talk about it—"

"This is the place." Merren pointed across the street at a low-slung shop with a white-painted wooden front and windows screened with rice paper. The sign above the door proclaimed it the YU-SHUANG NOODLE HOUSE, home to a proprietary recipe for ginger-pork noodle soup.

Kel felt his stomach tighten, but he was in no mood to show his nerves to Merren, or even to acknowledge them to himself. They went inside. A silk curtain hung in the entryway; ducking past it, Kel found himself in a wood-paneled room where a row of cooks, dressed in red, tended steaming pots of soup and curry. The air was redolent of green ginger, scallion, pork broth, and garlic. A water-color map tacked to the wall, its edges curling, showed the continent of Dannemore from a Shenzan perspective, with Castellane marked out as the Kingdom of *Daqin*. The greatest detail was reserved for Shenzhou and its neighbors, Jiqal and Geumjoseon. Kel thought of something Bensimon used to say: *We are each the center of our own worlds. Castellane may believe itself the most important country in Dannemore, but remember that Sarthe, Malgasi, and Hind all think the same about themselves.*

Kel had been in shops like this before. They tended to stay open late into the night, which made them attractive to Conor's friends. Using a technique he'd learned from Jolivet, Kel scanned the room without making it obvious that he was doing so. The place was about half full, and Jerrod was indeed there—alone, seated at a wooden booth in the back of the shop.

The top halves of the booths were open fretwork, with a geometric design. Through the latticed squares, Kel could see Jerrod was wearing a black linen coat over a hooded tunic, his silver mask gleaming in the dim light that filtered through the rice-paper screens.

It was as if someone had held a lit taper to his skin. Kel recalled all at once the stinking alley behind the Key, the pain in his side, his chest. Jerrod looking down at him, only his mask visible, his face hidden in shadow.

Kel's anxiety bled away into a cold fury. He felt nothing at all as he walked up to the long rosewood counter, placing his order in Shenzan. The cooks seemed surprised and even a little amused by his command of their language; they chatted a little, while Merren looked bored, about the intricacies of their recipe, and the way Kel wanted his food prepared. As he reached over the counter, Kel could not help but wonder if Jerrod was watching; he studiously ignored him as he ordered ginger tea for Merren (everything else had meat in it, which Merren wouldn't eat), paid, and headed for Jerrod's table, Merren muttering in his wake.

No one gave either of them a second glance as they approached the back of the shop. The owners must be used to Jerrod entertaining a stream of visitors, if he was doing business here. Presumably the restaurant got a cut of whatever deals he made.

It was only when they had reached his booth that Jerrod looked up. If he was surprised, there was no way to tell it: Jerrod's eyebrows quirked, though his expression was otherwise hidden by his tarnished quarter-mask. It was as if someone had laid the palm of their hand, in a silver glove, over the left side of his face, covering his eye and the upper part of his cheek. Was it hiding burns or scars? Identifying marks of some kind? Just an affectation, meant to alarm?

"I didn't think I'd be seeing you again," he said with remarkable composure. His gaze slid from Kel to Merren. "Merren Asper," he added, his voice taking on an entirely different tone. "Do sit down."

Merren and Kel slid into the booth across from Jerrod. The table between them was gnarled wood, sanded to smoothness, stained here and there with the marks of old burns and spills.

Jerrod, smirking, sipped his tea. The mask made it difficult to tell what he was thinking, but he seemed to be looking over the rim of the cup at Merren. There was something curious in his eyes— almost admiring.

Kel said, "Were you not expecting to see me again because you assumed I'd died in that alley?"

"I learned soon enough that you hadn't," said Jerrod. "Word gets around. I'm glad to see you looking better, Anjuman. It wasn't anything against you personally."

"So, now you do know who I am," said Kel.

Jerrod inclined his head. "You're the Prince's cousin, who had the misfortune to look a bit like him and borrow his cloak on your night out in Castellane." He glanced at Merren. "In fact, we followed you from Asper's flat to the Key. We wondered what the Prince of Castellane was doing visiting a dank building in the Student Quarter."

"It isn't dank," Merren said indignantly.

"But now I'm wondering what the Prince's cousin was doing visiting a dank flat in the Student Quarter. You do know your friend here"—he gestured at Merren—"has been spotted going in and out of the Black Mansion? That he seems to run errands for the Ragpicker King?"

"I can see how that might trouble you," Kel said, rolling his eyes. "Proximity to crime, I mean."

"I am not a cousin of House Aurelian," Jerrod pointed out. "Whereas you are, yet you seem to favor the more . . . seedy sides of Castellane."

"Some of us are drawn to sin," Kel said darkly, and noted Merren shooting him a glare. "And some of us are stupid enough to try to kill the Crown Prince of Castellane in an alley."

Jerrod shook his head so violently he dislodged his hood. It fell back, uncovering a head of tousled, brown hair. "We weren't trying to *kill* anyone. It was only a matter of money owed. And the money is still owed, by the way."

"I thought we could discuss the matter," Kel said, as a waiter carrying a tray approached their table. "Look, I've bought you dinner. A show of good faith."

Jerrod's eyebrows went up just as a server arrived at their table carrying a steaming tray. Two copper bowls were set down in front of them, followed by small ladles, ornately enameled with flowers and dragons. Soup was served from a vast pitcher of noodles and broth, and garnished with the traditional shavings of ginger, garlic and scallion, topped off with a rice cake and a dash of spiced oil.

Kel picked up his ladle and dug in. There was an art, in his opinion, to consuming noodle soup: One needed to get the right blend of broth, meat, and garnish into each mouthful. He glanced at Jerrod, who had not yet taken a bite. Finally Jerrod shrugged, as if to say, *Well, we're eating out of the same pitcher, what's the harm?* He picked up his ladle.

"I'd like to meet with Beck," Kel said. "Discuss this with him."

Jerrod swallowed his soup, then chuckled. "I don't have to ask, because Beck would never agree. He doesn't meet. Not with anyone." He cast a sideways glance at Merren. "Well. Maybe he'd meet with you, if you were interested in crossing sides. Working for Beck. He likes attractive people."

Merren raised an eyebrow.

"Beck's being awfully reckless," Kel said. "Trying to start a war with the Palace. What does he have to back up his threats besides a pack of criminals from the Maze?"

"He's got more than that," Jerrod said, and frowned, passing a hand across his face. He was starting to sweat. Kel could feel it, too, the first prickles of heat along his own skin.

"Well, what he has had better be an army and a navy, because that's what Conor has," said Kel.

Jerrod tapped the fingers of his free hand on the table. He had large, square hands, with bitten fingernails. "Prosper Beck has a good reason for doing what he does, and a better knowledge of his own position than you do."

"I want to talk to Beck," said Kel, setting his ladle down. There was a faint buzzing in his ears. "In person."

"And I said you can't." Jerrod set down his ladle. He looked exasperated, and . . . in pain? Merren looked at him with a sudden puzzlement, followed by a shocked realization. "Besides. Why should I do you any favors?"

"Because I poisoned you," said Kel. "The soup. Is poisoned."

The ladle fell from Jerrod's hand. "You *what*? But we shared the soup—"

"I know," Kel said. "I poisoned myself, too."

Both Merren and Jerrod looked equally stunned. "You *what*?" Jerrod demanded.

"I poisoned myself, too," repeated Kel. "I told the chefs it was a spice I'd brought from home, asked them to add it to the soup. Not their fault. They didn't know." His stomach cramped, sending a bolt of pain through his abdomen. "Merren didn't know, either. My fault—nobody else's."

"Kel." Merren was white about the mouth. "Is it *cantarella*?"

Kel nodded. His mouth felt dry as sand.

"Ten minutes." Merren's voice was flat with fear. "You have about ten minutes before it's too late."

"Anjuman—" Jerrod gripped the edge of the table, fingers whitening. With an effort, he said, "If you poisoned yourself, there's an antidote. If there's an antidote, you have it with you." He started to rise. "Give it to me or I'll cut your fucking head off—"

"The more you move around, the faster the poison spreads through your system," said Merren, almost automatically.

"Anjuman, you bastard," Jerrod breathed, sitting back down.

The collar of his shirt was dark with sweat. Kel could feel the same fever-sweat prickling his own spine, the back of his neck. There was a dull, metallic taste on his tongue. "You're insane."

"I can't disagree with that," Merren muttered.

"What," Jerrod said, with tight control, "do you want, Anjuman?"

"A promise that you'll set up a meeting for me with Prosper Beck."

The vein in Jerrod's neck was throbbing. "I can't promise that. Beck might refuse."

"It's your job to convince him not to refuse. Not if you want the antidote."

Jerrod looked at him; when he spoke, he sounded as if he were being slowly strangled. "Every minute you delay, you're risking your own life. Why not take the antidote yourself? Make *me* beg for it?"

Kel didn't feel like grinning, but he did it anyway. "You need to see how far I'll go." His hands were burning, his tongue numb. "That I'll die for this."

Jerrod's face was pinched around the mask. He said, "You really would?"

Merren leaned across the table, white-faced. "He's willing to die," he said. "He might even want to. For Aigon's sake, just *agree*."

Jerrod looked at Merren. "All right," he said, abruptly. "I'll get you a meeting with Beck."

His hand shaking, Kel drew one of the two phials of antidote Merren had given him out of his shirt pocket. Began to twist off the top. His throat was tightening. Soon he wouldn't be able to swallow at all. He tipped the open phial of antidote down his throat—sweet, licorice, the taste of *pastisson*—and flipped the second across the table to Jerrod.

Almost immediately, the buzzing in Kel's head, the pain between his shoulder blades, began to subside. He watched through blurred eyes as Jerrod, having emptied his own dose down his throat, slammed the empty phial down on the table, hard enough to crack the glass. He was breathing as if he had been running, his eyes fixed on Kel. When he spoke, it was a low growl.

"Many would say that a promise extracted under duress is no promise at all."

Merren groaned faintly, but Kel met Jerrod's gaze. "I know you work out of this shop." He gestured at the mostly empty restaurant, the chefs behind the counter studiously ignoring them. "I know how to find you. I have the power of the Palace behind me. I could get Jolivet to shut the Maze down. I could follow you to every place you go after that, and shut every one of them down, too. I could follow you like death at your heels and *ruin your hellspent life*, do you understand me?" He was gripping the edge of the table, his fingers white, the metallic taste still bitter at the back of his throat. "Do you?"

Jerrod rose to his feet, flipping his hood up to cover his hair. He looked down at Kel, expressionless. Kel could see his own reflection, distorted, in Jerrod's silver mask. "You could," Jerrod said, "have just led with that."

"But would that have been as much fun?"

Jerrod muttered something, likely a curse, and stalked out of the shop. After a long moment of utter silence, Merren scrambled to his feet, pushed past Kel, and walked out the door after him.

Kel followed. Merren hadn't gone far; he was only a few steps ahead, striding angrily along the road. Jerrod was nowhere to be seen, which was no surprise; he'd doubtless vanished down one of the many side streets that branched off Yulan Road like veins off an artery.

Kel didn't care. He had nearly died, but only nearly; everything was brighter, harder, sharper than it had been before he'd swallowed the *cantarella*. The world shone like the gloss of light on a diamond.

He had felt this before. He remembered the assassin at the Court in Valderan, how Kel had broken his neck, the small bones crunching under his fingers like flower stems. Afterward, he hadn't been able to be still, but had paced back and forth across the tiled floor of Conor's room, unable to slow down long enough for the Palace surgeon to bandage his shoulder. Later, when he'd taken off his shirt, he'd found that his blood had dried on his skin in a maze of spiderwebbed lines.

He caught hold of Merren's arm. Merren looked at him, startled, blue eyes wide as Kel drew him around a corner, into the shadows of an alley. Kel pushed him up against a wall, not hard but firmly, his hands tangling in the fabric of Merren's black coat.

Merren's cheeks were flushed, his mouth downturned, and Kel again had the thought he'd had in Merren's flat: that he could kiss him. Often when he was like this, when he was high on the exquisite agony of surviving, sex (and its auxiliary activities) could bring him back down to earth. Sometimes it was the only thing that could.

So he kissed Merren. And for a brief moment, Merren kissed back, his hands on Kel's shoulders, fingers curling in. Kel tasted ginger tea, felt the softness of Merren's mouth against his. His heart pounded *forget, forget*, but even as it did, Merren wrenched his face away from Kel's. Shoved him back with surprising strength. "No," he said. "Absolutely not. You tried to *kill yourself.*" He sounded as if he couldn't believe it himself. "You took poison. On purpose."

"I was not trying to kill myself," Kel protested. "I was trying to break Jerrod. I had the antidote—"

"And only my word that it worked!" Merren tried to straighten his jacket. "It was an insane thing to do. Insane and suicidal. And I won't—"

"I had to do it," Kel said.

"For who?" Merren demanded, a little wild-eyed. "Andreyen didn't ask you to do that. He wouldn't. Did you do it for yourself? For House Aurelian?" He lowered his voice. "You love your Prince; I see that. I thought it was half a joke, this Sword Catcher thing, when I heard it. Who'd do that?" He bit his lower lip, hard. "My father killed himself," he said. "In the Tully. They weren't going to hang him. They would have let him out in a few years. But he chose to die and left me and my sister to fend for ourselves on the streets."

"I am sorry for that," said Kel, torn between sympathy and defensiveness. What he'd done was dangerous, yes, but so was Ji-An shooting arrows at Crawlers, and Merren wasn't shouting at *her*. "But I am used to putting myself in danger, Merren. In fact, I'm going to need more of that *cantarella* antidote from you. It worked excellently well." Catching sight of Merren's expression, he added hastily. "It doesn't mean I'm going to do that again. I don't *want* to die—"

Merren flung up his chemical-scarred hands. "You don't value your life. That's a fact. So why should I?"

He walked away, boots throwing up puffs of bone-dry dust as he stalked out of the alley. Speechless, Kel watched him go.

Kel returned to Marivent via the West Path—a limestone track which wound up the side of the Hill through low-lying green shrubs: juniper and wild sage, lavender and rosemary. The sharp green scents helped cut through the fog in his brain, the lingering aftereffect of the *cantarella*.

He had a sneaking suspicion he owed Merren Asper an apology.

The wind had kicked up by the time he reached the Palace. The flags atop the ramparts snapped in the brisk air, and white squalls danced across the surface of the sea. In the distance, Kel could see half-drowned Tyndaris sharply outlined against the sky. Boats bobbed like toy ships in the harbor, their rhythm matching the sweep of waves against the seawall. Far in the distance, rain clouds were gathering at the horizon's edge.

After greeting the guards, Kel slipped through the West Gate and went looking for Conor. There had been a Dial Chamber meeting this morning, but surely it would be over by now? They needed to talk, though Kel was dreading the conversation.

He was halfway to the Castel Mitat when he passed Delfina and stopped to ask her if she'd seen the Prince. She rolled her eyes in the way only a lifelong servant of the Palace could. "He's in the Shining Gallery, playing whatsit," she said. "*Indoor archery.*"

Indeed, the doors of the Shining Gallery were standing open. From inside, Kel could hear laughter, interspersed with what sounded like breaking glass. He ducked inside to find that Conor, Charlon Roverge, Lupin Montfaucon, and Joss Falconet had set up a make-shift archery range inside the elegant, high-ceilinged room. They had lined up bottles of wine along the high table on the dais and were taking turns shooting at them with arrows, with whoever wasn't doing the shooting laying bets on the outcome.

Broken glass was strewn everywhere, amid puddles of multicol-ored wine and spirits. No wonder Delfina was annoyed.

"A hundred crowns says Montfaucon misses his next shot, Char-lon," drawled Conor, and Kel felt a rare feeling—a flash of real anger, directed at Conor. *You owe Beck ten thousand crowns, a debt you haven't yet paid. What are you doing, betting a hundred on something that pointless?*

Montfaucon took his shot, and missed. As Conor cheered and Roverge swore, Falconet turned and saw Kel standing in the door-way. "Anjuman!" he cried, and Conor glanced over. "You weren't at the Dial Chamber meeting."

"He doesn't have to be," Conor said, and Kel realized that Conor was, though hiding it well, very drunk. His smile was slightly off kilter, and his hand, where he leaned upon his longbow, un-steady.

Falconet winked. "Where were you? Caravel?"

Kel shrugged. There was a chorus of whistles, and Montfaucon muttered, "Lucky bastard." Kel wondered what they'd say if he told them he'd spent the afternoon not in the exercise of sybaritic plea-sure but rather poisoning himself in a noodle shop with two crimi-nals.

Of course, he didn't. Instead, he hopped up to sit on one of the

long tables where, as a child from the Orfelinat, he had first laid
eyes on the nobility of the Hill, and told them he'd been at the
Arena, learning new fight techniques.

This had the desired effect of distracting the group. Roverge,
Falconet, and Montfaucon peppered him with questions, several of
the answers to which he had to invent on the spot. They were all a
little drunk, he realized, though none as much as Conor. The whole
room stank of a sickening mixture of sweet liquors and jenever.

"What were we talking about before Anjuman got here? Ah,
yes, the lovely Antonetta Alleyne," said Roverge. "Whether she
might consider a bit of bedsport with someone now it seems clear
she'll never trap Conor into marriage."

The rage that boiled up in Kel's throat threatened to choke him.
"That was her mother's plan," he said flatly. "Not hers."

"True enough," Falconet said, taking the bow from Roverge,
who had just missed a bottle of yellow *cedratine* by a hairbreadth and
didn't seem pleased about it. "Pity Ana hasn't a brain in her head.
She'd be a good match otherwise."

"She doesn't need brains," said Montfaucon, leaning against the
great fireplace. He'd set his bow aside for the moment. "She's worth
millions, and she's ornamental enough."

Roverge chuckled, and sketched a voluptuous female form with
his hands. "If I married her, I'd keep her flat on her back, pumping
out little Roverges, all swaddled in silk."

Kel forced down the sudden, almost overwhelming urge to
punch Roverge in the face. *You used to play pirates with her,* he wanted
to say. *She once chased you around with a sword until you burst into tears,
after you insulted her mother.*

Kel realized then that he had always framed the past as the time
Antonetta changed: changed how she behaved, changed the way
she treated him. But now, listening to Roverge and Montfaucon
and Falconet, he thought: *They* were the ones who had changed.
When Antonetta had suddenly *curved,* her new body all breasts and

hips, it was as if she had become something else to them—something foreign and negligible, easy to mock. They had forgotten she was bright and clever. No, it was more than that. Her cleverness had become invisible to them. They could not see it.

At some point, alone, she had made the choice to turn that invisibility to her advantage. He thought of the way she had disarmed Conor in his room; it had been skillfully done, but it was not the sort of skill Charlon Roverge could see. In fact, Kel had to admit, he had not, until now, seen it himself.

"Then propose yourself as a match to House Alleyne," Kel said to Charlon, through his teeth. "With all you have to offer, they could hardly say no."

Conor's lips twitched. Roverge, though, was oblivious to the sarcasm. "Can't," he said. "My bloody father promised me off at birth to a Gelstaadt merchant's daughter. We're just waiting for her to finish her education. In the meantime, I'm free to play." He leered.

"Speaking of play," said Montfaucon, "I hear Klothilde Sarany arrived last night. I thought she might enjoy a small and tasteful gathering at House Montfaucon."

Roverge looked puzzled. "Who?"

"The Malgasi Ambassador," said Falconet. "Do try to keep up, Charlon."

"If you intend an amorous connection with her, I'm impressed," said Conor. "She's terrifying."

Montfaucon grinned. "I like a few scars." He blew a smoke ring. "You're having dinner with her tomorrow night, Conor. You could bring up the matter of the party . . ."

"I am not inviting Klothilde Sarany to a party whose only guests are you and her," said Conor. "She would be rightfully annoyed."

"That's why I'm inviting the rest of you," said Montfaucon, gesturing expansively. "Come one, come all. Wine will flow, there will be beautiful dancers and less attractive but highly skilled musicians . . ."

Montfaucon *was* famous for his parties. They went wrong as often as they went right, but were always a spectacle. There had been the time every guest had received the gift of a basket of snakes (Antonetta had fainted and fallen behind one of the sofas) and the time Montfaucon had planned to arrive atop his balcony in a hot-air balloon that became entangled in the trees instead.

"She's not here to attend your party, Montfaucon," said Roverge, ungraciously. "She's here to try to talk Conor into marrying the Princess, Elsabet—"

There was a crash. Falconet had let an arrow fly, shattering a bottle of *samohan* from Nyenschantz. Everyone ducked as glass flew in all directions. The floor was littered with shards, and some of the tapestries boasted long tears. Queen Lilibet was going to be furious.

Joss offered the bow to Conor, whose turn it was. Roverge, eyes glittering—he'd bet against Falconet making the hit—said, "Well, Conor. If this marriage business is still troubling you, you should talk to my father. He gives the best, most objective advice."

"Charlon," Kel said as Conor's expression stiffened, "whatever happened with that upstart merchant that was troubling your family? The ink-makers?"

Roverge scowled. "We took them to court. They had the temerity to argue before the Justicia that ink and dye are quite separate things."

"Aren't they?" said Conor, taking aim with the bow.

"On the contrary, they are the same! And the judges saw it our way, of course." *With an ample bribe*, Kel thought. "The Cabrols have left Castellane with their tails between their legs. They'll be lucky if they can set up as shopkeepers in Durelo." He spat. "I don't think they'll trouble anyone from now on. You're welcome."

He swept a bow just as Conor let his arrow fly. It hit the bottle of jenever, sending more glass flying and filling the room with the scent of juniper. Roverge, as always inattentive to the mood of his companions, clapped Conor on the shoulder. Montfaucon went to take the bow as Roverge continued chattering on about ink and dye and the destruction of the Cabrol family.

The table shifted; Falconet had seated himself beside Kel. He wore black velvet today, the silk pile enlivened with a luminous silver weave. Falconet was not like Conor or Montfaucon—he presented himself well but clearly lacked their fascination with clothes and fashion. Kel often wondered what it was that did interest Falconet. He seemed to regard all activities with the same casual amusement, but no real preference.

"So," said Falconet, glancing at Kel's shoulder. "How did you get injured, then?"

Kel cut his gaze sideways. "What makes you think I did?"

"People talk. But . . ." Falconet spread his hands wide. "We needn't discuss it if you'd prefer not to."

"I got drunk," Kel said. "Fell off a horse."

Falconet smiled. Everything about him was sharp—his cheekbones, the angle of his shoulders, even the cut of his smile. "Why in gray hell would you do such a fool thing?"

"Personal reasons," Kel said.

"Ah." Falconet was watching Montfaucon, who was engaged in wagering with Roverge. "As I said, we needn't discuss it." He leaned back on his hands. "Conor had mentioned that he was thinking of going to Marakand, but he seems to have abandoned that idea."

He was only running away from Prosper Beck. "Yes, he has."

"That's a pity," Falconet said. "I visit my mother's family in Shenzhou often, myself." This was something Conor and Joss had in common: Neither of their mothers had been born in Castellane. "But I take it that perhaps he has gotten more serious about getting married."

"Really? I hadn't gotten that impression."

"Well, it makes sense. The right marriage would bring a great deal of gold and glory to Castellane. If I may share a thought . . ."

"You will, whether I give you permission or not," said Kel, and

Falconet grinned. Joss was among those rare nobles who treated Kel as a person separate from Conor. Kel knew perfectly well this didn't mean Falconet had his best interests at heart, but it was interesting, all the same.

"If Conor has come to consider marriage, and I think he has," said Falconet, "he ought to consider the Princess from Kutani."

"I thought you were a backer of Sarthe. Or is this sudden enthusiasm for Kutani related to your holding of the spice Charter?" The Falconet fleet circled the world, delving deep into Sayan and Taprobana for cinnamon and pepper. But Kutani was known as the island of spices for good reason. Its shores were perfumed with cassia and clove, saffron and cardamom, each one precious and expensive.

Falconet shrugged. "Just because something is good for me, it does not hold that it isn't good for House Aurelian. The spices of Kutani are valuable, and will serve to enrich the coffers of Castellane. But I have had the privilege not just of visiting Kutani but of meeting Anjelica Iruvai. She is far from some empty-headed royal. A bandit uprising once threatened the palace in Spice Town while the King was away; Anjelica directed the army herself and put down the threat while the Princes cowered. The people adore her. And—well, you've seen her."

"Yes," Kel said drily. "Or I have seen the work of some very imaginative artists, at least." He glanced over at Conor, who was laughing as Charlon Roverge arranged a tower of *palit* bottles to form a new target. A few servants had ventured into the gallery and now scuttled about, picking up the broken glass that littered the room. Montfaucon looked on as he always did, dark eyes unreadable.

Kel glanced at Falconet. "Might I ask you something?"

"You may always *ask*," said Falconet. "Whether you will get what you ask for is anyone's guess."

"It is information," Kel said. "I overheard the Queen refer to Artal Gremont as a monster. Have you any idea why, or why he was exiled?"

"Hm." Falconet seemed to be considering whether to answer, for so long that Kel assumed he had settled on *no*. Then he said, "He was never exactly upstanding, is what I've gleaned. But it seems he conceived a passion for a guildmaster's daughter in the city. He could not offer her marriage, of course. But he did offer to make her his official mistress, for a decent sum." Falconet examined the shining half-moons of his nails. "Alas, her father was a respectable sort. Wanted his daughter married, and had no interest in bastard grandchildren. Gremont had the father thrown in the Tully on a trumped-up charge and took the opportunity to . . . *use* the daughter."

Kel felt sick to his stomach. "He raped her."

"Yes. And the father killed himself in the Tully. But he'd had friends among the guilds. There was talk of going to the Justicia. So Artal was sent away, and the scandal died down. Some money was settled on the daughter, for her pains." Falconet sounded disgusted by the whole business, which was, Kel thought, to his credit.

"The daughter," Kel said. "Was she Alys Asper?"

Falconet whipped round to look at him. "You *do* know more than you let on," he said. "Don't you?"

Before Kel could reply, there was a tap on his shoulder. It was Delfina. "My apologies, Sieur. Gasquet wants a word with you."

Kel hopped off the table. "You understand," he said to Falconet. "The chirurgeon demands my presence."

"Of course." Falconet inclined his head. "Your injuries, the sad result of falling off a horse for personal reasons, must be seen to."

Kel followed Delfina out into the courtyard. It was no longer drizzling, though the courtyard still smelled of it—the richness of white flowers, the green scent of damp earth and limestone, the sour-sweet marriage of sea and rain.

She turned to face him beneath a dripping arch. "I've a note for you, Sieur."

She handed over a folded piece of paper. Kel scanned the lines quickly before looking up at Delfina, who was watching him without curiosity. "So Gasquet *doesn't* want to see me."

Delfina shook her head.

"Who gave you this note, Delfina?" Kel asked.

She beamed, her face blank as paper. "I really couldn't say. So much happens in this Palace, one simply cannot keep track." She bustled off toward the kitchens.

Kel glanced back down at the missive, its ink already beginning to smear with the dampness of the rain.

Meet me at the gates of the Sault. You owe me. —Lin

The people of Aram had gathered together to hear the words of their Queen in their time of greatest need and fear. Already the armies of the Sorcerer-Kings were massing on the plains beyond Aram.

With Makabi beside her, Queen Adassa stood before the Ashkari people and spoke unto them. "For many years our land has been at peace while those around us have warred," she said. "But that time has come to an end. The wicked and the power-hungry are bringing war to us, and Aram must answer."

And the people cried out, for they were in fear for their families and their lives, and they said, "But Queen, Aram is such a small country, and with such power ranged against us, how can we prevail?"

And Adassa said, "Sorcerer-Kings such as Suleman know only how to take power by force. They do not understand that which is freely given." She stretched out her hands. "I cannot command you to share your strength with me, that I might wield it against our enemy. I can only ask it of you."

But though her words were bold, in her heart she was afraid. Perhaps none of her people would wish to share their strength. Perhaps she would stand alone before the armies of the plains.

But Makabi said, "Take heart," and so then the Queen threw open the doors of the palace, and as she sat upon her throne one by one each of her people passed before her. Not a one stayed back: not the very young or the very old or the sick or the dying. Each came and offered a word to increase the power of her Source-Stone—a word that they gave up willingly, a word that, after it was offered, they could never speak again.

And that was the gift of the people of Aram.

—*Tales of the Sorcerer-Kings*, Laocantus Aurus Iovit III

CHAPTER FOURTEEN

Lin had been waiting outside the gates of the Sault for more than an hour by the time Kel arrived. She was grumpy; it had been drizzling, on and off in bursts. For the first hour, at least, she'd had Mariam's company; they'd perched on the edge of a stone cistern, with Mariam watching eagerly for a sign of the Marivent carriage. She was delighted at the chance to lay eyes on the Prince's cousin.

"He's part Marakandi, isn't he?" Mariam had asked. She'd had a bag of speculaas—spiced cookies from Gelstaadt—open on her lap and was munching happily. Sugar had been forbidden to the Ashkar in Malgasi, and Mariam had an insatiable sweet tooth.

"Yes." Lin had answered slowly; she supposed she wasn't entirely sure. The Prince had Marakandi blood through his mother; Kel did look very much like him, so she supposed it was possible, even probable. Still. She hated lying to Mariam, even about small things, and she'd been forced to do so repeatedly these past days.

"I remember Marakand," Mariam said, a bit wistfully. "Such beautiful fabrics there. Silks and satins and brocades, all woven with these gorgeous patterns. I remember seeing a procession of the Kings once, in Kasavan. The courtiers were all wearing green brocade edged with saffron silk that looked just like flames—"

The Kings. Marakand had a double throne, currently occupied by two brothers. Queen Lilibet was their sister. If she had not come to Castellane, Lin wondered, might she have sat on one of those thrones? Or had her chances of queenship been greater here than in her mother country?

Mariam sucked in a breath. Lin looked at her friend, startled, and saw that she had gone bone-white. She was staring at something out in the Ruta Magna. Lin looked, but saw only a tangle of the usual traffic, damp pedestrians darting under stone arcades to avoid the drizzle. Among them was a massive dark carriage painted a deep charcoal gray, its lacquer top gleaming with rain. As it passed, Lin caught a glimpse of the blazon on its side: a black-and-gray wolf, teeth bared, ready to pounce.

"Mariam?" She put a hand on her friend's arm. Felt her shaking.

"The *vamberj*," Mariam whispered. She bolted to her feet, spilling her spiced biscuits into a puddle.

"Mariam!" Lin called, but her friend had already fled back into the Sault, leaving Lin torn. She wanted to go after her—she could not imagine what the shock of seeing a Malgasi carriage, all these years after she had barely escaped the *vamberj* soldiers, must be like for Mariam—but Lin could not chance missing Kel. He could not enter the Sault to find her, and if he thought she had abandoned him at the gates, he might not help her again.

Her worry over Mariam did nothing for her ill humor, though. By the time Kel arrived in the Marivent carriage Mariam had so wanted to see, Lin was as irritable as she was damp with rain. She clambered into the carriage, avoiding Kel's hand, and settled onto the seat opposite him, tucking the lank tendrils of her hair behind her ears.

"I see," Kel said, offering her a warm cloth from a basket at their feet—it took her a moment to realize it was for drying her face—"that rather than my physician being summoned to my side, I have been summoned to hers."

"Hmph," Lin said, scrubbing at her hair with the cloth. It was nice to be dry. "I needed someone to take me to the Maze."

"The Maze?" Kel looked surprised, but pushed open the window on his side and relayed the information to the driver. The carriage began to move slowly through the cordon of waggons and pushcarts snarling up the Ruta Magna. "Why me?"

"You are the only one of the *malbushim* I know who owes me a favor."

"Really? Kel settled back into his seat. "I'm the *only* one? What about Antonetta Alleyne?"

"Demoselle Alleyne is a respectable young lady," said Lin. "She'd be horrified if I asked her to take me to the Maze. Whereas I am sure you and the Prince's other friends spend plenty of time there, engaged in all sorts of unsavory activities. Besides—I rather think I've asked enough of her."

"I was surprised you were able to convince her to sneak you into the Palace," Kel allowed.

Mariam would have been disappointed in his outfit, Lin thought. He was dressed plainly, in black broadcloth and a white shirt, though the embroidery at his cuffs and collar must have cost more than Lin made in a month.

"It was easy," said Lin. "She fancies you."

Kel looked utterly surprised. *Men*, thought Lin. "She only has eyes for Conor," he said.

"I saw the way she looks at you," said Lin.

"She would never dare to even think on it," said Kel, and there was a new harshness to his voice. "Her mother would disown her."

Lin, realizing she had touched a nerve, thought it best to change the subject. "Perhaps." She discarded the now-damp cloth. "But as an Ashkari woman, it would be illegal for me to be in the Maze after sunset."

"Everything in the Maze is illegal," Kel pointed out.

"It also wouldn't be safe. Lawlessness does not protect me, even from unjust laws. Both are bad. Alone, I would be easy prey for a criminal in the Maze. If I am with you, it will be assumed I am like you. *Malbushim*."

"You said that word before. What does it mean?"

Lin paused. The word was part of the Old Language of Aram, and such a part of her daily vocabulary she had forgotten it would be foreign to Kel. "It means non-Ashkar," she said. "Well, literally, it means 'clothes.' Just clothes, like a jacket or a dress. But we use it to mean empty clothes—no one wearing them. No one inside."

"Empty suits," mused Kel. "No souls inside?"

"Yes," she said, and blushed a little. "I don't think it's true, by the way. About the souls."

"Not *literally*," he said, in a gently mocking tone. "Speaking of respectability, what is it you want in the Maze?"

"The Ragpicker King asked me to find him a book there," she said. "In exchange, he will let me use the equipment in the Black Mansion to distill medicines—like the kind I used to treat you."

"Can you not do that in the Sault?"

"Most of the medical apparatus in the Sault is off limits to women. It was only with great reluctance that they allowed me to become a physician at all."

"That's ridiculous," Kel said firmly. "You are clearly an excellent physician. And I say this as an unbiased observer whose life was not recently saved by your skills. Obviously."

"Obviously." Lin smiled. "How do *you*, Sword Catcher, know the Ragpicker King?"

"He offered me a job," Kel said. "I told him no, but he's very persistent."

The carriage jerked to a stop. They had arrived.

An old stone archway, once a monument to a long-past naval battle, marked the entrance to the Maze. They dismounted from the carriage—Kel offered his hand to Lin again, to help her down, and this time she took it—which would wait for them here; the streets of the Maze were too narrow for it to carry them inside.

For the first time, Lin passed through the arch, following Kel, and was inside the Maze. She could still see the glow of the Ruta

Magna if she looked back over her shoulder, but not for long. The narrow, smoky streets swallowed it up.

The city's lamplighters did not come here, any more than the Vigilants did. Instead, cheap torches—rags soaked in naphtha and wrapped tightly around wooden poles—blazed in metal holders clamped to pockmarked walls, much of whose paint had long been eaten away by salt air. The sense of being pressed down by darkness was profound, with the high warehouse walls and thick, rising smoke blotting out the moon and stars.

The place smelled of old fish, discarded rubbish, and spices. Houses where many families clearly lived had their doors thrown open; old women sat on the steps, stirring metal pots with long spoons over open cooking fires. Passing sailors carried metal bowls around their necks, and would hand them over, along with a few coins, for a ladle of fish stew.

The fires added their smoke to that of the torches, making Lin's nose tickle. It was hard to see anything clearly between the smoke and the crowds. Faces loomed up out of the shadows and vanished again, as if they belonged to lively ghosts.

Out of self-preservation, Lin stayed close by Kel's side. If she mislaid him, she doubted she could make her way back out to the Ruta Magna without becoming hopelessly lost. He walked with confidence, so her teasing had not been entirely misplaced. He *did* know his way around the Maze.

"Look out." Kel indicated a puddle of something blackish red, which Lin dutifully stepped around. He gave her the sideways smile she was beginning to realize was habitual—the one that seemed to say *I take nothing too seriously*—and said, "What do you think? Is the Maze what you expected?"

Lin hesitated. How to say that it was strange to her, because they did not have poverty like this in the Sault? She had been to poor houses as a physician, but this felt different. It was a place that had been left to consume itself without the interference of either charity or Law. She could see, through grimy windows, whole families sleeping on the floors of crowded, narrow houses. Poppy-juice addicts, their heads lolling as they dreamed, sat propped against walls, passersby stepping over them as if they were sleeping dogs. Old women kneeling in doorways shook metal cups, begging for coins.

"It's crowded, but it feels abandoned," she said.

He nodded, as if calmly observing the truth of what she'd said. He was awfully calm in general, she thought. She supposed it was the nature of his job, pretending tranquility in situations where he had to lie and lie and smile while he did it.

She wondered if he was lying to her when he smiled.

"I assume whatever book Morettus wants, it is something no reputable bookshop would carry," he said.

"It is a book about magic." Lin skirted around a Shenzan sailor sitting in the street, his left sleeve rolled up. A thin man in a Hanse-atic soldier's jacket was carefully applying a tattoo to his arm, using a tray of dye and heated needles. It was a crocodile, its tail looped around the man's arm, its scales done in brilliant green and gold. "I cannot say anything more."

"A book about magic," Kel echoed thoughtfully. "Dangerous stuff, indeed."

Lin eyed him sideways. Waves of sea air were rolling in, making her shiver, mixing with the spice-and-smoke scent of the Maze. They passed a salesman hawking bottles of a dark liquid he promised would clear up pox scars and "improve the quality of passion." Lin cast him a disapproving glare. She knew such men; there was no more than colored water in the bottle.

"Do you know what Morettus is planning to do with the book, if you find it?" Kel said.

"I don't think he wants it for himself, exactly," Lin said. "I think he wants me to have it. To learn from it how to better mix magic and medicine."

"Interesting," Kel said. "Perhaps he's ill. Or knows someone who is."

Lin had been too busy thinking about Mariam to consider such a theory. The Ragpicker King seemed well enough to her eye—too thin, and perhaps too pale, but in a manner that suggested intensity and overwork, not sickness.

Kel smiled—the smile of someone recalling a memory. "There was a game I used to play as a child, at the Orfelinat. *If you had magic, what would you do with it?* My best friend, Cas, and I used to say we'd use magic to become the most powerful pirate kings of all time. That gold would fly off the decks of other ships and into our coffers."

Lin could not help but laugh. "You dreamed of becoming a lazy pirate?"

She could not help but picture him as a little boy, before he'd learned that preternatural calm, that sideways smile. A little boy like Josit had been, all skinned knees and messy hair. She *liked* him, she thought. He was hard not to like—self-deprecating, funny, clever. She could see why Prince Conor had been so desperate for him to live.

They had reached the central part of Arsenal Road, the Maze's main thoroughfare. Drink and drugs for sale had given way to sex. Scantily dressed young men and women, lips and cheeks rouged with paint, sat in the open doors of brothels, or crowded in front of glassless windows, calling out to passersby. A man in a blue soldier's uniform stopped in front of one window. After a lively exchange with a crowd of girls, he crooked his finger at one—a slim young thing with dark hair and freckles. She came out of the bawdy house and smiled at him, holding out her hand. He counted coins into her palm under the light of a naphtha torch before leading her down a nearby alley.

Lin had thought they would disappear into the shadows, but they were still visible when he stopped and lifted the girl up against a wall. He slid his hands up under her skirt, burying his face against her neck. Her bare legs dangled around his hips as he unbuckled his trousers and thrust into her with a feverish desperation. Lin could not hear them, but the girl seemed to be patting his shoulder as he moved—an almost motherly gesture, as if to say, *There, there.*

Lin felt her cheeks flame. Which was what she got, she supposed, for standing and staring; Kel had stepped away for a moment to drop a coin in the cup of a young boy in a torn jacket several sizes too big. He'd only been gone for a moment, but when he returned, he took a look at Lin's face, glanced down the alley, and smiled wryly. "That's what they call 'a half-crown standup,'" he said. "Cheaper if you don't pay for a room. And no," he added, "I don't know that from personal experience."

"It's just . . . Well, it's not like the Temple District, is it? The courtesans there have their health checked by physicians regularly. For their *own* protection," she added, knowing she probably sounded extremely prudish, "as it should be."

"To work in the Temple District is to be a courtesan," said Kel, sounding uncharacteristically somber. "To work here in the Maze is to be desperate." He seemed to shake off the seriousness, like a heron shaking water from its feathers. "Come. We're not far from the market."

They fell back into step together. Lin said, "You told me the Ragpicker King keeps offering you a job. A job doing what?"

"Spying for him, as far as I can tell. He wants to know what's going on with the Charter Families. He has some eyes on the Hill, but not in every room."

"And spying on the Crown Prince, too, I'd imagine. Which seems awfully dangerous."

"It doesn't matter. I'd never do it, regardless." Kel exhaled and looked up at the stars, which were largely invisible behind the torchlight's glare. "I feel as if everyone keeps asking me why I won't betray Conor," he said, and Lin felt a jolt, as she always did when the Prince was referred to so casually. He was Crown Prince Aurelian; surely it was odd for him to have something so simple as a given name. "He isn't the one who came and got me from the Orfelinat. He isn't the one who made me a Sword Catcher. And if I hadn't become a Sword Catcher, I'd likely have ended up here." He indicated the Maze with a gesture. "When I was twelve, I fell off a horse. Broke my leg. They were worried I'd limp, that my gait would never match Conor's after that. They were ready to put me out on the street. Conor said if I did wind up with a limp, he'd break his own leg with a hammer. In fact, he said he'd do it if they sent me away, regardless."

Lin found herself staring. "So what happened?"

"I healed without a limp."

So the Prince never had to follow through on his promise, Lin thought, but she couldn't bring herself to say it out loud. It was an awful story, but Kel had told it as if it were a fond memory. A moment of grace in a strange and brutal life.

"I shouldn't have told you that," he said, ruefully. "It's probably a state secret. But fuck it. You know everything already."

Lin was too surprised to respond, but it didn't matter. They had reached their destination. Arsenal Road curved away from the city here, deeper into shadows where warehouses and shops were jumbled together like discarded toys. Here a square opened out, one side backed up against the Key; Lin could glimpse the shine of light on water through narrow gaps between the buildings, and hear the crash of waves.

Lining the inside of the square were tables—some of wood, some of boxes stacked hastily together, a cloth thrown over them—on which various objects were displayed. Lin hurried to investigate.

Here were things dredged from the bottom of the sea, blasted into the water by the force of mage-fire during the Sundering War. For the first time, Lin saw magical writing that was not *gematry*. Elegant scrollworked letters, winding around a carved wooden box, stamped on the hilt of a rusted dagger. She drifted over to look as a saleswoman in a Hindish *satika* snatched up the dagger and brandished it proudly. "It is no ordinary dagger," she said, in response to Lin's curious look, "for it cuts not skin or flesh, but emotions. It can cut through hate or bitterness and end it. It can cut through love and put it to rest."

"Lovely," said Kel, materializing out of nowhere, and putting on a *rich, distracted merchant's son, slumming,* voice, "but not what we need. Come along, my dear."

Lin rolled her eyes—*my dear* indeed—but followed him to another table. Here were bags of herbs, tied up with ribbons, and handwritten spells, which Lin knew at a glance were nonsense. Cards for fortune-telling, and all sorts of objects—weapons and pendants and even compasses—set with bits of Sunderglass.

Lin's heart sank into her shoes. She was a fool to have come here. There was no *real* magic at this market, no forbidden lore. Just a heap of glittery, useless nothing, like the contents of a magpie's nest. She wanted to smash a window, to scream.

As she turned away, she caught a glimpse of a book with a familiar red-leather cover. She dashed to look at it. It was indeed one of Petrov's. But her heart fell as she turned it over, and then the next, and the next. Nowhere among them was the book with the rayed sun on its spine. Only a collection of books about interpreting dreams and reading palms, and a few tomes on *gematry—The Mysterious Power of Alphabets,* one was titled—no doubt forbidden among *malbushim,* but of no use to her.

"This batch of books interests you, I see?"

Lin looked up to see that the junk dealer had made his way to her. He was a tall man in a brass-buttoned coat, with a reedy voice and a quantity of graying ginger hair.

"I sought one book in particular," she said. "The work of Qasmuna."

"Oho," he said. "An expert in the area of grimoires, I see." Lin bit her tongue. "There was a Qasmuna volume among these," he added, with a gesture toward the remaining books. "It was, I fear, snapped up immediately by a discerning individual."

"Who?" Lin said breathlessly. "Maybe they'd be willing to sell it to me."

The dealer grinned. He was missing several teeth. "Alas," he said. "My customers depend on my discretion. Perhaps something else . . . ?"

"These books belonged to a friend," Lin said, abandoning pretense. "His landlady sold them when he died. Have you nothing else that might have belonged to him?"

She felt foolish immediately. There was nothing trustworthy about the dealer; he would surely dig up his worst, most worthless volumes and attempt to exploit her presumed grief to sell them to her. She was about to turn away when he drew something out from beneath the table and said, "This did not belong to your friend. It does, however, mention Qasmuna. It is a different sort of book— not spells, but history."

Lin turned back to examine it. It was an old book, bound in pale leather gone gray with time. TALES OF THE SORCERER-KINGS was stamped upon the cover in gilt, as was the author's name: LAOCAN-TUS AURUS IOVIT.

"A historian's attempt to explain the Sundering," said the dealer. "When the Empire fell, most copies were destroyed. Not all of them, though. A rare item—ten gold crowns."

"Not worth it," said Kel, who had appeared at Lin's side. "I've read it. A bit of history, and then a great deal of praising various Emperors for their generosity and wisdom in putting various magicians to death. And we're off."

The dealer glared after them as she and Kel walked away.

"You didn't need to insult his book," Lin said peevishly.

Kel shrugged. "I will send him a letter of apology. I have been very well versed in etiquette." He looked down at Lin. "I'm sorry he didn't have what you wanted. Is it very important?"

"Yes, I—" She spoke almost without thinking. "I have a friend. She is dying. I would do anything to heal her. Perhaps there might be something in this book I could learn that would help her." She looked up at him. "I suppose that is my state secret."

"I am sorry," he said, and suddenly she wanted to cry. But she would not cry in front of him, she told herself fiercely. She liked him, oddly enough, but he was still a *malbesh* and a stranger—

Something flashed in the corner of her vision. A familiar gesture, a familiar face? She was not sure what it was that had caught her attention, but she turned her head, and when she did, she saw Oren Kandel.

He was moving among the various tables of objects, glancing from one to the next almost indifferently. He wore nothing that would mark him out as Ashkar. His clothes were merchant's clothes, linen and gray. His mop of dark hair nearly hid his eyes, but at any moment he would look up—and see her, and recognize her.

"I know him," she whispered, just loud enough for Kel to hear. "He is Ashkar."

"And he knows you?"

"We all know one another." She pressed herself back against the wall. "He'll see me," she whispered. "He'll tell the Maharam."

As if he'd heard her, Oren raised his head. He began to turn—and Lin found herself caught up, her body blocked by Kel's. His arms were around her. She looked up in surprise and saw the moon reflected in his eyes. "Look at me," he said, and kissed her.

For all that it was swift and bewildering, it was gentle. His lips captured hers with expert ease, his hands rising to cup her face. She knew he was hiding her, hiding her features from the man who might otherwise recognize her. The touch of his scarred palms was rough and soft at the same time, like the flick of a cat's tongue.

She let her head fall back against the cage of his hands. She had been kissed before, at the Goddess Festival. It was the one time of the year one might kiss and not have it be a vow or responsibility—or a shame if it was discovered. But that had been a quick peck on the lips, not like this at all.

He kissed like a noble, she thought. Like someone who had done this many times before because he was allowed to; because he lived in a world where kisses were not promises, where they were as common and bright as magic before the Sundering. There was something expert, if dispassionate, in the way he explored her mouth, sending small sparks rising up along her nerves, like the embers of a disturbed fire scattering brightness. A sort of heat suffused her body; her knees shook, and her hands, too, where she held the lapels of his coat.

When they drew apart, it was to the sound of whistles and cat-calls. She glanced around, half dizzy; Oren was gone. Kel acknowledged the attention of the crowd with an imperious nod that reminded Lin, with a dark kind of shiver, of the Prince. Would kissing the Prince be anything like kissing Kel?

She shoved the thought instantly from her mind. The crowd having lost interest, Kel began to draw her around a corner, back toward the wider part of Arsenal Road. "You're all right?" he murmured. "I'm sorry. It was all I could think of."

"Really? *That* was all you could think of?" Lin touched her hand to her mouth. Her lips still tingled. It had been a very forceful sort of kiss.

"It really was." He sounded rueful. "I apologize if it was terrible."

He looked sheepish as a puppy who had been caught chewing a slipper. Lin couldn't help smiling. "It wasn't terrible. And thank you. If Oren had seen me . . ." She shuddered.

"So," he said, "do you wish to try to discover who bought this book Andreyen is seeking? You are not wrong that it might be possible to buy it back—"

Lin froze. She had seen a shadow detach itself from a group of other shadows and approach them—a man, face hidden in the dim light.

The man was of medium height, wearing a coat with a multitude of buckles across the front. Most of his face was hidden behind a mask of tarnished metal. From the little she could see, Lin guessed that he was young, and the thickened scar tissue around his right eye suggested he had been in quite a few fights.

Kel exhaled. "Jerrod," he said.

"Sorry to interrupt whatever this is," Jerrod said, indicating Lin in what she felt was an insulting and dismissive manner, "but that appointment you were seeking? It's now."

Kel looked annoyed. "I suppose you've been following me around?"

"Obviously," said Jerrod, as if Kel were very stupid for asking. Clearly there was no love lost between the two of them.

"Prosper Beck wants to see me now," Kel said. He glanced at Lin. "Beck is like the Ragpicker King, but worse."

"How rude," said Jerrod.

"Why do you want to talk to someone worse than the Ragpicker King?" Lin asked, puzzled.

"I don't want to," said Kel. "I have to." He turned back to Jerrod. "Can I bring her with me?"

Jerrod shook his head. "No. Only you."

"I can't leave my friend here," said Kel. "Let me bring her back to the—to our carriage, and I'll return and meet you."

"No," said Jerrod. Lin had the feeling he rather enjoyed refusing requests. "Come with me now, or the deal's off."

"Then we're back to where we were in the noodle shop," said Kel. "I'll harry you unto death, et cetera, et cetera."

"Gray hell," muttered Jerrod. "I should have killed you when I had the chance. Wait here," he said, and disappeared back into the shadows.

"He seems nice," Lin said.

Kel, looking harried, half smiled down at her. "He isn't an easy man to deal with. But he's my only conduit to Beck."

"Is he a Crawler?" Lin asked.

Kel looked surprised. "How'd you guess?"

"Chalk dust on his fingers," Lin said. "I had a patient who was a Crawler once when he was young. He told me they use it for grip." She hesitated. "Was he one of the ones who—"

"Attacked me in the alley?" Kel said. "Yes, but I'm working on not holding grudges. Besides, it was a mistake."

Jerrod returned before Lin could ask what that meant. This time he had a carriage with him—a small, nearly impossibly light-looking vehicle with open sides. A young woman with close-cut dark hair sat in the driver's seat. She had chalk dust on her fingers, too.

"Prosper Beck offers you the use of a carriage and driver to bring your friend home," said Jerrod, in a tone that indicated that this was the most generous suggestion anyone had ever made. "Take the offer or leave the Maze."

Kel's brow furrowed. He started to protest, but Lin cut him off. "We will take the offer."

She clambered up into the carriage—easy enough; it was low to the ground, light as if it were intended for racing—and settled back into the seat. Kel leaned in. "Are you sure?"

She nodded. The Qasmuna book was not here. She felt empty and weary and wished only to go home and remake her plans. She would not give up, but she could not bear more of this tonight. There was also a thread of anxiety in her chest, still, about Mariam. Surely it would be best to check in on her.

Kel stepped back. "Take her to the gates of the Sault," he said to the driver. "Do not stray off course."

"Indeed, do not," said Jerrod. "Or he'll poison you."

This produced an alarmed look from the driver. She raised the reins, clucking to the horses, as Lin wondered what on earth *that* meant. She recalled Merren, the pretty boy at the Black Mansion who'd called himself a poisoner. Surely, she thought, as the carriage began to move through the tangle of Arsenal Road, that could not be a coincidence? It was as if every thread led back to the Ragpicker King somehow, like the threads of a web all led to the spider in the center. Was she an observer of the web, she wondered, or was she, too, a fly?

When the last of her people had passed before her, and her Source-Stone could hold no more power, Queen Adassa climbed to the top of the tower of Balal, and there her heart sank, for outside the city walls she could see the massing of the armies of the Sorcerer-Kings. She cried out then for Makabi, saying, "My right hand, you must now leave me. Leave me, and save our people."

Makabi did not want to leave his Queen, but he did as she commanded. He rallied the people of Aram and told them that their Queen would hold the armies off while they made their escape. "The land of Aram, we must abandon," he said. "It will be consumed in the fire of war. But the spirit of Aram is the spirit of its people, and it shall live on as we carry it with us."

With great mourning, the Ashkari people were led by Makabi to the uncharted western lands.

— *Tales of the Sorcerer-Kings*, Laocantus Aurus Iovit III

CHAPTER FIFTEEN

Kel followed Jerrod in silence down Arsenal Road. (He felt a little foolish—he ought to have simply assumed that when he entered the Maze, one of Jerrod's Crawlers would have reported on his presence. The Maze was Beck's territory, after all.)

Eventually they reached a warehouse whose windows had been blacked out with paint. Jerrod led him inside and down a long corridor that seemed as if it had been decorated in stripes; Kel realized, upon a closer look, that the weathered paint was simply peeling away in long strips. Curls of paint lay scattered on the floor, crunching under their boots like dried leaves. From the far end of the hall came the glow of moving lights and the sound of voices.

The corridor ended abruptly, opening into an enormous room. Here Kel paused a moment to stare. Glass lanterns hung from a roof that disappeared into darkness, dimly illuminating dozens of tables scattered across the rough wooden floor of what was clearly an abandoned shipbuilder's manufactory, back in the days before such work had been moved out of the city to the Arsenale. An array of rusting hooks, on which sails had likely once been stretched to dry, hung from the ceiling. The hulking shadow of a half-built ship gazed down at an upturned crow's nest, around which six or seven men played *lansquenet* with gleaming mother-of-pearl chips. Presumably, they would be traded for money at the end of the night.

Not everyone in the place was engaged in gaming. Men and women in dark-blue velvet moved among the crowd, taking money and dispensing gambling chits and fresh bottles of wine—Beck's employees, clearly. A few young men cavorted among dinghies piled with cushions, drinking abnormally bright-green *pastisson*, the kind that produced waking phantasms. One slept against a rusting anchor, the bottle clutched against his chest, a blissful smile on his face like a child's. They were more finely dressed than the average inhabitant of the Maze, in gold-cloth and silk, jewels gleaming at necks and fingers. As Kel did not recognize any of them, he guessed they were rich guildsmen and merchants, not inhabitants of the Hill.

Though, he mused, what would keep Montfaucon or Falconet away from such a place? Or Roverge, or even Conor? Though Conor claimed he had never met Prosper Beck, that did not mean Prosper Beck had not observed *him*.

Ships' berths, gutted out of their old homes, were stacked against one of the walls. Diaphanous curtains half hid them from the main floor; as they passed, Kel was aware of movement behind the curtains. Figures, writhing in the small compartments—muffled gasps and rustling, the occasional gleam of light on bare skin or dark velvet.

"The doxies here work for Beck," Jerrod said as they crossed the room. "It pays well, and we Crawlers protect them. As long as you keep spending money at the tables, their services are free."

The edge of a diaphanous curtain twitched back. Kel saw a girl: pale-purple curls, an indigo velvet mask. An arm looped around her from behind, a hand sliding down into her bodice. Her eyes fluttered shut as the curtain fell back in place.

Kel thought of Silla, and of Merren. Of Lin. He had been kissing far too many people lately, he thought. He was in danger of becoming some sort of romantic bandit from a Story-Spinner's tale, of the *he kissed her, then vanished mysteriously into the night* variety.

He'd enjoyed all the kissing—kissing Lin had been surprisingly pleasant—but knew enough about himself to realize he was seeking something he had not yet found.

Nothing about the berths here enticed him, regardless. There was something a little desperate about such public debauchery. As he and Jerrod headed toward a velvet curtain at the far side of the room, they nearly collided with a young Malgasi sailor as he staggered by, rolling down the sleeve of his copper-colored jacket. Not before Kel caught sight of the puncture marks along his forearm, though. They looked fresh. The boy glanced at him briefly; his pupils were vastly dilated, like black dinner plates. This was how it started, Kel thought; soon enough he'd be one of the emaciated addicts staggering around the Maze.

"So, is this Beck's headquarters?" he asked as they ducked past the curtain and found themselves in a stairwell. Rickety steps led upward. Lamps swayed from hooks on the walls. Stacked crates of bottles with bright-green labels that proclaimed it to be SINGING MONKEY WINE. A peculiar name for a vintage.

Jerrod led the way up. "One of many," he said. "Beck's not like your Ragpicker King, with his Black Mansion and his pretensions of being a *gentleman*. He owns a score of buildings, each running a different business, and moves among them. A manufactory one day, an old temple another. It's clever, really."

"And how'd you end up working for Beck?" Kel asked. They had reached a small landing.

Jerrod, though, seemed to have run out of patience with small talk. "None of your business," he said, shouldering open a door whose rusty hinges screeched like an owl.

Another short corridor before Jerrod led Kel into a room that seemed to have once been an office. It had a nautical feel to it, the walls painted dark blue and hung with dusty maps of faraway ports. A carved walnut desk took up most of the room.

On one side of the desk was an empty wooden chair; on the other sat a man who glanced quickly from Kel to Jerrod and nodded. "Good," he said, in a guttural voice. "You brought him."

So this was Prosper Beck.

Beck was a big man—much bigger than Kel had somehow imagined. Barrel-chested and broad-shouldered, he had a thickened nose that looked as if it had been broken more than once. Dark stubble shaded a lantern jaw. He wore an elaborate coat of scarlet-and-silver brocade that seemed somehow at odds with a neck the size of a tree trunk and fists the diameter of dinner plates. In fact, Beck overall was the opposite of what Kel had pictured.

Well, that was what one got for making assumptions.

Kel studied him, wondering what to say. Long ago, when he had first been learning *etiqueta* at Marivent, he had complained to Mayesh that he did not understand why he needed to memorize the hundred different ways to greet foreign nobility, the correct way to deflect questions without giving offense, the different bows appropriate to different occasions.

"Politics is a game," Mayesh had said. "Manners give you the tools to play that game. And it is a game as deadly as any swordfight. Think of etiquette as a sort of armor."

And so Kel, in his mind, put on his armor of manners. The greaves and gauntlets of polite smiles, the vambraces of careful answers that gave nothing away, the helm and visor of unreadable expressions.

"May I sit down?" he asked.

Beck indicated the seat across from him. "Sit."

Kel settled himself in the wooden chair. It was uncomfortable. He was aware of Jerrod, standing against the wall, arms crossed. He was not foolish enough to think Jerrod was the only observer here, the only one ready to leap to Beck's defense should Kel prove troublesome. Though Beck looked as if he could defend himself.

"You are the Prince's cousin," rumbled Beck. "Anjuman of Marakand. What message does the Palace have for me?"

"I do not come on behalf of House Aurelian," said Kel. "Only on behalf of Prince Conor. And he does not know I am here. No one does."

There, Kel thought. He had laid out a vulnerability, like a card on the table. He was unsupported by the Palace. He was alone.

"Ah," said Beck. "Are they aware of Conor's debt? The ten thousand crowns?"

"Only I am aware," said Kel. "Once the King knows, the situation slips beyond my control. One does not know what he will do. But he has an army at his disposal, not to mention the Arrow Squadron."

Prosper Beck smiled a little. "You are threatening me, but sideways," he said. "Amusing. Now let me ask: Why are you doing all this for Conor Aurelian?"

"Because," Kel said, carefully. "He is my family." *Surely criminals understand family.*

"You and the Prince are close, then? You're in his confidence?"

"Yes."

"Then it would surprise you to hear that he repaid his debt this morning?" said Beck, eyes glittering. "In full?"

Kel's breath caught in his throat. He thought of his armor. *Remember your visor, the mask you must wear.* He kept his expression neutral as he said, "The whole ten thousand crowns?"

Beck looked smug. "So you are surprised."

"I am surprised," Kel said, "that, having been paid by Conor"—he refused to say *repaid*—"you agreed to meet with me at all."

Beck sat back. His gaze flicked over Kel. His eyes were dark, opaque as metal. "You poisoned Jerrod. I thought that was . . . interesting. It made me interested in you."

Jerrod cleared his throat.

"Though the Prince's debt may no longer be an issue," Beck said, "I admire a person with nerve, which you seem to have. And I am sure you wish to know where the money I used to set up my business came from. Specifically, who on the Hill gave it to me. A person who wishes very much, let us say, to destabilize the monarchy. It was their idea"—he smiled thinly—"that I buy up Conor Aurelian's debts. And they gave me the money to do it."

Kel's heart slapped against the inside of his rib cage. "Why would I believe," he said, "that you would turn against your own patron?"

Beck snorted. "Why wouldn't I? If they happen to wind up in the Trick, I keep the whole ten thousand crowns, not just a cut of it."

"You're offering to tell me who on the Hill is betraying House Aurelian," Kel said. "But you have not said what you want in exchange."

"Antonetta Alleyne," said Beck.

In the ensuing silence, one could have heard a feather strike the floor. Kel thought of his imaginary armor, but it did not help. Rage was running through his veins like wires through a puppet. He glanced at Jerrod—as if Jerrod of all people would be any help—but Jerrod was at the door, conversing in a low voice with a boy in a blue velvet suit.

"Specifically," said Beck, as the boy slipped back out of the room, "a necklace that belongs to Antonetta Alleyne. A gold locket, shaped like a heart."

"It can't be worth that much," Kel said, without being able to stop himself. "Why—?"

"It's what is inside it that I want," said Beck. "A piece of information."

"Information that could hurt her?" Kel asked.

"She is far too rich and protected to be hurt," said Beck, dismissively. "And the information I have could well save your precious Prince, even your House Aurelian." He sat back in his chair. "Get me the necklace. Then we'll talk."

"And if I don't get the necklace?"

"We won't talk. And you came here for nothing." Beck shrugged his big shoulders. "I've nothing else to say. Off you go, Prince's cousin."

Kel rose to his feet. Beck was watching him with his odd, metallic stare. *What the hell*, Kel thought. He might as well ask. Abruptly, hoping to catch Beck off guard, he said, "Where did Conor get the money to pay you?"

Beck raised his hands, palm out. "Don't know," he said. "Don't care. One odd thing—he paid me in Sarthian *lire*." He chuckled. "Not that it matters. Gold is gold."

"We ought to get down to the floor," Jerrod said to Beck. "There's some kind of fight brewing over a hand of *lansquenet*. Things are turning violent."

Beck rose to his feet and, without another word, followed Jerrod out of the room. Kel watched him go. There *was* something odd about Beck, something that did not seem to quite match up, but he could not quite put his finger on it, and Jerrod and Beck did not seem to be coming back. After some time spent sitting alone in the room, Kel got to his feet and shrugged.

"Well, all right then," he said. "I'll show myself out."

When Lin returned to the Sault, she felt as if she had traveled much farther away from home than simply the Maze. She was absurdly pleased to see the place again, and wondered if this was how Josit felt when he returned from the Gold Roads. (She suspected not; he was always happy to see her, and Mariam, but retained an air of guarded wistfulness about him, the sense that while his body might be in the Sault, his mind was voyaging still.)

She went immediately to the Etse Kebeth, the House of Women, and found Chana in the kitchen. Chana shook her head when she saw Lin. "Mari's asleep," she said. "She was in a bad way. I had to give her passiflora tea to calm her down." She narrowed her eyes. "What did you say to her?"

"Nothing," Lin protested. "She saw a royal Malgasi carriage on the Ruta Magna. It gave her a shock."

"Ah." Chana played with the beaded fringe that edged her cuffs. "I had thought perhaps it was something about the Tevath. The Goddess Festival." She shook her head. "I had not thought of some-

thing so very painful. It took Mariam so long to feel safe in Castellane. To see a Malgasi carriage here . . ."

"She said something about the *vamberj*," said Lin.

"They were the Queen's own guard in Favár," said Chana.
"They covered their faces with wolf-face masks in silver, and hunted
the Ashkar in the streets as a wolf might hunt a rabbit." She shuddered and gestured to Lin to come closer. "Darling girl," she said,
giving her a one-armed hug around the waist, "you have been out
in the city so often these past days. Be careful."

If only she knew, Lin thought. She dropped a kiss on Chana's
wrinkled forehead and made her way back out into the night. As she
crossed the Sault, heading toward her home, she glimpsed the shine
of lanterns and realized, with a pang, that today had been the day of
Mez and Rahel's wedding ceremony.

She hurried to the Kathot. It was still alight. Round glass lamps
hung like pendant moons from the boughs of the fig and almond
trees. The damp paving stones were strewn with the petals of red
and white roses, as were the steps of the Shulamat.

Long tables draped in fine white linen bore the remains of the
wedding feast—half-empty glasses of wine; crumbs of sweet bread and
cake. Lin closed her eyes. She could picture it all: Mez and Rahel in
their finery, arms around each other; the Maharam with his staff, giving
thanks for the blessings of the Goddess: *joy and gladness, loving couples,
mirth and song, close communities, peace and companionship.* There would
have been gifts: silver blessing cups, made in Hind; gold incantation
bowls from Hanse. From Marakand, leather prayer books studded
with semiprecious stones. It was traditional that the wedding gifts come
from far-flung places, as a reminder that the world was full of Ashkar,
their sisters and brothers. They were not alone here in Castellane.

Lin felt suddenly lonely. She had thought perhaps she would go
to the House of Women when she returned from the Maze, to see
Mariam, but it was too late; she did not want to wake her friend.
Instead, as she left the Kathot, she found her feet pointed in a very
different direction.

As always on the rare evenings that Mayesh was present in the Sault, he was sitting on the porch outside his small, whitewashed house, enclosed in a cloud of lilac pipe smoke. His heavy rosewood rocking chair had been a gift from a Shenzan emissary; when Lin was very small, she had liked to run her hands over the intricate carvings of birds, flowers, and dragons.

In the moonlight, Lin climbed the porch steps. Her grandfather watched her from beneath his thick eyebrows, seeming not at all surprised to see her. "Were you at the wedding?" she asked, perching herself on the porch railing. "Mez and Rahel's?"

Mayesh shook his head. "I was at the Palace," he said. "The Ambassador from Malgasi required greeting."

There was a time when Lin would have been angry. Of course he had not been there, she would have thought. That was Mayesh, ever more dedicated to those outside the Sault than he was to those within it. But she could not summon that anger now. She herself had forgotten Mez's wedding; she herself had stood among the remains of the feast, the ghost-memory of the happy dancers, realizing that the river of life in the Sault went on, and she stood on the banks, watching from a distance.

"I heard you've been making trouble again," said Mayesh. "Bothering the Maharam about access to the Shulamat, is it?"

"I suppose Chana told you."

"I am too much of a diplomat," said Mayesh calmly, "to reveal my sources of information."

It took Lin a moment to realize he was joking. A grandfather who made jokes. *Well.* "I thought you didn't even like the Maharam."

"It's not our job to like each other," said Mayesh. "It's our job to serve the Sault, albeit in different ways." He set his pipe down. "You are rather like your mother," he said, and Lin stiffened. "You never stop pushing, refusing to accept things as they are. You are always *fighting.* For something else, something better."

"Is that a bad thing?"

"Not necessarily," Mayesh said. "The Sault is a good world, but it's a small one. That's why I became Counselor."

"The Sault was too small for you?" Lin intended to sound contemptuous, but the question came out as curious instead.

"I had a sense," Mayesh said, "of how small we were, and because of that, how vulnerable. We serve our roles as Ashkar—remaining in the Sault, providing small magics to the people of Castellane, but never being of them. Content to give counsel to others on the topic of laws that do not apply to us, rights that are not ours. There is only one voice that speaks for the Ashkar outside the walls, only one raised to defend our people in the halls of power."

"Your voice," said Lin.

"The Counselor's voice," said Mayesh. "It need not be me. It has not always been me. I will not be Counselor much longer, Lin. At some point, I will need to train a replacement. Perhaps someone clever enough to get themselves into Marivent against the Prince's will. Perhaps someone else who finds the Sault a little bit small."

Lin blinked. Surely she was misunderstanding him. He was looking at her very steadily though, the reflection of the moon a pinpoint light in each of his pupils. "You mean . . ."

Mayesh rose with a groan, settling his hands in the small of his back. "It is late, and time for an old man to seek his bed. Rest well, Lin."

It was a dismissal.

"Rest well," she said, and let him go. On the way back to her house, as she passed through the Kathot, she spied a small gray mouse, nibbling on a crumb of honey cake. It glanced up as she approached with tiny, fear-bright eyes.

Worry not, little mouse, she thought. *We are neither of us sure of our welcome here.*

Kel had intended to stop on his way back to the Palace to leave a message for the Ragpicker King. He told himself now, as he turned his steps toward the Hill instead of the Warren, that he would reach out to Andreyen soon; he needed to puzzle through what he had learned in the Maze first, and above all, needed to understand how Antonetta Alleyne could possibly be involved.

Upon his return to Marivent, Kel found the Palace was dark, only a few lamps burning in the upper windows of the various buildings. The single window of the Star Tower was ablaze with light, like a narrow eye gazing down on Castellane. Kel imagined the King in his tower, watching the stars, guarded by Fausten. He had underestimated the little man, he thought, recalling that Jolivet had once told him that the smallest serpents were the most venomous.

Kel trudged across the wet grass of the Great Lawn, nonplussed and bone-tired. Prosper Beck had not been at all what he had imagined. That sense of wrongness, of something being off about the man, nagged at him. He wondered, too, if Conor had been puzzling over where he'd gone, or if he'd been drunk enough not to notice. Kel hoped Falconet had taken him seriously when Kel had said: *Keep him distracted.*

Lost in thought, he nearly bumped into a carriage that had been left inside the courtyard of the Castel Mitat. It was massive and dramatic, shiny with dark lacquer, its sides sweeping up in the shape of great, dark wings. It seemed to crouch there in the moonlight, hunched and waiting, like some black beast of the night. Upon the doors was the silver blazon of a snarling wolf.

Malgasi, Kel thought. So the Ambassador had arrived. He thought of what Charlon had said: *She's here to try to talk Conor into marrying that girl, the Princess.* And he had been right enough, in his clumsy way. They would be swarming soon enough: Malgasi now, then Kutani, Sarthe, Hanse, and the rest. All of them, he thought, with a weary smile, underestimating how stubborn Conor could actually be.

Kel trudged up the stairs of the Castel Mitat to the rooms he shared with Conor. There were Castelguards posted at the door, as usual; Kel nodded at them and slipped inside, closing the door soundlessly behind him.

Conor was asleep on his bed, a shaft of moonlight falling cross-wise upon him. He was in shirt and trousers and, for some reason, one shoe. Kel half wanted to shake Conor awake, to demand of him the manner in which he had somehow managed to pay off his debt. But curled half upon his side, his arm beneath his head, Conor looked young and careless in sleep, and vulnerable. *Wrists, eyes, throat:* Kel was acutely aware, as he sometimes was, of all the places Conor could be hurt.

When they were younger, Kel had felt every bruise on Conor's skin as a weight of guilt, a failure on his own part to protect, to be the Prince's shield, his unbreakable armor. That had been a time when he had thought Conor kept no secrets from him. He knew better now.

Conor rolled onto his back with a sigh, though he did not wake. Kel sank down upon his own bed, staring into the dark. Had it done him any good to uncover Conor's secret—the debt, the connection to Prosper Beck? Conor had repaid the money without his help, and Kel had learned nothing from Beck.

Not yet, at least. And if he wanted more information, he would have to betray Antonetta. But that pathway was a dark one. Was it not part of his duty to Conor to betray Antonetta—to take her necklace if that meant he might learn more about protecting House Aurelian? Was that not where his duty lay, even if he did not like it?

He lay awake late into the night, his thoughts running in circles. One thing he was sure of: For the first time, what he knew his duty to be clashed with his own sense of what was right. Curious—he had not realized Kel Saren still had his own sense of rightness, buried under everything he had learned since his first arrival at Marivent.

The Sorcerer-Kings looked upon the small figure of Adassa atop her tower, and they laughed. She was but one person, they said among themselves, and they were an army; she was young, and they were experienced. It would not take long to destroy her.

But the fire of the Source-Stone that Adassa held was greater than any they had imagined, because its power came from willing sacrifice. As the armies of the sorcerers threw themselves against the walls of Aram, they found the very land turned against them: Pits of burning fire opened at their feet, and walls of briars sprang up from the ground to block their steps. Whirling pillars of sand and fire scoured the desert and scattered their soldiers.

For two days and nights this battle raged without slowing, and Adassa remained upon the tower of Balal, and it seemed she would never tire. The sorcerers came to Suleman and they said, "This cannot be won with magic alone. She is a woman, and she loves you. Go into the city and climb the tower and strike her down with your sword. Then we will have Aram."

— *Tales of the Sorcerer-Kings*, Laocantus Aurus Iovit III

CHAPTER SIXTEEN

Kel spent most of the next day feeling as if he were being driven slowly mad. For some reason, he had thought that the moment Conor had the opportunity, he would be eager to tell Kel that he had repaid his debt to Prosper Beck.

But it did not seem that was the case. To be fair to Conor, there was little opportunity. When Kel woke in the midmorning, Conor was seated at the small porphyry table, his hands outstretched as one of the housemaids painted his nails in alternating shades of silver and scarlet. He was also in the middle of arguing about something with Mayesh, who was pacing the floor.

"Lowering tensions with Malgasi would be ideal," Mayesh was saying. "But we do not want to find ourselves too closely bound to them. Their ways of doing things are antithetical to Castellane's."

"I thought we merely wished to secure the promise that we could continue to use the trader roads that run through their country," said Conor, flexing his fingers as the housemaid put away her little pots of paint. "Beyond that—" He winked as he saw that Kel was awake and sitting up. "Good morning," he said. "It is early yet, and already you owe me; I prevented Mayesh from waking you an hour ago."

He certainly *looked* at ease, Kel thought, as someone who had recently paid off a large debt might. But then Conor was an expert at projecting an air of ease, whether he truly felt it or not. A few weeks ago, Kel would have said he alone had the skill to see through Conor's pretenses. Now he was no longer sure.

Mayesh looked dour. "One forgets," he said, "quite how long it takes to prepare for these state dinners. Kel, get yourself up; the tailors will be here any moment to fit you and Conor for your evening clothes."

Kel yawned and began to clamber out of bed. "I had rather hoped everyone had forgotten I'd agreed to attend in the first place."

"Not a chance," said Mayesh. "Lest it slip your mind, Sena Anessa, the Ambassador from Sarthe, will also be present. As she is fond of Kel Anjuman, you will be in charge of distracting her while the main business of the event—smoothing relations between Castellane and Malgasi—goes on unhindered."

She is fond of Kel Anjuman. Not, *she is fond of you.* But Mayesh was right, Kel thought, as the tailors arrived, and Conor got lazily to his feet. Kel Anjuman was not Kel himself. Sena Anessa did not really know him, but a construction of him, and that was where her fondness lay.

"I told you you couldn't get out of it," Conor said. He grinned the way he once had when he and Kel had been young and had been caught stealing tarts from Dom Valon's kitchens—amusement mixed with unrepentance.

Mayesh excused himself, and the tailors went to work, fluttering around both Kel and Conor like anxious doves. Clothes, too, were political in the world of the Palace. Conor had to be fitted for an outfit that would pay tribute to Malgasi while retaining the honor of Castellane. He could not wear the silver and purple of Malgasi, obviously, but neither could he wear red. A deep burgundy had been settled on: a silk shirt, a fitted, gold-embroidered waistcoat of wine velvet, trousers of linen and brocade, and wrist-cuffs of blood-red rubies. He had been discouraged from wearing his swan-feather cloak, and was displeased about it.

Kel was given far more neutral colors to wear: pale grays and blanched linens, the colors of ash stirred into cream. They were colors that said: *Pass me over; do not see me.*

He buckled his leather vambraces, with their cleverly hidden blades, beneath the sleeves of his dove-gray coat, despite complaints from the tailors that it would ruin the lines of his clothes. "It is a state dinner, Sieur Anjuman; surely you do not need these weapons!"

Kel only stared coldly. "I would prefer to keep them."

Even after the tailors left, hurrying to make the last alterations to the clothes before evening came, there was no chance to speak to Conor alone. Kel took himself to the tepidarium while Conor was attacked on all sides: his hair trimmed, his eyes smudged with kohl (which would please Lilibet), his jewelry and coronet chosen, and a series of small stars painted in silver along his cheekbones. Kel was relieved to escape all that; Conor had a reputation to keep up, but no one much minded what Kel Anjuman looked like as long as he was respectably attired and clean.

By the time the tailors returned with the final iterations of their clothes, Domna Talyn, the Palace Mistress of Etiquette, was there, reminding them both of key phrases in Malgasi they would need to know that night—how to greet the Ambassador, how to send regards to Queen Iren Belmany, how to inquire after the well-being of Princess Elsabet. "I learned a phrase from a Malgasi gentleman the other night," Conor said, adjusting his glittering crown among the dark waves of his hair. "*Keli polla, börzul.*"

Domna Talyn gasped. "That is *obscene*, Monseigneur."

"But it does show a command of the language, I think," said Conor, looking innocent. "Don't you?"

At this point, Kel gave up. He was not going to have an opportunity to speak to Conor on serious matters tonight, and Conor was not in a serious mood regardless. He would wait until tomorrow and try to pry the truth out of Conor then (without giving away his own knowledge) and in the meantime, consider tonight a dead loss.

He did not regret that decision now. Despite Lilibet's graciousness, her committed decorating, and the efforts of Dom Valon's kitchen in pleasing the palates of the visitors, tension hung like a cloud in the Gallery, and seemed only to be rising. It was no time to be pondering matters of Beck and debts and the Ragpicker King; Kel's attention was needed in the moment.

The dinner had begun well enough. Lilibet had outdone herself with the decorations, draping the room in the Malgasi colors, and Ambassador Sarany had been delighted. (It helped that all evidence of Conor's indoor archery game had been cleared away; even the rents in the tapestries had been mended with impressive speed.)

The high table had been brought down from the dais that was its usual home and placed in the center of the room. Sheer curtains of mulberry silk drifted against the walls, softening the look of the stone. Every shade of the Malgasi color was represented somewhere, from the chairs upholstered in crushed burgundy velvet to the porcelain plates decorated with fat plums. Lilac jade vases overflowed with heliotrope and lavender, and the wine-colored glass goblets had been provided to Lilibet directly by House Sardou, sourced from their warehouses along the Key. Around the handles of the knives and forks, serpents made of amethyst curled, their diamond eyes glittering.

Their seats around the table had been carefully assigned as well. Kel was beside Sena Anessa, who seemed more amused by the decorations than offended that Sarthe's presence had been ignored. Conor sat across from Ambassador Sarany, near the head of the table, where a chair had been left empty for King Markus.

Along the wall behind the King's chair were ranged several members of the Arrow Squadron—including, to Kel's surprise, Legate Jolivet, who usually chose to remain where the King was, but had placed himself here tonight, where he could stare at the Malgasi Ambassador with a stony expression.

Things had begun to go sour when Lilibet explained that King Markus was too deep in his studies to attend. "Some new star system," Lilibet had offered airily, the emeralds at her throat catching the light when she moved. "A matter of great import for scholars, of course, though perhaps less for those of us who must live on the earth."

Sarany had looked furious. Kel understood now why Conor had said he found her terrifying. She was tall and very thin, perhaps forty years old, with a narrow, predatory face. Her dark hair was pulled back tightly, held in place with a dozen glittering pins. Her eyes were deep black, almost cavernous in her bone-white face. Yet despite her extreme spareness, her stare was hungry, as if she wished to devour the world. "Surely you are joking."

The Queen only raised a plucked, arched eyebrow. Conor tapped his fingers idly on the arm of his chair, and Kel realized how long it had been since he had seen anyone respond to the King's absence from official events with surprise. Everyone knew that this was how the ruler of Castellane *was;* one simply accepted it.

"What about Matyas Fausten?" said Sarany. She had only the faintest accent. An accomplished diplomat was likely to speak nine or ten languages fluently. Conor had managed eight, Kel seven. "Will he be here?"

"The little astronomer?" Lilibet seemed puzzled.

"He is Malgasi. I knew him as a tutor at the Court in Favár," said Sarany. "I would like to see him again."

"We could certainly arrange that," said Lilibet, recovering her equilibrium quickly. "I know he was an instructor at your great university . . ."

"The Jagellon," said Conor, and smiled without any emotion at Sarany.

She looked back at him with her hungry eyes. "In Malgasi, learning is treasured," she said. "Free education is provided to our citizens at the Jagellon. Among our royal line we number many polymaths. You will find Princess Elsabet a fine match for your own quick mind."

It was a peculiar thing to say. Peculiar enough that Kel wondered if she had misspoke in uttering the world *match;* usually diplomats were far more subtle than that in angling for a political marriage. Elsabet Belmany *had* been included in Mayesh's list of potential royal alliances, but still, it was strange for the Ambassador to broach the topic with such . . . careless conviction.

Sarany continued to enumerate the Malgasi Princess's many fine qualities to a puzzled-looking Conor: She could hunt, ride, paint, and sing; she knew eleven languages, and had traveled all over Dannemore, and didn't Conor think travel was the best broadener of minds? Meanwhile, Sena Anessa had opened a conversation with Kel about horses, and whether it was really true that the finest came from Valderan, or were the horses of Marakand rated too low?

Kel had begun to develop a headache as he tried to follow both conversations; fortunately one of the cleverly hidden doors in the walls, usually concealed by a tapestry, opened, and out came a line of servants bearing pitchers of iced wine and sorbet, and silver platters of quince, cheese, and savory pastries.

The iced wine was rose-colored and tasted faintly of cherries. The chatter at the head of the table seemed to have at last turned to the opening of a direct road between Favár and Castellane. It would facilitate trade, Conor said, and naturally it would also pass through Sarthe. Lilibet suggested the three countries share the cost of building the road. Sena Anessa seemed interested. Ambassador Sarany continued to stare at Conor. Every once in a while her pink tongue would emerge from her narrow mouth and flick swiftly into her goblet, curling up a tiny swallow of wine.

"In Sarthe, we, too, believe that travel increases wisdom," said Sena Anessa, smiling beatifically. "I just journeyed with our own Princess Aimada to the Court of Geumjoseon in Daeseong. Such a charming place. Their customs are so different from ours, but so fascinating."

"Are they not preparing for a royal wedding now?" inquired Lilibet. "I believe I had heard as much."

"Indeed," said Anessa. "Crown Prince Han, the King's second son, is soon to be wed."

Sarany wrinkled her forehead. "Is this the heir?"

"For now, yes," said Conor. "If I recall, succession in Geumjoseon is not determined by age. The King selects the favorite of his children and names them heir."

"It does lead to a great deal of *jostling*," said Anessa. "But rather exciting. Han is marrying into the noble Kang family, which may displease his father. They are quite wealthy, but scandalous."

"Ah, yes," said Lilibet. Her dark eyes sparkled. She always enjoyed gossip. "Didn't a daughter of the Kang family slaughter a dozen or so of another noble House? The Nams, I believe?"

"It is all a bit of a fairy tale," said Anessa. "It is said that the Nam family was already gathered for a funeral when the Kang girl climbed over their garden wall and murdered the lot of them. After which, she vanished in a black carriage—some say it was drawn by two dozen flying black swans. I am sure *some* of the story is true, but clearly not all of it. Anyway, Prince Han seems not to mind."

"What's a little bloodbath between friends?" Conor said. He was playing with the crystal stem of his goblet, but as far as Kel had noticed, he had not been drinking much. "Myself, I applaud the bravery of the young Prince of Geumjoseon. I would be afraid to marry into a family of murderers, lest I be next."

Ambassador Sarany smiled, though it was less a smile than a stretching of lips. "Getting married is always an act of bravery and faith. Especially when it represents the merging of two great powers."

Sena Anessa cleared her throat, clearly irritated. "My dear Queen Lilibet," she said, "where is Mayesh Bensimon? I always enjoy his sage advice."

Before Lilibet could speak, Sarany tapped her fork sharply against her plate. "I had nearly forgotten," she said, "that you have an Ashkari adviser to the throne, do you not?"

"Indeed," said Conor, "in the tradition of Macrinus."

Sarany's lip curled. "I noticed you have a very active Sault. There are so *very* many Ashkar in the streets here. Don't you find they spread criminality and disease?"

There was a blank silence; even Lilibet, normally poised, looked stunned.

Conor's eyes had begun to glitter dangerously. "On the contrary," he said. "The Ashkar are skilled healers who have saved many Castellani lives, and they are among our more Law-abiding subjects. Of the few hundred criminals in the Tully, not one of them is Ashkar."

"You are young and naïve, *Ur-Körul* Aurelian," said Sarany coolly. (Even with his limited Malgasi, Kel recognized the word for "Prince.") "You are fond of Bensimon—or you believe you are, at least. The Ashkar exert a sort of pull, a power that draws you to them. It is part of their evil."

"Evil?" The word broke from Kel; he knew better than to speak out, yet he could not help himself. "That seems a severe term. They are, after all, only people who pray to a different sort of God."

"And practice *gematry*." Sarany's gaze swept over Kel and dismissed him. "In Malgasi, we believe all magic is sin. We have made our lands *Aszkarivan*—free of Ashkar. In doing so, we ushered in a new phase of prosperity for our people."

"Was that because they enriched themselves with gold stolen from the Ashkar who had fled?" Conor said, and now his eyes were glittering in a truly dangerous way.

Kel could not help but remember the Dial Chamber meeting where Mayesh had said calmly that there were no Ashkar in Malgasi. No one had paused to ask the Counselor why, he realized. No one had thought about it; no one had seen it as important.

Sarany was looking at Conor, her nostrils flared. Kel could feel the energy in the room changing. It had spiked upward, from tension to anger. He wondered if he should rise and go to Conor, but at that moment, to his surprise, King Markus strode into the Shining Gallery.

With him was Fausten. Neither had dressed for the dinner, precisely, though the King wore a heavy velvet cloak over his usual plain tunic and trousers. It was clasped at the throat with a thick gold chain from which hung an elaborately carved pendant ruby. Fausten, a step behind the King, wore his astronomer's cloak of silk and glass. Kel could not help staring at the little man; the sight of him made Kel feel sick with rage, and the fact that he ignored Kel completely, his gaze sliding over him as if he were not there, did not help.

Markus was stony, bland, and calm as he approached the table and took his seat at the head. Lillibet was staring at him, lips parted in surprise; Conor was expressionless, but his hand was clenched around the stem of his wine goblet.

As Fausten positioned himself behind the King's chair, Kel noted there was something very different about his demeanor. Where he was usually cringing and sycophantic, now he seemed eager, eyes bright and darting. He seemed to be vibrating with excitement as he bowed in the direction of Ambassador Sarany, greeting her in Malgasi:

"Gyönora, pi fendak hi líta."

It was a breach of etiquette for Fausten to speak before the King did; Sena Anessa looked taken aback, but Sarany only smiled a thin smile and turned to the King. "I am so glad, *Körol* Markus," she said, "that we have the favor of your presence."

Markus? Kel shot Conor a look; Conor only shrugged.

The King inclined his head. "I know my duty," he said, with the tone of a man who was going to his own execution, and knew it, and knew he must not falter on the road to the gallows.

Very strange.

Ambassador Sarany did not reply, but stared at the King openly with a deeply peculiar expression. There was an edge in it, as of hunger—and something else as well. A sort of longing, almost desperate. Lilibet was watching her over the rim of her wineglass, her expression a mixture of vexation and disbelief.

"How kind of His Highness," murmured Anessa into the awkward silence, "to make a special effort to see us."

The King looked up and down the table, his face expressionless. Despite his rich cloak, there was a tear in the sleeve of the shirt underneath which must be causing Lilibet agonies of embarrassment.

"I have not heard words spoken in Malgasi in many years," he said, "nor seen the wolf blazon. It brings back . . . memories."

Kel saw Conor's eyes darken. Even before he had retreated to the Star Tower, the King had never spoken of his time as a foster at the Court in Favár.

As if sensing a change in his mood, Sarany turned to Conor. "Perhaps your father has told you of the beauties of Favár," she said. "The Erzaly River, the *Laina Kastel* palace—but to hear of something is never quite the same as seeing it yourself, is it?" She clapped her hands together in artificial delight, as if she had just had an idea. "Perhaps, Prince Conor, instead of our *Milek* Elsabet journeying to Castellane, you could come to us? Elsabet could be your guide to the city. No one knows Favár and its history better. And you simply must tour the harbor at night. The people of the city cast floating lamps upon the water; it is a sight to behold."

Conor tossed back the dregs of his rose-colored wine. There was almost no food on his plate. *Damn Sarany*, Kel thought. *She must press and press on this Elsabet business, like a finger pressing a bruise.*

"I get seasick," Conor said.

"What he means," said Lilibet, "is that his duties here compel him. It is a shame. I am sure he would love to see your city."

Sarany ignored this. "You must also visit our *Kuten Sila*, the Bridge of Flowers. It is a monument to the marriage of Andras Belmany and Simena Calderon, and known as the Bridge of Peace, for that union brought an end to many years of bloodshed. A marriage can heal many wounds, even those of long standing."

Kel could stand it no more. "Our own King Valerian never married," he said, "and he was known as a great peacemaker."

For the first time that evening, Ambassador Sarany looked at Kel. Her gaze said, *You are prey, but too small to interest me.* "And there was a bloody civil war when he died," she said.

"Arguably," said Conor, "that would have happened anyway."

Sarany looked directly at Conor. Something flickered in her gaze—there was a flash of anger, but that hunger remained there, too. She said, her voice dark and sweet as chestnut honey, "My dear *Ur-Körol* Aurelian. Might I give you some advice?"

"I am dreadful with advice," said Conor. "I so rarely take it. It is a besetting sin."

His tone was casual but his hand was in danger of crushing the stem of his wineglass. Sena Anessa had abandoned any pretense of speaking with Kel and was staring from the King to Conor, and back again.

Sarany said, "I have known, in my travels, many young lords and princes. In love with fun and adventure and ease." She made a face that indicated she was familiar with none of those things. "Those whom the Gods have blessed with a royal position inherit much from their fore-bears. Nobility and power, certainly, but also responsibility. Also *debt.*"

The King looked at Sarany as if, in her face, he saw the gallows.

"I owe no debt to Malgasi," Conor said, and Kel saw an ugly smile flash across Fausten's face. He wanted to get up and throttle the astronomer until he told what he knew.

"Oh, but you do," said Sarany. "Your father might not have told you, but long ago you were promised to Elsabet Belmany. Before either of you were born. It was a union written in the stars." And she looked at Fausten with her narrow, predatory gaze, the force of which made him shrink back a little.

Conor had gone an ashen color. "Promised? What nonsense is this?"

"Markus." Lilibet's voice was chilly calm. "Say it is not true."

"A King does his duty," King Markus said. "Conor's duty is to marry Elsabet Belmany. To unite the blood of Belmany and Aurelian. The stars have foretold it. It must be so."

Conor knocked over his wineglass, spilling rosy liquid across the tablecloth. The servants at the door exchanged glances, then vanished back into the kitchen.

"For *months*," Conor snarled, "we have been discussing the nature of the union I must enter into: which countries, which nobles, which alliances. And you have said *nothing*. I take it Bensimon does not know, nor my mother, nor Jolivet. You have lied to us all—"

"There was no lie," hissed the King. "Let the Council of Twelve bicker and barter. See where their alliances lie. It does not matter what they say, or do. What is written in the stars cannot be undone."

"No, my lord," said Fausten, in a voice like a chant. "Oh, no, it cannot. Never."

"Enough!" It was, of all people, Sena Anessa. She was on her feet, her crown of white hair trembling with indignation and rage. "Enough of this ludicrous discussion. It is too late for *the stars*." She spoke the words with contempt. "*Prince* Conor, in the name of the agreement that exists between us, put a stop to this—this—*misunderstanding*, before the Ambassador from Malgasi is further embarrassed."

"*Embarrassed?*" echoed Sarany, her voice rising. "What is this? I demand to know."

There was an awful moment of silence. Conor looked down the table—not at Anessa, but at Kel. There was something like an apology in his eyes. It sent a dart of fear up Kel's spine.

"Conor, *jun*," said Lilibet. An endearment, one she rarely used. "What is all this about?"

Conor flung his napkin onto his plate. He looked around the table with defiant eyes. "It is really very simple," he said. "I am already engaged. To Princess Aimada of Sarthe."

Ambassador Sarany's mouth fell open. Lilibet looked stunned, Sena Anessa vindicated. Kel felt as if his mind had gone blank for a moment. How could Conor have done this? Or, if he were honest, how could Conor have done this *without Kel knowing*?

"There you have it," said Anessa. "The contract has already been signed."

"*Conor*," said Lilibet, urgently. "*Is this a joke?*"

"No," said Conor. "It is not a joke."

Lilibet whirled on Anessa. "This may well not be binding," she said, "given that neither myself nor the King knew anything about it."

Anessa's smile soured. It seemed clear she had not been aware that Conor was making this agreement in secret, without the agreement of the King or Queen, though Kel imagined she would deny it if asked. "My dear Queen Lilibet," she said. "Prince Conor is not a child. He can make his own agreements. We have his signature, his seal, and we have already delivered the dowry payment."

The words flashed like lightning behind Kel's eyes. What was it Beck had said? About being paid in Sarthian gold? "Ten thousand crowns," he said, then clamped his lips together; he had not meant to speak at all.

But Anessa was crowing. "See," she said. "Even his cousin knows."

"Fausten," Sarany hissed, her blood-red lips twisted into a grimace. "You lying *traitor*."

The King looked between Fausten and the Malgasi Ambassador, his brow darkening. But Legate Jolivet—Jolivet looked directly at Kel, and for a moment, Kel felt pierced by his disapproval. In Jolivet's eyes, Kel should have not only known Conor's plans, but been able to stop them.

Fausten began to tremble. "I did not know—"

"You swore," Sarany snapped. "You said it was all in order, that Markus was in agreement, that the marriage would proceed."

Fausten looked at Conor with real hatred. "No one knew the Prince would do this. No one could have expected. *Cza va diú hama*—"

It was not my fault.

Markus turned his head slowly. It was like watching the head of a statue grind in a slow, impossible circle, shedding granite dust as it moved. "You said nothing was unexpected, Fausten. You said everything was there in the stars if one knew how to read them. You told me you were sure."

Sure of what? Kel wondered. *Of the marriage, of more than that?*

Fausten seemed to have shriveled in on himself, like a frightened beetle. "It isn't fair," he wailed. "I could not have known. I have done everything asked of me—"

"You," Sarany hissed in disgust. "You cheap little tutor who thought you could enrich yourself by meddling in politics. You will be dealt with." She looked at Conor. Her eyes were dead as the jeweled eyes of the spider in her ring. "You will not break the contract with Sarthe?"

"I will not," said Conor. "I have given my word."

Sarany's lip curled. She rose from her chair, facing the King. "Your son has betrayed you," she said. "And betrayed his own nature. He does not deserve to be joined with the great House Belmany." She swept the room with a contemptuous gaze. "We offered this alliance because of the deep connection we thought we had forged with House Aurelian when Markus fostered at our Court. I see now that our trust was misplaced."

"This is no favor you offer us," snapped Markus, and there was a light in his eyes Kel had not seen for many years. "This is to your advantage, always your advantage. Fausten lied to me at your bidding. And yet you behave as if you are entitled to not just a place at my table, but my blood. You would cage my son as you caged me."

"*Cage* you—?" Sarany began, her eyes flaring with rage, but she stopped herself. Straightened her back. "I see the stars have turned your mind. You are to be pitied, Markus," she said coldly. "House Belmany has better prospects than you and your debauched son."

She whirled and stalked from the room. Her bodyguards, who had been waiting by the door along with the Castelguard, scrambled to follow.

"Debauched? How rude," said Sena Anessa, rather cheerfully.

But if she were indeed cheerful, she was the only one. Conor sat unmoving, his finger circling the rim of his wineglass. Lilibet's mouth was set in a hard line. The King had returned to staring into the middle distance. And Kel was wishing he could be anywhere else in Dannemore.

"Sena Anessa," said Lilibet. "Would you mind excusing us? I do not think anyone is in the mood for a meal now."

Gracious in her victory, Anessa rose and inclined her head. "Of course. I understand that all issues of family are complex, Your Highness, and statecraft equally delicate. But I am sure we shall be able to arrange these matters to everyone's satisfaction, very soon."

She left, even as carriage wheels sounded on the gravel outside. The Malgasi delegation departing, no doubt.

Kel was conscious, very conscious, of the vambraces on his wrists; of the blades hidden therein. They had been no use to him this night. There had been danger, but not the kind that daggers could disarm.

"Father," Conor said, setting down his wineglass. "I can explain—"

But the King was not looking at his son. He was rising to his feet, his gaze fixed on Fausten, who had frozen where he was, a beetle pinned to a board.

"Was any of what you told me true?" the King demanded hoarsely. "Could you read the stars? Did they speak to you? Or were you only reciting to me scripts that had been written for you by the Malgasi Court?"

"N-no," Fausten whispered. "It was written—it may not come to pass now, but that does not mean it will never come to pass—"

Markus slammed a fist down on the table and Fausten cowered back. The King said, "Lies. Sarany called you a traitor. She believed you loyal to her—because you were. Everything you told me was what the Malgasi would have me believe. That is treason. You will go to the Trick. There, you will think on what you have done."

Terror flashed across Fausten's face. Kel could not help but pity him, even as he recalled that Fausten had threatened *him* with the same imprisonment. It was an awful irony, but not one he could enjoy. "No, no, I have always been loyal. If it were not for me you would have died in Malgasi when you were a boy. I made them understand how they would benefit, if they let you go—"

"Silence." Markus snapped his fingers, gesturing for Jolivet, who approached the table swiftly, flanked by two Castelguards. Fausten seemed to have shrunk in on himself, like a mouse under an eagle's gaze. He made no protest as Jolivet ordered the Castelguards to seize him; they dragged him from the room as he hung limp between them, his elaborate cloak trailing on the ground behind him like the tail of a dead serpent.

There was a sour heat in Kel's belly; he felt as if he might be sick. He tried to catch Conor's eye, but Conor's gaze was flat, unseeing. He had gone inside himself, as he had when he cut his hand open at the Caravel.

"I never did trust Fausten," said Lilibet. "Horrid little man." She looked at her husband with a sort of puzzlement; Kel could not help but wonder what she truly thought. Was she glad that Markus had been disabused of his dreams about the stars? Did she hope he might return, speak sense again, as he had tonight? Or did she hope otherwise? "Malgasi should not have approached this through Fausten, nor tried to twist your will, my dear," she said. "But the situation is not a disaster. A Princess of Sarthe is a perfectly rational choice for Conor—"

The King did not seem to hear her. Abruptly he caught his son's face in his hand, forcing Conor's gaze up to meet his own. "You may think you belong to yourself," he said, "but you do not. I thought you knew it. Nevertheless, you will learn it now."

He dropped his hand. Kel was on his feet, but Conor, bruises rising on his skin where his father had gripped him, shook his head minutely. *No. Stay.*

"Jolivet," the King said. "Take my son. You know what to do."

x x x

"Chana must be thrilled that you're helping with the festival after all," Mariam said.

They were in Mariam's bedroom. Seated on a pile of cushions, Mariam was embroidering a micromosaic of seed pearls onto the bodice of a sea-blue dress that spread out around her like a pool of water. Lin, at Mariam's small worktable, was fulfilling her promise to Chana Dorin—carefully tying off small packets of herbs with ribbons, creating the luck sachets carried by eligible young girls on the night of the Goddess Festival.

"What do you mean, *after all*?" Lin scoffed. "I was always going to help. It's my last Tevath."

"You were always going to hide in the physick garden until Chana gave up," said Mariam. "You only agreed because she made you feel guilty. I can tell because you make a horrid face every time you finish one of those sachets."

"I'm just so bad at it," Lin said ruefully. "And I'm not used to being awful at things." *Because you choose to only do the things you think you'll be good at*, said a small voice in her head. "I'm already dreading the Goddess dance. You *know* I'm not graceful."

Part of the Festival's ceremony required the eligible girls—all unmarried women between the ages of sixteen and twenty-three—to participate in a silent, complex, ritual dance. It was actually quite beautiful: As children in the Women's House, they had practiced its fluid movements each week. Lin was sure she could do it blindfolded, entirely from memory. Which didn't mean she could do it *justice*.

"Don't be ridiculous, you're a fine dancer," Mariam said. "Anyway, your grandfather will be pleased, won't he? Now that you're getting along with him better, I'm sure he'll be proud—"

"He won't see any of it," Lin interrupted. "Tevath falls on the same date as Ascension Day this year. They're having a massive banquet up at the Palace, which I gather Mayesh is required to attend. He won't even be in the Sault."

"Oh," Mariam said softly. "Lin—"

But before she could say anything else, there was a knock at the door. When Lin went to answer it, she found Chana Dorin there, wearing a worried expression. "There's someone at the gates for you, Lin," she said.

"A patient?" Lin demanded. But of course, it must be a patient; who else could it be? Her mind raced. She had not been expecting any emergencies, any babies being born. She'd have to get her medical satchel, change her clothes if there was a chance. She was wearing an ordinary day dress, spring green and slightly worn around the sleeves and hem. She'd had it for years.

Chana's eyes darted to Mariam, and back to Lin. "Yes, a patient," she said, though Lin was puzzled—what had that look been about? She was even more puzzled when Chana bundled her out of the room and placed a satchel in her arms, draping a shawl around her shoulders. "You'll have to hurry," she said. "Everything you need ought to be in there."

"Chana," Lin hissed, looping the strap of the bag over her shoulder, "what's this about? Why the secrecy?"

Chana gave her a dark look. "You ought to blame your grandfather. Now go. Hurry along."

Lin hurried, feeling slightly resentful. *Blame your grandfather?* This must have something to do with the Palace, then. Had Kel fallen ill? Gotten injured again? It was all very odd.

She found Mez at the gates, with Levi Ancel, a good-natured young man who'd grown up in the House of Men with Josit. "You lead an exciting life," Mez noted as she ducked through the gates. He was laughing, but Lin fretted a little, inside. To be summoned to the Palace once had already attracted the attention of the Maharam. For it to happen twice . . .

But then she saw Kel, and those worries faded. He was standing in the shadow of the Sault walls, near the old cistern. He seemed unharmed, at least, but looked ragged around the edges somehow, like a smudged drawing. She was instantly worried.

"Kel." She drew close enough to him so that she would not be overheard—she suspected Mez and Levi were still watching avidly from the gates—but not so close as to cause chatter. He was dressed quite finely in silk and linen, all shades of pale ash and smoke and dark soot. His coat was silver linen, the sleeves slashed open, as was the style, to show the shirt of raw silk beneath. He was not wearing his talisman. "Are you all right?"

His pupils were wider than they should have been, his mouth compressed in a tight line. "It's not me. It's him."

She looked at him blankly. It was a hot night; the air felt thick and heavy. She could see the lights of the Broken Market in the distance. The moon hung overhead, a copper penny, yellowed at the edges. "You mean . . ."

"Conor," he said, in a low voice.

She almost took a step backward. "Kel, he forbade me to come to the Palace. If you want an Ashkari physician, we can find someone else—"

"No." His eyes were wild. "It has to be you, Lin. I'm asking. If it isn't you, it won't be anyone."

Name of the Goddess. Lin knew the answer before she gave it. *For a Physician should not question whether a patient is enemy or friend, a native or a foreigner, or what Gods he worships.*

"All right," she said. "I'll go."

His shoulders sagged with relief. "We must hurry." He indicated the black carriage loitering in the road. "I'll explain on the way."

Once inside the carriage, she relaxed minutely. At least Mez and Levi weren't watching. The inside was richly upholstered, cushioning the shocks as they rolled over the pitted surface of the Ruta Magna. Outside the windows, the blaze of naphtha torches created halos of light that cast a blurring softness over the edges of landmarks. Shops and bridges, balconies and flagstones dissolving into a soft wash of gray and black.

Lin said, "Are you quite sure about this, Kel? You didn't hear Prince Conor when he ordered me out of Marivent. He was quite furious."

"I am very sure." A muscle jumped in his cheek. "You are skilled. Very skilled, as I am in a position to know. But there is more than that at work here. You are coming at the express request of Lilibet, because you are Mayesh's granddaughter. She believes she does not need to worry that you will tell anyone what you have seen."

"Lilibet—the Queen?" Lin was stunned. "Kel, you are frightening me a bit. If the Prince has injured himself in some foolish way, surely that cannot be—"

"He did not injure himself. He has been whipped."

Lin sat back, openmouthed. "Who would whip a Prince of Castellane? Are they in the Trick now?"

Kel said, tonelessly, "It was a royal order. He had to be whipped."

"I don't understand."

Kel looked at her in a sort of agony. The angle of the carriage indicated to Lin that they had begun to climb the Hill. She was suddenly desperate to know what had happened. Surely no one would whip the son of House Aurelian with true severity. The body of the Crown Prince was almost holy. He was precious, irreplaceable.

"Conor," Kel said, "displeased his father. The King felt he should be made to understand his duty. He ordered Legate Jolivet to whip him until he lost consciousness."

Lin curled her hands into fists to keep them still. The story seemed incredible. The way Mayesh had always described King Markus—distant, dreamy, studious—did not seem to match this behavior at all.

"And the Legate—he agreed to this?"

"He had no choice," said Kel, almost unwillingly. "Jolivet has always disapproved faintly of Conor, and the way he lives his life—and me as well, by extension; he considers us both a pair of wastrels—but he cares for Conor. He did not wish to do what he did."

"Has this," Lin whispered, "happened before?"

"No," Kel said. He ran his hands through his hair, agitated. "We were in the Gallery. Conor had angered everyone—gray hell, I don't think there was anyone who wasn't furious, but still—the

King had Jolivet take him to the Hayloft, the room where we train. I went, too; no one stopped me. And Lilibet ran after, calling for Jolivet to stop, but the King's orders supersede all others. It has just been so long since he has given any." His breath quickened. "I thought it would be symbolic. A lash or two over his jacket, to show him he'd done wrong. The King was not even *there*, but Jolivet had his orders. He knew them—and had known them a long time, I think. He made Conor kneel. Whipped him through his shirt, until the shirt came apart like wet paper." He made a dry, retching noise. Clenched his right hand tightly. "Five lashes, ten, then I lost count. It stopped when he was unconscious." He looked at Lin. "There was nothing I could do. I am meant to be Conor's shield, his armor. But there was *nothing I could do*. I told them to whip me instead, but Jolivet did not even seem to hear."

There was a metallic taste in Lin's mouth. She said, "The Legate had his orders from the King. You could not have made him disobey them. Kel—where is the Prince now?"

"Our room," Kel said. "Jolivet carried him there. Like he carried me, when I came to Marivent."

"And there was discussion of finding a physician?" Lin could see the white glow of Marivent, swelling outside the windows, as if they were nearing the moon.

"None of the Palace staff know what happened. The Queen was afraid to summon even Gasquet, as the news would travel so quickly through the Hill. That the King had whipped Conor. That there was discord in the House. That Conor had been shamed."

"I do not see anything shameful about it," said Lin. "If there is shame, it is the King's."

"The Charter Families will not see it that way. They will see it as weakness, a crack in the foundation of House Aurelian. I told the Queen about you—that you had healed me before, that you were Bensimon's granddaughter. That you wouldn't talk. So she agreed to let me fetch you. She is Marakandi; they have a great faith in Ashkari physicians."

"I won't know," Lin said. "I won't know what I can do until I see him."

She knew, though did not say, that whipping alone could kill a man. Blood loss, shock, even damage to the internal organs. She thought of Asaph and the long fall down the cliffs to the sea. Did they—the Queen, the Legate, even the King—understand what had been done? Surely they had never seen whip scars, that ugly grid of pain and trauma that ached long after the wounds had healed.

"I know," Kel said, as they passed beneath the North Gate. "But if it were not you, Lin, there would be no one. No other physician who could attend him. I—"

So I am not the best, just the only, she thought, but she was not angry. How could she be? It was so plain in Kel's face that there was more than duty here, more than obedience that had been drummed into him through years of training. It did not matter how much she believed that, in his place, she would resent Prince Conor, even hate him. She was not in his place. She could not understand.

The carriage had come to a stop in the courtyard of the Castel Mitat. Kel threw the door open, leaping down to the ground, and turned to help her down after him. "Come," he said. "I will bring you to him."

Sulemon passed over the city walls and into the land of Aram, and found it deserted. Many of its great buildings, its temples and libraries, its gardens and marketplaces, lay in ruins, but while he saw much destruction, he did not see death: The people of Aram were gone, the city and the land uninhabited. Adassa had held off the sorcerers long enough for her people to escape.

In fury, Suleman climbed the tower of Balal, his stone burning like a flame at his side. And when he reached the top, he found the Queen waiting for him.

It seemed she could barely stand. She had been worn away like a candle burned down to the wick. He knew then that she was dying, that she had used all she had—the power in her stone, and then her own power—to hold off the enemies of her people.

"What have you done?" he cried. "You have blackened the land, and your city lies abandoned. Where have your people gone?"

"They have escaped," she said. "Far beyond your reach."

But Suleman only shook his head. "Nothing is beyond the reach of sorcerers, and when you are dead, we will hunt your people down and make them slaves through the generations. You have won nothing."

And Adassa felt despair.

—*Tales of the Sorcerer-Kings*, Laocantus Aurus Iovit III

CHAPTER SEVENTEEN

The first thing that struck Lin when she walked into the Prince's apartments was the smell of blood. Coppery and bright; not old blood, but new.

Kel, beside her, tensed. She was not sure if it was the blood—there were streaks of it on the floor, even the print of boots in a drying pool of it—or the fact that Queen Lilibet was there, seated rod-straight in a chair beside her son's bed, her green skirts stained at the hem with blood and dirt. Around her throat and wrists and forehead were emeralds set in gold; they blazed like the eyes of the Ragpicker King.

And on the bed, the still, tensed form of the Prince. The thickly embroidered damask hangings had been drawn back, and Lin could see that he lay facedown on the coverlet, his head on his folded arms. He still wore elaborate velvet breeches, and soft leather boots; gems flashed on his fingers, and at his wrists—a peculiar contrast to the bare expanse of his back, which had been torn to bloody strips.

She could sense that he was conscious—clinging to it, perhaps, half dazed, but she sensed his awareness that she was there, though he did not move as she approached. Lin could feel her heartbeat in her fingertips, beating the words: *the Queen. The Queen herself.* Yet at the same time, her mind had focused, narrowed in on the Prince, on his wounds. Her physician's training overrode all other things, lending her the necessary emotional distance to do what was required.

She noted that on the night table by the bed were soap, bandages, towels. A silver bowl of water to wash her hands. Someone had prepared for her arrival. That was good. Where would she unpack her satchel? On the bed, she decided: It was vast, and even the Prince, not a small man, took up only a portion of it.

The Queen touched her son's hair once, lightly, her ringed fingers flashing among his wet dark curls. Then she rose and came down the few steps—the bed was on a sort of raised plinth—to where Lin and Kel stood.

"A woman," Lilibet said, looking Lin up and down as if she were a horse at the Fleshmarket. "I have known many Ashkari physicians—they treated me throughout my childhood—but have never seen a female healer before."

"Will it be a problem, Your Highness?" Lin asked.

"No. If it were a problem, I would not have summoned you." Lilibet Aurelian was beautiful, up close, in a way that commanded attention. There was nothing soft about her beauty. It was a beauty that seemed made of bright pieces, like glittering tesserae that came together to form something almost frighteningly magnificent: a great archway or spired castle. "As a woman, you will have worked twice as hard to get where you are. That pleases me. You have two tasks here. Make sure these wounds do not become infected or spill a poison into his blood. And do what you can to see he does not scar too badly."

"I will do what I can, as you say," said Lin. "But"—she glanced once at the Prince's back, the weals dividing his skin—"there will be scars. Almost undoubtedly."

The Queen nodded curtly. "So, let us not waste time. Ashkari physicians do not like to be surrounded and bothered while they work; that much I know. Kellian, accompany me. We will wait downstairs while she tends to my son."

And they were gone, leaving Lin slightly stunned. Usually she had to work harder to clear the family from the room. She had expected to be, as Lilibet had said, surrounded and bothered while she worked. Had mentally prepared herself for it. Now she was alone with Prince Conor, and that was much stranger.

She could not deny that she was afraid. Of him, of the situation. She was so small in the face of all that was the Palace and its inhabitants. But then, for fifty years, her grandfather had come to Marivent nearly every sunrise. Had talked with these people, worked with and for them, demanded their concentration, even their respect. And though she was not Mayesh, she had her own skills. Did not the *Book of Makabi* say: *The skill of a physician shall lift up his head; and he shall stand before nobles?*

Forcing herself to be calm, she climbed the steps to the massive bed. The Prince still did not move, but his breathing intensified. It was ragged; seeming to snag on every inhale, like cloth snagging on a hook. Lin set down her satchel, quickly washed her hands, and returned to the bed. The first thing to do was to clean away the blood from his back, to see clearly what she was dealing with. It would not be easy, given his condition.

She sat down beside him, the mattress sinking a little under her weight. His shirt had not been removed, she realized. Rather, it had been whipped to pieces, and blood-soaked scraps of silk clung to his arms, his waist.

Very gently, she began to sponge away the blood from his bare skin, using a damp towel. The Prince's body tensed, his back arching. Breath hissed between his teeth.

Then he spoke, and the sound jolted her. "You must be enjoying this," he said, turning his head to the side to avoid speaking directly into the mattress. "It must please you."

There was strength in his voice—more than she had expected. As a physician it pleased her, but there was bitterness there, too, sharp as poison. Perhaps it was the bitterness that was keeping him alert. Strength came from strange places.

Lin slowed the movement of her hand. "Cleaning up blood? Why would that please me?"

"Because—*ah!*" He winced, and lifted himself on his elbows. The muscles in his arms bunched beneath the torn and bloodied silk. "You don't like me. We've been over this."

"If you did not want me as your physician, you could have protested," she said.

"I did not feel like arguing with my mother. It is not something I enjoy at the best of times, and I would not call this the best of times."

He looked over his shoulder at her. His eyes were fever-bright, the pupils too wide. *Shock*, Lin thought. "I could give you morphea—"

"No." He fisted his hands in the sheets. "No morphea. I want to feel all of it."

Gently, she continued to dab away the blood, revealing the wounds beneath. "If you are doing this to show that you are brave, I should tell you honestly, this is the easiest part of what I must do. These wounds are bad. You will be screaming like a dying seagull soon enough."

He made a muffled sound that could have been a laugh. "I am not trying to impress you, Mayesh's granddaughter. I wish to feel the pain so that I remember it. So that I remain angry."

It was a more interesting answer than she had expected.

She had cleaned away most of the blood; the towel was soaked in red. She could see the angry stripes across his back now, some crisscrossing each other. Bits of white silk were embedded in the long cuts.

Jolivet had done this before, she thought. He had known to keep the lashes high on the back, over the blades of the Prince's shoulders, where the kidneys would not be damaged.

Still, it felt incongruous, almost grotesque, this destruction of what had clearly been so beautiful. The shape of him, unclothed, was all clean lines, perfect as a drawing in an anatomy book showing the ideal of the human form. Strong shoulders, tapering to a slim waist. His breeches hung low on his hips. The back of his neck was a vulnerable curve. Black curls, soaked with sweat and blood, clung to the skin there.

She reached for a jar of *theriac*, a clear salve that would calm pain and prevent infection. Taking some onto her fingers, she said, "When I was a child, I was angry at Mayesh. He had separated my brother and me, after our parents died. He felt his responsibilities here at Marivent prevented him from looking after us." She began to smooth the salve onto his back. His skin was hot to the touch, smooth where the lacerations had not torn at him.

"Go on," he said. He had turned his head so he could look up at her while she spoke. She could see his face clearly now. Kohl was smudged madly around his eyes, as if he had wept black tears. "You were angry at Bensimon?"

"Yes," she said. "Because he ignored me, you see. He was busy here on the Hill. I was so angry I would hit things and tear at them. Curtains and scarves. Other children." She smoothed the salve as gently as she could over the lattice of cuts that feathered like wings across his shoulders. "All that anger never amounted to anything, though. It never changed the situation. It never brought him back."

"Bensimon did that?" The Prince sounded genuinely surprised. "I never thought of him as someone who could neglect a responsibility."

No one wants to be a responsibility, Lin thought. *They want to be loved.* But she would hardly say such a thing, to him of all people. She put away the salve and began to remove amulets from her satchel.

"Well, I have had vengeance upon him for you," said the Prince, in a low tone. His voice was rougher than Lin remembered it—though one would expect someone in pain to sound different. "Though I did not intend it. When he arrives at Marivent tomorrow, and discovers the ruin I have wrought, he will despair."

Will he? I am not sure he can feel despair, Lin wanted to say, but held back. She was not sure she still believed it was true. She had taken out the amulets: talismans for healing, for blood loss. Talismans to prevent infection. They would help, but the scars . . . he would have such terrible scars. Like great claw marks, forever slicing across his back. *Forever spoiling his beauty*, said a small voice in the back of her head, but those were not a doctor's thoughts. Her doctor's brain said other things. That she ought to use lunar caustic, to make sure he did not begin to bleed again, but that the lunar caustic would worsen his scarring. That such scarring caused pain, the tightening and disfigurement of skin. He might never move properly again, for all of his life.

"Your mother," she said. "She seemed insistent that you not scar—"

He laughed shortly, and winced hard with the pain of the laughter. "A scarred prince is a scandal," he said. "Criminals are whipped, not princes. My father is angry I have disappointed him; he has written the words of his disappointment across my back in blood. But when the blood is washed away, there will be scars that require explanation. My mother does not want to have to make those sorts of explanations."

"You think it is just vanity on her part?" *Perhaps she, too, does not want to see something beautiful, something she made, disfigured. Perhaps she fears the pain the scars will bring. Or perhaps you are right, Monseigneur, and she only fears potential embarrassment.*

"I think it is practicality," he said, and caught his breath. "Your hands—"

"I am sorry." She was being as gentle as she could, but her stomach felt as if it were turning circles as she touched him. She should not be surprised, she thought. Though every patient was meant to be the same to her, she could not forget that she was laying her hands on a Prince. The blood that mixed with the salve on her skin was royal blood.

She drew her hands back, just for a moment—and felt it. A hot, needle-pain against her chest, like the sting of a wasp. Just where the brooch pinned inside her tunic touched her skin . . .

She seemed to see the image of the Source-Stone behind her

eyelids, as she had the night she'd healed Kel. The smoke moving in the depths of it, like steam rising from the surface of well water.

And she heard the whisper, in her mind. But not a whisper, now. Stronger than that. A voice—stern, genderless, unidentifiable. The voice of the stone itself.

Use me.

"Stay still," she said, in a distant voice, and laid the first amulet across his skin. As she did so, she set her left hand over her heart, where the brooch was pinned inside her jacket.

Heal, she thought. But it was more than a thought. In her mind's eye she clearly saw the word drift again through the smoke of the stone, but this time it broke into its component parts, into letters that were numbers, into an equation as complex and simple as a star.

Something pulsed beneath her left hand, like the pulse of blood in a heart. It seemed to quiver through her palm, unfurling tendrils through her veins. She opened her eyes.

Nothing had changed. The red welts across the Prince's back remained, the edges of the cuts as angry and visceral as before. She felt a dull anger at herself. Whatever she had thought she was doing, it had not worked.

Still, she could not bring herself to use the lunar caustic. She reached for more amulets, the flat metal cool between her fingers. She began to place them, one after another, atop the welts on his back.

Through all of this he had not spoken. He winced now, as the talismans touched his skin, arching slightly off the bed. She could have slid her hand into the gap between the clenched muscles of his stomach and the sheet beneath.

She did not know why she had thought that. He was rigid, awaiting the touch of cold metal. She said, "I am sure Mayesh will not be in despair. You could not have *wrought so much ruin* as all that."

He gasped an almost-laugh. Sweat had begun to bead along the hollow of his spine, at the base of his neck. "Oh—you would be—surprised. I am not good at many things, but"—he winced—"ruination is one of them. And bad planning. I am good at that as well."

She laid down the next talisman. "You could tell me what happened," she said. "Perhaps it is not as bad as you think."

He had relaxed slightly. He was still tense, but he was no longer holding his body rigid, off the bed. "I suppose I might as well. You will hardly be complimentary, will you, or tell me I am brilliant, and have made only the best decisions, as Falconet or Montfaucon would do."

"I think I have been very clear," she said, "that I will not."

He brought his forehead down to touch his clenched hands. When he spoke, it was in a near-monotone. "Prosper Beck," he said. "I owed him a great deal of money. It does not matter why, only that I was surprised to learn of it, and that it was a legal debt. I had spent the money. I owed it." He winced, swore, as she laid a talisman across a particularly bad cut upon his shoulder. "I was able to send messages to him. I thought he would demand interest. Instead he began to demand that I do things for him."

"Did Kel know?"

"No. The favors were demanded while he was recovering. And I did not want to worry him. At first I ignored Beck, but he knew when I did not. Finally, I did the first thing he asked. It seemed harmless enough. I was to put an emetic in a bottle of wine and give it to Montfaucon and Roverge. They spent the night vomiting, but assumed it was because they were drunk. It certainly wasn't the first night either of them had spent being sick."

"And did Beck know?" She laid the next talisman.

"He knew. And he sent another demand. That I kill Asti. My horse. But that—I could not do that." There was a defensive note in his voice, as if he thought she would judge him for foolish softheartedness. But in fact, it was the most she'd ever liked him. "I realized it would never end. He would continue to request things—some foolish, some brutal, some humiliating. I knew I had to pay it all back, at once. End the whole business. I went to the Sarthian Ambassador. We agreed in secret: I would marry the Princess of Sarthe in exchange for a dowry in gold, to be paid in advance."

Lin was a little stunned. She had not expected something so immense in its consequentiality. A secret union between Castellane and Sarthe? There would be many in the city who would hate the idea, many who loathed Sarthe with a passion. "The Princess—" she began.

"Aimada. I have met her before; she is agreeable enough, and sensible. She will not expect much from me, I think."

He sounded exhausted. Pain was exhausting, Lin knew; it wore out the soul as well as the body. But there was something else in his voice. A weariness that spoke to a death of expectation. If he had wanted more than a marriage brought about by blackmail, he would not now have it.

"Ten thousand crowns," he said, almost drowsily. "The cost of a Prince, it turns out. I realize I have been a fool; you need not tell me. I ought to have gone to Bensimon. Asked his advice. Told him the truth."

Lin placed the last talisman on his back. "I will not tell you that you have made good decisions," she said, drawing back her hands. "Clearly, that is not the case."

"Gray hell," he muttered into his clenched fists.

"But had you gone to Mayesh, he would only have told your father. And you would likely be in the same situation, or one very similar."

Between the black of his lashes and the darker black of the kohl, his eyes were very bright silver. He said, "But I would not now be getting married. Which I do not want to do."

"But you were always going to have to marry for statecraft, were you not? People like you do not marry for love."

"You have been listening to too many Story-Spinner tales," he muttered.

"Am I wrong?"

He narrowed his eyes. "No."

Aimada. I have met her before, he had said. *Aimada.* A pretty name. Lin could not picture her, could picture only a sort of drawing in a storybook of a princess in a ribboned crown.

Lin stood up, went to the silver bowl. Touched the surface of the water with her bloody hands, red threads spinning out from her fingers like thread from a loom.

"Wait," the Prince said.

She turned to see him, chin on his folded arms. The talismans gleamed in long lines across his back, like the scales of a dragon.

"I will take the morphea," he said, "but you will have to give it to me. I cannot move."

She did not ask what had changed his mind. She retrieved an ampoule of morphea from her satchel and came to the head of the bed. She had to make a space among the velvet pillows, batting them aside as if they were overly curious kittens, so she could kneel down by his head.

She took several grains from the ampoule and hesitated. Usually she would place the grains upon the patient's tongue. She had done it with Kel, unthinkingly. But she wavered now; there was something about touching the Prince so familiarly, so intimately—

He looked up at her through black lashes thick as fringe. She could see the flecks of blood across his cheekbones, a bruise rising on his jaw. He was waiting for her. Waiting for the surcease from pain she could offer. She steeled herself and reached out, cupping his chin in her hand, brushing the grains of morphea across the indentation in the center of his full lower lip.

"You have to swallow them," she whispered.

He licked across his lower lip with a flick of his tongue. Swallowed. Looked up at her, a somber light in his eyes. "You should not feel sorry for me, you know. Feel sorry for the one who has to marry me."

It would take a few moments for the morphea to work, she knew. Best to distract him. She said, "Why should I feel sorry for you? I doubt I will marry for love, either. Or marry ever." She tucked the ampoule into the pocket of her dress. "I am a woman and a physician. No respectable Ashkari man would marry me. I am too peculiar."

"Peculiar?" The corner of his mouth turned up. "I don't think I've ever met a woman who describes herself as peculiar before."

"Well, I am," she said. "I am an orphan; that is odd enough. I demanded to be allowed to train as a physician; also peculiar. I have only one friend. I do not participate in most dances, most festivals. Oh, and when I was a little girl, I was a terror. I pushed Oren Kandel out of a tree once. He broke his ankle." She knew these names, these words, would mean nothing to the Prince, but it did not matter. She was talking for the sake of talking, to quiet and to soothe. His eyes were already growing unfocused, his breathing more steady. As his eyes closed, she told him of her meeting with the Maharam, her hope to seek Qasmuna's book in the Shulamat, how he had refused and how she had kicked Oren's carefully collected pile of sweepings on her way out.

"That does sound like you," he said, drowsily. "You seem to have a problem containing your temper."

"Is it wise to annoy me when I have a satchel full of needles and knives?" she said, in her sweetest tone. She wondered immediately if he would be angry—it was so difficult to know how much familiarity was allowed, how much humor. King Thevan, the current King's grandfather, had once had an actor executed for performing a satirical play about him.

But the Prince only smiled wearily, and said, "What now? The morphea will put me to sleep soon, I expect."

"Yes. You should rest." She hesitated. "I ought to stay here with you tonight," she said, finally. "To make sure the talismans are working, and that the bleeding does not begin again."

He was very still. "No woman has ever spent the night in this room," he said. "No one has, save Kel and myself."

"If you would rather I go, I could see if Kel, or the Queen—"

"No," he said, quickly. "It would be irresponsible of you to leave. I could bleed to death."

"May the Goddess prevent that," she replied, a little stiffly. She slid off the bed, leaving him lying surrounded by pillows, his back a map of red and silver. At the door, she paused, glancing back at him, now just a shadowy figure on the bed.

Heal. She let the word whisper itself inside her mind. Raised her hand to touch the brooch one more time; then let it fall, and went out into the corridor.

She found the Queen standing just outside the Prince's room, her hands folded in front of her. Emeralds winked at her throat. She did not seem to have been pacing, or to have been doing anything other than standing perfectly still in the center of the hall. It was unnerving. And where was Kel?

"I sent Kellian off to rest," said the Queen, as if she had read Lin's mind. "He was agitated. In such situations as this, I prefer calm."

Rest where? Lin thought. But of course there would be dozens of bedrooms in a place like this. She felt a flash of worry for Kel, no doubt lying awake, alone in the dark, worried for his Prince.

"Physician," the Queen said, a little sharply, "tell me of my son."

What if I said he had died? Would I be thrown from the cliffs, food for the crocodiles, like Asaph was? And what if I were to ask why you had allowed him to be whipped, why you hadn't stopped it? Was there truly nothing you could have done?

Lin bit back hard on her thoughts. They were as useless as panicking at the sight of a wound. She said calmly, "There will be no muscular or internal damage, and the bleeding has been stopped. Those are the most important things. I have placed talismans on the wounds that should assist in healing."

"And scarring?" asked the Queen. "How bad will it be?"

"I cannot know that until morning, when the talismans are removed." Lin steeled herself. "It is likely there will be some . . . blemish."

The Queen's expression tightened. Lin's heart skipped a beat, but Queen Lilibet only said, "You, girl. Do you have children?"

"I have not been so blessed, no," Lin said; it was her rote response whenever anyone asked. She did not bother expounding: *I do not have a husband, I do not know if I want children.* No one who asked was truly that curious.

"Here is the thing you should know about children," said Lilibet. Up close, it was clear to see that the Prince's looks came from his mother: He had her black hair, her lush mouth at odds with those fine, almost too-sharp bones. "Children make you helpless. You can have all the power one can imagine, and if you cannot keep them safe from themselves and the world, it does not matter."

Lin inclined her head, not sure what to say. "I ought to remain with the Prince tonight. Make sure his condition is stable."

The Queen nodded. As Lin turned toward the door of the royal apartment, the Queen said abruptly, "And if you do have children, physician—"

Lin looked back over her shoulder. Lilibet was not looking at her, but into the distance, as if recalling some past event.

"If you do have children, make sure to have more than one."

By the time Lin returned to the Prince's side, he was asleep. She sat down in the chair the Queen had vacated earlier. This was the physician's task that required the most patience, and in which Lin sometimes thought one stood closest to the Goddess. To sit beside a patient as they slept through the night, waiting for a break in fever, a change in condition. Holding their *alor,* their life force, in your mind, willing it to stay tied to the body.

Of course there were times it did not succeed, and death came as a thief in the night to steal away the physician's work. But Lin preferred to think that death was not always the enemy.

She took the copied pages of Qasmuna's book from her satchel. She had managed to translate most of the words, and put the pages into a sort of order. Reading them again, she told herself, would surely bring more of its precepts into clarity. She would study a few sentences, then check on the Prince. Study a few more, check again. In this manner she planned to get through the night.

But she found it hard to concentrate on the words. It was so strange, to be in this room, alone with Prince Conor. This room, where he had grown up, where Kel had grown up. What had it been like when they were little boys, she wondered. Had they sat on the floor and played Castles? Josit used to roll about play-fighting with his friends like puppies did. Had they done that? Had they talked about what it meant for Kel to be the Sword Catcher, or had it been so ingrained a part of their lives that there was no need to discuss it any more than they needed to discuss that the sun would come up the next morning?

There were books on the nightstand; Lin had noticed them when she had gone to wash her hands. The Prince had been a figure in her life for all of her life, yet she had never thought about whether he read books or not. If these were anything to go by, he liked tales of travel and adventure. If he were awake, she thought, she could read aloud to him. Being read aloud to was calming for patients. But he was deep in the slumber of morphea and shock, his eyes moving rapidly beneath his smudged lids.

For so many years she had hated him. She had not thought of him, in that time, as someone who read, whose fingers curled in slightly when he slept. Who had a cluster of freckles on the top of his shoulder. Who had a white line through one of his eyebrows— a scar or a birthmark? Whose mouth lost its cruelty when he slept.

She wondered if she still hated him and decided that it did not matter as far as this night was concerned. He was her patient still.

She would remain with him, as his physician; she would stay awake until the last watch of the night had passed.

In the night, Lin slept, and as she slept, she dreamed that she was someone else. A man, climbing the high side of a mountain.

The paths had long ago fallen away, and now there was only rock, cracked and uneven. His hands were torn and bleeding, but he kept on, moving ever upward, for he was acting on the orders of the King, and to return empty-handed would mean death.

He was nearly at the summit when he found the entrance to the cave. He breathed a sigh of relief. The prophecy had not been false. On hands and knees he crawled into the dark crevice, dust and gravel irritating his bleeding hands.

He did not know how long he had been crawling when he saw it. Gold, all gold, and of a brightness that seared into his eyes. He cried out in Malgasi: "Hi nas visík!" And knew in that moment that he was blind, that he would never see anything again save that light, that radiance, and he did not grieve his sight, only reached out his hands toward the burning . . .

It was morning when Kel came back to the royal apartment. After Lilibet ordered him away, he had gone into the small blue room down the hall where he slept sometimes when Conor was with a girl, though the girls never stayed the night.

He had tried to force sleep to come. He visualized his peaceful place: the ship on the sea, the mast swaying in lazy, sunlit wind, white foam on the water below. But this time it had not calmed him. He had continued to see, over and over, the whip rising and falling, the blood oozing from Conor's back. Conor shuddering without making a sound.

Eventually, he had fallen into a black and dreamless sleep, only waking when sunlight was spilling through the east-facing window, turning the airless room into a roasting oven.

Conor. He was on his feet and out in the corridor before he'd shaken the sleep from his brain.

He'd half expected Lilibet to be there, but the hall was deserted, ghostly. He crossed it quickly and entered the room he shared with Conor. The light here was softer, laying a pale gold glaze over the odd tableau that met his gaze.

Lin was asleep in the chair beside Conor's bed, her arms hugging her satchel like a child with its arms around a pillow. Conor's bed was empty, a mess of tangled sheets, mud and blood. It glittered as if dusted with sequins. As Kel approached, incredulous, he saw that the shining spangles were Ashkari healing talismans, scattered across the coverlet.

"Lin." He shook her shoulder and she bolted awake, the satchel slipping out of her hands. He caught it before it hit the floor, tossing it onto the bed. "Where's Conor?"

She scrubbed at her eyes, blinking. A great deal of her red hair had escaped from its braids and curled in a halo of fiery strands around her face. "The Prince?" She stared at the empty bed. "He was here—at dawn, he was here, I looked—" She said something else, a blur of words in Ashkar, her face creasing with worry.

The door of the tepidarium opened then, and Conor came into the room.

He was barefoot and shirtless, a towel over his shoulders. Loose linen trousers were cinched at his hips. He had clearly washed, for his hair was damp, and his face clean of blood and kohl.

"Conor," Kel said. He was furious—at Conor, for not treating his injuries as serious. At Lin, unreasonably, for falling asleep. And behind the fury, beneath it, was puzzlement. He had seen Conor's wounds; how had Conor managed to get out of bed, much less walk across the room at all? "What are you doing? You should be—"

Conor put a finger to his lips, as if to say, *Hush.* There was a glint in his eyes, almost mischievous. Kel and Lin exchanged a baffled glance. Lin looked as if she were about to jump out of her skin.

There was real fear in her eyes, and worry; it moved Kel's own anxiety up a notch.

"Prince Conor," Lin began, her voice shaking slightly, and Conor drew the towel from his neck and turned around, presenting his back to them. Kel heard Lin give a little gasp; her hand flew to her chest, just above her heart.

Conor's back was a broad, smooth unblemished expanse of skin stretched over flexible muscle. No mark remained there, not even a healed scar. There was no sign of any wound. No sign he had ever been whipped at all.

And in that moment of the Queen's great despair, her magic seemed to falter. She could no longer hold back the armies on the plains. The walls began to splinter, and as the enemies of Aram poured through, the city began to burn. All was flame: the sky, the rivers and lands of Aram, the palace itself. Soon Aram would be only ashes.

She turned to Suleman. "You have left me no choice," she said.

Flame burned in his eyes. "What can you do to me? I will always be more powerful than you, as long as there is magic."

"But now," Adassa said, "there will be no more magic."

And she reached out with all the strength that had been gifted her by her people, with the power of each word they had sacrificed in her name. She reached beyond the stars, and she tore free the Great Word of Power, without which no spell could be cast, and she cast it into the void. And she herself followed it into the void, for the power of the Word was so great, it burned away all about her that was mortal. The Queen was no longer the Queen; she was magic itself, and magic was gone.

—*Tales of the Sorcerer-Kings,* Laocantus Aurus Iovit III

CHAPTER EIGHTEEN

It was the day of the Sarthian Princess's arrival in Castellane, and Kel wished he had not been seated among the Charter Families. Their chairs had been ranged upon a raised platform in the middle of Valerian Square, and he could not help but feel that everyone who had gathered to see the Princess arrive was staring at them curiously: from Montfaucon, resplendent in a yellow brocade doublet with vertical stripes of black silk, to Charlon and his father, both glowering in fury, to Gremont: richly dressed but asleep as usual, and snoring at the sky.

Falconet, seated next to Kel, wore dark-blue velvet and a pleased expression. Kel recalled Polidor Sardou's words during the last Dial Chamber meeting he'd attended. It seemed long ago now. *Joss, your sister is married to a Sarthian duke. You are not objective in this matter. An alliance with Sarthe would likely benefit your family.*

As always happened with Falconet, beneficial things seemed to simply fall into his lap. He waved languidly at the crowd in the square, clearly not bothered by the attention, before turning to Kel. "And how is our mutual friend, the Prince?" he murmured. "I have heard little from Conor since news broke of his felicitious engagement. But then, it has not been long, has it?"

Falconet's expression was blandly curious, but mischief lurked in his eyes. Kel did not believe it was a *malicious* sort of mischief, but it was clear Falconet found the situation slightly amusing, as he found so many things.

"No," Kel murmured back. "It has been just a fortnight." It was hard for him to believe himself—it seemed a lifetime, not two weeks, since Conor's engagement had been discovered. Now Princess Aimada was due to arrive in Valerian Square and be presented to the people of Castellane in less than an hour's time.

Even Conor seemed stunned by the rapidity with which everything had been arranged. Sena Anessa, clearly furious that the King and Queen were not more pleased about their son's marital plans, had left Marivent with a dark determination in her eyes. During the weeks since, each day had brought a new whirlwind of developments: arrangements for the Princess's arrival, for her welcoming ceremony, for the drawing up of contracts between Sarthe and Castellane. Each day, royal guards from both Courts galloped back and forth through the Narrow Pass, messages in hand. Should the wedding be held inside or outside? How many ladies-in-waiting would the Sarthian Princess require? How well did she speak Castellani? Would she need a tutor? Would she prefer to decorate her own apartments or have Queen Lilibet do it for her?

Kel had somewhat hesitantly asked Conor whether this meant it was time for Kel to move into his own rooms in the Castel Mitat. Conor's eyes had blazed for a moment before he said, "Why bother with that? Most married royal couples keep to their separate rooms. I don't see why things need to change."

"Because," Kel had said, "you'll need an heir, Conor. And that means—"

"I'm familiar with the process." Conor's tone was dry. "I suppose it's a matter of asking Aimada whether she wishes that process to take place in her apartments or mine. Either way, there seems no reason to consider moving you now."

So Kel had let it go, while hoping that if he were to be ejected from the room he shared with Conor, he would at least be given enough notice to relocate his things. He understood Conor's desire that things not change, but Conor's desires were often at cross purposes with what was practical.

Meanwhile, Lilibet had set herself to calming the Charter Families, who were predictably enraged that Conor had gotten engaged without consulting them. Not all of them had turned up for this, the official welcoming of the Princess. Falconet was here, and the Roverges; Cazalet, always politic, had come, as had Gremont, Montfaucon, and Uzec. Lady Alleyne was conspicuously absent, as was Raspail, furious at the spurning of Kutani. Esteve and Sardou were also pointed in their absence.

Even the people of Castellane seemed a little stunned. After years of pleasing speculation as to who might be their next queen, it seemed to them that things had been decided with a disappointing lack of fanfare. They had gathered behind the barriers separating them from the central square—where a sable carpet had been spread over the flagstones, and a curtained pavilion draped with asphodel erected as a temporary shelter in which the Crown Prince might, unseen, wait for his bride to arrive—but they seemed more curious than enthusiastic. They had the general air of a traveler who, after a night of drinking, wakes with the strong suspicion that he has been robbed of something, but is not sure what.

It did not help that Sarthe was widely regarded with the contempt with which countries generally regarded their nearest neighbors, rather as Shenzhou despised Geumjoseon and Malgasi loathed Marakand. Across the square, near the steps of the Justicia, stood a group of agitators dressed in makeshift ensembles cobbled together from old military uniforms—ragged jackets and shako caps with tarnished badges, even a ratty but voluminous admiral's coat—chanting, "Death before union with Sarthe!" One, a tall fellow with ginger hair, called out: "The only good Sarthian is a dead one! String 'em up outside the Tully!" as he swept before him a handmade banner showing the lion of Castellane pouncing upon the eagle of Sarthe.

Charlon Roverge, half asleep in the bright sunlight, cheered faintly.

"Charlon," said Kel, "we are not on their side. We are on *Conor's* side, and thus in support of a union with Sarthe."

"I can't help it." Charlon yawned. "I am easily persuaded by enthusiasm."

Falconet threw a glove at him just as there was a slight commotion among the guards surrounding the steps up to the Charter platform. A moment later, the platform swayed and Antonetta Alleyne appeared, looking around anxiously.

Kel felt a tight heat in his chest, as if he'd swallowed a burning ember. Gone were Antonetta's soft pastels and yards of lace. Her dress was silk, a deep-violet color, inset with black lace through which tantalizing flashes of skin could be glimpsed. It clung to her body before flaring out at her hips in a trumpet shape; the neckline plunged, creating a startling V of white skin against the black of the fabric. Her hair was loose, a river of dark gold, needing no ornament but its color.

Around her throat gleamed her locket, the carved heart dangling between her breasts. Kel glanced away—he didn't want to think of Prosper Beck right now, nor did he want to stare openly at Antonetta. (Well, part of him did, but it was not a part that he usually allowed to rule his will.)

"Someone," muttered Montfaucon, leaning over the back of Falconet's chair, "wants to show Conor what he'll be missing."

Antonetta lifted her chin. She was alone; Lady Alleyne was nowhere to be seen. Antonetta strode down the platform's central aisle and, to Kel's surprise, sat down beside him. Her skirts spread out around her, spilling onto his lap in heavy, weighted folds of silk.

Joss, on the other side of Kel, grinned at Antonetta. "I see Lady Alleyne's tastes have undergone something of a change."

Antonetta simpered. Perhaps that was an unkind characterization, Kel thought, but no—Antonetta was gazing at Joss with a meant-to-be-adorable little smile playing around her mouth. Definitely a simper. "Why thank you for noticing, Joss," she said. "You're *too* kind."

Falconet grinned before turning to start up a conversation with Montfaucon. Behind them, Kel could see Charlon, staring at Antonetta with hungry dark eyes.

"Kel," Antonetta muttered. The simper was gone; her hands were clenched in her lap. "You don't mind me sitting beside you, do you? I can trust you not to leer."

Kel felt instantly ashamed. He *wanted* to look at Antonetta, wanted to fill up his eyes with the sight of her. A wayward curl of her hair had become caught in the chain of her necklace; he wanted badly to reach over and free the silky strands from their imprisonment.

He felt hot, itchy, and foolish, as if he were fifteen years old again, offering her a ring made of grass in the cool shade of the Night Garden. He had lost himself in fantasy then; he had not realized how little it was he really had to offer. He recalled the night of her debut ball, after it was over, lying awake in the room he shared with Conor.

Do you think you'll marry Antonetta? he'd asked, his voice tight. *Her mother wants you to.*

Conor had scoffed. *Of course not. She's like a sister to me, Antonetta.*

Kel had been unguarded in that moment. Conor had been kind to him, but that was Conor; Kel did not plan to be unguarded like that again.

"I know your mother," he said, glancing at her. "I know she didn't pick out that dress."

"My mother," Antonetta said, twirling her fingers in the fabric of her skirt. "She had something of an *episode* when she heard Conor was marrying the Sarthian Princess. She threw several vases and a carved bust of Marcus Carus. Then she told me she was tired of dressing me and I could wear whatever I wanted since it no longer mattered." Something like a glint of real amusement flashed in her eyes. "Mariam made this. She seemed delighted to be free of my mother's . . . instructions."

"I assume that's why Lady Alleyne is not in attendance today," Kel said. "She does know she's courting controversy with the royal House?"

"She does. She is at home lying in a darkened room; she sent me out to save face for House Alleyne. No one can say we did not attend the welcoming of the Princess—not when I am here to represent us."

Kel lowered his voice. "That seems cruel," he said. "Whatever your mother's schemes, did she not know you cared for Conor?"

Antonetta looked up at him. The posy-drops in her eyes had turned the pupils to the shape of tears. Kel recalled Lin saying to him in her matter-of-fact way, *Antonetta fancies you.* He'd had a hard time hiding his reaction from Lin: the tension in his muscles, the speed of his heartbeat. It had stayed with him until he kissed Lin, which had forcibly wrenched his mind back to the present.

And now here was Antonetta, sitting beside him, smelling of lavender oil. It felt familiar, as if he had stepped back in time to one of the many parties where they had sat together on the staircase above, watching the goings-on and gossiping about the adults. It was strange: She seemed back in his life, but it was nothing he could trust to last. And though she might not have changed as much as she pretended, she *had* become someone other than the person she had been at fifteen. They all had. And he was not sure he knew the person she was now.

"Caring was only my mistake," Antonetta said. She put a hand up to her throat and for a moment toyed with her locket. It seemed a deeper gold against the rose tint of her skin. "Not hers."

Kel resolved to tell Lin she was an idiot next time he saw her.

A servant in pale-green livery came up onto the dais and whispered something to Montfaucon, who announced: "The carriage from Aquila has been spotted coming through the Narrow Pass. It won't be long now."

A stir went through the Charter Families. Antonetta frowned and said to Kel, "Do you know why the Prince made this decision so suddenly? He seemed so reluctant to marry. And now"—she gestured toward the flower-strewn square, the flags of Sarthe and Castellane draping the lions in front of the Justicia—"this?"

Kel was well aware that more ears than just Antonetta's were awaiting his response. "I believe," he said, "that Sarthe made an offer that was impossible to refuse."

Joss laughed sharply; everyone else was silent. Charlon and his father continued to glower in the direction of the square. Kel wished he could see Conor, but the Queen and Prince remained inside the draped pavilion, its damask curtains firmly closed. A hollow square of Castelguards had been set around the pavilion; within the guarded area, Kel could glimpse the figures of Jolivet and Bensimon, deep in conversation. Nearby stood the royal carriage—gold lacquer for a royal event, with a red lion blazon on the side.

It all made Kel uneasy. There had been no discussion of him accompanying Conor at the welcoming ceremony, or appearing in his place. Even Legate Jolivet seemed to feel this was something Conor must do alone, with no Sword Catcher to stand between himself and the world. There was a ceremonial, almost religious, aspect to this event: *You will be meeting your future queen*, Lilibet had said to her son, *and you must be there as who you are, the embodiment of House Aurelian, its blood and bones. This may have begun in lies, but it cannot continue in pretense.*

At least there were Castelguards everywhere. Some, in ordinary street clothes, had even been scattered among the crowd, to monitor the chatter of the citizens and prevent any violence. Along the roofs of the buildings—the Justicia, the Convocat—crouched highly trained marksmen armed with steel-tipped arrows.

Kel wondered if, under other circumstances, the King might have argued in favor of the Sword Catcher's presence; after all, Kel's very existence at Marivent had been Markus's idea. But since the night of the disastrous state dinner with Malgasi, and what had happened next, the King had hidden himself away in the Star Tower. Kel had gone one evening, half wondering if he could speak to the King now that Fausten was locked in the Trick, but the doors had been guarded by the Arrow Squadron, and Kel had turned away, unsure whether there was much of a point in trying to speak to Markus. It was easy to imagine that all his ravings about debt had been about whatever Fausten was pouring into his ears regarding Malgasi, and not about Prosper Beck at all.

It was still strange to Kel that Fausten, who had been such a constant presence beside the King in all the time Kel could recall, was now in the Trick, and no one—not Bensimon, not Jolivet, not minor Castelguards like Manish or Benaset—seemed to know what was happening to him. Kel and Conor had watched from the top of the North Tower, seeing the single light illuminating the topmost window of the prison tower, but had not caught a glimpse of anyone coming or going. Conor insisted that the King was likely planning to use Fausten as a pawn in further dealings with Malgasi, but Kel had his doubts.

Kel had not forgotten the look in the King's eyes—cold, inhuman—when he had ordered Fausten to the Trick, and then Conor to be whipped. Kel had not forgiven Markus for the whipping; the fact that Lin had healed Conor completely did not excuse the King's actions, though Kel kept that thought to himself.

He, Lin, and Conor had decided that Lin's handiwork would be kept a secret. Lin, pale with surprise, had not seemed to have wanted it known that she had healed the Prince overnight, and Conor had desired as little fuss about the whole business as possible; the more people who knew about the healing, he reasoned, the more would hear about the whipping. So Lin had re-bandaged his torso, and for a week or so he had walked stiffly before discarding the ruse, pointing out to Kel when he did that generally people found injuries and illnessses awkward and distasteful, and were glad for the chance to forget them. And indeed, the few who knew the truth—Jolivet, Bensimon, Lilibet—had asked no further questions.

Antonetta now elbowed Kel lightly just as three gleaming carriages rolled into the square, accompanied by a flourish of trumpets: a large, royal cabriolet flanked by two smaller companions. Falconet waved casually at the cheering crowd, who had perked up at the promise of spectacle. Some were clapping. Kel thought for a moment he caught sight of a flash of foxglove behind the barricades. He raised an eyebrow—though, of course, Ji-An was hardly the only person in the city who wore the color violet. Still, he wondered if Andreyen Morettus was somewhere here, watching. He suspected so.

The Castelguards began to move aside to allow the Sarthian royal carriage to draw up before the pavilion. Jolivet seemed to be giving orders, while Bensimon approached the pavilion, parting the curtains to lean inside; a moment later they were thrown back, and Conor stepped out onto the sable carpet.

Montfaucon whistled through his teeth in reluctant admiration. It was true, Kel thought, that one could often tell how bitterly miserable Conor was feeling by how spectacularly he had dressed. Today Conor's despair had taken the form of a waistcoat of dark-blue sueded leather with sapphire buttons. Under the waistcoat was a silk shirt; over it, a gold-frogged jacket with a high, embroidered collar. His trousers had been cut narrowly so high black boots could be fitted over them; his white lace cuffs spilled like seafoam over his hands, which sported rings on each finger. The coronet that encircled his dark curls was gold, with rubies set in the band.

Another small cheer rose from the crowd: They were pleased at the beauty of their Prince. It was a point of pride. They cheered again when Lilibet emerged to stand beside her son, her posture regal, her long black hair braided with emeralds.

Conor stood with his shoulders back as the doors of the Sarthian carriage opened. Kel felt a strange mixture of pain and pride: Conor was facing this, the consequences of his actions, with his head held high. At the same time, Kel hated that it was happening, even as a young woman stepped from the Sarthian carriage.

She was tall, with long chestnut hair, held back by a hoop of bronze. She wore a close-fitting black tunic and trousers, and a gold sword—safe in its scabbard—hung at her hip.

Antonetta made a puzzled noise. "An unusually dressed Princess," she said.

"She is not the Princess, Ana," said Falconet, lazily. "I recognize her from the Court at Aquila. That is Vienne d'Este, one of the Black Guard."

The Black Guard. Kel knew of them. They were nearly mythical: an elite unit of the Sarthian army who gathered intelligence for their King. They were also trained assassins, some of the best in the world, though that fact was never publicly admitted.

Vienne stepped aside as the carriage door opened again and Sena Anessa emerged, holding a young girl by the hand.

Not a young girl, Kel amended. A child. She could not have been more than eleven or twelve, her thin, dark-brown hair tied back with ribbons, her dress a modest lace kirtle, overlaid with a velvet pinafore. Around her forehead was a thin gold circlet.

The coronet of a Princess.

The crowd had fallen utterly silent. Roverge sat forward. "Well," he said. "She's awfully short."

"What in gray hell," Montfaucon muttered, as the trumpets sounded another flourish and Sena Anessa presented the small girl to Conor. Even from a distance, Kel could see the smile on her face as Conor and Lilibet stood frozen in shock.

"Well, fuck," said Falconet.

"Joss," Kel hissed, "what *is* this? What's going on?"

"That's not Aimada," said Falconet. He looked as unhappy as Kel had ever seen him. "That's her younger sister, Luisa. A Princess, yes, but she's all of twelve." He shook his head. "Double-dealing bastards. They've switched out one sister for another."

Antonetta looked stunned, everyone else, clearly furious.

"How did this happen?" demanded Cazalet, his usually beatific round face creased in fury. "Did no one look at the marriage contracts? Did *Bensimon* not examine them? He would never make a mistake like this—"

"It may not matter what the contracts say," snapped Montfaucon. "The language of those things is hundreds of years old. It may *provide* for a substitution to be offered, in the case of the illness or death of the first Princess."

"I assure you," said Falconet, "that Aimada d'Eon is not dead."

"She could be impure. Even pregnant," Uzec suggested, then shrugged at Falconet's glare. "It was only a thought."

"This is a deliberate public provocation," said Benedict Roverge. "A planned humiliation. They are trying to force House Aurelian's hand, trying to incite a conflict, even a war—"

"War with Sarthe will only happen," said Antonetta, "if Conor allows it. It is all in how he receives her."

Kel saw the others look at her in surprise. He felt a flash of irritation—did they really expect her to giggle inanely every moment of her existence? Antonetta, for her part, clamped her mouth shut into a firm line.

"How *can* he receive her?" snapped Benedict. He gestured toward the frozen tableau in the center of the square: Anessa, presenting the child, who was beginning to squirm. Conor, unmoving as a statue. "She is a child, and this is an insult."

"Antonetta is right," drawled Falconet, "which is not something I often say. It is a matter of saving face. He cannot spurn her in front of the crowd."

"So they slap us, and we cannot slap back?" said Benedict. "How is that good strategy? How is that *fair*?"

"It is not fair to make the girl pay for this, either," said Antonetta. "That poor child."

Enough. Kel stood up and vaulted over the railing of the dais, nearly landing atop a gawking Castelguard. He darted through the loose crowd of milling musicians, the girls with their baskets of flowers, everyone hesitating, unsure of what to do next. As he reached the square of sable carpet, one of the Arrow Squadron moved to stop him.

"Let him by," said Jolivet. His narrow face was expressionless, but Kel could see the banked fury in his eyes. As he took Kel by the arm, he glanced back toward the dais. Kel turned to see that, one by one, the Charter Families were leaving the square. The Roverges first, then Cazalet—guiding the blinking Gremont—and even Joss Falconet, until only Antonetta remained, loyally in place, alongside Montfaucon, who, Kel suspected, just wanted to see what was going to happen.

Jolivet guided Kel toward Conor. Kel was half aware of Bensimon, at the Queen's side, politely telling Princess Luisa that this was the Prince's cousin, come to greet her.

Kel reached Conor, laid a hand on his arm. It was rigid under the fabric of his coat. He seemed locked in place, as if his body had turned to iron or glass. He did not look at Kel, but he leaned into his hand slightly, as if his body recognized the familiar touch.

"Bow to her," Kel whispered. Conor flicked a glance toward him. He could tell that what the Prince wanted was to explode in fury. He could feel the rage running through him, and knew he had to contain it. Whatever happened, however Sarthe's betrayal was dealt with, it could not be dealt with here and now. Roverge had been right when he'd said it could provoke a war.

Vienne d'Este had put her hand on the shoulder of the little Princess, a protective gesture. (She was also glaring at Conor, for which Kel could not blame her.) She was awkward, Luisa d'Eon, pinned in that odd age between endearing childhood and adult beauty. She did not share her sister's unusual red hair, rather hers was a lank, colorless brown; her shoulders were bony. She was looking at Conor as if she were wonder-struck by him, her mouth a little bit open.

There was a terrible sympathy in Kel's heart. He knew it was pointless; his sympathy would not help her. No one could help her. She was a pawn in a game of Castles that spanned countries.

"You can deal with Sarthe later," he murmured into Conor's ear, speaking in Marakandi; he doubted very much Anessa spoke it, and certainly Luisa would not. "This is not the child's fault. She is barely older than I was when I came to the Palace. Be *kind*."

Conor did not respond, did not look at Kel—but he did step forward, finally bridging the gap between the two groups: Sarthians and Castellani. He swept an elaborate bow at Luisa's feet. If it was a little *too* elaborate, a little too pointed, the little girl did not notice. She smiled, bright and wide, and clapped her hands together. When Sena Anessa whispered to her, she hurriedly curtsied, then Bensimon stepped forward to present something to Luisa.

"*Un regàlo dal Prìnçipe*," he said, indicating the gift was from Conor. There were a few faint cheers from the crowd, though there was still a great deal of confused milling behind the barricades. Still, this was at least *normal:* the bowing, the presentation of gifts. Sena Anessa was grinning. Kel wanted to kick her.

Luisa tore open the small box and seemed delighted to find a brooch in the shape of a lion, its eyes small chips of ruby. "*Che beo!*" she cried. Pretty.

Kel looked at Vienne d'Este. With her smooth olive skin and curling chestnut hair, she looked far more suitable to play the part of a Princess than her charge did. "Does she speak Castellani?" he asked, indicating Luisa.

"She does not," answered Sena Anessa. "But she is a quick study and will learn."

Conor looked at Anessa with a polite smile. His expression was gracious, his voice calm, as he said, "What have you done, you bitch?"

Anessa sucked in a breath. Oblivious, Luisa smiled happily up at Conor, seeming more relieved than anything else. It was clear she had been dreading meeting some awful foreign Prince, and had found instead a figure out of a Story-Spinner's tale, graceful and handsome in lace and silk.

At least she had that, Kel thought wearily. She would think herself lucky, for a time.

"Monseigneur Aurelian, you agreed to marry Princess Aimada

of Sarthe," said Anessa coldly. "I think you will find that Princesses of Sarthe are given many names at birth. Most are never used, but still, they are official. Here, for instance, is Princess Luisa Estella Matilde Aimada d'Eon. I think you will find that fulfills the requirements of the *contract*."

She snapped out the word *contract* as if it were a curse. Behind her, Kel saw Bensimon slip away, and wondered where he could be going.

"This is revenge," Lilibet said. Her eyes were chips of black ice. "But my son did not break his promise to you."

"He lied by omission," began Anessa, and then the musicians began, belatedly, to play. The air was suddenly full of music and Luisa, who had begun to look worried, laughed in delight as the flower cannons were set off, one by one, and a thousand flowers, gold and violet, searing pink and deep scarlet, flew into the air and spun like a whirlwind.

Petals fell like rain. The crowd was cheering. Bensimon returned from his pilgrimage to the musicians, and he and Jolivet and the Arrow Squadron began to usher the various royalty and diplomats into their carriages.

"Do you wish to go back with the Prince, then?" It was Jolivet, at Kel's shoulder. The grooves in his cheeks, alongside his mouth, looked as if they had been cut there by knives.

Kel shook his head. "I can't. I rode Asti here. I'll bring her back."

"Lucky you," Jolivet murmured. A moment later he was gone into the royal carriage with Conor and Lilibet; it began to roll out of the square, followed by the smaller fleet of sky-blue carriages from Sarthe.

The crowd had begun to dispense. Flower petals still spun in the air as Kel crossed the square, looking for Manish, with whom he had left Asti. He felt numb, a faint ringing in his ears: The whole business had not taken that long, perhaps half an hour, and yet it had upended even the fragile expectations of what was to come in his future—and Conor's.

He found Asti where he had left her, beside the Convocat. Manish, wearing a hooded black cloak, was holding her reins. Which was odd; Kel recalled the young groom as wearing the red livery of the Palace, and it was far too hot for a cloak to be comfortable. He narrowed his eyes, his hand going to the blade at his hip, just as the "groom" threw the hood back and a spill of black hair, half contained with peony clips, was revealed.

Ji-An grinned at him.

Kel sighed. "I thought I saw you in the crowd. Should I even ask what you did with Manish? If you've killed him, I will be vexed. He always lets me in the West Gate."

"I certainly have not. I bribed him," Ji-An said, indignantly. "I am not a lunatic, unlike some people who go around poisoning themselves."

"Have you bribed my groom just for the chance to insult me?" Kel said. "Because I am already having a terrible day."

"I *noticed*," said Ji-An, with the air of someone who has come into a piece of excellent gossip. Kel did not have the energy to tell her that this was more than gossip, this was people's lives, and he doubted she would care if he did. "Regardless. It's been a fortnight since you've been to the Black Mansion. No message, either. Rather as if you'd vanished."

"I'd no idea you cared."

"I don't," Ji-An said. "But the Ragpicker King does. The last we heard, you were going off to speak with Prosper Beck. Then— nothing."

Kel ran a hand through his tangled hair. "Beck had nothing interesting to say."

"I rather doubt that," said Ji-An drily. "And Andreyen would want to judge the situation for himself. *I* think . . ."

Kel tensed, half waiting for her to say: *I think Prosper Beck offered you the chance to do something for him, in exchange for information, and you're considering it.*

"I think," she finished, "that you have been so caught up in the rather ... *startling* events regarding the Prince that you have forgotten all about us, down in the city."

"Perhaps so. But that *is* my duty." Kel sighed. "I have to get back to the Palace. Can you take a message to Andreyen?"

"No," Ji-An said, moving easily to block him from reaching for Asti. "He needs to see you. Face-to-face."

"I have no time for a journey to the Black Mansion—"

"Luckily," Ji-An said, "you needn't make one. The Ragpicker King's carriage is just around the corner."

"Of course," Kel muttered. "Of course it is."

Things had changed, he mused as he followed Ji-An, still leading Asti, around the Convocat to the road that ran behind it. There was the familiar shining black carriage with scarlet wheels, which would once have given him pause. Now he felt a weariness with the world as Ji-An swung the door open and ushered him inside.

There he found Andreyen waiting for him, Gentleman Death in his black suit, with his silver-headed cane and narrow green gaze. It was odd, Kel thought, that Andreyen seemed to carry the cane with him everywhere, though as far as he could tell, the Ragpicker King had no need for it. "Well," he said. "Sarthe has certainly chosen a unique method of retribution where it comes to your Prince."

Kel exhaled. "I suppose I should not be surprised. You always know too much."

The Ragpicker King hummed with amusement. "Only bits of the puzzle. I have put them together myself. Rather clever of young Prince Conor to arrange for Sarthe to provide him the gold he needed to pay off his debts. Rather less clever not to gain the approval of the King and Queen first. He is lucky Markus seems to have lost interest in worldly things, or he might be facing punishment from more than just Sarthe."

Kel studied the Ragpicker King's face, but there seemed nothing hidden in it, no second meaning to his words. He felt a wave of

relief—the secret of Conor's whipping, it seemed, had been successfully contained.

"I'm well aware of that," said Kel. "But I doubt you sent Ji-An
to fetch me because you wanted to discuss Sarthe."

"True. I want to know about Beck. Did Jerrod bring you to him?
What did he say to you?"

"I did speak to him," Kel said, carefully. "I do not think he is the
danger the King spoke to you of in his letter."

Andreyen's eyes glittered. "Has Beck gotten you on his side, then?"

"No." Kel supposed he should be afraid. He knew there was
more to Andreyen than the slightly absent, friendly enough façade;
he had caught glimpses of it here and there, in moments when the
Ragpicker King was unguarded. But he was too tense, too weary to
be anxious. "I have been watching the nobles of the Hill for fifteen
years now," he said. "They are no different from your criminals.
There are the schemers and the plotters, the ones willing to go
along with a plan for expediency's sake, and then—then there are
the opportunists. Beck is an opportunist."

Andreyen shifted his grip on his cane. "Go on."

"I do not know where Beck came from," said Kel. "I can tell you
he is not a noble. I made several deliberate mistakes when discussing the nobles on the Hill with him, and he neither cared nor noticed. For someone like him, there is no real benefit in playing
about with business on the Hill. Beck wants to run gambling dens
and bawdy houses in the Maze. He admits freely to being funded by
someone important, but is uninterested in their eventual goals."

"Someone important," Andreyen echoed. "Someone in the Palace?"

"On the Hill, at any rate. Someone who set Beck up in business
and put him in the position to play the game of debt with Conor."

"What do you think that was meant to accomplish? Not simply
to gain a bit of interest payment, surely."

"I think it was meant to humiliate House Aurelian, and put
them in the position of going begging to the Council of Twelve."

"Or it could have been an attempt to draw out Markus," said Andreyen. "Force him to act."

"I don't think either outcome is of real interest to Beck," said Kel. "I am inclined to believe him when he says he has a patron on the Hill who wants to cause trouble for the Aurelians. Not because I trust him, but because it makes sense."

"Why tell *you*, though?" Andreyen said, his narrow fingers tap-tapping at his cane. He was looking at Kel in that unnerving way of his, as if he could see directly through him.

Because he wants something from me. Antonetta's necklace.

Kel pasted his blankest, most Court-appropriate expression onto his face, and said, "I do not get the sense he likes the man who funded him much. He seems to feel that now that he has his own money, he no longer needs a patron, but I doubt his patron shares that view. I think he hopes I will discover who his patron is and cause trouble for him, perhaps get Jolivet to shut him down completely. And Beck will be free of obligation."

"I see," said Andreyen, and Kel had the unpleasant sensation that Andreyen did indeed see, far more than Kel wished he did. "What are you going to do next?"

"Look out for the patron," said Kel. "Beck gave me no clues, but perhaps he or she will slip up in some way."

He tried to look blank and credible; years of practice had given him an excellent face for card playing, but the Ragpicker King's eyes were razors, cutting through the fragile edifice he'd built to protect himself. Still, he would not mention Antonetta or her neck-lace. He could not bear the idea of bringing her before the Rag-picker King's searching gaze.

"Perhaps the King sensed a betrayal coming from someone on the Hill. From Beck's patron, or from Fausten."

"Alas," said Andreyen blandly. "So many options. If not Beck, then Beck's patron. If not the mysterious patron, then the Malgasi tutor." He spun his cane in his hand. "I take it that you have not tried to speak again to Markus of his letter of warning?"

"The King is inaccessible," said Kel. "You must trust me on that point. Besides, I half suspect that whatever danger he spoke of was some fever dream fed to him by Fausten and his lies about the stars."

"But the Council are not loyal, are they? Not save where it is expedient. Merren always keeps an eye on old Gremont; it seems he's been attending a number of shady meetings in the Maze district. Perhaps you might have a word with him about that."

"Artal Gremont left a mess behind him when he fled Castellane," said Kel. "Now that he's returning, most likely old Gremont wants to clean some of that up. Besides, what does it matter to you, what benefits the Palace?"

Andreyen regarded him coolly. "I am a businessman, Kel, like any trader on the Gold Roads. I benefit from the stability that is provided when the machinery of Castellane runs smoothly. There may be flaws in the system—flaws I exploit—but the alternative is chaos, and chaos is the enemy of business. Chaos might profit Prosper Beck, but it does not profit me."

"It is not my job," said Kel, "to help you profit."

"Then perhaps think on what your job is," said Andreyen. "Not just what it is now, but what it will be. Now you protect the Prince, but when he is King you will be the head of the Arrow Squadron. You will be Legate Jolivet. And it will be your task, as it was his, to go to the Orfelinat and select from the frightened children there the next Sword Catcher. The next *you*. And it will kill a piece of you to do it."

Kel put a hand against the carriage door, meaning to swing it open, but could not bring himself to do it. The brightness of the sunlight outside seemed to stab into his eyes.

From behind him, the Ragpicker King said, "I tell you, you cannot protect your precious Conor without my help."

Just what Beck said, or close enough. "I have never needed your help before," said Kel. "I do not need it now."

"Then perhaps it is Fausten you should speak to," said Andreyen.

"Fausten is in the Trick. No one can get inside while there's a prisoner there."

"Not no one," said the Ragpicker King. "And I think you know that."

Kel turned his head to look at Andreyen, who regarded him through the gloom with a cool, hard gaze. There was nothing of empathy in it, or the careless friendliness he so often wore like a disguise. "You're asking too much," said Kel. "There are things I will not do."

"For me, or for House Aurelian?"

"House Aurelian is my duty," he said. "For a moment, it seemed our goals were aligned. Now I think they are not. You are correct that the nobles are not loyal, but there is nothing new to that. I shall guard the Prince as I always have; if there are deeper issues on the Hill that intrigue you, you have your own spies. You do not need me."

"I see," said the Ragpicker King. "Is that to be the end of our connection, then?"

"I would prefer," Kel said carefully, "that it did not mean enmity between us. It is just that our business seems concluded."

"Perhaps," said the Ragpicker King softly, and if Kel did not quite like the tone in his voice, there was nothing he could say; Ji-An was rapping on the carriage door. When the Ragpicker King swung it wide, she gestured toward the square.

"There's a fight breaking out," she said. "Looks like the anti-Sarthe crowd are stirring up trouble. The Vigilants will be along any moment."

"That's all right. We're done here," said Andreyen easily, though Kel could see that he was far from easy in his mind. "Kel was just leaving."

Kel clambered down out of the carriage. Ji-An had been right, of course; he could hear a dull roar from the direction of Valerian Square, coming closer. It sounded like waves surging in on the tide.

Ji-An handed him Asti's reins; the horse nuzzled at Kel's shoulder, clearly puzzled by all the goings-on. "So, will we see you again?" she said.

"If I learn anything interesting. That remains to be seen." Kel stroked Asti's neck as Ji-An turned away, starting back toward the Ragpicker King's carriage.

"Kang Ji-An," he said, without being able to help himself.

She froze but did not turn around. "What did you say?"

"What's this I hear about a bloodbath between noble families in Geumjoseon? A girl who climbed a garden wall and slaughtered a whole family, then escaped in a black carriage?"

Still, Ji-An did not move. It was as if he were looking at a statue carved from obsidian: black hair, black cloak. Without turning around, she said, without a touch of mockery or humor, "If you mention that to me again, I will kill you."

She said nothing else, only climbed up onto the driver's seat, leaving Kel to watch the carriage vanish down the street.

With the Great Word gone, all the works of magic were undone. Suleman cried aloud in despair, his body crumbling into dust, for magic had kept him alive far beyond a human life span. And thus it was that the other Sorcerer-Kings, too, became dust, and the workings of their hands were destroyed: The great creatures of magic that they had created, the dragons and manticores and winged horses, all vanished like smoke on the air. Their weapons of war turned to ash, and their palaces fell away, and the rivers that they enchanted into being dried up. Islands sank beneath the sea. Magicians tried to speak the Great Name of Power, but they found they could not. Every book that had contained the name now had a blank space where it had been.

And this was the Sundering.

— *Tales of the Sorcerer-Kings*, Laocantus Aurus Iovit III

CHAPTER NINETEEN

*F*lames licked up the sides of the stone tower. All around was burning. She could see the remains of the great city, thousands of feet below. All blackened stone now, and wood petrified by fire.

Above, the stars. Glimmering, untouched, they burned but could not be burned. She yearned to reach out to them, within them, and take hold of it. That which she knew hovered in the emptiness. The Word.

But he was almost here. He was climbing the tower's side, clinging like a shadow to the uneven stone. She had to wait. Until he was here, his glimmering Stone set in the cross guard of his sword.

She saw it then. A movement at the lip of the tower, where stone met sky. Two pale hands, flexing and grasping. Lifting his big body up, until he had hauled himself over the edge, was on his knees with all of it behind him: the sky rising above, the city fallen below. She heard him hiss her name as he rose to his feet, hand on the pommel of his sword, his long black hair falling to hide his face, but still she could see his eyes. Still, she knew him. Would always know him—

"Lin?"

Lin jolted awake, a sharp pain darting through her hand. She blinked at Merren Asper, sitting across from her at his worktable in the Black Mansion, his pale eyebrows uplifted.

"Did you just fall asleep?" he said.

Lin looked down at her hand; she'd been clutching her brooch, the edged setting digging into her skin, leaving faint red lines. She slipped it into her pocket and tried to smile at Merren, who was stirring a thick black concoction with a glass pipette. The images from her dream still clung to the perimeter of her vision: shadow and fire.

"I haven't been sleeping much lately," she said, half apologetically. It was true enough. When she did sleep, she was troubled by wild dreams. Often she stood atop the tower of Balal and looked out upon the burning plains: Over and over she watched dream-Suleman approach her, and felt herself racked by a desire that left her body aching when she woke.

Sometimes she dreamed that she flew among mountains in the shape of a raven, and watched an old man hurl books into the sea. She had not dreamed again the dream she'd had at the Palace, where she had crawled into a cave halfway up a mountain and seen a blinding, fiery light. She'd asked Mariam the meaning of the words *hi nas visik*, and been surprised when Mariam had told her they meant: You are real.

"It is a sort of expression of incredulity," Mariam had said. "As if you cannot believe what you are seeing."

And Lin was troubled. How had she known Malgasi words in her dreams that she did not know in her waking life? But she could not think too much on it. Ever since the night she had healed the Crown Prince—so thoroughly, it seemed, that it was as if he had never been whipped at all—her whole mind had been focused on the way she had seemed to be able to use Petrov's stone (no, she should not call it that; it was *her* stone now) to accomplish something beyond anything she had ever accomplished before. Beyond anything she had heard of *gematry* accomplishing before.

She could still recall the image that had appeared before her mind's eye as she stood by Prince Conor's bedside: the swirl of smoke inside the stone, the appearance of that single word: *heal*. She could feel the pulse of the stone in her hand.

And she could still feel the stone go cold in her hand. Ever since that night, it had lost all its color and life. It had gone a milky, flat gray color, like a dull pearl. No matter how she angled it, she could no longer see depth in the stone, nor the suggestion of words.

She had tried again, with Mariam, regardless of the change in the stone—asking Mariam to lie down as the Prince had done, and concentrating on the healing talismans Mariam wore at her neck and wrists. But nothing had happened. It was driving her mad. Why had it worked on the Crown Prince, but not Mariam? And it had worked on Kel, too, she knew now, speeding his healing, though not as impressively as it had done with Prince Conor. She still remembered the feeling that the stone *wanted* her to use it, the burn it had left on her skin after she had treated Kel. Yet it had done nothing like that again with any other patient, though she always wore it when she did her rounds.

She did not understand it. And she was still without the one thing that might help her understand it: Qasmuna's book.

In the past fortnight Lin had been all over Castellane in search of it. She had met with several unsavory charlatans who had promised they had the book, or something like it, but they had never had the real thing—only silly, pasted-together "spell books," filled with chants and rhymes meant to "bestir love" and "enhance beauty" and no mention at all of any way to actually *access* magic, to draw it up out of oneself and save it, so that it could be used without killing the practitioner.

This morning, she had taken time away from her search out of necessity: The Etse Kebeth was full of girls and women preparing for the Tevath, and it had been impossible to use the kitchen there to mix up her cures and remedies. So she had come to the Black Mansion, where Merren had seemed only too pleased to have company in his workroom. He looked up as the noise of a dull cheer came from outside, wrinkling up his nose in momentary puzzlement. "Something's happening now, isn't it?" he asked. "Is the Prince getting married?"

"Not married," Lin said, gently. She had come to regard Merren as something of an innocent savant. He loved his potions and poisons, yet seemed to regard the rest of the world through a gauzy, fond bemusement. "The Princess from Sarthe, whom he's meant to marry, is arriving today. They're welcoming her in Valerian Square."

"Oh," Merren said brightly, and went back to stirring his black-brown concoction.

Lin had passed through the crowds on her way to the Black Mansion that afternoon; they thickened like cream at the top as she neared the center of the city and Valerian Square, where the Crown Prince would today be welcoming his Sarthian bride.

It ought to have been a festive day. Lin still recalled her mother telling her about the arrival of the young Princess Lilibet in the city, thirty years ago. Crowds had lined the Ruta Magna, cheering as an open chariot carried her into the city. Now that she had met Queen Lilibet, Lin could more easily picture her as her mother had described her: black hair flying, her lips painted red as lacquer, a green silk cloak fastened at her bare shoulders with emeralds, green fire blazing in their hearts. More emeralds burning in her crown; the citizens of Castellane had thrown red pomegranate flowers and dark-purple tulips, the flowers of Marakand, in her path and shouted, "*Mei bèra,* the most beautiful!"

They had been proud then, of the woman who was to be their new queen, of the beauty and fire she would bring to their city. But there was none of that pride now. A few balconies bore sprigs of white lily, the flower of Sarthe, but the general mood seemed— well, *bemused* seemed the best word for it.

The news of the betrothal had broken over the city like a storm. Lin heard little about it in the Sault, where the activities of the Aurelian family were only considered interesting if they affected the Ashkar. Prince Conor was not *their* prince; he was merely an important personage in Castellane. *Their* prince was Amon Benjudah, the Exilarch, currently traveling the Gold Roads with the Sanhedrin.

Lin, however, had gotten an earful from her patients, especially

Zofia, who seemed to have a personal dislike of Sarthe. "Such a disappointment," she had grumbled, waving an old cutlass in the air. "What a waste. Such an attractive Prince, and such a dull person to marry."

"You don't know that," Lin had said. "She might be interesting, the Princess."

"She's from Sarthe. They're all dull, or dishonest, or both," Zofia had said firmly, and her opinion seemed shared by the general populace. Some of Lin's patients had complained that the marriage would give Sarthe too firm a toehold in Castellane; that they would take advantage of access to the harbor, that they would insist everyone take up their fashions and wear uncomfortable hats.

Lin had listened, and nodded absently, and thought of the Prince. *You should not feel sorry for me, you know. Feel sorry for the one who has to marry me.*

And she did feel sorry, a little, for Princess Aimada d'Eon. But she felt more sorry for Conor Aurelian, which was uncomfortable, to say the least. She had always thought she would not feel sorry for him if he fell down a well and got stuck there, and now, here she was, feeling a regretful twinge every time she thought of him, which was too often.

She had heard not a word from the Palace since the morning when Kel had woken her and they had both seen Prince Conor whole and unscarred. Kel had sent a note a few days later thanking her, and a book about Sunderglass that she was reading now. He had told her that Queen Lilibet had been pleased with her handiwork and that Prince Conor was healing as might be expected.

This, she knew, was a bit of code. Lin had waited anxiously to see if either Mayesh or Andreyen would mention Conor's miraculous healing to her. When neither did, she had been forced to admit that it seemed their plan had worked: The few who knew the Prince had been whipped at all did not know he had recovered from the effects overnight. And as the days went by since that strangest of events, she began to feel more and more as if that night had been cut out of the unbroken line of the rest of her days. It lay somehow beside or athwart them, as if they were memories from someone else's life that she was somehow able to examine.

It seemed almost impossible to her that she now shared a secret with the Crown Prince and his Sword Catcher that no one but the three of them knew. Mari was aware Lin had been summoned to the Palace, of course, as was Chana, but Lin had said that it was only to treat a servant's burned hand, and if Mariam did not believe her, she did not show it. She had not told a soul of the whipping, of the strangeness of that whole night. Listening to the Prince talk, telling him secrets of her own, even touching him—as a healer, of course, but still, with gestures of startling intimacy—that she had brushed her thumb across his *mouth* . . .

She caught her breath at the memory, just as Merren looked up: The Ragpicker King had come into the room. He really did move with a catlike silence, as if the soles of his shoes were padded. Lin had begun to get used to him gliding about the Black Mansion, often coming in and out of the workroom to see what she and Merren were doing. He never badgered them about it—he seemed more interested in simply satisfying his curiosity than seeking results of any particular sort.

He looked rather haggard today, however, his face white and strained between his black curtain of hair and the starker blackness of his jacket. (As always, the same: black frock coat, narrow black trousers, gleaming onyx boots.) He was followed by Ji-An, who was tugging on a pale flower petal that had become snagged in her hair. She hopped up on the stool beside Lin's. "I saw our mutual friend in the square today."

Merren glanced up. "Kel?"

Ji-An twisted around to look at him. "Yes, and half the Charter Families, and of course, the Aurelians. All there to welcome the Sarthian Princess who will be Castellane's next queen."

Ji-An was grinning like someone who knew a secret. Lin said, "Ji-An, did something happen?"

"Another loveless marriage between heartless monarchists consolidating power," said Merren cheerfully. "Was she pretty, at least? The populace will respond better to this whole mess if they're assured of a glamorous queen."

Lin braced herself. There was some part of her that did not want to hear how beautiful Aimada d'Eon was, how alluring, how elegant—

"She's a *child*," said Ji-An, with glee.

Merren looked puzzled. "The Prince agreed to marry a child?"

"He agreed to marry a Princess of Sarthe," said Andreyen. "Who was, it seemed all agreed, to be Aimada. But—"

"But it wasn't *her*," interrupted Ji-An. "They sent her younger sister instead. All of eleven or twelve years old. The looks on their faces—the noble families, the Aurelians—was priceless."

Lin reached into her pocket, wrapping her fingers around the stone in its setting. She had found that holding the cool, heavy weight in her hand was soothing. "The Prince," she said. "What did he do?"

"The only thing he could," said Ji-An. "Went along with it. But he stood there stiff as a plank for ages first. Kel had to shake him out of it. Then he behaved himself well enough."

"Clever Kel," Andreyen murmured. "That was, indeed, the only thing that could be done. An interesting move from Sarthe. Whether they will do more to signal their fury remains to be seen."

"Rather hard on the Prince." Merren frowned. "That heartless monarchial bastard," he added.

"My grandfather," Lin said, slowly. "He was there, wasn't he?"

"The Counselor?" said Ji-An. "Yes, indeed. Didn't look too pleased, either. I imagine the Palace has quite a day of diplomatic antics ahead of it."

"They'll manage something. They always do," Merren said, lifting his pipette out of the dark liquid. He eyed it a moment before licking it thoughtfully.

"*Merren*," shrieked Ji-An. "What are you doing?"

He looked up, blue eyes wide. "What? It's chocolate," he said. "I was hungry." He held the pipette out. "Would you like to try it?"

"Certainly not," said Andreyen. "It smells of wet weeds." He frowned. "Lin. Walk with me. I wish to speak to you."

Both Merren and Ji-An watched curiously as Lin, trying to hide her surprise at being summoned—because it *was* a summons, however politely phrased—rose to confer with the Ragpicker King.

He waited for them to be out of earshot of the workroom before he spoke. Lin listened to the hushed thump of his cane on the Marakandi rugs as they walked. She found it soothing.

"There are murmurs that someone else in Castellane is searching for the Qasmuna book," he said. "With great dedication, I hear."

"Just now?" Lin said. "Since I've started looking for it?"

He nodded. "Rumor has it they're offering a pretty penny."

"I'm sorry," Lin said. "If I've been looking for it too clumsily, if I've stirred up interest that shouldn't have been stirred up—"

"Not at all." Andreyen dismissed her concerns with a gesture. "In my experience, it is often useful to stir things up. Perhaps whoever is looking for the book currently has been made nervous by hearing about *your* search. Perhaps these nerves will lead them to reveal themselves or what they know."

The smile he fashioned filled Lin with relief that she was not on the Ragpicker King's bad side, or standing between him and what he wanted.

"The junk dealer I spoke to in the Maze told me it had been purchased by a 'discerning individual,'" said Lin. "Perhaps this individual has put it about that they have this item to sell, and thus we are seeing evidence of interest in buying the book beginning to make itself known . . ."

"Perhaps," said Andreyen. "I admit I have not fully educated myself as regards the dark underground of antique book dealing. Vicious folk, I've heard." He pushed open the door to what she now knew was called the Great Room, with its massive stone fireplace and comfortable furniture. It was clearly an often-used room; someone had left a book facedown on the arm of a chair, and a plate of half-eaten biscuits balanced on a tabletop. "Usually, though, I get word of it when someone in Castellane has something interesting or illegal to sell. This time, I heard only of the person looking to buy."

"But no word who they are?"

The Ragpicker King shook his head.

"I could ask for permission to seek the book in the Shulamat again, but the Maharam made his position fairly clear," Lin said.

The Ragpicker King picked up the silver incantation bowl on the shelf near the fireplace. Lin felt a sort of itch when he touched it, a desire to tell him to put it down, that it was a precious thing to her people. But she would only be a hypocrite if she did; it was not as if her current connection to the Ragpicker King, with everything he stood for, would not have horrified the Maharam and the Sanhedrin far more. She wondered if he had ever employed someone Ashkari before. He seemed as if he knew more about what went on inside the walls of the Sault than most. But then it was in his interest to know things, and any one of her people who worked with him in secret risked their place in the community. As she was doing.

"There are certain men," said Andreyen, gazing into the bowl, "who, when in positions of power, err on the side of inflexibility."

"You are in a position of power," said Lin.

The Ragpicker King set the bowl down and grinned. "But I am very flexible. Mostly morally."

Before Lin could reply, there was a stir outside the room. She heard Ji-An protest, and then the doors burst open and a familiar-looking man stalked in, glowering. Dark-red hair, black eyes, dressed like a merchant's son. Lin remembered him now: the man who had been here the first time she came to the mansion. He had wanted—

"My black powder," the man snarled. "It was supposed to arrive two days ago. I've been patient—"

"Bursting into my home, pushing past my guard?" Andreyen said, green eyes narrowing. "You call that patience?"

"My apologies," said Ji-An, who had followed the young man into the room and stood at alert, her hand halfway inside her jacket. "I couldn't stop him without killing him, and I wasn't sure that was what you wanted."

"Unnecessary, Ji-An," said Andreyen. "He is rude but overall harmless. Ciprian Cabrol, if you want to talk with me, I suggest you make an appointment."

"I haven't got the time," Ciprian protested. "Ascension Day is in four days."

"Astonishing news," said the Ragpicker King. "I've always said I should keep better track of major holidays." He crossed his arms. "I've a meeting going on, in case you can't tell."

Ciprian Cabrol shot a single glance at Lin. "Irrelevant. She's Ashkar, who will she tell? My powder—"

Andreyen rolled his eyes. "Ciprian, this is Shenzan black powder we're discussing. Surely you understand the importance of transporting it *carefully*. Besides. The Roverge ships will be in the harbor for another two weeks."

Roverge ships? Lin felt her eyes widen. The Roverges were a Charter Family, dangerous to be at odds with.

"But it needs to happen soon—on Ascension Day," Cabrol insisted. "At the stroke of midnight. All the nobles will be gathered for that banquet. Roverge and his rotten son will be there. I need them to see my vengeance written in fire across the sky. The harbor will shine as though the lights of the Gods have returned. As though their magic still burns across the waters."

"That was surprisingly poetic," murmured Ji-An.

"You are being very theatrical about all of this," said Andreyen disapprovingly.

"Says the man who goes about in a black carriage with wheels painted the color of blood," said Ciprian. "Theatricality has its purpose. After what they did to us—driving a family from their home for daring to own a small business selling ink—"

"It wasn't *that* small a business," said Andreyen. "Honestly, I'm surprised, after what's happened, that you and your family are still in Castellane. The Vigilants—"

"My family is in Valderan for now," said Ciprian. "Only I am here. And I'm safe enough." He glowered. "I expect that powder tomorrow morning," he said, and stalked out of the room. After a moment, Ji-An followed him, no doubt to make sure he made directly for the exit.

"This business with Cabrol and the Roverge fleet," said the Ragpicker King. He looked down at Lin, eyes unreadable. "It is not information you can share. Do you understand? Not with anyone in the Sault. Not with Mayesh Bensimon. Cabrol is rude and careless, but he is a customer. And I have a certain interest in him getting his way."

"One question," said Lin. "Will there be people aboard those ships? The ones Cabrol wants to blow up?"

"No," Andreyen said. "Everyone will be in the city, celebrating Ascension Day. And they're moored halfway out to Tyndaris. Besides, that night is your Tevath, isn't it—your Goddess Festival? You and yours will be safe in the Sault."

"I am a healer," said Lin. "I would have difficulty keeping a secret that I knew would lead to injury or death, whether the victims were Ashkar or not. But the fleets of the Castellani nobility are not my concern. Besides," she added, thinking aloud. "If I were to tell anyone, how would I explain how I had come by the information without revealing things I do not want to reveal?"

"Like your association with me."

"You must know a great number of people who do not wish to reveal their association with you," said Lin.

"Indeed, and I find we all get along handily. In the meantime . . ."

"I know," Lin said. "Keep looking for the book."

Later, after she had left the mansion and was on her way back to the Sault, she glanced over at the harbor, a strip of blue in the distance. How odd it would be if Ciprian Cabrol succeeded in his mad plan, and sometime during the Goddess Festival the gold light of his explosions illuminated the sky over the harbor.

But that was what it was to be Ashkar. Whatever happened inside the Sault, they would always be surrounded by *malbushim*, by their machinations and their madness. If Cabrol managed to enact his plan—and Lin had her doubts—it would be the most exciting thing that had happened at a Tevath in some two hundred years.

Kel had returned to Marivent to find that Conor and Lilibet, Bensimon and Jolivet, were locked away in the Shining Gallery with the delegates from Sarthe. He could hear shouting from behind the doors. He tried to get close but was shooed away by Benaset. "Not your place, Anjuman," he said. "Jolivet told me expressly to make sure you stayed away. Go amuse yourself elsewhere."

Kel was furious, but he restrained himself. He headed back to the Castel Mitat to collect his thoughts; besides, he could at least change out of the wretched velvet coat he'd been roasting in all day. (Lilibet's desire for him to represent Marakand in velvet and brocade was rarely practical where the realities of Castellani weather were concerned, and it had been a depressingly beautiful day, the sky arching overhead like a dancer in pale-blue satin, the sea a sheet of unbroken teal-green glass.)

He expected to find the courtyard of the Castel Mitat empty, but it was not. The small Princess, Luisa, was there, playing along the edge of the tiled fountain. Kel and Conor had done the same when they were children; on hot days, it was a good way to cool down. The memory sent a piercing sadness through Kel: for his old self, for Luisa now.

With her was the bodyguard, Vienne d'Este. She did not seem at all bothered by the heat. She was walking alongside Luisa as the girl bounced a ball against the statue of Cerra in the fountain's center, catching it as it rebounded and giggling when it splashed into the water.

They both turned to look at him: Vienne with a cool suspicion, her eyes flicking down (*So there's a blade in your boots*, he thought, *I know your tricks, bodyguard, though you will not guess why I do*), while Luisa glanced at him, smiled, then frowned and said in rapid Sarthian, "*Mì pensave che xéra el Prìnçipe, el ghe soméja tanto.*"

"She thought you were the Prince," said Vienne. "She says you look very like him."

Kel turned to Luisa. "*Cosin.*"

Luisa smiled her gap-toothed smile. "*Dove xéło el Prìnçipe? Xeło drìo a rivar a zogar con mì?*"

Vienne retrieved the ball from the fountain where Luisa had dropped it. "The Prince can't come now, darling, he has business. I am sure he'd rather be playing."

That's probably true, Kel thought drily, *though not in the way you mean.*

"I'm Kel Anjuman," he said. "I'm at your service, and, of course, the service of the Princess."

He swept a bow, which seemed to delight Luisa. Vienne, holding the red ball in her hands, seemed less charmed. "Well," she said. "If you wish to help, truly—"

Kel raised an eyebrow.

"The quarters we have been given were decorated for someone much older than Luisa," she said, rather stiffly. "If you could find some old toys, perhaps, or a few pretty things she might like—that would be helpful."

It was clear on her face not only that she was the Princess's bodyguard, but that she loved the girl like a little sister. She had handed off the ball to Luisa, who was dancing along the fountain's edge. The hem of her pinafore was draggled by water and mud.

Kel wanted to say, *I know what it is like to love someone and be sworn to protect them, someone who has so much more power than you do, but whom you cannot save from the consequences of that power.*

But Vienne would simply have thought he was mad. At least Luisa seemed entirely unaware that there was a political firestorm raging around her—one that had wholly to do with the fact that her arrival was a disappointment. That she was unwanted.

Kel promised to see what he could do, and trudged upstairs to his rooms, a great weariness weighing him down.

The moon that night was blue. An unusual moon, said to augur the approach of confusing events. Kel, up in the West Tower, watched as it rose, turning the sky to a deeper indigo, the sea to moving lapis. Even the sails of the ships in the harbor appeared tinted with blue, as if seen through the lenses of Montfaucon's blue spectacles.

The long and terrible meeting in the Gallery dragged on; Conor had not yet returned. Lilibet seemed pleased that Conor had been pulled into her world of Palace negotiations and foreign interests, tellingly happy to have him at her side. Kel could picture what was going on: Bensimon and Anessa shouting at each other about what happened, about contractual points and details. Jolivet and Senex Domizio ready for talk of war. But he was, of course, just guessing. What he did know was that the King was not in attendance. Light glowed in the window of the Star Tower, and occasional smoke rose from the chimney.

He was not sure if he ought to be surprised, or angry at himself for being surprised. What else had he expected, when the King had not even gone to Valerian Square to meet the new Princess? For so many years, the Palace had put about the story: The King was a philosopher, an astronomer, a genius. His study of the stars would result in discoveries that would be passed down through generations, adding to Castellane's glory. They had put it about so thoroughly that Kel had believed it himself, because it was easier to believe it than question it.

He guessed now that Conor had never believed it, but had never discussed it, either. He had allowed the Palace to play a game in

which the King was sensible but eccentric. But Fausten's presence
in the Trick—a spike of dark-blue steel now; Kel could see it rising
against the night—belied all that. He could not help hearing Andreyen's voice in his mind: *Perhaps it is Fausten you should speak to.*

But Fausten was in the Trick, and no one was allowed in the
Trick, save the Arrow Squadron guards and the royal family themselves.

In the end, Kel supposed, he did it because he was tired of feeling useless, tired of imagining what was going on in a room he was
barred from. Among people who, save one, would not want him
there. And because he no longer trusted the King. He had already
put Fausten in the Trick, and had his own son whipped. If it were
not for Lin, Conor would be bedridden still, and scarred forever.
What else might Markus do, and why, and when?

He was supposed to protect Conor at all costs. And if that meant
protecting him from his own father, then that was the situation he
found himself in. *I am the Prince's shield. I am his unbreakable armor.
I suffer that he might never suffer.*

As if in a dream, Kel went down the spiral steps and to the wardrobe in their room. Not to his wardrobe, but Conor's.

He dressed in black. Linen trousers, silk tunic, fitted waistcoat.
Vambraces beneath his sleeves. Low black boots and, of course, his
talisman around his throat. Lastly, he lifted a simple coronet from
its black velvet box. Placing it on his own head felt like a crime,
something impermissible, though he had done it dozens of times
before.

But not without Conor knowing. Never without Conor knowing.

He slipped out of the Castel Mitat, finding the courtyard empty,
though Luisa's red ball was floating in the fountain like a water-
swollen pomegranate.

The blue moon cast a ghostly air over the Palace grounds as Kel
made his way through gardens and gates, past the closed doors of
the Shining Gallery, past the Little Palace, the Castel Pichon, where

Luisa's apartments had been prepared. The wind had kicked up, carrying the scent of eucalyptus and a freight of dried leaves and headless flower stems.

Long ago, he and Conor would sneak out of the Castel Mitat on nights like this. They would raid Dom Valon's kitchen for tarts and pastries; they would swim in the reflecting pool in the Queen's Garden. Huddle in one of the cliffside follies with a bottle of brandewine swiped from the cellars and pretend to like the taste of it. Pretend to be drunk, giggling, until they really were drunk, and had to guide each other back to their rooms before dawn, each too drunk to hold the other one up, but they tried regardless.

He remembered Merren saying, "I thought it was half a joke, this Sword Catcher thing, when I heard it. Who'd do that?" By Law, Kel knew, his loyalty was owed to House Aurelian, but in reality it was given to Conor. Conor, the only person who had ever really known what Kel's life was like, what made up his days—and in exchange, he knew Conor the same way. In fact, no one knew that Conor but him: the boy Prince who could only have a little brandewine before it made him sick, who cried when his horse (a bay stallion who hated him) broke its leg and had to have its throat cut by Jolivet. Who fretted that the world was so big, he could never see all of it, though he had never been farther than Valderan.

The Trick rose up before Kel's eyes then—a blue-black needle of marble, threading the sky. He slid the talisman down the chain around his neck so it lay just above the open collar of his shirt. He approached the front doors of the Trick, two wooden half-moons banded with iron. Outside them were stationed a group of three Castelguards; they sat at a folding wooden table, playing *yezi ge*, a Shenzan card game.

They shot to their feet at Kel's approach, their faces paling. "Monseigneur," said one, apparently the bravest. "We were— everything has been quiet, no sound from the prisoner—"

What were they afraid of? Kel wondered. That he—that

Conor—was checking to make sure they had shown alacrity in the performance of their duties? They were guarding one weak old man in a prison no one had ever escaped from.

Kel tried to imagine a Conor who would interrupt his own evening to come down to the Trick and shout at a group of guards for lazing about on duty. He failed.

"Gentlemen." He fought the urge to incline his head politely; Princes did not bow to soldiers. "I've come to see the prisoner. No"—he held a hand up—"there is no need to accompany me. I prefer to go alone."

As they melted away, ushering Kel into the prison tower, he had to hide a smile. It had been so easy. And it felt good, it always did, to put on power like a cloak of invulnerability from a Story-Spinner's tale. The trick was to fight against enjoying it.

It was a calculated risk, he thought, as he began to climb the tower steps, coming here as Conor. There was always the danger the guards would gossip about his visit, and another Palace denizen would point out that Conor had been in some sort of diplomatic meeting. But he was betting that the gossip about Sarthe and the new Princess was juicy enough to distract them from anything else.

Kel had been in the Trick recently enough, but only during the day. The narrow spiral staircase he climbed now looked deeply shadowed, illuminated only by the occasional hanging carcel lamp, casting spidery shadows against the stone walls.

When he reached the top, he found it equally dark. There was only one lamp. Thankfully, there were windows set high in the walls through which pale-blue moonlight poured, making the Sunder-glass bars of the cells glow as if they had been carved from opals.

He walked the narrow aisle until he found Fausten's cell. It was the only one with the door closed, though for a moment Kel thought it was empty. Then he realized that what he had taken for a heap of rags in the corner was the King's old adviser, crouched against the wall.

He was in the same clothes he'd worn when the guards had dragged him out of the Shining Gallery, only they were filthy now, the constellations sewn onto his cloak now a scatter of bright beads across the floor of his cell. The stink of piss and old sweat was rank. There was something else under it, too, a metallic smell like old blood.

Kel approached the cell reluctantly. He was no longer thinking about fighting the enjoyment of power. He was asking himself why he had thought he could do this.

Fausten looked up, his face a pale smudge in the dimness. He blinked into the shadows. "My—my lord," he stammered. "My King—"

Kel flinched. "No. Not the father, but the son."

A faint look of cunning flashed across Fausten's face. "Conor," he breathed. "I have always been fond of you, Conor."

A faint nausea twisted in the pit of Kel's stomach. "Fond enough to sell me to the Malgasi without a word to me of whatever bargain you had made?"

Fausten's eyes glittered, ratlike, in the half dark. "I did not sell you. There is no profit for me in any of this. Your father made this bargain, long ago."

"But why?" said Kel, and when Fausten did not answer, he said, "My father spoke to me some time ago of a danger. A terrible danger he believed was coming to Castellane, and to me. But he would not say what it was."

"Why ask me?" said Fausten. "I am but an old man, thrust unjustly into prison. All I have ever wanted to do was protect your father. You know I do not belong here."

"I'd know it better if you answered my questions," said Kel. "Was the danger my father spoke of some machination of the Malgasi Court?"

"The Malgasi Court," Fausten echoed scornfully. "All you think of is politics. There are greater forces at work than any worldly powers."

"Please, spare me your talk of the stars," said Kel. "I have seen how helpful that was to my father."

"Your father," said Fausten, in a hollow voice. He wobbled to his feet. He came closer to the bars, taking small delicate steps, as if he were picking his way among flowers. Though there were certainly no flowers here. "I have always been loyal to your father," he said, catching at the Sunderglass bars. "The Court of Malgasi is a cold, cold place. When your father was there, he was only a boy, a fosterling, a third son and ignored. He was open to any voice that whispered to him. And whisper it did."

"Who whispered to him?"

Fausten's rhuemy eyes wandered. "*Atma az dóta*," he muttered. "It was not his fault. He did only what he was persuaded to do."

Atma az dóta. Fire and shadow. "What did my father do?"

Fausten shook his head. "I promised. Not to tell."

"It was something bad," Kel said, dropping his voice. Low and confiding, as if he were speaking to a child. "Wasn't it?"

Fausten made an inarticulate noise.

"What I don't understand," said Kel mildly, "is why, if my father committed some terrible malfeasance in Malgasi, was Ambassador Sarany so determined that I marry Elsabet?"

"Iren's daughter," said Fausten. His eyes had begun to roll from side to side. "She was so beautiful, Iren. But then the fire left her, her light all dimmed, and she was only fury. Why does she want you to marry Elsabet? For the same reason Iren let your father live. Because she prizes your blood. Your Aurelian blood."

Well, of course. Every noble family prized royal lineage. Kel felt like grinding his teeth together with frustration. "Fausten. If you do not tell me what the danger is that my father spoke of, then I cannot intervene with him for your sake. If you *do* help me—well, then, perhaps I can convince my father you were acting in his interests. That you were not merely a puppet of the Malgasi, manipulating him at their whim."

Fausten made a gasping noise. "It is not so simple," he said. "Nothing is so simple." He turned his rat's eyes on Kel. "The danger is not the Malgasi Court. It is far closer than that."

"In the city?" Kel said.

"On the Hill," said Fausten. "There are those who would see House Aurelian destroyed. I thought a union with the Malgasi Court might prevent that. They are strong, ruthless. Perhaps I pushed the King too hard toward it. Perhaps—"

"Perhaps you should have told me," said Kel. "You expected me to have no will of my own. That was your mistake."

"Many are my mistakes," said Fausten.

"Amend them now," said Kel. "Tell me who is the danger on the Hill."

"Look to those close to you," said Fausten. "Look to your Council. To the nobles. Look to your Sword Catcher."

Kel went cold down to his bones. "What?"

There was a crafty light in Fausten's eyes, as if to say, *I have caught your attention now, have I not, Crown Prince?* "Just as I say. Your *Királar* will betray you. I have seen it in the stars."

"My Sword Catcher is loyal to me," Kel said. He was conscious of the awful irony of the situation, but he bit back on it; he could not waver in front of Fausten. It would only make the situation worse.

"He is loyal to you now. One day there will be something of yours he wants badly enough to betray you for it. And you will hate him then. Hate him enough to wish him dead."

"But what—"

"Envy. Envy is the great poisoner. I would have told you before, had I thought you would listen—"

"Enough." Kel's temper snapped like a twig. "It is easy enough to see you are trying to manipulate me. To drive a wedge between me and my Sword Catcher, so I will put my trust in you instead, as my father did. Do you think I could possibly believe you now about what you say you see in the stars? Are you that much of a fool?"

It was too much; he had pressed too hard. The little man gave a cry and curled up on the filthy ground, hugging his knees to his chest, rolling among the broken beads. Nothing Kel did or said could budge him.

And to be fair, Kel was only too eager to get away. Away from the stink of the Trick, away from the words buzzing in his brain. *Your Sword Catcher will betray you. And you will hate him then. Hate him enough to wish him dead.*

And thus did the time of the Sorcerer-Kings come to an end. Though the people of Dannemore were glad to be freed from the tyranny of those Kings and Queens, that freedom had been bought at great cost. Great devastation had been wrought upon the land, and after the Sundering came a time of darkness, during which the people, with righteous rage, fell upon and destroyed every artifact of magic they could find. The only magic that continued to exist in Dannemore was the *gematry* of the Ashkar, for it did not require the Name.

But there was not always to be darkness over the world. Before the Sundering, the people had turned away from the Gods, preferring to worship magic and those who practiced it. But now Lotan, Father of the Gods, set Marcus Carus, the first Emperor, upon the Imperial throne, and he brought beneath his rule all the warring kingdoms and united them, and he created the Gold Roads that spanned all the lands of the Empire and even beyond them, east into Shenzhou and Hind. And now the benevolence of the Emperor shines through the land, and justice has replaced tyranny, and trade has replaced war. All praise the Emperor, and the lands over which he presides, which shall never be divided!

— *Tales of the Sorcerer-Kings,* Laocantus Aurus Iovit III

CHAPTER TWENTY

K el had a bad moment when he returned to the rooms he shared with Conor and saw that the Prince had returned from his meeting. It was dim; the lamps Kel had left burning had for the most part been snuffed out. A fire in the grate provided some illumination, as did the blue moonlight that pervaded the room with an eerie glow.

But the door to the tepidarium was closed, and Kel could hear the sound of water. Swiftly, he moved to the wardrobe and divested himself of Conor's clothes. With shaking hands, he carefully returned the gold coronet to its bed of velvet. He slammed the wardrobe door shut, and by the time Conor had emerged from the tepidarium he had yanked on a linen sleep tunic and trousers.

Conor came out blinking, still in the clothes he had worn earlier that day, though the fur-lined jacket was missing. He had clearly splashed his face with water, and his black hair was wet, his heavy gold crown, rubies and all, dangling from one finger.

"Kel," he said.

He did not sound surprised to see him. He did not sound much of anything but tired. Kel could not remember the last time he had heard Conor sound so exhausted. He started to cross the room toward Kel, then seemed to give up and slumped down on one of the divans, letting his head fall back against the cushions.

He looked exhausted as well, bruise-blue shadows under his eyes, his boots unlaced, the blue paint on his nails picked away to a mosaic of cracks. He did not move, but his eyes tracked Kel as Kel came across the room and sat down across from him.

Kel remembered a time when Conor's pains and distresses could be soothed by a trip to the massive playroom in the Castel Mitat. There they had built walls out of blocks, and made a fort, and there had been toy Castelguards and dolls to staff it. They had played games with Falconet and Roverge and Antonetta until one day Falconet had made some comment about being too old for this sort of foolishness, and the next day it had all been gone, replaced by a sitting room full of elegant divans and silk pillows.

Antonetta had cried. Kel recalled holding her hand; the others had mocked her, but her grief over the vanished dolls—who had been characters, truly, with their own histories and names—was his own grief, one that her voluble sadness allowed him to keep hidden.

It was only later that he wondered if it had been wrong to let her bear the mockery for what he, too, felt. He supposed that he had been punished for it: In the end, she had been the one to tell him that it was time to grow up.

"I wondered where you were," Conor said, "when I got back."

Kel hesitated, but only for a moment. He had not meant to keep the night's activities a secret, but he had no choice now. *I went to see Fausten, disguised as you, and he said I would betray you. That I would take something important from you and you would hate me.*

Perhaps Conor would laugh it off. In fact, it was most likely he would, but he often laughed off exactly what bothered him the most. Fausten's words were already eating at Kel like acid. What would they do to Conor—especially now?

"I was walking around the grounds," he said. "They wouldn't let me into the Gallery."

"Bensimon wouldn't let anyone into the Gallery. Roverge tried to muscle his way in, but Jolivet had the Arrow Squadron march him out."

"He won't like that," said Kel.

"Probably not." Conor didn't sound as if he cared one way or the other.

"Con," Kel said softly. "Have you eaten? Had any water, at least?"

"There was food, I think," Conor said, vaguely. "They brought us things. There was a great deal of wine, though Senex Domizio may have drunk most of it. He called me a *buxiàrdo fiol d'un can*, which I don't think he would have done if he was sober. I'm fairly sure it means 'lying fucker.'"

"Bastard," Kel said, through his teeth. "You didn't lie. You made a deal, and you stuck with the deal. They're the liars—"

"Kellian," Conor said. He rarely used Kel's first name; he did it now with a sound in his voice that was like pain. "I know."

"Is there no way out of this?" Kel asked.

"There is no way out of it. The Sarthians are firm. I agreed to marry a Princess of Aquila with the name Aimada; there is no provision that it had to be her *first* name." Conor smiled a ghastly smile. "In the end, Anessa simply kept pointing out that this was a transaction, a marriage of kingdoms; there had never been any pretense that this was a love match. What does it matter in the end, she kept saying. And that should I accept Luisa, we would have the gratitude and alliance of Sarthe, whereas if I sent her back, we would have war."

"They have been wanting war for some time," said Kel. "Perhaps this is only an excuse to bring it."

"Perhaps," Conor said quietly. "I am not a very good prince of Castellane. I doubt I will be a good king, either. But I cannot deliberately bring war on my city. I suppose even I have my limits. Or perhaps I am only being selfish." He rubbed at his forehead, where the crown he had worn all day had left a red mark behind. "If I had been more clever, perhaps I could have prevented what happened at that dinner, with the Malgasi woman. But regardless, Anessa was there. She saw how far our house is from being in order." He flicked his gaze to Kel. "If you ask me, that was the moment when Anessa hatched this plan. She did not want to give Aimada over to a household in chaos. She is their crown jewel. But Luisa—Luisa is worth less to her."

Kel said nothing. There seemed nothing to say.

"I suppose at least there is one consolation," said Conor. "It will be a long time before this is a real marriage of any sort. Ten years perhaps." He smiled crookedly. "So you needn't move out. Although I suppose if my father dies and you replace Jolivet, you could petition for your own quarters. Quite grand ones, I imagine."

"I don't care about my own grand quarters," Kel said gruffly. It had been a long time since he had heard Conor sound so bleak.

He thought again of Antonetta, all those years ago. She had not wept for lost toys, he thought. She had wept for all the ways things were going to change, that she did not want to change.

He rose and went to sit by Conor, the cushions sinking under them, their shoulders bumping together. Conor hesitated a moment before leaning hard into him, letting Kel take his weight: the weight of his weariness, his despair. "The Charter Families are going to be furious," Kel said.

He felt Conor shrug. "Let them be. They'll learn to live with it. They know what's good for them, in the end."

Kel sighed. "I'd take your place in this, too, if I could."

Conor leaned his head against Kel's shoulder. His hair tickled the side of Kel's neck; he was deadweight, like a sleeping child. "I know," he said. "I know you would."

The hours of Third Watch had come by the time Mayesh Bensimon returned to the Sault. Lin, sitting on her grandfather's front porch, watched him trudge across the Kathot, head down, his hair white under the blue light of the moon.

He had not yet noticed she was there, she realized. He did not know anyone was watching him. Lin could not help but recall a night two years ago. It had been Third Watch, just as it was now, and she and Josit had been walking beside the southern wall, where it bordered the Ruta Magna and the clamor of Castellane outside. The sounds of the city had carried through the air: the rush of foot and wheel traffic on the roads, the cries of pushcart vendors, someone bellowing a drinking song.

They had both been startled to hear the creak of the iron gates—why were they opening, so late at night? They were even more startled a moment later when Mayesh strode through them, tall and thin in his gray Counselor's robes. Lin thought that she had never seen her grandfather look so weary. His face had seemed to sink into harsh lines of grief and exhaustion as the gates closed behind him with a clamor that rang through the night.

Lin and Josit remained in the shadow of the wall, reluctant to reveal their presence to Mayesh. Lin had wondered what he had been grieving for—what had so troubled him up at the Palace that day? Or was it simply the nightly reminder that no matter what help he was to the Blood Royal up on the Hill, he would still spend every night of his life behind locked gates?

But she and Josit did not approach him, and did not ask. What would they say? He was, in truth, nearly a stranger to them, in every way that mattered.

She was not sure what she thought now. She had come here because of what had happened in the Square; Ji-An had said Mayesh had been there, and she knew he would not have had a pleasant day. He prided himself on planning and control, and this was something very much out of his control, and contrary to his plans.

And he might have news of the Prince, said a small voice in the back of her head. *How he is reacting. If he is all right.*

She told herself firmly that this was a voice she should not listen to, and fixed her attention on Mayesh, who had come halfway up the stairs of his own house before stopping. He had clearly seen her, sitting in his rosewood chair.

"Lin," he said. It was half a question.

She stood up. "I was worried about you," she said.

He blinked, slowly. "I thought you were your mother for a moment," he said. "She used to wait for me, here, when I returned from the Palace late."

"I would guess," Lin said, "that she was worried, too."

Mayesh was silent for a long moment. The night air was soft and lifted Lin's hair, brushing it across her cheek. She knew she had her mother's hair, those same fiery strands she had tugged on when she was a child.

"Come inside," Mayesh said at last, and went past her to the front door.

It had been years since Lin had been inside her grandfather's house. It had not changed much, if at all. It was still spare, plainly furnished. There was no clutter or mess. His books were lined up carefully on their shelves. A framed page from the *Book of Makabi* hung on his wall; it had always puzzled her, since she had never thought of him as a religious man.

He sat down at his plain wood table and indicated that she should join him. He had not lit any lamps, but there was enough pale-blue moonlight to see. Once she had seated herself, he said, "I see you've heard what happened. I suppose everyone has."

"Well," she said, "everyone in the city. Perhaps not everyone in the Sault, yet. I heard it from a patient."

"I would have thought you'd be pleased," he said. "You have no fondness for the inhabitants of Marivent."

It must please you. What the Prince had said to her, when she'd first seen his wounds. It had stung a little, and stung again now.

"I was thinking of you," she said. "You are the Counselor for a reason. You stand for the Ashkar before the Winged Throne. The Maharam does his work here in the Sault, and so he is seen and appreciated. You do your work on the Hill, and so your hand is invisible. But I have begun to believe that . . ."

"That what? That I might actually be doing some good for the Sault? That in protecting this city, I am also protecting the Ashkar who live in it?"

"Hmph," she said. "I do not need to praise you, if you are going to praise yourself."

He barked a humorless laugh. "Forgive me. I may have forgotten how to recognize recognition itself."

"Do they not appreciate you, then, up on the Hill?"

"I am necessary to them. But I do not think they consider it often, any more than they consider water or sunlight or any of the other things they cannot manage without."

"Do you mind?"

"It is how it should be," he said. "If they thought too much about how they needed me, they might begin to resent me. And to consider: Is it only me they resent? Or all Ashkar? Malgasi is not the only example, you know. Not the only place we have been driven from, after thinking ourselves safe." He shook his head. "This is too grim a discussion. I am disappointed today, yes, and angry, but I will survive. Castellane will survive. An alliance with Sarthe is not such a terrible thing."

"So it is true," she said. "They presented the Prince with a little girl, and now he must marry her?"

"They will not marry yet," he said. "She will live in the Little Palace, and be tutored there, and likely encounter the Prince only on occasion. After eight years or so, they will marry. It is strange, but most royal marriages are strange. It is countries that marry, after all, not people."

"But you're disappointed," she said. She knew she was reaching for the answer to a question she had not asked, and could not: *How is the Prince?* He had resigned himself to one thing, and now must face quite another.

"In myself," he said. "I should have seen the signs of this. What

Conor did, he did out of desperation. He was ashamed to go to the Treasury for what he needed, so he hatched this half-cocked plan with Sarthe—" He shook his head. "But he has had no proper guidance. Jolivet teaches him to fight, and I try to teach him to think, but how do you learn to be a king? From the king before you. And if that cannot happen . . ." He looked at her. She could not see his eyes clearly, only the bluish reflection of the moon. "Have you given any thought to my suggestion?"

"About finding the Sault too small?" Lin said. She put her elbows on the table; Chana Dorin would have been annoyed. "If that was a suggestion, you will have to be clearer about what you mean."

"Don't test me, Lin. The Ambassador from Sarthe threw a plate at me today, and I am an old man."

She smiled in the dark. "Very well. You are asking if I would like to be Counselor after you. And . . ." *And yes I would, but to be the Counselor to the King that this Prince will become, to be with him all day every day, is an idea that should repulse me. If it does not repulse me, is that not a reason not to do it?*

"I have worked so hard to become a physician," she said. "I do not think I could give it up to be Counselor to House Aurelian, and I do not know how I could do both."

"I think you could," he said. "When I said you were the best physician in the Sault, it is not only because you had the best scores on the tests."

Lin had not been aware he knew of her scores. Perhaps Chana had told him?

"It is because you are always challenging yourself," he said. "You have pushed past so many barriers set up to stop you, and I can tell you from my own experience, once you conquer one challenge, you will want another. You will hunger for it."

And Lin realized he was right, if not entirely in the way he thought. Magic. That was what she hungered for. To bring light back to Petrov's stone, to feel that pulse again, that surge of power through her blood. *If I were the Counselor to Marivent, what could I not reach out and find? Qasmuna's book, surely. Others like it. Nothing is forbidden to those with enough power . . .*

"House Roverge is holding a welcoming party tomorrow night," said Mayesh. "It was meant to be a welcome for Princess Aimada. They have planned it all this past fortnight, and do not intend to cancel now; it will simply be for Princess Luisa instead. Just as the Palace is still planning their Ascension Day festivities, only they will call it a celebration of the union between Sarthe and Castellane instead. I do not think they are even changing the decorations."

"House Roverge," Lin said slowly. "Theirs is the dye Charter?" Mayesh nodded. "I have heard rumors of them," she added, recalling what she had overheard in the Black Mansion. "That they recently used their influence to drive a family of ink merchants from Castellane. It seems they are bothered by even a hint of competition. But surely that is not really in the spirit of the Charters?"

Mayesh snorted. "Profit is in the spirit of the Charters," he said. "But yes, the Roverges are especially ruthless in their pursuit of it. Even the other nobles look upon them with some mistrust. As for their treatment of the Cabrols, it was abhorrent, and if I were them, I might worry about revenge."

Lin felt as if she were holding her breath. If she were to tell Mayesh what she knew—but she could not; her talk with the Ragpicker King had made that clear. She had indicated to him that she would not say anything about Cabrol's plan, and she knew if she did, he would see it as a betrayal. Besides, the thought of trying to explain to Mayesh how she knew what she did made her feel ill.

In the end, this was not Ashkari business; the Roverges were *malbushim,* and it seemed they had done dreadful things. Some part of her wished to lay the moral puzzle of it at Mayesh's feet and have him sort it out. But it would not be fair to him. The less he knew about the whole business, the better.

"Are you worried about revenge, *zai*?"

He shook his head. "That is for the Roverges to concern themselves with. I am concerned with the affairs of House Aurelian, and with the place of the Ashkar in Castellane. That is as far as my remit extends."

Lin felt a faint sting of relief. Not only did her grandfather seem uninterested in the idea of revenge against the Roverges, he seemed truly to not want to know more. It was part of their being Ashkar, she thought: There was always that layer of something like glass between them and the doings of the outside world.

"If they are so unpleasant," she said, as lightly as she could, "must we then attend their party?"

Mayesh chuckled. "Parties are rarely about who throws them," he said. "It will be a small affair, just the Charter Families and the guest of honor. It will be a good opportunity for you to observe them all. To imagine what it might be like to work among them. Accompany me there, and you can give me your answer afterward."

A party on the Hill. As a child, Lin had taught herself not to want to follow Mayesh to the Hill, to see what he did, to be a part of his life and his duties. But here he was, offering what she had told herself she would never ask for—and not just offering, *asking*.

"But," she said, and she knew she was about to say yes, "I have nothing to wear to a party on the Hill."

For the first time that evening, her grandfather smiled. "Consult with Mariam," he said. "I think you'll find that you do."

After the Sundering and the destruction of Aram, Judah Makabi was named the Exilarch, the leader of the exiled Ashkar, who had no longer any home. He led the Ashkar to the west, where they wandered in the wilderness for generations, during which time Makabi remained young, and did not die, for the blessing of their Queen was upon him.

Every time they settled in a new place, and the inhabitants of that place learned that they were practicing *gematry*, they would be harried and driven out, for in the dark days after the Sundering, magic was considered a curse. The Ashkar began to become restive. "Why must we wander?" they asked. "Our Queen is gone, and our land as well, why must we continue to practice *gematry*, which marks us as outcasts?"

—Book of Makabi

CHAPTER TWENTY-ONE

Are you quite sure about this?" said Kel.

"Quite sure about what?" Conor braced a booted foot against the interior wall of the carriage as it nearly lurched into a ditch. The recent rain had left the roads on the Hill pitted with holes. Kel would vastly have preferred that he and Conor ride Asti and Matix the short distance to the Roverges', but Luisa, it seemed, did not know how to ride a horse. For Conor to arrive without her would not be protocol, so carriages it was. When Kel glanced out the window, he could see the lacquered d'Eon carriage following theirs, like a faithful blue beetle. "Am I sure about my outfit? I have never been more sure of anything in my life."

"Not the outfit," Kel said. "Though now that you bring it up, it is a bit much."

Conor grinned ferociously. He had decided, for reasons Kel could not fathom, to attend the party dressed as the male incarnation of Turan, the God of desire. (Usually depicted as clothed in silver and gold, Turan could appear as male, female, or androgynous, depending on the God's mood and the necessities of the situation.) Conor's breeches and frock coat were of heavy gold fabric, shot through with silk-wrapped threads of contrasting silver. Silver painted his lids, and more glittering powder dusted his cheekbones.

If one looked closely, one could see that the cuffs and lining of his coat had been embroidered with human figures engaged in what could euphemistically be termed "acts of love." Whatever tailor had been tasked with producing the embroidery had embraced their task with enthusiastic creativity. No position had been depicted more than once. (It was lucky for Conor, Kel thought, that the Queen had declined to attend the party, citing a headache.)

"I have no doubts about my outfit," said Conor. "The Hierophant is always complaining the royal family does not do enough to honor the Gods. Surely he'd be pleased."

Kel thought of the grim-faced Hierophant and snorted. "You know he wouldn't," he said, "but that is not what I meant. Only— poor Luisa. She is hardly prepared for the silk-clad vultures who populate the Hill."

"Is anyone?" Conor shrugged. "You were thrown in among them when you were only ten years old. You managed."

"I was not being presented to them as their future ruler," Kel pointed out, "but rather as your orphaned cousin from Marakand, whom they might pity. They will not pity Luisa." *They will hate her as a symbol of the scorn of Sarthe.*

"Speaking of Marakand," Conor said, "there is a saying with which my mother has always made sure I am acquainted. *The jackal that lives in the wilds of Talishan can only be caught by the hounds of Talishan.* I believe it means," he added, "that you cannot defeat what you do not know."

"And you cannot win a game you do not play," said Kel. "Luisa is too young to play Charter Family games."

"But she is not too young to see the board on which the games are played," said Conor. He smiled, eyes flashing silver under his silver-painted lids. "I am not going to change who I am, or what I do, because of an engagement that will not be a marriage for another seven or eight years. If Sarthe insists that Luisa remain in Castellane for all this time, they might as well understand the world she will inhabit, and the people she will know."

"And perhaps they may see the wisdom of letting her finish out her childhood in Aquila?" said Kel—more a question than a statement, but Conor only smiled and glanced out the window as the carriage came to a stop in the Roverges' courtyard.

The house of the dye Charter occupied a coveted position on the Hill, built half into the cliffside, with a view of Poet's Hill. Mount Cicatur rose behind the Academie, its face threaded with glimmering veins of Sunderglass. The sun was setting now, as they left the carriages, turning the Sunderglass the color of copper. To Kel it looked as if a bolt of lightning had speared through the mountain and been frozen there, a fiery reminder of a force long past.

The house itself was as grand as might be expected, and far more in the style of the old Empire than Marivent. Tall pillars supported an arched roof, and the front doors were reached via a broad marble staircase. Statues of the Gods lined the rooftop's edge, gazing down benevolently—Aigon with his sea chariot, Cerra with her basket of wheat, Askolon with the tools of his forge. Long ago there had been a statue of Anibal, lord of the underworld, but some past Roverge had removed it, considering it bad luck. The result, Kel thought, was somewhat odd—twelve Gods could be spaced out evenly, but eleven looked somehow lopsided.

The courtyard out front was full of carriages already, with footmen in the Roverges' teal livery seeing to the horses. Several of them cast covert glances at Conor: partly, Kel guessed, because he was who he was, and partly because of the sheer luminosity of his clothes.

They were quickly joined by the convoy from Sarthe. Sena Anessa and Senex Domizio were polite but unsmiling, wearing patriotic blue. Vienne d'Este—somber in her Black Guard's uniform—looked as grim as if she were attending her own funeral rather than a party. Luisa, lost in a bell-shaped dress covered in lace, ruffles, and ribbons, seemed delighted by Conor's appearance in a manner that her companions clearly were not. She pointed from Conor to the statue of Turan on the roof, and eagerly showed him her hands, wiggling her fingers back and forth.

Conor looked puzzled.

"You can talk to him, you know," Vienne said gently. "He speaks Sarthian."

Luisa smiled. As they moved in a group toward the front doors, she explained that she liked the color of Conor's nails, painted to resemble silver mirrors, and that she wanted her own the same color.

"Well, that's easy enough," said Conor, never one to deny another the opportunity to experiment with fashion. "We can have a cosmetician sent over to the Castel Pichon tomorrow."

"That would not be at all appropriate," said Sena Anessa frostily, and Luisa scrunched up her face. Before the situation could escalate, however, the liveried servant at the door caught sight of them, and soon they were lined up to be announced as they entered the house: Conor first, then Luisa (with Vienne beside her), then Kel and the Ambassadors.

Shouts and cheers greeted the entry of the Prince, which died away as Luisa entered, pressed tightly to Vienne's side. "*Ostrega! Xé tanto grando par dentro*," she whispered. Gracious, it's such a big place.

Indeed, the first floor of the Roverge mansion was a vast space, dominated by a wall of windows looking out onto a stone terrace and the city below. Nearly all the furniture had been removed, making the space look even larger. What remained was a temple to the worship of dyes: Brightly colored fabrics covered the plush divans scattered around the room and trailed gauzily from curtain rods. More consideration had clearly been given to impact than harmony. The textiles on display were a wild combination of deep cinnabar and blue, bright mustards and greens, tangerines and violets. Servants, moving through the room carrying trays of iced wine, added to the riot of color—they were dressed in indigo blue, gamboge yellow, poppy orange, vermillion red, poison green, and blushing coral.

Kel could hear Sena Anessa muttering that her eyes hurt. It was a great deal to take in, Kel thought, but it was also a display of power—a reminder to the Sarthians present that in taking on Castellane with this alliance, they took on the Charter Families as well, each one a fiefdom in their own right. The party might look like a carnival, but the message was clear: *Reckon with our kingdom.*

"Sena Anessa? Senex Domizio?" One of the serving girls was approaching their party, her head bent respectfully. She had on a red silk shift, the kind noblewomen wore under their gowns as a layer between the expensive fabric of their gowns and their skin. Her arms and legs were bare, save for a pair of white lace stockings. If she had been on the Ruta Magna, she would have been arrested by the Vigilants for public nudity. "Sieur Roverge craves the honor of an audience with you."

The two Ambassadors exchanged quick whispers with each other in Sarthian. As they did, the girl looked up, and Kel realized with a shock to his gut that he knew her. Knew her well, in fact.

It was Silla. Her red hair had been braided around her head, her lips lacquered dark scarlet. She winked at him before composing her features again into an expression of blank politeness.

Conor knocked his shoulder into Kel's. "Look," he said, under his breath. "Roverge must have emptied out the Caravel."

Kel looked, and cursed himself silently for his previous lack of observation. The servants were all as scantily dressed as Silla—in light shifts for the women, tight breeches and flowing shirts for the men—and all were courtesans. He recognized the young man who had been telling fortunes the last time they had been at the Caravel. The night Kel had met the Ragpicker King.

Their brief conference finished, the Sarthian Ambassadors de-camped without a word, following Silla across the room toward an alcove where Benedict Roverge was holding court from an arm-chair of violet brocade. Vienne, watching them go, shook her head in disbelief. "Oh, those *idiots*," she said. "Always their own interests first, never Luisa's—"

"Oh, hello, *hello*," piped up a cheerful voice. Antonetta was sail-ing toward them, and Kel had never been so relieved to see anyone. She wore a close-fitting gown of teal-green silk, cut daringly low in the back. Her hair was spilling out of the jeweled clips meant to restrain it, loose curls falling to cup her cheeks and brush her bare shoulders. When she bent to smile at Luisa, Kel saw the gleam of her gold locket, swinging on its chain. "Are you the darling little Princess?" she said, in passable Sarthian. "You look just lovely."

"I see Demoselle Alleyne's mother is no longer selecting her clothing," Conor said, in a low voice, as Antonetta handed a spar-kling hairpin to Luisa (while Vienne looked on, bemused). "A marked improvement, I would say."

Kel felt a prickly tightening of his skin. Antonetta turned briskly toward Kel and Conor. "Now," she said. "Why don't you let me bring her around, make the introductions? I know just the girls for her to meet and, really, I'm not sure you can say the same." She turned to Vienne. "Boys," she said. "They're just *impractical*."

Vienne looked stunned, as if the prospect of being asked to con-sider the Prince of Castellane and his cousin "boys" might be too much for her. "Luisa is a bit shy—"

"Oh, don't worry, all she needs to do is smile, and if she can't do that, everyone will just assume she's intellectual," said Antonetta, in a bright tone that belied the cynicism of her words. "Now, I swear I saw a tray of sweets around here somewhere, delightful cakes and things; I'm sure one of the rather naked servants had one. Come along, we'll find them."

"Interesting," said Conor, as Antonetta set off, Luisa tugging her by the hand. Vienne followed, looking more than a little dazed.

"I wonder if Ana sees something of herself in the girl. She, too, will have little say over who she marries. Ana might be flighty, but she's got enough of her mother in her to be a force of nature when she likes."

Now that Conor was no longer with the Sarthians, party guests were beginning to sidle closer—Cazalet was lurking, no doubt hungry for tidbits about any new trading deals with Sarthe, and a group of young noblewomen stood not far away, casting glances at Conor. Since the Princess from Sarthe had turned out to be a child, the position of mistress to the Crown Prince was clearly an open one for at least the next eight years.

She's not flighty. But all Kel said was, "She enjoys saving people, I think. At least, she used to. Remember she always like to lead the rescue expeditions when we played pirates. She even saved Charlon when we buried him in that pit."

"That *was* a good time," said Conor. "Come—it appears we're being summoned. And I have a plan for the evening."

They started off in the direction of Montfaucon, Joss, and Charlon, who were waving toward them from a cornflower-blue silk divan.

"What plan is that?" Kel said.

"I want to get so drunk I entirely forget who I am." They had reached the blue divan. Joss was lounging among the textiles, while Montfaucon and Charlon perched on the back. Joss slid over— a movement that caused a tidal surge of colored pillows—to make room for Conor and Kel.

"I see you've rid yourself of the child," said Charlon, who was wearing a yellow-and-black-striped suit that made him resemble a gigantic bee. He spoke carefully, which meant he was tipsy, but not yet slurring-his-words drunk.

"Excellent," said Montfaucon, who was not drunk at all. His dark gaze roamed the room with a restless curiosity; his posture said, *I am waiting for something interesting to happen.* "Now we can enjoy ourselves."

"I thought we were enjoying ourselves before," said Joss. He plucked a glass of wine from the tray of a passing servant. Flicking open the clasp on his ring, he tapped three drops of poppy-juice into the pale-red liquid and handed it to Conor. "Drink," he said. "I'd imagine it's been a while since you've been . . ." He paused as if searching for the right word. "Tranquil."

Conor stared down at his own fingers, silver-tipped, wrapped around the stem of the glass. Kel wondered if he were hesitant—but it seemed not. A moment later, he had downed the contents, licking a spilled drop from his thumb.

Charlon had signaled another servant. Montfaucon and Falconet both took glasses; Joss looked over at Kel, indicating his own ring. "And for you?"

Kel refused the poppy-drops, taking only the wine. It was one thing to drink alongside Conor (always carefully, always less than he did). That was a sort of protective camouflage; to refuse wine would only bring questions. But poppy-drops made all the world seem as a dream, as if everything were happening at some distance, behind a wall of glass. As a Sword Catcher, they would render him virtually useless.

Conor sighed and relaxed back into the cushions. "You are always there in my time of need, Falconet."

Joss grinned. One of the serving girls sauntered by dressed in a shift of saffron silk with indigo stockings. As she bent to pluck the empty wineglass from Conor's outstretched hand, Kel recognized Audeta, the girl whose window Conor had broken at the Caravel.

She appeared to harbor no ill will. "Boys," she said, smiling at them all. "Domna Alys will be hosting a party at the Caravel late tonight and into the morning. She wished me to extend an invitation." She glanced at Kel. "Silla especially hoped to see you there, Sieur Anjuman," she added, and darted off, her stockinged feet soundless on the marble floor.

"And Anjuman conquers, without having done much of anything," said Charlon. "As usual." There was an edge to his voice.

Kel imagined he hadn't much liked Conor's praise of Joss, either; he was looking peevish.

Kel raised his glass in Charlon's direction. "Perhaps we have forgotten to thank you, Charlon," he said, "for an excellent festivity."

"Indeed," murmured Conor. He was half sunk among the cushions, his eyes heavy-lidded. The poppy-drops would be softening the edges of everything for him, muting the brightness of all the colors, letting them run together like paints in the rain. "There are those who would say that throwing a party for a child and staffing it with courtesans would be wildly inappropriate, but not you. You have forged ahead, a true visionary."

"Thank you." Charlon looked pleased.

Montfaucon snorted, and said, "Joss, do we—"

"Wait." Falconet held up a languid hand. "Who is *that*? With the Counselor?"

Puzzled, Kel glanced over and saw that Mayesh had just come into the room, looking as he always did in his gray robes and heavy medallion. Beside him was Lin.

He had to blink to be sure it was her. She wore a deep-indigo velvet, against which her hair seemed a fiery crown. The dress was not in the current, fashionable style of heavy skirts clipped back to show a narrower column of contrasting material. It was all the same velvet, shot through with a few glittering strands of silver, the hem sweeping around her ankles like waves. The bodice was tightly fitted, shaping her slight body into distinct curves, the tops of her pale breasts swelling above the neckline. She wore no jewelry that he could see, but the lack of adornment only seemed to accentuate the delicate slant of her collarbone, the line of her throat, the curve of her waist where one might lay a hand while dancing.

Kel heard Charlon say, in a surprised tone, "Is that Bensimon's granddaughter? She's attractive. Doesn't look much like him."

"If by that you mean she does not have a long gray beard, Charlon, you are observant as always," said Joss. He narrowed his eyes.

"Interesting that Bensimon would choose to bring her here, to-night. Is this her first visit to the Hill?"

"No," Conor said. He had sat up and was half sitting forward, his gaze fixed on Lin. Mayesh was introducing her to Lady Ro-verge, and she was nodding along politely. Most of the women at the party had their hair dressed high, held in place with glittering pins like Antonetta's. Lin's was loose, cascading down her back in rose-colored curls. "She's been to Marivent, I believe."

Montfaucon, alert to every nuance, gave the Prince a sideways look. Conor was still looking at Lin, a low fire in his gray eyes. Kel had only seen him look like that before when he hated someone— but he had no reason to hate Lin. She had healed him, tended him, spent the night sitting beside him. The three of them shared a se-cret only they knew. The last thing Kel could recall Conor saying to him about Lin was that he owed her now.

Antonetta had come over to Mayesh with Luisa and Vienne in tow. Introductions seemed under way. Luisa was smiling shyly and fidgeting; Kel could not help but think that Conor had been wrong when he'd said Kel had managed the Hill easily as a child. He'd managed, but he'd been a gutter rat from the streets of Castellane, used to lying and fighting and scheming to survive. Luisa had none of those skills.

Lin bent to say something in Luisa's ear, the line of her body graceful as she moved. Joss said, "I wonder if Mayesh would intro-duce me to his granddaughter."

"Probably not," said Conor shortly. "He knows your reputa-tion."

Joss laughed, unperturbed. Montfaucon said, "She'd never sleep with you, Joss. It's against their Laws to go with those who aren't their kind."

"Forbidden fruit is the sweetest," said Joss airily.

"Who's talking about fruit?" said Charlon. "It's her arse I'm looking at. And it's never forbidden to look."

"But it might be unwise," said Montfaucon. "Unless you want Bensimon to kill you."

"He's an old man," Charlon said, with a touch of a sneer. "I hear they know all sorts of tricks, Ashkari girls," he added. "Things they don't even know about at the Caravel—"

"Enough," said Conor. His eyes were half closed; if he was still looking at Lin, Kel could not tell it. "The lure of a new face certainly has an effect on you lot, doesn't it? There are a hundred girls here you ought to find more interesting."

"Name one," said Joss, and as Conor began to tick off names on his fingers, Kel rose and crossed the room to where Lin stood beside the Counselor.

Lin saw Kel rise and come toward her across the crowded room; by the time he had reached her side, Mayesh had excused himself. The younger crowd, those near the Prince's age, were here in the main room, he had explained. Those he wished to speak with—diplomats, merchants, Charter holders—were by and large in the back rooms, drinking and betting money on games of chance.

Lin did not protest. There was no point; her grandfather did as he liked and always had. It was a relief to see Kel, though. He was smiling—that smile of his that always seemed to have a hint of reserve to it. She suspected it had something to do with always playing a part, and never quite being able to be himself. Every smile had to be weighed and calculated, like goods for sale in the market.

"I didn't expect to see you here," he said, bowing over her hand. It *was* a nice custom, she thought. He looked handsome and formal in a deep-green velvet cutaway coat, with gold buttons in the shape of flowers. Marakandi green, she thought, for the Prince's Marakandi cousin.

"My grandfather thought it would be a good idea for me to know a bit more about those he spends his days with."

Kel raised his eyebrows. "But he didn't remain to introduce you around?"

"I do not think you will be surprised," Lin said, "to hear that he believes in teaching children to swim by tossing them into deep water."

"And these are deep waters indeed," Kel said. She followed his gaze and saw that he was looking at Antonetta Alleyne, who looked stunning in a teal creation of Mariam's. She was still with the small Princess from Sarthe, Luisa, and her guard, the tall, elegant woman with the burnished hair. This did not surprise Lin. She had learned in her short time with Antonetta that she was someone who liked to take charge of a situation, especially when it came to looking after people.

"That's the girl the Prince is going to marry, then," Lin said. It was not a question. She had already been introduced to Luisa. It had been strange to put a face to the tale: the trick of Sarthe, the little Princess nobody wanted. "That poor child."

"I hope there is pity in your heart," Kel said quietly, "for both of them."

Lin glanced over at the Prince, who had not moved from his seat since she'd arrived. She'd wondered for a moment if he might come to greet her, but had dismissed the thought quickly enough. He was settled among his friends—a threesome whose names Mayesh had given her when they had entered the room. Falconet. Montfaucon. And Roverge.

Roverge. The family whose house and party this was; the family who had driven the Cabrols to dreams of revenge. She had thought it would not trouble her to stand in this house and know that the Roverges faced the destruction of some portion of their fleet, but she found it made her uneasy. And yet it was impossible for her to tell—and who would believe her, even if she did? Who was she? A little physician from the Sault.

She was no one. There was no reason for the Prince to go out of his way to speak to her, either. Not wanting to betray that she had even thought of it, she looked at him only out of the corner of her eye. He did stand out: Among all the bright rainbow of colors, he wore gold and silver, the shades of metal. Like a steel blade, she thought, laid among a display of colorful flowers.

"It is hard to pity a prince," Lin said, and she might have said more—that the Prince himself had told her he was not to be pitied, that instead she should pity his intended—but at that moment, the Prince's ginger-haired companion—Roverge, son of the House— jumped down from the divan he'd been perched on and strode toward the center of the room.

There was a screen there, painted with a design of herons in flight. As the young Roverge approached, the screen slid back, revealing the musicians who had been playing through the evening. Beside them stood two rows of what Lin could only guess were singers, their hands folded. They wore gold slippers and what Lin at first thought was smooth gold cloth. She realized, as the firelight flickered over them, concealing and revealing with its touch, that it was not cloth at all, but paint. They were naked, men and women both, painted head-to-toe with gold paint that mimicked, on their skin, the clinging folds of silk.

A murmur ran around the room. Guests craned their heads to get a better look at the entertainment. Vienne d'Este pulled the little Princess, Luisa, closer to her side, her mouth a thin line of annoyance.

It was quiet now, everyone watching; Charlon Roverge made a flourishing gesture, and the gold-painted vocalists burst into song.

It was a low tune, and sweet. An *auba*, a song meant to evoke lovers parting at dawn.

"Well," Kel said, in a low voice, "at least they can sing decently."

"Would anyone have noticed if they couldn't?" Lin whispered back.

Kel smiled a little but said, "You'd be surprised. It takes a great deal to shock this bunch—or even to intrigue them."

"I see," Lin said. She stole another glance at the Prince, sideways. He was looking at the singers but—indeed—without a great deal of interest. "That's—rather sad."

The song ended. There was a smattering of light applause. Charlon Roverge cast a glance across the room; he was looking at his father, Benedict, who seemed to be observing the entertainment with a peculiar intensity. They both had an unpleasant look about them, she thought, and recalled her grandfather saying that even the other nobles of the Hill mistrusted them.

"Tonight," Charlon said, loudly enough for his voice to ring off the walls, "we herald the dawn of a new alliance. Between Castellane and her closest neighbor, the honorable land of Sarthe."

The hairs on the back of Kel's neck prickled. He could not have said why, precisely, but he did not like this—did not like Charlon giving the welcome address, instead of Benedict. Did not like the tone of his voice when he spoke. The words were polite enough— Kel would have bet Prosper Beck's ten thousand crowns that Benedict had forced his son to memorize them—but there was an expression on Charlon's face Kel knew, and disliked. A sort of gloating look.

"Indeed," Charlon went on, "the haste and eagerness of Sarthe to cement this union, which has surprised us all, must certainly lie with the many advantages that will accrue to both our lands when we are joined in political matrimony. Sarthe, for instance, will have access now to a harbor. And we . . ."

He let his voice hang. There were a few titters; Kel could see the Sarthian Ambassadors, some distance away, glaring daggers.

"Did he just imply there's no advantage to Castellane in this marriage?" Lin murmured.

Kel wondered for a moment if he should run at Charlon, knock him over. He could plead terrible inebriation. He would garner some sympathy; he doubted there was anyone at this party who hadn't wanted to hit Charlon at some point or another.

But it would not stop things, he knew. Conor was the only one who could prevent this, and he was stonily silent, arms extended along the divan behind him, staring straight ahead.

"Well," Charlon smiled, "*we* will have the opportunity to learn more of the arts and culture of Sarthe. Who among us has not admired their music, their poetry?"

There was a confused murmur. If this was an insult, it was a poor one. Even Senex Domizio looked more puzzled than enraged.

"In that spirit," Charlon said, "please approach, Princess Luisa d'Eon."

Luisa looked up at Vienne; she had clearly recognized her name, and realized that somehow what was going on now was about her. Vienne said something to her softly, and together they came up to Charlon, in the center of the room. Luisa dropped a curtsy, her hair ribbons bobbing.

"Princess," Charlon said, in very stilted Sarthian, "a gift for you," and took from the inside of his jacket a thin gold box. He handed it to Luisa, who looked uncertain.

"We had all heard, for instance," said Charlon, as Luisa fumbled the box open, "that the Princess of Sarthe, Aimada d'Eon, was a skilled dancer. While she is not here, we have been assured by the good Ambassadors from Sarthe that her sister Luisa is just as skilled in every area as she is. In fact, we have been assured, they are as good as interchangeable."

"Gray hell," Kel muttered. Luisa had opened the box, and taken out what was inside. Frowning, she unfolded a black lace fan with a gold-lacquered grip.

"I believe your sister has one like it," Charlon said, not bothering with Sarthian now as he looked down at the girl. "Surely, then, you must know what to do." He stepped back. "Dance for your Court, Princess."

"He must be joking," Lin whispered. "She's just a girl, and she's shy—"

"He's not," Kel said, grimly, just as the musicians began to play.

As the tune rose up, rapid and sweet, the room exploded with the chant: "*Dance! Dance! Dance!*"

Luisa looked around uncertainly. The guests must have appeared a blur to her, Kel thought, of bright coats and dresses, rapid gestures and hungry faces. He could see Antonetta among the crowd; she had her hand over her mouth, as if she were stunned.

Kel looked at Conor. He had not moved, only Kel could see his hand curled against his side, and thought of what he had said in the carriage: *If Sarthe insists that Luisa remain in Castellane for all this time, they might as well understand the world she will inhabit, and the people she will know.*

Vienne tried to pull Luisa toward her, but Sena Anessa, looking at her across the room, shook her head warningly. Vienne let her arms fall to her sides. Kel could imagine what they were thinking. It was just a dance, and to run forward now to intervene would only underline how much of a child Luisa was, how unsuited to this position and this place. And they were, after all, the ones who had put her here.

Luisa began to dance. It was uncertain, awkward: She turned in a circle, the fan clutched in her hands. She was not following the beat of the music at all, only moving blindly, and in the flicker of the firelight, Kel could see the brightness of tears on her cheeks.

He felt Lin, beside him, tense. A moment later she was stalking across the room, her skirts swirling around her; she pushed through the crowd to where Luisa stood, shaking, and put her hands on the girl's shoulders. "That's *enough*," she said, her voice rising over the music. "This is ridiculous. *Stop.*"

The music stopped instantly. The sudden silence was like a shock of cold water; Lin felt herself suddenly incredibly exposed, the center of a room full of staring strangers. Where *was* Mayesh? She had been looking for him ever since Charlon Roverge had begun speaking, but she had not seen him among the crowd.

With a squeak, Luisa dropped the fan, pulled away from Lin, and ran over to the side of her guard, Vienne. *Good,* Lin thought. *Let her go where she feels safe.* She glanced over at Charlon, who was looking at her with an expression that reminded her of Oren Kandel—the sulky resentfulness of a boy whose game has been spoiled by a girl he had taken little note of before.

At least, Lin saw with relief, Vienne—accompanied by Kel, who was directing her—was hurrying Luisa out of the room. Whatever else happened, the girl would not be tormented further.

A mocking whistle cut through the silence. Lin looked to see dark-eyed Joss Falconet looking at her with amusement. "Charlon," he said, "it seems the Counselor's granddaughter thinks she has the right to interfere in the evening's entertainment. Are you going to stand for that?"

He dropped a wink at Lin, as if to say: *It's all just amusement, just a game, you know.*

She did not smile back. Of course he thought games were amusing; people like Falconet were the players of the game, not the pawns on the board.

Charlon looked over at his father, as if for help, but none seemed forthcoming. "No," he said gruffly. "I . . ." He cleared his throat. "Counselor's granddaughter," he said. "You have deprived us of our entertainment this evening. How do you suggest it be replaced?"

Lin suddenly felt close to snapping at him. At everyone in the room. A bunch of terriers, deprived of the rat they were tearing to pieces. "I'll take her place," she said. "I'll do the dance instead."

A stir among the crowd. She heard someone laugh: Lord Montfaucon, she was nearly sure. She was glad Kel had left the room. He was the only one here likely to have regarded her with sympathy, and she did not think she could stand it.

"Really," said Roverge, and as he looked at her, she could see the sneer on his face. "What do you know of Sarthian dancing, Ashkari . . . girl?"

"Let her do it."

The room went still. Prince Conor was still leaning back among the cushions of his divan, as if utterly relaxed. In fact, he looked almost sleepy, his eyes half lidded. Silver and gold dust glittered on his light-brown skin, where the angular bones of his face caught the light.

"Let her do it," he said, again. "It will be something to amuse us, at least."

Lin stared at him. In that moment she could see nothing in him of the young man whose wounds she had tended, who had said to her bitterly, *Ten thousand crowns. The cost of a Prince, it turns out. I realize I have been a fool; you need not tell me.*

His face was blank, a wall; his eyes narrow silver crescents below silvery lids. Beside him, Falconet was looking at her with curiosity, anticipation. The Prince's face did not show even that.

Charlon shrugged, as if to say, *As the Prince requests.* He signaled, and the musicians behind the screen began to play. The tune seemed to Lin to have changed: No longer pensive and playful, it was slow and dark, the occasional bright note lancing through like a shaft of light piercing the darkness of an unlit street.

Though perhaps it was only her own jangling nerves, Lin thought, as Charlon, having retrieved Luisa's dropped fan, presented it to her with an exaggerated bow. He backed away, eyes narrowed. He was not pleased with her, Lin knew. She had spoiled his game.

Now he wanted her to give him another one. They all did. Her only allies—Kel, her grandfather—were not in the room. She could, she supposed, simply run away. Flee House Roverge. It was hardly as if they'd set the dogs on her.

But then they would *win*. The Hill, the Palace, would win. And she would have managed only a few hours in this rarefied air before being shamed and defeated.

She raised her chin. Snapped the fan in her hands open, the black lace brilliant, laced with bright threads. She knew only one dance. She had never bothered to learn another, never been *required* to learn another. And she had never been grateful to have learned even the Dance of the Goddess. Not until this moment.

She let the music—different as it was from the music of the Sault—wash over her. She began to move, holding the fan as, in the dance, the girls of the Sault held their lilies. She turned, her body sweeping into the movements of the dance, the room blurring around her, vanishing. She was in Aram now, and it was overrun. Armies clashed on the barren-blasted plains, under a sky that was always dark. Lightning speared the clouds overhead. The end was very near.

She danced her terror, her excitement. She danced the howl of the wind through the broken walls of her kingdom. She danced the blackening of the land, the dim red light of the sun.

He approached, the Sorcerer-King who had once been her lover. The man she had trusted above all others. She wanted him with a fierceness that seemed to outpace the fire, the storm. She danced that fierceness now: her broken heart, her longing, the passion she still felt.

He begged her to stop, then. She was not to be a fool; to destroy magic would destroy him, who she loved, and destroy her, too. All he wanted was her, he said. He would put aside everything else: magic, power, kingship. She would be all he needed.

But he was not to be trusted.

Lin danced the last moments of Adassa—her defiance, her power, blooming like a flower of fire. She danced the shudder of the world as magic left it, draining from the earth, the rocks, the sea. She danced the grief of the Goddess as she stepped into darkness: The world was changed forever, her lover lost, her people scattered.

And lastly, she danced the first fingers of sunlight as they burst across the eastern horizon. The sun rising at last, after months of darkness. She danced the beginning of hope, and the glory of defiance. She danced—

And the music stopped. Lin stopped, too, hurled back into the present. She was gasping, utterly out of breath; perspiration ran between her breasts, stung her eyes. She was aware of eyes on her: everyone in the room watching. Charlon's mouth was open.

"*Well*," he said, "that was—"

"Very interesting," said the Prince. His arms were outstretched along the back of the divan; his eyes raked Lin with a sort of bemused curiosity. She was suddenly very aware that her hair was plastered to her temples and the back of her neck, her dress clinging to her damply. "I had always heard the Ashkar were not particularly good dancers, so that was acceptable, considering."

A murmur went through the crowd; a few titters. The Prince was smiling, a cool little smile, and she suddenly hated him so much that it was as if she were back in her vision, on the tower, choking on smoke. Her whole body seemed to burn with hatred for his arrogance, his contempt. For the fact that he clearly saw her as a joke, a plaything.

And she hated that because he was beautiful he was loved and forgiven, no matter what he did. He would always be wanted. The whole world wanted him. She could feel a violent trembling in her hands, utterly at odds with her healer's instincts: For the first time since she had been an angry child, she wanted to slap and scratch and claw. To wreck his pretty face, to stop his sideways smirk.

With a gasp, she hurled the black fan across the room. It hit the floor and skidded to the Prince's feet. "I hope," she said, her voice shaking with rage, "that you have been recompensed for your lack of entertainment. For, as you say, I am unskilled, and have nothing more of myself to offer."

She caught a look of surprise as it passed across the Prince's face, but she was already turning away. Pushing past Charlon Roverge, she strode from the room. Her grandfather had been right. These people were monsters. Let all their ships burn.

x x x

"Lin. *Lin*. Stop."

It was Prince Conor's voice. He had followed her, through the winding corridors of the Roverge mansion. She could not believe he had followed her. Perhaps he planned to arrest her, for throwing the black fan? An assault on royalty, they would surely call it.

She whirled to face him. She had fled the main room without knowing where precisely she was going—all she had thought was *out, away*. Away from the titters, from the people who had seen her dance, from the look on the Prince's face.

But he had followed. And now he had caught up with her in one of a set of deserted and interconnected drawing rooms that seemed to occupy the front of the mansion, each one decorated in a different color scheme. This one was blue and black, like a bruise. A carcel lamp glowed overhead, its flame striking sparks off his rings, his circlet. He seemed to loom over her, reminding her again how tall he was. Up close she could see his dark hair was in disarray, the black-and-silver kohl around his eyes blurred into luminous shadow. His eyes were a very dark pewter color. He said, in a voice of controlled fury, "What are you doing here, Lin? *Why did you come?*"

Even through her rage, the question set her back on her heels. "After all that," she said. "*That's* what you want to ask me? You know Mayesh is my grandfather. You know he brought me—"

He waved this away, with a short, sharp jerk of his arm. "You're a *physician*," he ground out. "You healed Kel. You healed me. I have been *grateful*. But now you come here, like this—"

His gaze dropped to her dress. She felt it like a touch, the fierce drag of his eyes over the neckline of her gown, her collarbones, her throat. She had always thought of contempt and loathing as cold emotions, but now they seemed hot, radiating off him. If she were not so furious, she would have been afraid.

"Oh?" she spat. "You mean I should know my place. Stay in the Sault, not presume to think I might be welcome, or allowed, on the Hill."

"Don't you understand?" He caught hold of her. She tensed up immediately, even as his gloved fingers dug into her upper arms. She could tell he was something more than drunk. He had always been unreadable, but now she could see too much in his face. The yearning printed plainly there, the hunger to insult her, to belittle her. "This place," he hissed. "The Hill—ruins things. Things that are perfect as they are. You were honest. This place has made you a liar."

"You dare call me a liar?" She could hear the fire in her voice. "The last time I saw you, you made a pretty show about how guilty you felt. How you'd gotten yourself into this situation, how I should pity your bride. I thought you meant I should pity her for the situation you found yourself in, but you meant I should pity her for the way you planned to treat her."

"Touching," he said, in a low voice, "that you believe I have *plans*."

She reached up and caught at his wrist. Soft velvet, crisp lace, the heat of skin underneath. She said, "Perhaps you have no plan. Perhaps your only goal is to be a selfish bastard who treats his wife-to-be abominably."

His grip tightened on her. "The commerce in this city is gold, Ashkari girl. But the commerce on the Hill is cruelty and whispers. If the Princess does not learn from me and mine, she will learn it from worse tutors."

"So you are cruel out of necessity," she said, her voice dripping sarcasm. "No—out of *kindness*. And what is your excuse for humiliating me?"

"I have no excuse." He was so close she could breathe the scent that clung to his clothes: a mixture of spice and rosewater. Like *loukoum* candy. "Only I wanted to see you dance."

She tipped her head back to look up at him. His lips were stained faintly red with wine. She remembered placing the morphea drops on his tongue, the soft heat of his mouth against her fingers. "Why?"

"To dance is to drop your guard," he said, and there was a harshness in his voice that made her believe him. He meant what he was saying; in fact, he hated saying it. "I thought I would see you without that wall you have built around yourself, like the walls of the Sault. But you were only further away than ever. All I could see was how little you wanted from me," he added, and there was a loathing in his voice that was directed entirely at himself. "You have wanted nothing from me since the moment I met you. You are and have everything you need." He dipped his head; his breath stirred her hair. The scent of wine and flowers. "You do not look at me as if I have any power over you."

She stared at him wonderingly. How could he think that? Power—he had all of it. Was armored in it. Wore it like his shining rings, like the strength of his body, the gleam of the circlet crown among the dark curls of his hair. "And that makes you hate me?" she whispered.

"I told you to stay away from me," he said. "From Marivent—I was clear I did not want you there—" He lifted a hand, slowly, almost as if he could not believe what he was doing. He laid it against her cheek, his hand soft but callused at the fingertips. Her hand was still wrapped around his wrist. She could feel his racing pulse. Imagine his heart, frantic as her own, driving his blood. "I *did not want you*," he whispered harshly, and kissed her.

He slanted his mouth over hers fiercely, parting her lips with a hard flick of his tongue. She twisted away from him—or meant to. Somehow he had pulled her against him and she clawed at his shoulders, digging her fingertips in. He groaned as she clung to him, almost tearing at the material of his jacket, and it was not simple hatred she felt, it was betrayal. She had *liked* him, that night he had been whipped. She had been unguarded. And then, tonight, he had been like *this*.

His right hand was in her hair now, fingers tangled in its thickness. He kissed her and kissed her, as if he could draw breath out of her and into his own lungs. She bit his lower lip hard, tasted blood, salt on her tongue. Arched up against him, into the sharp ache that was suddenly all she wanted.

His free hand stroked along her throat, his fingers finding the edge of her dress's neckline, where her breasts rose to press against the material. She heard his breath catch and was not prepared for the piercing ache of desire that shot through her. She had never felt anything like it. Perhaps only in her dreams of smoke and fire, where everything burned.

There was a step in the corridor. Lin felt the Prince freeze against her, the hardness of his body suddenly gone to stone. She felt her cheeks flame hot and slid away from him, along the wall—by the Goddess, what if it was Mayesh, looking for her? She smoothed her dress down, frantically, but the step in the corridor faded.

No one was coming into the room.

She looked at the Prince. "Lin," he said, and took a step toward her again.

She flinched away. She could not help herself. Her legs were still shaking, her heart beating like a panicked bird. She had never been so close in her life to losing control. Some part of her, a part she could not question or understand, had wanted to draw his hand down, to the rise of her breasts, to that place between them no one but herself had ever touched. Had wanted him to touch her more, and deeper.

It was madness, and the realization that she was as vulnerable as anyone else to the lures she had always thought foolish and shallow— beauty, power, royalty—was more than shameful. It was true what the Prince had said. The Hill ruined things, and this was the path to ruination.

He had seen her flinch, pull away. She did not catch the moment his eyes went hard, like chips of diamond. Only heard the distance in his voice as he took a step back and said, with a cold calm, "Aigon. I must be drunker than I thought."

The arrow in her belly dug deeper, a stab of pain. Lin raised her eyes to his and said, "My grandfather brought me here because he thought I might be interested in taking over his position someday. He wanted me to know what it would be like to be among those who call the Hill their home, to work among them. Now I know. I know, and I hope never to return."

And she strode out of the room, without looking back.

Kel had taken Vienne and Luisa to a small drawing room, where Lady Roverge sometimes received daytime visitors. The first time Kel had ever been drunk had been in this room; Charlon had unearthed his mother's secret cache of cherry jenever, and they all took turns making themselves thoroughly sick. Even Antonetta.

They had been the same age then that Luisa was now—twelve years old. Thinking themselves adult, but so very much children. Kel suspected Luisa did not consider herself an adult, and was likely the better for it. She had clearly hated being the focus of attention at the gathering, and was much happier here, curled onto a sofa with Vienne, who was reading aloud from a colorfully illustrated book of stories of the Gods, translating into Sarthian as she went. Seeming to sense Kel's gaze on her, she looked up, one hand ruffling Luisa's hair, and smiled.

"You need not stay," she said. "It is enough that you brought us here and away from all those—people." She rolled her eyes. "They are bad enough at the Court in Aquila, but your nobles here are even bigger—"

Kel grinned, despite himself.

"Bastards," she finished, primly.

"I'd be careful with that. They're quite fussy about their bloodlines around here," Kel said. He knew he should return to the festivities, knew he should join Conor, make sure he'd not drunk more of Falconet's poppy-drop wine. Knew he should check on Lin, though he was confident she could manage Charlon. But there was something calm and pleasant about this small room, something that reminded him of the quiet times of his childhood, the moments of rest between study and training when he and Conor lay before the fireplace in their room, seeing the shapes of distant countries in the flames, planning their future travels.

"And they aren't in Marakand?" Vienne said. She looked at him curiously. "I am sorry. I know you are a noble, but—you seem so much more like me than you do like them."

"Oh, I assure you," Kel said, "I am like them. Well, not as stupid as Charlon, perhaps—"

Vienne shook her head. "I sense that you do not just accompany your cousin, the Prince. You guard him, look after him, as I do Luisa. And yet you left him tonight to help us. So for that, I am grateful."

She was right. He *had* left Conor—and what was more, he had not even thought about it. He had wanted to protect Luisa against something he had grown so used to, he doubted he would have noticed at all weeks ago. It was easy for him to think of Montfaucon and the others as Conor's friends—careless but harmless, the sort of people who threw pies off towers. But carelessness could be a knife, sharpened by boredom as steel by a whetstone, turning it to cruelty.

Conor would not see that. He would not want to think his friends cruel, or that they did not have his best interests at heart. There were so few people in Conor's life that he could trust at all, and he had known them so long—

"*Here* you are." Antonetta had appeared at the door, smiling, though her eyes were anxious. "Kellian, Sieur Sardou has been looking for you."

"Sardou?" Kel was puzzled; he couldn't remember the last time he'd spoken directly with the lord of the glass Charter.

"He seems to have something to say to you." Antonetta indicated her puzzlement with a shrug. "Honestly, this is the *strangest* party."

Kel could not say he disagreed. With a nod to Luisa and Vienne, he left the room with Antonetta.

"Is she all right, the little girl?" Antonetta said, leading the way back toward the party. Kel could hear the sound of it rising as they approached, a dull tidal roar. "I suppose it's good that children forget things so quickly. I wonder if she even really understood what was going on." She made an impatient noise, which Kel realized was directed at herself. "I ought to have stopped Charlon . . ."

"Lin did," said Kel. "It's all right, Antonetta."

Antonetta's jeweled sandals clicked on the marble floor. "She danced, you know."

Kel stopped dead. They were in a wide corridor that ended in a beveled-glass window, looking out over the drop to the city below. "*Lin* danced?"

"She said she would dance in Luisa's place, and so she did. But it wasn't really a Sarthian dance, it was . . ."

"Lin," Kel said, again. "*Danced?*"

Antonetta nodded. "Do keep up. I told you she did! But it wasn't like any dance I've ever seen before. It was like—she looked beautiful, but she was daring anyone to think she was beautiful. It was as if the dance said, *You will want to touch me, but you will lose your hand if you do.* I wish I knew how to dance like that." Antonetta sighed. "I'm probably explaining it wrong. You look like you don't believe me."

"Not disbelief. Surprise," Kel said as Antonetta opened a door and strode through it confidently. He followed her into a narrow stone hallway. A few more turns—the light dimming as the wall lamps became fewer—and Kel barked his shin on something solid and square.

"Oh, dear," Antonetta said. "I seem to have gotten us lost."

Kel almost laughed. It was ridiculous. The whole evening had been ridiculous. They were in a low-ceilinged space, full of wooden crates, some of which had bills of lading, laboriously written out, nailed to them. The floor was damp stone, and spiderwebs drifted like white flags of surrender in the corners. A single taper affixed to the wall offered what little light there was.

He leaned against a pile of crates. Whatever was in them must have been heavy; they didn't shift. "Perhaps it's not so bad to be lost," he said. "If you didn't want to return to the party immediately, I wouldn't blame you."

Antonetta leaned against the crates beside him. Her locket, her hair, gleamed in the darkness. "I thought I would be more troubled by Conor getting married," she said slowly, "but I feel nothing but pity for that poor little girl. And the way they treat her—"

Conor has his reasons for what he does, Kel thought. But he found, unusually, that he did not wish to think about Conor at the moment. Instead, he said, "You cannot be surprised at it. We know these people, and how they are. They will not be merciful because Luisa is a child."

Something flashed behind her eyes—a glinting, sharp thing. If it was a memory, it was not a good one, and she said nothing about it.

"You have been kind to her," Kel went on. "More than I would have expected. And you were kind when you brought Lin to me, after I was injured, though I may not have acknowledged it. I know you disguise your intellect, by intention and design. But why also disguise your kindness?"

"Kindness and weakness are twinned, or are seen as such on the Hill," she said. "I recall long ago when Joss was kind. When Conor was kind. No longer. It is a defense as much as an affectation."

"Conor," Kel said, slowly. It seemed he was to think about him, whether he wished to or not. "If you think he is not kind—then why did you want to marry him?"

"I am not sure kindness is relevant to princes. And like all princes who have thus far faced little in the way of great conflict, he does not yet understand that being royal is easy enough. It is ruling that is difficult."

"Wise," said Kel. "But not an answer. And being royal is not so easy."

"You will always defend him," said Antonetta. "It is true that I've always known he would marry for advantage, not for love. And I suppose I thought, *Why not me, then?* You see, marrying him would have given me something I wanted very much."

Kel braced himself. "What is that?"

"The silk Charter," she said, to his surprise. She was not looking at him, leaving him staring at the curve of her neck, where the flickering candlelight caressed it. "You know I cannot inherit it from my mother. It will pass into the hands of my husband when I marry. But if my husband were the King—"

"He cannot hold a Charter," Kel said, realizing.

"Yes. I would remain in control of it."

"Was this your plan all along? Or your mother's?" Kel asked, remembering the long-ago party where she had first told him she intended to marry the Prince.

"My mother has always wanted me to be queen," said Antonetta. "I believe she thinks it would be a sort of ornament to the Alleyne name. I want the silk Charter. I suppose our desires converged."

"I had not thought you so interested in power," said Kel.

Antonetta spun to look at him so quickly that her hair flew in strands of spun gold around her face. "Of course I am interested in power," she said hotly. "Everyone is interested in power. Power allows us to chart our own course, make our own choices. And look at my other choices, Kellian. They are few and constraining. I feel them close in on me like the walls of a labyrinth." She tugged at the locket around her throat. "That is what is fascinating about you," she said. "You don't seem to want anything at all."

"Of course I want things." His voice sounded rough to his own ears. They were leaning into each other, he realized. As close as they had been all those years ago, behind the statue at her debut ball. When he had realized how far away from him she had gone.

But now she moved closer to him. Deliberately. A step and another step, bringing her head to just under his chin. He could feel the heat of her body, smell the heady scent of her perfume and her skin combined. See where the silk of her dress clung to her breasts, to the curve and dip of her waist, pulling tight across her hips.

She looked up at him. She looked nervous, and there seemed no artifice in it, no affectation. She laid a hand on his shoulder. It was a light touch, but it sent heat spiraling through his body. Through the pounding in his ears, he heard her say his name, *Kellian*, and without being able to help it, he reached to touch her.

His hand found the indent of her waist. He could feel a line of silk-covered buttons rough against his palm as he held her there, his hand resting just above the flare of her hip, as if he meant to balance her in a dance. The silk felt just as he pictured under his fingers, though he had not properly imagined the warmth of it, heated by its contact with her skin, nor the ache he would feel at the warmth and curve of her, a pressure in the back of his throat, in his belly. There was a haze in front of his eyes. All he could think of was drawing her closer.

And then she winced.

"Ana—are you all right?" He drew his hand back, a little awkwardly.

"It's nothing," she said, but she was white around the mouth. If there was anything Kel knew when he saw it, it was pain.

"You're hurt," Kel said, a faint buzzing in his ears. "Antonetta, tell me—did someone harm you—"

"No. *No.* It's nothing like that."

"Tell me," he said again. "Or I'll get Lin, have her look at you."

Antonetta pushed out her bottom lip the way she had when she was young and they had refused to let her pretend to be the head of the Arrow Squadron and give them all orders. "Oh, all *right*," she said, and twisted about, as having some odd sort of convulsion. It took Kel a moment to realize she was flicking open the row of small buttons that ran down the side of her dress, from just beneath her arm to her waist.

"There," she said, turning so that he could see her bare side through the parted silk, the smooth curve of her waist into silk-covered hips. Along her rib cage was a short, angry-looking cut—a dark-red line against pale skin.

Kel knew pain. He also knew sword wounds.

"A blade made that cut," he said. "How?"

"Sword practice," she said. "I used to love sword training when I was a girl—maybe you remember, though it's all right if you don't. I had to cease training when we all stopped being friends and my mother took over everything I did. She said no one would want to marry a girl who could swing a sword. But I missed it, and sometimes, now, I sneak away and train down in the city. My mother knows nothing about it. But when I do it, everything else falls away—the pressures of marriage, of etiquette, of being an Alleyne. I am just Antonetta, who is learning to fight."

"Can I touch you?" he asked. She looked surprised for a moment before nodding. He traced the cut lightly with his fingertips; her skin was warm, but not hot. No fever or infection, then. Just a crimson line, an incongruous mark in the context of silk and softness.

His blood was heating again. He told himself not to be a savage; she was injured. And yet her skin was like the silk on which her family had built its empire. He did not want to stop touching her.

"Talk to your dressmaker," he said. "Lin is discreet. She won't tell anyone. But you must have this bandaged. In the meantime, wash the cut with honey and warm water. When I have been injured before—"

"Have you been injured often?" she asked, looking up at him with wide blue eyes.

Kel froze. He had almost mistaken himself, almost forgotten that she was not talking to Kel Saren—she was talking to Kel Anjuman. A lazy, minor noble of Marakand, who lived off the kindness of House Aurelian, and had no reason to bear a multitude of scars.

Years ago, Antonetta had told him to make more of himself. And he was more than she knew. He had resented her for her artifice, for showing a false face to the world. Yet he'd never acknowledged that he was doing the same thing. He had become so used to lying that it was not simply second nature; it was first. Everything he told her, even when it was the truth, had a lie at its heart.

Lady Alleyne had been right all those years ago, but not for the reasons she thought. There was no future for him with Antonetta. There was no future for him with anyone.

She seemed to see a change in his face. She looked away, biting her lip, her hands suddenly fluttering nervously. "We ought to go back," she said. "Can you help me do up my dress?"

He did not want to do it. It was dangerous to be so close to Antonetta. Even now, the urge to take her in his arms was overpowering; she would be soft and hot to touch; he could take her by her silk-covered hips, lift her up against him. Stop the ache in his heart and his body with sensation so powerful it obliterated all thought.

No. He was not Charlon; he could control himself. Could behave as if nothing was troubling him, as if he had no weakness where she was concerned. He had acted more difficult parts.

He turned to the row of tiny buttons that required his attention, and focused on pushing them through their small silk loops, rather than focusing on Antonetta. She stood very still, bracing herself against the crates in front of her; as Kel glanced up, he saw the label on one of them flash white in the dimness.

Antonetta looked over her shoulder at him. "Is everything all right?"

"Just fine." As he rose to his feet, he settled her tousled hair around her shoulders, his hand brushing the clasp of the gold chain at the back of her throat. "Do you think . . ."

"What?" She turned around, her face open, questioning. His stomach felt sick with wanting and guilt.

"I could speak to Conor," he said. "Even Mayesh. See if there's a way to protect your Charter so you could hold on to it, even if you don't marry."

She smiled at him, luminous in the dark. "That's not necessary. I'm not entirely out of ideas yet." She glanced around the room. "I've realized—I do know where we are. Come along."

He followed her from the room. A series of twisting corridors brought them back to the party, where a peculiar sight met their eyes. The room, with its divans and flowing curtains, was mostly empty: The terrace doors had been thrown open and the guests were outside, crowded up against the stone railings.

"I must find Conor," Kel said.

"Sardou can wait," Antonetta agreed, and Kel slipped into the crowd. The night air was cool, the mingled scents of different perfumes—musk and flowers, the bite of juniper—clashing in an olfactory war. As he came close to the edge of the terrace, he realized why the guests were here. Down below, at the foot of the Hill, a crowd had gathered. Kel could see little of them in the torchlight, but recognized their makeshift banners, the lion of Castellane pouncing upon the eagle of Sarthe.

Their chanting rose up, faint at this distance but still audible, like thunder over the mountains. "*Death to Sarthe! Better blood than alliance with Sarthe!*"

But Kel could not concentrate on Sarthe, or questions of uneasy alliances between countries. In the room with Antonetta, he had seen the label on one of the Roverges' boxes flash out at him. *Singing Monkey Wine*. He had not forgotten the odd name. The same brand of wine, the same sort of boxes, that Prosper Beck had had in his office.

Could the Roverges have some connection to Beck? Could Benedict be his patron? It was a thin connection, but enough to push Kel to do what he had done next.

Now he opened his left hand and glanced down at the gold locket in his palm. Antonetta had not even felt it as he slipped it off her neck. That same sickness of guilt came back as he stared down at it. This was what Beck had demanded of him, what he had sacrificed the little that was left of his sense of honor for. He felt suddenly sick at the idea of turning it over to Beck without knowing what was inside it. He knew what Beck had told him, but had no reason to trust it; what if it contained something that could truly damage Antonetta, or her reputation?

Without another conscious thought, he snapped it open. And stared. There was nothing inside, only an empty miniature frame where a small painting or illustration might be placed. Surely Beck had not charged him with this task only to have him retrieve an empty locket?

And yet. The locket was oddly light in his hand, for an object made of gold. He thought of the false bottom to Conor's cabinet, where the poppy-drops were concealed, and pressed down hard with his thumb on the gold frame.

With a click, it slid to the side, revealing a small hollow space beneath. Inside it was a woven circlet of some kind of dark, rough twine, with fraying edges . . .

His heart seemed to stop in his chest. It was a ring. A ring made of grass, the long pale grass that grew in the Night Garden. It was the gift he'd given Antonetta so many years ago, before her mother had warned him away from her. Before she had changed.

He snapped the locket shut, his mind buzzing. Someone was coming up behind him; he turned, trying to school his expression from shock into a mild curiosity.

It was Polidor Sardou, wearing a brightly dyed doublet of rich brocade. "The protestors only say what everyone feels," he said. He looked sallow, unwell, his eyes shadowed. "It is an insult, what Sarthe has done." He glared past Kel, in the direction of the Sarthian Ambassadors, who stood with Mayesh. Senex Domizio seemed impassive, but Sena Anessa was clearly furious. "And House Aurelian tolerates it."

"House Aurelian has no choice." Kel saw Conor, then, emerge from the house. He was smiling, seemingly careless, and not alone. With him was Silla, her red hair bright as candle flame. "You wanted to talk to me?" Kel asked, tucking the locket carefully into his sleeve.

"Indeed. There are always choices," said Sardou. "I hear you walked away from that farce of a welcoming ceremony in the square. You showed your loyalty then."

Kel looked at Sardou in surprise. *You showed your loyalty.* Loyalty to whom? It had never occurred to him that his leaving the dais might be interpreted as anything other than what it was: a desire to go to Conor. But it was clear that some had seen it as an expression of indignation.

"If you ever wish to discuss," Sardou began, "potential *options*— pressure that could be brought to bear, perhaps, in certain places, where this *marriage*"—he said the word with disgust—"might be discouraged . . ."

Kel could not help but think of Fausten. "There are those who would see House Aurelian destroyed," he said in a low voice.

Sardou recoiled. "*Destroy* House Aurelian? I have no such goal. I wish to strengthen them where they are weak."

Kel looked at him in the shadow-shifting darkness. He knew he should stay, pressure Sardou, try to discover more. But he felt a sudden revulsion for all of it—for the Ragpicker King, for Prosper Beck, for the lies he had told Conor, for what he had just done to Antonetta. For having looked inside the locket at all.

Antonetta had worn the locket necklace since she was a child; she could easily have placed the ring inside it years ago and forgotten all about it. But it did not change the fact that he was most likely the last person she would ever want to know it was there. He could not escape the feeling he had violated more than her trust. And then there was Prosper Beck. Why on earth would the crime lord care about the dried-up remnant of a long-gone crush?

But is it long gone? whispered a voice in the back of his head. *Did your heart not skip a beat when you saw the ring, hidden away? Does it not mean something to you that she kept it, all these years?*

Kel was well practiced at ignoring that small voice, the one that wished him to know more about himself than was practical or wise. He pushed the thought away, concentrating on Sardou.

"I shall remember what you've said," Kel said, carefully, "as the words of a loyal man who wishes to protect his Prince and his King."

"Indeed."

Kel took a step back. "But I must go. Conor will be looking for me."

Sardou's smile turned brittle. "Of course."

Kel felt Sardou's eyes on him as he left the terrace and went back into the mansion, where he found Antonetta in conversation with one of the brightly dressed courtesans. She turned to smile at him as he approached. "Everything all right?" she said.

"Yes, only hold out your hand," he said, and when she did, he set her locket gently in her palm. "You dropped this," he said.

"Oh, how lovely!" said the courtesan, leaning in. "What do you keep inside it?"

Kel felt his stomach lurch as Antonetta flicked the locket open. "Why, nothing. It's a pretty bauble, but I don't keep anything in it. I just like people to think that I have secrets."

Lin dreamed again of the tower that night. This time she did not have to wait for Suleman to arrive; he was already there, standing at the tower's edge, the black and red storm clouds coalescing behind him. When he came toward her, she saw the winking gleam of his Source-Stone in the hilt of the sword belted at his side.

He held out his arms to her, and this time, for the first time, she let him pull her close. Pull her down, so that they were both lying on the rough stone top of the shaking tower. When she drew him on top of her, she felt the relief of it. She had wanted him so much— had loved him, and love did not disappear when hatred bloomed. Rather, her hatred seemed to feed her passion, as if she were watering a monstrous plant with poisonous water.

She tore at the front of her dress, baring her skin to the thundering sky. He kissed her bare breasts and she arched up against him. His mouth was hot on her skin, the only warm thing in a world of distant flame and icy wind. She clutched at him, drawing him closer, closer still, her hand lowering to grip the hilt of his sword.

She pulled it free with a single motion, driving it into his back even as her legs wrapped around him. And when he gasped, she did not know if it was pleasure or pain, only that his blood was hot against her as it ran out over her bare skin, burning scarlet as the eye of the storm . . .

After generations, the people of Aram found a peaceful settlement. They began to build, and to raise their children there, until the king of a neighboring land heard that they were users of magic, and came to them at the head of an army, saying, "If you swear fealty to me, and use your magic on my behalf, I will not slay you."

And the younger of the Ashkar said, "It is worth it, for peace, to do this thing."

But Judah Makabi remembered their Queen, and he remembered, too, what happened when kings used their people as tools to do magic. And in despair he went away from the settlement, and into a cave in the mountains. And he cried out to his long-gone Queen Adassa, saying: *We have always been faithful to you, O Queen, we have always been your people. Do we die in your name or do we give our fealty to another?*

It was then that Adassa appeared to Makabi in a vision.

—*Book of Makabi*

CHAPTER TWENTY-TWO

Sunlight woke Kel, lancing through the window glass and, it felt, directly into his eyeballs. He rolled over, wincing. It seemed that despite his best attempts, he'd managed to down enough alcohol the night before to give himself a hangover.

He sat up, the sheets tangling around his waist. He could guess by the angle of the sunlight that it was about noon. He glanced over at Conor's bed, but the curtains were drawn tightly. Whatever hangover Kel had, Conor's was likely twice as bad.

After Antonetta had revealed her empty necklace, Falconet had appeared and spirited Kel away, telling him that he had to accompany Joss to the drawing room where Charlon had stripped off his clothes and was allowing one of the courtesans to paint him gold; the small group that had gathered to watch were taking bets on when Charlon would be rendered unconscious by the paint fumes. Conor had been there, smiling a glittering, hard smile; he had pressed blue wine into Kel's hand, and Kel recalled little of what had happened after that.

He stared up at the ceiling. Like a tickle in the back of his throat, or a sore tooth, the thought of Antonetta's locket was a botheration he could not quite ignore, as he could not ignore the pounding in his head. The grass ring inside—why had she kept it, and kept it so close to her? Was it a sign that she had missed their friendship as much as he had? A fond memory of a long-gone time? Had she placed the ring there years ago and forgotten it was there?

Or was it something else? He thought again of what Lin had said. *Antonetta fancies you.* And then, *Antonetta does not know me. Not me as I really am.*

And then there was the matter of Prosper Beck.

Why had Beck sent him to retrieve—at some risk—a locket that contained nothing inside it save a dried-out loop of grass? Did Beck even know about the ring's false bottom, or had the whole business been some sort of test? Had someone else already gotten to the contents? But Antonetta had clearly expected the locket to be empty. Had she removed the contents herself? If there was one thing he had learned during these past strange weeks, it was not to underestimate Antonetta as she seemed to wish to be underestimated.

He swung himself out of bed; there was, after all, only one person who could unknot this knot. And he could explain any absence from Marivent as the need to take a walk and clear his head. Perhaps he would stop at the kitchens and ask Dom Valon for a serving of his hangover cure before he headed down into Castellane. Maybe ask for an extra helping of white vinegar. After last night, Kel felt as if he needed to be cleansed, inside and out.

Kel was just stepping into a pair of linen trousers when there was a rustle from behind the heavy velvet drapes that shielded Conor's bed. A pale hand parted the curtains, and a distinctly feminine leg followed.

So there was a girl in Conor's bed. It was hardly the first time. Kel cast about for a shirt while a slim, white-clad form slipped between the curtains, closing them carefully behind it. She exhaled and shook her head, sending a fountain of dark-red hair tumbling over her shoulders, and for a moment, Kel's heart stopped.

Lin?

He must have made a noise, for she jumped a little and turned around. When she saw him, she smiled. "Ah," she said. She was wrapped in a white sheet; it hung to her bare feet. "Fancy meeting you here." She flicked her dark gaze up and down him with a grin; he was still shirtless. "I applaud your choice of outfit, Kel."

"Silla," he breathed. There was relief mixed in with his surprise, and some annoyance at himself: How could he *ever* have thought it would be Lin? She had made it clear enough several times that she didn't care much for Conor. "What are you doing?"

"I should think that much would be obvious. I'm looking for my clothes."

Kel pointed. The red dress she had been wearing the night before was tossed over a chair back next to Conor's bed.

"Why, thank you, *Sieur* Anjuman." Apparently deciding that since it was just Kel, it didn't matter, she dropped the sheet, stepping out of its white folds like a mermaid out of seafoam. Kel flushed a little, not because she was naked, but because her body was so *familiar*. He had learned her body as one might learn a piece of music, its rhythm and inflections, the vibration of its low notes, the sharp trill of the higher range.

Silla slipped the red dress on and began to do up the laces in the front. She peered at Kel from beneath her eyelashes. "You don't *mind*, do you?" she said. "I hadn't seen you in so long. I assumed . . . and he *is* the Crown Prince."

Somewhere in the distance, outside the room, Kel could hear the sound of laughter. A child playing. He pressed his fingers to his eyes as if he could hold back his headache.

"I don't mind," he said. "He treated you well enough, I assume?"

She kicked her feet into her red satin slippers and padded across the room to him. "Perfectly well," she said, and kissed his cheek. "But thank you for worrying about me." She tilted her head. "Now, is there a . . . discreet way out of this place?"

Kel searched for a shirt while giving her directions to the Sea Path, and told her what to say to Manish at the gate. She disappeared in a swirl of red hair and redder satin. He did not know why he had imagined she was Lin. Lin was tall, while Silla was slight; Lin's hair was dark auburn, streaked with lighter strands of copper, while Silla's was bright as scarlet paint.

But Lin had been there last night, and he had thought there was something about the way Conor looked at her—but it could just have been rage. Conor was bitterly miserable these days. Miserable enough that Kel could not be angry at him about Silla.

And indeed, Kel thought, having located boots and shirt and run his fingers through his hair to tame it, Silla was free. He had not paid to reserve her only for himself. Still, Conor knew . . . He *knew* . . .

Though what he knew, Kel could not put his finger on exactly.

The sound of laughter grew louder as Kel made his way downstairs and into the courtyard. He found it empty save for Vienne and Luisa, who was scampering up one of the walls rather as if she were a Crawler. Vienne stood under her, her arms outstretched, wearing her Black Guard uniform—and looking far more comfortable than she had the night before. "*E si te scavalca 'l muro, alora, cosa fatu, insemenia?*" Vienne said in Sarthian. *And if you get over the wall, then what, you silly girl?*

Luisa looked over and saw Kel. Startled, she lost her grip and tumbled off the wall; Vienne caught her while Luisa pealed with laughter. Kel had worried Luisa would be troubled by memories of the night before, but she seemed to have recovered. She giggled while Vienne set her on her feet, then ran over to Kel and began to rattle away in Sarthian so fast he could barely follow it.

"She's glad to see you," Vienne said drily, "and she wants you to know that she's had a Castles board set up in her rooms, if you want to play."

"*Me piasaria zogar, 'na s'cianta,*" Kel said, and would have said more, but Vienne—not sharply, but firmly—said, "Luisa, *cara*, go pick some flowers for the *Prìnçipe Marakandi.*"

Luisa skipped off to begin denuding a marigold shrub of its

blooms. It was a cool day, for Castellane, with a wind off the ocean that shook the petals of the flowers.

"You are her new favorite person," said Vienne. Sunlight glinted off her chestnut hair. Kel was aware of the weapons she was carrying: a short-sword at her side, and almost certainly daggers in her boots. "Do not worry; the position comes with few responsibilities."

"Ah," Kel said. "Well, Conor will win her back. He always does."

"It doesn't really matter, does it?" said Vienne. "Whether she likes him or not, this business will all go forward regardless."

"I suppose." Kel's head felt as if it were splitting under the hot sun. "Still, I want to apologize. To you, to her. The way Conor was last night—he isn't usually like that."

"*Verità?*" she murmured. "I will tell you, as a bodyguard, I am trained to observe people. To watch their reactions."

That's nothing I don't know about. But Kel kept his eyes wide, voice neutral. "And last night someone reacted oddly?"

"No one reacted oddly," said Vienne. "No one seemed surprised by your Prince's behavior at all."

"Really?" said Kel. "He is not usually dressed like the God of love, or drinking quite so much. All right," he admitted at her doubtful expression, "dressing as the God of love is just the sort of thing he likes to do, and he often drinks when he is miserable."

Vienne shook her head slowly. "You're his cousin, aren't you? So I don't suppose you'll answer me honestly if I ask you something."

"I'll do my best," Kel said, warily.

"Is he going to be unkind to her?" She glanced at Luisa, who was busy murdering tulips now. "I mean truly unkind to her, not just neglectful. I need to know what to be prepared for."

"No," Kel said, quietly. "He can be careless and capricious, but he is not cruel by nature."

Vienne nodded slowly, but Kel was not entirely sure she believed him.

"He is angry and resentful of the situation. It is not the fault of the Princess Luisa, but he is disappointed. And feels he has been humiliated, publicly. It is not the Princess's fault that she is just a child, but . . ."

"But she is just a child," said Vienne, with the ghost of a smile. "So she thinks this is some sort of romantic game, or adventure, like a Story-Spinner's tale. But I know differently."

She turned restlessly to look at her young charge, who had grown absorbed in reading the inscription on the sundial. "She does not know everything that this takes from her," Vienne said, her voice low and passionate. "Her childhood. The freedom to make choices for her own life, decide her own path, love who she chooses to love—all of that. Falling in love, the beauty and the pain of it, she will never experience, and she does not even know it."

"Aside from childhood, those same things will be taken from Conor, as well," said Kel. "And he *does* know it."

For a moment, there was a look in Vienne's eyes—as if she understood him, sympathized with him, if not with Conor. She might not know he was a Sword Catcher, Kel thought, but she understood they were both caretakers, in their own ways.

"What about you?" Kel said. "I cannot imagine this is what you would have chosen for yourself, either. You are the Princess's guard, so this is effectively a sort of exile. Do you think, in some years, after she—after they marry, you will be able to return to Aquila?"

She looked past him, squinting against the sun. "I will not return to Sarthe unless Luisa does. I am not only her guard; I have sworn an oath to protect her that will last as long as she lives. Where she goes, I go. It is my calling. I suppose that is hard to understand."

"Not really," said Kel. "I understand it perfectly."

Luisa had come running up to them, her curls bouncing. "Look, I caught a bird, a pretty bird!" she cried in Sarthian. And indeed, in her cupped hands rested a small red bird with yellow markings on its wings.

"A scarlet tanager," said Conor. "Something of a lucky creature here, considering its colors are Castellane's."

Kel looked up in surprise; he had not noticed Conor emerge from the Castel Mitat, which was atypical. Usually he was more at-tuned to Conor than that.

Luisa gave a little gasp, and the scarlet tanager flew out of her hands. It seemed she was not as disenchanted with Conor as Kel might have guessed. He wore a black velvet coat with gold frogging and a more-than-fashionable amount of white lace at the cuffs and collar. Around his throat was a pendant: two birds shaped out of gold, holding a ruby between them.

"*Maravejóxo*," Luisa sighed. Vienne, barely perceptibly, rolled her eyes.

"Princess Luisa," Conor said, switching to Sarthian. "I imagine you might like to see my mother's garden. It is far more grand than this one, and there are peacocks."

Luisa seemed delighted. Vienne was still looking at Conor rather narrowly, which he was ignoring. Kel could see he was not about to offer any apologies for the night before. He said, "Kellian, would you show the Lady Vienne where to find the Queen's Gar-den? I would myself, but I have an appointment in the city today."

An appointment? Kel wasn't aware of such a thing, but he couldn't ask now, in front of Vienne, which was doubtless the reason Conor had chosen this moment to announce his plans. He gave Conor a sharp look, but Conor only looked decidedly innocent, his gray eyes wide.

"Benaset will accompany me," he said to Kel, which seemed to be his way of offering reassurance. And it *was* a bit reassuring; there was a limit to the trouble Conor could get into with Jolivet's right-hand man watching him. "And I believe tomorrow night is the great banquet? We welcome our new Princess on Ascension Day." He turned to Vienne. "I trust Luisa has everything she needs?"

Luisa, understanding the word *Princess*, and her own name, smiled at him. Vienne said, "You would have to ask her lady's maids, but I believe she is well prepared, yes. I trust the banquet will be more—appropriate—than last night's entertainment?"

Conor's smile did not waver. "Oh, indeed," he said. "My mother has been planning it for weeks now, and everything she does is exactingly appropriate. I do not think, Lady Vienne, that you will find anything in the way of surprises in the Shining Gallery. Or at least," he added over his shoulder, as he left the courtyard, "one hopes that what surprises there are will be pleasant ones."

"I'm not surprised Demoselle Alleyne decided to look after the little Princess," Mariam said. She was sitting on Lin's bed, wrapped in a shawl. She was pale, but there was bright color in her cheeks—put there, Lin suspected, by her excitement over Lin's tale of the party at the Roverge house. It was why Lin was telling it, despite her reservations. "She's quite a bit kinder than most of those ladies up on the Hill. That's the thing about being a seamstress," she added. "You are all but invisible to the nobles, and they forget you are observing their behavior." She leaned forward. "So what happened after Roverge demanded that the little girl dance? Did the Prince stop him?"

Lin sighed inwardly. She was barefoot, wearing a plain gray frock. When she had come home from the party last night, she had scrubbed every last bit of paint from her face, and nearly torn off her beautiful indigo dress in her haste to be rid of it. She had gone to bed still furious, and dreamed—well, she could hardly remember what she had dreamed. It had been a version of the dream she had often now, about the last moments of the Goddess, only it had ended very differently from the others. She knew it was just a dream, no more—the story of Adassa's last moments was well known to all Ashkar—but she had woken trembling and damp with sweat, her skin so hot she had needed to sit before her open window for nearly an hour before she could lie down again.

All she wanted now was to forget about the entire night, but Mariam was hungry for details, and Lin wanted to make her happy. "Well, he didn't, to be honest," she said, and immediately felt a bit guilty; Mariam only wanted to hear things that were happy or scandalous or both. "But someone else stepped in to dance instead, so the evening could continue."

"Who was it? Oh, never mind, I don't remember who half those young nobles are anyway," Mariam said cheerfully. "Anyway, it seems entirely an inappropriate sort of party to throw for a twelve-year-old. When I was twelve, all I was interested in was playing tricks on the boys in the Dāsu Kebeth."

Lin laughed at the memory, but sobered quickly. "The thing is, the Castellani nobles were expecting a twenty-year-old Princess, and they simply haven't bothered to change any of their plans. I imagine it would seem too much like accepting what Sarthe has done. There's some sort of welcoming banquet tomorrow—their Ascension Day celebration—that will be nothing but speeches in a language Luisa doesn't speak. She'll be horribly bored."

Mariam furrowed her brow. "Are you going to the banquet?" At Lin's surprised look, she added, "I thought Mayesh might be bringing you to more events on the Hill—"

"No," Lin said. She thought of the quiet ride home in the carriage from the Roverge house, Mayesh watching her with sharp eyes, clearly waiting for some sort of reaction from her, some verdict on the party. But she had said nothing until they reached the Sault. Standing in the shadow of the gates, she had said, "I will tell you if I think there is a point in my returning to the Hill."

He had not asked questions, only nodded and let her go.

"I won't be at the banquet, don't worry," said Lin. "It's the same night as Tevath."

"It's all right. If you'd rather go to the party."

"Mari," Lin said sternly. "I'd rather be at the Goddess Festival, with you. It's our last year."

"I just feel as though you've gone off into a wonderful story," Mariam said, with a smile that held a wisp of sadness. "A party with the Charter Families. The Prince himself there. In a Story-Spinner tale, you'd already be secretly engaged to him."

Instead, he kissed me, then flung me away and said he must have been drunk, Lin thought. *Ever so romantic.*

"In a Story-Spinner tale, that would mean I'd be about to be kidnapped by pirates so he could save me," Lin said, crossly. "Mari. The Prince is of the *malbushim.* Even if he weren't the Prince, I couldn't—he is not like us. You must notice," she added, "that none of the girls in the Story-Spinner tales, even if they are peasants, are Ashkar."

The hectic color in Mariam's cheeks bloomed, and Lin felt suddenly guilty. What on earth was the point of telling Mariam to face reality when dreams and hopes of some grand event were what she had to sustain her?

"Mari, I'm sorry—"

There was a knock on Lin's door. The two women exchanged a startled look. "It's likely Mayesh," Lin said, rising to her feet; she padded barefoot to the door and threw it open.

On the threshold stood Oren Kandel, looking as if he were attending his own funeral. With him were two Castelguards, in red livery, both squinting against the bright sun. And between them was Prince Conor Aurelian, all in black velvet, wearing a gold coronet.

Lin's mouth opened in shock, but no sound came out. She had only just seen the Prince last night, but he had been in his own world, his own element, among the people of the Hill. She thought of his cloak of white-and-gold brocade, and the metallic ink around his eyes. He was more quietly dressed now, it was true, but that still meant many flashing rings, gold paint on his nails—and that *crown.* For him to be here in the Sault, looking up at her calmly from her own front steps, was for reality to have folded itself in half. She could make no sense of it.

"Oren?" she whispered, almost regretfully; it was a dark day indeed when she had to ask Oren Kandel to explain what she was looking at with her own eyes.

"The Prince of Castellane is here to see you," mumbled Oren.

This, Lin thought, was the least helpful thing he could have said. From behind her, she heard a squeak. Of course; Mariam was watching from the doorway of her room.

In fact, it was not just Mariam. Lin's neighbors had begun to pour out into the street, and were staring in the direction of her house. Mez and Rahel, hand in hand, were gaping from their doorstep, and Kuna Malke, her baby girl balanced on her hip, was on tiptoe on her porch in order to see better.

For the first time, Lin locked eyes with the Prince. His were the shade of clouds, unreadable. She said, "If you seek my grandfather, Counselor Bensimon, he is not here, my lord."

Before Prince Conor could answer, there was a patter of quick steps. Mariam appeared at Lin's side, her cheeks bright red. "Monseigneur," she exclaimed. "I am Mariam Duhary, and it would be the honor of my life to sew a cloak for you—"

"You're the one who made Lin's dress last night?" Prince Conor spoke for the first time. Something in Lin's chest jumped when he said her name like that: *Lin*, not *Domna Caster*. It was familiar; too much so. She saw Oren notice it, too, and scowl. "Kel told me. Lin's friend with the needle."

Mariam glowed. "Lin spoke of me to him?"

"Of course she did. You're very skilled." There was real warmth in his tone, and though Lin knew it had been trained into him, it remained affecting. "I would like to speak to Lin for a moment alone. It is a matter of state."

He managed to say it as if he were asking Mariam's permission. She glowed brighter, and nodded. "Of course, of course," she said, bolting down the stairs of Lin's house and nearly knocking into Oren at the bottom.

"We will keep watch, Monseigneur," said Benaset. He, too, descended the steps, where the guards had set about shooing off Oren. Oren seemed to have decided that the better part of valor was to pretend that he had always planned to escort Mariam back to the

Women's House. Fortunately for him, Mariam was in too good a humor to wave him off.

Rahel and Mez were both waving energetically at Lin, but she had no chance to wave back, had she been so inclined. The moment Benaset was gone, the Prince had closed the door of Lin's house behind him, plunging the room into dimness. Lin wondered if she ought to go and pull the curtains closed over the windows, but no—that would simply set tongues to wagging even further, and it wasn't as if one could easily see in without coming straight up to her house and pressing one's face against the glass.

"That man who guided us to your house," the Prince remarked, his gaze sweeping lazily over her living room, "has he a dog?"

"Oren?" Lin wanted to wrap her arms around herself. She felt oddly exposed, as if the Prince could see all of her: It was close enough, in a way. Here were her remaining books, her crumpled dress over the back of a chair, her breakfast plate still on the table. Open to his gaze, like a corpse on an anatomy table. "A *dog*? No, why?"

"I was wondering if it had died recently. He seems the most depressing person I have ever met."

Lin was not sure if she should sit down or stand up. She settled for leaning against the wall. She was abnormally conscious of her bare feet, of the plainness of her dress, of her unbraided hair. Loose, the copper curls fell to the middle of her back. "That's Oren. He's just like that, always has been. What are you *doing* here, Monseigneur?"

"Don't call me that," he said, rather sharply, and she inhaled a breath; was this going to be like last night? Was he going to be strange, half furious, unpredictable? "I would prefer that you call me Conor. As your grandfather does."

She stared at him. "I can't do that. I'm not a royal or a noble, it would be too"—*intimate*—"too familiar. What if someone over-heard?"

"Familiar," he said, his lips quirking at the word. "I came, Domna Caster, because I understand that last night I may have alarmed you by kissing you. I don't remember it *well*"—he waved a hand, as if shaking off a cobweb—"but I assure you there was no meaning or malice in it. I kiss a great many people."

Lin blushed. She had not mentioned that part of the evening to Mariam; in fact, she had not mentioned a great deal of what had happened—not Luisa crying, nor her own dance, nor her angry words, nor Prince Conor's fury when he had followed her from the room. And certainly not what had happened then. "I truly hope," she said, "that you did not really waste your royal morning coming here to tell me something I already knew."

Something in his eyes flashed. It was not anger, though she might have expected that. He had been angry the night before. It was something more like a passionate puzzlement, as if he were trying to solve an equation and coming up short.

"All right," he said. "You are correct enough. I did not come here merely to apologize for kissing you."

She looked at him directly. That always seemed to make a difference, she thought—when she could catch his gaze with her own, when she could make him look at her and *see* her. She did not think many people sought his gaze. The studied gaze of a royal might uncover any sort of secret; it might unsettle, might remind a member of the Charter Families that, though they were nearly as powerful as Gods, they were not.

Their gazes met, held. In the dimness of the room, his eyes seemed the brightest thing before her, save for his crown, a ring of fire. She said, "Then why are you here, Prince Conor?"

He drew something out of his jacket. A square something, that looked like a ragged brown package. "You called me a selfish bastard last night," he said, "but would a selfish bastard gift you this?"

He held the object out to her. She realized it was a book, its leather cover tattered and worn. As she took it from him, her hand shaking slightly, she recognized the title, half faded from the spine: *The Works of Qasmuna*.

"Ohh," she breathed. She began to flip through the pages, frantically—even as she felt how soft they were, and fragile, under her touch. Words, so many words, and drawings—of stones that looked like her own, in various stages of brightness—and numbered columns that could be instructions—

"I suppose I should have expected this," said the Prince drily. "Your grandfather has never thanked me for anything, either."

Lin forced herself to look up from the book, remembering suddenly what Andreyen had said. *There are murmurs that someone else is searching for our book. With great dedication, I hear.*

"*You're* the one who's been searching the city for this?"

She was still clutching it to her chest, like a little girl with a new favorite toy. She saw a smile tug the corners of his mouth.

"I've turned Castellane upside down looking for it," he said. "I finally hunted it down in the collection of a trader who'd found it in the Maze. He was about to take it to Marakand, where collectors will offer great sums for this sort of thing. I persuaded him he'd make more money selling it to me."

"But—why did you do this? How did you even know I wanted it—?"

"You mentioned it. That night at Marivent."

And she had, she realized, the night of his whipping. She had told him all about the book, the Maharam, the Shulamat . . .

Only she had not thought he was really *listening*. But he had been, it seemed. Something hot flared inside her chest. Gratitude—but she had never been comfortable with gratitude, and it came now edged with panic.

"But what does it matter to you," she said, "that I was looking for it? I do not need to be paid, I have told you that before—"

He was no longer smiling. "Yes," he said. "You refused the ring I offered you in recompense for healing Kel. You would take nothing for healing me. But that does not mean I do not owe you. And I despise being indebted."

She drew herself up, knowing she must look ridiculous, barefoot and tangle-haired and stubborn. "What difference does it make? You are a Prince—one might say you cannot owe anything to someone like me."

"But you know that is not true. You saved me. You saved my Sword Catcher." He took a step forward, closing the space between them. Lin could not move away; the table was directly behind her. "And as long as I owe you, I cannot forget it. I think of you—of the debt I owe you—and I cannot rid my mind of the thoughts. It is like a fever."

"And now you wish me to heal you again," Lin said slowly. He was so close—not as close to her as he had been the night before, but she could see lighter flecks of silvery white in his eyes. "Of the fever that is myself. Your debt to me."

"It is a sickness," he whispered. She felt his breath stir her hair, and a tide of goosebumps flooded across her skin. "I need my thoughts back. My freedom. You ought to understand that, physician." He flicked his glance to the book in her hands. "Everyone wants something," he said. "It is the nature of people. You cannot be that different."

Her hand tightened on the book. A part of her, that did not want to give him what he wanted—that did not, if she had to admit it, want to be ordinary in his eyes—wished to thrust it back at him. But she thought of Mariam, of Mariam's bright eyes glowing at the thought of making a cloak for the Prince, and she could not do it. It would be madness.

She set Qasmuna's book down on the table. Turned back to look at him. "There," she said. "I've taken it. Does that mean you can forget all about me now?"

He was breathing quickly. If he had been her patient, she would have laid her fingers against the smooth skin of his throat, would have pressed in lightly, feeling his blood pulse beneath her fingertips. Would have said, *Breathe, breathe.*

But he was not her patient. He was the Prince of Castellane, and he leaned in close to her then, putting his lips against her ear. She clutched the edge of the table behind her, feeling a hot tide flood through her belly, her legs. His voice was rough in her ear. "I," he said, "have already forgotten you."

She stiffened. Heard him inhale sharply, and then he was gone, whirling away from her. She stayed braced against the table as the door slammed shut behind him.

Lin closed her eyes. She could hear the commotion outside as he exited her house; presumably everyone who'd just heard that the Prince of Castellane *had come to visit Lin Caster* was now lining the street, satisfying their curiosity. She wondered what would happen if she told them that he had simply come to settle a debt. She rather doubted they would believe her.

Kel turned through the crumbling stone arch and made his way down Arsenal Road. He had never been in the Maze during the day before. Like the flowers in the Night Garden, it came awake only after sunset.

Most sights were improved by bright sunlight and a blue sky overhead, but the Maze was not among them. The harsh illumination showed all its ragged edges and filthy corners, without the shadows of night to blue them to softness. Drunken nobles stumbled home after a night of carousing, stopping to vomit against the walls of abandoned shophouses. The doors of poppy-houses stood open, revealing bare wooden floors on which addicts twitched, the morning light stirring them out of dreams and into painful consciousness. While the brothels that lined the road were still open, there were few customers trickling in and out of the doors. The doxies who worked through the nights sprawled comfortably on the balconies in tunics and knickers, drinking *karak* and smoking hand-rolled cheroots from Hind. Food stalls set up in between the buildings served bowls of Shenzan rice porridge topped with fish or fruit to sailors who lined up, carrying the dented metal serving bowls they kept in their packs; they were often to be seen cleaning them conscientiously at various public cisterns.

He nearly passed it without recognizing his goal: the warehouse with the blacked-out windows where Jerrod had brought him the other night.

It was hard to believe that the cracked façade hid a lively cabaret within, at least during nighttime hours. The place seemed utterly silent and deserted. Kel was aware of curious eyes on him as he knocked on the front door. There was no answer, so he tried the handle and found it unlocked, but stuck in its frame; wood warped often here, so close to the sea and the humid air. Kel shouldered it open and stepped inside.

The long corridor he remembered was nearly lightless, illuminated only by window spots where the black paint had chipped away. Kel made his way silently to the enormous main room. It was empty, the glass lanterns, nearly all unlit, swaying over a floor scattered with overturned tables and broken bits of furniture. Abandoned mother-of-pearl gaming chips gleamed like sequins against the dusty floor surrounding the upturned crow's nest.

Kel ran up the stairs, taking them two at a time. He found, as he had expected, nothing at all. The warehouse seemed as if it had been deserted for years; the room in which he had met Prosper Beck was entirely emptied, even the boxes of Singing Monkey Wine gone.

He made his way back downstairs, trailing a hand along the wall to keep himself oriented in the gloom. Prosper Beck moved his headquarters from place to place often, he knew, but this was more than that. This place had been looted of its decorations, abandoned utterly. Something had happened.

He paused in the main room, where a single velvet cushion lay on the floor, a rip along the side releasing a small gust of white feathers. He thought of Antonetta's gold locket, shining empty in her hand, and a wave of rage went through him, mixed with a frustration so intense it felt almost like despair.

Putting a booted foot against the pole of the crow's nest, he shoved as hard as he could. He'd half expected it to wobble, but instead it went over so quickly that Kel had to jump back to avoid being hit as it toppled, slamming into the warehouse floor with a force that sent dust and splinters into the air like a sandstorm.

"*Beck!*" Kel looked up, at the empty hanging hooks, at the lightless interior windows of the second floor. "*Where the fuck are you, Prosper Beck?*"

"Kel."

Kel turned. Standing in the stairwell was a familiar figure in black Crawler's gear. His silver quarter-mask gleamed, as did his boots. His hood was up, drawn close about his face, but Kel could see that he was frowning.

"Jerrod," Kel said.

"I thought they taught you better manners than that," Jerrod said, "up at the Palace."

"Manners don't interest me at the moment," said Kel. "I want to see Beck."

Jerrod came into the room a little more, glancing with interest at the wreckage of the crow's nest. "Haven't we been through this once? Beck has expressed no desire to see you a second time. You aren't that charming."

"I want to know why he's been wasting my time."

Jerrod hopped up onto an overturned table, his legs swinging over the side. "Couldn't get the locket from the girl, could you?"

"I got it," Kel said shortly. "But it was empty."

Jerrod glanced up at the ceiling. "So you snuck a peek inside? Beck won't be pleased."

Kel hesitated. He could mention the grass ring, the false bottom of the locket. But it seemed a betrayal of Antonetta, as well as a piece of strategic information he did not yet wish to share. If Beck did not know about the ring, there was no reason to be the one who told him. And if he did, then what had been the point of all of this? What was he after?

"You care about his opinion. I don't," said Kel. "Antonetta

opened it herself. And it's been driving me mad since. Why would Beck send me to retrieve an empty necklace for him? He told me there was information inside, but that's hardly Antonetta's way of doing things. What sort of information? Is this something to do with her mother—" Kel cut himself off impatiently. "And then it occurred to me. Beck *wants* me to be driven mad with pointless questions. He wants me to be gazing over at the locket and the Alleynes, so I won't be looking somewhere else, somewhere he doesn't want me to look. All of which had led me to come here and ask: What does he *really* want?"

Jerrod kicked his heels like a small boy sitting along the harbor seawall. "Well. You aren't going to find out."

"I *will* see him. You cannot stop me."

"You are welcome to see him, if you can find him. Because I cannot."

Kel went still. "What do you mean?"

"I mean he's gone. He's left Castellane."

"You're lying—"

"I'm not." Jerrod gestured around the room. "You can confirm it with your friend the Ragpicker King if you like. I'm sure he's heard the buzzing by now. The Maze is no longer Beck's, and likely Andreyen will want to march his own people in soon."

Kel thought of Mayesh. *Odd. One does not usually willingly take leave of a position of power.*

"Beck was thriving here," Kel said. "Why leave so suddenly?" He narrowed his eyes. "On the other hand, he was planning to betray his patron, someone of importance on the Hill. Did that patron discover Beck was hoping to stab him in the back?"

Jerrod threw up his chalk-powdered hands. "You're thinking too small, Anjuman. I don't know who Beck's patron was—there is some information it is better not to possess. I have been happy in my ignorance. But I do know one thing. You are thinking of your Prince and your House Aurelian, as you always do, while Beck was thinking of the whole of Castellane."

"What did he know of the whole of Castellane? The Maze does not represent it, any more than the Palace does."

"He knew enough to leave you a message," said Jerrod. "Which, by the way, is the only reason I came when you called for Beck. Because he knew you would come, and he asked me to tell you this when you did." He looked thoughtfully at the palm of his hand, as if there was a message scrawled there. "'Trouble is coming for the Hill, Anjuman, and Marivent will not be exempt. You have no idea how bad it will get. Blood will run from the height to the depth. The Hill will drown in it.'"

Kel felt the back of his neck prickle. "A warning indeed," he said. "But Beck is not concerned for my welfare. This could be another game he's playing, couldn't it?"

Jerrod smiled enigmatically. "Some people are only convinced by empirical evidence, I suppose. You need not heed anyone's warnings, Anjuman. Feel free to fuck around and find out yourself."

"Right." Kel started for the door. Halfway there, he stopped and turned; Jerrod was still seated on the overturned table, his mask gleaming like a quarter-moon. "Would you tell me one thing?" Kel said. "Why didn't you kill me? That night your Crawler stabbed me. Once you realized I wasn't Conor. Didn't you worry I could make some kind of trouble for you?"

"You've made plenty of trouble for me," Jerrod said shortly. "The answer is simple. I saw Ji-An on the wall. She seemed invested in keeping you alive, and I didn't want to go directly against the Ragpicker King."

It was a sound enough reason, but it didn't sit quite right with Kel. Something about the whole situation gnawed at him. Abruptly, he said: "You're not going to tell me anything really useful, are you?"

"No," Jerrod said pleasantly. "I've discharged my last responsibility to Beck. Time for me to look for other work. Perhaps I'll see if your Ragpicker King is feeling generous. He could always use another good Crawler in his employ."

"He's not *my* Ragpicker King—" Kel began, and nearly laughed. He was letting Jerrod get under his skin, and to what end, really? "You know what? Go ahead. I'll let him know you send your regards."

"Send my regards to the pretty poisoner, while you're at it," Jerrod said. "He isn't the only one waiting for Artal Gremont to return to Castellane, you know."

And he grinned.

As Kel approached Scarlet Square, he recalled how sure he'd been, the last time he had spoken to Andreyen, that he had severed their connection. That he owed Andreyen Morettus, inheritor of the title of the Ragpicker King, nothing at all.

And yet here he was, feeling a sense of near-relief as his feet carried him through the Warren to the Black Mansion. Jerrod had been very convincing, but Kel had known a great many convincing people. He thought of the Council, sitting around the face of their great clock, each one untrustworthy, each one convincing in his or her own way.

Of course, Andreyen, too, was not to be trusted. But the key was not trust, Kel thought. The key was knowing in what ways someone could be trusted, and in what ways they would lie. And Kel did not think Andreyen would lie about this.

The garden in the square's center was brilliant green in the sunlight. As Kel approached the mansion, he saw the door swing open, and Merren and Ji-An, wearing her foxglove jacket, came down the stairs to meet him. He saw Ji-An close the door firmly behind her. So he was not going to be let inside, Kel thought. Not yet.

"Does he not want to see me?" Kel said as Merren sat down on one of the middle steps. He wore a yellow jacket, stained at the cuff with something green and dangerous looking. Kel thought of Jerrod: *Send my regards to the pretty poisoner.*

Merren might sprawl, but sprawling was not in Ji-An's nature.

Back straight, she raised an eyebrow at Kel and said, "If you want to see Andreyen, he's not here."

"I can wait," Kel said.

"All day?" said Ji-An. "You might not have heard, but Prosper Beck has gone. The Maze is unguarded. Andreyen has some strategy to work out."

"So it's true," Kel said. "Beck's really left?"

"Like a shadow in the night," said Merren cheerfully. "All his people left wandering about, looking for someone to tell them what to do."

"I don't suppose you know anything about why," said Ji-An, looking closely at Kel. "*You* talked to him."

"I'd like to flatter myself that I charmed him into telling me all his plans," said Kel, "but I doubt it. Jerrod said he fled because he knew of a danger to Castellane, but—"

"But Jerrod Belmerci cannot be trusted," said Ji-An.

"Mmm," said Merren. "Really? More so than any other criminal?" He turned to Kel, ignoring Ji-An's surprised look. "Was that what you wanted with Andreyen? To tell him about Beck?"

"More to confirm that he was gone," said Kel. "Andreyen came to me asking me to look into Prosper Beck. But that investigation seems finished. So—"

"So you're done," said Merren. "Now that Prosper Beck is gone, you're done with us and the Black Mansion?"

"I think Andreyen hoped for more from Kel than just that," Ji-An said, clearly aware that Kel was watching her, but addressing her comments to Merren. "He said there was more for Kel to do on the Hill. That he wasn't finished."

"And yet," said Kel, "I find myself tired of tangling with business in the city and on the Hill. My loyalty is with the Palace. With Conor. I should never have tried to do more than that."

Merren raised his face to the sun. "I admit," he said, quietly, "I hoped you might know something about Artal Gremont. About when he was coming back."

Kel wondered for a moment if he should mention what Jerrod had said about Gremont—but if Artal had other enemies, he doubted that was something Merren didn't already know. "I can get word to you as soon as I hear of his return," he said. "But that's all."

He thought of Roverge, of the wine, of Antonetta's locket, of Sardou's peculiar overtures. But it had all taken on the quality of chasing clouds or shadows. There would always be another nobleman exhibiting suspicious behavior. Another scheme on the Hill, another corrupt secret to be uncovered. It was the way things had always been. Power and money, the getting and the keeping of them, was the realm of kings and princes—those on the Hill, or down in the city. They were not his realm, and the further he went down this path, the further it would take him from Conor.

"I am sorry," Kel said to Merren, "that I tried to poison myself in front of you. It was discourteous." Merren looked surprised as Kel turned to Ji-An. "And I am sorry if I pried into your personal business. We all have our secrets and are entitled to them."

Ji-An smiled, just the corner of a luminous smile, like a glimpse of the moon through clouds. "A carriage drawn by black swans," she said, "does sound glamorous."

Kel bowed to them both—the sort of sweeping bow he would have offered to a foreign dignitary. "Good luck," he said, "with your criminal endeavors. And give my regards to Morettus."

As he left the square, he was aware of Ji-An and Merren watching him go. He wondered if he should have said something about Jerrod's intention to seek employment at the Black Mansion, but suspected that there would be many such seekers in the next days, as the world of the city—and perhaps the Hill, as well, in ways unseen—rearranged itself around the absence of Prosper Beck.

In the vision of Makabi, Queen Adassa showed herself to him, and he was aware immediately that she who he had once known as a human woman had become something else. She appeared in the shape of a maiden, but a maiden woven of *gematry*, of shimmering words and equations like chains of silver. And she said to him, "Do not despair. You have wandered in the wilderness for so long, but you are not unprotected. I am no longer your Queen, but your Goddess.

"My earthly body was destroyed but I am transfigured. I will watch over you and protect you, for you are my chosen people."

And she showed to him a sword, upon whose cross guard was etched the image of a raven, the wise bird whose shape Makabi had once taken at the behest of her who stood before him now. "Tell all my people what I have told you, and that I will prove myself to them: Go forth tomorrow against this interloper King and face his army. and you will be victorious, for I will be with you."

And when the sun rose the next day, Makabi rode at the head of the army of Aram once more, and the Aramites were victorious, though they were outnumbered ten to one.

—*Book of Makabi*

CHAPTER TWENTY-THREE

K el decided to take the long way back to the Palace to give himself a chance to think. This meant the Sea Path. As the city fell away below, Kel could not help thinking of what Jerrod had said: *You're thinking too small, Anjuman. You're thinking about your Prince and your House Aurelian, like you always do.*

Jerrod had meant it as a criticism, but to Kel it had been almost a relief to hear. A reaffirmation of his purpose, which was to protect Conor. His place was by Conor's side, and both the Ragpicker King and Prosper Beck had tried to bend that loyalty and duty to further their own ends. His proximity to the Prince would always prove appealing to those looking for an advantage; he wished he'd been taught to guard against that sort of approach the way he'd been taught to guard against swords and daggers.

He had not realized that there was a gap in his armor: not the desire to involve himself in matters on the Hill, but rather the desire to be around people who knew him, knew him as he *really* was— not as Conor's false cousin, not as a suit of armor that sometimes wore the Prince's face, but as Kel—orphan, observer, Sword Catcher. It was a need he had never known he had. A dangerous need to have . . .

He had reached the part of the path where it curved around the side of the hill, hiding the city behind it. Kel was always struck by the beauty of this part of the trail, where the green hill fell away to the sea. The ocean was an ink-blue road today, flecked with small boats. They cut white paths through the water, Tyndaris rising behind them, its towers like the fingers of a hand reaching out of the sea. The air tasted of salt and promise.

He thought of Vienne then, and how she had said that he guarded Conor as she guarded Luisa. As if she had sensed some quality about him that betrayed his true work—a quality that Falconet and the others, for all the years they had known him, had never observed.

The path slanted steeply upward here, the last quarter mile to Marivent, and Kel could see the sea cliffs appear, and far above him, the shadow of the walls. And then, below the path, appeared a strange sight. A wooden platform, cantilevered over the sea, jutted from the hill below him. The Sea Path continued above it and the space below the path was recessed, meaning the platform must emerge from a hollow dug into the mountain. Kel did not recall seeing the platform before, but surely it could not just have *appeared* out of the mountain?

There was a flash of red and gold—the uniforms of Castelguards, bright as flames. Two of them appeared on the platform, as if they had simply walked out of the mountain. Pinned between them was a struggling man, his arms bound behind him. His hair was a wild tangle, his straggling beard matted with blood. His face was bruised, his eyes swollen half shut, but he wore his fine cloak, embroidered with tiny beads that glittered in the sunlight. Beads that marked out the shapes of constellations: the Lion, the Harp, the Twins.

It was Fausten.

He must have been dragged here from the Trick. Perhaps he had fought the guards who came for him. Perhaps he had expected them, and they had beaten him regardless.

The guards turned to each other, speaking in quiet voices; the wind off the sea muffled the sound, in any case. Kel could hear his own breath, harsh in his ears, but nothing more.

He crouched down behind a scrubby growth of thyme. He could try to scrabble up the path or down it, but that would bring him more plainly in view of the platform below. He was hidden here, his own verdant clothes camouflaged among the hill's greenery.

His view, straight down, was clear. He almost wished it wasn't. Fausten was struggling, though he made no sound. He kicked out at one of the guardrails, then froze, his terrified eyes darting to and fro as a new figure stepped out onto the platform.

King Markus. He looked very big against the sun, his gold circlet glittering against his pale hair. His cloak was clasped at the shoulder with a heavy silver brooch, and his hands were, as always, covered with black gloves. A pace behind him came Jolivet, his posture rigid, his face expressionless.

To Kel's surprise, the Castelguards immediately released Fausten, who sagged to his knees. Both guards vanished back into the mountain. Jolivet remained a few yards away, as though keeping himself at a remove: a witness, rather than a participant.

Markus reached down to catch hold of his adviser by the front of his cloak, hauling him to his feet. He pulled him close, and over the sound of the sea, the screaming of the gulls, Kel heard him shout in Malgasi: "*Miért árultál el? Tudtad, mi fog történni. Tudtad, hony mi leszek—*"

Why did you betray me? You knew what would happen. You knew what I would become.

Fausten was shaking his head. "Your medicine," he cried, answering not in Malgasi but in the language of Castellane. "Only I can make it. If you kill me, your sickness will be worse. You know what is coming, my lord, *you know what is coming—*"

The King roared with rage. He caught hold of Fausten, wrenching him to his feet. Fausten screamed, over and over—high sounds that matched the crying of the gulls. Fausten's feet were bare, Kel saw. They drummed against the wood, leaving bloody streaks behind.

It seemed like forever, but Kel knew it was likely only a few seconds. Fausten struggled as the King, inexorable, stalked to the platform's edge. Gripping the thrashing man with black-gloved hands, he lifted him as if he weighed no more than a pair of boots and flung him over the guardrail.

Fausten fell, hurtling toward the sea like a bird shot out of the air.

His body hit the waves. There was a soundless splash, and then his head appeared, a dark dot riding the surge of the water. He seemed to be screaming as the sea roiled around him. A black shadow rose up under him and Kel's stomach surged into his throat. Dark, knobbled green heaved itself through the dark blue; a vast mouth yawned, lined with discolored, knife-sharp teeth. Even from a distance, Kel imagined he could see the thing's eyes: yellow and rolling as the jaws snapped shut, blood pulsing through razored teeth. A howling scream, a last, helpless thrash, and a great blot of scarlet spread like a stain over the surface of the ocean.

The crocodile vanished with the surge of the waves. Fausten's head still floated atop the water, the red stump of his throat no longer joined to his body. Then the shadow beneath the water curved back around and the head, too, was pulled down.

Everything seemed distant, as if it were happening at some remove. Kel dug his fingers into the dirt. He could hear nothing now but the wind in the branches of the scrub pine and his own harsh breathing. He watched as the King dusted off his gloved hands and stalked back into the mountain.

He was followed a moment later by Jolivet, who had watched the scene unfold without moving, a silent witness. As Jolivet passed out of view, he looked up, as if alerted by a movement. His eyes met Kel's. They were chips of ice, chill and dead.

You will be Legate Jolivet, the Ragpicker King had said. *And it will*

be your task, as it was his, to go to the Orfelinat and select from the fright-
ened children there the next Sword Catcher. The next you. And it will kill
a piece of you to do it.

A moment later, Jolivet was gone. There was a deep groaning sound from within the mountain, the rattle of gears and pulleys. The platform began to recede, sliding back into the Hill; in seconds, it was gone, along with any evidence that anything unusual had just happened. As Kel rose to his feet, he saw that even the surface of the sea where Fausten had died was smooth again, an unruffled expanse of blue-green silk.

Kel started back up the path to Marivent. He felt numb, as if he had been dosed with morphea. When he had to stop halfway to the walls to vomit among the rosemary and lavender bushes, he was more surprised than anything else. He had not even realized he felt sick.

He must have seemed normal enough to the guard at the gate, who let him in with a friendly word. He stopped in the courtyard of the Castel Mitat to splash water on his face. His heart was racing as he made his way up to the rooms he shared with Conor.

Conor was there, sitting in the window embrasure. He looked up when Kel came in. There was something about him that seemed different—he was smiling, and there was real relief in it, as if he had been divested of a weight on his shoulders. The last time Kel could remember Conor smiling like that was before he had found out about Prosper Beck.

Kel hated to have to shatter that expression. But Conor needed to know; it was not something he could keep from him. "Con," he said, his voice rougher than he'd expected, "there's something I have to tell you. It's about your father."

It was Second Watch, and there was not enough moonlight to read by; Lin, with a sigh, rose to light the lamps. She had been sitting at her kitchen table all afternoon and into the evening, translating Qasmuna's book and taking careful notes.

Not *in* the original book, of course. She wouldn't have dared to write in it, and besides, the pages were already loose in the binding, the paper soft with age, almost powdery under her fingertips.

Lamps now glowing, Lin returned to the table and her cold cup of *karak*. There were, of course, still passages she didn't understand, so she planned to bring the book to the Black Mansion tomorrow; surely among the forgers and thieves Andreyen employed, someone must be able to translate Callatian. She suspected Kel could do it, if it came to that.

There were many passages in the book about how magic was used for healing. The first of them followed what she had learned about Source-Stones: Magicians in the past had been able to use their powers to heal, but were limited by the power they could themselves expend without dying. Those able to store energy in stones were able to do more. When Suleman (the betrayer, the traitor) created stones that could hold limitless energy, the ability to heal became, also, nearly limitless. *A man would fall dying on the field of battle*, Qasmuna wrote, *and the sorcerer-healer would come and raise him up to fight on; even if his wounds could not be healed, he would still fight.*

It was a chilling image, and gave Lin pause. She even had to rise to her feet, and make a circuit of her room, before returning to the book. Every power *can* be used for evil, she reminded herself. But she would not do so. She wanted only to heal Mariam. But her stone seemed dead, and had since she had used it to heal Conor. And while she had known that there was a way to put her own power into the stone, to imbue it again with strength, she had not known how to do it.

According to Qasmuna, as Lin read painstakingly on, the issue was one of binding. A Source-Stone needed to be bound to its user via a series of steps. Some seemed simple, while others involved words that, even with her dictionary, Lin could not yet understand. There were also places in the manuscript that Lin found blank—sections, she guessed, where the Word itself had once been written, and had vanished when the Goddess removed it from the world.

Still. There was enough for her to try binding herself to her stone, and why not now? Why wait?

Her eyes fixed on the page in front of her, she took the stone, embedded in its silver setting, in her hand. She laid her hand against her chest—as the book bade her to do, and as she had done instinctively when she healed Prince Conor—and closed her eyes.

Against the darkness of her lids, she imagined the stone as her heart. Imagined it set into her chest like a jewel that was also a living part of her. That pulsed with light in time to her heartbeats.

For a moment, she felt wind in her hair, and smelled the scent of smoke. She saw the top of the tower in Aram, and Suleman, rising to his feet, his stone pulsing at his chest—

Her eyes flew open. Her heart was hammering almost painfully, as if she had run flat-out until she could run no more and must crouch down, gasping for breath.

Her hand ached. She opened it, stared down at the stone in her palm. It was still pale, milky as a blind eye, but was there something moving in it now? A swirl, down in its depths, like the first rise of smoke from a fire . . . a whisper, in the back of her mind.

Use me.

A sharp rap on her front door. Lin jumped to her feet, flipping the tablecloth across Qasmuna's book to hide it.

"Lin!" A familiar voice. "It's Chana. Mariam—"

Lin flung the door open. Chana Dorin stood at her threshold, her broad face creased with worry.

"It's bad, Lin," she said, in answer to Lin's silent question. "She's been coughing up blood. And her fever—"

"I'm coming." Lin slipped the stone into the pocket of her tunic, caught up her satchel, and stuffed her bare feet into a pair of embroidered slippers Josit had brought her from Hind. She followed Chana out into the night, her heart hammering as they raced through the dark streets of the Sault.

She found Mariam in her bed at the Etse Kebeth, racked with uncontrollable coughing. She held a bloody rag to her mouth, and more rags were littered on the bedspread. She was pale as starched linen, drenched in sweat, but she still managed to glare at Chana.

"You shouldn't—have bothered Lin—I'm fine," she gasped. "I'll be—fine."

Lin clambered onto Mariam's bed, already unbuckling her satchel. "Hush, darling. Don't talk. Chana—tea, with feverfew and willowbark. Quickly."

Once Chana had left, Lin wrapped a shawl around Mariam's shoulders, despite Mariam's coughing protests that she wasn't cold. There were streaks of blood on Mariam's chin and neck, blackish red.

"It's always worse at night," Mariam said, hoarsely. "It . . . goes away."

Lin wanted to scream in anger, though she knew it wasn't Mariam she was angry at. It was the disease. The blood on the rags was flecked with foam: It was coming from deep within Mariam's lungs, carrying air inside it.

"Mari," she said. "How many nights? How long?"

Mariam looked away. Sweat shimmered on the sharp divide of her collarbones. The room smelled of blood and sickness. "Just make me well enough to go to the Festival," she said. "After that . . ."

Lin caught Mariam's thin wrist. Squeezed it gently. "Let me try something," she whispered. "I know I keep saying that. But I think there's a real chance this time."

Some part of her knew it was a terrible thing to keep asking—to keep raising Mariam's hopes and then dashing them. But the voice in her head was louder: *You have the book now. You're so close. She cannot die now.*

Mariam managed a weak smile. "Of course. Anything for you, Linnet."

Lin reached into her pocket and drew out the stone.

Use me.

Holding it lightly in one hand, she placed her other palm over Mariam's heart. She could feel Mariam watching her as she let her mind spin away into that space of smoke and words, where letters and numbers hung shining against the sky like the tails of comets.

Heal, she thought, picturing the word in all its separate components, and then in its completeness, the pieces of *gematry* flying together to form the concept, uncovering the truth of what language had been formed to hide. *Heal, Mariam.*

"Oh!" Mariam's gasp broke the silence, and the shadowy world fled from Lin's vision. Mariam had a hand on Lin's shoulder, and her huge dark eyes were wide. "Lin—it feels different."

"Is the pain gone?" Lin demanded, not daring to hope.

"Not entirely—but it's much less." Mariam took a breath—still a shallow one, but less ragged than before.

Lin reached for her satchel. "Let me examine you."

Mariam nodded. Lin retrieved her auscultor and listened to Mariam's chest—the terrifying clicking and bubbling noises had faded. Lin could still hear a faint wheezing when her friend inhaled deeply, but at least she *could* inhale deeply. Some color had come back to her pale face, too, and the beds of her nails were no longer blue.

"I'm better," Mariam said, when Lin straightened up. "Aren't I? Not healed, but better."

"It really seems like it," Lin whispered. "If I try again, or try differently—I need to look at the books again, but Mari, I think—"

Mariam caught at Lin's hand. "I'm well enough to go to the Tevath, aren't I? However long this lasts?"

Lin bit back an assurance that of course this would last. She could not be sure, and knew she should not raise Mariam's hopes unreasonably. But her own hope felt as if it were pressing against the inside of her chest like a bubble of air. For so long, nothing had worked to help Mariam—to have helped her at all, even just a bit, seemed a reason for optimism.

And more than that. It seemed a reason to believe that all she had done, all the choices she had made with Mariam's healing in mind—perhaps they had been the right ones? She had reached the limit, she knew, of what she could do with the knowledge she'd gleaned. But there was more to be learned from Qasmuna's book . . .

"Lin?" Chana appeared at the door, looking apologetic. "I'm not sure about the tea, Lin, could you look at it—?"

Lin felt a wave of impatience. Chana knew perfectly well how to make willowbark tea. She slipped her brooch into her pocket again and followed the older woman to the kitchen, where a kettle was boiling away on the stove.

"Chana, what—?"

Chana turned to face her. "It's not the tea," she hissed, waving away Lin's question. "I just heard. The Maharam is at your house. With Oren Kandel. They're looking through your things."

"*Now?*" Lin felt faint. She had expected some sort of reaction from the Maharam to Prince Conor's visit, but had been anticipating being called to the Shulamat, or perhaps even waylaid and scolded in the street. For the Maharam to enter an individual home without permission spoke of a situation he believed to be extreme indeed.

"I must go," she gasped, and fled, Chana's worried look following her to the door. Lin raced back through the Sault, cursing herself for not having hidden the Qasmuna more carefully. She could have taken it with her, rather than merely slipping it beneath her tablecloth. She had been foolish, careless. She was shivering with anxiety as she passed through the Kathot, where long tables were already set up in preparation for the Festival tomorrow night. Silver braziers of incense hung from the trees, and the air was redolent with the smell of spices.

When she reached her house, she saw that the front door was flung open, yellow lamplight spilling out into the street. Shadows moved against the fabric of her curtains. She raced inside, only to feel her heart tumble into her slippers.

It was as she had feared. The Maharam stood by her kitchen table, from which the cloth had been removed. Oren Kandel stood beside him, looking smug; his smile widened when Lin came into the room.

Laid out on the table, like a body ready for the autopsy knife, were all her books—Qasmuna's tome, of course, and the pages the Ragpicker King had given her. Even the scatter of mostly useless books on medicine and spells she had bought long ago in the market, or at Lafont's, were there—everything she had collected in the desperate hope she would find answers among their pages.

Lin lifted her chin. "*Zuchan*," she said. The formal term for a Maharam; it meant He Who Communicates the Word. "This is an honor. To what do I owe this visit?"

The Maharam struck the floor with his staff, nearly making Lin flinch. "You must think me quite an old fool," he said coldly. Lin had never seen him look like this: the rage on his face, the *disgust*. This was the man who had sentenced his own son to exile for his studies into the forbidden. Lin felt a small sliver of ice lodge in her spine. "The Prince of Castellane comes marching into our Sault, our sacred place, because *you* invited him—"

"I never invited him," Lin protested. "He came of his own accord."

The Maharam only shook his head. "Your grandfather, as much bad as there is to say about the man, has never made the denizens of the Palace feel that they are entitled to enter here. The Crown Prince of Castellane would hardly have come marching up to your door had you not let him think he was welcome to do so."

"I did *not*—"

"How long has he been giving you books?" the Maharam snapped. The rage in his voice was a pure flame; Oren seemed to be lapping it up, like a cat with spilled milk. "You came to me, asking to see the books in the Shulamat, but you were not satisfied with my answer, is that it? So you went behind my back, in defiance of the Law?"

"The Law?" Lin's voice shook. "The Law says that above all things, life matters. The life of our people matters, for if we were gone, who then would remember Adassa? Who would open the door for the Goddess to return?"

The Maharam gazed at her coldly. "You say those words, but have no idea what they mean."

"I know what they mean to a physician," said Lin. "If we are offered the means to save a human life, we must seize it."

"You speak of the Law? You, who have never cared about it?" said the Maharam, and for a moment, Lin saw a flash of the dislike he held for Mayesh, and knew that he hated her in part for that. For being her grandfather's blood. For, like Mayesh, finding the Sault too small for her desires, her dreams. "These books will be confiscated. And when the Sanhedrin comes, this matter will be put directly before the Exilarch—"

"*Zuchan*," said Oren, hoarsely, and Lin turned to see Mayesh ducking through the low doorway. She wondered if he had just returned from Marivent; he was in his Counselor's robes, his medallion shining on his chest. The lamplight carved deep shadows under his eyes.

"The Exilarch?" he said, mildly enough. "That seems extreme, Davit, for what amounts to no more than a misunderstanding."

The Maharam looked at him with loathing. "A *misunderstanding*?" He swept a hand toward the books on the table; Lin saw her grandfather's gaze flick from Qasmuna's book to the Maharam, an odd expression flashing across his face. "At least one of these dates to the time of the Sundering. The Goddess alone knows what sort of forbidden magic it details—"

"I doubt Lin has even had time to peruse it," said Mayesh. He was utterly calm. Calm as his job had trained him to be, calm in the face of crises through five decades of serving the Palace. "It is, as I said, a misunderstanding. I brought her to Marivent to consult on a medical matter, as you know, and the Prince, in his gratitude, took this volume from the Palace library and decided to make a gift of it. He believed it a medical tome she might enjoy. A mistake was made, but not intended; I cannot imagine you, Maharam, would think it wise to throw that error back in his face by punishing the very one he meant to honor."

The Maharam's mouth worked. "He is not *our prince*," he said. "Our prince is the Exilarch, Amon Benjudah. Conor Aurelian has no authority here."

"But outside these walls, he does," said Mayesh. "And outside these walls is all the world. There was a Sault in Malgasi, you know. Queen Iren Belmany knocked down the walls and seized the Ashkar inside. By the word of the Law, it may be true that House Aurelian has no authority here. But in practice, those in power can do what they like to us."

His eyes bored into the Maharam's; Lin could not help but feel that there was some communication here that she and Oren were not privy to; that more than the present moment was under discussion.

"Then what do you recommend, *Counselor*?" said the Maharam, finally. "She keeps these books, and the Law goes begging for justice?"

"Not at all. The books shall be confiscated, and reviewed when the Sanhedrin comes, if you like. Lin won't care. She never asked for the book in the first place." Mayesh turned to Lin, and the meaning in his eyes was unmistakable. "You don't mind, do you?"

Lin swallowed. *Blood on the rags on Mariam's bed, streaks of blood on her hands.* Then Mariam telling her the pain was better. What she had done had not fixed Mariam forever; she knew that. But with only a few hours' reading of Qasmuna's book, she had done something she had never managed before—she had *helped* Mariam, using magic. To give up that chance now was more bitter than the taste of blood.

But she knew what had to be said.

"No," she whispered. "I—don't mind."

There was a moment of silence. Finally, the Maharam nodded. "The Law is satisfied."

"That's *all*?" Oren cried. "You're just going to take these stupid books away from her? Isn't she going to be punished? *Exiled?*"

"Now, now, young man," Mayesh said. "Don't overexcite your-self. The Maharam has spoken."

"But—"

"She is young, Oren," said the Maharam. "She will learn better. The Law can be merciful, too."

Merciful, Lin thought, bitterly, as the Maharam directed Oren to gather up her books. They seemed a pitifully small pile in the end, as Oren, glaring furiously, marched out the door with them. The Maharam lingered a moment longer before he, too, departed.

Lin sank down in a kitchen chair, all the strength gone from her legs. She was trembling suddenly, her body shaking with frustra-tion. It was unfair, so very unfair—

"That could have been much worse, Lin," said Mayesh. "Had I not been here, had the Maharam not been in a generous mood—"

"A *generous* mood?" Lin flared. "That was generous?"

"For him. He has a special hatred for this sort of thing, even the hint of interest in medicine that is not Ashkari medicine. And as for magic, the study of it"—he shook his head—"he would never have let you keep those books, and he might have done worse."

"We are supposed to save lives," Lin whispered. "How is that something he does not understand?"

"He understands it well enough," said Mayesh. "In his mind, he is weighing the life of one against the lives of many. If the *malbushim* thought we were practicing forbidden lore—"

"It is the Prince of the *malbushim* who gave me the book in the first place!"

"Do you think Conor had the slightest idea what it was he was giving you?" Mayesh said. He did not sound angry, only tired. "I assure you, he has never given this sort of thing any thought; he has never had to. You refused the first thing he of-fered, so he wanted to offer something he did not think you could reject. It was a challenge, and he wanted to win it. He does not like to lose."

Lin stared at her grandfather. "You know him so well," she said.

"I suppose that is because you spent every day of his childhood with him, as you did not with me, or with Josit."

It was a low blow, she knew. He did not flinch, but his eyes darkened. "Conor Aurelian is dangerous," he said, heading for the door. He turned on the threshold to look back at her. "In ways that he does not even understand, he is dangerous. You were right to refuse the first gift he offered you. You should have refused this one, as well."

When the battle was done, and victory secured with blood, the people of Aram fell to their knees in thanks. And before them appeared a white doe, and spoke to them in the voice of Adassa:

"Once, in another land, I was your Queen, but now I am your Goddess. You are my people. You will no longer be Aramites. Instead, you will be known as the Ashkar: the people who wait. For there will come a time when the Ashkar will be needed. You must be preserved, you must continue, until that day. You must become a people of all nations, so that if one community of Ashkar is destroyed, the others shall survive. You must be everywhere, though none of these places will be home."

"But what of you, O Goddess?" cried Makabi. "Where will you be?"

"I will be all around you and with you, my hand on your shoulder to guide you, and my light to lead you. And one day, when the time has come, I will return to you clothed in the flesh of a woman of the Ashkari people. I will be once again your Queen, and we will rise in peace and glory."

And then the Goddess ascended into the heavens, and as she went, she took Makabi's hand and brought him with her, and she gave his sword to his son and named him Benjudah, son of Judah, the next Exilarch. All Exilarchs from that day forth would be descended from Makabi, and would carry the name Benjudah and the Evening Sword, the gift of the Goddess.

Thus dawned the new age of the Ashkar.

—Book of Makabi

CHAPTER TWENTY-FOUR

Lin stared stonily at the wall as Chana Dorin helped lace her into her Festival dress. Her eyes burned from sleeplessness, but she had not cried. Not even after Mayesh had left the night before and she had been alone in her house. Not even when she looked at the few dusty bits of old paper that were all that remained of Qasmuna's book. Not even through the long hours of the night when she blamed herself. How stupid had she been, imagining the Prince's visit would go unremarked? That the Maharam would not investigate? That Oren would not have spied on her?

She had tried again to create a spark within the stone, using her own visualization and energy. It had not worked. The stone had flickered only dully, and she had exhausted herself badly enough that she had fallen asleep with her head on the kitchen table.

While she slept, she dreamed. The dream was vivid, as had been all her dreams since the stone came into her possession, but for a change she did not dream about the tower and the desert, the last battle of Aram. Instead she dreamed of the harbor of Castellane and the sky over it painted with white fire. And in her mind, she heard Ciprian Cabrol's words, though not spoken in his voice:

I need them to see my vengeance written in fire across the sky. The harbor will shine as though the lights of the Gods have returned. As though their magic still burns across the waters.

When she woke at dawn, her eyes felt as if sand had been poured into them. As she went to splash water on her face, she thought of Mariam, of the Maharam, and of her dream. The beginning of an idea had taken root inside her mind. Perhaps there might be a way to get Qasmuna's book back after all.

"Stop it," Chana said now, her hands moving efficiently in Lin's hair. "I can hear you scheming."

"As can I," agreed Mariam. She was sitting on her bed in her shift, her dress thrown over the footboard. When Chana was done with Lin, she would begin on Mariam: lacing her dress, braiding her hair into an elaborate, flowery coil. These were the things Lin and Mariam's mothers would have done for them before the Goddess Festival, if they had had mothers. Chana had stepped in to fill that gap years before, as she had filled so many. "It is not your fault, Lin. I'd like to tell the Maharam *exactly* what I think of him, taking your books like that. But tonight is the Festival, and we cannot let him ruin our fun."

She broke into a cough and Lin whirled anxiously. She had arrived at the Etse Kebeth at first light to see Mariam, who, to her relief, had slept through the night and was feeling much better. "Good days and bad days," Chana had muttered as she let Lin into the house. "This is one of the good ones, praise the Name."

Mariam waved off her anxiety. "I'm all *right*," she protested, and indeed, she did look better than she had in some time. Lin knew why—and only prayed the effect of the small magic she had done would last Mariam at least through the night and into tomorrow. "Just angry. The Maharam would never have done this to one of the male physicians."

Lin had only told Chana and Mariam what she had to, that the Maharam had confiscated a number of her medical books that came from foreign lands. By the direct word of the Law, it *was* forbidden to study non-Ashkari magic, but Mariam was right in saying that it was a Law that was largely disregarded. Would the Maharam have taken all the rest of her volumes had he not been so angry about Qasmuna's book? She could not say, but her anger sat inside her belly, cold and hard. Anger . . . and a resolve that was growing every moment. The Maharam had insisted she attend the Tevath, after all. And attend she would, in the full spirit of the occasion.

"There." Chana patted her hair. "You look nice."

Lin glanced at herself in the mirror—the same reflection she had seen yearly since she had turned sixteen: a girl in a blue dress, her red hair coiled into a long thick braid, apple blossoms artfully woven in among the plaits so that they appeared to grow there naturally. She would draw those flowers from her hair, one by one, during the Goddess Dance, and fling them to the ground until she and every other girl present danced on a carpet of petals.

"My turn." Mariam got out of bed, smiling. As she took Lin's place in front of the mirror, there was a knock on the door. It was Arelle Dorin, younger sister of Rahel. She was already in her blue Festival dress, her hair half braided, her cheeks flushed with excitement.

"Mez says there's a patient of yours at the gates," she said to Lin. "Seems like it's important. Here, don't forget to take one of these with you," she added, handing over a sachet of herbs on a slim blue ribbon. "You made them, after all!"

Promising Chana and Mariam she'd be back shortly, Lin set out for the Sault gates. The day was bright and warm, the wind blowing toward the sea. It carried with it the scent of flowers. They were everywhere in the Sault: roses in baskets hanging from tree branches and windows, lilies woven into wreaths pinned to doors. The Kathot would be even more spectacular with blossoms, but Lin avoided it: Maidens were not meant to enter the square on Festival day until the sun had set.

There were more flowers at the gates. Lilies and roses, as was customary (for the Goddess had said, *I am the rose, and the lily of the valleys*), as well as flowers that grew naturally in Castellane: bright lantana and dull-purple lavender. Mez wore a wreath of fig leaves in his hair and grinned at Lin as she approached.

"Don't know who it is," he said, pointing. "They won't get out of their carriage."

It was a plain gray barouche, the kind of conveyance one could hire if one had a little money to spend, but not enough to purchase a carriage of one's own. The driver was a bored-looking old man who didn't raise an eyebrow as Lin, in all her finery, strode up to knock on the carriage door.

It opened just a little, only enough for Lin to see who was waiting for her. A moment later, she had flung herself into the carriage, slamming the door shut behind her.

"You," she whispered. "What are you doing here? Haven't you got a banquet to go to?"

Conor Aurelian raised his eyebrows. "Not until tonight," he said. "Do you only own that one dress?"

"Did you only have one copy of that book you gave me?" Lin snapped back.

Conor, who had been slumped in a corner of the carriage, sat up, looking at her with what seemed to be genuine puzzlement. He was as plainly dressed as she'd ever seen him, in gray trousers and a black linen jacket with frogged silver clasps up and down the front. He wore no circlet, no crown; he could have been any merchant's son, if he had not had one of the most recognizable faces in Castellane.

"You're dissatisfied with the book?" He was frowning a little. He rubbed at his neck, and she realized he was wearing none of his usual rings. She could see the shape of his fingers, long and delicate, his palms lightly callused. Couldn't *anything* about him be ugly? "You said it was what you were looking for—"

"I'm not dissatisfied with the book." She took a deep breath. "Today, your Ascension Day, is also an important day for my people. It is the day of our Goddess Festival. I should not be here with you; I should be in the Sault. So if you please, Monseigneur—why are you here? Is there something you require from me?"

He sat up straight. Leaned toward her. His gaze flicked down, briefly; he must have noticed how hard she was breathing. As if she'd run a mile. He said, "I wish to consult with you. As a physician. As someone who I know can be trusted to keep a secret."

A weariness went through Lin. More concealments, she thought, more secrets she could not tell to Mariam, or to anyone in the Sault. And there was no concern for the weight of them on her, or what they might cost her. She was only a useful tool: a physician who would not, could not, speak. "You are ill?" she said.

He shook his head. There were shadows under his eyes, dark as the linen he wore. They made her think of candlelight and poetry, of long nights spent studying old books, though she knew better. He was probably hung over.

"What do you believe madness is?" he said. "Is it a question of illness, or is it, as the Castellani believe, a weakness or corruption in the blood? Is there such a thing as a medicine that might treat it?"

Lin hesitated. "There could be," she said. "I do not believe madness, as you call it, is corruption. Often it is a wound borne by an injured mind. Sometimes it is indeed an illness. The mind can be sick just as the body can. But medication—I have never heard of treating an illness of the mind with medicine."

"But there might be something in all those books of yours," he said. "All those volumes the Ashkar have, that we lack access to—"

All those books of yours. It was as if the freezing-cold ball of anger in her belly was melting in his presence, sending icy slivers of unthinking rage through her veins.

"I have no books," she said.

He flushed, his eyes darkening to pewter. "Do not toy with me," he said. "What I am asking of you, it is important."

"Is someone dying?" Lin said. "Are they desperately ill?"

"No, but—"

"Then it will wait for another day." Lin reached for the carriage door.

"Stop." He sounded furious. "Lin Caster—"

She whirled on him. "Are you giving me a royal order to stay and speak with you about whatever you wish to discuss? Regardless of my duties, my responsibilities?" *My only and single chance to take back what is mine?* "Is that what this is?"

"Do I need to?" he said, in a voice as dark as bitter syrup. "After I gave you that book? Are you really so ungrateful?"

Lin looked at her hand, where it rested on the carriage door handle. She felt detached from it, as if it did not belong to her. As if she were looking at her own body from the outside. She said flatly, "That book. Yes, you brought it to me. You walked into the Sault with a bevy of Castelguards, making sure to attract as much attention as possible, making sure every eye would be on you, and you brought it to me."

"It was an honor," he said. There was something in his voice she could not identify. It was not anger, which she would have expected, but something else again. "I was honoring you. As your prince—"

"All these years you have known my grandfather," she said, "and still you do not see or understand his people. You are not *my* prince. You are the Prince of Castellane. A city I do not live in—a city I am *forbidden* to live in, save I keep myself walled off from it. You came into the one part of Castellane in which I am at home, and you brought the worst kind of attention upon me. You could simply have had a messenger deliver that book, but no, you had to show off, prove that you were being gracious to someone so far below you." Her voice shook. "And the moment you left, the Maharam came and took the book from me and confiscated it, because it came from *you*. And now—"

She stopped before she could say *And now I will lose Mariam. Unless . . .* The tears that had not come the night before were threatening now, her eyes burning painfully, but she would not cry in front of him. She would not.

She reached for the handle of the carriage door and tugged on it. To her horror, it stuck. She felt herself freeze as he reached around her, his gloved hand sliding over hers as he grasped the handle. She could feel the strength in him, the lean arch of his body.

He had not moved to open the door. She was in the circle of his arm: She could feel the rough softness of his linen jacket against her. Feel him breathing in short, caught breaths. He wanted to touch her, she knew. She could not help but remember kissing him at the Roverge mansion; even now, in the depths of her rage and despair, she knew that whoever had interrupted them had been all that had prevented her from doing anything he wanted that night. She had wanted it, too.

"I thought," she whispered, "that you were going to forget me. Forget all about me."

"I can't." His voice sounded as if it were being pulled taut. "A malady. Which is ironic, since you are a physician. If you had medicine that could make me forget you—"

"No such thing exists," she said.

"Then I am cursed," he said, "to think only of you. You, who think I am a loathsome person. A vain monster who could not resist showing off, and in doing so, has made you wretched."

Lin stared at the carriage door handle. It appeared to be growing and shrinking in size, as her vision blurred. "I think you are a broken person," she whispered. "Since you have been given whatever you wanted, all of your life, and never been told no, I don't see how you could have been anything else. I suppose it is not your fault."

There was a short silence. He withdrew his arm from around her, moving stiffly, as if he were recovering from an injury.

"Get out," he said.

She fumbled for the door handle, nearly falling when the carriage door swung open. She tumbled out into the street, and heard him call out, hoarsely—but he was only shouting to the carriage driver. The carriage lurched off, the unlocked door swinging. A hand emerged, caught the door, slammed it shut; the carriage vanished into the traffic on the Great Southwestern Road.

Heart hammering, Lin made her way back to the gates, where Mez was waiting. He looked at her in concern. "You're awfully pale," he said. "Someone really ill?"

"Yes," Lin said, her voice seeming to echo, some distance from where she was. "But they've been ill a long time, I think."

"Well, don't let it ruin the Festival for you," he said, kindly, and tapped at his forehead. "I nearly forgot. You're popular today, Caster. Someone left this note for you, earlier."

He handed over a folded sheet of vellum, sealed with wax. She thanked him and walked away, running a thumb under the seal to break it. When she opened the note, she saw familiar, cramped handwriting. The Ragpicker King's.

Remember, stay away from the harbor this midnight. You never know where a stray spark might land.—A. M.

She crumpled the note in her hand. She had not forgotten about Ciprian Cabrol's black powder. It was time to send a note back to the Ragpicker King, telling him that she had acquired Qasmuna's book, and though it had been taken from her, she now had a plan to get it back.

When Kel woke up, Conor was not in his bed. This was unusual, as Kel was almost always the earlier riser. Still, he had had a restless night, tossing back and forth as he woke over and over from dreams of Fausten's screams, and red blood spreading across the surface of the ocean.

It was already nearly afternoon, and a quick look out the window told Kel that preparations for the evening's festivities were well under way. He frowned—tailors, boot-makers, jewelers, and the like would all be arriving shortly to make sure Conor would be impeccably turned out. As much as Conor might not be looking forward to the banquet, he would be unlikely to miss having every stitch of his attire fussed over. Frowning, Kel threw on clothes and went in search of the Prince.

He looked first in Conor's favored hiding places—Asti's stable, the Palace library, the Night Garden—but found no trace of him. As he wandered, preparations for the banquet went on around him. The trees were draped in yards of blue and scarlet fabric, and lanterns in the shapes of apples, cherries, and figs dangled from their branches, waiting to be lit at nightfall. Waggons rolled by, piled with ceramic plates, silver vases, and what looked to Kel alarmingly like whole trees. The doors to the Shining Gallery had been flung open, and servants raced back and forth from the kitchens and the storerooms, carrying everything from piles of green silk to what appeared to be a life-sized jaguar carved from sugar pastry.

So he returned to his bedchamber. Later, he would wish he had kept wandering around the grounds, possibly until the next day, but by the time he stepped through the door it was already too late. Conor's closets had been torn open, and his clothes scattered on the floor. Queen Lilibet was pacing back and forth, stepping occasionally on an embroidered waistcoat or fur-trimmed hat, keeping up a stream of curses in Marakandi. Mayesh had stationed himself at the window, his lined face more haggard than usual.

Both started at the sight of Kel, their faces momentarily eager before relaxing in disappointment.

"It's *you*," Lilibet said, marching across the room toward him. "I don't suppose you have an explanation for this?"

She thrust out a folded note. This, Kel knew, could not be good. He took the paper with a feeling of deep foreboding and unfolded it to see Conor's familiar spiky hand slashing across the page. He read:

Dear Mother,

I have decided not to attend the welcoming banquet this evening. I wish to reassure you that I have thought deeply about the issue, and the many very good reasons I ought to attend. Please do not imagine it an ill-considered decision when I say that I will not be attending because, frankly, I do not want to. I leave it in your capable hands to manage my absence. If it will trouble you, I suggest you cancel the banquet. If not, it is my opinion the banquet could be held perfectly well without me. If you really consider it, this entire engagement and wedding could proceed perfectly well without me there, to say nothing of the marriage. My part could as easily be played by an empty chair.

If you demand to find me, I will be in the Temple District. I have heard that they occasionally throw orgies, and while I have never attended one, I find myself suddenly curious. If nothing else, it should be an education in how to manage a party involving a large number of guests.

All best, yours, etc, etc,
C.

"Gray *hell*," Kel said, forgetting not to swear in front of the Queen. "He's serious?"

Lilibet snatched the note from his hand. "Don't pretend as if you didn't know," she snapped. "Conor tells you everything; surely he would have mentioned *this*. I'm sure he thought it was the wittiest sort of joke, that stupid boy—"

"No," Kel said. For all the bite to Conor's letter, there was nothing about it that made Kel think it had been penned by someone who was amused to be writing it. It was bleak, no doubt informed by the knowledge of Fausten's death, not that Kel could say that. "I do not believe there is any chance Conor imagines this a joke."

Lilibet pressed her lips into a thin line. She looked to Mayesh, who was gazing at Kel, his eyes seeming to bore into him in a way the Queen's had not. "*Think*, Kel," he said, his deep voice gruff. "Something must have happened, to so affect Conor's attitude, and so suddenly—"

Surely he cannot want me to say it, Kel thought. To mention the execution of Fausten, carried out by the King's own hand. *But he must imagine I know nothing of it, unless Jolivet told him I was there. Jolivet saw me—*

"Counselor. My lady," Kel said. "The Prince has been miserable. Of *course* he has been miserable. That ought not to be a surprise to either of you." He looked to Lilibet, who glanced away, her right hand toying with the emeralds at her throat. "But he has been *resigned,* not rebellious. I cannot speak to what is in that letter. I do not understand this sudden change. Only that he must be unhappier than we have all thought." He spread his hands wide; he was only telling the truth. He did not know where Conor had gone, or why. "I blame myself."

Lilibet muttered something that sounded very like, *I blame you, too.*

"Leave him be, my lady," said Mayesh. "Kel is the Prince's Sword Catcher, not the guard of his emotions."

Lilibet had started pacing again. She wore a dress of dark-green velvet, to match the emeralds at her throat; her black hair was lacquered into coils. "I am sure he thinks me very cold," she said, half to herself. "As if I would want my own son to be in despair; I could never want that. If I could have shielded him from the consequences of this mistake . . ." She glanced at Mayesh. "The King must not know. About tonight. He will not be at the banquet, but still."

Her tone was brittle. Kel thought of the King lifting Fausten over his head, as easily as if he were a bag of feathers. Thought of the blood in the water, the slick green slide of the crocodile beneath the waves.

"It would be preferable," said Mayesh, "if no one outside this room knew. Which means we cannot postpone the banquet. Sarthe would take it as an insult if we did, besides."

"You could say Conor was ill," Kel suggested. "Surely they would have to accept—"

"They would not believe it," said Mayesh. "They are already very much on edge. The Roverges' display the other night did not help."

"Much as I'd like them to take that ridiculous child and go

home, it would mean severing the last amiable ties we have with Sarthe," said Lilibet. "If they wished, they could harry us at will at the Narrow Pass, cut off half our trade, murder our people—"

"That will not happen," said Mayesh. "The evening's plans will go on, with Conor in attendance." His gaze rested on Kel, who had guessed, the moment that Mayesh said the banquet could not be postponed, what would happen. He could have protested, he knew; he also knew it would make no difference if he did. "My lady, let us ready the attendants. Kel, fetch your talisman; we have only a little while to get you ready."

It had been a long time since Kel had taken Conor's place at a Court event—years, he thought—but there was, at least, a rhythm to the pantomime. Kel let himself fall into it, even as his thoughts raced.

He went to the tepidarium first, where he scrubbed his body with handfuls of flaked lavender soap, and used the strigil to shave himself clean. (Conor would never appear anywhere in public with even the shadow of a beard.)

When Kel emerged, stripped down to nothing but the talisman at his throat such that he appeared a perfectly naked Conor in truth, the Prince's attendants had been summoned and now swarmed around him like fashionable bees. His hair was dried, curled, and perfumed, his hands rubbed with scented lotion. He stepped into the clothes held up for him: a shirt of bleached cambric, the sleeves wrapped with gold thread, with a cuff of gold embroidery around the neck. A hip-length black velvet doublet with bands of gold brocade, trousers of the same material, and tooled-leather boots. An overrobe of gold brocade, lined with the fur of white lynxes. A ring on each hand, set with jewels the size of plover's eggs: an emerald on his left, a ruby on his right. Lastly, the Prince's circlet was set on his head: a plain gold band that always left a mark across Kel's brow when it was removed at the end of the day.

His talisman remained, tucked down under the neck of his shirt, now invisible even to those who knew he was wearing it.

Their task complete, the attendants melted away like ships vanishing at the horizon, and were replaced by a somber Mayesh. Kel gazed at the Counselor wearily. Mayesh wore Ashkari gray, but his tunic was silk, belted with silver, and a heavy silver Court medallion hung around his neck.

He nodded curtly at Kel. "You're ready, then?"

Kel nodded. The city clock had already chimed seven, but Conor was expected to be late; it would not matter. He followed Mayesh into the hall and through the corridors of the tower into the passages underground that connected the various sections of the Palace.

Only now did he let himself wonder: Where *was* Conor? He'd told the Queen that Conor had been gritting his teeth through the last few days, and that was true, but he could think of nothing that would have made it so much worse, to drive him into the city. There were parts of Conor where he could be hurt, chinks in his armor where he could be wounded, but he could not fathom what could have hurt him so terribly as to drive him from Marivent at such a significant time. He must know that though the Queen would be furious, it would make no difference in the end; his absence would be patched over, and the marriage would go on, unstoppable as weather or taxes.

They emerged into the small room that had struck ten-year-old Kel as so wondrously full of books. It was familiar now, unremarkable. There were far more books in the West Tower library.

Kel could hear the dull roar of the party through the golden doors that led to the Shining Gallery. He moved toward the doors, only to be stopped by Mayesh with a hand on his arm. "Let me see your talisman," he said, and looped a finger below the chain, drawing it out from under Kel's shirt. He ran a finger over the etched numbers and letters, murmuring under his breath in Ashkar. Kel did not know the words, but he had heard Lin murmur something similar over him, that night he had nearly died. A prayer for safe-keeping, or luck?

Mayesh tucked the talisman back under Kel's collar, and said, "I know you are worried for him." As always there could be only one *him*. "Set it aside, for now. You can help him best that way."

Kel nodded. His heart was beating hard; he could feel it in his fingertips, that sense of anticipatory tension he felt every time he faced the world as Conor. The last time it had been on the steps of the Convocat, with the crowd roaring for him. He wondered if this was what soldiers felt, the moment before stepping onto the field of battle: a mix of fear and a strange exhilaration?

Except his battlefield was the floor of the Shining Gallery, his foes any who might doubt that he was Conor. His strengths were not blades or *couleuvrines*, but pretense and careful obfuscation. Conor was not here, but he paused for a moment at the door as the guards announced him, his hand on the lintel, and spoke the words of the ritual silently in his mind.

I am the Prince's shield. I am his unbreakable armor. I bleed that he might not bleed. I suffer that he might never suffer. I die that he might live forever.

Only Conor was not here to say: *But you will not die.*

Perhaps that was the reason that a sense of wrongness clung to Kel, like a spiderweb to his shoe, as he stepped into the Shining Gallery. He was aware of Mayesh, not far away, moving into the crowd toward the Queen; he was aware of the noise of the party, a roar of heightened chatter mixed with the tap of boots on marble and the clinking of glasses.

There was no *reason* for Kel to feel a sense of wrongness, at least none that he could see. He smiled automatically as the musicians in the gallery—a wide balcony of carved wood reached by a flight of marble stairs in the corner of the room—greeted his entry with a flourish of harp and violin.

He realized now why he'd seen waggons carrying trees across the Palace courtyards; Lilibet had transformed the center of the

Shining Gallery into the secret heart of a forest. An irony, Kel thought, as no such forest grew in Castellane, nor among Marakand's deserts and mountains. And yet it was such a forest as anyone might recognize immediately: the heart of an old tale of princesses and huntsmen—a place of curling leaves, strange flowers, and the harp-song of birds.

Living trees had been arranged throughout the room, their trunks and branches painted with lacquer until they shone like the polished goldenwood floor. The red apples that dangled from the trees were carved garnets; the berries that grew among the thickets of greenery artistically arranged about the room were lapis and onyx. The leaves that scattered the floor were green silk. Animals had been cunningly crafted of sugar *pastillage*, colored with royal icing—white ermine scampered among the leaves, sugar birds perched among the boughs, and a leopard, native to the island kingdom of Kutani, gazed from the shadows with eyes carved from jasper.

At the far end of the room, where the forest ended, the great carved table had been restored to its accustomed dais. It was empty, save for old Gremont—sitting wearily in a low chair—and, near the head of the table, Princess Luisa. Beside her was Vienne d'Este.

Apparently the Sarthians had decided not to risk Luisa mingling with the party guests. Dressed in white lace, her hair tied back with a ribbon, she was whispering to Vienne, who was no longer wearing the clothes of the Black Guard, but a simple dress of gray silk with pinked sleeves, through which silver-threaded linen was visible. Her hair was unbound, a riot of chestnut curls. She seemed to see Kel looking at her across the room and shot him a glare; it startled him for a moment until he recalled that she thought he was Conor.

He grinned at her; it was what Conor would have done. Luisa, glancing up, caught the tail end of the grin and smiled happily. Down the table from her, old Gremont snorted and settled more comfortably into his chair. For a moment, Kel seemed to hear Andreyen Morettus whispering in his ear: *But the Council are not loyal, are they? Not save where it is expedient. Merren always keeps an eye on old Gremont; it seems he's been attending a number of shady meetings in the Maze district.*

Though it was hard to picture Gremont in the Maze district, or at a suspicious meeting. Especially when it came to staying awake for one. He wondered if Merren's understandable obsession with the Gremont family was prejudicing the Ragpicker King. Gremont did not seem a credible threat, especially when compared with many of the other Council members—Sardou, Roverge . . . Alleyne.

He looked then for Antonetta. He did not know when she had become one of the first people he searched for when he entered a room, only that it had somehow happened. Nor did he have any trouble finding her in the Gallery: His eyes snapped to her as if he had been trained to discover her among crowds, the way he had in fact been trained to see the gleam of weapons, the shift of a suspicious movement.

She stood beneath the shadow of a tree that was hung with golden berries. Her dress, too, was gold, as were her high-heeled slippers. She was not wearing her locket.

His heart seemed to tighten under the layers of velvet and brocade that protected it. She *always* wore the locket. Where was it, and why had she chosen to leave it off? He desperately wanted to ask, but knew he could not. Conor would not have noticed the locket or the fact that it was missing: not because he was not observant in general, but because he spared little thought for Antonetta.

As for Antonetta, she looked, unusually for her, desperately sad. When she raised her eyes and looked at him directly, he saw a sort of relief in her gaze, and something that felt like a shared secret that passed between them.

His heart lifted, and fell again. It was not him she was sharing this secret with; she thought he was Conor. But what kind of secret could Conor have with Antonetta?

A crowd passed in front of him, cutting off his view of Antonetta.

It was Lilibet and the entourage currently following her. Dripping wit and jewels, she was charming House Uzec, House Cazalet, House Raspail, and House Sardou with equal enthusiasm.

Kel knew his duty—or at least Conor's duty. He flung himself into the flock of nobles, engaging with them as Lilibet did: asking Esteve about a team of horses he had just purchased, soliciting Uzec's advice on what wine might be served at next season's Solstice Ball, and listening to Benedict Roverge extol the virtues of his fleet of dye-ships, currently berthed in Castellane's harbor.

Kel was conscious of the Queen's eyes on him even as she went to speak with Jolivet, who wore his full Court uniform of red and gold, a sash of gold braid across his chest. He stood before a painted silk screen, which was no accident. Lilibet never liked shows of military force at celebrations; she felt it broke the mood of revelry. But the Legate insisted there be guards present. They had compromised. The Castelguard, when in attendance, remained concealed behind a screen, through which they watched the festivities unfold. Kel hoped someone brought them food on occasion.

"My Prince. Your mother has outdone herself with these decorations." It was Lady Alleyne, swathed in silvery silk, a moon to her daughter's sun. Was Liorada now following Antonetta's fashions? Interesting, if so.

"Thank you, doyenne." Kel bowed. "Though you should be telling her; she never tires of praise for her skills."

"If one is skilled, one should be praised for it." Lady Alleyne smiled, but her eyes were hard as the carved leopard's. She leaned toward Kel, her voice conspiratorial. "Congratulations on the happy event to come."

Which meant: *I see you are getting married, and not to my daughter. My resentment will be undying and evergreen.*

"Yes, congratulations," said Antonetta, who had come up to join her mother. She carried a glass of pale-yellow wine in one hand, and her dark-gold hair curled down her pale throat to meet the deeper-gold silk of her dress. She smiled at Kel, though it did not reach her eyes. "Monseigneur Conor—is Kel Anjuman here this night, by any chance?"

Kel was glad he himself had not been drinking wine; he would have choked on it. "I am quite sure he's here somewhere," he said. "I do have a difficult time keeping track of him."

"He's quite popular, you know, with many of the young ladies of the Hill," said Antonetta. "And some of the young men as well."

"*Is* he?" Lady Alleyne looked mildly intrigued—and, somewhat insultingly, surprised.

"I have heard his skills in the bedchamber are unparalleled," said Antonetta, her eyes gleaming with amusement.

Kel felt himself blush, followed by an acute sense of horror. Conor would never blush. He hoped the dim lighting hid the color. *Think about something else*, he told himself. *Picture something calming.* But his boat on the sea, with the blue water all around, would not come.

"Antonetta, *honestly*," exclaimed Lady Alleyne, looking scandalized.

"I *am* sorry," Antonetta said contritely. "I do say the silliest things! I've no idea why. Monseigneur, Lord Falconet had sent me to ask if you could come and speak with him. I know there is little time before the banquet begins, but he seemed eager to talk to you."

Kel looked across the room but did not spot Joss. "Where is he, then?"

"Somewhere in the make-believe forest, I believe," Antonetta said. "I will take you to him."

Kel knew that if it had been someone other than who he was pretending to be, Lady Alleyne would have protested; as it was, she looked annoyed that her daughter was doing a favor for Falconet. But she could not object, as it was also a favor for the Prince. She simply watched the two of them, narrow-eyed, as Antonetta led Kel among the lacquered trees. Gold and greenery pressed in around them until the Shining Gallery itself seemed to disappear, and they had wandered, like the protagonists of a Story-Spinner tale, into the heart of the forest.

Kel knew only a few layers of trees hid them from view, yet it felt surprisingly real: The floor was marble and not dirt, the fallen leaves cut from silk, and the birds perched among the branches were sugar and clockwork, but the sap that ran down the trunks of the trees was real, and scented like resin. He even thought he caught sight of a real bird's nest, no doubt transported by accident, perched high in the boughs above.

Antonetta leaned back against the lacquered trunk of an oak tree and looked up at him. At Kel—no, he thought; she was looking at Conor. The look on her face was for Conor. "I did not lie," she said. "Joss does wish to speak to you. Only I wished to speak to you first, and in private."

"It couldn't wait?" Kel was used to putting on Conor's haughtiness like a cloak; but now, with Antonetta, the cloak seemed ill fitting. Cinched so tightly at the throat that it was difficult to breathe.

Her eyebrows drew together questioningly. "Did you not get my message?"

Kel tensed. If Conor had gotten a message from Antonetta, he had not mentioned it. "I don't recall," he drawled, hating himself a little. "I get so many messages."

If he had thought she would look hurt, he was surprised; she merely looked annoyed. "Conor. It was important."

He took a step closer to her. Something seemed different about her. She wasn't flirting, he realized, or using the smile that was like an arrow in his heart. She was looking at him—at Conor—directly and steadily, with a clarity tinged with frustration.

For a wild moment, he thought, *Does she know it's me?* He had never wondered that before when disguised as Conor, or at least not for many years. No one saw past the illusion. No one cared to. He had relaxed into the truth that people saw what they wanted to see.

But the clarity of Antonetta's gaze undid him. She looked at him as if she knew him down to his bones, and he wished, knowing as he did so how dangerous it would be if that wish came true, that she did. That she would say, *Kellian*, and tell him she had recognized him the first moment she had seen him. Perhaps all those years ago, the first time he had ever sat down for dinner in the Shining Gallery, not sure which piece of cutlery to pick up with his shaking hands.

But that was ridiculous; she had only been nine. She could not have known.

He thought of the grass ring. If she did know who he was, he could ask her. The question had been in the back of his mind since he had learned the locket's secret, like the afterimage of a bright light printed against his eyelids. He said, "Antonetta—"

Antonetta glanced around, as if making sure no one was there to overhear them. "I told you in the note," she said, quietly. "It's my mother. She wishes to engage me to Artal Gremont the moment he arrives back in Castellane."

Kel felt as if the trees were closing in around him. "*Artal Gremont?*"

Antonetta looked stricken. "He is years older than me, but an alliance between our Council seats would please my mother—"

"He is a bastard," said Kel. "And not the usual sort of bastard we've all gotten used to ignoring here on the Hill. He is an exceptional bastard."

"Which is why I want your help, Monseigneur. There must be a way you can convince my mother to form another plan."

Monseigneur. Kel wished he were anywhere else; his ridiculous hope that Antonetta knew him through his disguise had been just that—ridiculous. He knew he could simply walk off—Conor had done stranger things—but more than he wanted to be away, he wanted to help Antonetta.

And yet there was little he could do. He was not himself; he was Conor, and must answer her as Conor would. There was nothing more important than preserving the illusion that he was the Prince. Even though it seemed to choke him as he said, "Your mother wants you to marry. Is there—someone else you wish to wed? I could per-haps try to turn her in that direction."

Antonetta took a deep breath. In the strange false-forest light, her skin seemed dappled with shadow and gold. Kel knew there had been a time that he had not found her beautiful, but he could not remember the shape of his thoughts then. "No," she said. "I would remain unmarried if I could. As my mother has since my father's death."

"I have no doubt she loves you," said Kel, "but you are a piece on a Castles board, as well. Asking her not to marry you off is asking her to sacrifice her queen."

Antonetta took a step toward him in the moving shadows. She laid her hand on his arm—he could not feel it, through the thickness of the material he wore, but the weight of her touch carried warmth with it. "You are kind," she said. "There are many who say you are not, but I know that you are. I know you can help."

And for a moment, he let himself be lost: in the touch of her hand, the look on her face, the scent of her lavender perfume. And the softness of her gaze, though he knew it had to be for Conor—whatever she felt for him—drew Kel in; he bent his head, brushing his lips across her cheekbone. She looked up in surprise. He could kiss her—her mouth was inches away; he could bury his hands in her hair and slant his lips against hers, and even if her kiss was for Conor, he would take it. It made him feel like a beggar, but in that moment, the idea had ceased to trouble him. He had been born a beggar in the streets; it was nothing new to him.

He felt her warm breath against his cheek. His mouth brushed hers; she started, and stepped backward, raising her hands to form a flimsy barrier between them. She looked at him wryly. "Conor," she said. "Are you really drunk this early in the evening?"

Set back, he blinked at her. "I thought—"

"No, you didn't," she said, calmly. "You know how I feel. I know how *you* feel. Let us not do anything silly."

"Conor!" The soft sound of rustling silken leaves broke the odd silence. Kel stepped away from Antonetta as a shadow flickered through the trunks of the trees. It was Joss Falconet. "Thank you, Antonetta, for finding him for me." He winked. "A personal matter has arisen, and I require his sage advice."

Antonetta inclined her head politely. "It was nothing," she said, and though Kel wanted to stop her, he could think of no reason Conor would do so. She set off alone through the false trees, and a moment later Joss was steering a bemused Kel toward the center of the room, where a massive sugar sculpture of Aquila soared toward the sky, perfectly detailed down to a working portcullis in the wall around the city. Flying from the top of the tallest tower were miniature flags of Sarthe and Castellane.

Hm, Kel thought. It was a conundrum. Conor would be very likely to nibble at least one tower, or possibly the city clock. It would, however, annoy both Lilibet and the Sarthian delegation. Deciding to choose harmony over verisimilitude, Kel said, "Joss. You have a personal matter you wish to discuss?"

Joss was as fashionable as ever. Posy-drops had turned his pupils the shape of wings, and a blue Shenzan dragon curled across the back of his silk tunic, wrapping its gold-and-cobalt tail over his shoulder. And yet he looked uncomfortable, which was unusual enough for Kel to note it. He lowered his voice before saying, "I wished to offer an apology, actually."

Kel looked at him in some surprise. Falconet was rarely serious; nor was he the apologizing type. "What for?"

"The party the other night. Charlon's mockery of the Sarthian Princess."

Kel glanced over at the long table, where a plate of sops— a sweet bread stuffed with jam made of peaches, pears, and cherries— had been laid in front of Luisa. She was offering one to Vienne, who was smiling and shaking her head.

"Luisa," said Kel. "Her name is Luisa."

"I wanted you to know that I had no idea what Charlon was

planning with that dance business. Neither did Montfaucon, though I think he found it funnier than I did."

"I'm sure he found it uproarious," said Kel. "I'm surprised to hear you didn't."

"I could see it bothered you," said Joss, looking at him closely. Kel had not wondered before if Conor had been bothered by Charlon's casual cruelty; he had assumed Conor had been too bitter, too angry at the situation, to consider feelings other than his own. But perhaps he had been unfair. Joss was observant, in a way Montfaucon and Roverge were not, and he knew Conor well. "I knew you didn't like it—and I wanted to tell you, whatever I might think of what Sarthe has done, whatever I might have wished was different, I am loyal to *you*. To House Aurelian, but more than anything to you."

"You mean," said Kel, "if I wish all of you on the Hill to make your peace with Luisa, you will do what you can to help?"

"Yes, though it will not be easy. There is a great deal of bad feeling toward Sarthe, and a great deal of rage over the trick they played. But," Joss added hastily, "I will try. I am cleverer than most of them, and I imagine I can sort them out."

"And you are modest," said Kel. "There's also that."

Joss grinned a little. "And there was something else I wanted to ask you," he said. "About that girl, Mayesh's granddaughter. The one who danced at Charlon's—"

He broke off with a look of surprise. Kel soon realized why; old Gremont had come up to them and laid a frail hand on Kel's brocaded sleeve.

"Might we speak alone for a moment, my Prince?" he said.

Joss bowed and excused himself, shooting a look at Kel that communicated clearly: *You'll have to tell me what this is about later.*

Kel turned back to Gremont, whose eyes were darting around the room; the old man seemed clearly anxious at the idea of being overheard. "Alone," he said, again, and cleared his throat. "If we could talk for a moment, perhaps outside . . ."

"Is this about Artal?" said Kel. He knew he should not ask—
Conor would not—but could not help himself. "Is he returning
soon?"

Gremont's eyes darted away. "Soon enough," he said. "In a few
weeks, I'd imagine. He had business to attend to in Kutani. It is not
Artal I wished to speak to you about," he added hastily. "It is something else entirely."

"My dear Gremont," Kel said, as gently as he could, "of course
I will be happy to speak with you." *About your meetings in the Maze?
If that is even true?* "But let us make it after dinner. It will be difficult
for me to get away just now, as I'm sure you can imagine."

Gremont lowered his voice. "My lord Prince. It must be soon.
It is a matter of trust, you see—"

"Of trust?" Kel echoed, puzzled, just as the bell that meant food
was to be served rang out. Guests began to swarm the high table,
and a moment later Mayesh was at Kel's side, smiling benignly at
Gremont. "Come, my Prince; you had better finish your greetings
and sit down, else no one will ever eat."

It was true enough; Castellani Laws of etiquette decreed no
noble could sit and eat until the Blood Royal did, though because
Conor thought the rule was stupid, he usually ignored it.

Gremont's face fell, but Mayesh was already steering Kel to the
high table. Kel mounted the steps, stopping to greet Senex Domizio and Sena Anessa. They looked surprised as he spoke of his delight at the thought of visiting Aquila, the Eagle City. (If nothing
else, Kel thought, Conor might as well get a trip out of this whole
business.)

As he made his way toward the royal seats, stopping for a moment to joke with Charlon and Montfaucon, he was conscious of
Mayesh watching him from across the room. The Counselor was in
deep conversation with Jolivet. The two men might dislike each
other, Kel thought, but they were bound nonetheless, to the service
of the King and the keeping of royal secrets. They reminded Kel of

the figures painted on the Doors of Hell and Paradise—one representing good, one evil, both tussling over the souls of humankind.

At last, Kel reached his place and seated himself beside Luisa. Vienne was on her other side; Lilibet was at the head of the table, some seats away, already in conversation with Lady Alleyne. Antonetta had been relegated to the other end of the table, across from Joss and Montfaucon.

Luisa looked anxiously at Kel. She had cherry jam on her cheek. Conor, he knew, would ignore her, but he could not bring himself to do it. "*Me scuxia*," he said to her, in Sarthian. "My apologies. A Prince has many duties."

"I was beginning to wonder if you were going to grace us with your presence at all," said Vienne, drily, in Castellani. "I had assumed you would spend this evening as you did the one at the Roverges', flirting and drinking."

Before Kel could reply, it became temporarily impossible to say anything at all as the food was served. There were plates and plates of the Marakandi dishes Lilibet favored: pigeon stewed with dates, capons cooked with raisins and honey, lamb studded with sour cherries and drizzled with pomegranate syrup. Alongside such delicacies were the recipes of Sarthe: cuttlefish in black ink, meatballs stuffed with dried cheese, chicken brined in vinegar, *passatelli* in herb butter.

There were expressions of pleasure up and down the table, but all Kel could think of was the first time he had visited the Palace. The wonder of the food—so much of it, and such variety—unrolling before him like an enchanted tapestry. How he had eaten until his stomach hurt.

Now it was just food, a source of sustenance without wonder. And he was not hungry. Though he was ignoring the tension he felt, it was still there, a coiled spring in his belly, precluding any desire for food.

He wondered if Vienne, too, was tense. Despite her clothes,

despite the rather calm circumstances, she was still guarding the Princess. He wished he could tell her he knew what that was like; instead, he said, echoing her words, "Drinking and flirting, eh?"

"Well, yes," said Vienne, spearing a raisin with her fork. "It is what you were doing—"

"I was speaking with Mathieu Gremont. He is ninety-five," Kel said, "and he runs the Charter for tea and coffee, though I rarely see him awake. I would not say I was flirting, however. He is frail, and such activities might kill him off."

Vienne looked a little surprised—it was probably more than Conor had ever said to her before. "I meant the other night—"

"But that was the other night," said Kel. Servants were moving down the table, serving from the platters. Kel reminded himself to make sure he took some of Conor's favorite foods: hare and candied ginger, capons stuffed with cinnamon. "This is tonight."

"Are we to expect it will be different, then?" said Vienne, who was trying to encourage Luisa to eat.

Kel said, "I am reminded of an old Callatian saying: 'If you look for faults, you will find them.'"

"And I am reminded of another Callatian saying," said Vienne. "'The measure of a man is what he does with his power.'"

"I was unaware," Kel said, "that it was in the remit of the Black Guard to take the measure of royalty. Also, if you wanted Luisa to eat, you shouldn't have let her consume an entire plate of jam."

Luisa, hearing her name, tugged at Vienne's sleeve. "What's wrong?" she demanded in Sarthian. "What is it you are saying? I will not be left out, Vienne."

"Look, do you see that tapestry over there?" said Kel, in Sarthian as well. He pointed at the arras that hung down from the balcony, screening off the alcoves beneath. "It is called *The Marriage to the Sea*. It is a ritual that the royal family must undertake, here in Castellane, to dedicate themselves to the sea that brings us so much. The King and Queen carry golden rings out into the harbor on a ship of flowers, and they scatter them upon the waves of the sea. That way we seal the sea's love of the city, and keep our-selves on her good side."

"It seems like a waste of jewelry," said Luisa, and Kel laughed. "I would rather keep the ring."

"But you would anger the sea," Vienne teased. "And what would happen then?"

Luisa did not answer; Lilibet had risen to her feet, a small silver bell in her hand. She rang it, sending a peremptory chime through the room.

The music from the gallery above faded as Lilibet—queenly, elegant, chin raised—gazed about her. Her emeralds glittered at her throat, her ears, on her fingers.

If any wondered where the King was, they knew better than to express that wondering aloud. His absence was an expected thing at this juncture; even the nervous Sarthian delegates could not be in-sulted by it.

"On behalf of Castellane," Lilibet said, "I offer welcome to the delegates of Sarthe, and to the Princess Luisa of the House of d'Eon."

Luisa brightened; she had understood her name, at least. *Poor child*, Kel thought, *to have come all this way at the whim of politicians.* It was like releasing a dove among hawks. Being engaged to Conor would not save her. There would be jostling for her favor, true, but many more hoping to see her fall.

"She welcomes you," Kel translated, and Luisa smiled. Lilibet was still speaking: of the eagle of Sarthe and the lion of Castellane, the union of fury and flame and the empire they would build to-gether of domination over land and sea.

Vienne reached for a decanter of rosé wine; Kel got there first, and passed it deftly to her. She gave him a narrow look. "You seem different," she said.

"Different than other Princes?" Kel said, flexing his ringed fin-gers. "More charming? Ah. More *handsome*."

She rolled her eyes. "Different than you were," she clarified.

"You have not been kind to *her*"—she glanced at Luisa—"these past days. Now you are all kindness and jests. Perhaps you have had a change of heart," she added, "though I do not credit it. I have never known a Prince who had a heart to change."

Luisa, tired of her companions speaking in Castellani, gave an aggrieved sigh just as Lilibet finished speaking.

"You must clap for the Queen's speech," Kel whispered, and brought his own hands together, though it was not quite etiquette for the Crown Prince to applaud. Luisa copied him quickly. The musicians began to play again, and the twang of a *lior* filled the hall as Lilibet took her seat.

Through the servants' doors under the arches, a stream of performers in bright silks and gold braid began to enter the room. Pleased murmurs ran up and down the table: These were dancers, called *bandari*. They wandered the Gold Roads, affiliated with no particular country or language, dedicated to their art. They wore tight-fitting silk jackets that ended just below the rib cage and low-slung trousers in sheer silk. Gold satin slippers completed the outfit.

They performed with their hair unbound and intricate belts of coins wrapped around their muscled waists. It was said that a *bandari* dancer saved a coin from each performance and looped it on a chain; the length of a belt indicated how long the dancer had been plying their skill.

The Court at Jahan had its own troupe of *bandari*, and Lilibet was a particular enthusiast of the art. She applauded as the dancers entered the room.

"Must I clap again?" Luisa whispered; Kel shook his head. The decorative trees and greenery had been rearranged to create a cleared space for the dancers to perform; he had an excellent view of the "stage" since the chairs opposite him were empty. "No need yet," he said. "Only do as I do, and do not worry."

He wondered if the sight of the dancers would bother her, considering what had happened at Roverge's party. She seemed only charmed, though, at the sight of them. Indeed, they were beautiful: lithe and carefully put together as if purpose-built for graceful movement. Unbound hair—fair and scarlet, black, and brown—cascaded down their backs.

Vienne was not looking at the *bandari* dancers; she was regarding Kel with the same puzzled look on her face. *I must stop being kind to the child,* he thought, yet he knew why he was doing it—it was what Conor had done for him, when he had first come to the Palace. Showed him which fork to use, told him when and how to speak. Luisa was a child, as he had been; he could not leave her to flounder.

Yet still, he felt a prickle at the back of his neck—as if the force of old memory had sent a shiver up his spine. He turned and saw a flicker of movement at the back of the hall. A cloaked figure had come in through the golden doors and stood regarding the room. His hood was up, shadowing his face, yet Kel knew his step, his gait, as he knew his own.

Conor.

Kel could only stare as the Prince made his way into the room. The dancers were still moving about, as were a few servants carrying bronze bowls of rosewater, apparently needed for the performance. Up in the gallery, the musicians tuned their instruments. No one—not even Jolivet or Mayesh—seemed to have noticed Conor save Kel.

All his life, Kel had been trained to do as Conor would do, anticipate his actions, guess his likely responses. Conor was in the shadows, but to Kel he was plain enough. He could tell that Conor was drunk—drunk enough to require a hand against the wall as he walked, steadying him.

But not so drunk that he did not know where he was, or what he was doing. He was making his way determinedly toward the high table, as if he intended to take his place there.

Kel could not bear to think what would happen then. He could excuse himself, he thought; he could slip into the Victory Hall, but even then—

Conor had reached the arras, was walking alongside it, one bare hand trailing along the tapestry of *The Marriage to the Sea.* Above him, the fast strumming of the *lior* signaled that the dance was about to begin. Luisa gave a gasp of delight as the lamps dimmed. Silver and black gauze scarves began to tumble from a hidden opening in the ceiling. The room was no longer a forest. It was the night: the iron of stars, the obsidian of the sky. The dancers, in their shining finery, began to move across the floor. It was a dance of constellations, Kel realized: The dancers would be comets, meteors, and asteroids. They would be the air that caught fire between the planets, the brilliant and unexplained debris of the universe.

They would be a *distraction.*

Murmuring something to Luisa, he slipped out of his seat, leaped silently down from the dais, and crept behind the high table. He slid along the length of the wall beneath the gallery, his every sense on high alert. Music poured through the room; the air was full of glittering scarves, and the dancers spun a glimmering path across the floor. Conor had paused, his back to the tapestry, to stare at them. Kel sped up, caught hold of him by the jacket he wore beneath his cloak, and dragged him behind the arras.

One carcel lamp illuminated the bare stone alcove behind the arras; the tapestry fell into place, concealing them, as Conor struggled for a moment.

"Con," Kel hissed. "It's me. *It's me.*"

Conor went limp. He sagged back against the wall, his hood falling away to reveal his face. He wore no crown, and his eyes were bloodshot.

"I'm sorry," he said. He wasn't slurring his words—he wasn't drunk enough for that—but he was half whispering. It was hard for Kel to hear him over the music. "I left you. I thought I was leaving them, but I left you."

Kel, still holding on to the front of Conor's jacket, said, "What did you think would happen? Though I suppose you didn't think. Conor—"

"I thought they'd cancel this fucking party," Conor hissed. "I thought they'd realize—I know this has to happen, it's politics, it can't be changed, but all this *pretense*, these lies that we're happy about it—that anyone is besides whoever stands to profit: a few politicians and merchants—" Kel saw the motion of his throat as he swallowed. "I didn't think they'd make you do this."

"This is my duty, Conor," Kel said, wearily. "My charge. I pretend to be you. Of course they'd make me do this. And you shouldn't be here."

Conor put his hands flat against Kel's chest. "I want to make it right," he said. "Let me switch places with you. I'll go out. Do my duty."

Kel wanted to ask him what had happened, why he'd left so abruptly and come back the same way. Why now, today? But now was so incredibly, utterly not the time. He said, "Con, you're drunk. Go back to the Mitat. Go to sleep. I'll tell you what happens. It won't be much."

Conor set his jaw. "Switch with me."

"It'll make everything worse," said Kel.

Conor flinched. And for a moment, Kel remembered back down the years, the boy with the light behind his eyes, who'd said to him playfully: *What was it like, then, being me?*

When had that light gone out? Had he noticed the moment? Conor's eyes looked like bruises in his face now, and there was a pinched tightness to his mouth. Half of Kel wanted to shake Conor, to scream at him; the other half wanted to stand in front of him, protecting him from every dangerous thing in the world. Not just blades, but lies and cruelty, disappointment and despair.

"I can make it better now," Conor said stubbornly. "Switch with me."

Kel expelled a breath. "Fine. *Fine.*"

Conor yanked off his cloak. His jacket. Kel could not remember the last time he had seen Conor dressed so plainly. He wore more elaborate clothes to practice fencing in the Hayloft. Kel drew off his overrobe and rings, lifted the crown from his head. It was a relief, not wearing it.

He handed them over to Conor, who flung them on hastily. "Trousers—" Conor began, doing up the clasps on the robe.

"I'm not taking my trousers off," Kel said firmly as he took off his amulet and slipped it into the pocket of the jacket he was now wearing. "No one looks at trousers, anyway."

"Of course they do." Conor slid on the last of the rings. The circlet glittered in his dark hair: It was amazing, Kel thought, what a difference a thin gold band made. It transformed Conor, not into what he wasn't, but back into what he was. "Otherwise, how do you know what's in fashion?" He looked down at Kel's feet. "Boots—"

But there was no chance to swap either trousers or footwear. From the other side of the tapestry, a sound cut through the music. A scream, high and terrible, and then another. The music stuttered, faltering.

Kel raced to the arras, twitched back the corner.

"What—?" Conor said, at his elbow, and they both stared: The doors of the Shining Gallery had been flung open wide, and dark figures were pouring through. Behind them, Kel glimpsed the night outside, the brilliance of stars, the lights of the Hill, and for a moment, he wondered if this was some sort of play, a part of the evening's entertainment.

Then he saw the flash of torchlight on steel, and saw a Castelguard crumple, a blade in his belly. One of the dark figures stood over him, a bloody sword in hand. Another sword flashed, and another, like stars coming out at nightfall, and Kel realized: This was no entertainment. Marivent was under attack.

Maharam,

You have asked me where your responsibility lies in the matter of the return of the Goddess. You ask if you will look into her eyes and see the flame of her soul. You yearn for wisdom and the gift of certitude, as do we all.

Be at rest, Maharam. This is not your burden. The Exilarch is not merely a title passed down through the sons of Makabi, it is a soul that is passed down, and the soul of the Exilarch will recognize the soul of the Goddess when she returns. In this matter there need be no question.

Your burden will be of a different sort. For when the Goddess returns, you must gather our people to rise up with their swords, for it will mean a great threat has come, not just to the Ashkar, but to all of the world.

—Letter from Dael Benjudah to Maharam Izak Kishon

CHAPTER TWENTY-FIVE

As Lin stepped out into the garlanded streets of the Sault, the air was heavy with the fragrance of roses and lilies. She paused a moment on the front step of the Etse Kebeth, nervously adjusting the lace at her cuffs and collar, smoothing down the lines of her blue dress. She touched the silk sachet at her throat, hoping it would distract from the pulse she was sure was beating visibly in her throat.

She had never been so nervous.

The door of the Women's House opened behind her, releasing a flood of laughing young women. Arelle Dorin smiled at her as the group went by, headed to the festival. Their excitement was warm and palpable; on another night, Lin would have found it infectious. Now she only clenched her right hand into a fist. Silently, she said to herself: *You can always change your mind, Lin. Up until the last moment, you can change your mind.*

The door opened again, and this time Mariam joined Lin on the steps. Her dress was a magnificent creation of pale-blue Shenzan silk, the cuffs turned back to show saffron-yellow *setino* lining, striped with black. Her hair, like Lin's, had been twisted into a thick braid dotted with flowers. Against the richness of her dress, her fragility stood out starkly: Rouge circles spotted the pale tops of her jutting cheekbones, and the stiff collar rose high around her thin neck. But the smile she gave Lin was as strong as ever.

"Our last Festival," she said, linking her hand with Lin's. "After this we will be officially old maids, I think."

"Good," Lin said. "Once one is an old maid, one can stop making an effort to be charming."

"I am astonished." It was Chana Dorin, joining them on the stairs. She wore her usual uniform: a gray tunic and trousers, and thick boots one could garden in. Her only concession to the importance of the evening was a silvery shawl Josit had brought back for her from the Gold Roads. "I had no idea you were making an effort to be charming, Lin."

"Outrageous," Lin said. "I am outraged."

Mariam giggled, and they set off together for the Kathot, Lin detailing as they went the many ways she planned to cease making an effort to be "maidenly" once this night was through. She would dress in only torn clothes, she told her companions, and wear only muddy boots. She would buy a pet rat at the market and walk it on a silk lead. She might get some chickens as well, and she would name them all individually, and tell anyone who inquired that she sometimes sat on the eggs to see if they would hatch.

"I am impressed," Chana said. "This *is* worse than your current behavior. Though not by much," she added.

"You should talk," Mariam said. "Your boots are always muddy, Chana."

Lin smiled at the good-natured squabbling, but only half her attention was on it. As they neared the center of the Sault, Marivent seemed to loom above them, hovering against the darkness of the sky, white as a second moon.

Tonight, Lin knew, was the welcoming banquet for the child Princess from Sarthe; it was why Mayesh would not be attending the Festival. In past years, this would have angered Lin—that her grandfather could not even be bothered to turn up for the most important religious event of the year in the Sault because his loyalty was to Marivent and not his people.

Now she was only glad he would not be there. She was not sure she could go through with her plan if he was watching.

They had reached the illuminated Kathot, brilliant as a live ember among banked coals. Lamps of hammered silver swayed among the branches of the trees, and candles burned in cups of colored wax paper all up and down the long tables with their coverings of white cloth.

Chana cut through the crowd, pulling Lin and Mariam after her. For once, Lin was glad to be led. She felt naked in the crowd, as if her intentions were surely visible on her face. *Stop it*, she told herself. These were all people she knew, all familiar faces. There was Rahel, laughing among the other married women; nearby Mez sat tuning his *lior* at a circular table, surrounded by several other musicians. In addition to the *narit*—young women like Mariam and herself, all in blue dresses—there were young men of marriageable age, awkward in rarely worn finery. They sprawled at long tables, joking with one another and drinking reddish-purple wine from silver cups that had been liberally distributed by the Sault elders.

The Festival was a celebration, Lin reminded herself; people were supposed to be relaxed here, and happy. She forced herself to smile.

"Stop that." Mariam shook her arm. "Why are you glaring?"

Chana had guided them to a space under the fig trees where they had a good view of the square. Directly in front of them was a cleared space scattered with petals, meant for gathering and dancing. At the foot of the Shulamat stairs a raised plinth had been erected. Upon it stood a purpose-built wooden chair intended for the Maharam, garlanded with flowers. When the festival was over, the dais and the chair would be broken down and burned, the sweet scent of almond wood filling the air.

"I'm *not* glaring," Lin whispered. "I'm *smiling*."

"You could have fooled me." Mariam ducked out of the way as

Orla Regev, another of the Sault elders, rushed up to Chana for a whispered consultation. *Someone*, it seemed, had garlanded the Maharam's chair with hyacinth flowers, when everyone knew they were supposed to be roses. Also, the wine had been put out far too early, and many of the older men were drunk, and some of the younger ones, too.

"Oh, poor dear," said Mariam sympathetically as Chana was whisked away by Orla, complaining as she went that the Maharam was unlikely to notice what kind of flowers were on his chair, and the Goddess, blessed be the Name, unlikely to care. "Why can't Orla leave her be to enjoy herself?"

"Because this is how *Orla* enjoys herself," Lin said just as a young man approached them, smiling. Lin recognized him immediately as Natan Gorin, Mez's older brother, the one who had just returned from the Gold Roads.

Like the rest of the young men at the Festival, he wore plain white cambric with silver embroidery, a crown of green spikenard leaves on his head. (For a moment, Lin was reminded of another crown, a gold circlet with winged sides, gleaming against dark curls.) His hair was coppery, his skin sun-browned. He smiled easily, extending a hand marked with the black-ink tattoos of the Rhadanite traders to Mariam.

"I happen to have a friend among the musicians"—he winked over at Mez—"and have been informed that the dancing is about to begin. If you would join me?"

Blushing, Mariam took Natan's hand. Mez greeted this with a trill of the *lior*, and a moment later the music had swelled, and Natan and Mariam were dancing.

A swell of happiness cut through Lin's nerves. She looked over at Mez, who was grinning. Had he asked Natan to dance with Mariam? It didn't matter, Lin told herself; Mariam was happy just to be dancing. Her face was shining, and in the moonlight she did not look the least bit tired or ill.

Other couples had begun to join them. Lin leaned back against the rough bark of the tree trunk, letting the moment carry her. There was laughter all around her, and the brightness of a community that was glad for an excuse to come together. Something cold snaked under her ribs, even as she watched Mariam. A feeling of dread.

You can't do this, said the voice in the back of her mind. *Not to all of them. The stubbornness of the Maharam is not their fault. And surely there is some other solution. Something less extreme.*

Though she had not thought of it, yet.

"Lin." She stood up straight; it was Oren Kandel, looking down at her somberly. He really was immensely tall. She felt as if she had to crane her neck back to see his face, which was set in somber lines. He was not wearing a leaf crown, like the other boys, and his clothes were somber, without embroidery. He said, stiffly, "Would you dance with me?"

Lin was too surprised to refuse. She let Oren lead her out among the other dancers, let him take her hand and draw her close. He smelled faintly acidic, like bitter tea. As he turned her awkwardly in his arms, she could not help but remember the last time she had danced. And made a fool of herself, she thought, Conor watching her with that bitter light in his eyes—

Not Conor, she reminded herself. The Prince. She was not Mayesh, to use his given name. Besides, he hated her now. She had told him he was broken, and he would be unlikely to forgive an insult like that.

"Lin," Oren said, and his voice was surprisingly gentle. For a moment, Lin wondered if he was going to say, *You look troubled*, or, *Why do you seem sorrowful, on such a joyful occasion?* "Lin, do you remember when I asked you to marry me?"

Lin winced inwardly and wondered why on earth she had thought Oren Kandel might have noticed she was unhappy. If he had not had all the insight and empathy of a slug, she might not have refused his marriage proposal in the first place.

"Yes, Oren," she said. "That sort of thing is hard to forget."

"Did you ever wonder why I asked you?" His dark eyes were brilliant as he looked down at her. "Though you are obviously unsuitable, and would make a very difficult wife for an ordinary man."

What was that expression Kel always used? And Merren, too? *Gray hell*, Lin thought.

"I had not wondered," she said. "Though, I confess, I am wondering now."

"I know you're angry at me," Oren said. "I helped the Maharam take your books." *And begged him to punish me more*, Lin thought grimly. "But I think you'll come to understand, Lin, that the things I've done have all been to help you, even if you couldn't see it."

"Taking my books does not help me, Oren."

"You think that now," he said, "but that is because you are corrupted. Your grandfather has corrupted you with his worldly values. He wants to make you like those women out there"—he jerked his chin toward the Sault walls, a gesture that seemed to encompass all of Castellane—"too proud, too arrogant, thinking they're better than we are. But I can save you from his influence."

"Oren—" Lin tried to pull away, but he held her fast.

"Reconsider my offer," he said. His eyes were still shining, but it was not with happiness. It was with a mixture of revulsion and desire that nearly turned Lin's stomach. He might have told himself he wanted to save her, she thought, but what he really wanted was to change her beyond all recognition. And she could not help but think of Conor, who—drunk as he had been, wild and uncontrolled— had told her she was perfect as she was. "I still want to marry you," he breathed. "I *want* to—and marrying me will raise you up in the estimation of the Maharam, of all the Sault—"

"Why?" Lin said.

Oren blinked for a moment. "What do you mean, why?"

"Why do you want to marry me?"

"Do you remember," Oren said, "when we were children, and we would play hide-and-seek in the gardens? No one else could find you, but I always could. I always found you in the end. You are lost like that now, Lin. Only I can find you. Help you."

A sour note sounded on the *lior*. Lin glanced over, saw Mez looking at her, his eyebrows raised, as if to say: *Do you need me to step in?*

"Lin," Oren said. "What are you thinking?"

She shook her head minutely at Mez, and turned back to Oren. "Just that I wondered if those were the words Sulemon used, when he was trying to convince Adassa to join with him and the other kings. *Join with me and I will keep you safe. I will help you. You are lost on your own.* Isn't that the sort of thing he said?"

Oren stiffened.

"Although," Lin said, "he probably at least told her that he loved her. And you haven't even done that."

The music had stopped. Mez must not have been able to stand it any longer, Lin thought, the way Oren was looking at her, and she could not blame him. Nor could she look at Oren anymore. His face was creased with anger, his eyes hard and bright as stones.

She walked past Natan and Mariam as she hurried away from the dancing. She took herself to one of the tables, found a silver cup of wine, and drank, letting the heat of the alcohol settle the vibration in her bones. Turning, she looked about but could not see Oren among the crowd. She let herself relax slightly.

Oren was not the Sault, she reminded herself. Most of them, her friends and neighbors, were not like that: not rigid or judgmental. They had empathy, like Chana. Compassion, like Mez. Wisdom, like Mayesh. (Yes, she told herself, it was all right to think it: He *was* wise, and cared about goodness, even if he was not always kind.) Most of the elders had not voted to exile the Maharam's son. It was the Maharam himself, in the end, who had cast the deciding vote.

Mez began to play again, this time a slower song, a sweeter refrain. Sparks from the lamps were flying up, salting the air with firefly light. Lin was hot from the dancing and the wine, but the space between her shoulder blades was clammy-cold.

She sat watching the dancing, the couples circling under the glowing lanterns. She did not know all their names, she realized—not the younger ones, who had not been in school with her and Mariam. It was almost as if she were observing a play, or a performance in the Arena. Some part of her ached. These were her people, their ways her ways. And yet even as one song blended into another and the moon glided across the sky, Lin did not move to join them but sat and watched, a spectator.

"Lin!" Mariam hurried up to her with Natan following, hands in his pockets. He had a nice smile, Lin thought, an easy smile. "How long have you been sitting here?"

Lin glanced over the walls of the Sault, at the Windtower Clock rising against the sky. To her surprise, some hours had passed; it had felt like only a few moments. Midnight was looming on the horizon.

Mariam said, "I saw Oren with you—"

"It's fine," Lin said quickly. "We danced, that's all." She turned a smile on Natan. "I had wanted to ask you—"

"If I saw your brother on the Gold Roads?" Natan said. "I did, actually. At a caravansary near Mazan. Josit seemed well," he added, hastily. "He told me that if I made it back here before he did, I should send his love to you both."

"Did he say *when* he might be coming back?" Lin asked.

Natan looked mildly puzzled. "I don't believe I asked him. He'd bought a pet monkey, though," he added. "Off a Hindish trader. It was stealing people's hats."

Natan, Lin was beginning to think, might be handsome, but was not that bright. "Hats," she said. "Imagine that."

Mariam shot her a chiding look, though she looked close to smiling herself.

"I doubt he had any news as exciting as yours," Natan said. "The Crown Prince, in the Sault? I doubt that's ever happened before."

Lin wondered if she should start telling people that Conor had come to see her because he had some terrible version of the pox and desperately needed treatment. That seemed, however, like the sort of untruth that would get you arrested by the Arrow Squadron.

"He was looking for Mayesh," she said. "That's all."

Mariam grinned. "Everyone says he's going to sweep Lin away to a life of luxury on the Hill."

Lin thought of the Hill. The brilliance of it, the colors. The way people spoke, as if every word were dipped in sweet acid. The way Luisa had wept in humiliation. The way Conor had watched her when she danced.

"Well, that's just silly," she said around the tension in her throat. "The Prince is as good as engaged, and besides, he would never marry an Ashkari woman."

"He wouldn't," Natan agreed. "There is no alliance to be made there. We are a people without a country, and kings do not marry people. They marry kingdoms."

Perhaps Natan was cleverer than she'd given him credit for, Lin thought.

"We do have a country," said Mariam. "Aram."

"I have passed through Aram, on the Roads," said Natan. "It is a blasted land. Nothing grows, and there are no resting places—the land is too poisonous to sustain life for even a short time. One must travel through without stopping."

The music paused. Lin looked quickly toward the Windtower Clock. It was thirty minutes to midnight. The ritual of the Goddess was about to begin.

She barely noticed as, with a polite murmur, Natan excused himself. The young women and young men were separating from each other, as the ritual required. Dancers vanished from the square, melting back into the crowd.

Lin's heart began to beat faster. She could feel her own pulse in her throat, her spine. It was starting. The ceremony. The Maharam had appeared at the Shulamat door.

He came slowly down the steps, carrying his walking stick,

which had been engraved with the name of Aron, the first son of Judah Makabi, and the numbers of *gematria*. He wore his *sillon*, woven of midnight-blue wool, the cuffs and collar gleaming with talismanic equations picked out in glass.

Beside him was Oren Kandel, staring straight ahead. If he saw Lin at all as he escorted the Maharam to his chair on the dais, he gave no sign.

Mez's *lior* trilled, a summoning chime. Mariam took Lin's hand, and together they moved with the other *narit* into the space before the dais. A crowd of girls and young women in blue dresses, their hair full of flowers, looked up as the Maharam took his seat in the garlanded chair. He gazed out over the gathered crowd, smiling benevolently. Lifting his walking stick, he laid it lengthwise across his lap.

"*Sadī Eyzōn*," he said. It was the Ashkar's own name for themselves: the People Who Wait. They did not speak it to the *malbushim*, to any outside their own company. "The Goddess is our light. She illuminates our darkness. We are in shadow, as she is in shadow; we are in exile, as she is in exile. Still, she stretches forth her hand to touch our days with miracles."

He raised his staff, which burst into flower: Blossoms and almonds bloomed from it, as if it were still a bough on the tree. The crowd gave its small gasp. Though it happened every year—in every Sault, at every Tevath, in the hand of every Maharam—it never failed to elicit wonder.

"Today," said the Maharam, "we celebrate the greatest of Adassa's miracles, the one that changed our world and preserved our people." His voice began to fall into the rhythm of a chant, the lilt of a story so often told, it had almost become a song. "Long ago, long ago in the dark times, when the Goddess was betrayed, the forces of Suleman rode against Aram. They expected an easy victory, but they were denied. The people of Aram, led by Judah Makabi, held off the Sorcerer-Kings of Dannemore, with all their might and power, for three long days and three long nights." The Maharam's gaze raked the crowd. Though they had all heard the story countless times, his eyes seemed to ask: *Can you believe this? This miracle of miracles?*

"And when at last the walls fell, and the enemy armies poured into Aram, they found it an empty land. Under cover of shadow, Judah Makabi had already led our people to safety. But Suleman knew the Goddess was not finished with her work.

"He raced to the top of the tower of Balal, the tallest tower in all of Aram. She was there, Adassa, our Goddess. There in all of her terrible glory. She was dreadful and wonderful to behold in that moment. Her hair was flame, her eyes stars. Sulemon cowered before her, but he could not flee, for her gaze held him fast. She told him, 'In striving for my annihilation, you have only ensured your own. The power you wield should not be wielded by any man, for it only causes destruction. And now it shall be taken from you.'"

Lin closed her eyes, slipping her hand into the pocket of her dress to touch the smooth surface of her stone. Oh, she knew this story. She knew it in her heart; in her dreams. The flames, the desert. The tower. This was what she had danced, on the Hill, in that terrible house of terrible people. This moment, when the Goddess, betrayed by her greatest love, snatched victory from her own obliteration.

"The Goddess stretched out her hand," said the Maharam, "and she plucked from the world the Great Word, the Name Unspeakable—and when it was gone, all the artifacts of magic it had made possible began to disappear. The Sorcerer-Kings were struck down where they stood, for all that had kept them alive was their own foul spells. The beasts of magic vanished from the world, and the armies of the risen dead crumbled away to earth. With the last of his power, as the tower of Balal turned to dust around him, Suleman reached for the Goddess. But there was nothing to touch. She had already vanished into shadow."

He sighed. And Lin thought: It was a measure of the power of the tale, of the Goddess herself, that his small sigh was audible. The crowd was that still, that silent.

The Maharam said, "It is a tale of great bravery and sacrifice, but you may be asking yourself, why are we here? Easy enough for the outsider to say: Sing a song of your Goddess, then, if in her you believe. For how shall we sing our Lady's song in a strange land? Long have we wandered, but we are not abandoned. Long have we waited, but we are not abandoned. We are scattered among the nations, yet we are not abandoned. For now, we make our home in our own hearts, and there we wait. For we are not abandoned. The Goddess returns, and leads us to our glory."

Whatever Lin thought of the Maharam, it did not matter. The old words still thrilled her down to her bones. She touched the necklace at her throat, her fingers tracing the words. *For how shall we sing our Lady's song, in a strange land?* Was Castellane then a strange land? She supposed it was. All lands were strange until the Goddess brought them home.

"Tonight, in every Sault, in every nation, comes this ceremony to pass," said the Maharam. "Tonight the question is asked and answered. Come now, *narit*, and stand before me." He rapped his flowering staff upon the dais. "Let her will be done."

Lin found herself moving to join the others, a slow river of blue snaking toward the dais as, above them, prayers were recited. Mariam wiggled through the crowd to stand beside her; there was a flush on her cheeks—rouge or nature, Lin could not be sure. She gave her friend a reassuring smile. *Easy, easy,* her mother had told her, long ago; *a formality, a ritual, that is all. When the Goddess returns, do you think she will wait until the Tevath to reveal it? No, she will come to us in a pillar of fire, on the spear of the lightning. One sweep of her hand will illuminate all the earth.*

It was not a swift thing, gathering so many people into an orderly line, and it was ten minutes to midnight by the time the Ma-

haram had begun the questioning. Lin could hear his voice as the
narit passed before him, one by one, lingering on the platform.
They answered the old question, their voices shy or sharp, confident or questioning.

Are you the Goddess Returned?

No, I am not she.

Very well, depart.

Six minutes to midnight. What if the Maharam did not call her
name in time? She touched the stone in her pocket again, lightly,
just to reassure herself with the feel of it. Someone added a load of
wood to the bonfire. Red-gold embers flew upward as Mariam
moved to take her place before the dais. The Maharam regarded
her with kindness, mixed with pity: *We allow you to be here, but only
as a formality. Surely one so ill, so weak, could not be she.* He said, "Are
you the Goddess Reborn?"

Mariam raised her chin. Her gaze was firm and clear. "I am
not."

She turned then, her back very straight, and went to join the
other girls who had already given their answer to the Maharam. Lin
felt a stab of pride that Mariam had not waited to be dismissed. The
Maharam had noticed it, too; as Lin came to stand before him, she
saw that his eyes were thoughtful. That thoughtfulness turned to
something else when he saw Lin. His pale gaze raked her from her
blue slippers to the flowers in her curled hair.

She kept her face blank, her hands clasped loosely before her.
She could still feel her own heartbeat in every part of her body. In
her fingers, her toes. In the pit of her stomach.

It was five minutes to midnight.

"Lin Caster," the Maharam said, "this is the last year you will
stand before me at the Tevath."

It was not a question, so Lin said nothing. She could sense the
gaze of the Sault on her. There was little suspense in it. No one
really expected an outcome different from every other Tevath they
had lived to see. But Lin—Lin could feel her hands shaking like

leaves at her sides. Only the long practice of patience that being a healer had taught her enabled her to cling to the semblance of calm.

"They say all wisdom comes from the Goddess," said the Maharam. Lin heard someone behind her whisper; it was unusual for the Maharam to say more than the required words of the ritual. "Do you believe that, Linnet, daughter of Sorah?"

Reminding me that he knew my mother. Lin gritted her teeth. Her knees were trembling, her palms wet with sweat. She said, "Yes."

The Maharam seemed to relax minutely. "My dear," he said. "Are you the Goddess Reborn?"

Long ago, when she and Mariam were young, they had swum together in the stone pools of the washing room in the Women's House. Diving underwater, they would call to each other, seeing if the other could understand their words through the rippling distortion of the water. She heard the Maharam like that now, as if his voice came down to her through echoes, as if she stood not at the bottom of a shallow pool but on the floor of the ocean.

Are you the Goddess Reborn?

She clenched her fists at her sides, so hard her fingernails bit into her palms, breaking the skin.

"Yes," she said. "Yes. I am."

They poured through the broken doors of the Shining Gallery, assailants dressed in ragged scraps of old military uniforms, red and black, their faces blank, featureless. In the jagged light of the swinging lamps, they had the look of creatures out of nightmare: They wore close-fitting caps, their faces painted in white and black greasepaint to resemble skulls. They carried a motley assortment of weapons: old axes, maces, and swords. One swung a banner above his head: the image of a golden lion, pouncing on an eagle.

And suddenly Kel was in the square, watching as the Castelguard dragged the group of vociferous protestors away. Their banners, stitched with the victorious lion, the bleeding eagle. Their shouts—repeated later at the Roverge house, when the Charter Families had listened from the terrace and laughed: *Death to Sarthe! Blood before union with Sarthe!*

They had not had their faces painted then, nor had they had weapons; they had seemed a little ridiculous, even. No longer.

Kel turned, grabbed Conor by the shoulders. Shoved him behind the arras. He yanked the dagger out of his boot. It wasn't much. Not enough to protect Conor, if it came to it. He glanced back, saw Conor with his back against the wall, eyes wide.

"Stay here," Kel snarled. "Stay *back*."

He dropped the dagger, kicked it across the floor to Conor. Turned back to the Gallery. It had been seconds, and the place was a melee. The silk screen behind Jolivet had come down, and the room was full of Castelguards. Half of them dashed toward the high table, moving to encircle the Queen and Counselor. Vienne had pushed Luisa behind her. She was screaming at the Castelguard, words Kel could not hear but could guess: demanding they protect the Princess, demanding they give Vienne a weapon, too.

The dancers had scattered. Some of them were hiding among the clustered trees of the false forest. Kel could see their bright clothes, like fireflies in the dark. The half of the Castelguard who were not protecting the high table had flooded into the center of the room, swords flashing. A second false forest, this one of steel.

They met the intruders with a clash, and Kel could smell blood in the air now, sharp and coppery.

The Castelguard whom Kel had seen stabbed in the belly lay nearby, on his back, eyes staring sightlessly at the ceiling. A silver-and-black scarf was caught in the branch of a tree overhead, flickering in the wind from the open door. Kel ducked and rolled, sending himself skidding across the floor as he'd done with the dagger. He fetched up beside the dead guard. He knew his face—one of the Castelguards who'd let him into the Trick to see Fausten. *May he pass through the door unhindered*, Kel thought, gripping the hilt of the blade embedded in the guard's belly. It came free with the sound of steel scraping against rib bones.

Kel rolled to his feet. Now he was armed. And—

"*Fuck*," he whispered. Because Conor had not stayed put, or stayed back, as Kel had told him. He had come out from behind the arras, dagger in hand, and as Kel watched, he flung himself onto one of the skull-faced assailants knocking him to the ground. He stabbed down, plunging the dagger between the Skull's shoulder blades. When he jerked the blade back, blood gushed, a scarlet spray across gold brocade.

Kel reversed course, and began to cut his way toward Conor. The floor of the Shining Gallery was a boiling whirlpool of white, black, and red. The red of Castelguards, the darker red of blood, slicking the floor. A Skull—it was hard to think of them as anything else—lunged at Kel, who parried and thrust, savagely burying his sword between the man's ribs. He crumpled, blood running from the corners of his mouth, mixing with the white greasepaint on his face.

Some of the nobles had joined the guards on the floor. Kel saw Joss Falconet brandishing his sword, a slim silver blade. Montfaucon had drawn a thin dagger from his brocaded cuff; Kel saw him slit a Skull's throat before plucking a half-full wineglass from a nearby table and downing the dregs. Charlon had waded in like a bull, un-armed but swinging his fists. Lady Sardou had produced a jeweled misericorde from the bosom of her dress, and was laying about her with ferocity.

In that moment, Kel knew he had been correct to always go armed to Dial Chamber meetings.

But where was Antonetta? He was used to having his entire focus be on Conor—whom he could see engaged in battle with a Skull, slashing away at his opponent without regard for the rules of swordplay Jolivet had taught them—and to have it split was disori-enting. But he could not do anything about it; Ana had taken up residence somewhere behind his eyes, and he could not stop them searching for her. Looking for the flash of gold silk among the teeming mass—

And there she was, a silver dagger in her hand. She was near the doors, her mother behind her, looking stunned as Antonetta dispatched a Skull who had come too close with a kick to the knee and a swift slashing cut to the shoulder. *Those secret sword lessons must be good ones*, Kel thought. The Skull collapsed, bleeding and clutching at his arm, as Antonetta dragged her stunned mother by main force out of the room.

A few were following—safety seemed to be outside, but the path to it was a bloody trek through flashing blades and mounting chaos. Kel was halfway to Conor now. His progress was slow, each step a bloody fight. He decapitated a Skull with the sweep of his blade, ducked low to sever the ankle tendons of another. He stopped short of cutting the man's throat. Better if some of them survived the night, a small rational voice in the back of his head told him. They would need to be interrogated. There was a *why* to all this, a why Kel could only guess at—

And then there was a shriek from the high table. Kel looked over and saw Sena Anessa stagger back. A black arrow protruded from her shoulder. *No, not an arrow*, Kel thought, rising to his feet, *a crossbow bolt*—

Anessa slumped, blood pouring down the front of her dress, and Luisa screamed. She was struggling in Vienne's arms and she pulled free suddenly—only for a moment, but it was long enough. Even as Kel turned to look, to see where the first bolt had come from, the second arrowed through the air. It plunged into Luisa's chest with enough force to lift the girl off her feet.

She slammed into the wall behind the high table. The bolt that had gone through her body must have lodged itself between two stones—later, it would be discovered that this was exactly what had happened—for it stuck fast. It stuck fast, and Luisa, who must have died the moment the bolt went into her chest, hung limply from it, dangling against the wall like one of the butterflies Kel had seen in Merren's flat, pinned to a specimen board.

Vienne let out a terrible, heartbroken, shrilling cry and flung herself at Luisa. Kel could not bear to watch; he turned and saw a flicker of movement out of the corner of his eye, partway up the wall—

The gallery. From what better vantage point might one shoot a crossbow?

Kel ran. For the first time in his life he ran not toward Conor, but after something else. He shot up the twisting marble steps, exploding out onto the gallery, only to find it empty of musicians. There were instruments here, lying scattered about, and chairs that had been overturned—by those who had fled, Kel guessed—but the gallery was empty.

Kel was about to turn and go back downstairs when he saw the window.

An ordinary sash window at the end of the room, it was open, its curtain fluttering in the breeze. Only Kel knew, from years of familiarity with the gallery, that this window did not look out on empty air. It led to the roof.

A second later, he was climbing through it. His boots hit the roof tiles and he nearly slipped. It was no darker out here than it had been in the gallery—the moon was bright, a white moon that cast a brilliant glow over the curve of the roof, illuminating the scattered palaces of Marivent. And outlining the figure standing in shadow at the roof's edge, gazing out over the city.

At its feet, a crossbow lay, abandoned.

Kel shouted, scrambling down the tiles. He was not sure, later, what he had shouted exactly. Something like: *Who are you? Who paid you to do this?* Something pointless, anyway.

The assassin did not move or seem to hear Kel. A slim figure, and tall, they seemed fitted into some kind of tight black uniform, flexible as a second skin. And yet Kel could not tell if the stranger was male or female, old or young, Castellani or foreign. Only that whoever it was seemed to have no fear of heights.

As he crept closer, the dark assassin turned toward him, slowly. Kel almost yelled aloud. The stranger had no face, or none he could observe. Only a smooth and featureless dark expanse. The black uniform, whatever material it was, covered everything entirely.

And yet, somehow, he felt strongly that the stranger was smiling.

"Sword Catcher." The voice was a low hiss. "*Királar.* You ruined my plans, you know. But do not be afraid. Tonight is not your night to die."

"How reassuring," said Kel. "And yet, you'll forgive me if I don't find you entirely trustworthy."

He took another step forward. He could not tell if the figure was watching him. It had no eyes, only pools of darker shadow amid the pale shadow that was its face.

"You stand upon the threshold of history, Sword Catcher," said the figure. "For this is the beginning of the fall of House Aurelian."

"And are you the architect of that fall?" Kel demanded, desperation and fury hot in his veins. "Will you buy their destruction with a child's blood?"

The figure chuckled. "The fall is all around you," it said. "Tread carefully."

And with unbelievable speed, the assassin caught up their crossbow and sprang. Not toward Kel, but off the roof's edge. The dark figure seemed to hang for a moment against the moon before hurtling silently toward the ground.

Kel raced to the edge of the roof, nausea roiling his stomach as he looked down, expecting to see a body crumpled on the flagstones, dark blood pooling around it.

But there was nothing. Only the empty courtyard, the ordinary shadows, the sough of wind in the branches of the cypress trees. He moved closer to the roof's edge—

You ruined my plans, Sword Catcher.

There must have been another crossbow bolt, one meant for Conor. *Death before marriage to Sarthe.* Cursing himself, Kel bolted back the way he had come.

He had only been gone a few minutes, maybe less than that. But by the time Kel returned to the Shining Gallery, everything had changed, because of Vienne.

He found out later that, a moment after Luisa's death, Vienne had leaped onto the high table, flinging herself at a Castelguard; they went down together, and when they rose, she had his sword in her hand.

She tore through the ring of Castelguards and lunged, her body making one long line with the sword, as if it were part of her. It sliced through the nearest Skull's throat; his head spun from his body. Blood spurted from the stump of his throat as he sank slowly to his knees, listing like a drowning ship. He hit the ground just as Vienne leaped from the dais and charged into the fray, heedless of the blood that soaked her silver slippers.

It was then that Kel came back into the gallery, racing down the stairs, his bloodstained sword in his hand. He looked first for Conor, and saw him with Jolivet. Conor's gold coat was slashed nearly to ribbons, the white lynx-fur lining stained scarlet with blood.

But it was not his blood, not his injury. He had found a sword somewhere, and still held it. Its blade was red-black. And he was staring, as everyone in the room was staring, at Vienne d'Este.

Never before had Kel seen one of the Black Guard fight. Vienne's sword blazed in her hand like lightning bursting from the palm of Aigon. She leaped and spun, cutting down Skull after Skull, leaving a trail of blood and innards behind her.

She was the north wind, the Wind of War. She was a comet formed of cold steel. She was Lady Death, with a blade that danced.

There seemed nothing for anyone else *to* do. Indeed, as Vienne fought, the Castelguards were ushering the rest of the nobility outside, through the broken doors. The room was swiftly emptying.

Kel saw the Queen escorted out, with Mayesh; Lady Gremont, white-faced with shock, walked between two guards. Falconet and many of the others refused to be escorted, but instead stalked out, heads held high, as if insulted at the suggestion that this was a matter for the Castelguard now and not for them.

Conor had seen Kel, across the room. He raised a hand, beckoned to him. Kel started across the room, stepping among the bodies, the slick-drying blood on the floor.

He heard a groan. Looked down. Saw the sleeve of a torn robe, gray hair. A white beard, speckled with blood.

Gremont.

Kel knelt down by the old man, knowing instantly and terribly that there was nothing he could do. The blade of a dagger protruded from the left side of Gremont's chest; the hilt of it had broken off, leaving only the blade, a broad sliver of steel, embedded in his body.

It was a miracle he was still breathing at all. Kel laid a hand on his shoulder. "Gremont," he murmured, the back of his throat burning. "Gremont. It's all right."

Gremont's eyes opened. They were blurred, rheumy. He looked up at Kel and said, "I told you—we had to speak. Urgent—"

He coughed. Kel stayed silent. Gremont thought he was Conor. He was not wearing his talisman, but still. It was dim and chaotic in the room, the man was dying, their eyes and hair were the same. It was understandable . . .

"Place your trust in no one," Gremont whispered. "Not mother, not Counselor, not friend. Trust no one on the Hill. Trust only your own eyes and ears, else the Gray Serpent will come for you, too."

The Gray Serpent? He must mean the Dark Guide, the serpent-headed boatman that met the dead at the door to the afterworld, and led them to the kingdom of Anibal.

"I did not know it would come so soon," Gremont wheezed. "The Gods forgive me. I did not know when it would come, that it would start tonight, but I knew. They came to me—I would not—I could not—"

His wheezing choked off in a gout of blood. Numbly, Kel clutched at the old man's shoulder. "Gremont," Kel said. "Thank you. You have done your duty."

If he had thought the words would comfort the old man, he had been wrong. Gremont's eyes rolled; he plucked once at Kel's sleeve, and died. Kel knew the moment it happened; between one breath and the next, he was gone.

"May he pass unhindered," Kel whispered, for the second time that night, and rose to his feet. As he did, he could not help but think of the Ragpicker King. Andreyen had begged him to speak to Gremont. Had he done so, would things now be any different?

He forced his mind back to the moment at hand. The world, not knowing Gremont was dead, had gone on. Vienne was fighting the last of the Skulls now, a big man with a nicked bronze blade. If there was blood on him, his black clothes hid it, but Vienne was soaked in the stuff. It flecked her cheeks like freckles, soaked her dress. She had lost one of her slippers, and her bare left foot was smeared with blood. She looked like a fiend from a dream, but there was nothing dreamlike about her actions. She ducked the Skull's blow, raised her own blade, and with a precision too swift to follow, cleanly sheared away the top of his skull.

He crumpled at her feet. Vienne looked around, as if in a daze, or waking from one. Kel saw her realize: There was no one left to fight. She was standing in the Shining Gallery surrounded only by a few Castelguards, the Legate, Kel, and Conor himself.

And the dead. Most assuredly, the dead.

She turned to look at the high table. Someone had lifted Luisa down, thank the Gods, and laid her on the table itself. She was very small, lying among the scattered plates; her white lace dress looked as if it had been dyed scarlet in blood.

"Sena d'Este," Conor said. His voice was low, urgent. Serious. "We will find out who did this. We will discover the ones responsible. Sarthe will be avenged. The Princess—"

"This is your fault," said Vienne. She said the words very carefully, as if each one were an effort. "She would not have been here if it were not for you. She should *not* have been here."

"No," said Conor. "She should not. But that part was not my doing."

But Vienne only shook her head, her eyes widening. "This is your *fault*," she said. And raising her blade, she charged at Conor.

Jolivet shouted. The Castelguards raced toward Vienne. Conor did not reach for his sword; he seemed too stunned.

There was a flash of silver. Steel slammed against steel; Kel had placed himself between Vienne and Conor. He did not even remember moving; he had been *there*, and now he was *here*, in front of the Prince, his body and his blade between Conor and a sword.

"Kel Anjuman," Vienne said tightly. "I will not tell you twice. Get out of my way."

He met her gaze. "It is as you said. I guard him, as you did Luisa."

Her mouth softened. He thought, for a moment, she might have heard him—but her sword turned to a silver blur in her hand and Kel staggered, blocking the sweeping blow. His ears rang as she forced him back; it was all he could do to defend himself. He had been trained, well trained, but he was not Vienne. She would drive him to the wall, and she would kill him there. There was nothing he could do about it.

He heard Jolivet say, "You cannot. She is Black Guard, Conor, you will die. Conor—"

Kel moved back, and back again. The wall was steps behind him. Vienne raised her blade—

And was lifted into the air, as if she were tethered to strings. She was flung aside, the sword clattering from her hand.

Kel heard Conor suck in his breath. "Father," he said.